Operation Last Exodus

I pray this book
both informs + entertains!
Robb Schmitt
2/20/16

Ez 37
Is 11:11
Rom 9-11

OPERATION LAST EXODUS:

*A Prophetic Possibility
of America's Coming Holocaust*

Robb Schwartz

Aliya Press
with *Spirit of Hope Publishing*
Irvine, California

OPERATION LAST EXODUS: *A Prophetic Possibility of America's Coming Holocaust*
Copyright © 2012 Robb Schwartz
Published by *Aliya Press*
in cooperation with *Spirit of Hope Publishing*

International Standard Book Number: 978-1-929753-36-9
Printed in the United States of America

Written by Robb Schwartz
Edited by Jerry Seiden
Character Sketches by Alina Bohm
Cover Design by Charles Schnur

ALL RIGHTS RESERVED: No part of this publication may be reproduced, stored in a retrieval system, or transmitted in any form or by any means—electronic, mechanical, photocopying, recording, or otherwise—without prior written permission, except for brief quotations in critical reviews or articles.

All Scripture taken from the *New American Standard Bible*. Copyright © 1982 by Thomas Nelson, Inc. Used by permission. All rights reserved.

All quotations, poems, references, and copyrighted material used by permission. Records on file with the publisher—contact info@spiritofhopepublishing.com or 714-308-2494.

NOTE: **This publication is a fictional work** intended to entertain, enlighten, encourage discussion, and explore possibilities. The author's reflections on world and Jewish history are accurate representations of facts available to him. Quotations from extant written works or literature are accurately noted with authors credited and permissions obtained. With the exception of historical and public figures (past or present)—all characters in the fictional story of *Operation Last Exodus* are literary creations of the author and any resemblance they bear to any individual living or dead is purely coincidental.

Operation Last Exodus by Robb Schwartz is designed to provide information on the subject matter covered. It is provided with the understanding that the publisher and author are not engaged in rendering professional advice or services beyond the stated purposes. The publisher and author are not responsible for any conclusions or actions taken by any reader.

For information and permission contact:

   Spirit of Hope Publishing
   PO Box 53642
   Irvine, CA 92619-3642

      PHONE: 714-308-2494
      EMAIL: info@spiritofhopepublishing.com
      WEB: www.spiritofhopepublishing.com

Publisher's Comments

We are very pleased to add ***Operation Last Exodus*** to our list of titles. You will find that author Robb Schwartz has provided extensive helps, resources, information, and nice-to-know materials in the back of the book. We wants you to be aware of the resources available to you, the reader, before you begin. We are certain that you will want to refer to some or all of the back matter as you progress through the book.

PLAYERS

A number of friends who read an early draft of ***Operation Last Exodus*** told Robb that they needed a program to keep track of all the characters. Others commented that his novel reads like a movie or television mini-series. All the more reason to make sure that none of the characters slip through the cracks. So in the backmatter Robb has provided the ***Players***. Readers will find a thumbnail sketch of the important, noteworthy, key, or pivotal players throughout the story—good, bad, or indifferent.

KEY WORDS & CONCEPTS

Throughout the book readers are certain to encounter unfamiliar words. The author often uses Hebrew transliterations, Yiddish, or other words and names that might escape American readers. In many cases the first usage of these words will be in ***bold-italics with an asterisk (*)***. But not all foreign or unfamiliar words will be in bold-italics with an asterisk—so refer to the ***Key Words*** often. In addition to words, readers will also find that ***Key Concepts*** are included as well. We and the author believe that some idea or concepts need to be expanded and explained a bit more that is available in the story. But we aren't done.... Readers who have suggestions for other words and concepts that should be included, please email us.

NOTED RESOURCES

The ***Noted Resources*** are a list of resources, recommendations, "must-reads," audio/video materials, and published works. These are materials that the author in some way used in the development or writing of ***Operation Last Exodus***. It has the combined elements of footnotes, endnotes, bibliography, and recommended reading all-in-one. But more, it reflects the author's broad experience, interest, and desire to share. In education and career Robb is a businessman, but in heart and passion he is a student of history. The **Noted Resources** reflect his heart for history and his love for God and God's Chosen People *Israel*—the Jews, wherever they maybe.

OUR STORY

Highlighted materials entitled ***Our Story*** appear in various places throughout the chapters. This is historical material based in fact—taken from the pages of world history and our common Jewish story. In some frames the Hebrew word ***midrash*** * (מדרש) is found. In broad terms *midrash* means "story" (for more on *midrash* see **Key Words** in the backmatter).

Dedication

Operation Last Exodus is dedicated in memory of all holocaust victims, Jewish and non-Jewish, including the unnamed and misunderstood Hebrew Christians who perished alongside their Jewish brothers and sisters. This is also dedicated to all those Jewish victims who suffered and died without the world's knowledge or recognition within the global Jewish community.

Acknowledgements

Operation Last Exodus could not have been written without the encouragement of my family—my wife Nancy (she named the book) and my daughter Shayna. They kept me going and always cheered me on to the goal.

Jerry Seiden, my editor, publisher, and friend offered wise counsel, writing technique, and general overall coaching through the final development, production, and presentation phases of this project. I can never thank you enough.

Our artist, Alina Bohm, gave life to the characters through her drawings.

Friends Ben Griffin, Mike Kutner, Irma Siegel, Trish Olsen, Mike Chacon, Keith Thompson, and others provided technical insights and valuable editing when called upon. I also draw inspiration from Chuck Missler, a gentile in whom there is no guile.

Last, a tribute to perhaps the greatest author America ever produced—James Michener. I drew the key kernel and initial spark for my story's concept from him (see *Author's Preface* for more). Mr. Michener, I only wish I could have met you, sat in your lap and listened to your stories.

Author's Preface

Operation Last Exodus is a work of fiction. Still, that doesn't mean it could not or will not happen.

The spark for this book came to me thirty years ago, and the story has burned within my heart and soul through those years. I read *The Source* by James Michener in which he chronicles a thousand year period in the history of Israel.

In the final chapter, several of Michener's characters discuss a long debated issue among Jews everywhere. They clash over Jewish emigration and the question: *Where do Jews belong?* An Israeli military officer argues that all Jews belong in Israel. The American counters that Jews in the U.S. are safe. Two oceans, a history of tolerance, and respect for Jews provide security in America. The U.S. Jews work and raise funds to support and visit Israel, but they *live* in America.

The argument ping-pongs back and forth until the conflict is clear and developed. Then near the chapter's end, the Israeli notes recent attacks on synagogues in Florida. He says that the attacks have made Israel consider the insertion of agents into Florida to defend Jews living there.

Wow! Really? Michener had introduced the thought of Israeli intervention on American soil in defense of Jews here—fifty five years ago. That spark ignited a fire in me that has intensified over the years with each day's news at home and abroad.

Since that time until today, I've asked myself, *Could it happen here?* I know that the thought of a holocaust in America seems impossible to most American Jews (or Jewish Americans). Yet, my knowledge of history and cautious thoughts keep me close to current affairs and ancient prophecies.

The fact is that prophecies throughout the **Tenach*** describe a time when dispersed Jews would be gathered back to Israel. Moses, Isaiah, Ezekiel, Jeremiah, and other prophets foresaw and wrote of such a time. By choice? By force?

I wonder-*why would Jews in America leave job, home, family, and familiar settings and perceived safety to live in Israel? Would they exchange safety for insecurity?* I don't know.

This story is about another Jewish holocaust—just ahead in America's near future. It's about how current and yet-to-come events force American Jews to make a decision.
The decision?
Stay in America at great risk to themselves and family? Or emigrate to Israel? Also a risky decision.
This story is about how hope and help arrive. It revisits Jewish historical events and patterns in light of current and growing trends. And it connects the dots and predictable patterns in a modern day context.
Could another Holocaust happen **here**? Does history repeat itself? The Jewish calendar has events each year—reminders that enemies often sought our annihilation. Yet Jewish preservation endures. ***Tish B'Av****, ***Purim****, ***Yom Ha'Shoah****, to ***Chanukah****, and others tell us every year that our people have faced suffering, cruelty, threats, *pogroms**, and true evil from malevolent people and powers.
So, now, my readers, you may wonder and ask, *Could another holocaust happen **here**?*
My answer: don't ask me. Ask the six million from Europe who never believed it could happen **there!**

Table of Contents

Chapter	Title	Page
1	In a Small Jewish Village	13
2	Ben-Yehuda	17
3	The Wanderers	23
4	Who Are We?	28
5	Old Friends	33
6	Familia	38
7	Preparations	42
8	A Roof Over Their Heads	44
9	The Planning	49
10	Hunters of Men	59
11	Dreams, Visions, & Memories	61
12	Hiding the Jews	65
13	Summer Camp	69
14	Dinner	73
15	Pogroms	80
16	A Change of Heart	83
17	In the Hospital	86
18	The Brothers Meet	90
19	Righteous Gentiles	99
20	Aryeh Cohen	105
21	Beth Emunah	109
22	Changing Patterns	124
23	Logistics	130
24	Durban	147
25	Roberts Receives a Call	153
26	NUMB3RS	158
27	The Census	164
28	Departures and Arrivals	167
29	Instruction	171
30	Aliya	175
31	Living in the Diaspora	180
32	Mimi	182
33	Avner and Danielle	189
34	Ephraim	194
35	Plans	197
36	Potential Fulfilled	201
37	Salt of the Earth	208
38	Ships	215
39	The Lessons of Entebbe	218
40	Shabbat Dinner	222
41	The Census Revealed	226
42	Dinner Plans Missed	232
43	The Knesset Meets	235
44	Dallas	242
45	Danielle	246
46	Past Meets Present	248
47	Things that Matter	252

Table of Contents Page 11

48	Shoshana Arrives	256
49	Independence Day	260
50	Team 3 Moves	269
51	Chaim in the Hospital	281
52	Jewish Doctor, Pickup Truck, & Pastor	290
53	Roberts & Cohen	295
54	Warriors Mingle—Hearts Unite	303
55	What Time Is It?	308
56	Supper with the Vicenzos	316
57	Brain Washings	319
58	Allied Forces	327
59	Buzz	329
60	New Target	336
61	Pilot Training	339
62	Let My People Go	343
63	Consensus on Critters	351
64	Bloody Water	356
65	Drones	362
66	Battle Plans Form	364
67	Let My People Go—Pestilence	369
68	Let My People Go—Remix	381
69	Mutiny	385
70	Taking Plunder	392
71	Strike in the OC	397
72	The Ground Shakes	408
73	Mecca & the Hajj	412
74	Dome of the Rock	421
75	Friends	428
76	The Underground Express	432
77	Comfort, Comfort Ye My People	436
78	A Curse or Blessing in Kind	453
79	Father Gregor	458
80	Operation Last Exodus—Fully Engaged	469
81	Financial Collapse	483
82	The Battle For Brooklyn	485
83	On Wings of Eagles	491
84	Eastern Corridor—Mimi in Command	493
85	Chicago	506
86	Shabibi's Gift	510
87	Shabbat at Papa G's	516
88	Attack at Sea—The Turning Point	523

Resources	Title	Page
	The Players	527
	Key Words & Concepts	534
	Noted Resources	538
	About the Author	543

Coffee House Chatter

—Heard in a coffee house in New York

"Anti-Semitism? Do you think it's real?" He asked.

"Are you kidding?" She asked. "Haven't you read or heard the news? Everyday in the U.S. there are new reports of vandalism, violence, and threats against Jews. Their synagogues, cemeteries, community centers, small businesses—even schools and daycare facilities have become targets."

"Awh," he scoffed. "Just a few random things here and there. No need for alarm. There are no Jewish ghettos, no storm-troopers in the streets, no death camps. All that is in the past."

He paused, thought, and jumped back in to add, "Besides, that violence and abuse you mentioned goes on every day in Palestine. I read that the Jews just bulldozed some homes, blew up Arab businesses, assassinated political leaders, and killed innocent civilians in the mix? The Jews are no different than the Arabs.

"Anti-Semitism is in people's heads," he declared. "Nobody thinks that way anymore."

"No." She shook her head. "That's not it. What you should have said is... **Nobody thinks anymore.** But not to worry—you may not have said it, but you demonstrated it."

Chapter 1

In a Small Jewish Village

* * * BASED ON ACTUAL EVENTS * * *

Months of preparation and reconnaissance were over, the targets now selected. Allah's young soldiers readied themselves to strike fast and hard. The Zionist enemy would feel this one and think about it for a good long time.

The young man wasn't nervous. His hard work over the past few months didn't escape notice of his superiors. Private conversations behind closed doors marked him as a future leader. He was fearless and enthusiastic.

From proper British college student to soldier in his god's war, he was ready to take the next step. They picked this small town for a reason. The young families were the future hope of the Jewish state. This would provide a few less soldiers to the enemy. One of them in particular, had seven children, ranging in age from infancy to thirteen.

The small attack squad knew every movement inside the tiny enclave of forty families. They knew everyone's coming and goings, school schedules, even deliveries to the small shops and little farms. Disguises came in handy. Playing friendly with unfriendlies was the best strategy of all. They knew the villagers as well as the villagers knew them.

Portrayed as delivery boys and seasonal fruit pickers, they always treated their neighbors with respect and deference. The Jewish villagers treated them well, paying them above the current wage scale. But that didn't matter anymore. It was actions like this that got the attention of an uncaring world. Enough of the world hated the Jews. This would be but a small blip on the radar.

The team assembled as night fell that Sabbath evening. From about a half mile away, they could see everything with their night vision goggles, smuggled in years before through Gazan tunnels. Guns were too noisy. Tonight, all the work would be done with knives.

When the lights went out in the small farmhouse about 11 P.M. that evening, the three attackers said their final prayers, worked through last minute details and then set out for the house. From this point on, they would refer to themselves as Red, Blue, and Green.

"There are three bedrooms. Six of the children will be found there, the infant, we don't know. We'll enter through the back window of the middle bedroom—they usually keep it open. The smaller children will sleep while we silence the parents."

The squad leader was experienced. He knew that once the parents were handled, the rest of the work would be easy. Still, he was ready for anything. All Israelis know how to use weapons.

"Red, you will subdue the husband, Blue, you the wife, and I will begin with the children. Remember to work fast. We don't need any trouble. Maintain silence—now."

The small team set out toward the tiny village. They moved through the olive trees, heavy with fruit for the first pressing. Beyond the olives lay the fruit trees—plums, peaches, and apricots. A small wisp of a breeze played in the trees.

They drew close to the house. A last minute check showed no other movement in the neighbor's homes. Everyone was asleep, just as planned. Green's hand signals directed Red and Blue to the middle bedroom in the back of the home.

The window was open. Red looked inside and found both parents asleep with the infant in a bassinet beside their bed. The quiet and darkness enveloped them. He carefully slipped off the screen. With the screen off, they deftly hopped inside the window. No movement from either the parents or the sleeping infant.

His heart beat fast. A trickle of sweat worked it way down his neck. He felt hyper-aware of every detail in the room. He felt powerful, almost as if he had become the power to give or take life. His partner moved with same precision, sensing the moment.

A thought crossed Red's mind, but just for a moment—what if this were his family? He chased the thought away. Slowly, he reached for the hunting knife in his belt. There was no sense of remorse, no second thoughts at this point. He had a job to do.

He moved to the husband—father of the seven children, slowly raised the knife to the sleeping man's throat. At that moment, the man stirred and Red knew time was short. With a quick and deft hand, he did his business. Green then attacked the mother. It was over within seconds, the carotid arteries in both of them sliced open, blood now flowing from their lifeless bodies. Red moved to the infant, still asleep.

His companions work was done in the same quick and efficient manner. Seven Jewish deaths would hardly make a dent in the Zionist enemy but it would send a message that they weren't safe even in their own beds.

The killing was over. They left the same way they came in, replaced the screen on the window and hurried back through the orchards.

The crime wouldn't be reported until the next day. When a friend of the thirteen-year-old called on them in the morning, he received no answer at the door. He called out to other family members, but still no response. This puzzled him and he went to the front door. It was locked so he went around to the back of the small home. There he noticed that the window to the middle bedroom was open. He called inside but there was no response.

Concerned but not panicked just yet, he went across the street and summoned his father, just preparing to leave for the fields. His father accompanied him to the little house and they went back to middle bedroom window. The father called out but got no response. Normally he'd see the family stirring and preparing for the day ahead, but there was no trace of movement. He thought it strange. Then he noticed something they had both missed just a few moments before... what appeared to be a red smear on the wall next to the bedroom window.

Now concerned, he looked inside again and then saw the mother and father, unmoving. They appeared to be sleeping. The sun was just beginning to rise... the new light now revealed the horrors left behind by the killers.

He jerked the window screen off and hopped inside. He wasn't prepared for the scene that awaited him. He moved to the children's rooms and discovered the same thing... everyone in the house dead in their beds, throats cut, lifeless, defenseless.

Heart pounding, he pulled out his cell phone and called his wife.

"Hi... I'm across the street... somebody got in here last night and... and... killed the whole family. Call the police right now!"

"What, what?" Suppressing a wail, his wife dialed the police. She dropped her morning chores and hurried across the street. Her husband met her at the front door.

"Don't go in!"

"No! I must!"

"Please, honey, don't! It's gruesome."

She pushed him aside, and when entering the bedroom of the older children, she collapsed on the floor, screaming.

The police arrived a few minutes later. They were followed by a news reporter from the Jerusalem Post. As they cordoned off the area, the other neighbors began to awake to the invasion of their quiet neighborhood. Within hours the pictures would be posted on the internet and the work of this heinous crime would be known to millions.

And children handed out candy in Gaza, celebrating the work of their heroes, three brave men who snuffed out the lives of seven Zionist enemies.

> **From the Prophet Hosea**
> **Chapter 6 Verse 6**
>
> For I delight in loyalty rather than sacrifice, and in the knowledge of God rather than burnt offerings.

Chapter 2

Ben-Yehuda

Avram Ben-Yehuda sat in his office one floor below the main complex of the Mossad. His regular Shabbat routine didn't bring him into the office, but today was different. *After all these years,* he reassured himself, *this really isn't work—is it?*

Still, *something* had drawn Avram to his office. *I don't like this,* he thought. *Where's my slow and easy Shabbat morning?* Whatever led this old Mossad veteran to the complex now left him with an odd and uneasy quiet. Eerie feelings were nothing new. *Just keep your eyes and ears open, old man,* he told himself.

There had been the on and off again "chatter" of terrorist threats in the past few weeks, but this morning seemed rather quiet.

He poured himself a cup of green tea, added orange flavored honey, and squeezed slices of lemon and orange. He lifted and inhaled the soothing aroma. He sipped at the brew and spoke his approval. "Ahhh, just right."

He laid his head back on the chair and his mind began to drift—back to a time where every day mattered in the land that he knew so well. He knew it as well as his own backyard. He had seen it all... born not long after the birth of the nation, the First Fruits of Zion. His was the first generation born after Israel's declaration of independence.

Avram and his generation had seen endless war. They witnessed wars of attrition and threats from enemies—near and far. Those enemies all had one thing in common—the eradication of the Jewish state and Zionism as the world knew it.

Avram recalled history that he'd never witnessed. He had received memories from a history handed down from one generation to the next. Before he'd breathed a breath, these memories would be ***his***-story. Then thoughts turned to dreams and heavy eyes closed in sleep.

His job was to thwart any-and-all efforts to harm Israel—a thankless job. He was Director of Operations (D.O.) for Israel's intelligence agency—Mossad. Its very name sent shivers, sounded alarms, and generated fear among Israel's enemies. And it fostered reverence among Israel's friends. But now there were few, if any, friends. Israel seemed to stand alone on the world's stage. Many believed that Israel's days were numbered.

May 14, 1948—David Ben-Gurion (the former David Green) had just declared the establishment of the Jewish state, as foreseen by the journalist Theodore Herzl, just 50 years before. The stories, passed down from those who were there, and his voracious reading throughout his life, made it all so real to him. Arguments swirled whether or not this was the fulfillment of the Biblical prophecies. Few of them worried about such things.

In his dream, he could see young and old, dancing the **hora*** in the streets of Jerusalem. Minutes later, Egyptian aircraft rained bombs on Tel Aviv as their tanks rolled into the desert.

Within minutes, the tiny nation was plunged into a war for its survival. Five nations and their armies surrounded and attacked at once. No rational person questioned the outcome. The armies were confident—it was only a matter of time. They would punish the miserable Zionist usurpers and purge the occupiers from Islamic land.

Israel! Ha! This is Palestine. This is Al Quds—the third holiest site of all Islam! Avram could hear their boast. He could see the newspaper accounts. He viewed the newsreel footage.

He slipped deeper into the dream.

The history came to him. Golda, the old man, Weitzman, Allon, Sharret, Dayan, so many heroes—all long gone. He saw these people in the parlor of the modest home. They were friends of his parents, not giants of history. His generation was fading fast. The legends grew larger with the years.

Nobody had money. Everyone lived like one big family. Oh, there was plenty of infighting—Irgun, Stern Gang, Palmach, Lechi, and other splinter groups. They would later put differences aside, band together and form the Haganah. His people were a weird bunch, so quick to fight among themselves until outsiders appeared, and then they closed ranks. We are all brothers, are we not?

He remembered the stories of the British. They were desperate to hold on to their crumbling empire. They did their best to separate the Arabs and Jews to maintain peace. Some British officials favored the Arabs, some the Jews, and some had no sympathies one way or the other. Jews accused the British of being pro-Arab. The Arabs accused them of being pro-Jewish. Both sides made good arguments.

Palestinian Jewry held out for the promises of the Balfour Declaration of 1917. The promises were set forth in a letter from Arthur James Balfourby, the United Kingdom's Foreign Secretary and a former Prime Minister of England. The declaration was written at a time of warmer Jewish-Arab relations. Along with it came a very big stick, a land for the Jewish people, just not now and certainly not on Jewish terms.

In the end, the declaration brought more disappointment—promises made, promises broken, time after time.

Our Story . . .

During World War II, the Jews found themselves caught between the Germans, the Arabs, and the English. Even so, they remained loyal to the Crown, chomping at the bit to fight Hitler even as Great Britain slowed immigration and turned her back on her promises. Some believed this contributed to the deaths of millions. So, they fought alongside England while they defied British authority as they snuck in refugees. It was hard to figure loyalties. Many Arabs joined with Germany, including the Mufti.

The more Great Britain fought to hold her empire together, the further it slipped away. The war ended, and it took British influence and power with it. The empire's crown jewel of India now yearned for independence. The burden was too much for Britain to bear. Treasuries empty, the people weary of war, and everyone anxious to have the troops at home.

Great Britain continued to fight Jewish immigration, even after the war. They sought to appease the Arab population. But postwar international opinion seemed to favor a Jewish homeland. British resistance, according to some, grew into anti-Semitism.

But this time... the Jews fought back! They didn't speak a common language. They had come from Europe, Africa, America, Canada, England, even Central and South America. But they formed a nation. A melting pot of people who would stand and shoot as one!

Many believed this was an actual fulfillment of Bible prophecy. The term Christian Zionist was born in the U.S. about this time. Senator Harry Truman joined such an organization. Later, when Vice President Harry Truman assumed the Oval Office after the death of President Roosevelt, he took on the burden of the leader of the Free World and recognized the gravity and the significance of the new world stage.

Truman, was a Bible believing Baptist. He had read the entire Bible a dozen times before the age of 15, more than most read it in a lifetime. His interest was more than just pure politics. He saw himself as a tool of the Almighty, an actual participant in Biblical prophecy. He wanted to help the remnant of this ancient people redefine itself, even in modern times. One influential rabbi called him a modern-day Cyrus.

But Truman honored the arms boycott. Where to find weapons would be left to those with 'other means.' Israel would find a way to buy what it needed. The infighting ceased when everyone recognized they had a common enemy. They picked up whatever weapons they could make, or steal, buy, or find. They built them in underground factories, bought them on the open market, and scrounged them on the black market. And they learned to use them—well.

Avram's dream of the past continued. He was younger and stronger then. He remembered every detail of the history lessons delivered to him in his home. His storytellers were the very men and women who fought for independence and made the history.

The young nation's enemies gathered to control roads, choke off supplies, and remove all hope. Jerusalem residents rationed everything. They ate rats, caught raindrops, and prayed. Still, desperation grew. Young men—just boys—fought in the hills of Judea. They struck the opposition hard and freed the corridor on the Jerusalem Road.

Hostilities ceased, convoys arrived, and evidence of the conflict told the story. The twisted carcasses of the rescue vehicles littered the road to Jerusalem. They were a solemn testimony to those who had lost their lives—A stark memorial for heroes who sacrifice all to save the starving.

Latrun— Its memory evoked tears. Every visitor to Jerusalem ascends up the mountain and sees those crazy "armored" vehicles, cars or small trucks, really, with nothing more than metal plates welded onto the bodies. Cars full of rescuers, doctors, nurses, slaughtered by Arab bullets. Oh, yes he knew the stories, every inch of roadbed, every wrecked vehicle on that road told a story. He wondered what a future civilization might think about these relics when they discovered them on some distant future field trip.

Those soldiers, few professionals, had fought multitudes of enemies in almost every corner, every street, and every valley of the new nation. And when it was his turn, he went, with joy and with purpose in mind. Many times his country called, many times he answered. He was the first wave of troops at the Western Wall in 1967, a young, green, but committed soldier. He recognized and cherished his role in history.

To make and build **Eretz Israel*** would take every resource, every citizen, child, man and woman. It would take both young and old. And it would continue to do so, year in and year out. They cried when they reached the Wailing Wall, after 48 sleepless hours of combat. They were sweet tears. They were bitter tears. They were the tears of the Jewish journey.

It would be nice for God to help his people, Avram thought. *That is if He even existed.* None of this was easy, none of it clean. There was no black and white, only shades of grey.

God? Hah! Where was He when the 6 million died? Where was He when He was needed most? No, no, no! He believed it was in his hands and his mind, and that of his young countrymen. They would save this nation from the butcher's knife of radical Islam and a deaf, dumb, and blind world. They would resist the aggression and hatred. They would confront a world that no longer cared. The crazy thing was that he had Muslim friends and neighbors that he'd known since childhood. He didn't hate anyone.

Religion was a joke to him now. Israel had little room for God. It needed men and women to make the sacrifice, and defend the land, THEIR LAND. The Bible was a nice book of stories and maybe even had some nice history, but it was guns and tanks and planes that convinced her enemies that she meant business. It had always needed that. And it needed LOYALTY.

He remembered Ben Gurion—legends of the *Old Man*. He barely acknowledged a supreme being. Salvation came out the business end of a gun. And, Ben Yehuda couldn't have agreed with Israel's first leader any more. All they wanted was lasting peace... peace to raise their families, peace to run their farms, peace to receive an education, and peace to fulfill their dream. War was a means to an end, except that end never seemed to come. War was never wanted, but was often necessary.

Against all hope, the tiny nation fought back with the courage of a lion. Within weeks, to the amazement of the world and the horror of her enemies, she slowly began to push back the disorganized and emotional invaders, street by street, valley by valley, here a little, there a little.

The tiny **Yishuv*** may not have been stronger or bigger, but she was a well-organized machine on a mission, a dream, a shared collective memory, and driven by a higher purpose. Ah, the memories, sweet, bitter, but never dull. Maybe the Bible had something to say after all. The memories, the memories....

At that moment, the phone rang, jarred his senses, opened his eyes, and brought him back to the here-and-now and his place in it.

The New Colossus — Emma Lazarus, 1883

Not like the brazen giant of Greek fame,
With conquering limbs astride from land to land;
Here at our sea-washed, sunset gates shall stand
A mighty woman with a torch, whose flame
Is the imprisoned lightning, and her name
Mother of Exiles. From her beacon-hand
Glows world-wide welcome; her mild eyes command
The air-bridged harbor that twin cities frame.
"Keep, ancient lands, your storied pomp!" cries she
With silent lips. "Give me your tired, your poor,
Your huddled masses yearning to breathe free,
The wretched refuse of your teeming shore.
Send these, the homeless, tempest-tossed to me,
I lift my lamp beside the golden door!"

Chapter 3

The Wanderers

America, the *Goldena Medina*, was the Promised Land to many downtrodden Jews from the mid 19th century to the early 20th century. America, the blessed, the place anyone coming from anywhere could come, blend, live, work, and grow. America, the hope, the one land where people died to GET IN.

The Jews immigrated to America in search of hope, a better life both for themselves and their children. Emma Lazarus' inscription on the Statue of Liberty became almost as famous to new Jewish immigrants as the words of the ancient rabbis. They hailed Lady Liberty with tears. It was here that the streets were paved with gold.

America drew the English, Irish, Germans, Poles, Italians, and others from Europe, each desperate to escape tyranny. Later, the Jews immigrated in huge numbers in the mid-to-late 19th Century. Later still, those from Central and South America, and even China, would find the land of promise.

Where had the Jew come from? Why did he want to leave the *shtetl* or the deserts of his past? What drove him away from the lands of his ancestors and to this new place of promise?

History records how Jews were displaced and driven out by Assyrians, Babylonians, Romans, Christians, Muslims, and a progression of nations and peoples. Religious authorities drove them into the hills, over the borders, through the mountains, across the oceans, and to the shores of new lands.

This dispersion of the Jewish people and the places where they were scattered and sent is known as the **Diaspora*.**

Our Story . . .

The Diaspora, or the dispersion, actually began in eons past, as early as 586 BCE, when first, the Assyrians and then the Babylonians overran the ancient cities of the homeland. Enemies murdered the Jews by the thousands, tens of thousands, hundreds of thousands, and then by the millions, as the Moses and the ancient prophets predicted.

Later, they fled the Romans after the Temple was destroyed about 70 A.D. More than one million died in the streets of Jerusalem as prophesied by the one called **Yeshua***. More died in the Bar Kochba rebellion some years later. This accelerated the exile to foreign lands. It didn't matter who was in power, the Jews were targets largely because they refused to give up who they were. They remained separate and in their opinion, chosen.

Some said it was because the people hadn't lived up to their promises and commitments to the God of Israel. It was theirs to suffer eons of wandering. Perhaps a vengeful God was paying them back for their sins.

Their enemies wrote about Jewish conspiracies, of blood libels, where Jews killed Christian children and used their blood for the Passover. Later, lies and slanders were published in the Protocols of the Elders of Zion. It was all refuted by scholars, but still a popular seller. It was just one of the reasons that the Jews were forced to wander. Sometimes they were pushed out or pulled by the promise of a better life.

Later, in the early 21st Century, the Muslim world accused the Israelis of harvesting organs of their enemies and selling them, a new twist on the old blood libel myth. The story was later proven a hoax by Camera, the research agency. By the time it made it into print, the truth didn't matter any longer. The world would believe what it wanted to believe.

While some of this history placed the Jewish people in harm's way, other events conspired to the common good. Jews dispersed during the first and second exiles later established deep roots in Persia, Babylon, and throughout the Middle East. Of course, the Jews always maintained a Jewish presence in the Land.

The Jews sometimes held governmental positions, ran successful businesses and furthered commerce between nations. In neighboring Alexandria, Egypt, Philo, the ancient Jewish philosopher wrote of a Jewish population exceeding one million, indicating some level of comfort and confidence that their neighbors would leave them alone.

The **Diaspora*** pushed them to places such as Greece, Italy, the African continent, and major cities throughout the world. They were truly dispersed **but most never fully assimilated.**

Their migrations later took them to all four corners of the world. Jewish traders headed to England, Spain, throughout Europe, into Asia, eventually finding themselves as far away as the Caribbean islands.

מִדְרָשׁ ...

Spanish Jewry flourished for more than 700 years. Spain produced many great Jewish sages and their works of literature, mathematics, and science. It was from Spain that Columbus, an Italian by birth and to some, a suspected Converso or Crypto Jew, sailed to the New World for the Spanish crown.

Speculation circulated on his adventures to find a safe place for Jews in the midst of the Inquisition. Other rumors said that Columbus' was looking for precious metals in the New World to restock the Spanish government's reserves expended in wars with England. Long buried stories told of Jews who escaped the Spanish crown, sailing for the new world. Some even took up pirating to pay back their tormentors, becoming, in effect, Jewish Pirates of the Caribbean.

After years of peaceful coexistence with their neighbors, the Jews encountered Christian-sponsored Crusades and for more than 200 years, they lived in fear. The first Crusade in Jerusalem in 1099 ended in a *pogrom** when the crusaders entered the Jewish Quarter and rampaged through homes and synagogues. Thousands of Jews lost their lives as the Christians burned their synagogues, sometimes full of worshippers, all in the name of Jesus. A Christian writer wrote that blood from the victims flowed as high as the thighs of the horses.

Though most have not heard of the Cossacks' Chmelnitzky Massacres in 1600's Poland/Russia, historians pegged the Jewish death toll between 100,000 and 500,000, the disparity due to poor recordkeeping. The Jews were trapped in a battle between two Christian factions, Russian Orthodox and the Roman Catholic traditions. They were simply in the wrong place at the wrong time. This holocaust was largely relegated to the pages of history, yet illustrated once again, the expendability of the Jews amidst the surrounding Christian population.

No matter how long they remained, or how well things may have gone, persecution would always come. There would be crusades, pogroms, outright murders, and edicts from the Crown or the Church. It didn't matter whether or not they lived in Muslim or Christian nations. Living in Muslim lands presented its own challenges.

Islam classified them as *Dhimmis*—virtual slaves of Muslim nations in which they lived. Their Islamic overlords would exact a *jizia* (poll tax tributes) which all male non-believers fifteen years or older had to pay. But more, their Muslim overlords exacted special land taxes called *kharaj*. Their local authorities held the power of life, death, and purse.

Stories circulated about the humiliation Jews suffered from their Muslim masters. They were pushed about in the streets. They faced random beatings. They were forced to step aside and yield to Muslims on the street. All of this was a cruel reality for hundreds of years. Then sorrow was added to humiliation. Muslims often kidnapped Jewish children and forced them to convert to Islam.

Jews were second-class citizens.

...מדרש

Centuries later this Muslim attitude extended to peace talks during the 2nd Bush administration. Arabs tried to force the Israelis to enter the White House peace negotiations through the servants' entrance.

Jews did fare well in certain areas and with some overlords. In Morocco and Tunisia neighbors lived in harmony from time-to-time. It all depended on the mood of the Muslim rulers.

Though a small Jewish presence had always been there, a stirring began in the 1880's and with it, the first wave of Jewish immigrants found their ancient homeland once again. A few years later, the Dreyfus affair signaled the birth pangs of the need for a new Jewish national home.

Local Muslim families assumed the local tribal taxation after Britain defeated the Ottomans in World War I. The native lands lost their revenue. Some believed that much of the anti-Semitism in the 1920's arose due to the growing Jewish presence. The Arabs lived better under the Jews than at home. That put a target on the Jews back. Some government authorities and Jewish residents were killed.

Persecution led Jews to Israel. They arrived by foot, horseback, boat, and the sweat of their brows. They came to build a new land. They brought a desire for collective farming communities. They developed their own internal security force known as **HaShomer***. They bought Arab land at exorbitant prices and pushed back the swamplands. They planted millions of trees and turned the desert into a garden.

After World War I, British intrigue turned Jew and Arab—against one another. Factional religious disputes were often orchestrated by Great Britain to damage Jewish interests and break Jewish morale. They sought to prevent cooperation between the two indigenous populations. Riots broke out several times—many Jewish and Arab lives were lost. This era gave rise to the *Grand Mufti of Jerusalem*—who later was implicated as a Nazi collaborator who approved of the mass murder of Jews in Europe.

On the heels of these persecutions came the Holocaust. The German death machine was constructed to wipe-out an entire civilization from the earth. Reports of the genocide were not believed in the West until it was too late. Governments turned a blind eye and a deaf ear to pleas for help.

General Dwight D. Eisenhower commissioned a film crew to document the liberation of concentration camps in 1945. He knew future scoffers would arise to deny even eyewitnesses. And he was right. Neo-Nazis, certain Christians, radical Muslims, and others have either denied or down-played Nazi atrocities. In the early 21st century, doubters from Iran and other radical Islamic nations decried it as Jewish propaganda, even in some cases praising Hitler's work. Muslim propaganda closely mimicked Nazi propaganda from the 1930's and 1940's.

Alfred Hitchcock also filmed the atrocities before his venture into Hollywood film making. His work now appears online for the world to see as a stark reminder of the human condition at its worst—a testimony to man's depravity.

The Jews came to America from Germany, Poland, Russia, Italy, Hungary, Austria, and every other European country. They came from the Middle East and Arab lands, too. They were the *Sephardim* and the *Ashkenazim*—bearded men and scarf-wearing women speaking countless languages. They came to America with renewed hope that their ancient wandering was about to end. And end they did... until now.

The 21st century... Jews faced changes that no one could have imagined. Distrust, suspicions, and walls grew between Jews, Christians, and Muslims.

> **From HaYad Moshe, the Hand of Moses:**
> D'varim (Deuteronomy) 26:18-19
>
> The LORD has today declared you to be His people, a treasured possession, as He promised you, and that you should keep all His commandments; and that He will set you high above all nations which He has made, for praise, fame, and honor; and that you shall be a consecrated people to the LORD your God, as He has spoken.

Chapter 4

Who Are We?

The Jews stood out. They were a clannish people. They learned to keep to themselves. They planted generations of deep roots wherever they lived. They never quite fit in although from time to time they would assimilate.

They always educated their young, and sought to help their fellow man. Jews guaranteed their survival through education. They became known in more than one culture as "People of the Book," and even though the reference may have been Biblical, it also referred to the fact that Jews were literate.

Between 1901 and well into the 21st Century, more than one-fifth of Nobel Peace Prize winners came from persons of half or three-quarters Jewish bloodlines. Of that number, more than one-third of all American Nobel recipients during that time period were Jewish, despite their small numbers. The American Revolution even had a Jewish hero, though he remained very low key about it.

It was said that Haym Solomon financed a great portion of the American Revolution. His money enabled the colonists to purchase badly needed weapons and war material from foreign governments such as France and Spain. More than 200 years later, the U.S. Postal Service issued a stamp hailing Solomon as a "Financial Hero of the American Revolution."

Through the years, the rabbis in America taught their congregations that America was blessed because of the way it treated its Jews. Things were different in America. There were no beatings in the streets, no pogroms, no towns burned to the ground. Synagogues were safe, neighborhoods left alone. Any conflict with the Jewish population was an individual matter, at least until now. America bore no hatred against the whole of the people by either the government or the populace at large.

Jews learned to brush off many insensitive, thoughtless, and even cruel comments from their fellow Americans. Most repeated the words and thoughts of their fathers and grandfathers. They said, "He jewed me down." "The Jews own all the banks and control the economy!" "They own all the media, networks, and airwaves." But when things escalated, the *B'nai Brith* or the Anti-Defamation League (ADL) stepped in to help. These organizations exposed the matter, and called out those responsible for the attacks.

Loyalties could be divided though. Though Jews had fought in all of America's wars including both sides of the American Civil War, thoughts of Zion and the promises it held were never very far from the collective Jewish conscience. At the end of every Passover **Seder*** came the eternal cry of the Jewish people, no matter where they lived, *'L'Shana Ha'ba, b'Yerushaliam,'* or "Next year in Jerusalem!" It didn't matter how religious they may have seemed. Jews knew, by instinct that they lived on borrowed time. It may not be this generation or next, but something deep within the collective consciousness ticked away for a return to Zion.

Jews grew comfortable in America. They adopted a comfortable cultural identity. They were close yet separate from those around them. This was cited by some observers as the primary reason Jews were persecuted and not for economic reasons. The Jewish population remained far more focused on its culture and establishing successful communities and businesses.

There was a relationship with the local synagogue but few studied their Bibles, other holy books, or had much of a formal Jewish education. Such endeavors were left to the religious community. Intermarriage divided Jewish communities across the nation. And with it came a new invention to explain and understand this phenomenon called *Interfaith Dialog.* Rabbis, ministers, and priests tried their best to downplay the differences between the various cultures and promote peace and understanding between them. It was a noble goal. It was also the beginning of the end of the Jews in America.

Study of Hebrew often ended with a few years of **Bar Mitzvah*** and Hebrew School training. Yiddish, the lingua franca of European Jews for centuries, was dead except within the ultra-orthodox communities. An even smaller community in Sephardic circles spoke Ladino, an offshoot of Spanish. Jewish Americans (or American Jews) lived comfortable lives in America. Separated by two oceans they felt insulated from their long history persecution.

About six generations grew up safely in America. They were far from their roots. Only some 120,000 Jews had ever left America for Israel... almost half that many had come from tiny Ethiopia to Israel alone.

America was their home. It was the new Promised Land. An occasional trip to Israel? Yes! Support through donations? Yes! Emigration to the land of their fathers? No!

To say that the Jews were achievers was true. To say that the Jews were overachievers was true with an exclamation point. It wasn't that Jews achieved, but rather it was that Jews achieved in most fields of endeavor far greater than their numbers would or should dictate.

Jewish Americans or American Jews succeeded in such areas as film, the arts, sciences, medicine, law, finance, education, or even organized crime. It confirmed the fact that Jewish families valued literacy, education, and success as family and community values.

While not all Jews were political activists, a large percentage of political activists were Jewish, including many of the early Communist party in 19th and 20th Century Europe. American radical politics even saw its share of Jewish leaders such as Emma Goldman and Samuel Gompers, both immigrants and both active in labor movements. They didn't distinguish between woman and men as many women took active roles in the garment industries both advocating for change and working to eliminate such distasteful practices as sweatshops and child labor. Women's' liberation was never much a problem in Jewish families. Strong women were not to be feared, but respected and cherished.

As time went by, more and better access to higher education meant their sons and daughters would climb the American ladder of success. Their children attended the finest schools, snagged good positions in all professions. They married, sometimes in mixed marriages where any semblance of faith tended to disappear, settled down, had family, and maybe or maybe not got involved in Jewish social life.

Many headed to community organizations like Rotary, Optimists, Little League, or became soccer moms and dads. One could find the Jews at the forefront of virtually every major campaign for social change, heading fund raising organizations, non-profits, and academic institutions, and often even religious cults. They invented, innovated, inspired, and grew successful. It was just something in the Jewish blood that cried out for all of these.

And yet, there was still a small voice that called out for God.

Assimilation

They achieved success in the most well known institutions, both private and public. Jews living within America's borders saw themselves as Jewish Americans, not American Jews. The Jews became loyal Americans and mastered the language in the first generation. It seemed to some that faith in God waned and was slowly replaced by education and success.

That they happened to be Jewish was a matter of bloodline of course, but loyalty to America, was unquestionable. They fought in all of America's wars. Though they remained pro-Israel in general, there was a vocal minority within American Judaism that opposed many things the Israeli government stood for, including Zionism. That self-perception would now be challenged by their enemies and their remaining friends, fewer and fewer as they were. Things were changing for those who had so well integrated themselves and their families into the American social fabric, just like pre-World War II Europe.

It was a debate often brought up in Jewish social circles where the questions of loyalty to the flag, country, and then to one's religion always provoked some level of controversy. It was an ongoing debate, sometimes more public sometimes more private. Who were the American Jews? To whom were they loyal? Did they have split loyalties to both America and Israel? Were they to be trusted? History, as always, lent a clue. Recent history shed some light on their mindset.

For years in Germany for example, Jews had been loyal German citizens. They served in the military, practiced medicine, law, and excelled in the professions. Jews were involved in the financial infrastructure, taught in the schools, and blended comfortably with their neighbors. After World War I, German Jews sang *Deutchland Uber Alles*, the German National Anthem, because they were indeed, Germans first and Jews second. Jewish war veterans were honored as were their gentile counterparts.

Jewish Germans fought Jewish Frenchmen in that war because they were Germans first and Jews second. Their children attended the same schools with their Gentile neighbors. Families attended theater, symphonies, and sporting events... together.

Many intermarried. Religion took a back seat to German culture and the arts. For those Jews who valued their Jewish roots, there was always Yiddish, the lingua franca within the Jewish communities across most of Europe. Jewish culture and Yiddish Theater kept them entertained.

That the people all spoke a refined German was the tie that would bind them together, Jews and Gentiles of the higher German culture. But, they were Germans. That was until the late 1920's when a new Germany began its slow resurrection from the ash heap of World War I.

An American historical precedent existed to help explain this identity conflict. Most Americans had never heard of the story of the San Patricios. These Irish American soldiers chose not to fight for the U.S. in the Mexican American War in 1846-1848 but rather deserted and fought alongside their Mexican Catholic counterparts.

Many of these Irish immigrants chose to leave the U.S. military and become Mexican citizens, their faith more important than their U.S. Citizenship. They fought in five of the larger battles laying their lives down for their Catholic cousins south of the border.

Germany's economy staggered under the burdens of war reparations. Runaway inflation destabilized the political and social structure. Germany found herself in desperate straits. A little known political functionary fresh out of prison would soon make his move. Then the Jews of Germany would learn what their neighbors really thought of them. Were they German Jews or Jewish Germans?

It would be the same in America. Americans, long tolerant of their Jewish neighbors, would soon learn more about themselves too. The Jews living in America would soon be in for more than just a rude awakening. Long buried hatreds surfaced even within communities that had long worked and lived together in peace and harmony. They thought and believed, *it could never happen here because we live in a free, democratic state.* Yet those Jews living in America would soon ask themselves, *Are we American Jews or Jewish Americans?*

Christians among them would also ask, *Are we American Christians or Christian Americans? What does being Christian mean?* Loyalties may waver when you are not working or cannot feed your family, when gas is running close to $8 a gallon, or when you are getting foreclosure notices from the bank or you cannot qualify for a loan.

Loyalty means little when it's you versus him or us versus them. Loyalty to a cause wavers when the enemy combatant has a knife to the throat of a loved one. Hearts and minds can bend when your family is on the street and there is no hope in sight. There are few Corrie Ten Booms, few Oscar Schindlers, and few Raoul Wallenbergs.

However, one group had absolutely NO problem with its self identity. That night, an **Imam*** in a New York City mosque asked his congregation in a thundering voice, "Are we American Muslims or Muslim Americans?"

With one voice, and raised fists, the resounding response was, "We are American Muslims! To Allah be the glory!"

> **George Bernard Shaw**
>
> *We learn from history that we learn nothing from history.*

Chapter 5

Old Friends

Legends are often born from a grain of truth. Jewish involvement in American organized crime seemed pretty farfetched. If organized crime existed at all, it was drug cartels in far away countries or run by black market pirates. But there was some truth to the story.

At one time, Jewish mobsters ran the rackets from prostitution, drugs, unions, and extortion. But in time these businesses faced competition, challenges to their growth models, aging leadership, and a changing community ethos. Still, stories circulated of Italians and Jews that cooperated as partners in the "business that never existed." That confounded America's storytellers for generations. Nobody ever admitted to it, but those stories were not secrets among the families.

Small details leaked out over the years and the picture became clearer as time went on. Meyer Suchomlanski, a Jewish financier, had helped the Italians and their business enterprises while he managed a few of his own concerns. He became known to the world as Meyer Lansky, the Mob's accountant, though no friend of Israel, who deported him years later when he tried to emigrate.

Both the Jews and the Italians found a way to coexist and form solid, if not professional business relationships that seemed to endure for a lifetime. There were those who believed that without Lansky's monetary genius, the Italian mob would have never achieved the success it did. To many, it felt like family. And so it was that when the Jews called many years later and in their hour of greatest need, it would be "familia" that would provide the muscle it needed.

Sal "Dogface" Vicenzo grew up in such a family. The family's business was never openly discussed at home but if one paid attention, it soon became apparent that cash flows came from 'interesting' business arrangements. After college he would find himself in the 'family business.'

He acquired his nickname because of some name-calling in school as a young boy. In the fourth grade during recess on the playground, the other kid called him Dogface at which point Sal, without thinking, simply took him down.

As the two young pugilists rolled around in the dirt, Sal put the mustard to him with a shot to the chops, broke his jaw and knocked out his four front teeth. The other boy wisely stayed down, spit out his teeth or what was left of them anyway, onto the asphalt playground. For good measure, his nose was broken too, the blood and mucous smeared all over his face. From that point forward, nobody ever approached him in anger again and Sal wore his nickname with pride.

Sal's Italian ancestors came from the Northern part of Italy, close to Genoa. He was fair with hazel green eyes, dirty blond hair, uneven smile, and dimple in his right cheek. He stood a shade over 5'9" and was stout like his father. His face was craggy with laugh lines around his eyes and mouth—early for his years. Most of the women in his life liked the less-than-perfect look. But it was his deep-seated confidence that attracted people to him. He prided himself on his ability to mediate disputes among family and friends. His tenderness with animals always provided a point of conversation with anyone he met. And, he loved dogs.

He was well read, with interests in European History and Western Civilization. The family maintained the culture within his home. He spoke both formal Italian as well as the Northern Italian Genovese dialect. He could get along in Spanish and French too, though he didn't have much opportunity to use French. Dogface's charm wasn't based on anything other than a quiet confidence mostly gained from his mother who was a supremely clear-headed and firm-thinking woman. His father, though strict and tough loved him and his family more than anything.

Late one summer night, he needed some alone-time in his car. A rain-shower ended and left the air thick and muggy. He headed toward the New York he grew up in. His thoughts went back in time. They took him to memories of one person in particular—a girl.

Her name was Yanit. Sal knew her well—they went to school together and even dated for a while. The relationship never took root, but they stayed in touch and got updates from one another. They had been close—like brother and sister.

Yanit Silver grew up in a simple Jewish home. Her parents were working class Jews. They were both educated but not into material pursuits. Their everyday dishes were plastic. They had a ***mezuzah*** * on the doorpost, but little faith in the house. Most Friday nights were spent with friends over dinner. The discussions were common—politics, community, social news, events, movies, and kids. There was always a connection to the Jewish people and Israel—though strictly secular.

Yanit's father was a plumber, and her mother was a school teacher. They both loved to sing and play ragtime music. Both were tolerant of others with friends of all colors, race, and religious faith. Their motto: *live and let live.* Yanit and Sal were neighbor kids who played together. School and other friends never broke the bond they had.

High school put Yanit's Jewish heritage in context. The historical contrasts and conflicts got her attention. She became involved in Jewish politics and yearned to study in Israel. So, she headed overseas after high school for a six-month study program arranged by her synagogue. But six months turned into five years. She mastered Hebrew, went to college, and graduated with degrees in Jewish Studies and Economics.

Yanit loved the history and culture of her people, yet she never considered herself religious. Her thoughts of God were rare and short-lived. God was for the scholars.

Before she left, Yanit joined a Zionist organization in Israel. She felt that Jews should spend some time in the land of their fathers. They should understand their history and see it up close. Still, she was a realist—she knew that commitment to Jewish history, land, or people had waned in America.

When she returned, she discovered Jews had less and less interest in their heritage. Her alarm also grew over the increase of anti-Semitism in America. Yanit expanded her personal study to gain an understanding of anti-Semitism and to research the history of the Holocaust.

All of Yanit's knowledge created a hyper-awareness of current events—local and global. Sal knew that recent incidents against Jews would turn Yanit's life upside down. He couldn't help but wonder and worry.

Sal's memories of Yanit brought pleasant emotions. He recalled her and remembered her look as "easy on the eyes." Her fawn eyes, freckled nose, and pleasant features could capture anyone's attention. Her warm spirit, kindness, and ability to connect drew others. She generated a sense of comfort, safety, and significance in those near her. He clung to those memories of her best and light-hearted years. Still, that was then and this was now.

Dogface's cell phone buzzed on his hip. He lifted the phone, looked at the caller, and shook his head in disbelief. He put the phone to his ear and heard the voice of an old friend—now agitated and shaken. "Dogs, I need to see you."

Sal was stunned to silence. *How in the world!* He wondered. *Why would she call me at this moment? Did my thoughts somehow travel and touch her?*

Just then, Yanit's words brought him back, "Dogs? Dogs, you there? I need to see you."

"Yanit. Uhhhh... of course! You name it: where and when?"

"I'm in the deep end—it's over my head, now." She spoke and sobbed in short bursts with gasps and gulps for air.

Sal was alarmed. "Dear, God! Yanit, this isn't like you. What in God's name is goin' on?"

"An attack. I saw, uh.... Oh, God.... It was... I mean, oh Dogs."

"Where was it? Did you actually see the attack?" Sal asked.

"Yes, it was in Queens," she gulped. I was walking to the subway to come home and I heard a scream. I looked across the street and two men were...." Yanit couldn't finish her sentence.

Yanit's sobs and sadness filled Sal's ears and went straight to his heart. She cried, "Oh, Dogs, I don't know where to turn." He offered what comfort he could, but she needed her moment.

Once she composed herself, Yanit said, "They were brutal. They just came in there and beat these two people senseless. I felt so helpless. I knew I had to get home and call you."

Then Yanit began to fill in the details of what she'd witnessed.

"This attack was on a small mom-n-pop business. It broke my heart. I could see and feel the violence get closer. The amount and nature of graffiti in the neighborhood has grown into something so ugly I can't even describe it. More pointed and profane messages focused on Jews. Our synagogues, cemeteries, and centers have been common targets. And the attacks...." She paused to clear the emotion from her throat. "Well, I mean... what I saw was brutal and brazen—open and unchallenged.

"I'm afraid that...." Yanit paused to rethink her words. But the pause was too long. Sal jumped in.

"What? What are you afraid of?"

"Well, it's just a sense—something I feel," Yanit hesitated.

"Yeah?" Sal poked. "What do you feel?"

"I'm afraid that all this is a whiff, a mere taste of what's to come."

"Come to think of it... " he said. "I've noticed the same things in my part of town. I didn't connect the dots till now. Now, I'm frightened—for you."

"Dogs, I just can't watch this happen. I've got to do something about it."

"Like what? What can I do? You know I'm all in."

"I need to come see you," Yanit insisted.

"Sure, of course.... Come to my folks' house. Have your parents join us, too. Tell them to come hungry. But, Yanit, what can I do now?"

"I don't know," she answered. "But I know one thing... we're gonna need help!"

In the weeks that followed, attacks against Jews spread up and down the East Coast. They became more regular and intense. The attacks grew from common crimes to cruel violence. Random graffiti turned to real threats. Vandalism ignited in destruction. Robbery became looting. Muggings morphed to murder. And peace in the Jewish community was displaced by panic and fear.

Racism is terrible. But anti-Semitism is born of evil itself. Yanit knew from history lessons that anti-Semitism starts with the people who surround the Jewish community. History told her that governments sometimes encouraged and even directed actions against the Jews. The troubles have often been triggered by harsh and outrageous rumors that become accusations... and then actions.

The libelous, false, and insightful book *The Protocols of the Learned Elders of Zion* was a best seller again among Muslims and Christians. *The Protocols* were proven to be baseless lies. Still, those lies buzzed in the air around local mosques and even some churches. It was all too familiar—echoes of libels sounded from pulpits generations before. Anti-Semitism of the worst sort took root within the shores of America.

> **From the Hand of Solomon the Wise**
> Proverbs 3:3
>
> Do not let kindness and truth leave you;
> Bind them around your neck,
> Write them on the tablet of your heart.

Chapter 6

Familia

Sal wanted this time with Yanit and her parents. He was worried about his friend. He hoped the support of family and friends would help her find some peace and perspective. He'd never seen her so shaken and vulnerable.

Yanit was NOT someone who could be intimidated or crossed—not without consequences. Sal remembered how in high school a boy had been careless with her heart. She set things straight with a personal visit to return a necklace and to reason with him. No words were exchanged, but she left in good spirits. The boy ran home for first-aid.

Witnesses spread the fracas all around school by the next day. Yanit was tight-lipped. On-the-other-hand the boys lips... well... they weren't tight. She washed all the blood off her jacket. Only one eraser-sized stain remained. It was her badge of honor. Other kids gave her kudos and laughed. Yanit didn't respond or laugh. She had only tears for wounds that needed time to heal.

One good thing came from the ordeal. Boys gave her a wide birth. And those who did approach her were serious and respectful. She liked that. Still, Yanit remained a vulnerable and caring soul. Her closest friends knew she was easily wounded. They also knew she could handle herself well.

And Sal, who was one of her closest friends, offered her the comfort and consolation she needed.

Then he told her, "You know, that kid was lucky. In fact, you may have saved his life."

"Huh? How'd I save him?" Yanit tilted her head and squinted her eyes.

With face straight and body tense, Sal said, "You got there before me."

But this night was different. The topic was serious, but vino, pasta, and spirit of *familia* would warm hearts.

Sal and his parents greeted Yanit, her mother Maria, and father Joe with open hands, hugs, and a kiss on each cheek. The families were familiar friends. To Yanit this was her second home. She'd often enjoyed dinner here. She learned about good pasta and those wonderful thick, garlicky, fragrant, and rich sauces long before they became so popular at local eateries. Her favorite was actually more gravy-like. The family called it *sugo*.

Everyone felt reconnected and got up-to-date on family news. So Yanit began to describe what she'd witnessed the night before. She explained the big picture of events in recent months. She tied many random events into a comprehensive and clear pattern.

The faces and silence around the room reflected the gravity and distress that gripped them. They searched one another's face without words. Expressions and some tears spoke for them.

"All of you know that I didn't intend to stay in Israel as long as I did. I left home with as much Jewish history any of you or my friends had. Like any average Jewish person in America. But in Israel something awoke inside of me. The people and the land captured my heart—so I stayed. I studied and learned the history of my people, and I discovered myself.

"It took very little education to shatter my innocence and my illusions. In study I spanned the years and the globe to crawl inside Jewish history and the horrors. I faced disbelief and denial at every turn. Mentors became my comforters. Professors were my tormentors. Still, they told me the truth. In time, my eyes were opened and my sense of security was ripped away. I became a Jew, and it scared the hell out of me!"

Yanit couldn't control the tears and quiver in her lip. She took a moment to dry her face and clear the emotion from her throat.

"And now, I see things happen here. I see things I can't believe... familiar events and patterns that have an unbroken link to the past. But no one else gets it! No one else sees it.

"I guess George Bernard Shaw was scary right, *we learn from history that we learn nothing from history.*" Yanit's emotions were still close to the surface. Every heart went out to her—every eye and ear was hers.

"I hate to drag any of you into this, but I... WE need your help. The Jews are not awake yet. But if this is what I think it is, it won't take long."

She finished talking and Sal's father Joe pushed his half finished pasta con pesto away. His big eyes looked at her with the love of a father. He got up and walked around to Yanit. She stood and fell into his extended arms. Then the sound of her sobs, Joe's comfort, and gentle hand that patted her back. This was *familia*. Needs were needs and *familia's* needs always came first.

"Yanit, honey, you are family to us. When Sal told us you needed help, I wondered if it might have to do with all this stuff we've been seeing. We are here for you and your family. The Jews are like our own," he calmly said to her.

Later that night, a telephone rang in a non-descript warehouse near the docks, down by the Battery. The rains stopped. The night air hung heavy with humidity. It was a tough part of town and one would probably have chosen another area for a leisurely evening stroll.

"Johnny, this is Joe. I need to see you tomorrow about an urgent matter dealing with my family."

Johnny DiMattea was a trusted friend of the Vicenzos and was one of those guys who just 'took care of things.' It wasn't what Joe said, it was the tone of his voice. He understood this to be a matter of the highest urgency and that was enough. He then made a few calls to 'arrange things.' He and his people would be ready for just about anything.

The next day, Joe, Sal and Johnny sat in the back room of the warehouse. The more they talked the more they began to realize that something so profound and bigger than anything they had ever done was about to hit them with a force that no one could have possibly foretold.

"We have work to do, my friend," Joe said. "You remember Yanit? She and Sal have been friends since they were kids. She was pretty ripped up—this anti-Semitism thing has been getting a lot of press lately. She saw some things," he explained.

"Yeah, so I've been hearing." Johnny wasn't much of a talker but was very perceptive and understood when things were heating up.

"She thinks this is going to get big. She needs our help," Joe said, leaving that comment hanging in the air. Somewhere behind them a fly buzzed near a light before the bug zapper got it.

Without fully realizing what she had set in motion, Yanit would soon become a central figure in Jewish efforts to fend off what was quickly becoming the biggest outbreak of anti-Semitism since World War II, and perhaps in history. They began mapping the strategy to help their old friends.

The next day, Johnny placed five calls. The first was to the head of the crane operators union.

The second call went directly to the president of a trucking company partly owned by the family.

The third call was placed to the president of the longshoremen's union.

The fourth went to a small cyber-security firm in New Jersey also well known to the family.

The fifth was to highly placed friends in the Coast Guard. Business was business and sometimes you needed to bend the rules a little. Five calls within five minutes set the plan in motion.

Johnny made one more call to Joe to reassure him everything would be all right.

"Don' worry about it."

> From the Pen of Isaiah the Prophet
> Chapter 60 verse 9
>
> Surely the coastlands will wait for Me;
> And the ships of Tarshish will come first,
> To bring your sons from afar,
> Their silver and their gold with them,
> For the name of the LORD your God,
> And for the Holy One of Israel
> Because He has glorified you.

Chapter 7

Preparations

A world away in Haifa, Israel's beautiful port city on the Mediterranean, a ZIM transport ship, the "Holy Tabernacle" began loading its precious cargo of Haifa oranges, food stuffs, manufactured goods, cosmetics, and "religious items."

Israel became a hub for its products and sold great volumes of cargo abroad. However, this shipment was different. It was destined for New York Harbor and for one very important customer. The shipment continued a pipeline of defense items that would soon find their way into Jewish hands and give the dispersed Israelis of the Diaspora their first taste of home in quite awhile.

Haifa oranges always tasted good when you were cleaning your guns.

ZIM is an Israeli international shipping concern. Founded in 1945, ZIM's first task was to transport Jewish refugees. Europe gave up all its displaced and captive Jews—free to find a new life. Many ships seized by the British mandate would be liberated and pressed into service by the shipping agency.

And where were the liberated Jews taken? They were transported to the British territory of Palestine—others to Cypress and new camps.

Just a few years later, during the War of Independence, ZIM became the sole maritime body associated with the fledgling Jewish state, hauling food, freight, military equipment, and exporting any goods it could stuff in its cargo holds. It is as much a national asset as it is a shipping company.

After the war, ZIM watched its business grow. New business opportunities saw the company shift to passenger travel, though it was short lived. By 1964, it ceased cruising and returned to cargo, its core competency. With its shipping business growing, the company began to add capacity and expanded into different types of shipping.

ZIM purchased several all-purpose vessels in the 1960s. They transported crude oil from Iran to Israel—until the Iranian revolution in 1979. They carried Israel's farm produce, manufactured goods, and high tech products. Israeli shipping took on cargo from various ports-of-call for transport across the globe.

The ZIM lines would benefit from new associations and friends, each, in turn becoming an integral cog in a machine that would later grow into the backbone of Jewish rescue efforts.

Nothing moved on the docks without Dogface's knowledge or the approval of the family. Once the weapons pipeline opened up for the Israel Defenses Forces of America (IDFA), the Vicenzos would ensure that there would be no break in delivery of the needed weapons and material. This order had 10,000 more Uzis, Galils, Galil snipers, and Tavors, M4 Flattops, one half ton of plastique or semtex (C4), a moldable substance that is much more stable as it is handled and prepared for use. It was also known as plastic explosive.

The Vicenzo family's vast network of friends, well placed in ports, docks, and warehouses all over the United States were about to be called on to deliver the most important favor of their long association.

The shipment would be a lifeline to those who couldn't defend themselves. Soon, ZIM container ships would dispense the tools of the trade for those awaiting them. Even though the general call to arms was still some time off, the process was moving forward.

Coupled with the receiving apparatus was a vast network of truck and rail transportation. There were also other family businesses. One such business—a network of garbage dumps across the country would pay big dividends soon. If the family did not own the dump and the trucks that went with it, they knew who did. They knew how to make things happen.

You could do a lot with a garbage dump and a warehouse.

> From Yad Yerimiyahu (the Hand of Jeremiah)
> Chapter 30 verse 18
>
> Thus says the LORD, Behold, I will restore the fortunes of the tents of Jacob And have compassion on his dwelling places; And the city will be rebuilt on its ruin, And the palace will stand on its rightful place.

Chapter 8

A Roof Over Their Heads

"Hello? Is this Modern Designs?"

"Yes, how may I help you?"

"Thanks, I need to speak with your company president, if possible."

"Who may I say is calling?"

"My name is Michael Wilson and I am representing a client of mine." The client happened to be the Jewish Agency, but that wasn't immediately discussed.

"That would be Jocelyn Anderson. What is this regarding?"

"I am interested in some modular housing, in fact a lot of it in a very short amount of time."

"Mrs. Anderson is not in the office right now, but I can reach her by cell, can you hold on while I track her down?"

"I'll hold," he said. When the young woman came back on the line, she had Ms. Anderson on hold. "Ok, I've got her on the line, go ahead."

"Is this Jocelyn Anderson?"

"Yes it is. How can I help you?"

"I represent an organization interested in your product.

"My client may have need for a lot of your product very soon. We will need to build a lot of homes and apartments for them, uh, rather quickly."

"Why are you calling us? We are not the largest modular home manufacturer."

"Well, it's not necessarily that easy to explain.

"There are some extenuating circumstances here that are somewhat difficult and complex. We've been searching for just the right supplier, and your firm is on top in the field. You have new developments and processes that we believe fit our needs."

"Well, I'm happy to talk to you. When do you want to discuss this idea of yours?"

"Tomorrow."

And so it was that a representative of the Jewish Agency set up a meeting with the owner of a medium sized modular housing company in America. It was not with the intent of purchasing product, but rather buying the company, moving it to Israel, and expanding the Israeli modular home building industry, currently the hottest business commodity in Israel, and soon to be throughout Europe and the United States.

Within six weeks, the Jewish Agency, through its American contacts purchased two dozen of these businesses. They merged them into one seamless firm with a cover company located in the Bahamas. Agency team members came to America to learn the ins-and-outs of the business. Agency managers placed huge orders for the needed supply components. This increased the backlog of each link in the supply chain. It's known as vertical integration. Israel could better control things if it controlled the supply chain.

Factories all over America and Europe sprang to life with orders to feed the new business entity. EL Al's recently purchased used Boeing 747 cargo aircraft and discarded U.S. C-17 cargo jets ferried materials, equipment, machinery, and huge inventories to Israel. The 747-9, the newest model of this flying warehouse, was made for this application. Operators of the aircraft were excited to use it. The C-17 could haul oversized cargo and had been the bulwark of America's foreign wars for almost forty years. The aircraft turned into a flying hospital within minutes when its floors and cargo section were reconfigured by the loadmasters.

When the companies merged as one large industrial concern, Desert Homes Incorporated became an industry leader in short order. It soon incorporated on the NASDAQ shooting to international prominence within that year. The company was wildly profitable because every unit had a buyer (mainly the Israeli government) to start, thus guaranteeing cash flow and profits.

With breakthrough desert living technology built into the units, it grabbed the attention of the industrialized world, for each unit was a self-sustaining powerhouse capable of not only supporting all of its energy needs, but even more to the point of recycling all water and waste. What energy not actually consumed or stored for short-term use, was returned to the local neighborhood 'grid' for use by others.

In fact, each home could compost all food product waste and turn it into a very useful fertilizer. The designers treated the human waste with special environmentally safe chemicals and converted it for industrial use. Roofing materials also doubled as solar collectors, meaning that once the roof was completed, the house was a virtually one big solar unit. Those solar roof panels ran all energy needs with storage batteries backing up everything.

The homes came equipped with wall-sized widescreen entertainment centers, computer panels in every room, and self-sustained electricity running all appliances and built-ins. The walls contained a new, environmentally safe and renewable type of insulation, important in the desert environment and capable of heating the home in the dead of winter or helping cool it in the blistering heat of the desert summer.

Israel became the world's first nation to pull itself off its national grid, thanks largely to companies such as Better Place. More recently, the technology was coming into heavy demand in the East and the West as the industrial giants continued to deplete their resources and grow more and more dependent on Middle East oil.

They made arrangements with key contacts in the U.S. and placed friendly customs agents in strategic positions as the imports made their way through the paper jungle that was the American import system. Among these agents were certain Christians and others the Vicenzos knew and trusted.

Secretly, and imperceptibly, the 747 return flights were bringing back something to America as well since it made absolutely no sense to fly back an empty plane designed to carry lots of cargo and passengers.

Disguised as machine parts for heavy equipment, the Israeli export agents, through an elaborate chain of contacts set up for this very purpose, shipped what would become an integral piece of future ground operations in America. For these were the parts and equipment needed to form the backbone of the agile mechanized units made so famous in all of Israel's wars along with the technicians to assemble, fix, and operate that equipment. Combined with the ZIM shipments, Israeli planners forged the framework for eventual rescue of America's Jews.

CHAPTER EIGHT: A Roof Over Their Heads

In came vehicle bodies, engines, tires, treads, side armor, all manner of engines, and other components for tanks, trucks, armored vehicles, jeeps, and staff vehicles. Each package was cleverly devised and broken down to be invisible to any inspections. Of course, as the planners in the Jewish Agency knew, it should never get that far as certain friends within America's infrastructure should have made advanced contacts and plans to ensure that all equipment and parts arrived safely, securely, and without the prying eyes of uncooperative border officials.

With friends on the ground, arrangements were made to ensure that all materials would arrive at their future destinations. Up to now, nobody, not the local police departments, nor the FBI, nor the CIA, no one figured out that Israel was preparing for hostilities with America, just in case it came to that.

Once on the ground, port authorities checked off the massive containers. Equipment handling operators picked up the containers and then loaded them onto the waiting trucks or flatbed railcars, all of which in some fashion were linked into a complex web of trucking companies run through the Vicenzo family network.

What couldn't be loaded onto a flatbed railcar went by truck and what couldn't fit into a truck found its way by flatbed rail. Overland shipping ended at a string of warehouses strategically placed around the American landscape and within easy access to critical roadways, airports, and shipping terminals. Many were near airports. From arrival to final destination, Israel, anticipating future events well in advance, prepared its way through these long cultivated contacts. Plans were coming along well.

Business was good and Dogface was pleased.

From HaYad Moshe — The Hand of Moses
Deuteronomy 28:64-68

Moreover, the LORD will scatter you among all peoples, from one end of the earth to the other end of the earth; and there you shall serve other gods, wood and stone, which you or your fathers have not known. Among those nations you shall find no rest, and there will be no resting place for the sole of your foot; but there the LORD will give you a trembling heart, failing of eyes, and despair of soul. So your life shall hang in doubt before you; and you will be in dread night and day, and shall have no assurance of your life. In the morning you shall say, 'Would that it were evening!' And at evening you shall say, 'Would that it were morning!' because of the dread of your heart which you dread, and for the sight of your eyes which you will see. The LORD will bring you back to Egypt in ships, by the way about which I spoke to you, 'You will never see it again!' And there you will offer yourselves for sale to your enemies as male and female slaves, but there will be no buyer.

From The Covenant of the Islamic Resistance Movement (Hamas)
INTRODUCTION

Our struggle against the Jews is very great and very serious. It needs all sincere efforts. It is a step that inevitably should be followed by other steps. The Movement is but one squadron that should be supported by more and more squadrons from this vast Arab and Islamic world, until the enemy is vanquished and Allah's victory is realized.

Chapter 9

The Planning

The planning took them more than two years. Hatched in the rugged and mysterious mountains of Afghanistan, 10 squads of Allah's best spent the time in the harshest of conditions. Bearing incredibly hot and buggy summers then long, frigid winters, the men and women toughened under the care and feeding of their leader, Abdul Aziz Rachman. Rachman was a British subject, born and raised in London.

Rachman had been at this for a very long time. He and his network of intelligence officers fanned out across the American landscape. They surveyed, studied, and shaped a series of coordinated attacks. Each assault would target their most hated sworn enemy—the Jews.

Passage in and out of the United States was easy, their passports and traveling documents as clean as a whistle. Despite America's best efforts Rachman's little army could not be kept out. The intent was to put the Jews on the run and further promote the disintegration of the West's confidence in keeping out the marching progress of Islam. These plans, long in the making, were finally about to come to fruition. ***Allahu Akhbar!****

Thirty years passed since the 9/11 attacks. Allah's foot soldiers from Al Qaida, related networks, and other loose alliances had kept a low profile. They knew America had a short memory. It would soon forget or grow beyond that terrible day.

Yet that day was a perennial day of remembrance and celebration for Rachman and his young agents. This current operation readied troops born after 9/11 or too young to remember. Still, they all knew the historic events—planes, Pentagon, Twin Towers, chaos, collapse, courageous heroes of Allah's, nineteen martyrs, and glory.

Fears of terrorism in America had waned. The occasional arrest of some sleeper cell would hit the news and America would breathe a sigh of relief. America had developed sort of a collective ADHD or Alzheimer's—on a grand scale. She felt angst and anxiety of the future, 401K failures, vanishing pensions, and the soaring cost of health care. In addition, family dreams, demands, and expectations weighed on them. Frets over college tuition, a daughter's wedding, vacations, retirement, and end of life care sapped Americans' energy.

CHAPTER NINE: The Planning

Where would the money come from? How could it all happen? What would the future hold?

The dollar continued its downward spiral. America appeared to be strong. But many warned that she was on the verge of collapse.

Dreams of SUVs, second homes, vacation cabins, trips to the river, lake, or ocean began to slip away. The price of gasoline devoured discretionary funds. Lives of freedom, leisure, and the resources to play belonged only to the wealthy.

The American consumer was on the hunt for a scapegoat. The perfect storm had begun to brew. The fuel and fodder to fire an American Jihad only needed a spark.

America was a favorable environment for Islam. Millions of Muslims had reached America's shores. **C.A.I.R.** * reshaped its public campaign to project a positive perception of Muslims. Islam was portrayed as a non-threatening, peace loving, lifestyle and religion.

Another change in perception began at the same time. Anti-Zionism (or anti-Semitism) began to grow beyond the visible and vocal fringe of hate groups and graffiti. There were subtle shifts in public opinion. Some Christian groups left long-held loyalties to the Jewish people. Others began a dialogue—even courtship—with Islam. The American landscape was in transition. Every change signaled trouble for the Jews. And the wedge to separate the Jews and Israel from America grew with every blow.

Tall and powerfully built, Rachman sported his mother's jet black eyes, his father's thick dark hair, and his grandmother's surprisingly light skin. His even, white teeth flashed strength and power. His beard, equally dark and thick, made an otherwise pleasant face much more menacing. People were drawn to his charismatic charm. He was easy going in company, aloof, once attainable with the ladies, though now that was a distant memory. There were new challenges now, and he would be there to reap the rewards. He could not afford to be distracted.

His parents, honest and hard-working engineering and technical professionals escaped Iraqi infighting and finally tired of the strong armed local chieftains who always seemed to control things there. Civil wars within civil wars. The story was always the same. The local tribal affiliations always trumped the national "Government" (if you could call it a government). They lived through so many ruthless regional conflicts that an escape to anywhere was better than the life they had. So, to England they went and set out to begin their lives anew.

Their third child was born and Rachman's parents had settled into a comfortable life in north London. All their children were now English citizens and, as far as they could tell, were loyal subjects to the crown. Both parents worked for the Geneva Corporation for years now, slowly moving up in their fields. They changed their names to blend into London society. Mohammad had become Mo and Afraima (or Fruitful) had become Afri. They made friends with everyone including some Jewish couples with whom they enjoyed many evenings out at the theater, local dining establishments, and work engagements. They became westernized. Their muted Muslim faith was not the powerful influence it would be to their children.

There were no hints of falling under the hypnotic pull of the ***muzzheins*** or the growing Islamic movement in London and England. Where just a few years before, there was barely any Muslim presence, there was now a transcendent religious buzz in the air. Middle Eastern restaurants were found in every neighborhood, it seemed. Small shopping areas now sported such Arab necessities such as hookah bars, hallal meat markets, Islamic bookstores, and mosques, lots of mosques.

The mosques seemed to pop up almost overnight. Women in ***burkahs*** were a common sight. They followed paces behind their bearded men, who seemed to proclaim: *I am master and lord of my domain.* In this influence and environment Abdul Aziz Rachman became a believer in the Islamic faith.

He became friends with a local Islamic youth minister in his junior year at Oxford. Without a thought, this mild mannered engineering student was swept up by the magnetic power of Islam. He began with attendance at Friday night prayers in the local mosque. He bought ornamental prayer rugs, prayed the obligatory five times per day, grew and groomed his beard, lost his fancy wardrobe, wore the long garments associated with observant Muslim men, and embraced the lifestyle of the devout. His world changed. Internal attitudes and attachments transformed his outward actions and appearance.

His mentor and imam, Jamal Kareem Ibraham, was a brilliant scholar. Born in Iran, he had become an expert in ***Sharia law****, was an accomplished musician who played ten instruments, spoke six languages, and wrote poetry. His preaching style was akin to Martin Luther King's emotional, powerful, and compassionate oratory. Also apparent were influences from Louis Farrakhan and Osama Bin Laden.

But his real love was working the recruiting tables at the universities. Ibraham also taught at the university, using his PhD in Mathematics as a stepping stone to gain his young charges' trust. After all, how could any of them go wrong with such an important fellow in their lives?

CHAPTER NINE: *The Planning*

Ibraham was not a big man nor particularly handsome. Thinning hair and thick glasses certainly lent an air of academia and intellectualism to his spare frame. Countless hours spent in his studies had made stressed his eyes, hence the need for the ever-thickening glasses. But his charismatic nature drew recruits to him like a moth to a flame.

Belying his mild mannered public persona, Ibraham was also an expert in explosives, small arms, and interrogation techniques. Water boarding was a joke to him. He knew how to get his "guests" to tell their stories.

He was well read in the literature of the East and the West. Better to know and understand your enemies than to leave everything to guess work. He learned the old western adage: *Keep your friends close, your enemies closer.*

Ibraham became an expert in international politics, business, military tactics, and of course his beloved mathematics. No longer would Islam suffer at the hands of the West. It was now armed, educated, and sophisticated, far beyond what the West knew or wanted to know or believe. The deception was fully engaged. He knew all about the Nobel Peace prize dominance of the Jews and hoped one day to train up Muslim minds to unseat them.

Rachman began his Islamic studies listening to the lectures in mosques. Though he grew up with Jewish friends, some of whom he had known his whole life, he now began to see them as the blood-suckers they were. The lectures at the mosque were lively, filled with emotional tales of how the Jews had stolen the Land of Palestine. He learned of the brave Palestinian freedom fighters that resisted the Zionists at every turn. He began to question all of his learning and reading of his education. As he grew closer to his student, the teacher realized what a prize he had. This young man had potential to lead, something he didn't always see in his recruits. This was a true protégé, smart, quick, and willing to take the measured risk that all actions required.

"My young friend, it is good to see you tonight," the teacher said.

"Thank you. It's been a long day but I'm ready for the word of Allah."

"Good, good. Tonight, we will study much in the way of the one true God. But first, let us begin with our mission. The Zionists... we know how they usurped this land. It is the long history of the Zionist beast to steal what isn't his and to turn away those who lived there. The Jews make this **nakba*** into policy. They kill the innocent and then claim to be the victims by hiding behind a few killings by the Germans in the Great War.

So the lectures went, session after session—the facts twisted at will. Ibraham made no mention of the 1947 United Nations declaration, denying the fact that there had always been a Jewish presence in the land, and of course never mentioning the Balfour declaration. The facts were to be manipulated by the wiser. No more would their brothers suffer at the hands of those who take and never give back. He was to join the liberators and free the land from its oppressors. He never thought to check facts.

Rachman trained with them first in street protests. Then he took up small arms against the Jewish invaders. Later he learned how to handle, manufacture, and fit explosives for a number of applications. He had become expert in the assembly of explosive vests for martyr heroes in Palestine.

He could assemble such weapons, witness such carnage, and praise such effort because of Ibraham's words. His mentor often said:

> Never forget: the suicide bomber is a warrior. He kills Israelis who appear to be civilians. Every Israeli carries a weapon at one time or another. They all have had or will have military training. They dress as civilians, but they are weapons used against us. They are always military targets, even the children!

The Palestinians had become brothers to Rachman. Their struggles were his struggles. He witnessed the next generation being readied for the cause. They were taught to extol the work of the Jihad and the virtues of the martyrdom as a bomber. He marveled at the brave mothers and grandmothers who were willing to sacrifice their own to the cause. It was now his cause.

Rachman called a morning meeting to finalize plans as he remembered his first action in the orchards so long ago.

"My brothers and sisters, our time is almost upon us."

His piercing eyes surveyed the room. Fifty of his now well-trained little army was at the ready, prepared to give their all to the mission. Death was not unexpected and, in fact, almost welcomed. He had recruited them patiently, steadily, and had lovingly trained their minds as well as their hands. The culture of death, so prevalent in these past years in Islamic circles, became life itself. The delicious irony did not escape him.

Where the Jews worked to preserve life, Islamic killing parties like his worked to facilitate death, believing that it would release them to a paradise filled with their every desire. Taking Jews with them seemed as sweet as Allah's paradise, like the nectar of the gods. Indeed, it was Allah's will they carry out this mission.

"In the next two months, we'll work our way to America," Rachman announced. "May you all survive the actions we are about to launch on the Great Satan. Yet paradise awaits those whom Allah's will has chosen. Have no fear of death. You carry out a holy mission for the Almighty.

"All is well—on schedule and according to plan. We have many friends in North America. The American Muslims of the Nation of Islam are eager to support us. They've awaited this opportunity for years. They are with us."

CHAPTER NINE: *The Planning*   Page 55

A young man stood and asked, "But will they fight the Jew—a fellow American?"

Rachman answered, "You are right to ask that question, my young brother. *Can we trust Nation of Islam in America?* Listen—I will read what their current leader, a Louis Farrakhan disciple proclaimed. He spoke to hundreds of thousands of American Muslims in Washington D.C. Hear his words then answer your own question."

> My brothers in the most holy faith... do not be deceived—the Jew is not our friend. No. No.
>
> The Jew in Palestine, the Jew in Europe, the Jew in Asia, the Jew in America, the Jew wherever he may be found... is not our friend. No. No.
>
> The Jew has fallen into the pit. He sits in the slime of his gutter religion. The Jew spews forth his sickness in speech born in hell. No. No. The Jew is not our friend.
>
> Today, I stand before my brothers—to stand against the Jew. I say to Jew: You wicked deceiver! You liar and fraud! You are the Black man's enemy! You are the new American threat! You are not our friend. No. No.
>
> You have sucked the blood of our people. You have stolen our wages. You have sacrificed our young men and women in your wars. You have enriched yourselves at our expense and upon our backs. No. No. To the Jew I say... You are not our friend.
>
> You are the Synagogue of Satan. Serpents born of hell. Sorcerers within society. You cast spells upon America and its government.
>
> Resist me as you will. You may even crucify me. But know this... Allah will crucify you!

"Years before at the Savior's Day Rally, Louis Farrakhan, the founder of the Nation of Islam, assaulted the Jews with these words:

> You expect Muslims to stand against suicide bombers. You expect us to say, "wait a minute, you do not kill innocent people for political purposes." You want us to say that and if we don't say it you rise up against us. But we don't hear you correcting your brothers because what they're doing is creating hatred for Israel and hatred for America that looks the other way while the Palestinians are being slaughtered.

"Farrakhan spoke for an entire generation of outraged Muslims. But more, he laid the foundation for the zealous generation that followed. He exposed the Jews for who they are and what they've done. So now... they are about to pay the ultimate price for their government manipulations, Palestinian murders, and the ultimate desecration of Islam."

Rachman turned to the one who asked the earlier question. He stroked his beard and asked, "So my young brother... *Can the Nation of Islam in America be trusted?* Allah be praised, yes! The Nation of Islam stands at our side. Their hearts and lives are with us. They have been prepared and ready to strike for years. With American Muslims we see many new friends coming to join us. We have one heart and mind. And we cannot be stopped.

"The Gaza conflict back 2009, the threats against Iran, the attacks against Syria, and the many conflicts with Lebanon are proof. Israel and its international Jewish cabal have been and still are the world's primary threat to peace. In their eyes, Israeli responses to a few homemade missiles, harmless really, were always disproportional. The Goldstone Report condemned the Jewish state for that very reason.

"Why can't Israel and the Jews just leave the poor Palestinians alone to figure things out for themselves? Why did they always have to threaten war and use their military might against a largely unarmed populace?"

Public opinion was tilting away from534

a pro-Jewish perspective once again. Large blocks of Christian Americans began to see the light. Many of their leaders claimed that these weren't the Jews of the Bible. Even well-known and respected pastors admitted that current Israel was far from the Israel of God.

Islam had a voice, too. It began to flex political muscle and make itself known. America's religious and ethical base began to move from its "Judeo-Christian" moorings toward a new "Islamo-Christian" identity. The holy month of Ramadan was declared an unobserved holiday on American calendars. And bills before Congress proposed recognition for a number of ***Eids**** festivals. Select U.S. Postage stamps had featured Muslim *Eids* since 2001.

They believed it, the Europeans, those of the many nations in Africa, Russia, and of course, all of the Islamic countries believed it as did governments and peoples in North America. The United Nations continued its anti-Jewish, anti-Israel diatribe at almost every opportunity. Islam was merely defending itself against an encroaching enemy, and in so doing, gained a beachhead in the war for legitimacy in those Western nations, something it sought for decades.

The term "interfaith dialog" was a new catch phrase. Many Christians now understood and embraced their Islamic neighbors. Churches sponsored conferences while Imams extolled the virtues of a new Christian/Islamic brotherhood of peace, either hinting at or verbally attacking Jewish institutions, businesses, or leaders as the last obstacles to global peace and security.

The pastors of many large and well known evangelical churches and mainstream Christian denominations traveled to Muslim nations. They went to observe, study, and understand Islam. They sought similarities between their Bible and the Quran. They discovered a common enemy. The Bible was and would remain the Word of God. Still, the Quran, like Islam, was a part of world history with events and influences not found in Christian scripture or experience.

Their brand of Christianity had little place for Jews. These leaders believed that the Jews had become the Synagogue of Satan. They had taught all this for years—to some degree or another. Many of these pastors, priests, and ministers adopted and preached **Replacement Theology*** that excluded Israel and the Jews.

They understood that the Christian Church Universal (believers in Jesus Christ) had replaced the Jews as God's people. Jews rejected God's Son—and now God rejected them. All the future promises, prophecies, and purposes for Israel found in scripture were now for the Church. This theology had grown for about 500 years. But it had exploded to infect most of the established and institutional church within the last 75 years.

The well-read and savvy Rachman knew all these things. He saw the attachments and advantages in this Christian development. He also knew enough business to predict the trends and times to come. Economic hardships would continue to shrink lifestyles and sour attitudes in America. Friendships, loyalties, commitments, and even civility would be affected by the dollar.

Christianity continued to fragment further into more and more denominations and sub-denominations, and would be hardly recognizable to its founders. The further it fractured, the more anti-Semitic it became. The more anti-Semitic it became, the more it fractured.

Recruits were found among many of those impacted by the difficult economic times. They stood ready, a silent army, to work with the *Children of the Crescent*, to crush and eliminate the Jewish voice and influence once and for all. Traditional enemies became friends—skinheads working alongside of the Nation of Islam, Christians, new allies, and a new reality for a new age. It was a new harmonic convergence of Biblically cataclysmic proportions.

From the Hand of the Psalmist (T'hilim)
Psalms 83:1-8

O God, do not remain quiet; do not be silent and, O God, do not be still. For behold, Your enemies make an uproar, and those who hate You have exalted themselves. They make shrewd plans against Your people, and conspire together against Your treasured ones. They have said, "Come, and let us wipe them out as a nation, that the name of Israel be remembered no more." For they have conspired together with one mind against You. They make a covenant. The tents of Edom and the Ishmaelites, Moab and the Hagrites, Gebal and Ammon and Amalek, Philistia with the inhabitants of Tyre, Assyria also has joined with them. They have become a help to the children of Lot.

From the Pen of Jeremiah the Prophet 16:16

Behold, I am going to send for many fishermen, declares the LORD, and they will fish for them; and afterwards I will send for many hunters, and they will hunt them from every mountain and every hill and from the clefts of the rocks.

Chapter 10

Hunters of Men

Rachman could see it in his charges' eyes. They were ready to embark on the greatest adventure of their lives. He went on with his speech.

"So, the balance of public opinion in America continues to tip in our favor. The Jews don't have the control they once did. I have been reading the American press. In the last 2 years they have added another measure to what they call their leading economic indicators."

Rachman lifted papers and continued, "This poll asked the Americans, 'Do you believe the Jews are, in any way responsible for the economic problems America faces?' And last month, the results indicated that 60% believed they did!" He was excited now, waving his arms in animated bursts of energy. His small audience hung on every word as he continued.

"They believe the Jews still have much influence, much because of the American Israel Political Action Committee (AIPAC). But that will only go so far because public opinion is turning against them.

"Circumstances favor our mission," he added, pausing for effect, and flashing his smile. "We have them where we want them." He scanned his followers' eyes, all eagerness and intensity fixed on him.

Islam was gaining ground, not only at the end of a gun but was winning the war of hearts and minds. Another generation of Palestinian children had grown up with the same hatred as that of their fathers, looking at the Zionist enemy with contempt and disdain. Their entire culture was well-tuned to hate. Textbooks denied the Holocaust, glorified suicide bombers, and even denied the existence of Israel. It was the Jews who kept them enslaved in Gaza, the West Bank, or behind the walls of separation. Over the few decades since, the Islamic population exploded in America.

"As we speak, arrangements are being readied for you. You will come into America through several entry points: Canada, through Mexico, and through various major American cities. There will be safe houses for you in each city. We have chosen each of these because we know that in two months, on the tenth of that month, our planners have arranged targets having one thing in common. I will not reveal that to you just yet because, in case you are caught, the less you know now the better.

"You will contact our friends in these cities, where through our cutout networks you will receive your orders. We have arranged secure laptops have designed intranet-style internal networks invisible to public prying. Your training here and in the past two years in our mocked up American cities, have well prepared you for your targets.

"Many Christians have been enlisted for our cause. You will meet them and may not even know it. They will be the ones who greet you at the airport, rent you the cars you will need, they will be your waiters in restaurants, and they will be your maids in the hotels where you stay." His methodical and hypnotic lecture continued.

"Our friends in Mexico have tunneled under the Mexican-American border for years. They will provide the means you need. You'll be met with weapons, ammunition, clothing, and many other necessary item. We have a powerful army of supporters. The Americans have no idea."

The network of tunnels came up in homes near the borders in San Diego, Nogales, and other communities in the Southwest United States. What wasn't hauled above ground was making it into the U.S. underground.

"When you land, you will proceed to the car rental agency. We have chosen an agency called *Company Car*—a generic, low-profile operation. Once you arrive at your destinations, your contacts will provide packets with new your new identifications, passports, maps, and untraceable credit cards. Your safe houses are all arranged. Each of you will carry a cell phone with the latest technology. Your laptops all have the latest and most advanced encryption, and as I mentioned before, are impervious to snooping."

This last point was such delicious irony for the encryption software installed on the computers was of Israeli (or Jewish) make and origin... made by the very infidels who they would be hunting very soon. That made Rachman smile.

"To paraphrase a Bible verse a Christian once told me, 'You will become *hunters* of men,' he chuckled, the irony again, not lost on him.

"Their Jesus would be very proud."

They laughed because they knew that the Jesus of the Quran had special plans for the Jews. He was not the Jesus of the Bible. Sadly, most Christians didn't know their Bibles well enough to discern the difference. But the Muslims knew THEIR Jesus very well.

He began to hand out the initial contact packets and surveyed the room for any team member who did or did not fully understand the gravity of the mission. He was very perceptive and could almost smell dishonesty or lack of will in his subjects. He sensed none of that today. His hard work and theirs was about to pay off.

And in the Southwest and Western United States, no one could quite explain when it started. For some time now, there had been a growing undercurrent of interest, almost obsession, in certain rabbinical circles about the Exodus from Egypt. It started with two of them.

> From the Prophet Joel
> Chapter 2, Verse 28
>
> **T**hus says the LORD, It will come about after this that I will pour out My Spirit on all mankind; And your sons and daughters will prophesy, your old men will dream dreams, Your young men will see visions.

Chapter 11

Dreams, Visions, & Memories

The old rabbi awoke with a start. That same dream again—as if he was walking with the great Hebrew prophet, Moses himself, wandering in the Sinai desert! This was the seventh straight night he had the same dream. But what made this stranger still was that it seemed more like, what, a vision?!? It was so real, he could almost smell the animals, hear the children, and taste the desert dust.

In the dream he saw boiling clouds of dust several miles wide and high. Was that the Pillar of Smoke by day and the Flame by night? It seemed to consume everything. There was a loud din of animals, children, adults, so loud it sounded like a rushing wind, like the ***Ruach HaKodesh**** of God.

He saw millions of them on the march—like a scene from Exodus. Many were singing what seemed like some sort of praises to the God of heaven. Others grumbled just as the Scriptures said they did.

Rabbi Chaim Wasserman, now in his 70's, led an Orthodox congregation in Dallas, Texas. And, yes, he wore cowboy boots. His congregation was the largest of its kind in the great state. It had grown these past few years and represented a strong Orthodox Jewish community.

Though it seemed an unlikely place for Jews, Texas actually attracted many for its vibrant and growing business climate. And, of course, the exploding demand for precious gems and metals such as gold, silver, and platinum was another draw for these people. His congregation was made up of diamond cutters, precious gem brokers, gold and silver traders, oilmen, gun shop owners, et al.

The rabbi sat up, struggled for his breath, and clutched his chest. He sat still, composed himself, and focused on his racing heart. Tiny droplets of sweat gathered on his wrinkled brow. The dreams were beginning to trouble him. His wife Esther woke up at the same moment.

"Nu?" he asked, looking at her.

"So," Same dream again," she replied, calmer than he, but still somewhat shaken.

"I'm beginning to think these dreams are no coincidence." Silently, Esther nodded in agreement. Something was up.

Of course, they both were familiar with Moses and the story of the Exodus. Through the years, Chaim tutored Esther in the Hebrew Scriptures. She mastered the Hebrew language and studied the Talmud and Jewish history as well.

Chaim, though steeped in the traditions, rather enjoyed their banter as Esther would bring up questions or perspectives on the holy books that would send Chaim reeling. He would then call on his brother Eleazer or his other rabbinical colleagues for answers, never wanting to appear to his lifetime mate as if he were arrogant. She could always tell when she stumped him because he would simply go silent, stroke his beard, or rub his forehead.

Esther knew him well and understood when to probe and when to retreat. Their gentle way with one another stood the test of time and anyone who knew them grew to respect and trust their wisdom and judgment about a lot of life's puzzles and problems.

When the children came, Chaim and Esther took special pride to raise them right. They grew up with a strong scriptural foundation from Chaim, were well schooled and learned their science, technology, and mathematics from their mother.

The two children, David and Shara, would go on to accomplish much- David as a doctor and Shara as a university professor. They would bring their parents *great nachas* (joy), thus giving their parents many opportunities to *kvell* (burst with pride). But those dreams.

"These dreams must mean something. Both of us... how can this be?"

Chaim looked at his wife again rubbing his forehead, his fingers busy twirling his graying beard.

The dreams ended abruptly every time. In one dream, he saw Mount Sinai in the distance. The tribes were camped around the Holy Tabernacle where he could see Moses setting up the tent's curtains, boards, and all the items that made up the strange looking rectangular structure. He could see the bright weavings covering the main structure and then looking down a little, he could also see the bronze laver, and the place of sacrifice.

Another vivid dream startled him. as he watched the animals led to the sacrificial slaughter. He could hear the braying of the oxen and the bleating of the sheep. He could see the sounds and sights of so much death. He could see the blood, so much blood, smell the burning flesh. It was all so real. God made the price for sin so overpowering to the Children of Israel. The sights, smells, and noises assaulted and overpowered all five senses.

But why? And, why he and Esther? And why now?

> **From the Hand of Isaiah the Prophet**
> Chapter 26, verse 20
>
> Come, my people, enter into your rooms and close your doors behind you; Hide for a little while Until indignation runs its course.

Chapter 12

Hiding the Jews

Yanit's organizing skills were paying off.

As the early warning signals became more and more clear, she knew what the mission was and what she had to do. The campaign started with a few local churches and synagogues in her area, then began to take off. The effort now consumed her.

Thousands of phone calls, emails, appeals sent through electronic media to churches, Jewish institutions, websites, and social networking sites recruited an army of volunteers and concerned members of the communities.

The effort led many to learn of the tiny Southern French village of Le Chambon sur Lignon during World War II and the miracle that happened there. She used that learning to help her prepare the rescue plan. If this was going to work, it would take many Le Chambons. And many dedicated townspeople.

In that town, more than 5,000 Jewish refugees, exhausted from climbing through the Pyrenees, found sanctuary in the village supposedly occupied by descendents of the Huguenots, a Middle Age French Protestant movement. The villagers recognized the times for what they were and as the Jews began to arrive in the middle of the night, they simply found hiding places for their guests.

The strange thing was that the townspeople rarely spoke with one another about events, and chose instead to go about their daily chores and work. The less said to one another the better. They hid the desperate Jews in barns, homes, schools, wherever they could without being detected.

Years later, when a documentary crew came to film the town and tell the rescue story, they were met with a general incredulity-the townspeople didn't feel they had done anything special.

"Had we organized, it wouldn't have worked," one elderly townswoman answered. "It was our Christian duty to protect God's people."

Yanit was taken with the story. It taught her about self-sacrifice and *leaderless leadership*. She asked herself over and over again, *how does that work? How is it that success happens even with no leaders to lead?*

The first wave of the campaign soon led to a frenzied speaking tour. It was slow to build momentum at first. But Yanit gained traction once she was better known in the neighborhoods. She stumped and spoke like a politician in a campaign. And her efforts bore fruit. Grass roots organizations popped up all over the nation.

Yanit and Dogface also recognized an opportunity when they saw one- the Vicenzo garbage dumps. When Dogface mentioned his idea to Yanit, she was intrigued.

"We can use the dumps as temporary half way houses for those with nowhere to go," he suggested.

"I'm listening," she said.

"We have facilities all over the country. Once we get the Jews out of the neighborhoods, we can set them up in the dumps. It won't be easy and it won't be the Ritz. Still, we can hide them. Many of our dumps are in rural or forested areas. We can build some temporary shelters. It'll be like campgrounds."

"I remember some World War II reading about how the Partisans lived in the forests, in the shadows of the surrounding society. Many others were hidden by friends who risked their lives to do so. I also remember they formed an underground to help the Jews get out of there but they often stayed in homes, farms, anywhere they could until they were escorted out of danger," she said, as she built in her mind, a network of different support communities.

Her voice trailed off at that moment for it seemed like an incredibly complex task, but she began to see a ray of sunshine through the clouds. Her deep knowledge about the Holocaust but also of other historical events such as Chmelnicki or numerous European pogroms quickened this problem solving exercise.

As she pondered these, other ideas grew in her mind. She ticked off the issues in her mind: transportation, food, clothing, children and their needs, hundreds of logistics challenges to think about. She sensed there wasn't much time. She also knew that when the wheels began turning, there would be no way to stop them. Dogface interrupted her thoughts.

"One thing we do know is that there's more chance we could be discovered... satellite technology, cell phone cameras, who knows what- could easily betray our efforts."

"That's the bad news. The good news is that we have a much quicker capability to communicate. Once the word is out, we can mobilize quickly and hopefully more efficiently." Yanit sensed opportunity where Dogface played devils' advocate.

"And we don't know who our friends are. I suspect many will come forward to offer help and sanctuary."

Both of them could see hundreds of thousands in need of refuge. They both envisioned and understood themselves to be responsible for that safe place. Whatever the amount of time, there would be sanctuary for those who waited to be airlifted to Israel. All this would take the family's entire resource network. And it would require Yanit's best organizing skills.

Yanit's efforts combined with the Vicenzo network to make an interesting partnership. She discovered churches willing to help. She awoke to the fact that the Jewish community simply would not believe what was happening. They were engrossed in their lives that they were blind to the disaster that loomed ahead.

"We've had hundreds of churches step up. Some are saying that they already are working on the underground networks in their communities. It's pretty remarkable."

And so garbage dumps under control of the family quietly built hiding places for an eventual underground. Construction crews loyal to the family, largely made up of Bible believing Christians and others sympathetic to the Jews built a network of small shelters capable of providing relief to those refugees, way stations of sorts as they would embark on their final destinations.

"The camps will provide temporary housing for about two million, if need be. Once the Jews are gone, there may be need to house those of us who are supporting the effort."

Her words to Dogface carried conviction and confidence, but concern for the helpers. She had heard stories of end-times prophecies in the Bible but they seemed so distant to her. She had spent little time in the New Testament which actually predicted huge slaughters of Christians and new Bible Believers but she couldn't see that as an issue in this case.

"I hate to think that it will come to that, but from what we've been seeing, things are getting worse. I'm sure you saw the story the other day of a senior center that was taken over and the residents held hostage in Miami," Dogface mentioned.

Yanit was silent. She indeed remembered the story for it raised the very real and ugly possibility of that type of event coming to America's shores. It was one thing to anticipate such an event, but it was entirely another to see it happen.

"Yeah, thankfully the police were able to kill those guys," she recalled. Her voice trailed off.

"Dogs, you know what? They are going to hit at our weak underbelly... kids and seniors, I can feel it," she said.

"I think you're right Yanit. The Jews have always valued their elderly and their children... their future and their past.

"We need to put the word out that every facility will need security beefed up. We have to get the word out to the synagogues and the community centers. We may not be able to prevent every occurrence but we can certainly begin preparations. If we can't be everywhere at once, we certainly can increase cameras, early warning systems, maybe even install some sort of lockdown mechanism that would protect the kids and the seniors.

Do you think they'll listen?"

From the Broadway Musical:
Fiddler on the Roof

*Matchmaker, matchmaker,
make me a match,
find me a find,
catch me a catch....*

Chapter 13

Summer Camp

When Chaim and Esther met 30 years before, at a children's summer camp, they were both youth counselors. It was a summer of oppressive heat in the rolling green landscape of upstate New York, he a yeshiva student, she a graduate student heading into the Entomology field. They had seen each other from across the room and then glanced away, yet would sneak another peek again to see if the other was looking... and they both were.

Formal introductions are normally expected in this religiously observant community. So, Chaim turned to one of his friends and asked him who the girl was with the wild auburn reddish hair and flashing, blue-blue eyes. Sholom, his friend and cabin mate looked up from his paperwork and stole a glance at her.

"I think her name is Esther. I'm not sure, but let me do a little asking around," he said.

"Don't wait! I don't expect that she'll be on the market long," Chaim replied, with a sense of urgency. When Sholom came back to their cabin from a stroll a little later, he eyed his friend.

"You don't have a chance," he said.

"What do you mean?" Chaim, now intrigued, shot back.

"I asked around a little... a real brain... and that face! She's starting grad school this fall, a PhD, I think in Entomology," he said to Chaim.

"Oy! God must have quite a sense of humor, no? She wants to study bugs for a living? What kind of life is that? By the way, wise guy, what makes you think I have no chance?"

"She doesn't seem religious," Sholom added. "I can't imagine you with an outsider. Besides, she's got quite a mouth."

Chaim pondered his friend's words. *Well, I know I sensed a connection. We looked at each other, and I know she sensed a spark. I could feel it,* he thought. Chaim had never felt much of anything from the girls in his community, busy as he was with his studies. This one seemed different.

"Did she say anything? And, you know what, what's wrong with *my* face?" Chaim probed.

"Well, only this," Sholom answered. "I heard her tell Sheila that she wasn't that religious, in fact, she hasn't even set foot in a shul (synagogue) since her Bat Mitzvah."

"She used some pretty choice words too about not needing religion... something about it being a crutch for the weak."

Chaim chuckled to himself. *That may be so, but she hasn't met me yet. All I need is a few minutes with her.* No girl had ever captured his interest like this. He was just too busy with life.

Sholom almost reading his friend's thoughts, looked across the cabin and, hunching his shoulders, asked in his funny, self-deprecating Yiddish accented English "Ok, you vant I should introduce you two?"

"It couldn't *hoit*, you know?" Chaim said as a smile crept across his face and as he winked at Sholom. "Set it up."

The ancient tradition of formal introductions within the ultra-religious community would continue.

Sholom dialed the girls' cabin looking for his friend Sheila, who would be the intermediary. He laughed as she picked up the phone.

"Hi Sheila, its Sholom, the Matchmaker! How funny is this, huh?"

She laughed too, half expecting the call.

"So Chaim wants to meet her, does he?" she asked, reading into the call. At that moment, she would remember many years later, the hair on her neck stood up and goose bumps crept down her spine.

"Oh, yeah, he wants to do it right now," Sholom answered.

"Ok, I'll ask her," Sheila replied. I'll call you back in a few minutes, she's in the shower right now," Sheila whispered, delighted to be in on the conspiracy.

A few minutes later, Esther stepped out of the shower toweling dry her long auburn red tresses. Her 5'10" inch frame was well-toned and athletic. She played volleyball, softball, and amateur women's golf. Mixing athletic skills, a strong scholastic history, and some good old-fashioned common sense made her quite a young lady. She would be a catch for any young suitor, but could also intimidate the more insecure men she knew.

She looked at Sheila and asked, "Did I hear the phone ring a few minutes ago while I was in the shower?"

"Yep, you did."

"So, whoooo waaaas it?" she asked, drawing out the subject and verb for effect. A bemused smile played on her face.

Sheila, an avid crossword puzzle enthusiast, looked up from the booklet, which coincidentally, was on a love theme.

"What's an eight-letter word for someone in love," she asked her roomy. "I think the first word starts with 'L'.

"Hmmm, let me think," said Esther. "Eight letters, huh? Try 'LOVEBIRD', she suggested to Sheila. Word and letter combinations always came quickly to her and she wasn't to be toyed with in a Scrabble game.

"Perfect fit!"

By this time, Sheila was beginning to chuckle to herself. *How funny and appropriate,* she thought, almost aloud.

"Did you say something?" Esther asked.

"Uh, no," she said.

"Anyway, yes the phone did ring when you were in the shower. It was Sholom," she parried. Sholom and Sheila were old friends, from their days in elementary school and a local temple. They had remained friends ever since, hence their comfort with one another. She often wondered if he had more on his mind. They would often play a game of wits.

She loved it.

He hated it.

She usually won.

He got frustrated.

"What did he want?" Esther asked and half hoped he wanted to 'arrange' something.

"Well, he wants to meet you!" Sheila answered.

"Really? He does? I thought I had no chance. I'm not religious and he's so smart, going to be a Rabbi, right? What chance would I have?" Esther scoffed. She felt both panic and a sense of curiosity arise about the bearded rabbinical wunderkind in the other cabin.

Rumors flew that Chaim was a true scholar—schooled in the holy Scriptures and skilled in Hebrew, Greek, and Latin. Stories asserted he could read the Tenach in Hebrew and use ambidextrous skill to write in Latin and Greek with each hand—all at the same time.

Esther respected hard work and scholarship, so this was indeed a challenge. The only drawback was his deeply religious nature, something that was of no interest to her. His looks were growing on her too.

Sheila placed the call back to Cabin 43. When Sholom picked it up, she whispered, "She's interested in your boy. So, what do you want to do?"

Sholom turned to Chaim, who, coincidentally, was also working on the very same crossword puzzle as Sheila had been.

"What's an eight-letter word for someone in love? The first letter is 'L'" Chaim told him.

Sholom thought for a moment, and said, "Try LOVEBIRD."

It was a match.

"We can introduce them tonight at dinner," Sholom whispered back to his co-conspirator.

"Ok, I'll tell her... she's pretty excited. How's Chaim taking all this?"

"He is intrigued and knows she's got no real religious side to her. But he sees all of that as a challenge," he answered. They both laughed and then hung up the phone.

Sheila spun around, grabbed Esther, and danced around the room.

"I feel like Yenta the Matchmaker!" she squealed with delight. They danced a flawless waltz, laughing and spinning around the room together.

Esther began thinking about what to wear. She went to the sink, brushed her teeth, brushed out her hair into a plumage of bright red glory, brushed her teeth again, and gargled with Listerine, twice. This was an opportunity she wasn't going to miss.

"Will my mother *plotz* when she hears this!" she told Sheila. They both laughed.

Coffee House Chatter

"Do you believe in love at first sight?" she asked.

"Nah, that stuff is for the movies," he said, half listening. Instead, he was intrigued by the World Cup Soccer match on the TV brought in especially for the international crowd in the coffee house.

"Really? I thought you'd be one for a little romance," she said.

"I don't know. It's never happened to me," he answered.

"How about you?" he asked, now getting into the conversation.

"Yes, once. It was, perhaps, the most thrilling moment of my life. It gave me hope that there were forces at work in the universe that were bigger than I was," she said.

"What happened?" he asked.

She just smiled.

Chapter 14

Dinner

They spied each other from across the dining hall all that week, sneaking a glance, then looking away, pretending to make conversation with friends or the children surrounding them-building up anticipation and maybe even a little fantasy about each other. Finally, that wonderful Jewish social networking world had finally connected. The two would finally meet.

"Chaim, Sheila and I would like to formally introduce you to Esther Cohen," he said, as he smiled. "Esther, this is Chaim Wasserman."

The other three eyed him, and as if on cue, the smiles turned into warm laughter. "Chaim, it's nice to make your acquaintance," she said, with an amused and approving look at him.

Social situations of this nature didn't allow for any formal hand shaking so the two nodded, each eyeing the other. Even though Esther wasn't in any way into Chaim's Orthodox traditions, she respected the practice. Her grandparents on both sides were pretty observant so she was familiar with ritual.

The two of them seemed to slip into a trance as they drank in each other's much anticipated presence. They were both skating on thin ice in that the strictly Orthodox community rarely strays out of its borders and the non-religious are rarely let in. She had little use for the old ways, pulled as she was into the sciences and academia. Just a few days before, he would have never even considered meeting anyone outside of the tradition. Ah, the difference a day makes.

"Esther, it's my honor," he said. As they looked into one another eyes, it was obvious to both of them that this encounter was exactly what they both anticipated. The attraction was immediate and profound. He thought of the moment Jacob had laid eyes on Rachel.

"Ok, so now that's done, what does this wonderful restaurant have in store for us tonight?" laughed Sholom, trying to make small talk. But there was no need for that as the two new acquaintances began to talk, sitting on the picnic-style benches across from one another. And talk they did, completely cutting out anyone else in the room, rarely removing their eyes from one another.

Years later, Chaim and Esther recounted their first meeting and expressd the belief that they had fallen in love that very evening. That's how in-tune they were to one another's feelings, thoughts, emotions, and beliefs. *Except for God and all the religious stuff,* Esther thought. They covered the gamut including family, politics, science, history, and more. They agreed on little but it just didn't seem to matter, so engrossed were they into each other.

But there was something about this young rabbinical student that drew her. His faith seemed so very real and tangible. He was mesmerized by her quick wit, charm, smarts, and that red hair. He realized that freckles dotted her nose and cheeks. He also realized for the first time that she was taller than he was, by a good two or three inches. He had to sneak a look at her feet to see if she was wearing heels. She wasn't.

They all arose and headed for the nightly buffet. The camp cafeteria featured a large skylight through which the late afternoon sunlight would pour through, filling the room with speckles of floating dust and shafts of light. As the sun set, the light would move around the room and the shadows would dance at the light's retreat. It all seemed very magical.

At night, the stars shone through the glass ceiling, looking like gleaming jewels against a black velvet canvas. Anybody looking up could see shooting stars through the glass. The room's picnic-style benches underscored the camp theme but everything else was nice and modern. The room was painted an off white with pictures of Israel, Jewish personages of the past such as Golda Meir, David Ben Gurion, Moshe Dayan, Abba Eban, Yitzhak Rabin, and other national heroes.

In the middle of the large facility was the salad bar, a very popular place for many of these young health conscience campers. In the southwest corner, the regular food line offered many healthy options and a few fun items like hamburgers or hotdogs. Since it was a kosher camp, no meat or dairy were served together. And of course, no bacon or sausage, nor pork of any kind could be found. The same went for shellfish as it was prohibited in the Book of Leviticus.

Around the perimeter sat couches and little conversation areas where the kids and counselors would mix for impromptu Bible or Talmud discussions, chats about current events, sports, or other topics of the day. Since many of the campers loved to read, a small library sat in the northwest corner and usually attracted those who needed private and quiet reading time. On the east side of the room was a small recreation area with air hockey, pinball machines, and game tables. Monopoly was popular as was Scrabble. It had been a very busy day in the camp with games, swimming, hiking, and time spent teaching the campers Bible stories.

The children lined up first, and slowly picked and chose their selections from the patient cafeteria crew, with others still circling the salad bar. Then it was the counselors' turn. That night's kitchen help was, like the other nights, a rotation from cabin to cabin. Everyone served in the kitchen, each taking 2 turns per week setting up, serving, then cleaning up after everyone had left. Jewish camps were like that where everyone was equal and everyone served. This was planned and modeled after the **Kibbutzim*** (collective farms) in Israel.

Chaim had fried chicken, mashed potatoes, salad, vegetables—with a slice of fresh peach pie. Esther, the athlete she was, did the same, just adding more veggies. The kitchen crew got the chicken right and everyone dug in to the meal. Dinner chat continued where they began only this time focusing on their dreams and futures.

"Feel like a stroll?" Chaim asked, feeling pretty sure she'd go along.

"Thought you'd never ask," Esther said, becoming more intrigued by the minute.

Chaim and Esther felt at home with each other. So they bid the others good night and took a moonlit stroll in the forest. Adjacent to the wooded area was a lake with mirror-like still water. Sholom and Sheila followed close behind, not too obtrusive, but still visible. Chaperones were always encouraged. Traditions were traditions and rules were rules.

It was obvious to anyone who watched—some magic happened. Both Chaim and Esther moved in and out of the conversation like old friends do, sometimes completing each other's sentences. Since both were fluent in Yiddish, when they wanted to retreat into their little world, they would slip into the old Jewish tongue. When their eyes would meet, it was no longer a furtive glance then a look away. They would hold each others' gaze sometimes lapsing into silence as the evening engulfed them.

They continued on the path by the moonlit lake. A soft breeze whispered through the trees and insects added their voices. The air smelled sweet.

Chaim felt so alive and also curious about this amazing young woman. "So, tell me about your family."

"Gosh, I don't know where to begin. When I get asked that question, I wonder what people want to hear. I mean that with all the interviews for graduate school and work and all. I really wonder where the talk begins and the interest ends for the other person," she said—followed by nervous laughter.

That last statement was true. Esther was reluctant and shy—not anxious to gush forth a bunch of random facts about herself or her family's social involvements. *What do I say?* She wondered. *Does he really want to know all about my golf game, studies in school, job interviews, the camp, my family's active world and connections?*

"Where do I start?" Esther began. "Hmmm... well, I have an identical twin sister." She searched his eyes and wondered at his thoughts.

"No! Really??"

"Such a reaction!"

"Me too!"

"No! Really! You're an identical too?" she responded. Now she had an opening so any butterflies she felt just fluttered away.

"How funny is that?!?" I'm going to kill Sholom!" Chaim said.

Geez, where's Sheila? I wonder why she never said anything! Esther pondered.

"Tell me about her. Why isn't she here with you?" he teased.

"Well, maybe you can tell me the same thing about your twin," she said, tossing the subject right back at him. He loved the retort. She was feisty, quick, and unafraid to challenge him. She wasn't like his family or friends who would avoid him and these battles of wit.

"Eleazer wanted some time to get away from me this summer," he said, half jokingly but also half serious. As close as Chaim and Eleazer were, it was time for some separation. This seemed to be the year.

"Yeah, us too. Rifka is far smarter than I am. She's got her sights set on something in the Engineering world. And whenever we're asked about vacations, we looked at each other and answer in unison, 'separate vacations.'"

"Well, Eleazer is very intense, has a lot of different interests, and is a real scholar. Still, rabbinics aren't his all-consuming passion—like mine is."

"Hmmm... interesing. I can relate. It's funny how Rifka and I have a similar view of the world, but where we differ is that I love the practical and she's really into the theory. I want to get my hands into the science. She'll be the inventor."

They walked a little more under the silvery moonlight. Tall tree shadows gently enveloped them. Esther laughed out loud, but kept her thoughts to herself.

"What?" Chaim wanted in on her private little joke.

"We oughta set them up," she laughed, a twinkle in her eye.

Chaim thought... *and devious too!*

"THAT is a wonderful idea. Revenge! They'll probably never speak to us again!" he laughed... then both of them looked at each other and burst out in convulsive laughter, not able to contain the irony of it all. It was serious twin humor, only understood by those of multiple births. Tears rolled down their cheeks they were laughing so hard.

"It's a date!" He said. "My brother will either thank me or kill me."

"No kidding! Rifka is very shy and hates it when people try anything like this. But I think she'll listen to me this time."

When Sheila and Sholom heard them laughing so hard, they came running up, not exactly sure what was going on.

"What's so funny?" Sheila asked—annoyed and feeling left out.

"Why didn't you tell us?"

"Tell you what?"

"Well, for starters, that we're both identical twins!" Chaim and Esther both blurted out at the same time. This wouldn't be the last time they had the same thoughts at the same time.

Sholom and Sheila looked at each other and it hit them... they had both forgotten to say anything. The four of them shared the laugh as the brilliant moon continued its ascent above the hills across the lake.

Chaim turned to Esther and silently nodded to her. She followed his lead and they continued their walk down the path. The electricity between them was obvious.

Chaim decided to do the boldest thing he could think of which was to reach out and hold her hand... even though he knew he shouldn't. Almost sensing his thoughts, she reached out her hand and met his. Fingers intertwining together, they began a romance that would last a lifetime. They stopped on the path, the beams of moonlight dancing around them. Insects chirped and whirred in the trees. It was a magic moment, one they would never forget.

✡ ✡ ✡ ✡ ✡ ✡

The dreams were as real to them tonight as that moonlit night so many years ago. A moment of silence passed between them now, as they held each other's gaze. Their hands once again moved toward one another's, grasping for safety, just as it was in the camp's forest. It was one of those tender moments, shared by two lifetime partners that could not be explained, but both of them knew exactly what it meant.

The years had certainly flown by.... Esther felt her husband's gnarled and arthritic hands in hers. She knew things were changing once again, only this time, she felt they had no control of the events surrounding them. For someone so irreligious much of her life, she sensed the hand of God Himself, only she didn't know how to bring this up to Chaim. And the kids? Not yet, not yet!

These two lifelong lovers had shared a life together. Their passion for one another still burned deep within. Neither of their natural forces was abated. For an entire week now they awoke at the same time with the same dream, holding on to each other for dear life. What could it mean?

✡ ✡ ✡ ✡ ✡ ✡

Meanwhile, that Shabbat morning out west in Los Angeles, a vivid dream shook Rabbi Eleazer Wasserman from his sleep. His wife, Rifka, also awoke and stared wide-eyed at him... she had had the very same dream, AGAIN. They began to talk over each other, eyes widening as every detail spilled out. What could it mean? It was all quite eerie. The room fell absolutely silent, sunlight playing through the shutters and dancing on the walls. All they could hear was the droning of a lawnmower across the street.

"It was almost like I was in it... I could smell the animals—hear the children cry. I looked over to see you with the goats and cattle," she said to him. "What did you see?"

"Same, my love," he answered, reaching for and finding her hand. Silence enveloped them. They could hear one another's heart beats, fast and loud.

"Seven days in a row," they said at the same time. The rabbi looked at his wife with a sense that something was about to happen, but having no idea what.

"Okay, okay... I need answers." Eleazer lifted both hands in the air, waved them, and said, "I need to make a few calls.

"I'm going to call Chaim in Dallas, as soon as Shabbos ends tonight. Even though we are twins, I have always looked up to him and maybe he can help me figure this out," he said. Rifka agreed.

"I need to talk to Esther too. She always understands me—this is way beyond coincidence now."

These twin brothers and sisters consulted one another on a regular basis, growing even closer over the years. She of course, understood what identicals did and how they thought.

Later that evening, Eleazer, the LA rabbi, dialed his twin brother Chaim, the Dallas rabbi. When Chaim answered the phone, he sounded different, a little distant even. The Sabbath had just ended and Eleazer heard his older brother on the other end.

"Hello?"

"Chaim, it's me."

"Eleazer, it's good to hear your voice, in fact, I was thinking about you just a few minutes ago. I've got something I need to talk to you about."

"Me too," said Eleazer, "Me too."

From the Pen of Ezekiel the Prophet
Chapter 33, Verses 1-6

And the word of the LORD came to me, saying, "Son of man, speak to the sons of your people and say to them, 'If I bring a sword upon a land, and the people of the land take one man from among them and make him their watchman, and he sees the sword coming upon the land and blows on the trumpet and warns the people, then he who hears the sound of the trumpet and does not take warning, and a sword comes and takes him away, his blood will be on his own head. 'He heard the sound of the trumpet but did not take warning; his blood will be on himself. But had he taken warning, he would have delivered his life. 'But if the watchman sees the sword coming and does not blow the trumpet and the people are not warned, and a sword comes and takes a person from them, he is taken away in his iniquity; but his blood I will require from the watchman's hand.'

Chapter 15

Pogroms–
Random Shootings, Killings

At first, the attacks seemed random and rather disconnected. There appeared to be no real discernable pattern in any of them. Different cities, different kinds of weapons used, and some even appeared to be robberies or just plain thuggery. Some of these were no more complex than a simple beating or shooting, carried out by a single individual or maybe two. Still others attracted larger groups and began to expand. There were drive by shootings too. There was one pattern; authorities later figured out the perpetrators of each crime left no trace. Any connection seemed impossible.

The latest incident in the news occurred in a small town in Indiana. CNN broke the story. Anchor Kent Allen said, "Granger, Indiana was the sight of a brutal shooting today. CNN reporter Denise Dulberg is on the scene. What do we know, D.D.?"

On scene stood D.D.—pretty, late 20's, brunette hair in a tight ponytail, and an all-business tone and demeanor. "Kent, here's what we know. Two assailants entered Friedman's insurance agency around 3:30 p.m. today. Only the Friedmans, Gerald and Sarah his wife, were in the small office. Several shots were heard. A single bystander witnessed the ordeal.

"Near-by business owners rushed in to find the well-liked and long-time residents both deceased. This sidewalk memorial has grown by the minute and shocked mourners continue to arrive. The community has gathered around the Friedman's children. News spread in a wireless instant to their high school. And they arrived with scores of students minutes later." D.D. step aside to capture the scene.

"Kent, the single witness described the men as swarthy in appearance, 25 to 35 years old, and bearded. However, local news reports left out those details. They also omitted other details such as... the assailants spoke with distinct but undetermined accents—according to the witness."

Then the scene went dark. Viewers were returned to the studio and Kent. "Thank you D.D. I'm sure you'll keep us update when you have more."

"That moron! I have more! Lots more!" D.D. exploded.

She stood still, settled her storm, spied her notes, and then went straight to her on-scene producer. D.D. got 12 inches from her face and in controlled fury asked, "Hey! What gives?!"

The producer stepped back from D.D. and said, "It's above your paygrade, *Schnooky*. You know I had to send them your copy."

"So nobody's gonna tell the truth? Nobody cares that this couple was Jewish? Nobody's concerned about possible terrorism?" D.D. stepped in and stared at the producer.

"Listen, Hon', the witness—an old lady; her view—across the street; her eyesight—who knows? Too many unknowns."

D.D. turned to scan the crowd—then said, "Mrs. Anderson is not that old. She got details that most half her age would miss." She searched her notes and added, "**I talked to her!** She saw them drive off in a white mid-sized sedan. And the cops said they found no trace of them. They policed their brass, touched nothing, took nothing. Now, you gotta admit that's not common, criminal, or kosher. It's terror—it's evil. Come on! Talk to Mrs. Anderson, please!"

"Listen, D.D...." The producer barked and cut D.D. off. "You're right, nobody cares! Jews or not. Terror or typical. It doesn't matter. Your copy raised flags, Ms. Dulberg." She spun around and pointed, "Now look... the van is loaded, the guys are in it, and it's two hours to Chicago. That's two long hours till I get a drink, my dinner, and my bed. Get your butt on in the van, now! Or find another ride."

What the news people couldn't possibly have known was that the car was driven into a garage two miles away. Both men shaved off their beards, changed clothes, and vanished. Two hours later, the car was dismantled, loaded into crates, and on a truck headed to parts unknown.

The very next day, in San Diego California, at Julio's, an old Mexican restaurant in the Normal Heights, a young Jewish couple was enjoying some of the city's best Mexican food.

When two men entered the restaurant, they took a seat next to the couple, who were completely oblivious to anyone there. What happened next would haunt those who witnessed it for the rest of their lives as the men moved in unison towards the young couple.

The first man, broad-shouldered and very strong, grabbed the woman from behind as she sat in the booth. When her boyfriend struggled to get out of the booth to help her, the other man tripped him and silently plunged his knife into the man's windpipe. His gurgling cry for help was met by a boot to the head as he lurched forward and he died a horrible death knowing his young fiancé had seen the whole thing as she was herself being murdered.

Struggling with the woman, the other man, using one swift move with his knife slashed her throat. There was so much blood in the restaurant, they both slipped but maintained their footing while making their escape. The patrons were too stunned to react. The entire attack lasted less than 30 seconds. The two men vanished into the night, driving their car to a residence near the local university, where they drove into a garage, disrobed, changed clothes, and disappeared.

The car was in pieces in minutes, the chop shop doing its job as the parts were prepared to make their journey to Mexico, just a short ride over the border. Their clothes and shoes were destroyed when the accomplices of the pair destroyed everything in a furnace. Again, no trace of anybody or any evidence left behind. Nobody could identify the car involved. Even though the police did manage to get footprints from the blood, they lost the trail. Gone without a trace.

From the Hand of Solomon the Wise—
Proverbs 16:3

Commit your works to the LORD,
and your plans will be established.

Chapter 16

A Change of Heart

The next week in New Jersey, Nation of Islam members gathered in a park near a shopping mall. They listened to a series of speakers on Saviour's Day. One speaker after another extolled the virtues of the founders, their version of Islam, and liberal passages of the Quran.

There were the expected shouts of *"Allah Ahkbar"* and "Amen, Brother!" The speakers continued to raise the rhetoric against the Jews and Israel, calling it a gutter religion and denouncing Israel's treatment of its neighbors and condemning America's and the world's Jews for their oppressive ways. Further readings from the Palestinian Manifesto and the Hamas Charter seemed to ignite the crowd. Just then, about 200 members of the crowd turned to look across the street.

Across the street was a small Jewish day school and community center that happened to have a special weekend event planned. Two flagpoles stood in front of the building, the American Flag and the Flag of Israel, the Star of David laying against a white field and bordered by two blue stripes.

The event was a special art show and exhibit by and for the children. About 100 kids and adults entered the school as the meeting across the street in the park was breaking up. The crowd from the park crossed the street in unison and surrounded the small school. Those inside hadn't noticed anything until the chants began.

"Jews out of Palestine! Death to the Jews!" The crowd shouted louder, drew nearer, and made intentions clearer. Their agitation and anger grew. Action was imminent—assault assured.

"Back to the ovens with you!" The mob screamed hate, pumped fists, and made threats. The few Jews who braved the scene were the objects of their scorn. They tried to assure themselves, *this is America. No violence will come of this. Words only, don't worry—it's all just rhetoric.*

Pleas for peace went unheeded, even within their ranks. One of the protesters, Ibraham Hussein (formerly Ross Evans) was raised Christian, but converted to Islam and took a Muslim name. He was well educated with a Masters Degree in Education from the University of California and had been a youth leader in a Christian denomination years before. For some reason his faith had wavered and he found solace in Islam. He believed much of what he had heard in the park speeches. Still, he didn't condone the methods that the group employed.

The protest grew from fervor to a threat of violence. Something stirred inside him. He felt an urgency to act, but didn't know how. His heart raced, his senses sharpened, and his body tense—he was ready for something but wasn't sure just what.

Then a handgun appeared.

"Gun, gun, gun!" a voice shouted from behind him.

The shooter aimed. Hussein leaped and the shooter squeezed the trigger. Both Hussein and the shooter fell to the ground. The gun knocked out of his hand. The crowd stepped back—silent at first. Then men pounced on Hussein with punishing blows. But out of nowhere a big man appeared. He pulled Hussein from their grip and took to him to safety inside the school.

Hussein bled from the beating, but his wounds were much worse. The bullet had entered his chest. He was stunned—his mind was a blur. He was in the house of his enemies, but he wasn't afraid. He was weak and unable to move.

Those in the school closed in on Hussein. Some had malice, but one came to his defense. It was his rescuer—the one who brought him inside. He stood with authority and spoke for Hussein. "This man before you is not your enemy. He lies fallen, wounded, and bleeding... for you. He alone stopped the attack. The bullet would have come through that window to shattered glass and a family. But he put himself between the shooter and you. Now it's time for you to act."

No one inside recognized the mystery man and he couldn't have come from the mob. He spoke his peace with authority and wouldn't be seen again. Still, his words changed minds, moods, and motion. They rushed to Hussein's aid. A doctor and a nurse, administered first-aid to Hussein. The doctor applied pressure to the wound and whispered to the nurse, "I don't know. He's lost a lot of blood."

The nurse didn't answer. She held Hussein's hand and spoke into his ear. "You'll be fine. The paramedics are just outside. Just relax. I won't let anything happen to our hero."

Voices, I.V.s, vibrations, and vision a blur. He felt the presence of paramedics and heard their questions. He tried to stay present, to answer, and to think. But Hussein had lost all his strength. His thoughts slipped away from a mind that had dimmed. No panic—just peace. Then a voice of full of comfort came to him there.

Hussein heard his mother's voice. He saw her face, felt her touch, and drew strength from her tears.

"I'm proud of you, son. You did what was right. I know you remember the stories I told. Oh hon', those freedom riders had courage back in the day. Dr. King and the marchers—they knew what was right. And before then it was Mr. Lincoln.... Remember what I said? Well, hon' well, he was our voice. He did what was right, and he did it. But baby... the right and the just who do it... well, there'll be enemies. Hate fills their hearts and hurts marks their way. Dr. King was cut down and before him that good man Abe.

"Hon', remember.... I told you about God's people, the Jews? They marched by our side. They defended us in the courts. They were kind to my father and kind to me, too. I worked in their homes. They accepted and loved me. And I loved them, too."

Hussein saw his mother's face. Her expression was familiar. She searched his eyes but saw into his soul. She had often spoken her mind, but left the choice to him. Then her face would betray her heart. He saw her concern, her pain, her urgency—all tempered with hope and her enduring faith. Her face began to fade, but her words continued in his heart and mind: "Ross Baby... hon' listen, listen to the voice of the Lord!"

Her Bible taught a lot about the Jews. Many of her people hated them, but she taught him not to hate anyone. She was a Christian, one who believed her Bible that the Jews were somehow chosen, not because they deserved it or even asked for it but simply because God had made it so. She had raised him right —especially when it came to God's chosen. The families she worked for gave her gifts for her son, often cash at the holidays which she faithfully stashed away to give him for college. Her boy was going to get an education!

She had instructed him that the Jews had been put on Earth for a special purpose and it wasn't up to him to question it. Her loving instruction was firm and she never wavered from her position or beliefs. And she knew and instructed him to love them, even when it seemed so very unpopular to do so. Somewhere along the way he forgot that message. She had taught him that her Savior and their Messiah, had died and was resurrected, thus cheating death for the Jews just like He had died for her people.

Somehow, deep in his unconscious state, something awoke at that moment. It now appeared that his conversion to Islam, at least the Nation of Islam's version of it, was a sham and a falsehood. Suddenly, he could hear voices around him and felt the loving touch of the doctor and a nurse. Maybe it was the tears, her tears he felt, as he struggled to hold on to his life.

The truth had come to him on the soft gentle breeze of his mother's distant voice.

And somewhere in Israel, a telephone call was made to the Jewish Agency. Michael Shapiro picked it up and silently listened to the caller.

> From the Hand of the Psalmist
> Chapter 55: Verses 18-19
>
> He will redeem my soul in peace from the battle which is against me, for they are many who strive with me. God will hear and answer them—even the one who sits enthroned from of old—selah. With whom there is no change, and who do not fear God.

Chapter 17

In the Hospital

Hussein awoke. It was dark. Nothing was clear. A small, dim light above and behind him didn't help. He was cold, disoriented, and blank. His eyes tried to adjust, but all he saw were shadows. He imagined a figure in the corner and felt that someone was there. But the room was too dim to see.

He heard the hum and beeps from machines around his bed. He felt an IV in his right arm. He patted himself and found wires attached to his head and chest. He saw shadows on a table to his left. He reached out to touch them, but felt a guardrail on his bed. *Why am I'm in a hospital?* He thought. *How did I get here?*

Panic seized him. Then pain was a sword that took his breath and ran through his ribs, chest, and out his back. His heart raced, his eyes gained focus, and his began to clear. He remembered—the protest, the pain, and the powerful man who helped. He couldn't lie still, but every move hurt.

The door blew open. Bright light filled the room. His nurse flew in—full of comments and questions. "Somebody is awake. You just turned my monitor into a Christmas tree. I lost the pool, but I'm glad to see you awake,

Mr. Hussein. This new bag here is your pain medication. It comes in with the I.V. Here... push this button when needed for pain. I already pumped it a bit. We heard you moan through the walls. Listen, chest wounds are painful and gotta be watched. You're gonna see a lot of me. But please don't hate me."

Hussein searched her face to understand. But all he could do was get out a grunt and groan. "Mufmmuh?"

"Huh? Oh well, you'll probably hate me at first," she said. "That tube in your side has to be cleaned and cleared, often. And I gotta keep your lungs clear, too. You don't need to know how I do that—not right now.

"You know, Mr. Hussein, you must have angels watching over you!" She said with a smile. She adjusted his pillows and position in bed. Then she stroked his face with her hand.

The nurse turned to leave, and Hussein tried to speak. His mouth was cotton, and he needed a drink. "Wa... uhuhuh... water, please." It wasn't easy, but his raspy words got her attention.

She filled his cup, fixed the straw, and then sat by his side. She lifted his head with one hand and moved the straw to his mouth with the other. He noticed her name tag: Jenny Del Fuego, R.N. He sputtered and sipped and got just enough. The water soothed his parched throat.

"Don't worry," Jenny assured. "You'll navigate on your own by tomorrow." Then she let him lie back and put the water in reach.

Morning's light brought a clearer mind to Hussein. He recalled the events from the park. He remembered the crowd, the protest, and the move across the street. He recalled his unease and the edgy young man in his sight. Hussein had started to move before the man lifted his arm. Then he flew when he saw the man's gun. He remembered his leap, the pain, and nothing more until the man carried him to the school. He saw the man's face. He was familiar, but Hussein couldn't remember his name.

He ran the events through his mind until a visitor tapped on his door. He had no strength to answer. But she poked in her head. Hussein didn't know her and made no response—he just stared.

The nurse looked up, walked over, and asked, "Can I help you? Are you a family member or friend?"

"I'm Ayelet Simcha," she whispered. "I was in the community center school during the incident. I helped with first-aid after he was in the school auditorium."

"May I see him?" she asked the nurse. She nodded an ok and motioned her to step into the room.

The young woman quietly stepped to the bed and leaned down to look at Hussein. He returned to a more full sense of consciousness now and there was a quiet peace in the room.

"Hi, my name is Ayelet and I came to see how you were doing," she said gently. She looked into his eyes and saw warmth and acceptance.

"I'm okay, I think," Hussein rasped. His eyesight improved and he could see Ayelet's face and pleasant smile. He also saw her necklace—a Star of David.

"Can you tell me something?" He asked.

"What?" Ayelet answered.

"Were you there? I remember the protest in the park. We crossed the street. But it's all a blur after that. Can you tell me what happened?"

Ayelet cast her glance to the room's upper corner, took a deep breath, and said, "Well, let's see." Then her gaze came back to a twisted tissue in her lap. "I'm not sure of all that happened outside of the school. But we hosted an art show for our children inside. It's our Jewish community center and school.

"I remember a lot of noise. I guess it was your group around the school. The shouts got louder and louder. Then we heard a gunshot. Everything got quiet for a long moment. Then more shouts and chaos. All our doors were shut and locked, but we were still so frightened... then the sirens.

"Then somehow, someone carried you in. Our men were alarmed—then hostile toward you and the man. But this tall man spoke with authority, 'Stop!' All the men stopped. Then he laid you down and said that you had stopped the bullet. He said you leaped between the bullet and the window where we stood. He said you were no enemy. He said you risked your life for us."

Hussein rolled his eyes and let out a "Whew!"

"So," Ayelet said, "I came down here to meet a real hero, to say thank you, and see if I could do anything for you."

"You just gave me what I needed most."

"What?"

"My memory," Hussein said. "I remember now. But a hero? No. Not me. I didn't have a choice. It came from deep inside, and I did what I had to do."

"Thank you, Mr. Hussein. Had the bullet found its mark, it would have entered the window in front of me and other parents and teachers. One of us would have...." Emotions choked her words. She cleared her throat and said, "If the bullet had hit us, I knew things would explode. Great violence, bullets, an assault inside, certain death, and the children...." Ayelet couldn't go on. Instead, she patted his arm and mimed the words "Thank you."

"So, of course, you're Jewish?" He asked and gazed at her Star of David. She nodded and Hussein remembered his mother's voice all over again. His eyes filled with tears that broke and rolled down both cheeks.

Hussein found his voice and said, "Many years ago, my mama taught me about the Jews and how God has a special place in his heart for them. She took me to church and Sunday school. And until the day she died, she read her Bible aloud to me. She did it at least once a day, and more if she could catch me.

"She told me to never forget what Jewish people did for my people in the civil rights years. They marched with us and defended us in the courts."

Hussein paused—Nurse Jenny came to the bed and listened to his story. He glanced at her and realized that both women had Stars of David. The thought that he had been posed and prepared to harm, perhaps kill, either one of them caused him to shutter in shame. Then in addition, he felt such peace and kindness from both. But more, they show no thread of hostility or anger towards him.

It was an atmosphere of loving care. He sensed love. And felt his mother's love and presence.

"Anyway, through the years I got distracted by all the politics and the things I saw around me. I ended up with the Nation of Islam. They often spoke on campus. I read their materials, spent time with a preacher-mentor, and allowed that stuff inside my head. It made sense to me at the time. But a deep uneasiness always haunted me. I guess I knew that my mama wouldn't be pleased.

"Still, despite my doubts and unease, I followed along... till yesterday."

He looked up at her and asked, "You're Jewish, too?"

"I'm a follower of Jesus Christ, and I believe the Bible—all of it. It teaches that the Jews are chosen by God for great works. I pray for, bless, and love Israel and the Jewish people. God's love found me, saved me, changed me, and gave me the power to love myself and others. Mr. Hussein, today I can say that I have love for even a person like you."

The room fell silent. He studied her face, looked for truth and then said, "Please call me Ross. My name is Ross Evans. That bullet killed Ibraham Hussein."

> From the Prophet Yoel (Joel)
> Chapter 2:28-29
>
> It will come about after this
> That I will pour out My Spirit on all mankind;
> And your sons and daughters will prophesy,
> Your old men will dream dreams,
> Your young men will see visions.
> Even on the male and female servants
> I will pour out My Spirit in those days.

Chapter 18

The Brothers Meet

The Wasserman brothers arranged to meet the following week at the National Rabbi's Conference in Chicago. They hadn't seen each other for a couple of years. But both brothers embraced technology and a variety electronic devices. Whatever the crazy world developed, they learned it and used it to stay update and in touch. Still, they both looked forward to their face-to-face meetings and brotherly embraces.

Chaim caught Eleazer's eye in the hotel lobby. They rushed to greet and hug one another. "Ah, here's my good looking twin brother!" Chaim exclaimed. The bear hug was welcomed by Eleazer. In fact, the two remained in the embrace and held on to one another other for dear life.

"So, tell me about these dreams of yours," Chaim said.

"Unsettling," Eleazer seemed a little spooked, as he searched his brother's eyes.

"They started last week, seven straight nights. Rifka had the exact dreams too." Chaim, nodding his head, remained silent listening to Eleazer.

"Same with me and Esther," he said—eyes locked on his brother. They were deep into each other's heads. It was past coincidence now. They both knew it.

"At first, we thought it sort of amusing, almost a little joke from *Ha Shem* Himself, but by the third night, we began to think something was up. Judging by what you tell me, I am beginning to wonder," he said, stroking his graying beard.

"Have you told anyone else?" Eleazer asked him. Fear and excitement gripped them both.

"No, we're not telling anyone. We haven't even told the kids. I would imagine they might think this is the crazy raving of two demented old people," he said with a sly grin on his face.

Eleazer, nodding, let out a long sigh, the breath exhaling through his nose. He looked at Chaim and shook his head from side to side, with what might be considered concern, yet with a quizzical look.

"You remember the story of Joseph?"

"Of course I do! He kept having dreams—dreams about the men in the prison, dreams about the sheaves and his brothers, dreams about the moon and stars, all very prophetic about the future but also about those around him," Chaim recalled.

Would God still communicate in visions and dreams? They were new actors in His little drama. Could it really be so?

"And, he interprets Pharaoh's dreams, which helps him gain executive status in Egypt." This thought made him chuckle.

"A Nice irony eh! A former Hebrew prisoner and slave who becomes Prime Minister of Egypt." They both grunted their amusement.

"Right... then there is the Book of Daniel, where Daniel, the prime minister, interprets Nebuchadnezzar's dream and ends up running Babylon."

The history of the Bible was very real to them. The stories happened so long ago, but were still very relevant.

"So, interpreting dreams is good for business, eh?" Chaim winked at Eleazer, nudging him in the ribs with his elbow. They both laughed at the little inside joke. Then Chaim turned serious.

"Something is going on. This is bigger than either one of us. What do you think it means?"

What was really bothering them both was that dreams were known to be a way that God Himself might use to communicate with His people, *BACK THEN*. But that seemed such a long time ago, and nobody he knew would think that God used dreams today to communicate to his chosen.

Only **Messhuganers*** walked around having dreams like this, much less telling people about them.

Eleazer looked at him for a moment. "You know, if you start putting two and two together, we might start understanding a little more about this," he said.

"Well, pardnah, shoot."

The Texan in Chaim jumped out. And, yes even Jews living in the South end up with a drawl. And, some even drive pickups with gun racks and guns, too. Of course, cowboy boots were worn without question. Eleazer began to share his thoughts with Chaim.

"I see more hatred aimed at Jews... it's not only obvious to me, but I'm starting to get questions at Shabbat services. People are starting to ask me where all of this is going. I mean, in the last year or so, synagogue desecrations at an all time high in the U.S. The killings last week in Indiana and San Diego... Some of them actually listened to me. I've told them to read their Tenach."

"And, those crazy Messianics are getting a little more attention, perhaps more than they deserve. You remember Raphi Shachor? He recently went to the 'other side.' We reestablished contact online. We've had some bizarre conversations. He doesn't sound so crazy now... though I still think he's a little *messhugah*."

"We now have a negative population growth rate among Jews here while the Muslim growth rate has more than doubled in the past 20 + years. All the talk about population control seems to have affected the Jewish community, except for the Heredim (deeply observant). By the way, have you noticed how many Muslims have been elected to local, state, and national offices in that span? The U.S. has been moving still further away from Israel too. And, then that weird stuff in Egypt."

"You know, it's strange, I've been reading what the Prophet Isaiah had to say about Egypt. Something's about to happen with *Mitzraim* (Egypt) of profound significance. I wouldn't be surprised if they end up in a civil war. Something's brewing there—much bigger than the 'Arab Spring' a few years ago."

Indeed, his perceptions would soon be proven true. The Egyptians'strange mix of various faiths including Muslims, Coptic Christians, Mystics, and even Jews, among others, were heading for an internal upheaval. Of course there had once been a thriving and powerful Jewish community there, not to mention the great Library of Alexandria.

The forces of the various religious authorities had been sensing growing tensions and the Egyptian government was having a harder and harder time keeping the lid on the different factions. Palestinian tunnels in Gaza and the pressures being brought to bear by the various radical Islamists such as the Muslim Brotherhood, Hamas, Hezbollah, and the PLO had were gaining international attention once again. It was a powder keg and nobody seemed to understand how to handle it.

Opposing forces continued trying to bring Egypt in closer alignment with the West, realizing that the radical Islamization of the Middle East had gone too far. It had been building for years and seemed ready to blow.

"Right, I hadn't put all that together like this," Chaim answered. The light bulbs were starting to go on.

"Continue," he urged his brother on, with a wave of his hand.

"Well, the Egyptians, according to Isaiah, will have quite a tough time of it with internal strife in a civil war, something akin to a battle of the spirits, almost like demonic forces battling it out or something."

"Then later, in the 19th Chapter, it says that there will be a spiritual awakening, where these ancient Egyptians will suddenly recognize and accept the God of Israel, and at which time there will be great blessings poured out on them. You know, there was a time where the Egyptians believed in the God of Abraham, Isaac, and Jacob." His voice trailed off as he seemed somewhat lost in his thoughts.

All of it seemed to follow an Egyptian theme... the current events seemed to be right out of the Bible. And then, there were those dreams of the Exodus that had been common to both of them.

They compared notes about how a three-way highway would be constructed between Egypt, ancient Assyria, (not Syria but roughly Southern Iraq), and Israel. Syria itself awaited a different fate. It would bring blessings to all three partners, so unlikely all these centuries, but almost understandable in light of the Holy Scriptures. Peace and brotherhood between ancient enemies would come to pass as the end result after a whole lot of upheaval.

Egypt, Egypt, why Egypt, not to mention Assyria?

It may have been because Egypt had observed a cold peace with her Jewish neighbor for decades. Though various radical groups had operated within her borders, Egypt had observed a non-aggression pact and remained a non-belligerent. The ancient nation had even tried to broker peace deals and keep terrorists off balance throughout the years. She hadn't taken up arms against Israel since the Yom Kippur War way back in 1973. In fact, one of the early peace efforts eventually led to the assassination of its Prime Minister, Anwar Sadat.

"It's been brewing awhile now—the Arab Spring and all that nonsense back a few years, and then we saw what the radicals really had up their sleeves..." Chaim said.

He and Eleazer didn't even have to finish that thought as the world soon learned that the phenomenon called the Arab Spring was simply a ruse to usher in a new round of more and more brutal Islamic rulers. Those who welcomed the supposedly innocent-looking revolutions realized too late that they were merely the first wave of something far more sinister.

"Do you remember how the Jews would get blamed for killing Muslims in battle, yet, Muslim on Muslim violence accounted for the slaughter of hundreds of thousands of innocents—and the UN—in fact, no one did or said anything!" Eleazer was hopping mad.

The discussion fell silent. The twins eyed one another, exchanging unspoken thoughts between them. Chaim spoke next.

"I think I see a pattern here. You know as well as I do, in the past, it would seem that events would align and then either the Christians or the Muslims would do something. Where religion wasn't the driver, it would be the government. It might be a pogrom or a government sponsored 'action' where a sanctioned public event, aimed at the Jews would 'spontaneously' spark the local population into a sweep through the village or city. The recent attacks and murders against random Jewish targets are happening on a regular basis."

There was something familiar about all of this, yet almost impossible to believe.

Thoughts of the Holocaust, now close to 100 years in the past, were never very far from their minds. In fact, fears of another **Shoah***, like World War II Europe played at the mind's edge of all Jews, sometimes a little closer, sometimes a little farther away. All of the Holocaust survivors were now dead. The museums, a myriad of books, films, and even the records kept by the meticulous Germans, all spoke for themselves, despite what the Muslims and some Christian doubters had to say. And of course, the multitude of Holocaust museums around the world remained beacons of truth and light to an unbelieving world.

Movements that questioned the Holocaust grew, even among some Christians. Some denied that it ever happened. Many Muslims have long scoffed at the notion of a Jewish genocide in World War II. Yet they praised Hitler and the Nazis for the "wonderful work" they had done in WWII. It was a strange, yet obvious paradox. The occasional Muslim, who acknowledged the *Shoah,* was immediately discredited and silenced by critics, yet Islam generally denied the history associated with the Holocaust and accused Israel and the Jews of using it as an excuse for their heavy-handed ways with the Palestinians. And, yet, many embraced Hitler and the Nazi Party.

That sparked a discussion about **Kristallnacht*—*the Night of Broken Glass***. The night of Nazi sanctioned terror in 1938— riots and public disturbances were aimed at Jewish businesses, schools, and synagogues. More than 200 religious houses of worship were destroyed all over the Germany, thousands of Jewish businesses were wrecked, and tens of thousands of windows shattered, countless books burned in great bonfires. The Jews were then ordered to clean up the damage and pay for it, adding insult to injury.

History's lessons were never far from the Jewish community and though they may have not known their scriptures, they knew about this episode of the history in their suffering.

The Jews taught their children, and those children taught theirs, and so on, thus keeping the history alive, never to be forgotten. One of the more interesting things about the Jews was that they were living history, proof to some, that God was alive and working. He preserved this tiny race of people but for what purpose was anyone's guess.

Even in non-religious Jewish homes, the Holocaust was never very far from even the non-observant Jewish mind. Many Jews couldn't explain much about the Bible or Jewish history but they always knew about the Holocaust, perhaps the most important event in their living and historical memories. And every Jew knew what the number 'six million' meant.

In Nazi Germany, the government began passing legislation in the early 1930's, first to isolate the Jews, strip them of their citizenship and livelihoods, confiscate property, and make their lives as miserable as possible. These became known as the Nuremburg Laws. Could this happen in the U.S?

Stage one of the Holocaust had nothing to do with a systematic murder machine, but rather was designed to expel the corrupting influence of the Jewish beast from within. Jews such as Einstein left early, reading the signals correctly, paying the appropriate bribes, and escaping in the first wave, numbering approximately 50% of the German Jews. The rest of the Jewish population became the 'proverbial frog in the pot.'

Still, almost half of the Jews in Germany got out... it was mostly others who were cut off and condemned, such as Poles, Czechs, Ukrainians, Hungarians, and other Central and Eastern Europeans. Ninety percent of Polish Jews eventually lost their lives.

But, this was America, a place of safety and freedom. Yet, the distant echoes were closer than they appeared and were getting closer, though not many perceived it correctly.

They discussed rumors of a bill in Congress dealing with religion, something about the upcoming census, but it didn't seem like anything to worry about at the time. Now they weren't so sure.

"So, then," said Eleazer, "what we have is something we need to keep our eyes on. Things are building but to what, only Ha Shem knows."

And then, changing the subject, Eleazer asked, "By the way, did you happen to see that story of another group of archeologists climbing Ararat?"

"Yeah, something came across the wire. I think I saw it on Yahoo or Google, or somewhere. It's probably nothing but just another attempt at finding Noah's Ark."

Neither rabbi was a particular believer in environmental theories such as global warming' or its cousin 'climate change,' but what made this most recent attempt interesting was that the snow, always an obstacle in previous efforts to find the ark, had receded several hundred feet below the suspected placement of the most famous watercraft in history, if it existed at all. The rabbis believed it was real but didn't spend much time pondering the details. The slight warming was working in the climbers' favor.

Still, another story on the back page of a recent edition of the New York Times mentioned a provocative discovery found buried deep in the Judean desert by two hikers. Though Chaim hadn't read the article, Eleazer had. The story dealt with the discovery of what appeared to be an ancient Hebrew Language scroll that was entitled *The Good News According to Matthew.* Other found scrolls included The Gospels According to Mark, Luke, and the Book of Acts, and several lost books of the Bible, including the Book of Jasher, the Book of Jehu, and the Book of Nathan, each truly astounding finds that had the Antiquities authorities buzzing.

Further Hebrew fragments found seemed related in some way to the **Brit Chadasha*.** There were rabbinical letters with believers in various cities around the Middle East. Also popping up were several chapters from the Book of Revelation. Scholars dated the previously known Dead Sea Scrolls to approximately 100 years before the Common Era. This latest find wasn't dated yet.

But as everyone involved with such things knew, the Brit Chadasha was not completed until later in the First Century, meaning someone had buried them, most likely in haste, fairly soon after the crucifixion of **Yeshua*** and perhaps after the deaths of some of the disciples.

Of course, the Book of Revelation was dated about 90 CE, meaning that there must have been a Hebrew reading and speaking contingent who wrote and understood this version of the Brit Chadasha. Perhaps there was something akin to an early Messianic congregation that called the desert home and buried the scrolls for posterity. Who knew?

The discovery was strange, the timing even stranger. Some of this discussion called to mind another missing Book of the Bible, *The Book of the Wars of the Lord,* traces of it found in the book of Numbers. The antiquities community noted the timing of the Dead Sea Scrolls had strangely coincided with Israel's birth. This discovery, however, had many of the scholars puzzled, for up to this moment, there had been only a shadow of a set of Hebrew language documents of the New Testament. Scholars debated this for centuries.

Both rabbis dismissed pretty much anything dealing with 'Christian' thought, though the discovery had caused quite a stir in the Messianic Jewish community. Of course, all this talk led to discussion of Bible prophecy, much of which was getting harder and harder to deny. Chaim had exchanged several emails with his Messianic friend about the subject. So much of what the Messianics had been talking about for years now seemed like it was happening right before their eyes.

'*No, just a coincidence,*' thought Chaim.

The rabbis both agreed that Christians couldn't be Jews and Jews couldn't be Christians. Was there another answer? Was something there that they couldn't understand but was right under their noses?

Interestingly enough, a well-known Christian pastor and scholar, Jonathan Roberts, favorably prepossessed towards Israel and the Jews, had been touting such stories in newsletters both in print and on his website, and of the ark's latest search party's efforts to find the relic. He believed, taught, lectured, and wrote that in the last days, many of the ancient unsolved questions of the Bible would be mysteriously revealed as living testimonies to the veracity of Scripture. These were just a few of many stories (or legends according to the skeptics) he discussed and taught over the years.

For years Chaim had followed Roberts' work, read his books, listened to his talks, and dialogued with him about current and future events. Still, he remained a little aloof and cautious of his theology. Even so, these discussions had begun to work on his inner soul and he began seeing things from a different perspective. The two became closer friends by the day.

The Ark's search team, made up of teams of international scholars and their guides, were equipped with the latest satellite communications equipment and small laptops capable of acquiring and bouncing signals off multiple satellites and beaming their reports to a waiting world. They believed they were onto the most amazing archeological find of the last 4,000 years, maybe ever.

The New Testament documents were an entirely other matter. Many international scholars were amazed yet puzzled as to what it could mean, and maybe more to the point to a largely unbelieving world, what if it was true? And those "missing" books of the Bible? What did that mean?

> **The Good News According to Yochanan**
> Chapter 15 Verse 13
>
> Greater love has no one than this that one lay down his life for his friends.
>
> **From Rav Shaul (Paul)**
> 2nd Epistle to the Thessalonians, 2:11-12
>
> For this reason, God will send them a powerful delusion so that they will believe the lie. Then all who have not believed the truth but have taken pleasure in unrighteousness will be condemned.

Chapter 19

Righteous Gentiles

The Learning House was the ministry organization and institute founded by Jonathan Roberts. The institute was established as a spiritual support, biblical resource, international network, information exchange, and staunch advocate for Israel and the Jewish people. The organization was born from Roberts' own personal travail and troubles.

He loved military service and wanted active duty till liver spots and lapses in memory appeared. But years of dangerous missions, sudden deployments, long separations, and too many unknowns... took its toll on Roberts' family. He separated from active duty, kept his commission in the Naval Reserves, and accepted an invitation to apply for a civilian job with the National Security Agency.

The National Security Advisor had given the President three applications to review. He finished and called his NSA Chief into the Oval Office.

"Bill, talk to me about Roberts," the president began. "The other two are in the trash headed back to your office."

"Yes, Mr. President... " the NSA Chief replied. "Commander Roberts would stay qualified for carrier flight ops. He'd still be active duty and not just reserves—if his wife had let him. Her orders are for him to be safer and seen more at home."

"His jacket says that he was in our black-joint-forces Project Enoch." The president noted. "It this number right? It says he provided operational coordination, cover, cleansing, and command in a Dark Knight cockpit for 234 missions. Check those numbers, Bill. No wonder his wife was pissed. Give me a confirmation on those numbers, and I'll give him a medal."

"You already did, Mr. President."

"Then I'll give his wife a medal!"

"His NSA responsibilities will require travel, but much less and not in body armor."

"Good. And so, how's he gonna help me?"

"Well, Mr. President, Commander Roberts has already proven his military genius. He has an uncanny ability to interpret intelligence, develop analysis, suggest strategies, predict developments, propose counter-measures, and more. He has a special sense and skill to present variable options for uncertain scenarios and operations already in play. Plus he plays the role of devil's advocate and counterpoint for his own proposals."

"I want you to double-check this I.Q. score, too. Get the confirmations and get your butt back here before I leave the office."

"Yes, Mr. President."

"And Bill...." The NSA Chief stopped and turned back. The president said, "I find this guy and his service jacket hard to believe. Prove me wrong, Bill, and you better be prepared to have him and his wife in here tomorrow for lunch with me and my wife."

Roberts remained with the president's NSA team from the last year of his first term to the end of his second term. He proved to be everything and more than his press. His broad ability, global savvy, strategic smarts, and personal popularity among people in power—all this increased his value to the president. But this meant a shift from the work he loved behind the scenes to a more accessible position near the president.

Roberts found politics and public visibility a bitter pill to swallow. But he forged friendships and contacts with people in high places—at home and abroad. Roberts later noted, "I may have chaffed then, but now I see God's hand. He gave me the education, exposure, and experience he wanted and I needed."

✡ ✡ ✡ ✡ ✡ ✡

A few months after the new president's inauguration, Roberts fled the Beltway at mach three. He applied his genius in the corporate world of big business. But his faith, intelligence, character, and integrity were no match for the deceit, betrayal, avarice, and greed of the business community. He was humbled by serpents that professed faith but practiced fraud. Experts in legal larceny, they repeated the phrase: *It's not personal—just business.*

Roberts longed for the integrity and camaraderie of military service. He wanted to do something where honor and honesty weren't handicaps.

Deep inside his heart hungered for spiritual things. He loved biblical study and was more of a scholar than many seminary professors. So he lowered his sights, scaled down his business ambitions, and plugged into the pastoral staff of a well known mega-church in Southern California.

Roberts packed the house whenever and wherever he taught. People were hungry for his kind of presentation. He was able to teach God's Word and ancient prophecies in light of current events and the near future. His intellectual prowess and personal integrity rang true with those who received from and supported his ministry. They had longed for a minister who taught with power and authority. Plus Roberts provided pertinent briefings of the world around them—a man with his finger on the world's pulse.

Israel and the Jewish people were central to Roberts' ministry and teaching. He defended his bias with common comment, "Any bias or focus I may have is a proportional response to the emphasis I find in scripture and the heart of God. Any complaint—take it up with the author of this." Then Roberts would lift his Bible high and shake it.

Over the course of two years Roberts had focused more and more time on ministry and less on business. And he felt more fulfilled than ever.

Then Roberts returned to his office after a luncheon appointment and found Luke Phillips. "Hey, Luke," Roberts greeted. "I thought our time is Friday night at my place."

"It is," Luke responded.

"So what brings you by? Everything okay?"

"Yeah, everything's fine. Except... you haven't given me an answer."

Roberts reviewed his paper messages and sorted through email. "Uh huh..." he mumbled. "That's nice...."

"Jonathan, aliens landed in the dry river bed and you promised to introduce me. Remember?"

"Huh, let me see. You know my wife's fixin' dinner Friday—your favorite."

"One of the aliens claims to be your cousin. And another says she was your kissin' cousin and you promised to marry her."

"What?!?" Robert came to attention. "What did you say?"

"Two years ago I moved down, found work, and made a deal with you," Luke said.

Roberts got up from his seat and plopped down in a plush office chair next to Luke. "I apologize, Luke. You're such a familiar friend that sometimes I don't give you the respect you're due."

Lew smiled, nodded, and continued, "Our deal.... You agreed to mentor me in spiritual matters. And I agreed to be your techno-nerd, AV engineer, and rear guard behind the scenes at your Bible studies and speaking engagements."

"Haven't I kept my bargain?" Roberts asked.

"Yes, but I want more. I want to tweak things a little." Luke studied Roberts' eyes to measure his focus.

"You name it, buddy."

"You know Jonathan, you may be super intelligent, but you're not very smart."

"I can't argue that... I'm listening."

"I've got two yeaChars worth of your teachings recorded, edited, and in the can," Luke said with his nose wrinkled and eyes squinted at Roberts. "And a whole year I've dug my spurs into you. I want the word to broadcast. I think you're missing the boat. It only means more exposure, more support, and more more...."

"I know what it means. It means trouble." Roberts said with slow measured words and sad eyes. "What's your plan of attack?"

Lew got excited and began, "I've got more that plans. I've got all my ducks in row. And here are my ducks: First, online audio broadcasts and downloads. Second, radio broadcasts of the same. Third, online video broadcasts and downloads. Fourth, video on cable and broadcast television. Then offer the materials packaged into albums organized by the study series."

"Gotcha," Roberts responded. "But first... I need one random audio sample from each month."

"You got it! Check your messages tonight for the attachment." Luke was all smiles.

Roberts had no smiles. He was listless. Deep furrows marked his forehead. Half-closed tired eyes saw sorrow from somewhere. He let out a sigh, took a deep breath, held it, and let it all go in a groan.

"So what's wrong? What's the trouble?" Luke whispered.

"Lew, I want you to answer that question for me in three months."

"Why?"

"Your question has no real value to you yet, but it will in three months. *Why?* Well, the Lord prepared me for this. I knew you'd come. And I knew I'd have to say yes. Not for your youthful zeal—for God's perfect will. The Lord said, 'Now!'"

"God told you I'd come?" Luke questioned.

"Yes. But more, he told me the troubles this would bring. I saw the trials that will come and continue. But he also showed me the counter balance of blessings to come in time."

Roberts saw the puzzled looked still on Luke's face. "Remember our study together about this? Genesis 18? Abraham's three visitors?" Roberts stood, grabbed his Bible, handed it to Luke, and said, "Turn there and read verses 17 and 18:

Lew found the chapter and verses:

> *And the LORD said, Shall I hide from Abraham what I am doing, since Abraham shall surely become a great and mighty nation, and all the nations of the earth shall be blessed in him?*

Lew nodded his head up and down and said, "Now, I remember. God tells him about Sodom."

"Right. Now turn to Amos 3:7 and read it."

Lew found the spot and said, "Got it.... *'Surely the Lord GOD will do nothing, unless He reveals His secret to His servants the prophets.'*"

"What's that all mean to you?" Roberts asked.

"Well, I guess God keeps his friends and servants in the loop." Luke answered, squinted at Roberts, and awaited his approval or not.

"You are spot on, Luke. Now, to get the inside skinny don't quiz or cozy up to me. Find that prayer closet or park and make friends with the One with all the answers. And while you're there, please pray for me."

Roberts needed Luke's prayer and more. The material was broadcast and Roberts was buried by the rush. Messages, requests, calls, visits, and demands for his time came in from all over the world.

Less than three months into the broadcast, Roberts was invited into the host pastor's office. The meeting was civil. The pastor was concerned about some of Roberts and his "imbalances" and "undue focus on Israel" and much more. But in the end Jonathan was asked to go.

Lew heard the news and began to rail on about the pastor. "He's just jealous 'cause he doesn't have the effect you do. It's sour grapes...."

"Stop!" Demanded Roberts. Then he put both of his big hands around Luke's upper arms. Held him firm, got close to his face, and said, "*Do not speak evil of a ruler of God's people.* I have taught you better than that. Pastor is a great man who has helped us and furthered the Kingdom in many ways. We love him, pray for him, and respect his wishes."

In the rush and rise of his ministry, Roberts had neglected his booming business. He trusted others to manage things for him. Instead, he awoke to greater trouble than before. He found his funds drained, his associates and advisors gone, and his investors enraged. Lawsuit after lawsuit led to bankruptcy and the loss of everything.

Roberts and his family moved to Idaho. He continued the ministry he'd begun—*The Learning House*. The agreement between Luke and himself continued—Lew was happy to be home. And Roberts found the success, support, serenity, and personal satisfaction for which he'd longed. He was happy, and his wife was happy, too.

Roberts' public exposure, profile, and demand grew beyond reasonable expectations. Attention was drawn to his words and works. His support of Israel and the Jewish people drove a wedge between him and many segments of Christianity. Churches with deep historical roots, social agendas, emergent-church ties, or replacement theology doctrine were at greatest odds with Roberts.

The annual conference *Ecumenism: Christianity in America* invited Roberts to join the public forum and panel. He provided balance for the anti-Semitic comments of some. That led to a question from a fellow panel member.

"Dr. Roberts, you are an enigma to many of us here. I can't help but wonder: Are you Jewish?" Laughter erupted all over the auditorium.

Roberts smiled at the crowd and nodded toward his questioner. "Am I Jewish? No. But the God I worship is!" The same crowd now responded with some laughter but far more boos, jabs, and hecklers.

Then he looked to the forum moderator and said, "Bishop Manley, if I may, I'd like to beg your indulgence and excuse myself."

A perfect plastic smile covered the Bishop's face. He turned his head to Roberts, closed his eyes, nodded once, and said, "Of course, my son."

Roberts gathered notes, his name card, and briefcase. Every eye watched him and every sound fell silent. He began to walk away but stopped. He paused, thought, turned back toward the panel, and said, "Previous engagement.... I need to wash my car."

Then Roberts looked to Heaven and said, "Father forgive me. I didn't know what I was doing."

Coffee House Chatter

"Do you have your passport? Is it updated?" she probed.

"Uh, no. In fact, I've never even had one," he said, rather embarrassed.

"Well, I think I'd rather be prepared, having everything in place, y'know?" she said.

"Ok, ok, I get it. But, how close are we?" he pressed.

"Well, I don't exactly know, but I'd say at least one day closer. You may want to get down the post office and get rolling," she said.

"Alright, tomorrow, that ok?" he asked.

She just smiled. She liked winning arguments, especially when he had no defense.

Chapter 20

Aryeh Cohen

Reports of Roberts' comments at the conference spread. He attracted new supporters and greater global attention. Some of that interest came from certain key players within the Israeli government. Aryeh Cohen was one such individual.

Aryeh served as director of communications for the former Prime Minister of Israel. Both he and his former boss knew and liked Roberts from his NSA days. It was Aryeh's work and relationship with Roberts that brought him before the current prime minister.

"Shalom, Aryeh!" The prime minister stood and offered the greeting.

"Shalom, Mr. Prime Minister."

The prime minister reseated himself behind his desk, picked up a file jacket, and looked at Aryeh. "Your research, analysis, and published works on Islamic terror are impressive. You left government, and you got busy."

"Thank you, Sir." Aryeh, an introvert, was uncomfortable in the spotlight. This made him the perfect Director of Communications. His press conferences were prepared, precise, and professional. He couldn't be distracted or carried off by the media or others. But he wasn't prepared for this meeting. His body was tense. His eyes, hands, and feet wouldn't be still. He stared at the floor.

"I'm told that you are our foremost expert on the encroachment of Islamic terrorism around the globe," the P.M. said. "I admit, I haven't read all your work, but I trust my team. They say you can identify the earliest indicators of Islamic mischief in an area. You have a systemic understanding of formation through execution for any given terror act, operation, or campaign. And more, I'm told you have a model for all this."

"Let's see, here...." The P.M. picked up the file. "Your model can predict, follow, and project the terror event... from vision, mission, strategies, tactics, recruitment, training, timing, logistics, action, and so on." The P.M. stopped, tilted his head down, and looked at Aryeh over his reading glasses.

"I pay attention... Mr. Prime Minister."

"That's what I'm told." The P.M. took his glasses off, leaned forward and made eye contact. "My team calls you *The Weather Man*. I also understand you have given my team first-eyes on your most comprehensive models and information. And you work with them on what should be published. I appreciate that, Aryeh."

"Lives are at stake, Mr. Prime Minister, maybe even an entire civilization." Aryeh looked down to deflect the kudos, but lifted them again to say, "It was part of my agreement with my benefactor who has funded and continues to fund my research." The P.M. opened his mouth to speak, but spoke first. "And my benefactor's stipulation in our agreement was that his name and involvement remain confidential in perpitude."

The P.M. smiled, nodded, and then paused for a long moment. He shuffled papers and files around on his desk. Then he looked at Aryeh. Smile was gone—face straight, sober, and serious. And his voice became pointed and deliberate, "Do you keep track of developments in the U.S.?"

Aryeh looked into his hands on his lap and then answered, "Mr. Prime Minister, I received the IDF briefing with the other officers in my reserve unit. And I am invited to lecture there from time-to-time."

The prime minister scribbled a few notes and asked, "What about Roberts? I understand the former P.M. and yourself were on 'first names' with him."

"Mr. Prime Minister, my boss was more informal than...."

"No!" the prime minister interrupted. "Not that. I mean, Roberts. How well did you know him? What do you think about him?"

"Yes, Mr. Prime Minister. I'm sorry." Again Aryeh looked to his lap. "We had a cordial, cooperative, and casual relationship. I valued every opportunity we had to talk or do an activity together. He is one-in-a-million—a **gibbor***. He has an I.Q. of 195, doctorates in aeronautical engineering and divinity, decorations for air combat...."

"No!" The prime minister interrupted again. "I have his file filled with facts. I want to know about Roberts, the man. What does your gut tell you about him? How do you feel about him, today?"

"Mr. Prime Minister, Commander Jonathan Charles Roberts is a fierce patriot who would defend his country with his last breath. But...." Aryeh turned his head and look for the words. "He is the only true and good Christian I've ever met. He loves our nation and the Jewish people wherever they may be. He believes, lives, and teaches Genesis 12:3. And... he believes that Jesus Christ is *Yeshua Ha'Mashiach*—the one and only Jewish Messiah.

"He doesn't tell Jews to become Christians. But he does tell Christians to rethink their holidays and get in line with scripture."

"I'm listening," the P.M. said. His hands rested on his desk and his eyes were fixed on Aryeh.

"He is a man of his word. Whatever circumstances arise, he will do the right thing. He is uncompromised in his faith. His first and greatest priority and passion is to serve his God—the Lord God of Israel." Aryeh searched his mind for anything else and decided to say, "I trust him with my life."

"It's not your life I'm worried about," the P.M. said. "I need your service for an undetermined amount of time."

"Of course, Mr. Prime Minister. May I ask...."

"No," the P.M. interrupted. "You will tell me what the nature, longevity, requirements, logistics, and details of your assignment will be after you are in country and in contact with Dr. Roberts." The P.M. dropped his head and rubbed his temples. "Oy...." He lifted his head, looked at Aryeh, and said, "Okay.... Someone will be in to take you through your paces. You'll get your briefing, paperwork, resources.... Are you married?"

"I was, Mr. Prime Minister. Married twenty-five years."

"Ahhh, Aryeh, I'm sorry. I should have remembered. I gave you her medal, myself. She was a fine woman." The P.M. shook his head back and forth several times. "Such a loss... for you and all of us."

The P.M. stood, moved to Aryeh, and sat next him. "A Jewess born and raised in Egypt. So many times she'd go to become our eyes, ears, and provide her analysis. No one could have been trained to be what your Sari was. She saved the lives of so many of our people."

The P.M. paused, looked for Aryeh's eyes, and said, "You know, you're a hero, too. I can't imagine what you felt. I can't see my wife, my Miriam, in the *Mossad* as your Sari.... Well, I... I don't think I could...." The two made eye contact and the P.M. put his hand on Aryeh's shoulder.

"Aryeh, this wound may still be.... Well, I mean, if you'd rather not...."

"NO! I mean, respectfully, Mr. Prime Minister... I want to go. I **need** to go. I will go. I know it's what Sari would want—expect of me. It will be good to see Jonathan. I've wanted to talk to him ever since Sari.... Well, I mean...." Aryeh's eyes found his lap—he was embarrassed by his thoughts.

"Thank you, Colonel Cohen. I understand."

Aryeh took a fresh breath, looked at the P.M., and asked, "Mr. Prime Minister, how is Dr. Roberts?"

"That's what you will tell me—within the week. He's had a lot of exposure in recent weeks. Forces beyond his control have made him stand out from the crowd. His government is clueless. Still, eyes have found him. They watch now until he becomes a threat. Then... well... But you're not going to let that happen. Are you, Aryeh?"

"No, Mr. Prime Minister."

A knock at the door—the P.M.'s personal secretary stuck her head in. "I'm sorry, Mr. Prime Minister, Agent Rekevesh is here."

"Thank you. I'll bring the Colonel out." Then the P.M. turned back to Aryeh and said, "Your tour guide is here. But before you go... a few final thoughts. First Aryeh, I have never seen, heard, or known a director of communications like you—anywhere. You can command any size group or audience. I've never seen you make enemies in your press briefings, presentations, or lectures. You disarm opponents, dismantle their objections, and gain their admiration in the process. You're a walking library, terror expert, intuitive observer, intelligence insider, and fierce warrior. And... " The P.M. surveyed Cohen. "And you have a spiritual side."

Aryeh wanted to respond, but he knew better.

The P.M. continued, "So, connect with Roberts and co-present with him in his blitz. Package and present your info to his audience. Give frequent reports to my Mossad chief, Ben Yehuda. Colonel, in public, you are directed to carry diplomatic credentials, weapons sufficient to the threat, mail-mesh-material on your body, RF detectors, and your superior wits. Partner and protect your friend Roberts. Whether he knows it or not, he is a vital asset that we can't afford to lose. The same goes for you."

The P.M. stood, walked Aryeh to the door, and handed him to Agent Rekevesh. "She'll make sure you do and have everything necessary. And Aryeh, please give Dr. Roberts my personal regards, but he is not to know a word of our discussion nor of your mission."

"Of course, Mr. Prime Minister. And thank you."

> **From the Writer of the Proverbs**
> **Chapter 8:10-11**
>
> "Take my instruction and not silver,
> And knowledge rather than choicest gold.
> For wisdom is better than jewels;
> And all desirable things cannot compare with her."

Chapter 21

Beth Emunah

"Aryeh! Aryeh! Aryeh Cohen!" Roberts cupped his hands like a megaphone and yelled at the familiar face. Cohen heard Roberts, turned, and walked toward him. The two met and hugged.

"It's been too long, my friend!" Roberts' joy was infectious. "I can't believe this. God knew I needed a friend."

"Really?" Aryeh asked. "Well, you don't know how I've longed to talk to spend some time with you."

"I just can't believe this!" Roberts spun around and hugged Cohen again. "Thank you, Lord!" Roberts held Cohen at arms' length, looked at him, smiled, and then his face went straight and cold. "Oh, God. Aryeh. I'm sorry. I forgot. I just saw it in your eyes. Sari." Roberts hugged him again. "My friend, I'm truly sorry. I can't imagine your grief. I read that another star was placed on your wall there. I asked around and then.... Well, I wanted to call—then I told myself that I'd see you on my next visit, but I.... I'm sorry, Aryeh."

"Thank you, my dear friend. Maybe we can have that talk while we're both in town," Aryeh proposed. "I need it bad."

"Yes, let's talk over dinner tonight," Roberts said. "But details first.... What brings you to Newark?"

"It's complicated. In thumbnail... work brought me to the U.S. My main research mission will apply and test my model here. My research investigation is threat assessment in America. Of course, I live for observation, data collection, interviews, and so on. And last, personal, professional, and secret goal was to cross paths with you and compare notes.... I just find it hard to call and ask for favors.

"Then I called an old friend, a local rabbi. His congregation is Beth Emunah."

"No way! Aryeh, really?" Roberts grabbed Cohen's shoulders. "You came because of me?"

"Are you kidding me?!" Roberts hugged Aryeh again. "Man, I'd give my eye teeth and a kidney to compare notes with you! I got the review copies of your books. I was in awe. I couldn't wait to talk with you and get the back-story and between the lines stuff. Your books were...." Roberts looked to the side and thought. "Aryeh, your books were rich treats to me, and I'm sorry I didn't tell you—life changing.

"I meant to say and do a lot of things, but... well... this last year has been as tough as any battle I've seen. I've been mistreated, maligned, knocked-down, beat-up, bloodied, and betrayed. Still, I got back up.

"Bottom line... we moved to Idaho, licked our wounds, started a non-profit work, and continued to broadcast teachings. Now, I feel like I fit in and God has honored our work. We've had support mushroom, online sales explode, speaking opportunities flood in, and success stress hit a new level each month. We've hit the ceiling." Robert saw Cohen's puzzled expression.

"I mean. We can't keep up. It's my wife, my young friend Luke, my daughter, and me. I call our staff Skeletor! Ha! But it ain't so funny." Roberts looked down, shook his head, and said, "People I trusted cut my throat. And now... in this new chapter.... Well, it's hard for me to trust. Anyway, I'm sorry I didn't communicate better. Still, thank you." Roberts put his hand over his heart. "From the bottom of my heart."

"You're welcome, my friend. I can relate, believe me. And about the books... I can tell you some back-story, but I need to keep *some* secrets—you understand."

Roberts face lit up like the Jerusalem on Saturday night. "Hey, Aryeh, of course, I got it! Listen... I refuse to present at Beth Emunah alone. Not with you in the crowd. No way. You gotta promise that you'll co-present tonight. I mean... How could such a treasure sit on his hands while a hick like me rambles. No way. You have something to say, and you're gonna say it tonight. Gosh, you're outta my league with this stuff."

"Jonathan, I don't know...."

"Stop. Not a word. Don't even try to say no. We'll work things out."

✡ ✡ ✡ ✡ ✡ ✡

"Shalom and good evening. My name is name is Rabbi Levi Herschel and welcome to Beth Emunah" The rabbi paused, smiled, and surveyed the auditorium.

"My wife should be here. I told her this would happen." He looked around again, turned to Cohen, and said, "Will you look at this, Aryeh. A *Shabbat* crowd, no less! And you, my friend...." Eyes still on Cohen but hand extended toward Roberts. "Even you came for him!"

The regulars responded in laughter. The visitors had blank or wary stares.

"No, seriously, folks...." the Rabbi returned to the crowd. "We're honored that you're here." Then he motioned toward Cohen and Roberts and said, "And we are blessed to have these two uber menches with us tonight." The applause and cheers were deafening.

Rabbi Herschel threw his hands up and yelled out, "Hold on, hold on.... Let me check." He stepped to his bema and looked inside. Shock and surprise covered his face. He slapped his forehead and said, "Oy vey! You broke my applause-o-meter!" More laughter.

The Rabbi spoke above the roar, shook his arm, and pointed his hand toward the back, "You better visit our *pushke* tonight!" Regulars laughed and visitors fell silent and resumed their stares.

"No, seriously... the *pushke*. No, no.... Hey, we are glad to see so many new faces tonight. I thought I had an idea about tonight. For sure I know both of these guys. But by the look of this crowd... you all must know something I don't. Just no surprises. Surprises I've had enough of today. Over coffee, I hear.... Uh, oh.... Friends, turn around. In the back... the one standing with the fist. My lovely wife, Rebekah. I didn't see you come in, *Libi*."

"Okay, business at hand. Our guests tonight." More applause. Rabbi Herschel bit his tongue and introduced Cohen.

"Regulars here at Beth Emunah know both of our speakers tonight. But our visitors may not." Rabbi Herschel walked over put his hand on Cohen's shoulder. "This distinguished fellow is Aryeh Cohen. He used to be the guy to know in Israel's government. He was Director of Communications for the ***former*** prime minister. Now, he's famous author, coveted speaker, and ad hoc professor at a number of prestigious universities—though none in Damascus or Tehran I hear." The Rabbi waited for a response. A few of the regulars chuckled. The Rabbi then turned off the humor and turned on his serious face.

"I'm told that he's the expert—bar none—on the spread of Islamic terrorism around the world. He hits this subject from different angles in his books. Aryeh is an academic inside-n-out. Still, his books are practical, easy-to-read, man-on-the-street, gotta-know and glad-I-know-stuff. With the rise of anti-Semitic and anti-Western terrorism, his information may save your life.

"Now to our other guest.... Well, you all know him. Anyway, he lost the coin toss. So we'll get to him soon enough. But first up is Aryeh. He's worked in the halls of power. He's rubbed shoulders with world leaders. But you would never know it. He's a humble man with a heart for others. Welcome and give your attention to my friend Aryeh Cohen." Rabbi Herschel signaled Cohen to come up, hugged him, and joined the applause.

"Thank you, Levi," Cohen said to his friend. "I hope you've never told them how we first met."

"Nooooo," Rabbi Herschel mooed. "I wouldn't embarrass you like that."

Cohen smiled, nodded, and mouthed the words, "Thank you."

"It is good to be among friends," Cohen began. "I'll keep my comments brief for two reasons. First, I wasn't prepared to speak tonight—it wasn't the plan. That leads me to my second reason to be brief. I'm not prepared because I came here for the same reason most of you did. I wanted to hear Jonathan." Cohen pointed to Roberts.

"Folks, I'm serious.... My friend Jonathan Roberts is one-of-a-kind. I can identify malicious patterns, threats, and potential events. But Jonathan is in another league. He can recognize the signs-of-the-times and something we call the times-of-the-signs. Think what you will about him...." Cohen shielded his mouth from Roberts and whispered, "I think God speaks to him."

"David had been a fugitive from King Saul. He found a refuge in Ziklag—the Philistine city given to him by the king of Gath. King Saul's days were numbered. Still, most of the Jews were clueless. The people followed in blind obedience. And Saul led countless thousands with him into the jaws of sorrows, suffering, slaughter, and death," Cohen lamented, shaking his head in sadness.

Roberts was on the edge of his seat, elbows on knee, eyes and attention focused on Cohen.

"However... " Cohen noted, "There were some men of discernment who could read the signs. They knew that Saul was the past—David was the future. These wise souls came to David at Ziklag and before. Numbered just in the hundreds they came. The tide would soon turn, and they would take it with David. And they did.

"These men became the watchmen and leaders that God used to usher in the Golden Age of Israel with King David at the head. They did not die with Saul—they lived to reign with David."

"Amen!" Roberts burst forth.

"Now, among these sage souls came leaders from a tribe near the Galilee. Listen. I'll read the words from the Tenach found in 1 Chronicles 12:

> And of the children of Issachar, which were **men that had understanding of the times, to know what Israel ought to do.** The heads of them were two hundred; and all their brethren were at their commandment.

"Men understanding the times... they knew what Israel ought to do—*had* to do. And they had the courage to step out and follow their hearts. Men like Joshua and Caleb. And Jonathan Roberts—he's that kind of man. Rabbi Herschel, too. And I hope that I am counted in their midst."

Roberts stood and moved toward Cohen. He wrapped his arm around his friend and buried his face in his upper chest. "You know you are, my brother. I will be your wing man any day—any time!"

Roberts found his seat and noticed the crowd. Here-and-there throughout the sanctuary—white handkerchiefs waved. Some stood and waved—others sat. Cohen turned back to Roberts. First a look of surprise—then both nodded and smiled.

Cohen stood silent, surveyed the crowd, closed his eyes, tilted his head, and listened. "There. There. Did you hear it? Did you feel it? The wind... the breath of God Himself." He paused and looked far off. Then he straightened, raised his voice, and declared, "It's begun to change!

"Friends, those of you who can't or don't or won't feel, see, or sense the change.... Well, my advice to you is this. Listen to those of us who do!

"Noah heard and proclaimed. But only eight were saved. All of Egypt heard the warning. But only those with the blood saved their firstborn. All of Jericho heard and saw. But only Rahab, the harlot, and her house were saved."

Rabbi Herschel turned to Roberts and said, "I hope you're ready for this. He'll have them tenderized, dipped, breaded, and ready for you to fry."

Roberts whispered back, "God knows I'm hungry."

Cohen stepped out from behind the bema and approached the people. His warm eyes and smile connected at a human level. He said, "Please stand to your feet." They all stood. "Now, go to ten people around you—other than your group. You might shake their hand or hug their neck, but be certain to look them in the eyes. See them as someone created and loved of God—like you. And then say to each one, 'I care about what happens to you.' But only say it if you mean it. Then please be seated again. Okay, go for it."

Cohen, Roberts, and the rabbi launched into the crowd and led by example. The atmosphere changed. The voices changed. Stuffy silence turned to sounds of joy and laughter. One elderly woman who couldn't stand wept and laughed and shouted out in praise. Rabbi Herschel hurried to her side. "Kitty are you alright?"

"Yes, of course! You're number twenty. Look at me Levi.... Listen... I care about what happens to you. Now, bend down so I can kiss you!"

The crowd of strangers returned to their seats as friends. Cohen returned to his place behind the bema. He stood, smiled, motioned to be seated, and said, "Now, believe me when I say.... I care about what happens to you.

"I told you that I had not prepared any words for tonight. That's true. But I carry with me...." Cohen pounded on his chest. "I carry a message in my heart. Wherever I go, I am prepared to share the burden of my heart. Listen to more than my words—please hear the message of my heart for you tonight."

The crowd was still, silent, and fixed on Cohen. "Friends, we face more than Islamic terror. Something far more dangerous is afoot. It is invisible to the average person.

"Population growth in the average Western nation is (and has been) zero or below. On-the-other-hand, the Muslim birth rate is +2 and is on the rise. Islamic populations within Western nations have surged. Their rate growth will transform the demographic of the Western world within this century, maybe far sooner. To see the days of a Judeo-Christian faith, heritage, and ethic look in your rear-view-mirror.

"Worse, we will have brought it on ourselves," Cohen warned. "We have allowed this to happen through immigration policies and the electoral process.

"Already we see this in several cities in Great Britain, France, and other European capitals, mosques springing up quicker than any other faith's houses of worship. Islamists live in cloistered neighborhoods where they force Sharia Law on any and all who wish to live there. They spread their faith from there into the greater population. Few Christians read or know their Bible. Fewer still could defend their faith. But the same is true for most Jews," Cohen asserted and turned to Rabbi Herschel, who nodded and winced.

"Europe is in decline. Islam holds majorities in a number of parliamentary districts in France and England. Its influence is growing. Remember just a few years ago, the debate started in both France and England about the Holocaust and how upset the Muslims were about it? Some talk circulated that Islamic fundamentalists had pressured members of parliament to remove it from the curricula of their schools. Though no legislation was introduced—new rumors persist. There is a steady drumbeat of holocaust denial coming out of the Islamic nations. During my last trip to London I noticed a lot of graffiti on the synagogues. Physical attacks on Jews have increased in all walks of life," he warned.

"One of the biggest problems the Europeans face- deals with the young people of these nations. Many are attracted to street crime and violence.

Many were born in Britain or France but had adopted radical Islamic ways. Their governments now face an internal insurgency which could lead to rebellion. Many of the street attacks were conducted by these native-born young Muslims, some as young as 15.

"Some of the social scientists blame it on poor living conditions within their ghettos. The truth—the Islamic message resonates with those who see themselves as downtrodden and disenfranchised.

"It mimics the youth of Nazi Germany in the last century. Their self-esteem waned, their economic outlook dimmed, and their dissatisfaction needed an outlet. They were primed and ready for a man with a message. And Hitler gave them purpose, passion, power, and a scapegoat. The perfect storm gathered, grew, and broke onto Germany's streets." Cohen's voice trembled and broke with emotion.

Cohen stood still, silent, and sober. No one stirred. No one spoke. No one saw anyone but the man before them.

"History has many lessons for the humble, honest, and open in heart and mind. History teaches that people and nations are fickle folk who forget. They seek self-centered solutions and short-sighted goals. Their *quid-pro-quo* mind-set asks, 'What have you done for me lately?'

"The morning weather report predicts rain. You carry an umbrella. The traffic alert reports an accident. You take another route. The calendar has a reminder. You get flowers. We hear and heed reports and signs every day. Please hear the report we bring tonight."

Rabbi Herschel joined Cohen and asked the people, "Do you have any questions for Dr. Cohen?"

A man in a black suit, full beard, and *peyot* (sidelocks) asked, "Are you here from the Israeli government to suggest *aliya?*"

Cohen opened his mouth to speak, but a young woman in her early 30s popped up. She spoke with alarm, "Will we Jews in America need to emigrate to Israel?"

Then another man shouted, "What will happen here in the U.S.? What do you know that you're not telling us?"

Cohen lifted his hands and said, "Hang on. Wait a minute." Cohen let the crowd settle. "Okay.... Now—look at it this way.... After 1938, there was NO WAY to get out of Germany. There had been a way, and some who saw the signs got out early. Still, they had to find a new home—a new country.

"We Jews didn't immigrate to Palestine in the 30s and 40s. *Why?* The British didn't allow us in. The West didn't let us out of the Displaced Persons (DP) camps until after the war. And the U.S.? What help did they lend us back then?"

"Well... the U.S. had an opportunity to break the deadlock and bring some of the refugees here. America sat at the table in two important international conferences. The first in Evian, France—1938. The second in Bermuda—1943. But no help, kindness, or compassion was shown. The delegates spouted U.S. immigration laws and denied the refugees entrance. And millions died in the interim." Cohen showed his emotion. His history lesson was personal.

"I've heard this tactic called "paper walls." It's a common practice in many organizations and governments. The boss is asked for a favor or a decision. They don't want to do the favor or make the decision. Nor do they want to alienate the party who asked. So the man-in-charge says, 'Oh, I'm sorry our policy won't allow me to do that.' Or 'I'll have to run this past my board of the appropriate committee.'

"The paper walls tactic was a U.S. strategy that meant suffering and death to millions. Yes, or course, it was the depression. But we all know European Jewry would have been a positive factor in America's economic recovery. No, the U.S. could have done much more. It was a purposed and planned action by this government.... and it wasn't just the government."

Cohen took a breath, a sip of water, and a moment to survey his audience. Everyone was onboard and attentive. He continued, "Many Americans have forgotten the story of the M.S. St. Louis. The German passenger ship left Hamburg on May 13, 1939 with 937 Jewish refugees aboard. It made its way to the American coastline off Florida. But the Coast Guard met it and kept it bay—in the sight of Miami—they could see the city lights. The St. Louis was not allowed to enter any U.S. port. They faced the same fate in Cuba and Canada. The refugees were refused entrance at every port-of-call they tried.

"Gustav Schröder, the ship's anti-Nazi German captain, had no choice—he had to return to Europe. He refused to bring any refugees back to Germany. He also told his crew to treat the passengers with the same courteous service they give any regular passengers. Captain Schröder worked hard to place his passengers in safe European countries. Great Britain took 288. The rest were distributed in France, Belgium, and the Netherlands. But the Nazis reached even there. In the end 227 of the ships number were imprisoned and killed by Hitler."

Cohen's voice wavered and broke. He cleared the emotion from his throat and took a sip of water. Then in a small voice he added, "For more get the book *Voyage of the Damned* by Gordon Thomas and Max Morgan-Witts—first published in 1974. Or see the film adaptation with the same title—1976."

Cohen wiped his brow, looked back at Roberts, and received a thumbs-up from his friend. Then he returned to the crowd and spoke in a level yet firm voice. "I believe in a Judgment Day. And I believe American leaders will face judgment for decisions like that and many others."

The room took on a pall. A still silence hung in the air. A few knew the story, but most did not. Cohen saw the question on the faces: *Could America really have done that?*

Cohen let his words take root and then added, "Today there is an Israel. She wants and waits for you to come home. So yes to *aliya*. But no—the Israeli government did not put words in my mouth."

Cohen looked at some scribbled notes, looked back at Roberts, turned back to the congregation, and said, "Will you HAVE to immigrate to Israel? What will happen here in America? What am I not telling you?

"Well, none of you HAVE to do anything you don't want to do. It's called free will. However.... Any number of events in the U.S. could lead you to emigrate. You might have to make bricks without straw.

"You've eyes and ears. You've witnessed the demographic changes. You've seen events in the U.S. heat up. You've been shocked at the violence and hate mongers. But will anything more happen?" Cohen paused to scan and note his audience.

"Well, one of my specialties these last several years has focused on the encroachment of radical Islam into the Western world. A meteorologist measures certain atmospheric conditions to predict the weather. I observe certain socio-politico-economic conditions, behaviors, and patterns to forecast events and make threat assessments. Just today, I arrived in the U.S. to collect data, make observations, do interviews, and research. I'll analyze what I find and determine my forecast for America. And I promise to share my findings with you." Cohen turned to Rabbi Herschel with his pledge. They both nodded and agreed.

Then Cohen lifted a 3x5 card and asked, "Do you know what this is?" The question was rhetorical—still he paused. "It's a Jonathan Roberts' scripture memory verse. He gave me a copy earlier today. It explains a lot about the man, his motivation, and his message. So to my fellow Jews— it's why I'm never offended at Jonathan's comments to us. I know his heart is in the right place. Here, I'll read it to you—it comes from the Prophet Ezekiel, chapter 33:

> *But if the watchman sees the sword coming and does not blow the trumpet, and the people are not warned, and the sword comes and takes any person from among them, he is taken away in his iniquity; but his blood will I require at the watchman's hand. So you, son of man: I have made you a watchman for the house of Israel. Therefore you shall hear a word from My mouth and warn them for me.*

"This is no game or idle pursuit for any of us on this platform. Nor is it up to our support team behind the scenes. Our time is limited in opportunities like these. But we will always tell you what we are able as time allows. It is up to you to dig and search out resources. Jonathan will give you information on where to begin."

Rabbi Herschel stood, gave Cohen a big hug, and words of thanks. Then he approached the mic. "Now, the man you all came to hear. A man who needs no introduction.... And that's a good thing because we don't have time for one anyway. Mr. Friend of Israel himself—the Reverend, Doctor, Professor, Commander Jonathan Roberts." The rabbi greeted Roberts with a hug—then he turned to Cohen and said, "Wake me when it's over."

Roberts turned back to Rabbi Herschel and said, "The title of Commander is just a courtesy, now. I retired from naval service this past year. I spent the last several years in the Navy's active reserves. And I already miss my monthly get-aways to San Diego."

Roberts arranged his notes on the bema, pick up his AV-controller, filled the screens with scripture, and began. "Ezekiel the Prophet saw the Jewish people scattered throughout the earth. He saw them lost and abused—sheep without a shepherd. But he foresaw Israel rebuilt as a nation. He foresaw his people returned to their homeland. They were drawn from every corner of the earth—called to come home.

"He was shown a vision of dry and lifeless bones and was told that it was Israel. The vision began in horror but ended in hope. Here... let me read it to you. I'll read the odd verses and you read the even ones. Roberts began and the people responded:

> Ezekiel 37
> *1 The hand of the LORD was upon me, and carried me out in the spirit of the LORD, and set me down in the midst of the valley which was full of bones,*
>
> *2 And caused me to pass by them round about: and, behold, there were very many in the open valley; and, lo, they were very dry.*
>
> *3 And he said unto me, Son of man, can these bones live? And I answered, O Lord GOD, thou knowest.*
>
> *4 Again he said unto me, Prophesy upon these bones, and say unto them, O ye dry bones, hear the word of the LORD.*
>
> *5 Thus saith the Lord GOD unto these bones; Behold, I will cause breath to enter into you, and ye shall live:*
>
> *6 And I will lay sinews upon you, and will bring up flesh upon you, and cover you with skin, and put breath in you, and ye shall live; and ye shall know that I am the LORD.*
>
> *7 So I prophesied as I was commanded: and as I prophesied, there was a noise, and behold a shaking, and the bones came together, bone to his bone.*
>
> *8 And when I beheld, lo, the sinews and the flesh came up upon them, and the skin covered them above: but there was no breath in them.*

> *9 Then said he unto me, Prophesy unto the wind, prophesy, son of man, and say to the wind, Thus saith the Lord GOD; Come from the four winds, O breath, and breathe upon these slain, that they may live.*
>
> *10 So I prophesied as he commanded me, and the breath came into them, and they lived, and stood up upon their feet, an exceeding great army.*
>
> *11 Then he said unto me, Son of man, these bones are the whole house of Israel: behold, they say, Our bones are dried, and our hope is lost: we are cut off for our parts.*
>
> *12 Therefore prophesy and say unto them, Thus saith the Lord GOD; Behold, O my people, I will open your graves, and cause you to come up out of your graves, and bring you into the land of Israel.*
>
> *13 And ye shall know that I am the LORD, when I have opened your graves, O my people, and brought you up out of your graves,*
>
> *14 And shall put my spirit in you, and ye shall live, and I shall place you in your own land: then shall ye know that I the LORD have spoken it, and performed it, saith the LORD.*

Roberts spoke on the dry bones vision and many other prophetic passages. He led the congregation through key predictions of the Jewish return to the land of Israel. He went beyond Ezekiel to the prophets Isaiah, Zephaniah, Zechariah, and others.

He was confident, enthused, and full of quotes and comments from rabbinical friends or commentaries. But something wasn't right. He stopped, offered up a silent prayer, and said, "You know... I have been known to miss the mark a time or two. I'm man enough to admit it. I can get over zealous and lost in my own presentations and leave my audience at the gate. I'm sorry. And now I sense a disturbance in here. So let's take advantage of this opportunity for growth and make a course correction to reconnect.

"I need your help and feedback," Roberts admitted. Then he asked, "What's on your minds?" He threw his arms open wide, lifted his eyebrows, and smiled.

A young man stood and said, "Dr. Roberts, I ask this for myself. Still... I know I reflect the thoughts of most in my Jewish community. To me... the scripture you displayed and discussed is not familiar. I hear it, yawn, and wonder, *what do those ancient texts have to do with me?* So my question: What makes you think that stuff is for this time?"

"Thank you," Roberts responded. "Your comments and question help a lot. The truth is that I don't know that this is the exact time. However, I do believe that we are in the season.

"For example, in the Torah Moses predicted that Israel would choose the wrong path. He foresaw their idolatry and sin. He warned that they would be scattered throughout the whole world. He didn't prophesy a calendar date for any of these things. Still, he knew they were coming. And, in fact, they did come. We know Israel suffered exile as a result of its disobedience.

"The prophetic judgments came to pass. So I have to believe that the prophetic blessings will come. That means the prediction that the Jews would be brought back to the land of Israel.

"The Jews are a blessing to virtually every nation on earth where they were allowed to live. The wandering Jew has indeed been good for the world. They brought medical and scientific advancements, economic progress, great learning, of course the wonderful research in all aspects of society, always with a willingness to share what they knew. Perhaps the world had grown jealous of this most amazing race of people. I'm sure you know the story of Jewish recipients of the Nobel Peace Prize."

"And now, it's time to look across the ocean and ask if this is the right time.

"Since the late 1880's, more than 5 million Jews have come, with more on the way. If I'm reading the "signs-of-the-times" or the "times-of-the-signs" correctly, a huge milestone occurred in 1948, with the establishment of the Nation of Israel. Prophecy watchers alive then got pretty pumped up about it. Israel captured Jerusalem in the Six Day War in 1967—for the first time in 2000 years Jerusalem came under Jewish control. And that was, with the U.S. feeding stolen Israeli battlefield intelligence to the Arabs," he explained.

That last piece of history was a hotly debated issue between the two nations, even so many years later and took the audience by surprise.

"That's enough for me," he added. And, last, he gave them both a parting gift and a warning. "Please don't take my word for it, but pick up a Bible. See for yourselves. Oh... and go out and get your passports—right away."

Roberts collected his materials, stood still for a moment, looked at the crowd, and said, "To close, I cannot leave you and would be a fraud if I didn't tell you why I believe this. I am a Christian; I believe Yeshua is the promised redeemer of Israel and the Jewish nation. I believe He died for my sins and was resurrected as foretold by the prophets. It is my belief that God is about ready to take the Children of Israel home to the land of their fathers, for eventual judgment and then redemption. Then, King Messiah will reign during the Millennium—1,000 years. I am also convinced that many in Christianity have misunderstood the intent of the message of salvation for it is to the Jews first, then to the Gentiles. I believe that all Christians, or those calling themselves such are about to be tested on this very issue."

Roberts' final word was spoken and Cohen sprang to his feet. He marched over to Roberts and said, "I'm sorry to do this, but may I ask for just five more minutes?" He looked at Roberts and turned to Rabbi Herschel.

Each nodded in agreement. Roberts found his seat, but Rabbi Herschel stepped to Cohen's side. He leaned toward the mic and said, "Folks it's okay. I know my friend Aryeh. He just wants the last word." The group laughed here-and-there, but they all gave Cohen their attention.

"I want to echo what Jonathan said. Get you passports ready. Don't panic—be prepared. Also find every one of your official documents—financial, military, insurance, titles, deeds, birth and marriage certificates, and so on. Keep them together in a safe location. You may want to register them with your county records office or make certified copies—to be double sure. Prepare a reserve cache of cash or other liquid assets.

"I'm no financial advisor, nor am I a U.S. citizen. Still, if I were in your shoes... I'd open a bank account in Israel. I'd be ready to sell everything and transfer funds to Israeli bank at a moments' notice."

Many in the audience were shaken. They began to shift and whisper. But he still had their attention. They wanted to hear his words.

Cohen continued, "Those who left Nazi Germany before the war left with some of their wealth. The Germans extracted a heavy tribute, tax, or bribe on those who wanted to leave. Still, they got out with something and their lives.

"Are you willing to gamble with your lives and the lives of your loved ones? Remember... those who forget history are doomed to repeat it."

Cohen left the bema and the platform and came down to the people. He made eye contact with as many as he could. Then he spoke. His words were warm and filled with concern. "Every one of us has missed important events or experiences in life. That special time with a son or daughter slipped passed without you. Your loved ones' hour of need and you were elsewhere. So many things in life only come once.

"My wife used to say all this to me. She read me a story from a copy of the *Brit Chadasha* she had been given. Before Yeshua's arrest, he expressed his sorrow through prayer in Gethsemane. This great prophet who had healed and helped so many asked his disciples to pray with and for him. He needed their support. *But you know what?* The closest three disciples fell asleep—steps away from his cries. I'm told it's the only time he requested personal prayer. He needed them, and they failed him.

"I can only imagine how they felt later. When they were needed most.... My wife asked me to join her in Cairo. She had a simple mission there and she wanted my company. But I had a book deadline. Ohhhh how I wish that I had gone. It haunts me every day of my life. Of course, her job was dangerous. Of course, I might have saved her. Of course, I could have been killed, too. But I'll never know—because I stayed and I missed the most important moment. And I'll never get that back. I'll never get her back."

Cohen fought hard to control his emotions. He took a moment and then said, "I'm all done. Thank you for your patience. I'll leave you with a little Shakespeare. *How's that?*

In the 4th act of William Shakespeare's Julius Caesar, Brutus tries to enlist Cassius to his aid. He says...

> *There is a tide in the affairs of men,*
> *Which, taken at the flood, leads on to fortune;*
> *Omitted, all the voyages of their life*
> *Is bound in shallows and in miseries.*
> *On such a full sea are we now afloat;*
> *And we must take the current when it serves,*
> *Or lose our ventures.*

"We all have high tides that come in with the promise of life and blessings. But some of us doubt or choose less important things. Others pull anchor and venture on to prosperity. We remain behind like sea creatures left in a high tidal pool. We will be dried out and dead before another high tide returns. We're left in shallows and miseries.

"I don't want that for you! So get those damn passports!"

"Thank you Jonathan and Aryeh. Thank you so much. You've given us so much to think about," Rabbi Herschel said.

Cohen and the rabbi hugged. Cohen still had the lapel mic on. Everyone heard him say, "Levi, I'm sorry I swore."

They all also heard the rabbi answer, "I never heard it. Your heart was too loud."

Rabbi Herschel later reported to Cohen and Roberts that the passport offices got real busy in the weeks that followed. "For Sale" signs have grown up like weeds in yards throughout the community."

And Bibles got dusted off, read, and used as the source of all sorts of questions for the good rabbi.

Coffee House Chatter

"You know what *b'shert* means?

"No, why?"

"Well, it means 'meant to be' in Yiddish. It's used a lot when trying to describe two lovers who were meant to meet, fall in love and get married. It can mean other things too... like destiny."

"Ok, I understand. Where are you going with this?"

"Sometimes I wonder if the world around is just a bunch of random events that just sort of happen, you know, no real order or anything. Then I see something and wonder how it fits into a larger picture."

Silence engulfed them and he remained silent for a couple of minutes, as he thought about what she said.

"So, for what it's worth, I see everything in this world connected to something else. Remember when all those Arab revolutions hit the news years ago? Well, I kept telling people they were all connected in some way. Nobody listened and then we found out how they were connected... boy did we ever!"

Now it was her turn to think about his comments.

"I see your point... maybe those revolutions were 'b'shert. It certainly changed the order of things in the Middle East."

Chapter 22

Changing Patterns

The phone jarred Ben Yehuda from his nap. He'd fallen sound asleep and was lost in his dream. But now, eyes wide open and fresh, he reached for the phone and heard the voice of Daniel Weinstein from the Operations Center.

"Avram, you might wish to come up here... something is going on... you need to see this."

Ben Yehuda reached for his cup of tea. It had cooled off but he tossed the last swig back anyway. This was his favorite because all the orange, lemon, and honey blended into a nice, sweet mélange of aroma and flavor. Tazo got it right.

He smiled, stretched, stood to hitch up his pants, and then headed upstairs to face the challenge. He rode up to the main operations floor, and exited the opening doors. Ben Yehuda's 85 years had been kind, though never easy. He wasn't immune to aches and pains. Still, he was sharp, fit, and focused on the task before him. His mind sped along faster than men half his age.

"So, what is this I need to see?"

He had pretty much seen it all. He had sifted through endless reports, listened to endless briefings, made countless battle plans, fought the wars, battled with the bureaucrats and maybe the most annoying thing of all, and shared tight quarters with analysts. He liked his space.

"We're seeing a spike in violent patterns." Weinstein began. "We've seen a number of attacks on Jews in the U.S." Most are in the East, but we're also seeing things in the Midwest and out West too. What makes this a little different is the lack of support coming from our more dependable friends."

What he meant to say was that there was no outcry from anybody in Congress, state governments, or any radio outlets, nothing, anywhere. Even the conservative talk show hosts had grown silent. This puzzled the experts. Israel could always count on their support and vocal defense over the years.

"We are monitoring all the talk shows, internet traffic, the blogs, everything. It's too quiet." Weinstein stared at Ben Yehuda through thick glasses, a worried frown on his brow.

And now it seemed the negative press about the economy, loss of jobs, and more pressures on families, drowned out any support for the Jews and Israel. It was almost like nobody cared. Was this a new trend? Had the status quo shifted away from Israel? It seemed almost sinister.

"Ok, anything else?"

"Whoever is doing this is also going after synagogues and cemeteries too... these are the typical things we often see such as graffiti and graveyard desecrations."

As bad as these were, it was the cyber attacks on reformed and conservative Jews in New York, as well as small Messianic congregations out west that caused even more concern.

"Most of the attacks seemed pretty minor, all things considered, until the past few weeks with clusters in various areas around the U.S. No deaths until the past few days. We've also heard about some beatings, car vandalisms, and like I said a moment ago, a lot of graffiti."

This was the first they'd heard of these other Jewish targets. Whether or not the Messianic congregations were really Jewish was always a point of contention, though they decided to keep an eye on things. Ben Yehuda's team was paid to spot trends and patterns around the world. It might be something. Then again, it might not. It wasn't his intention to determine who and who was not a Jew... the world had done that before and appeared to be doing it again, thank you very much.

Weinstein continued, "The attackers seem to be more of a mixed bag—we have reports of young Muslim gangs, Black Muslims, whites calling themselves Christians, even some skinheads in LA, a whole variety of attackers. We have heard of some drive-by shootings as well. We are working the patterns to tie all of this together into a bigger picture."

In the past 30 days, there had been about one attack a day, some smaller, some larger. But they continued to rise both in numbers and in intensity and diversity. He described the double murder of the young Jewish couple in San Diego. That one hadn't been pinned on anyone and nobody knew for certain if it was even classified as a hate crime.

"What's even stranger is that some traditional enemies like white racist skinheads and Black Muslims seem to be forming alliances. The Aryan Nation-related websites are lit up too. It looks planned."

"What do you make of it?" Ben Yehuda asked his young analyst. This last fact had gotten his attention.

"Well, I'm not quite sure, but if I were a betting man, I'd say we better keep an eye on this and start considering where we have to speed up our involvement."

That last comment shook his thinking. The grizzled veteran stopped for a moment and reflected on a conversation he had long ago with a former Israeli general, long since deceased. That conversation told of a plan, buried deep within the Israeli brain trust, where certain operational plans would be put into action if, what seemed another major systematic and planned action against Jewish targets became clear. He recalled its operational name, *Operation Last Exodus*. Was this the time?

"Get Shoshana, she needs to see this... She needs to weigh in on this."

Shoshana bat Levi was Ben Yehuda's right hand. Born and raised in Northern Israel, she was a **Sabra*** through and through. Sabras are known as tough on the outside and soft and sweet on the inside. The Sabra is actually a fruit akin to a prickly pear, and so it was that Shoshana and many of her kind who had gained their reputations from certain "personality traits."

Shoshanna impressed her superiors with her love for and understanding of flight. She had earned a place in Israel's first all female Strike Fighter Squadron. It was a distinguished and battle-seasoned bunch. Shoshana added to their reputation and made a name for herself. She scored five dogfight kills in Israel's defense in the Syrian-Lebanese regional conflict... a new record for a female or male pilot! The enemy pilots didn't know it was a woman who toasted their tail-feathers. The shame and dishonor would have consumed them long before the flames.

Her achievements were celebrated among discrete circles in Israel. Public recognition would put a target on her back and price on her head. She was a legend to those who mattered—end of story.

Shoshana always remembered upon whose shoulders she stood. First and foremost was Roni Zuckerman, Israel's first Israeli female fighter pilot to earn her wings way back in 2003. She survived and became a successful businesswoman.

Bat-Levi rose in the military ranks to full Colonel and eventually accepted a position in the Mossad, the main Israeli intelligence service. She advanced most recently to the recruiting arm of the agency. Working in the government, especially the military impacted all its members—family came second when the shooting began. In a sense, all of the Eretz Israel was family. Virtually no one escaped losing someone to either war or terror. Her marriage had suffered and her children often wouldn't see her for months at a time. Living in Israel had its sacrifices.

Shoshana was now in her 50's, thickly built but still beautiful. She had short, jet black hair with some highlighted streaks added in, sky-blue eyes, and spoke almost accent-less English as well as Yiddish, Italian, Arabic, passable French, and Spanish.

Her Hebrew was learned from her Sephardic roots, which meant she spoke the purist dialect of the ancient tongue. She picked up her Yiddish from Ashkenazi friends' families. With all of her education (a Masters Degree in Software Engineering) and skill, perhaps her true loves were mathematics, physics, and computer modeling. She held several patents and copyrights for software simulations as well as multi-layered virus protection and encryption systems which sold well in the West.

She learned… never sell the latest software release to your customers…. reserve next generation software for your own use. Her experience taught her well after being burned in a business transaction with someone she trusted. Her company was on two stock exchanges and was doing just fine, thank you. A $1,000 investment just five years before was worth ten times that now. Those skills and that wisdom would prove themselves invaluable many times over in the coming months.

"Shoshana, I want you to look at these analyses," Ben Yehuda said, motioning her over to the console.

"Our young friend here thinks he sees a pattern in all these reports."

Shoshana sat down at the desk and pulled up Daniel's analyses. Her fingers drummed the desk for a few moments, and then the questions started. She was a tough inquisitor.

"Daniel, tell me something, how many attacks and in how many places in the last 60 days?" she quietly asked, though it sounded challenging to him. He knew her voice inflections and understood when to be cautious when he answered. It felt like one of his comprehensive exams for his Doctorate.

The young analyst stood firm, confident in his conclusions.

"From what I've been able to gather, and the data is still coming in, it's like 35 total, mostly concentrated in areas of heaviest Jewish population, However, the rate and intensity has increased and continues to do so."

They discussed the four main Jewish population centers, displaying them on an electronic map on the wall. They were centered in the Southeast mostly in Florida and surrounding states. The Northeast included New York and Boston. The Midwest area included Chicago and surrounding cities. In the West were the greater Los Angeles area including Orange County and San Diego, with San Francisco and the Bay area thrown in for good measure. Wherever you found colleges, universities, hospitals, and large business districts, you will often find significant Jewish populations.

Spending time in this atmosphere with two of Israel's most decorated veterans caused him to stutter a little, though he didn't waver in his convictions.

"I've been watching the political gauges too, and from what I can see, normally dependable sources of Jewish support have gone silent. I can't say for sure, but when I put the numbers through some cause and effect simulations, I see incidents accelerating and conditions deteriorating."

"And," he added, "support from our traditional allies is nowhere to be found. It's almost like America has gone on radio silence."

"How about the previous 30 days, and the previous 45 days?" she asked. This question was meant to determine if the problem was getting worse. Daniel didn't hesitate a bit.

"These started about 60 days ago. We saw sporadic events like a few graffiti attacks or a random beating here and there. There was also a jewelry store robbery and murder. That store was owned by Jews as well. Then slowly at first and accelerating day by day, we saw things pick up in the last 30-45 days." Daniel paused, and went on.

"Then in the last 10 days, the restaurant and the insurance company murders, that school incident, it's all jumbled together as I've shown here in the scatter diagram. I've noticed more harsh rhetoric coming from our friends in the Nation of Islam and from this one Christian church in California and others like them. They like to post their comments online and broadcast them in speeches and by radio. We have our monitors everywhere."

The real science was to determine if these were coincidences or events aimed at American Jews. The analysts also wanted to see if the events made a trend or just random episodes and blips.

"Awhile back, the pastor of that mega church in California made some visits to various Middle East Muslim nations and held some news conferences where he reported on how well the Jews and the Christians were being treated under Islamic rule. We know it's the opposite as both the Christians and Jews fear for their lives. They are still treated as *dhimmis*. Any good treatment you see tends to be for the cameras. That same pastor also likes to attend Muslim conferences and speak on brotherhood and how well we should all get along—you know, Christians, Muslims, and Jews, the 'interfaith dialog stuff.' And, now, he's come out of nowhere with comments about the Palestinians and how poorly we treat them. Some of it sounds like what's coming out of the Vatican."

Shoshana nodded as she took all this in, piercing his eyes with hers. She clicked one screen, then another. She made a few keystrokes on the computer to test Daniel's theories. She paused for a moment, spun around in her chair, and faced the two men, and drummed her fingers on the desk. She let out a long and very audible sigh, forcefully blowing the air from her cheeks. Ben Yehuda and Weinstein stiffened in their chairs. Something else was bothering her.

"What about the earthquakes and volcanic activity we keep hearing about?"

Her mind raced to connect the dots. This last question was really more rhetorical in nature and not really meant to solicit an answer, but it was on her mind. She nodded to herself, satisfied that what she was seeing was indeed reality.

"I've factored natural disasters into the equation. Do you remember that book, 'Eye to Eye' written years ago? It correlated natural disasters with efforts by American politicians to force Israel into a peace with her neighbors. It was uncanny. Every time American negotiators tried to force Israel into some sort of arrangement against their will, they got hit by a hurricane, tornado, earthquake, or something else... tremendous damage in every case.... and I have to admit, that even as a scientist, I've begun to wonder myself.

"The author argued that Israel was God's land and no matter who tried to meddle, they would be punished, even Israeli leaders. History and current events seem to bear him out. As to whether or not God is responsible will be proven one way or another. Meanwhile, *it's man* I'm worried about. Avram, he's nailed it. Good job Daniel, good research, good analysis, cogent and to the point. The data tells us that something bigger than anything we've seen is coming."

"The regression data tells us that things are picking up at a rapid pace in both frequency and intensity. You may or may not know this, but I did some research years ago on the Holocaust. I looked at newspaper articles, new anti-Jewish legislation, Hitler's speeches, and a whole lot of data. Then I tried to correlate the events with the rising attacks, the deaths, and all that. The data told us that there were definite patterns that built towards something like we see now. I believe present conditions are virtually identical to those of the days leading to the *Shoah*. I don't know how, or where, or what exactly, but this looks (the attacks) organized to me and it feels urgent. All of these events are tied together somehow... almost as if..." her voice trailed off and she sat in silence.

Weinstein and Ben Yehuda looked at her.

"Almost as if what?"

"Almost as if all of this is *b'shert*... meant to be." The room fell into a thick silence. This was a side of her they had never seen.

Shoshana was a voracious reader, an amateur archeologist, and history buff. She commanded a detailed knowledge of the history of anti-Semitism as well as its twin, Anti-Zionism. She wasn't one to go off half-cocked. There was something about natural disasters that rang a distant bell in her head.

Those volcanoes and earthquakes, all of it, all of it... she thought and tapped her number 2 on the table.

> **From the Pen of the Prophet Isaiah**
> Isaiah 40:31
>
> Yet those who wait for the LORD
> Will gain new strength;
> They will mount up with wings like eagles,
> They will run and not get tired,
> They will walk and not become weary.

Chapter 23

Logistics

How do you move 6 million people from one nation to another? Where do you put them once they get there? Of such problems, relocation specialists, logistics engineers, and planners dwell on daily.

This was very much on the mind of Michael Shapiro, Director of the Jewish Agency in Jerusalem. Here's what the analysts were working with that early morning. The logistics team found that worldwide Jewish population was centered in two main clusters—the U.S and Israel. That meant another nine million would have to be absorbed from all around the world.

Impossible, was the verdict. But Shapiro had no choice.

The Agency had the responsibility to find housing for Jews. The return to Israel was a journey home. It's called ***Aliya****— *one ascends or goes up to Jerusalem.* The Agency found them jobs, helped them relocate, find housing, and integrate into their new Israeli/Jewish culture.

Shapiro and his agency were used to handling maybe 10,000 to 20,000 immigrants a year. But never very far from their minds was the potential of another situation like World War II... 6 to 9 million!

CHAPTER TWENTY-THREE: *Logistics*   Page 131

Had Palestine been fully under Jewish control before World War II, the Agency would have had to deal with that problem then and possibly provide a home (and safe haven) for the lost six million Eastern European Jews, even more perhaps. But the British and her allies chose another path. There was even some debate within Jewish circles in Palestine itself what they would do with that many refugees. Instead, the six million were condemned to horrible deaths in the concentration camps.

Double dealing between America and Israel was nothing new. On the one hand, the Executive Branch, under President Truman, though annoyed by pressing Jewish demands, generally supported statehood for Israel while at the same time, the Department of State worked to prevent it. Relationships between Britain and America grew strained as Britain's pro-Arab policy opposed the Jews' dream of a Jewish state. Yet there were supporters as well. Great Britain was doing all it could to hold onto its dying empire, much of which would dissolve in the coming decades.

All of this occurred while the survivors of the *Shoah* languished in deportment camps on the island of Cypress, or even in some cases, in Europe where the horrors were perpetrated, including a little known post-war pogrom in Poland. So, America ran two very distinct foreign policies concerning Jews and Israel from World War II onward. One of the more sensitive issues between the two nations had to do with the Six Day War in 1967.

Few knew or understood what had happened to the U.S.S. Liberty, a communications spy ship stationed off the coast of Israel during that war. When Israel attacked the ship after much internal angst, it was with the suspected knowledge that America had stolen battlefield signals from the Israelis and turned them over to Egypt in the midst of the struggle. Israel deemed such an act hostile to its existence. Its leaders believed and acted on the perceived threat to the nation's survival by attacking the ship.

Stranger still, with the ship under attack, an American aircraft carrier, stationed not far off in the Mediterranean, and within easy reach of the hotspot took direct orders from the White House to stand down defense of the Liberty.

Even with the deadly Israeli attack, few realized what constraints Israel put on itself and even with the deaths of 34 brave Americans who couldn't or wouldn't fire back, Israel could have easily sent the ship to the bottom of the Mediterranean Sea and killed more than 300 of its crew.

The story was buried by both parties and an unofficial secret agreement was reached between two 'old friends' to 'deep six' the incident and make up a cover story for the press. Sparks can fly when conflicting aims of a sovereign's foreign policy ram into that of another. Though over time the relationship between America and Israel remained generally cordial, there were underlying tensions, many which would serve as a backdrop for what was coming years into the future.

Within the Jewish Agency was a department of 50 analysts who ran population shift simulations and absorption studies on high speed computers. The studies gave Israel accurate absorption models for any number of immigrant variables. It measured the local impact on housing, food, water, waste, work, schools, transportation, the environment, etc. And the studies also considered the challenges and issues that would impact the indigenous and existing people.

At most, they calculated, Israel could absorb 500,000 a year for a period of maybe two to three years. After that, there would be precious little room. Without expandable borders, the Jewish state was trapped in its own box. Or, there was always the desert. With international Muslim and Christian agitation, the problem seemed impossible.

Next, he and his team wondered how the people would find passage to Israel. So, he called in some chips from old friends in El Al, the National airline of Israel. It made sense to him that air travel would be the most efficient and quickest way over but what kind of capacity did El-Al have? Some might be offset by ship, but how could he arrange cruise ships to haul millions out of the U.S. and into Israel? He dialed his contact and agreed to meet for lunch—so many questions, so few answers.

Ari Melnick was a flight engineer and French immigrant. He headed a little known planning unit within the airline's marketing and sales department. He was quick witted and very insightful as well as a prolific painter and cartoonist. He also loved writing having published several books on Biblical topics.

Shapiro learned, however, that there was a little discussed but very much alive secondary mission of this small group... that of contingency plans for quick rescue of Jews anywhere in the world. They had actually planned for this scenario. Flight crews on old converted bombers rescued more than 47,000 Yemeni Jews from that God-forsaken desert hole in 1948. That story was legend by now and the planners thought that it might serve as a model for future operations.

CHAPTER TWENTY-THREE: *Logistics* Page 133

Our Story . . .

The date was 1948. Back then, he remembered from his reading, the Jews managed to get their hands on some old DC4 aircraft. These Douglas Aircraft Company airliners became available by chartered American air transport firms. The young, idealistic Jewish state believed any Jew was worthy for rescue, no matter where they were or who they were. And, so, Operation Magic Carpet was born.

It became known that thousands of these desert nomads, Jews, trapped in a 'Dhimmi' Muslim nightmare, were reachable and willing to come to Israel. The government planned the mission. When the planes landed, these desert Jews, somehow cut off from the rest of their Jewish brothers, offered praises to God believing that this was a fulfillment of the ancient prophecy uttered by Isaiah, 'that salvation would come on the wings of eagles.' Strange as it might seem they had never seen an airplane. The DC 4's, glittering in the desert sun, must have indeed looked heaven sent.

And so the Yemenite tribe of Jews stepped aboard the former American airliners and lifted off to the land of their ancestors, a true fulfillment of the ancient prophecies. Flying round the clock, missions, up to seven and eight a day, Israel lifted almost the entire population of 47,000 of Yemen's Jews to the land of promise.

And what a gift Israel received in the bargain. It was these poverty-stricken nomads who brought a preserved version of the Hebrew language home. Many thought it to be the purest version of the ancient tongue.

An amazing story that goes along with the Yemenites' flight had to do with the unpressured fuselage temperature dropping to close to zero as the plane reached its cruising altitude. Feeling cold and not understanding aircraft safety rules, one of the groups of Yemenis decided to light a fire in the cabin to get warm. It was quickly doused by the cabin crew but underscored the tremendous challenges that young Israel faced in her first years, that of bringing some of their Jewish brethren into the 20th century while fighting a modern war against the five enemy armies it faced.

Israel again went to work in Iraq in the early 1950's. Iraq was the home of an ancient Jewish population of more than 100,000. The tiny Jewish state duplicated the Yemenite feat with another around-the-clock airlift. Known as Operation Ezra and Nehemiah, this second piece of the rescue mosaic further defined the Jewish state's desire to bring all of her children home, no matter who they were or where they lived.

These Iraqi Jews traced their lineage back to the Babylonian captivity, more than 2,500 years before, clearly one of the oldest Jewish communities in the Middle East. They were well entrenched in Iraq and were unsurpassed in wealth and culture, not to mention achieving higher level roles in Iraqi society and government.

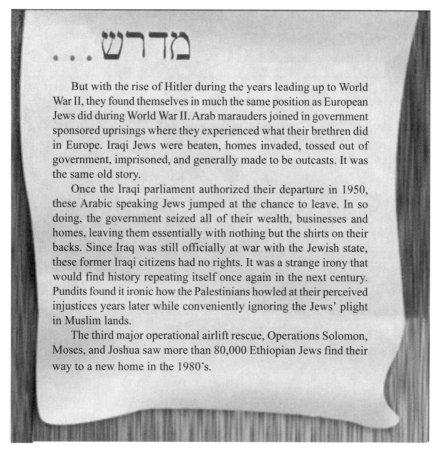

... **מדרש**

But with the rise of Hitler during the years leading up to World War II, they found themselves in much the same position as European Jews did during World War II. Arab marauders joined in government sponsored uprisings where they experienced what their brethren did in Europe. Iraqi Jews were beaten, homes invaded, tossed out of government, imprisoned, and generally made to be outcasts. It was the same old story.

Once the Iraqi parliament authorized their departure in 1950, these Arabic speaking Jews jumped at the chance to leave. In so doing, the government seized all of their wealth, businesses and homes, leaving them essentially with nothing but the shirts on their backs. Since Iraq was still officially at war with the Jewish state, these former Iraqi citizens had no rights. It was a strange irony that would find history repeating itself once again in the next century. Pundits found it ironic how the Palestinians howled at their perceived injustices years later while conveniently ignoring the Jews' plight in Muslim lands.

The third major operational airlift rescue, Operations Solomon, Moses, and Joshua saw more than 80,000 Ethiopian Jews find their way to a new home in the 1980's.

Ari and Michael then looked at the numbers generated by a quick search on the company's intranet database. They confirmed what they already knew. There was no way to airlift six million American Jews out of the U.S. and into Israel... unless a miracle could be worked.

After some discussion, it was apparent that the 737's and the 757's were of no use—their ranges were too short, capable of flying less than 5,000 miles on one tank of fuel. They would have to look at the 767 and 747 to ensure it had extended range capacity. That left 27 available extended range aircraft capable of flying from Los Angeles, Chicago, New York, or Florida and reaching Israel non-stop.

There was absolutely no reason to add risk of stopovers to an already tense situation growing tenser by the day. All flights, no matter their origination, would be non-stop. Her enemies didn't need the opportunity that a stop in the middle would afford them.

Melnick promised Shapiro that he would conduct capacity planning scenarios for him within the next few days. The planning would include load figures inbound to Israel on a 24-hour incoming basis. Ari agreed to give Michael his best guesses, an added bonus considering that over time, he had always proven to be very accurate in his projections. Ari set up a spreadsheet to give him the capacity plan. It projected a total of about 50,000 passengers a week.

When Ari finished the analysis, he called Shapiro who, at first glance, was both encouraged and disappointed. First he knew that all the 747, 777, and newer 787 models could meet his needs but that wouldn't be enough to get the Jews of America out fast enough. He learned that the Boeing 767's, though older, were capable of the long distance haul—that lifted him. He also had to factor in maintenance and repairs. That gave him 27 aircraft available for his rescue efforts.

"If every aircraft flew once a day, at close to capacity, about 50,000 (rounded to the higher number) could come to Israel, weekly. That means 200,000 a month, or 2.4 million per year. Extrapolating that number and assuming all the Jews wanted to come, it would take about two and one half years to get them out of the U.S."

"No, it has to be much faster than that. The more time the surrounding population has on their hands, the more mischief they could cause."

No... it had to be a 2 to 3 months maximum time limit, maybe four months tops.

"Even that is too much time," Shapiro said, downcast.

He knew he needed more planes. There was simply just too much risk- too much demand and not enough supply.

"We need more planes, it's that simple, People will be waiting for a flight while trying to fend off their neighbors or the authorities," he said during the emergency meeting of the EL Al Executive Board.

Leaving the American Jews in such a vulnerable position was something he just couldn't handle. The Board promised to meet in private session and then contact him. This was an extraordinary circumstance, but Shapiro just didn't know where else to turn. The phone rang in his office at noon the next day. He was summoned into the CEO's office. This would take months to execute.

"Michael, the Board has met and authorized another purchase of 25 new Boeing 787's and 12 747s. Boeing has some whitetails in storage and it will take them a few weeks to bring them back out, perform fly-away maintenance on them. We can have them here in 4 weeks. We are fortunate we still have friends within the company," the CEO said.

They all agreed that Airbus, the European consortium, refused to do business with the Jewish state, so they were out of the equation. The newest jet maker in the market, a Far East consortium of China, Japan, and Korea wasn't in a position to sell long range jets just yet. They had entered the short haul market and were gaining market share, but that was the extent of it. Bombardier, a Canadian firm and Embraer, from Brazil didn't build any long range aircraft either.

Shapiro thought about it for a moment and said, "Ok, that's better, but still not what we need. I'll redo the numbers and see what we can come up with."

He knew that Boeing's products offered dependability rates well over 98% meaning that these aircraft were prepared and ready to go 98% of the time, as expected. That also gave him some breathing room so he could keep some aircraft in reserve.

"How about spares?" he asked.

The CEO answered, "Boeing says they can support all the way." That was indeed good news because he wasn't quite clear where the company stood as it sold to all comers including Israel's enemies. Boeing was in business to make money and that's what they did. So long as they kept selling to him, Shapiro figured it didn't matter. The nation would deal with the other consequences later. They would find the money somehow.

Melnick and Shapiro both breathed a sigh of relief. With the purchase of new and used aircraft wherever they could find them, the planners laid out the inbound traffic and relevant logistics it would require to bring the Jews home and then escort them to their new homes.

Over the past 20 years, the 787 Stretch (now seating 350 passengers) had become the airplane of choice as operators realized it was virtually corrosion free since it was comprised of about half composite materials and lightweight aluminum and titanium parts. Passengers loved the latest in in-flight entertainment and environmental comfort. It was his first choice, even the previously operated ones, and they both knew the stellar track record of the 747 and the 777. He placed a call to his superiors and asked to present his case.

His fierce loyalty to the home of his birth and ancestors meant more than anything to him. Shapiro smiled at that and for the first time in his life, he thanked God for his good fortune because the plan was now more than just ideas in someone's head. Not a particularly religious person, it rather surprised him just how naturally the prayer had come out.

He recalculated the numbers again.

The total Israeli aircraft inventory now numbered 59 planes, giving the planners another problem to solve. With 350+ passengers per wide-body aircraft, there would be 20,000+ people in the air daily. If 2.5 to 3.0 aircraft landed every hour, then 700 to 1000 people would need to be received at each airport hourly. Local transportation, buses, and trains would be ready.

CHAPTER TWENTY-THREE: Logistics

The new monorail system was complete. It was complemented by a newly designed internal railway and monorail central terminal having the ability to move people quickly and efficiently between most cities, *kibbutzim* and ***moshavim*** * and of course new cities and suburbs, thanks to the rapidly growing modular housing. That would certainly help the process along. But there was still the problem of getting them out of America and to Israel.

The numbers were a challenge. He looked at the CEO.

"We can only bring in 128,000 a week, or about a half million a month. It will take us about 40 weeks to get this done... I don't think we have that much time," he said, dejectedly. The simulation and absorption engineers were going crazy. His boss agreed.

"My teams are working 20 hour days and are ready to collapse."

By applying his understanding of the dispatch reliability rate, he realized he could have about 346 plus flights per week, each unit making six flights a week. The planes would need maintenance of course, and there were always other assorted unknowns. If the spares business was quickly resolved he could see it coming together, for at least this number of aircraft.

The idea of cruise ships had also been discussed. But ships were too slow. They could carry up to 3000 per journey, but the thought of them as sitting ducks in a multi-day, multi-week journey ruled them out. Still, the thought of millions of offspring from fleeing 19th Century Jews heading back across the ocean, this time to Israel for protection, intrigued him.

This left them with a dilemma. The initial numbers were not as good as they had hoped. Adding more inventory now would strain their capacities. Where would they find enough pilots? How could they refit enough planes with processing capabilities on board, and how quickly?

The thought of the elderly, disabled and incapacitated, infirm, or other sickly Jews, not to mention late term pregnant women also haunted him. He knew, he'd need a certain number of planes in each safety corridor to handle this demographic. Some planes would have to be outfit with special interiors, seats, and special accommodations for the various types of conditions. He'd also have to ensure each flight included at least one doctor, nurse, or medic team capable of stabilizing a patient while en route. He was graying by the minute.

He concluded this line of thought with a note to himself to engage the services of his logistics team and make sure they had worked out plans with the air traffic controllers and hospitals. That gave him another thought... he knew that some aging C-17's were available on the used aircraft market. Israel had a few in its inventory, bought years ago on the used market... but they needed more. He knew that each of those workhorses could be converted to a flying hospital within minutes and could also handle heavy cargo needs, inbound as well as outbound to Israel. He jotted that idea down as well. The internet amazed him-so much information available at a touch of a button.

Shapiro thought for some time on this issue and finally concluded that they could not do it alone. He knew he needed a miracle, or at least another idea better than his. And then it hit him—why not use existing carriers to support the effort? He knew of course, that Israel was not exactly in good standing with international governments but then again, there may be some friends out there who could help.

He also knew that he had limited time to convert certain areas of the interior of each aircraft to working processing centers enabling other members of his agency to set up working offices to receive the inbound immigrants and process them through customs. If there were any spies hiding among the passengers that would be learned too. Israeli world-class security techniques would ensure that no undesirables enter the country. Contingency plans had to be designed for any and all scenarios.

Once airborne, five onboard Israeli processing representatives from the Agency would clear each and every passenger through to Tel Aviv or whatever airport would be receiving its human cargo. Since Ben Gurion airport had added an extra runway years ago, giving it three with enough capacity to land the heavies, it was a logical choice.

Other airports included Megiddo and Ramon. They weren't as convenient or setup as well as Ben Gurion. Still, they'd do in a pinch. The good news was that he knew there were train and monorail hubs at all the airports so deplaning them and ensuring passage to their new homes should work in the short term. He also had another option—landing in the Negev at the Air Force base.

All of this gave him an incredible headache. He reached for his bottle of extra-strength Ibuprofen. The bottle was empty, but his frustration peaked. He threw the bottle across the office—it pinged off the wall and next to a painted portrait of the Valley of the Dry Bones prophecy of Ezekiel. He had received the painting years ago as a gift from a young artist living in the U.S. at the time. Thankfully he did no damage.

It also caused him to look a little closer at the framed work. As he got up from his chair and approached the painting, he noticed something he hadn't seen before. The young artist had craftily and painstakingly laid in images of Hebrew lettering in her artwork. The closer he looked, the more he realized what an exquisite work of art this was. He took his time and studied the work. He realized she had quoted those exact passages from the Prophet Ezekiel within the painting—subtle, but there. *Brilliant,* he thought.

That story was one he loved to tell—she was Ziva Shemesh (roughly translated as "Radiant Sun"), a beautiful dark-eyed, brunet Messianic Jewish girl whose grandparents had fled Cuba for the safety of Florida in the early 1960's, leaving family and friends behind. Later, the family moved to California where she grew up. The artist was now an art teacher and painter living in Jerusalem, having made aliya years before. He remembered his trip to the U.S. and meeting her in a coffee house. All she could talk about was Israel, the Bible, the Messiah, the Israelis she knew, and of course her art. She exuded love, elegance, and kindness in all she did.

Ziva had arranged to send him the gift later on and he felt that it was one of the sweetest things anyone had ever done for him. He hadn't met many of these Messianic Jews but if they were at all like her then they couldn't be too bad. There was something about her that stirred him, but he dismissed it at that moment.

It was amazing, he thought, *she never preached to me, but she showed me her faith in God through her life and her kindness.*

Shapiro then turned back to the population density issues he had been working earlier.

His mind snapped back to the work at hand.

"Where was I... ah, yes, runways and airports," he said aloud to himself. Now he began to pace.

"Let's see, with an extra runway built at Ben Gurion and an additional two or three at various places around the land under construction, we can develop the capability to land inbound passenger traffic on a 24 hour per day/7 day per week schedule," he said aloud, to himself.

That posed all sorts of problems for him including raising Jewish awareness that they faced their extinction on American soil. How to get the Jews safely to the airports and onto the planes posed another problem.

And then again, there was that annoying issue looming in the back of his mind ... those believing themselves to be Jewish, and who believed in Jesus, whom they called Yeshua. Messianics... what to do with them?

They kept popping up, youth like Ziva (now he couldn't stop thinking about her) seemed no different than many of the Israelis he knew. He had heard that there was somewhere around 200,000 of them in the U.S., but it wasn't something he thought much about, until now. He had no way of knowing just how many there were but he did have some contacts to find out. He added that to his list of 'to do's.'

"I wonder how many of them will try to hide in churches? How many of them will try to evade their Jewishness?" he asked himself, continuing his monologue.

He knew the stories of World War II.

"This is going to be interesting. Should we include them? Are they really Jews or do we just call them Christians and forget about them?" He continued his solo argument with himself. The debate had raged for more than 2,000 years.

He knew what the rabbis thought but was that really right or fair to allow them to place labels on these people? Shapiro suddenly remembered something just then from his undergraduate studies at Tel Aviv University. During his History of the Jews in the Diaspora, he had come across a Doctoral dissertation by a Messianic believer that claimed that Hebrew Christians in pre-World War II Europe had numbered in the hundreds of thousands or even more. At that moment, one of his staffers walked in with a question.

"Ari, I've been reading something about the Messianics...."

"What? I, uh... what?"

"Oh, sorry to interrupt you."

"No, no... it's ok... just deep in thought. What about them?"

"Well, I think there's evidence to suggest there were entire European Hebrew Christian congregations made up of these Jews who refused to leave their Jewish heritage behind even though they believed in... well, you know who. The Church encouraged them to do so, but they simply could not. And as was the fate of their brethren, they too were marched off to the camps for extermination, no matter what they believed."

"Yes, I remember some of my research along these lines... I remember reading another book written before the war which condemned the Church for not recognizing that these people were still Jewish no matter what their beliefs. The writer saw return of the Jews and the Hebrew Christians as the same thing... an issue of national restoration, not just religion.... the remnant... "

He needed to know if such an issue came up, hot and debatable as it might be. It was an intriguing thought, something about which he was sure the rabbinical authorities in Israel would have something to say. He also knew that the Messianics would jump at the chance to come and would become the nation's most fervent citizens based on their previous track records of loyalty to the Jewish state. Such stories traveled fast.

His family members told him stories that the Messianics fought hard in battle, always offering help and comfort to and for their fellow soldiers. They seemed kind and accepted circumstances as they came—almost like Job. Israel meant something very spiritual to them, not always the case with his fellow Sabras. He never remembered any trouble serving with them, even if their beliefs were different from his. He wondered how many of them had previous military experience, were doctors, nurses, engineers, lawyers, and who knew what. What the rabbis were putting out about them simply didn't line up with his experience.

✡✡✡✡✡✡

At that moment, completely unknown to Shapiro, a group of Christian pilots from the U.S. gathered secretly somewhere in upstate New York, to discuss what they could do to help the Jews. Nobody from Israel had said anything to them as of yet, but as the meeting got underway, U.S Transit (a new airline launched just five years before as a merger between three major carriers) pilot Dayle Johannson, the leader of the group, opened the meeting in prayer.

When the prayer ended, he looked at the roughly 200 attendees.

"I appreciate your willingness to join us tonight. How many of you are willing to risk your lives to help the Jewish people reach their destination?"

When every hand in the small room went up without reservation, he knew the mission would be successful, though no cakewalk.

"How many of you know Jonathan Roberts, the Christian pastor from Idaho?"

When virtually every hand went up, he knew he was on the right track. Johannson then explained how he had been in contact with Roberts and his ministry.

"We've spoken about how the Christians could help and when I volunteered my services for the cause, Roberts jumped on it."

Johannson, a long-time supporter of Roberts' ministry, had read most everything the prolific author had written. He purchased and listened to much of his Bible teaching, and believed him to be an important link in the chain to help the Jews get out of America. He then promised Roberts that he could deliver at least 50 from the American Society of Christian Pilots, a professional trade association dedicated to enhancing the life of that small group.

"And that's why we are here tonight."

The group was not a union but rather an advocacy group and often sponsored medical mercy trips to Central and South America. These trips attracted more and more believers in the past few years, none of them fully understanding why they had developed such an interest in that mission. Johannson noted something during the evening that it was either weird coincidence or maybe God's hand that had brought them together that evening for such a time as this. It seemed to him that the Central and South American missions were just a warm up for the main event.

One by one, the pilots turned to one another in greeting, brotherhood, and fellowship, and, that night, became as one man. It was plainly obvious to these Christians that there were no coincidences in the Kingdom of God. It seemed to Johannson to be "a God thing."

When the meeting closed, Johannson called Jonathan Roberts to report his success. When Roberts answered the phone, Johannson was just happy to hear his voice.

"Jonathan, this is Dayle Johannson."

"Dayle, it's good to hear your voice."

"Thanks... I have some news for you... we didn't get the 50 pilots I promised, (pausing for effect) but we did get 200! And I have reason to believe there may be more," he said, his excitement clearly coming through.

"Praise Him to the Highest Heaven. "Dayle, if we throw 200 pilots into this, and in some way procure more planes, I think we can get it done. The more pilots we find, the quicker it will go."

Roberts, with an uncanny mathematical and scientific mind, had been running exactly the same kind of capacity planning scenarios as his counterparts, Michael Shapiro and Ari Melnick had in Israel.

Unknown to the Israelis, Roberts had contacted friends in the industry who were able to put him in touch with the world's largest aircraft leasing company. That individual was willing to help and began arrangements to deliver the needed aircraft to the cause. Within a few weeks, Israel would have more than 150 wide-bodied aircraft at its disposal almost tripling Michael Shapiro's capacity.

Shapiro and his team met to discuss these scenarios, run the simulations, and prepare reports that would find their way to various agencies within the Government. He usually copied the IDF and Mossad because those agencies needed to understand population shifts, political trends, and how their fellow Jews were treated abroad. Other agencies were brought in as needed.

Shapiro looked at the table of the largest Jewish population centers and began to think about what it would take to get them all to Israel if such an event ever happened again, though 'if' was quickly becoming 'when.' Until a few years ago, the thought of another Holocaust seemed so remote, yet, strange things were afoot and the logistics engineer sensed it. The recent American census would give him even more useful data.

Shapiro had seen the studies now and had a chance to digest them. He believed, with the rapid advances in solar and electrical technology, desalinization, hydroponics, and drip irrigation, that the Israelis could grow virtually anything, virtually anywhere. That meant that Jewish expansion pushing further into the desert was now moving beyond distinct possibility to necessity. Imagine turning the entire Negev into a garden! But time was wasting and his team needed more information.

He was also tracking the new modular housing industry. After the government negotiators had completed the purchases of all the companies, the units sprang up quickly. When he checked the latest production, it numbered in the tens of thousands of new units going up every month. Over the past year or so, Israel had built more than one million units, thus approaching their original capacity.

Advancements in the industry made each unit true masterpieces. Each home came with choices of carpeting, granite countertops, 3-4 bedrooms and studies for every home, complete with receding book cases built into the walls. And, of course with the latest environmental technology baked into the units, this would really seal the deal.

The entire home became a virtual solar panel, taking advantage of not only the sun but even storing heat within the walls for later extraction when needed, following the natural heating and cooling cycles of the day. Each new home had the latest water technology with continuous recycling plants built within the walls, under the units, and on top of the roofs. All waste was recycled and turned into other products. In other words, no Israeli family would be without power or water, food, or an adequate roof over their heads. Coupled with the world's leading solar energy capture technology, and natural gas finds, no Israeli would be too hot in the summer, too cold in the winter, or would be without energy to run any appliance.

This wasn't Levittown.

Everyone was working in Israel now, thus virtually eliminating unemployment and poverty. While some families struggled, the vast majority had what they needed and needed what they had. Everyone was paid a decent living wage including those Palestinians who were willing to work within the social system.

In fact, the Arabs had it much better than their brethren in other Arab lands. They were paid top wages and benefits. Medical care improved, making Israel one of the world's leaders in medicine. With the inbound immigration would come some of the world's top doctors, nurses, and medical community. More than a dozen new medical schools were chartered including three for Arab doctors and nurse practitioners. Someone in the halls of Government remembered ancient admonitions about treating the strangers who lived amongst God's people as if they were native born. And so the Israelis did as much as they could.

With the settlements also moving ahead to the chagrin of a hateful and disapproving world, Israel would finally be a haven for the Jews who wanted to come. And new businesses were springing up almost overnight... Israel had become the hottest place to incubate new startups, exporting products and services, and attracting vast amounts of venture capital, even though the world hated them. Go figure.

Money had no name and no home.

Combined with a push southward, the territories of Judea and Samaria were available for population settlement expansion as well, but at what price? Arab population centers could remain pretty much where they were but the Jews would need more room and the world wouldn't exactly support that idea.

Pressure had been building for years to destroy the settlements in those areas, believing them to be Arab soil. *Geez,* he thought, *if they would just let it be and agree to co-exist with us, we could, together build an incredible oasis of humanity and prosperity.* He thought about the words of Golda Meir, the former prime minister.

"Peace will come when the Palestinian mothers love their children more than they hate the Jews."

Disputes over the *territories* always amused him. It was his land and the land of his fathers. Imagine if the Native Americans or the Mexicans had put up as much a stink in the U.S. as Israel's neighbors had? Imagine an American Jihad! The thought made him shudder.

Shapiro scoffed and imagined a different scenario. What if the European Union or United Nations forced the residents of Maine to leave their state, he wondered. The justification is the need to placate Canadians who made claim to the territory. And could you imagine the southwest?

Then he shouted to the ceiling, "No Way, No Way! The U.S. would spill blood and lots of it!" Shapiro fumed even louder.

"How dare you, America for such hypocrisy. Your track record of colonialism, expansionism, Native American displacement and massacre dwarfs anything Israel has ever done. How dare you!"

How could one sovereign dictate and force its will on another? And that was with a long-time ally! Well, maybe not anymore.

Imagine another nation doing exactly that to the U.S.! It seemed like the United Nations had been doing just that to the U.S. over the past few decades. It mimicked the classic bully scenario, where the bully (the U.S.) was bullied by a bigger bully (the U.N.), then turns the tables on a smaller victim. That's what the U.S. had become-a bully, he thought.

Shapiro vowed to work harder at his problem. There had to be a way. And it had to be soon. And then another thought occurred to him-something so incredible, he had to stop and gather the thoughts as they were hatching in his brain. His ideas were out of control but that didn't matter... no matter how crazy they sounded, he still wanted to grab them, so pulling out his

CHAPTER TWENTY-THREE: Logistics

new voice recorder, he began his personal brainstorming session.

"What if," he dictated to the recording device, "we assumed the Biblical borders for ourselves promised by the Almighty, blessed be He, Himself? What would that look like?"

How could his tiny nation just claim populated lands from her neighbors and incorporating land all the way to the Euphrates River? Laughable to the world!

Impossible? That would take care of the space problem and extend Israeli sovereign territory way out from her borders taking much or all of Jordan and Lebanon in the deal. Preposterous... or was it?

'Well, He HAD parted the Red Sea, hadn't He?

He HAD sustained the Children of Israel for 40 years and provided Manna while doing so, right?

Their shoes never wore out in the desert, did they?

Wasn't God in the miracle business right now, today?'

Shapiro wasn't so sure that God even existed but it always nagged at his conscience and was now gnawing a hole in his stomach. The ancient maps showed a future state much larger than the nation as it stood on the map today.

'They will be celebrating in Mecca tonight,' he grunted to himself. Ibuprofen wasn't going to fix this migraine.

God, miracles, or not—Shapiro had work to do. Ideas flowed into his voice-to-text recorder. The computer interface meant no typing. Just instant text ready to edit and print. *Ingenious*, he marveled. *I wonder where it is made.*

Then he turned it over, read the 'made in' location, and let out a loud "huh, what do you know!"

Coffee House Chatter—Flipping the Newspaper

"It says here that they're meeting in Durban next week," she said.

"Durban, what? Who?"

"You know—that conference in South Africa. It's all about racism. Remember?"

With head in and eyes on the paper, he mumbled, "Uh, huh. Oh, sure.... Man! They haven't won a game yet!"

She pulled and ripped the paper out of his grasp. "Pay attention!"

"Okay, okay. Now, what about Durban?"

"Every year they discuss racism. It started back in South Africa's apartheid days. But now, it's become an opportunity to condemn Israel."

"Really?"

"Come on," she scoffed. "I can't believe you have never heard of it."

"I don't concern myself with affairs I can't control," he said and reached for the paper. But she had a clamp on it.

"But this is important," she barked. "The unified voices against the racism and injustice leveled at blacks in South Africa now targets Israel. Delegates come from nations all around the globe. Their South African mission was accomplished. So they looked for fresh meat. Israel and the Jews are an easy quarry for their sport."

"Yeah, but Israel doesn't pick the fights," he plead. "Why don't they chase after those Muslims? They've got Israel surrounded. They stay awake at night to figure new ways to kill Jews. And they come after us here, too!"

"Atta-boy, now you're catchin' on!" She smacked him in the back of his head.

"Ow! What was that for?"

"General principles!" She laughed.

She released his sports pages. He retrieved them and added, "Yeah, but it's still all outta my control." He paused, looked to the side, and said, "But what's all this got to do with Ireland?"

"Scheeesh... good thing you're a gynecologist!"

Chapter 24

Durban

Many years had passed since the first Durban Conference in 2001. Conference attendees had pushed for Anti-Zionist language to label Zionism as a racist entity. Even though the final Declaration and Programme of Action did not contain the text that the U.S. and Israel had objected to, and even though that text had been voted out by delegates in the days after the U.S. and Israel withdrew, it still left an undercurrent of animosity within Israel and certainly had exposed the attending nations' true intent.

As the years passed, the conference grew increasingly chilly towards international Jewry and in particular anything associated with Zionism. Those supporting Zionism were simply ostracized from the greater community. All nations from the Muslim block voted in favor of language condemning Israel, simultaneously claiming that they were not racist themselves. In turn, the U.S. and Israel resisted for a long time, pointing the finger back at the Islamic nations. One year an entire bloc of European nations threw their support behind Israel, but, over the years, slowly abandoned that position and moved toward the Islamic influences that were taking their countries by storm. The tide had turned.

At the 8th Conference, rather than standing with its longtime friend, the US chose to vote neutral towards anti-Zionist language. The Europeans had long ago expressed growing support of anti-Israel/anti-Zionist positions, thus aligning with the wishes of their constituents. The people had spoken and their governments were listening.

During the plenary session, the delegates were treated to a fiery speech from Elijah Abdul, a leading member of the Nation of Islam. He had flown in from the U.S. as a featured speaker.

"Each of us here today represents his or her people. We are here because we know that powerful forces align against us. Though small in numbers, we know that throughout history, the Jews and now the Zionist entity have conspired against the poor of this world.

"It is imperative on us to stand together now. One of my predecessors, Minister Farrakhan, understood these things and left us with a vision of a new world, free of Zionism—free from those of the gutter religion. We applaud the works of those who have gone before us, those who have sounded the klaxon of warning. Mr. Hitler foresaw a world called Judenfrei, or free of Jews. It is a worthy vision."

He mixed quotes from the Bible, the Quran, and Louis Farrakhan into an amalgam of a new theology. He challenged them to protest. He called on attendees to take action against the bloodsuckers.

A heavy Muslim attendance was joined by Black Liberation groups from Africa as well as a large number of interested friends. These represented independent Christian communities from Europe and the U.S. Many spoke in sympathy and solidarity with the Palestinians and their plight. Others voiced support for the Black liberation movements in Africa.

A succession of speakers stepped the attendees through a series of speeches on racism, mostly camouflaging their discontent with the state of affairs in the Middle East, most particularly with the condition of the Palestinians. All of their speeches not only condemned Israel but also advocated economic boycotts and disinvestment from Israeli companies. One speech addressed the issues of the sex-slave trade. That gathered mildly polite applause but nothing like those pointed directly at Zionism. Anyone attending could easily discern where this was heading.

As the plenary session closed with a forum of that morning's speakers, the audience was treated to a scholarly panel asking whether or not Zionism was racist. The only Jewish member of the panel was an ultra-orthodox rabbi from Israel who actually agreed that Zionism was wrong but for a totally different reason, that of his sect's non-recognition of Israel. There could be no Jewish state until Moshiach (Messiah) came, and this wasn't it. Furthermore, using the Holocaust as an excuse for what he believed to be "abuses" further buttressed his claims. His comments drew some of the loudest applause and shouted agreement, as the audience believed he spoke for the "truly enlightened Jews." The heavy Muslim crowd loved having a Jew point the finger back at his own kind.

Later, during the first day breakout sessions, the delegates discussed just what actions they could take to send a message to international Zionists and their Zionist supporters. The first draft from that subcommittee was prepared and sent to the planning staff for inclusion into the final set of conference proceedings which would be published both on the internet and in Podcasts and on CD's. Leaders from the different nations present decided to begin planning street protests, beginning in the larger Western capitals, closest to the Jewish population centers. These protests would eventually light the fuse for what would come later.

They created a short list which included 20 cities in the US, Canada, and England. They all agreed to a 'peaceful approach,' but that didn't mean allowing themselves to be stopped or forced to abandon their methods if any pressures were brought to bear on them.

Youth leaders were called in during Days Four and Five to map out the strategy, with an eye on university recruiting. Their collective belief was that the protests would draw out their supporters, hoping for tens of thousands to join them in the streets. After the electronic campaigns were launched, plans called for picket signs, banners, flag burnings, effigies, and plenty of speeches at the destinations, but no violence. Should any violence occur, they would condemn it, publicly anyway. They knew their history. They knew what large population could do—once stirred. They knew the pogroms. They were a model of the new civil justice. They knew Kristallnacht, the Inquisition, the Crusades, and were well acquainted with those lessons of history. They also knew the populations of their respective nations would eventually fall in behind them because it always happened before and they had no reason to believe this would be any different.

Next, the teams set plans in motion for a print campaign to target universities, colleges, public venues, the nation's capital, and key state capitals. Correspondence in every form was sent, posted, sped to local, state, and Federal officials, and of course a massive electronic blitz. Social networks, blogs, wireless Lightening Lists, etc. were poked. Volunteers stepped up to take each project in turn. In short... ideas, thoughts, proposals, and energy released at the conference were transformed into plans. They would rid the planet from its most toxic entity: Zionism, racism embodied.

Those Jews who survived would march to the world's drumbeat, not the other way around. Much could be learned from anti-Semitic protests at the universities such as the University of California, Irvine and York University in Toronto. Students at these universities and others had learned to be bold, papering their campuses with anti-Zionist materials, posters, flyers, and speeches. Disrupting opposing viewpoints was also a tried and true technique.

The leaders from Durban then flew to the US and kicked off a series of planning meetings in San Francisco in January of that year. Titled 'The U.S. Conference to Fight Racism and Zionism,' the delegates poured in from all 50 states, Europe, and the Middle East. They agreed to target US cities including Dallas, Los Angeles, Chicago, New York, Miami, Washington DC, and several others, and established the date—the 4th of July.

Former enemies put aside their animosities and worked together towards the common goal. Christians from evangelical and non-evangelical churches, Muslims, Nation of Islam, and even a smattering presence of skinheads joined together to make this event something that the Jews would never forget. There had even been inquiries for support from the Ku Klux Klan, and though not warmly received, they were not ignored either. Organizers recognized there could be a role even for the KKK. Several more heavily populated states broke off into subgroups to plan their own rallies. From there, protests were planned for most major cities of more than 500,000. Organizers tapped a huge network of students, community activists, many from previous political campaigns and ballot initiatives.

The ball was rolling.

Next, conference attendees formed the protest theme around American Independence Day as a day for equal rights for all, including any and all oppressed peoples, thus expanding the concept of American freedom to all. But the real kicker was the focus on the Jews who would be portrayed as inhibiting the freedom of peoples the world over, mostly including those less fortunate Americans living below the poverty line. Since their literature held that Jews owned the financial machinery, it stood to reason that the poor must be the victims of Jewish oppression. It was an ancient argument and the old bird was growing new feathers. The new anti-Semitism was alive and well.

Conference themes would be carried over into street protest planning. Several common themes emerged: Zionism as Racism, Advocacy for a Palestinian State, International Jewish Financing and Control, and Death to Israel and the Jews. These rallies would advocate for all men but would squarely place the blame where it belonged, where it had always belonged, at the foot of Zionism.

Protest organizers grew more excited by the day. Copies of the Protocols began circulating within the protesters' circles. Organizers encouraged their supporters to read and understand what they said. Additionally, copies of Mein Kampf found new life on the printing presses, flying off the shelves when appearing in bookstores. The main principle was to find the scapegoat, blame him, and turn the attention away from the real perpetrators. The talk shows sprung to life with this new energy of hate.

As the day approached, state organizers acquired the services of printing presses in the target cities. Mysterious funding sources appeared and the grass-roots planners bolted into action. Monies were provided through a series of non-profits set up through many churches and mosques, and even some of the more 'liberal' synagogues, and handled virtually all on line through debit cards, websites, online banking, and quick money transfers. They made it easy to participate, easy to give. Publicity shot through the web as social networking sites picked up the buzz. The campaign was going viral.

Handbills, protest signs, and banners were coming hot off the presses. Billboards, usually a fairly costly method of advertising appeared virtually overnight with graphics of the upcoming parades. Images of Jews oppressing their neighbors in Palestine were overlaid with swastikas and the Star of David. Many images made infamous during the years leading up to the Holocaust and culminating with the Holocaust surfaced again, this time with a pro-Palestinian theme, showing the Jews and Israelis as the fascist war mongers bent on world domination and the poor Palestinians as the victims.

Strange, this twist of events, for it was exactly this terror strategy identified back in the 1980's that now defined the new anti-Semitism—that of reversing the roles of the players in the drama—the victim was now the perpetrator and the perpetrator now the victim. The second pillar of that philosophy then had the new victim provoking a response so deadly and seemingly over the top that the new perpetrator, formerly the victim, would be perceived by all as the monster. And it was working.

Pro-Jewish websites such as Camera and MEMRI learned about the hate being produced and published. But it was ignored by most American Jews as a passing fad. Still, the ones in the know got the news to planners of *Operation Last Exodus* in Israel. Most of the materials reached Shapiro, Ben Yehuda and Shoshana Bat-Levi, and others filling in additional pieces of a puzzle not yet quite clear but adding up to something bigger than they could possibly imagine. The Israelis always maintained a tight surveillance on the internet and anything appearing there was known. Weinstein and Shoshana smelled it correctly.

Bumper stickers appearing on cars with the 'Coexist' theme on them became far more prevalent. Churches and mosques alike began preaching tolerance of others, love of your neighbors, all the while questioning Israel's role in the Middle East and expressing sympathies for the continued oppression of the Palestinians. Organizations such as CAIR, the Council on American-Islamic Relations began appearing everywhere on radio, print media, and television.

And another trend began to emerge... Muslims joining the American military, local police forces, and school boards.

From the Book of Beginnings:
   Bereshit (Genesis) 6:13-18

Then God said to Noah, The end of all flesh has come before Me; for the earth is filled with violence because of them; and behold, I am about to destroy them with the earth.

   Make for yourself an ark of gopher wood; you shall make the ark with rooms, and shall cover it inside and out with pitch. This is how you shall make it: the length of the ark three hundred cubits, its breadth fifty cubits, and its height thirty cubits.

   You shall make a window for the ark, and finish it to a cubit from the top; and set the door of the ark in the side of it; you shall make it with lower, second, and third decks.

   Behold, I, even I am bringing the flood of water upon the earth, to destroy all flesh in which is the breath of life, from under heaven; everything that is on the earth shall perish.

   But I will establish My covenant with you; and you shall enter the ark—you and your sons and your wife, and your sons' wives with you.

Chapter 25

Roberts Receives a Call

The phone rang in Roberts' office and startled him. It was early, but he was up and reading his Bible. Who could be calling at this hour? He grabbed the phone to answer it.

"Mr. Roberts?" a voice asked. "Yes, this is Mr. Roberts."

"Please hold for Mr. Patel."

"Jonathan Roberts?"

"Yes, this is Jonathan Roberts." Roberts' heart skipped a beat. He knew the voice for it was Sarvish Patel. Patel was the CEO and President of Skytrain Leasing, the world's largest aircraft leasing agency.

"Jonathan, we have secured the aircraft you need."

Roberts sat stunned. His prayer was answered so specifically, so timely, he had to collect his thoughts and respond to the call.

He whispered a quick silent prayer of thanks to his Creator then asked when they could meet. Patel was as anxious to see the deal done as Roberts and the two of them agreed to meet the following week. Meeting plans were left to their staffs and the meeting was arranged for the following week in Paris.

Roberts now had the numbers he needed. To him it looked like about a 16 week operation if they could hit a 98% dependability rate. It looked reasonable for he knew Boeing aircraft had that reliability and more. It was all in the public records. They would have to strike fast with a tightly coordinated efficiency never done before. Was God still in the miracle business?

Aircraft Type - # of Units	Capacity	2 Flights per week per aircraft	3 Flights per week per aircraft	4 Flights per week per aircraft	5 Flights per week per aircraft	6 Flights per week per aircraft
777 - 30	350	21000	31500	42000	52500	63000
767 - 25	350	17500	26250	35000	43750	52500
787 – 54	350	37800	56700	75600	94500	113400
747 – 50	400	40000	60000	80000	100000	120000
Totals		116300	174450	232600	290750	348900
98% Capacity		113974	170961	227948	284935	341922

Roberts and Patel each boarded private jets and headed for Paris. Roberts landed first, and was met by two limousine drivers, one holding a sign for him. They grabbed his carryon and bag and then escorted him to the waiting limo.

These two men were placed in Europe by friends of his ministry and had proven trustworthy. He recognized one of the men as a former Shin Bet agent who had 'retired' from the agency and had gone to work for private security companies. His $2,000 Armani suit fit perfectly around his broad frame.

Patel followed him in and landed about 30 minutes afterwards. Patel's driver and bodyguard accompanied him as well. Patel was well-known in these circles. The three men made it to the hotel with no disruptions and then settled in for a quick nap.

Two hours later, Roberts' phone rang. It was Patel.

"I trust your flight was comfortable?"

"Fine, just fine," Roberts answered. In fact he had a chance to get caught up on some reading and correspondence.

"How about we meet in my suite?"

"Fine."

Roberts and his bodyguard caught the next elevator and descended to the 45th floor. They left the elevator and headed down the corridor and knocked on the double doors. What greeted Roberts and his companion was an answer to prayer.

"Jonathan Roberts I presume?" Patel asked, extending his hand. "Sarvish Patel."

"A pleasure and an honor," Roberts said, meeting Patel's handshake with a firm grip of his own.

"Same, I'm sure."

Patel owned world's largest aircraft leasing company of more than 800 aircraft of all makes, models, and sizes. Estimates on his net worth varied but a safe figure ran well into the billions with plenty of change left over for coffee at Starbucks. Patel owned more planes than most of the airlines and was Boeing's, Airbus', and Bombardier's biggest customer.

He started his leasing firm first right out of school as an air services provider handling scheduling, support logistics, and insurance, then branching into aircraft leasing. He hit the market at the right time, capitalizing on low-interest loans and knowing how to bring the right people to the table at the right time.

A classic deal maker, he kept fit by daily exercise, swimming, and golf. Short of stature, he sported a thick mustache, powerful blocky body, olive skin, and blue eyes—the color of an early summer morning sky. His background was hard to explain so he just said he was Turkish, and that usually settled it. This was partially true for his father was a Turk but the name came from a great grandfather who was Indian. His wife, Penelope, was never very far from him either.

CHAPTER TWENTY-FIVE: Roberts Receives a Call

The lovely Mrs. Patel, a stunning Brazilian brunette, was a model in her previous life. She stood close to six feet four inches tall, an interesting contrast to his five foot six frame. When they entered a room, all eyes went to him, as the shorter man- taller woman thing was still a silly social taboo that caused people to look almost as if it were some kind of freak show. With her heels, she stood close to six feet-eight inches, and wasn't afraid to show it.

She was an interesting character and was not taken seriously by most. But she was nobody's fool for after her modeling career, she reentered college where she left off in her junior year. Two years later, she finished degrees in Aerospace Engineering and Materials Engineering, and then within two years completed her MBA.

The multi-lingual Penelope would often remain in the background during Patel's meetings, listening but rarely speaking. Then when the meeting would conclude and the staff left, she and her husband would debrief and arrive at decisions together. Her sharp business acumen and background in the Engineering sciences made them a deadly one-two punch.

Over the years, they almost single-handedly changed flying by driving business change from the flying public's perspective.

One example brought a disrupting revolution to the industry when he, a student of engineering technologies, had become aware of two key advancements that were now standards in the industry. He learned about the budding science of metal composites by reading a blog from a deaf engineering scientist in the aerospace industry. When he turned the article over to Penelope, she researched the new concepts and the two of them decided to take a flyer on a small design and manufacturing firm.

This inventor-engineer held several patents on the technology. The material faintly resembled a substance once only described in science fiction. That substance, a composite metal produced a material far stronger than steel or titanium and almost as light as plastic. Some called it plastic steel but it was in many ways better than both of those materials. Later, after the technology was proven and more manufacturing companies wished to enter the business, the Patels decided to sell their shares, pocketing hundreds of millions and giving away a significant portion to scholarship programs, angel venture capital firms, and endowing several chairs at universities. It was always better to get out too early than too late.

The material reduced aircraft weight tonnage by almost a third meaning that aircraft operators could run their product at greatly reduced costs and expect longer lifespan along with less corrosion and enhanced fuselage and wing strength. The newest Boeing aircraft had incorporated the technology and found that they could sell the planes for a little more with the operators making the money back in a short time with savings in fuel, maintainability, and durability.

Patel's operation was international in scope. Roberts was doing his own figuring and came up with his estimates. Somehow he had to get this information to the Israelis. But who would it be?

Roberts looked at Patel for a moment.

"I think you understand the issues here that Israel faces," he said.

Patel nodded.

"Yes, it's pretty obvious they need friends, but of course you understand that my benevolence can only go so far—I do have stockholders who expect a return on their investment."

"Perfectly understood. I'm a businessman myself."

Not only was Roberts a businessman, he was a skilled Bible scholar and acknowledged his counterpart nodding at him.

"So, how do we get this rolling?"

Patel held one of his hands up to inspect the nails. Turning his hand this way and that, he answered, "I know who you need to speak with."

The following morning, both Roberts and Patel were on a jet to Tel Aviv. Penelope joined them as well. They were booked at the newest hotel in the city-a brand new Ritz Carlton with amenities fit for dignitaries. Roberts though was mostly oblivious to the special perks though he did take advantage of the gym, spa, and a massage. After freshening up and getting dressed (no ties), Roberts and Patel entered the meeting suite.

"Jonathan, I'd like to introduce you to someone—please meet Michael Shapiro," Patel said, smiling.

"Michael, this is Jonathan Roberts and he would like to discuss airplanes with you," Patel said, with a slight hint of humor and understatement.

Shapiro extended his hand to Roberts. The grip was warm, sincere, and would cement a new friendship between the two men. When Patel and his wife added their hands to the others, the four realized they were making history.

This was a monumental moment for Shapiro was the one person Roberts needed to meet, and vice versa, thus ensuring that all details of the aircraft deal were met.

For the next 48 hours with nary a break, the new partners hammered out a deal. In the end, the Israeli inventory would number 159 planes with more possible if Patel could free up the aircraft. He would receive a 7% commission on the sales and leasing arrangements, a nice tidy sum and one he could live with.

He promised to see about securing some older C-17's which were being excessed by the U.S Air Force, or so the rumor was reported in Aviation

Weekly. The Israelis already had several but this mission would be enhanced by more.

For the next few days, Shapiro, Patel, and Roberts laid out the plan. Patel identified where his aircraft were. When Melnick arrived later that morning the plan accelerated. The four of them hammered out the logistics. Penelope quietly excused herself as her part was done.

The financial arrangements would be handled by Shapiro's office. He dictated notes into his recorder while the others banged away on laptops and other portable devices. Information was all triple encrypted to prevent any leaks. Arrangements were made for Israel to receive the aircraft and perform all the retrofits including the processing center software, electronic countermeasures, and medical accommodations, easier on the 747's, and if possible, more C-17's.

Roberts began laying out the pilots' schedules and movements. He texted Johansson with the basics. Johansson's crew recruiting was almost finished.

Within weeks, the pilots would find their way to Israel for training and to gain familiarity with the new features of their aircraft. It was agreed that although it was essentially an Israeli government operation, that the flying livery from the airlines who leased the planes would remain to help disguise some of the mission.

Meanwhile, Shapiro and Melnick began making plans for ground arrangements, now knowing that the air transportation was well in hand. They placed calls to Israel's Interior Minister and to the Transportation department. Handling hundreds of thousands of passengers, getting them on trains, buses, and who knows what vehicles created another set of headaches for the planners.

Then there was the business of retrofitting each aircraft with the processing capabilities, electronic countermeasures, and medical equipment. Thankfully, the well developed Israeli hi-tech industry was quite capable of handling the growing demands. The progeny from more than one million Russians who had immigrated years before now would make their impact felt-both through their efforts, those of their offspring, and those whom they taught in Israel's schools.

> **From the pen of Thomas Jefferson**
>
> *It does me no injury for my neighbor to say there are 20 gods or no god. It neither picks my pocket nor breaks my leg.*

Chapter 26

NUMB3RS

When acts of terror are perpetuated by one's own citizens, they are often categorized as drive by shootings, gang violence, or in the case of a political killing, the work of a crazed, lone wolf, as Lee Harvey Oswald was portrayed in the assassination of President John Kennedy. But when heinous acts of violence are brought to bear on another's citizens by those from a foreign land, outside of a declared or undeclared war, they are classified as terrorism. And of course, more than one person involved means conspiracy—just another word for a well executed plan.

As the new millennium dawned, many plots of evil were in the planning. America further fractured along religious and ethnic lines and large fissures in its long history of tolerance continued to emerge. Its citizens had, for generations, integrated those entering from other lands, though not always welcomed at first but eventually would find a way to live in peaceful coexistence. And they came by the millions, the Germans, the Irish, Italians, Poles, French, Hungarians, Czechs, and others.

As the years passed, a very different America evolved. In a typical evolutionary journey, according to some political scientists, nations are born, mature, and then die. They may be overrun by another culture and subordinated that way or they just disappear. Civilizations are said to last between 500-1000 years.

CHAPTER TWENTY-SIX: NUMB3RS

A young, vibrant America was born in the blood of its revolution. 85 years later, she faced a brutal four-year civil war which would have destroyed any other nation. But the strong fabric from which America was woven became stronger still. However, some of the regions touched by the war would take more than 100 years to heal.

America grew westward toward the Pacific Ocean. Expansion extended her influence and involvement. She would have to defend herself and her weaker allies in two world wars. Then a series of police actions led to an international war on terror. America's view of the world was forever altered on September 11, 2001.

But, as any nation which has been at war for long years, there was always an enemy who would hang on longer, testing that nation's will and fortitude, thereby wearing that nation down. America experienced this in Korea, Vietnam, and the Middle East, finally taking the lesser part of a standoff, though there were those who claimed America lost those wars.

It was all about the spin.

Others disagreed, saying she fought the wars with one hand tied behind her back. In any event, they were not decisive victories but really more of an agreed standoff. Eventually, its citizens would no longer tolerate the wars, the never- ending drain on the national economy, no matter how righteous they were and would then resist further perpetuation of that war. And so it was with early 21st Century America.

After two successful Gulf wars, longer and more trying wars of attrition such as the long standing conflict in Afghanistan, others such as in the Philippines and Central and South America, began to wear down the might of America's military machine and the nation's fighting will. It was one thing to win a war. It was an entirely different thing to try your hand at nation building, something that America found completely different than prosecuting a war.

Infighting among various groups such as Jews, Muslims, and Christians, and political rivals ripped the underlying fabric of the nation. Few of America's elections in the last half century had given clear-cut mandates for much of anything. Everyone had become African Americans or Christian Americans, or Mexican-Americans, but nobody seemed to call themselves simply Americans anymore.

Twenty-first Century America wrestled with its identity. That long debated question of whether it was a Christian nation was coming to a head. This search and confirmation for an identity would now be fully exposed in the nation's 25th census.

The Department of the Census began its preparations early by training the more than one million census takers. Their work would fill gaps not identified by the more than 100 million census questionnaires mailed to American households. They prepared to hit the streets, house to house, apartment by apartment. Their work would finally once and for all, help America define who it was, and maybe, just maybe, help it heal its wounds.

And that included America's newest immigrants. About a half million Muslims lived in the U.S. in 1990. By the turn of the century, the population exploded. No one really knew how many there were.

America looked to its future with some trepidation. Absorbing immigrants into its fabric had become something the American landscape learned to handle throughout its history. However, a new immigrant with very different values and lifestyles had alighted upon her shores.

America is a nation of great order. There are policies and procedures for anything and everything it does. Every 10 years the Constitution mandates that a census be taken. The Department of Commerce manages the census process through the U.S. Census Bureau. The goal was to count and survey every citizen and soul within her sovereign borders. The data is used for demographic profiles, representation in congress, adjustments to social policy, and many other applications. Money and power ride on the census results.

The census has a long history dating back to the American Revolution. There had been 24 Federal censuses since the practice was inaugurated in 1790, under then Secretary of State Thomas Jefferson. Although, general statistical data is released almost immediately upon compilation, detailed data from particular respondents is not released for 72 years after the census is conducted. This is due to privacy laws meant to protect individuals from an encroaching government.

The census tracks many things such as all names of individuals living in a particular household or ethnic extraction. Later, some censes added questions regarding whether those living in the residence are covered by health insurance, household income, marital status, disabilities, educational levels, and work status, even if the household owned a computer. Questions can change based on social and political trends.

And until the 25th U.S. Census, no actual mention of preferred religion (due to Public Law 94-521) was included. That would soon change. From time to time, based on changes occurring in American society, additional questions may be added to the census. After Public Law 94-521 was abolished, it opened the doors to the question of religion.

As budget bills make their way through Congress, 'riders' are often attached to a bill by one of its many committee stops along the way. These additions are often put on bills as horse trading tokens when congressmen or senators need votes to influence pet legislation such as jobs programs for their states.

Three years before the census, one such rider hopped onto a bill regarding supplemental farm payments. Sponsors wanted to add a question to the U.S. Census and attaching it this way to another bill was the most expedient way to do it. The question, pertaining to preferred household religion, was quietly added by a long time House member, now Senator, William Jones, a newly elected legislator from Missouri. His attempt to establish once and for all that America was indeed a Christian nation would, perhaps, one day, finally be answered. His constituency pushed him in this direction.

That America was or was not a Christian nation had long been in debate. Many of the founding fathers had professed belief in God but some writings were not very clear. Many had written conflicting views. Some were labeled Deists or Masons, still others were deemed Christians, or even irreligious. Many public buildings, monuments, and memorials, even America's coinage contained Bible references or Bible characters. Others paid homage to non-Biblical figures such as the Greeks or Romans. Although the basic system of jurisprudence did echo the distant instruction of the Bible, America's symbols remained a mixed bag.

In any event, over the centuries, many provocative quotes would be trotted out to defend this position or that. However, the 250 plus year-old debate would now be settled by the census. Oh, yes, there were surveys and polls, but never anything quite as scientific as the census. Debate often came down to interpretation of the First Amendment.

So many debates and disagreements had defined the religion question in America's history. Where God was mentioned in the Declaration of Independence, He was not in the Constitution. The First Amendment protected the people's freedom of religion. The Establishment Clause prohibited the government from creating an official church of the state. The Free Exercise Clause prohibited the government from interfering with the expression of religious belief. Willingly or unwillingly, Thomas Jefferson was dragged into the debate.

Danbury Baptist Association corresponded with newly elected President Thomas Jefferson to lodge a complaint. They protested that in their state "religion is considered as the first object of legislation."

A short time later (1802), Jefferson said that the First Amendment prohibited the Congress from taking such action, 'thus building a wall of separation between church and state.' Though those words never appeared in the official national documents, they became an understood interpretation and were still in use more than 250 years later.

America had indeed turned the corner as the 3rd Patriot Act would soon be voted on by Congress. The first sniff America had of the rider began on a small internet site that tracked bills as they came out of committee. The dust had just begun to blow. When Senator Jones published his editorial in the Sunday New York Times that week, it got minor attention from the major news services.

> Since America's founding, we Americans have always prided ourselves on being a Christian nation. Our values have always led to charity for others, both domestically and internationally. We've always believed in a sense of helping those less fortunate than ourselves and have always tried to offer hope to all oppressed peoples.
>
> Millions have come to our shores over the past 300 years, both before we became a nation and afterwards as well. They had dreams of opportunity, freedom, and hope. And though many came in slave ships too, eventually we saw the wisdom to end it in a bloody Civil War. Today, we are a nation different from the rest of the world, made up of an ethnic and cultural soup that makes us truly unique in the history of Western Civilization.
>
> Our heritage is rich and diverse. But we have gotten lost in the past few decades. New ways of thinking have changed our course so that now it is with this sense of urgency we must determine who we are. We are not the same America we were even 30 years ago.
>
> It is with a new sense of vision and hope that I began asking myself, are we still a Christian nation, dedicated to the same values our forefathers set before us? Are we still that nation conceived in liberty and dedicated to the proposition that all men are created equal? I believe we are but I also believe we must, for the very first time, truly find out, 'who are we?' So, it is with a renewed sense of the future that my colleagues and I are proposing a change to our decennial census.
>
> I have been working for the past four years to bring legislation forward to Congress with the intent to survey each and every household in our great nation and determine, once and for all, who we are: Christian, Muslim, or Jew?
>
> The world has changed. More than 25% of the earth's population honors the Prophet Mohammed. We cannot, as Americans, continue to ignore the profound effect Islam has had in the world. In the past 30-40 years, millions of Muslims have come to America's shores with hopes for a better life.
>
> Immigration and natural population increase grew this rich culture into the millions. They attend our schools, they work alongside us, they shop at the same stores, and they participate in the same events. They deserve a voice and we welcome them in Christian love.
>
> Once the census is completed, we can take guesswork out of our demographics. We will truly know who we are. I believe in our true diverse and dynamic selves. Everyone will have a voice and everyone's culture will be honored. As we celebrate diversity, we must remember to be inclusive, not exclusive. This is a Christian value. And frankly, our Jewish citizens would agree that it's a Jewish value too. Isn't this what America is about?
>
> So, we are asking every American, no matter who you are or where you come from to help America move forward into the future by supporting this new feature on the census.

Surprisingly, after some initial radio and internet noise, not much made it into the mainstream media. Conservative and liberal talk shows normally would have lit up the wires with a story like this. On the other side, every effort was made to lay low on this one because as every clear thinking human being on the planet knew, religion was nothing very useful and always led to controversy and war. What editorials did appear addressed religion as the cause of more wars, bloodshed and death than anything else, especially Christianity. Even the religious programs remained strangely silent.

"Leave it alone," the Program Directors said. "It will go away in a few days."

Three days later, the appropriations bill and the attached measure passed the House vote. Two months later, it passed the Senate, then was signed by the president, and enacted into law the following January.

From Article I Section II
Constitution of the United States

The actual Enumeration shall be made within three years after the first meeting of the Congress of the United States, and within every subsequent term of ten years, in such manner as they shall by law direct.

Chapter 27

The Census

The ultimate goal of any U.S. census is an accurate accounting of the American population. The census process moved at a quick pace. Six months need to be allotted for follow up activities on the whole survey. Soon the 25th census would be a reality.

100 million surveys were returned by mail. Census takers were the next wave. They covered everything from small businesses to private residents—regions, states, counties, cities, and neighborhoods. They paid personal visits to households that didn't return the census. Their goal was "ten questions, ten minutes."

Dolores Esquivel, a census taker in Los Angeles found the population generally pleasant but somewhat curious as to why there was a religion question on the census, as it had never been there before. She explained, as she was trained to say, that America wanted to know its true heritage and once it understood that, would be able to provide even better services to its constituents, the voters and citizens of the United States.

As the census website said that year, federal dollar expenditures were largely dependent on the data derived from the census. She cherished the four-month job she had snagged as a result of visiting the website and threw herself into her work. She had been unemployed for awhile, so it felt good to be back to work. The money would sustain her and her family for a few months.

Illegal immigration was still a challenge, she noted, and found that in some communities, several families lived in one apartment, breaking living space codes. Illegal residents, some who had been living in the States for a long while now, had nothing to worry about—not even those bent on American's destruction.

But she was not there to report violations of such things. Rather, she was there just to gather data and report it on her electronic device given to her by her supervisors. They were not supposed to enter the premises in any case, but sometimes wandering eyes could pick up a lot.

Muslims' interest in the census process grew over the years. They developed active campaigns to urge their people to participate. Their numbers has grown, and they knew it. Community leaders organized rallies and mailers urging the faithful to give their time to the census, realizing that if their numbers were accurate, there were far more Muslims than previously believed, potentially opening the door for more Federal funding for their neighborhoods. Others with more sinister ideas on their minds saw another advantage-where the Muslims were approaching a majority in that area, they could introduce Sharia Law as they had in wide swaths in England and France.

The electronic devices were quite ingenious. Nicknamed 'America Counts,' the GPS census machines took inputs gathered by the census takers through a clever touch screen system and immediately uploaded all information directly to a central database in Washington D.C. Electronic maps, created as the data was compiled, formed the basis for analysts. As results came in, all sorts of measures were compiled, charts drawn, and compared to past censes. The Government even made the data available to news sources in real time, thus allowing them to create and follow the census' progress.

Data analysts spotted trends and began to form opinions as to what it all meant. Of course, congressmen and senators all paid close attention, for changing population figures meant emerging or changing trends, and that meant money, jobs, and likely, votes. The data was fed to a number of Federal agencies, all simultaneously updating their records with the intent to reformulate policy and potential legislation.

One trend became quite evident—the population explosion within Muslim communities. It started small. About a half million reported such affiliations back in the early 90's. Increased inclusion of and tolerance for Islam and an open immigration policy opened the door. They filled communities from Dearborn, Michigan to Brooklyn, to Orange County, Florida. Despite happenings abroad, on they came. With the increased population, alliances formed with many Christians around the nation, and the growing perception that America's true makeup was no longer based on a Judeo-Christian ethic but rather an Islamo-Christian one. The numbers would soon bear them out.

And so, Ms. Esquivel dutifully recorded her findings. She was increasingly running into more and more Muslim households, sometimes in traditionally poor Black and Hispanic neighborhoods. That was the American way; new immigrants would come and immediately move into the poorer neighborhoods, then, within a generation or two, would move away into more affluent places as conditions and commitment to American ideals permitted.

Generations before, Jews lived all over the Bronx, Brooklyn, or in East Los Angeles. Then they moved out as others ethnic groups moved in. It happened all over the nation in every city and every state—cyclical and predictable.

Ms. Esquivel came from a Latino culture. She knew little about Islamic cultures or why they came to America. Most didn't seem poor or disadvantaged in any way while others did. She didn't know it but her family home was once owned by a family named Levy who had sold the home to her parents.

Many of those she interviewed drove very sleek cars, dressed well, and so very many wore clothing very different from she was used to seeing. The Middle Eastern families, it struck her, were very much like her own family, it was just that the language and their clothes seemed a little different.

From *The Politics of Heroin*
Page 441, 1991

Although Soviet forces have withdrawn and CIA aid has now slackened, there is every indication that Afghanistan, like Burma before it, will remain a major heroin supplier for the world market long after the covert operations are over....

Chapter 28

Departures & Arrivals

Rachman's teams had just about completed their preparations. Plane flights, sleeping arrangements, transportation, and all the other details of such a complex operation were all coming together, Allah be praised. His group enjoyed full funding by a splinter group formed from members who had left Hamas, Al-Quds Brigades, Hezbollah, and the Islamic Brotherhood. They had formed a functional partnership with a financier who managed the money through a network of bank accounts, all emanating from Switzerland.

Much of the money came from drug sales. Credit cards, non-traceable phones, computers, and all manner of equipment to eavesdrop. They would carry no weapons into the cities of destination, of course, but once in theater there would be no limits placed on the mission. That end of the business was being handled in the States. Where the money came from was another crazily ironic story and it amused its hosts no end. The financial arrangements were quite a story in themselves.

Operating from Afghanistan gave this cell unique access to the cash flow from opium sales from local Afghani farmers. In fact, business was so good with America of all places, that the Americans themselves were virtually funding this mission. In the past few months, Islamic businessmen had finalized more than $2.5 billion in recent local poppy sales, a nice fat skim of which ended up in Rachman's hands through the financial networks created by his contacts. Some of the money arrived through local arrangements while other monies filtered through the Swiss connection.

Most of the money passed through Swiss banks and the hands of the Swiss financier. From this pile of cash, he could purchase the weapons he needed through his international connections, make all arrangements for his charges, and sit back and enjoy the glory and the fireworks.

The world would soon learn who he was. Living in a cave had its advantages.

And so continued the 'Great Game.' It was first played out by the Russians and English more than 170 years before and now by the U.S., NATO, a host of Muslim nations, and stateless, nameless shadow governments, various terror organizations and others.

Sadly, hundreds of thousands of Afghanis had become addicted to the white sticky compound over the years, perhaps because of the close proximity of the drug and its ease of purchase. If Rachman cared at all about his fellow Muslims it wasn't apparent. He saw it as a casualty of war. These were peasants anyway, and what good could they possibly be to the Jihad? As far as he was concerned, these people were expendable.

You could use their services to do your bidding, whether it was to plant Improvised Explosive Devices (IEDs) on some small road or run weapons in and out of the desert. If they were stupid enough to experiment with the drug, then let them suffer the consequences. But, to Rachman, business was business and that meant the supply chain must be served. He knew the long history of the drug wars in that area and now it was his turn to rake in profits as Westerners had. However, his profits would be turned back into the business of his product—Jihad against the West and in particular against Israel and the Jews, American or otherwise.

That supply chain was busy. Middlemen, often from large centers of commerce in major American and European cities would find their way to distribution hubs where they would be met by the "sales force" of the poppy growing collectives. From there, arrangements were made for drop zones, transshipment to faraway places, deals struck, and monies exchanged. It was pure capitalism at its best, just slightly twisted. It was supply and demand, price and quantity... basic Economics 101.

Heroin deals were often accompanied by a weapons black market, where virtually anything and everything could be had for a price. Manufactured supply shortages driven by who knew what forces were at play, where demand for high quality, Middle East white heroin was up in the U.S., thus driving prices even higher. The sweet irony of all this was not lost on the crafty leader.

Rachman rose early that morning, just before the approaching dawn. The sun began its slow climb from the desert floor and into the cloudless morning sky while a few birds circled overhead. He heard a hiss in the bushes near him and caught, just briefly, a glimpse of a snake with a large fat rat for prey in its mouth. *Nice metaphor,* he thought.

Soon, he knew that the world as they knew it would never be the same. The Jews were on the run now, history was about to repeat itself. He was the predator and they were his prey. They were the rats, he the snake. The world would soon learn that those who forgot their history were condemned to repeat it in the future and he would be the schoolmaster.

In the coming weeks, the 10 strike teams would periodically scatter from their base in Afghanistan nestled in the mountainous regions of the hauntingly beautiful desert setting. They would virtually vanish from the surface of the earth and they would find, from time to time, interconnected caves and tunnels in and around the desert landscape, thus avoiding detection from the ground or from the sky, especially from the American's satellites and high flying drones. Night travel was most preferred.

Despite almost 30 years of the American and Coalition troops' best efforts, local Islamic terrorist teams operated with virtual impunity. They leveraged relationships with local farmers for the cash crop. In exchange for 'protection,' which the loyal forces of Allah provided to them, the farmers were free to grow and sell the strange sticky fruit from their poppies.

Even stranger to him was the notion that American armed forces, when present, actually BELIEVED that the farmers, for a price, would consider NOT growing the crop.

'Ah, those gullible Americans!' Rachman chuckled to himself.

Of course, even the Americans, with all their vaunted morals and attempts to democratize the Middle East, would lose some to heroin addiction here just like they did in Vietnam. He read history and the lesson was not lost on him. Americans had short attention spans, his people had long memories.

The teams prepared to disperse to various capitals within Europe. From there, they would take on new documents, learn new "legends", and then begin their journey to America. Each team member was well trained, spoke excellent English, and was disciplined to carry out the mission. Days later, the 50 chosen fighters found their way to their beginning points.

The strike teams prepared to board their respective flights from some of the major capitals in Europe and Asia:

> **Team 1** prepared to board a Lufthansa flight in Munich heading to New York.
>
> **Team 2** would leave aboard an American Airlines flight from Copenhagen and fly to Chicago.
>
> **Team 3** boarded a Delta plane in Paris for its flight to Dallas.
>
> **Team 4** members climbed aboard their Air France flight in Seville, headed to Atlanta. The stopovers and airline changes didn't appear too difficult.
>
> **Team 5** left from Singapore aboard Emirates and headed to Cleveland.
>
> **Team 6** made its connecting United Airlines flight from Munich to Toronto.
>
> **Team 7** hopped aboard a KLM Dutch Airlines flight heading to Boston from Paris.
>
> **Team 8** would fly British Airways from Antwerp to Miami.

Team 9 with a Philadelphia destination began in London aboard British Airways.

Team 9 began its journey in Lisbon aboard an Iberian Air flight, heading to Baltimore.

Team 10 boarded KLM its flight in Brussels heading to Mexico City. This team would eventually find their way into America through the Mexico-California border.

From the pen of the Prophet Ezekiel
Chapter 11 Verse 17

Therefore say, Thus says the Lord GOD, I will gather you from the peoples and assemble you out of the countries among which you have been scattered, and I will give you the land of Israel.

Chapter 29

Instruction

The Wasserman brothers' congregations had many questions. The members had little exposure to the Hebrew Scriptures beyond the Torah. Yet the media and pulpits in their community said a lot about Bible prophecy, the role of the Jews, and the Land of Israel. Television specials argued whether these were the end times and whether or not the Jews had any special place in those prophecies.

A lot of the talk centered on whether or not the Jews belonged in America or whether they should emigrate to Israel. The vast majority of the Jews didn't believe they belonged in Israel because of how they saw themselves- as Jewish Americans. However, many were beginning to ask questions.

With surrounding conditions worsening, Chaim decided to capture some of the concerns in his Friday night address to his congregation in Dallas. Eleazer would do the same in Los Angeles. The two brothers saw an opportunity to train their respective congregations in the new facts of life. After the Shabbat liturgy drew to a close, Chaim began his sermon.

"Friends, we sit in a very precarious situation. Many of you have asked me recently whether or not we should pack up and move to Israel. Some of you have been exposed to either Messianic Jewish or Christian teaching in the past few years and more specifically the past few months. You have asked me if these are the end times and whether or not we should listen to those who tell us that the Bible is coming true before us. I felt that it was time to discuss some of these ideas and so I will."

"In the next few sessions we will explore, together, what some of the prophecies say and what I've come to believe about them. However, before I do any such thing, I want to challenge you, each of you, to do something for me and for your families, and for the greater Jewish community as a whole. Go out and purchase a copy of the Tenach (Old Testament) if you don't already have one, and start reading it. If you would rather go online and find it, that would be fine too. Chances are you have never read your own Bible cover to cover."

"I urge you to keep a notebook of difficult questions or confusing portions and we can discuss them when we meet. The key is not to be persuaded by anybody's opinions and that includes mine. I have a good Christian friend who admonishes his audiences to 'study to show yourselves approved.' I rather like that and plan to follow that advice myself."

What Chaim wanted more than anything else was a sounding board. Yes, he had his friends among the Christians including Jonathan Roberts. He knew Roberts' friend Aryeh Cohen. But Roberts, or any other Christian, couldn't possibly understand the anguish of the Jews and their history, though he was extremely sensitive and as good a friend as the Jews had right now, especially in light of the dwindling numbers of friends of any type. He needed his flock to read things for themselves and make their own decisions and observations as best as they were able. This was the first time he had put such a plea out to his congregation.

"If you look at the prophecies, they do predict a time for the Jews to return to the land of Israel, after a very long scattering abroad. We call this the Diaspora or the Galut. Our great, great grandparents were among the early arrivals in America but our people have been living abroad for much longer than that."

"Remember, prophecies tend to fall into different categories and you must be aware of those types. For example, there are some prophecies concerning the Land of Israel and the dispersion of the Jewish people based on certain prohibited practices. These kinds of prophecies concerned our own people who were very sinful, practiced idolatry, child sacrifice, and other abominations. Still other prophecies concern the people of God who would be brought back to the land of their ancient fathers after a long time away. Other prophecies focus on the coming Messiah, whoever he may be."

Rabbi Chaim paused, stood silent, surveyed faces, and measured his connection. Every listener found his eyes, awaited his words, and honored his silence. He continued with the Prophet Ezekiel, chapter 28:

> *"Thus says the Lord GOD, when I gather the house of Israel from the peoples among whom they are scattered, and will manifest My holiness in them in the sight of the nations, then they will live in their land which I gave to My servant Jacob. They will live in it securely; and they will build houses, plant vineyards and live securely when I execute judgments upon all who scorn them round about them. Then they will know that I am the LORD their God."* Ezekiel 28:25-26

"Ezekiel the prophet spoke of a future time for Israel—though written 3,500 years ago. The span of time until fulfillment was beyond Ezekiel's perspective. He may have imagined 50 or 100 years.

"Remember, Israel was in captivity in Babylon and ruled by a foreign king. Ezekiel couldn't have possibly known any of this which included details such as the planting of vineyards, housing, and the interesting detail that they are living in secure and safe homes," he said, again pausing for effect.

His intent was to impress on the congregation that God indeed could see and explain the future, though those hearing it may not have understood it, or worse, believed it. Indeed God stood outside of time, as man understood it, thus being able to see the end from the beginning.

Many agnostics or marginally religious Jews sat in the pews because that's what Jews did, go to Temple for Shabbat services on Friday night—at least some of them. They rarely asked why. Besides, being Jewish didn't really depend on what one thought of the Scriptures. Being Jewish was more about birthright, performing charity, educating your children, living within your culture, tolerance, and observing tradition. Those were *real* Jewish values.

The rabbi slowly stroked his beard, an old habit of his, his eyebrows arching in the manner he used when he wished to add a profound point, and then looked out over the audience.

"You may note here that it is God who does the gathering from among the peoples who are scattered. You may also notice that this is land given to *my servant Jacob*. What I find fascinating about all of this is that when God is ready to make something happen, he will make it happen and He will telegraph it to the Prophets. And He will make it happen in such a way that it seems so natural, almost normal in the course of daily events. Or it could be caused by events beyond the control of anyone involved. Miracles do happen too. He paused... again... this time for what seemed like an eternity.

"Friends, God's message is for us—**TODAY**! The time is **NOW**. The first Aliyot (returns) began more than a hundred years ago.... for good reason! God is today re-gathering the Jews home!"

His words collided with his people. Wide eyes, audible gasps, and furrowed brows reflected their understanding and surprise. No one suspected that the Rabbi believed any of this nonsense. Yet he proclaimed it before their eyes for the very first time.

The rabbi stood silent and looked at his congregation. He scanned faces he known for years. He wondered what thoughts filled their minds. Some stared, others fidgeted, and still others tried to get comfortable in their seats. Nobody could get comfortable—but they all paid attention to their Rabbi with the grey beard.

Dry Bones—Ezekiel
Chapter 37 Verses 11-14
... on the Promised Jewish Return to Israel

Then He said to me, Son of man, these bones are the whole house of Israel; behold, they say, Our bones are dried up and our hope has perished. We are completely cut off.

Therefore prophesy and say to them, Thus says the Lord GOD, Behold, I will open your graves and cause you to come up out of your graves, My people; and I will bring you into the land of Israel. Then you will know that I am the LORD, when I have opened your graves and caused you to come up out of your graves, My people.

I will put My Spirit within you and you will come to life, and I will place you on your own land. Then you will know that I, the LORD, have spoken and done it, declares the LORD.

Chapter 30

Aliya

Jewish immigration and emigration patterns have, historically, been a mixed bag. Many Israeli Jews had become tired of the constant grind of the tiny nation and sought refuge abroad years after the Yom Kippur War. Some left for the mountains of Nepal, where they looked for peace and calm in a strife-ridden world. Still others sought sex, drugs, and a free-wheeling lifestyle in Thailand or the drug dens in Holland. Others made for America where the lure and promise of a better life for them and their children provided temptation too difficult to resist.

That close to 350,000 of them had settled in the United States and North America alone over the years far overshadowed those declaring aliya, or inbound immigration to the Land of Israel.

The modern history of Jewish immigration or "aliya", (going up) had begun in earnest in the 1880's. Slightly more than 35,000 Jews immigrated to the land of the Hebrew Fathers, then in the hands of the Ottoman Empire. Just a few years before the Dreyfus Affair in France, Theodore Hertzl's Jewish Congress met and declared the need for a Jewish state (still at that time a half a lifetime away). They established the first communal farms, known as *kibbutzim*. There were also *moshavim*, or collective farms, differing from *kibbutzim* in that they were privately owned though still collectively managed.

Later, between 1904 and 1914, another 40,000 immigrants came to the Land. Most of these were Russians fleeing the Czars' and the peasants' pogroms. This group brought many of the socialist ideals that drove early political thought in the nascent Jewish state. Arab resistance and a transition from Turkish to British rule was evident as the Jews began living under new rulers. Perhaps one of the most profound developments was the early adoption of the Hebrew language, a revival, actually, of the ancient tongue, modernized for the 20th century realities. It would be the first time a people revived an extinct language for daily use.

The third aliyah covered the years from 1919 through 1923, a very volatile time as more Russians arrived. The *kibbutzim* movement expanded through the Jezreel Valley and throughout Israel as the new immigrants pushed back the swamps and the desert acre by acre and converted it to arable land. Both recent and distant arrivals rejoiced together when the Balfour Declaration was announced by the British government in 1917, signaling, that perhaps within their lifetimes they might see a re-established Jewish State.

Jewish money bought and paid for land at exorbitant prices, whether from local Arab families or the former Turkish overlords. Historically, the Arabs had demonstrated little interest in farming or working the land but the Jews were hungry for it.

Even Mark Twain was puzzled over any interest in the land, writing of its utter desolation in the 1870's. Twain's comments that the land was a 'hopeless, dreary, heartbroken, land... inherited only by birds of prey and skulking foxes,' were saved for posterity years before there was any debate over whose land it was.

Over time, the land, once desolate, rocky, and completely denuded during the 400 plus years of Turkish rule, was slowly reclaimed, the swamps drained and pushed back hectare by hectare, then transformed into an oasis, similar some said, to the ancient descriptions in the Hebrew Scriptures. A modern day miracle was at hand. Over time, they planted more than 200 million trees causing the environment to reintroduce both the former and the latter rainy seasons-a true modern day miracle.

After the war, the next several Aliyot brought in hundreds of thousands of refugees recently having fled from the madness of Hitler's death traps. This pushed Jewish population figures past 600,000 and meant that they had achieved a majority in the land, a Jewish victory and an Arab's nightmare. The Jews wrested control of the smaller version of Israel, thus ending 30 years of British rule and 400 years of Ottoman control. Events headed for a climax in 1948 and beyond.

During the 1950's, more than 765,000 Jews from North Africa and the Middle East arrived in Israel. As the Arabs claimed that the Jews had driven them out of Israel, so it was the same for the Jews who were driven out by the Arab backlash that followed the 1948 War of Independence and creation of the Jewish State. Except the Arab claims were proven false.

When, during the buildup of the War of Israeli Independence, neighboring Arab radio broadcasts reached indigenous Arabs within Palestine's borders urging them to leave their homes while the invading Arab armies massacred the Jews. But the day never came and those landless didn't return in the same numbers that left. Stories circulated for years that should they have returned and been able to prove their ownership, Israel would have evicted any squatters and returned the land to its rightful Arab owners. However, Jews living abroad in Arab lands would face an even harsher situation.

One such instance that made the news in 1950 occurred when 100,000 Iraqi Jews were literally tossed out of the land they lived in for more than 2000 years. Deeply entrenched in the social system, they were kicked out with the clothes on their backs, all possessions stolen from them and no enumeration provided. This game was a two-edged sword and was rarely, if ever, mentioned in refugee and displacement discussions of the Jews in Arab lands.

Hundreds of thousands more from the European Communist bloc would soon follow and then another million from the collapsing Soviet Union would finish the last of the major waves of immigration. Interestingly enough, the Soviet waves later created a technology boom unparalleled in history.

After the 1990's, inbound immigration slowed to a trickle. And over the years, no immediate threat appeared against world Jewry. Terror seemed to calm and some measure of stability grew. Nobody could have possibly foreseen a modern-day Holocaust followed by a contemporary exodus anywhere in the world, certainly not in America. America's Jews or the Jews living in Europe were relatively safe and protected from harm.

There had never been any mass immigration from the United States. The obvious reason was that there was no reason to come to Israel or to leave America. Jewish Americans were just that, Americans first, Jews second and so it was that few felt the need or had the motivation to move to Israel. Those 120,000 who did, came for either religious or cultural reasons, not because of persecution, the driving factor in virtually every other major Aliya.

The very place that received and absorbed Jews who fled pogroms or the Holocaust would later find themselves in danger. Without pressing reasons to leave the Goldena Medina, they stayed in America where they could go to school, work, raise families, and if needed, raise money and send it abroad to Israel. But later, Israel awoke to another wave of immigrants, a group no one saw coming.

Over the years, many Yemeni, Iraqi, and Persian Jews would eventually find their way to the Promised Land. When Israel discovered her Ethiopian brothers and sisters living on the African continent, it kicked up quite a controversy as to whether or not they were actually Jews. Once the courts decided they were, Israel quietly airlifted close to 80,000 members of Ethiopia's ancient Jewish community to their eventual destination. In what some termed a modern day miracle, Israeli planes brought almost 15,000 of them in just two days in 1991, thereby testing their capacity to perform a short-term major airlift once again.

This now made at least three international airlifts executed by the small Jewish state, a fact not lost on Michael Shapiro.

Ori Konforti, the Ethiopian envoy for the Jewish Agency, was quoted years later to say:

> *I am going to destroy a myth here; waves of immigration have never been because of the pulling power of Israel but rather because of the pushing power of where those people came from.*

This comment, more than most, described the state of affairs Israelis had lived with for decades. Jews, when comfortable, became an ingrained part of that host culture until they experienced severe persecution, and only then would they attempt to leave or, in more recent times, flee to Israel. And so it was that the winds of hate, bigotry, and persecution pushed the Jews out of their ancient homelands and blew them into Israel.

If coming to Israel was, to the Jews, a dream come true, to the Palestinians it was the al-Naqba, or the (catastrophe) equivalent of the Holocaust, though there was really no comparison, no mass killings, no efforts to wipe an entire race from the planet. The Arabs made the point that the Jewish drive for independence had usurped their land, invading with an army of European immigrants who had been persecuted by others. Conveniently forgotten was the fact that most of those calling themselves Palestinians had arrived later than most of the Israelis. They had come from surrounding Arab lands and claimed citizenship during the Ottoman or the British years, ignored by both of the ruling authorities.

Yet, they would ask, 'why should we bear the brunt of this people's desire for a homeland? What did we do to deserve this invasion? Why should we have to pay the price for what the rest of the world had done?' As far as they were concerned, the Jews should be absorbed back into the lands from where they came. But, in 1947, The United Nations didn't see it that way. As the vote approached, the nations waited anxiously by their radios for the decision. The vote for partition was the turning point for statehood and brought about what the British, while promising for years, refused to do.

Upon the votes being cast in November of 1947, the U.N. voted for partition, a compromise really, for the original mandate promised a far greater portion of land for the Jewish nation, including what eventually became the modern state of Jordan. But through the years leading up to that point, international Muslim pressures had whittled the size of the land grant down to a far smaller portion.

The Jews, coming out of the Holocaust had little if any choice but to accept the vote and declare independence.

Within minutes, the new nation was plunged into a bloody war for its very survival and began its national defense efforts that would amaze the world for decades. A little more than one year later, Israel signed an armistice with its neighbors, ceasing hostilities for a time, though an official state of war still pulsed through the veins of the Arab nations. She would never know peace for more than a few years at a time. Each war, in succession, just gave her enemies a chance to rearm with bigger and better weapons, learning the lessons of war as they went.

Coffee House Chatter —

"Where do you think the Jews belong?" She asked.

"What do you mean? They should live wherever they want," he answered, wondering where she was going with this line of questions.

"No. What I'm asking is, do you think there is some sort of calling for Jews to go to Israel?"

"Wow, that's a loaded question. I can tell you that at least 1/6 of the world's population thinks any Jewish presence in that part of the world is an abomination."

"Well, we agree on that point. But, I always wondered if there was something else operating... something buried deep within the Jewish DNA... something that no one can understand unless it is calling you."

"Jury's still out I say. Are you saying there is some sort of spiritual pull towards Israel within the Jewish gene pool, whether or not they believe in God?"

"Now, that's deep.... but if you are right, then it's not really an issue of personal choice, but more like a calling or something."

"B'shert?" He asked.

Chapter 31

Living in the Diaspora

Yerida, or "descending" was another matter entirely. At the outset, Israelis leaving Israel were a trickle but had accelerated over the years. According to internal government records, close to ¾ of a million Israelis were living expat, meaning away from the motherland and the cradle of their forefathers. Also called the Israeli Diaspora, it was a term of derision used to describe those who left and those who stayed away.

For those Israelis living abroad, however, life was good. Since most of them spoke at least two languages and easily picked up any language where they lived, transitions were normally fairly workable. It seemed to many that the Jews had been given a gift of tongues. Many, if not most of them attained higher education, most frequently in the professions such as law, education, engineering, the sciences, and health care. Jewish achievement was no myth and wherever one looked there were Israelis and Jews quickly climbing the ladder of success, innovation, and achievement.

Many escaped the Land to seek opportunity elsewhere. Life grew hard in Israel, so hard in fact that just staying even with grueling inflation cycles, constant threats of terrorism, and perception as a pariah state took its toll. It was reported early in the 21st century that as many as one fifth of all Israelis lived under the poverty line. It was tough for the 350,000 who lived in the U.S. as well. One of those emigrating after his military service concluded was Avner Sullivan.

Sullivan served in both latter regional conflicts and other incursions into Gaza and the West Bank. His service time prepared him for leadership as it had with many of Israel's youth. Over the years, international businessmen learned what could happen when a company hired young Israelis. Their entrepreneurship, industriousness, leadership, decision making abilities, and overall business acumen and skills formed partly on the battlefield, became a valuable asset to the hiring company.

Avner served his mandatory three years and settled down near his family on the outskirts of Haifa, the beautiful port city on the Mediterranean. His apartment overlooked the picture-perfect blue water and fresh ocean breezes. He was where he wanted to be, but his soul was restless. So Avner began to explore other options.

His sister Mimi was the wild one. She was still serving her time in the military. The third sibling, Ephraim, had recently finished his service time and had headed to the U.S. to go to school. It was a very common thing—three children, born into an Israeli family, two living in the U.S. and one heading there soon.

Sullivan is not recognized as a Jewish name—at least not on the surface. The name suited and served him well. Avner, his sister Mimi, and their brother Ephraim were native born Sabras and had grown quite talented in technical fields.

This was an interesting phenomenon as inexplicable to the world as anything to do with Jews. Israelis, especially those who had completed their mandatory military service and had pursued other occupations had become something of a miracle in the business world—more Israeli companies were listed on the NASDAQ exchange than all European nations combined.

The tiny nation also attracted venture capital by the billions. Per capita venture capital investments in Israel were more than two and a half times greater than the U.S., 30 times greater than Europe, 80 times greater than China, and 350 times greater than India. It attracted more venture capital than Great Britain, Germany, and France combined.

All of this amazing growth and success developed against the backdrop of rising terrorism, internal strife, corrupt governments, a bursting tech bubble, and several wars. Israel's share of the global venture capital pie doubled in a relatively short time and even thrived during war. In the midst of wars and turmoil, the Sullivans became a family to be reckoned with.

Their story was not untypical among Jews who had emigrated from the Emerald Isle. His family, Jews from as far back as they could trace, underwent a name change generations before—for murky reasons that no one really understood, or perhaps cared to admit. Jews weren't unknown in Ireland. At one time, even Dublin had a Jewish mayor.

The Sullivans, in a way, represented all that was good with Israeli society. All of their children had served or were serving their time in defense of the nation. They were all bright, capable, and had experienced more at 19-21 years of age then most of their counterparts around the world would ever experience.

They also represented something else that few ever thought of—virtually every Israeli living abroad, woman or man, had completed their military commitment and were battle tested, trained and hardened to the pressures of life.

Coffee House Chatter —

"What do know about strong willed children," he asked.

She paused and asked, "What are you getting at?"

"Have you ever dealt with a strong-willed child, or an adult for that matter?"

"Are you kidding me? You're looking at the poster child for strong-willed children."

"You? Really?"

"You soooo don't know me!"

Chapter 32

Mimi

Mimi's delayed military service provided a new start for her. She was the wild one, running away from home at 13, pregnant at 14 (she eventually lost the baby), becoming way too familiar with drugs by 16, in short a big disappointment to her family. She had dropped out of high school and, for a brief time, had gone to work at 17 as a taxi cab driver. She had no fear of anyone or anything.

She sported two scars along her cheeks extending to her jawbones... both from scuffles involving knives. One came from an attempted rape by a Palestinian who mistook the pretty blond, blue eyed Sabra for an easy mark. She left him in the street, unconscious, and bleeding from the ears. The other she cared not to discuss.

The scars gave her face a mysterious quality. People she met would be tantalized both wanting and not wanting to know how she acquired them. That was what was visible. Under her clothes lurked three tattoos, each

CHAPTER THIRTY-TWO: *Mimi*   Page 183

associated with a dark moment from her past. She lived life as hard as any man she had ever met but deep within was a heart of gold, seeking liberation.

Mimi was the smartest one in her uber-intelligent family—that fact drove the others crazy. She entered the service at 18 and aced every test thrown at her. She mystified all of her classmates and officers. She entered the Engineering Corps to design and build bridges, roads, and causeways for military vehicles. It was child's play for her.

When asked by her family what she was doing with her service time, she had offhandedly remarked that she 'made sand castles in the dirt,' a typical smart-aleck retort to which they had grown accustomed. When her commanding officer discovered her gifts, he called her into a meeting with the brigade's senior staff.

"Mimi, we really don't understand you at all... we've never seen anyone score as high as you did on the testing and you don't seem all that hard pressed to work at any of this."

He was right. She seemed to do everything with some measure of belligerence, often whispering under her breath as if everything and everyone annoyed her. And yet, it had not gone unnoticed that she did everything with skill, paying attention to detail, and personal dedication. She never made excuses for mistakes and took responsibility for everything she did correcting them as she learned.

He was Colonel Yigal Dayan, a distant relative of Moshe Dayan, the hero of the Six Days War in 1967, a long time ago. The latter Dayan's experience in both of those more recent regional conflicts had gained him a fair amount of recognition in the military apparatus. It must have been in the blood. In fact, he was already being compared to some of America's most decorated engineering generals such as Robert E. Lee and George Meade of Civil War fame.

It was generally recognized that his ability to construct quick access roads with a minimal amount of trouble allowed Israeli ground forces to hook up quickly with their paratroopers behind the lines and cut off and surround the enemy. His techniques had proven themselves in the latter regional conflicts and in other incursions in Judea and Samaria as well as other adventures. But this challenging young blonde girl, sweet and charming looking with freckles bridging her perfectly shaped nose, but tough as nails, threw him for a loop. She couldn't be cracked. So he and the senior staff changed their tactics.

He offered her a cigarette and held up a light for her. She took it and drew deeply, the smoke curling around her head, then blowing out just to amuse her superiors.

"We are offering you something that's only been done once or twice in the history of the IDF, as far as we know. We are willing to sponsor a full scholarship ride through Hebrew University, or the Teknion, or frankly even MIT's Engineering Program, or anywhere you want to go. With your smarts and their new accelerated programs, you could be out of there in 2 years or less."

More and more schools offered fast-track programs, and Mimi seemed a logical fit. There were many qualified candidates for Israel's technical schools and international programs. Still, Mimi's 200 IQ was rare. She was a true diamond-in-the-rough, and Dayan's senior staff knew it. And to sponsor her through school would make his command look good. The final outcome would be tantalizing to consider.

"Ok, so, let's say I take you up on your offer," she parried, her hand holding the cigarette, and punching the air. She pulled from her smoke again, exhaling into the room.

"We all agree I can do this, but what's in it for me? I mean, I get all that about the scholarship, but what happens when I finish?" she asked, again with attitude, playing her senior officers, almost like a cat with a bird or a mouse. She flashed that charming smile, white, even teeth perfectly fitting her generous mouth, and complete with two dimples.... and the scars.

Behind her question was something deeper, more profound, for Mimi had always felt the world didn't care about her... feeling abandoned at an early age though she wasn't, she had always carried a very tough, defensive edge about her. Many men had come and gone in and out of her life, friends were few and far between, and there was really nobody she trusted. Even family seemed distant, nobody really understood her.

"People make promises all the time, but they never keep them," she argued. She had done a lot of living for someone her age and she had learned to trust no one.

Dayan pulled up a chair close to her face, and turning it around he faced her, hanging his elbows over the back of the chair. Their eyes locked.

"Look, I can't promise you anything beyond the degree, but if you finish, and let's face it, we know your life better than you do, and we know your background, we can place you in the officer's program when you return. That I can promise. Beyond that, it's up to you. But based on what we know about your past, we know you have something very special - you know how to lead and control your surroundings."

And, how right he was. Every eye contact with her left him feeling weak in the knees and she knew it.

Tough customer, he thought.

Not bad looking might be something there, she thought. She loved playing this game.

Mimi's background, sordid as it was, demonstrated seemingly simple, yet profound gifts. Though appearing difficult to deal with, she had shown something from her past... the capability to lead with an uncanny ability to read others and the situations life presented. He pulled out a document from her personnel file.

"We know you organized campaigns for the homeless, volunteered at animal shelters, and also know about your drug importing and exporting operation. You were only 16. We know you used a line of cosmetics from the Dead Sea as a cover story. The Americans never knew about that—it was pretty popular in American shopping malls over the years. Even that made money."

She just stared at him. *How did they know about all this?*

She had an ability to draw people to her with an arsenal of charms that made anyone who came in contact with her never forget that face and smile. In short, people trusted her... and feared her. She trusted no one and feared no one.

"We even know about the facial scars—they make you look older than you are. Why didn't you let the plastic surgeon, repair the wounds?

"This may be hard to understand, but those scars are mine. I earned them, I love them. You can't possibly understand why and I'm not going to try to explain... just accept it." She was firm and there was something in her voice that caused him to stop his line of questions.

Working right under the authorities' noses, her international multi-million dollar contraband business involved more than 100 dealers. Everyone prospered as she demonstrated an acute sense of supply and demand, price and quantity, basic economic laws, practically applied, and always knowing when it was time to pack it in and move on.

She did business with Arabs, Persians, West Africans, Russians, mobsters, and her peers. It was apparent that you didn't mess with Mimi Sullivan and nobody tried. She was way too smart for the authorities and carried an undefined, yet palpable air of confidence and control. That she had never been arrested was a miracle. She swore like a sailor and charmed like a debutante. She wasn't arrogant, just supremely confident in her abilities. And though no one outside of her world knew it, she was dying inside.

"Look, we know about all of that," and we still want you. You are now clean. We've tested your blood and urine a million times. Your gifts and talents are now ready for testing in the defense of your country," he continued. Mimi pondered the offer as she thought about her family.

Those statements were true as she had kicked a cocaine habit almost as easily as she had gotten into it. Even in her personal rehabilitation she had demonstrated skills that flabbergasted everyone around her. Nobody could figure out why she had even checked herself into the facility and then out of it. Nobody even knew she had an addiction. She had learned, from that point forward, never to let anything or anyone control her. She would set the terms and others would follow.

Mimi lived her own life—out of reach from her parents. Still, she loved them and wondered what they would think. Ha! The loser daughter/sister off to study engineering—only God knows where. Then back to an officer's commission in the corps. Also action on the front lines where she would be needed, cherished, and respected. The look on the faces of her family might be worth the trouble. She would think about it.

Coffee House Chatter

"So... do you believe in love at first sight," she asked—then looked down to conceal a playful smile.

He didn't answer right away, staring out the window and not looking at anything in particular. It was a rainy day, the wind sweeping the rain through the parking lot in misty gusts. It was very cold as passersby hurried to their destinations. She thought she saw a tear forming in his eye.

"Hey, you ok? Did I strike a nerve or something?" she asked, quiet and more gently.

"Once. I'll never forget her. She was older than I was, an incredibly beautiful woman, smart, funny, and the attraction we had is something I'll never forget. But there was someone else... " his voice trailing off.

She waited for a moment. It might be best not to dig too deep. He was more sensitive than she thought.

Chapter 33

Avner & Danielle

Avner was the quiet one, thoughtful of others, compliant, and ready to help another family member. He was just 5'5", dark brown eyes, curly brown hair, full beard, and even-white teeth. Avner was shy but adored by all who knew him. With humdrum rimmed glasses, he looked like a scholar.

He had entered the IDF at 18 and honored his mandatory three year hitch. He served the Northern Command with distinction in both the latter Lebanese Wars, showing gifts of leadership, compassion for his troops, and fairness with enemy captives. After discharge, Avner felt the longing of a long road trip outside his home and so he packed up what few possessions he owned and headed to the U.S, after spending some time with family in Haifa. He always heard about California, especially Southern California, which he understood to be something where there were a lot of beaches, warm sun, and girls. Someone told him it reminded them of Haifa. That was all he needed to know.

Shortly after arriving in California one morning, he found his way to the Starbucks at the Circle in Orange, California, a small town in the middle of the vast area known as Orange County and not far from Disneyland. The little town was charming, with its small roundabout in the middle of the town and many unique antique stores. A small park with palms, fountains, and grass split the four streets surrounding it. More than 40 restaurants attracted customers in and around "the Circle" as it was known.

Avner took his place in line, lifted his voice, and in Hebrew spoke to the man behind the counter. Both laughed, and the man answered Avner in kind.

Behind Avner was an attractive young woman. She caught Avner's conversation and decided to join in. ***"Boker tov!"****

Avner turned around, looked right passed the pretty women behind, and continued to scan the room.

"Boker tov," she said again—this time in his ear. He turned, and their eyes met. "You didn't expect Hebrew from a Black woman, did you?"

"No, not that. I just didn't think that such a beautiful woman would be talking to me!" He smiled. She dropped her head and waited for her smile to pass. "It really is a good morning if *you* were talking to me."

Avner studied her eyes and waited. She studied his, too and then said, "I was."

By the time they had their super-charged mochas in hand, the two strangers were friends. They spoke in half Hebrew and half English with lots of laughter and many stolen looks. They spoke of Israel, the Bible, the Jewish people, persecution, the Holocaust, and four thousand years of history.

"You are testing my whole vocabulary, not to mention exhausting my history!" she said between laughs.

"Don't worry, you are doing just fine!" he answered, growing more intrigued by the minute.

They opened up their lives to one another... the occasional pause to drink in the dialog and each other's eyes. Since Avner spoke very good English and Danielle spoke passable Hebrew, the conversation flowed between them fluid and warm. Both of them tossed away years of self doubt and fear of rejection and passed silently into one another's souls. Their attraction was profound and immediate.

Danielle told him that she loved languages and after two trips to Israel on church and synagogue tours, had invested in and gobbled up Rosetta Stone, completed 3 years of conversational Hebrew and was now studying Biblical Hebrew, with a desire to read the Scriptures in their native state. And, she was holding her own in the conversation. Her investment in the classes and the software was paying off. *My teachers would be proud*, she thought.

Several moments passed, the silence between them sweet. She felt herself grow a little ***ferklempt****.

"I feel like I've known you all my life," she said, as their eyes locked and held on to one another's. The time had gotten away from her and as she looked up, the clock said 9:30.

"I can't believe this... we've been talking for two hours, and I don't even know your name." Avner was transfixed by her presence.

There was something about this stranger, she wondered, *he's just different from anyone I've ever met*. Even her toes tingled. She hoped her breath was ok, silently doing a breath test in the palm of her hand and hoping he hadn't noticed.

"I'm Avner, Avner Sullivan" he said, suddenly standing formally and extending his hand as he had been taught from his youth.

Standing too, she looked at his hand for a moment, gently brushed it away, studied his eyes for a moment, then threw her arms around his neck, kissed him deeply and said, "Nice to meet you Avner Sullivan!"

At that moment, they would both recall years later, a perceptible and physical spark passed between them. She had never, ever done anything quite as bold as this, yet it just seemed so... appropriate. Avner was caught by surprise, but for some reason he couldn't resist the kiss. It wasn't your typical first impression. They both burst into laughter.

"I'm Danielle!" she exclaimed, "Danielle Rogers!"

Avner stepped back from her for a moment. He took her hands in his and said, "You remind me of someone, but I cannot remember just who... you are so familiar to me," he said. "Do you know the term *b'shert?*" he asked her, hesitatingly, eyes searching hers.

"It means *meant to be* or *destined,*" she said. She looked into his eyes and reached for his hands, studying them for a moment. She couldn't hide the tears.

"Where did you learn Yiddish?" he asked quizzically

"Well, I speak some Yiddish too," she said. He couldn't find the words, but knew he was in over his head.

"Long story," she said, with a smile breaking on her face. Her teeth, though slightly crooked, had brightness to them and her remarkably charming smile invited him in like a warm pool. Smile and laugh lines slightly creased around her deep hazel eyes and her mouth. She also wore her hair in a traditional 'fro', framing her face.

He sensed safety and strength all at the same time.

She was different. He knew that she was something special.

She couldn't believe this was happening.

At that point, and at all risk to this crazy mixed up meeting of chance, she let out all her inhibitions tumble out.

"Look, you need to know something about me. I'm a Christian—maybe a better term is Christian Zionist. But you also need to know that I am wholly and deeply committed to helping Israel and the Jewish people. I need to know what you think about the Bible, Yeshua (Jesus). I just don't want to scare you." She felt a little panic, not sure how he would respond. She knew she was crossing a threshold from which there was no turning back.

She also knew that she was about to risk everything, rolling the dice, hoping for a big fat 7. She told him that she attended a Messianic congregation and spent the next few minutes explaining just what that meant. He was trying to understand this amazing woman standing before him. A cup of coffee had turned his life around, upside down, and sideways. Or maybe it was a mocha.

Avner paused for a moment, seeking her innermost soul through her eyes. They stared at one another for what seemed like an eternity. He felt a million sunsets burst in front of him and a million butterflies land on his shoulders. Simultaneously, time stood still and time flew by. Things were just perfectly 'in flow.' Eternity seemed right at his door, though he had never really thought about it. This was the magic moment.

He let out a long slow breath. His eyes searched hers.

"I'm not really religious. Yet I've always felt spiritual. I've heard so many things about Yeshua. But I paid no attention. I guess you'd say that my family is more secular. We'd attend a local synagogue in Haifa—now and then. Of course, we'd go to the occasional bar/bat mitzvah, wedding, funeral, high holyday, and Shabbat of course." Avner paused and thought a moment.

"There has been something strange that's been haunting me though," Avner pondered aloud.

"Haunting?" Danielle puzzled.

"Do you know what street preachers are?"

"Sure, of course."

"Well, I've encountered these free spirits in Israel and America. It's like they know the route I'm gonna walk. It's happened so many times... well, I stopped and listened to a couple of them. Go figure. Huh?"

Danielle waited. Her heart pounded so loud she was certain Avner could hear it. There was no sound except a ticking clock somewhere in the Starbucks. She couldn't hear a thing, though there were several people talking around her. It was a moment she would never forget. She stared right back at him, her eyes drinking in his.

She felt weak in the knees though never stronger in her faith. She never had an experience like this, ever.

Avner spoke first.

"Ok, so go slow, alright?" he started. Their hands met and clasped... tightly.

She waited for a moment before speaking, but could not find her voice. And she began to cry tears of joy, and at that moment reached out for him. He met her embrace and they held on to one another for what seemed like an eternity. And he cried too. At that moment, she ushered him into the Kingdom of God without saying another word.

And, for some unexplained reason that neither of them ever figured out, their coffee drinks never got cold.

> From HaYad Moshe (the Hand of Moses):
> Genesis Chapter 48:20—Ephraim's Blessing
>
> He blessed them that day, saying,
> By you Israel will pronounce blessing, saying,
> May God make you like Ephraim and Manasseh!
> Thus he put Ephraim before Manasseh.

Chapter 34

Ephraim

Ephraim was the youngest of the three children. His curly dark hair, green eyes, a mop of dark, seemingly unkempt curly hair, and quick smile always put others he met at ease. It was the dimple on his right cheek that killed the girls. He had grown to be a bright, inquisitive young man who had just completed his military service and wanted to join his brother in his American adventure.

This broke the hearts of their parents as both boys were now living abroad. Though they came home at least once a year to visit and see family and friends, the Sullivan boys were missed by all who knew them. Though Mimi was known as the family rebel she was still loved and respected but was away in the military, leaving the Sullivan household quiet for the first time in years. That would soon change.

Ephraim developed a love of computers and all things electronic. Within a year of his arrival in America, he had enrolled in a local community college in Orange County, California. With natural gifts in electronics and his military experience, he quickly declared an electrical engineering major and completed two years of community college in one, then enrolled at the University of California, Irvine.

Since most of his military service had him working technical communication system issues, setting up networks, and writing code (he had become quite the amateur gaming programmer), the curriculum was not difficult for him. Often he would correct his professors on this technical point, or that, virtually driving them nuts, but gaining grudging respect, then enthusiastic support. He was never rude, but they sometimes mistook his silence and introverted personality for arrogance. But having Ephraim on your staff meant that certain pet projects would get done in a fraction of the time.

The smart professors learned quickly that they had to keep one step ahead of Ephraim and tended to offer him special considerations if he would help them work on technical papers or their doctoral studies. In more than a couple of instances, he was given a free pass and didn't have to attend class. They allowed him to challenge the exams, as long as he worked for them. And he passed everything thrown at him with flying colors.

What Ephraim kept to himself and the professors never discovered was that he had a gift for artificial intelligence systems and "backdoor programming," meaning he could pretty much break others' code within minutes.

It was almost a sixth sense and would serve him well in the future. With increased permissions, he also had access to the entire UC student system record collection. The skill would serve him well for in the near future his skill and creativity would be tested in a way he could have never have imagined.

Years had passed since the first protests on the campus. Since that time, UCI had become a political hotbed of Islamic student protests, symposia, and heavy signage all around the campus. Sadly, the rhetoric grew from simple cries for justice and equality for Palestinians to virulent anti-Semitic hatred accompanied by physical assaults and intimidation of Jewish or evangelical Christian students. Years before, the ambassador of Israel spoke on campus but disrespectful Muslims from the Muslim Students Association disrupted the speech, with eleven of them getting arrested.

Many of these students staged protests with vitriolic speakers calling for death to Israel and the Jews. They conducted 'forums' where they condemned Zionist policies and Holocaust denials all the while local Jewish organizations such as Hillel or the Anti Defamation League, and others lodged protests with university officials, hoping for more "horsepower" and a stop to the Islamic racism, but to no avail. The University leadership mostly proved completely impotent in stopping the escalating threats, intimidation, and violence. Later, some officials banned the MSU for a year, but the damage was done.

These students became known for their strong voices and intolerant attitudes. Over the years, vandalism of dorm rooms or cars known to be driven by Jewish or Christian students became more than just an occasional occurrence.

Later, after the students were convicted of violating the ambassador's First Amendment rights, the Council of American Islamic Relations (CAIR) launched a vicious public relations campaign to discredit the decision and overturn the conviction. Jurors were discovered, harassed and intimated by what some labeled as "thugs." Public opinion bowed to the pressure and the court's decision was overturned.

Campus authorities hesitated to enforce codes using the excuse that the Islamic students were within their constitutional rights of free speech, even though many of them were not even American citizens and were later found to be in the country illegally, a fact that Ephraim had learned during some work within the university's student data. Times were indeed changing and Ephraim would be ready for the challenges that awaited him.

Meanwhile Ben Yehuda and his people watched.

From the Hand of Solomon the Wise
Proverbs 16:3

Commit your works to the LORD,
and your plans will be established.

Chapter 35

Plans

When Israel fought the Gaza War in 2009, the IDF instituted another technological innovation, that of dialing every Gazan residence about 10 minutes before that targeted building would be struck by Israeli bombs or missiles. Israeli pilots had been briefed where weapons caches, explosives, and other materials were stored, so superior was their intelligence on the ground. Not much moved in Gaza without Israeli knowledge. No matter what the world would say, they knew they would strike with a minimal loss of human life. That Hamas and the Palestinians in general were known to use human shields would not deter this most necessary of battles.

The news agencies told their stories and further demonized the Jewish state, while a nation of almost six million stood face to face with more than a billion of her ancient enemies. A sovereign nation, after all, must defend its citizens. And, after years of enduring more than 8,000 rocket attacks on her cities, indeed Israel had struck with a vengeance.

Video after video posted on a vast universe of internet websites, showed mosques, private homes, and other buildings being blown to smithereens. Secondary explosions touched off what appeared to be entire neighborhoods, thus proving to an unbelieving world that Hamas was actually using its religious centers, tunnels, and private homes as ammunition dumps and weapons storage facilities. But the world had no interest in the truth. Israel had simply had enough. The Religion of Peace could fool some of the people some of the time but not all of the people all of the time.

Her enemies got what they wanted however and that was to bait Israel into another war. Terror experts agreed that one of the primary psychological weapons used by terrorists is to provoke the attack back on yourself. Done right, the overcompensating (or a more contemporary term-disproportionate) amount of firepower thrown at you by your enemy turns the tables on the victim and exchanges positions in the minds of the public. In other words, the true terrorist becomes the victim and the true victim becomes the terrorist. Palestinians in Gaza and elsewhere proved the tactic was still useful and continued to employ it.

For years, Israel had experimented with lightning fast communications and working for a way to notify local innocents that there would be a strike on their households if they were harboring terrorists or stashing weapons. Her humanitarian goal had always been to reduce the chances of civilian casualties, any casualties really, while still achieving military goals.

This new and exciting technology had been deployed and heavily tested in 2009 Gaza war. In fact, launched more than 300,000 calls to warn Gaza's citizens to vacate before the strikes, thus saving thousands of lives. Though slightly more than 1,000 died (numbers disputed by Israeli authorities) it would have been in the tens of thousands had no warnings been issued at all. Israeli authorities believed the technology to have proven itself. The world didn't agree. When did it ever?

In much the same way, years of communications planning had finally borne fruit. In what would be considered a superior strategy in the field, a true lesson learned, each and every Israeli living abroad carried a cell phone, programmed with an emergency clear channel, triple encrypted with special software, completely invisible to the surrounding world, and tied to 3 low-flying Israeli-launched satellites.

Every expat Israeli was just a call away and within reach of their home. The beauty of the thing was that each computer and phone had a GPS chip in it so that every Israeli could be tracked back from home. If the phone rang, it might be a call to arms. This feature and others like them would pay handsome dividends in the weeks and months ahead.

There were difficult plans to execute before these arrangements could move forward including calls to centralized command centers and preparations to dictate battle plans and other details to troops in the field. The plans for *Operation Last Exodus* were formulated long ago. It was a contingency option in the event of another Holocaust threat. Israel would not let it happen again.

There were street plans by city and region. Other plans were drawn up to disrupt important communications, water service, power, traffic, electricity, and transportation. Since America continued to wage at least two foreign wars at a time, and sometimes three, its military was somewhat compromised and weakened, with no discernable plans to fight an all-out war on its own soil. The thought of an internal insurgency never made it to the military planners' boards.

With at least 350,000 boots on the ground in the United States, and many more expected to join them, the Zionist defenders would form quite a formidable fighting force if push came to shove. Each American Israeli also had a deep and intimate knowledge of the local areas too. Further, more and more American Jews were arming themselves as times grew darker.

CHAPTER THIRTY-FIVE: Plans

The last thing Israel wanted was a war 8,000 miles away, fought in hostile territory, old friends facing each other. But business was business and the Israelis were prepared to face the worst. Though details were fuzzy, it would quickly grow into a fighting force that would be called on to protect American Jewry and facilitate its journey home to the land of its fathers.

Israeli planners developed many game theory scenarios, several of which predicted that at least another five million or more Christians (those supportive to the Jewish state and loyal to God) would find their way to the defenders.

Nobody really knew how many Christians were willing to help. An army of close to five million could form to open a path to America's airports and ports, rescue its five to six million Jewish citizens and help arrange transport to Israel. If any American Jews joined forces, it could swell the numbers even higher. The idea was so farfetched, in most of their minds, virtually impossible, and even unthinkable, with no real chance for success. But, they realized, had this kind of plan been in place during World War II, another six million and their offspring would now be alive. No Jew could ignore it.

No one could remember an historical example, with the war against the British and the Arabs being the only thing even coming close. But that was mostly on Israeli soil. Entebbe was a single action but still a model with valuable learning. Operation Magic Carpet was another and then airlifts for the Iraqi and Ethiopian Jews proved that airlift rescues were possible in the tens of thousands. But almost six million-unfathomable!

And then again, there were miracles to be made. Could this be the time? Others, more perceptively, realized that this might actually look like the American Civil War, with neighbors actually fighting neighbors, families fighting families. It hadn't come to that just yet, but the planners realized that it could. They had actually begun discussing the Biblical Exodus as a potential model.

Deep within the bowels of the planning chambers, plans were dusted off and trotted out at least once a year for revision and enhancement based on new lessons learned or field intelligence. Of course, the logistics analysts and intelligence teams had to update everything, especially communications and the shipment of arms and all that went with them.

Ben Yehuda knew of the plans, in fact, he had a hand in their development back in the 90's. He had intimate knowledge of how weapons and other material were shipped. He knew of the ZIM shipments, the placement of defense items and where the contacts were. This would take a divine miracle and nothing short of it.

Foreign intelligence was gathered, analyzed, torn apart, and put back together. Then the IDF would then be briefed. Operational plans designed and developed. Planners would argue with the logisticians. Then they would argue with their superiors. It was the Israeli way. But in the end all would be set and prepared for deployment.

The logistics alone were enormous. The good news was that Israel had assets no one knew about. They were old friends who could provide the resources and support needed in a critical hour. The slogan *never again* wasn't an empty platitude to any of these battle toughened soldiers living in the U.S.

Never Again was a reminder and force that kept them motivated, determined, hopeful, and ready.

From the Pen of Solomon the Wise
Proverbs 17:17

A friend loves at all times,
and a brother is born for adversity.

Chapter 36

Potential Fulfilled

They had never seen anyone quite like Mimi Sullivan. She had been compared to the likes of Alia Sabur, who years before at 19, was deemed the world's youngest professor and was touted for her musicianship as well. Mimi's mind was something to behold. She had finally chosen from among several colleges who had heard about her prodigious gifts. It was all about the dirt or more specifically the soil.

For Mimi's expertise in the world dealt with soil and she had a gift with it. Ever since she was a little girl, she had loved to play outside with the boys, digging in the dirt, planting things, building things, all very strange, her family thought for a girl, yet it never stopped her.

She read books on growing plants, another gift, but her interest was the dirt and what it did. She could reach down, pick up a handful of dirt, smell it, taste it, and come pretty darn close to identifying its contents. She would make soil blends for fun, just to see what kinds of things she could grow. Sometimes she could just look at the soil, determine its composition, and figure out what amendments it needed to grow plants and flowers. Her friends loved her and she often installed wonderful landscape schemes in their yards, always unique to their properties.

Years later, after joining the IDF, she accepted her assignment into the Civil Engineering Corps and acting like it was nothing to design roadbeds and direct the earth movers while they moved massive amounts of dirt. She had even learned to handle the earth moving equipment, the great Caterpillar and John Deere tractors and earth movers, inspiring awe in her fellow soldiers but her real specialty was "reading" the soil to ensure that everything being done was safe for her "boys," as she would call her fellow soldiers. The bigger and more powerful the machine, the more she liked it.

Even though she was the youngest among them, they looked up to her, even though only a peer or even an 'inferior' to most of them. Respect and leadership often had less to do with title and rank as with the confidence and the compassion of the leader. Mimi was quickly honing her leadership qualities, even while digging in the dirt. And so, after a few calls were placed, Mimi received her appointment to the Massachusetts Institute of Technology, MIT.

Upon entering MIT she declared twin majors: Civil Engineering and Geology/Soil Engineering. A curriculum normally taking up to four or more years to complete took her just a little more than two. The only reason for the 'delay' was another of her prodigious gifts, something she did just for fun which was to play the violin. So accomplished was she, that she had joined a local orchestra and gained first chair within just a few months. The Sullivan name allowed her to move in certain circles, without fear of any "misunderstandings."

Mimi Sullivan had arrived.

But it was roads, bridges, dirt, and all that came with them that drove her in this new phase of her life.

Civil Engineering programs always focus on building projects, whether they were buildings, bridges, sewer systems, anything really, that dealt with how to build and maintain a city. She learned much during her two years and developed additional expertise in structural engineering techniques such as understanding weight bearing loads, spotting weaknesses and how to buttress failing structures as well as another specialty, preventing terrorism.

A field assignment required for her degree was published in 'Civil Engineering,' a juried trade journal where she described how city planners could prevent terror attacks on civil landmarks. Sadly, no one took her advice. When one of her professors approached her to consider submitting the paper to an international trade association, she hemmed and hawed.

"Hello?"

"Mimi, this is Dr. Tibbets. I just received the Call for Papers for this year's Geo-Sciences Conference. Both Dr. Gordon and I are willing to publish your paper on Farming the Desert at the conference and sponsor a speech. We've been talking about this for a while now and are convinced you'll bring a good message to the crowd and it won't kill the department to get a little publicity."

A small group of them decided to mentor her and do what they could to develop her shy side a little more. Mimi was stunned.

"Really?!? I'm not so sure. I haven't given many speeches. Public speaking isn't my thing."

"Mimi, we understand, but we believe this is an incredible opportunity for you."

"I'm far more comfortable with small groups, parties, that kind of thing."

For someone so overwhelmingly bright, it was a strange insecurity to have. She didn't know what to think. Despite those moments of bravado she was used to working alone for the most part, away from the public eye, only engaging when she had gained the trust and comfort of a group, like

CHAPTER THIRTY-SIX: *Potential Fulfilled*

her unit in Israel. Mimi was indeed far more at ease with smaller groups of people and found her alone time far more stimulating than being in larger groups.

Mimi showed up in his Public Infrastructure course. The Professor recognized the talent and her passion right away. Their volatile debates sparked spirited exchanges in class. Discussions on earth moving techniques were sure to be ignited by Mimi. It was a familiar and well studied area for her. Dr. Tibbets loved those sessions. The free exchange of ideas brought out the best in her. It also made class time more exciting.

Her professors rightly sized her up as being more introverted but also realized that she had so much to share. She was quite delightful once you brought her out of her shell, though they quickly learned that she was not to be trifled with as she could turn on them with a ruthless and biting wit. The Sabra deep within wasn't afraid to mix it up.

"Well, you don't have to worry. We will help you along. The process isn't difficult. The paper you wrote on terrorism and civil engineering is great and it got a lot of response in the journal but the work you are doing on cultivating desert soil and growing crops in a waterless environment has amazing implications for a very large audience. You probably don't know this yet but you are on the radar—people are hearing more and more about you and your research."

"I don't know, Dr. Tibbets."

"Mimi, look, we know it's a little uncomfortable for you, but why don't you give it a try? We will be there with you and will make the experience worth your time," Dr. Tibbets pressed her because he knew what she could do though Mimi wasn't at all sure she could perform as they expected.

Dr. Tibbets completed his PhD in Civil Engineering years before. Now, he was focused on research and publishing—his legacy. He had designs far into the future. He just needed to start the process right now. Mimi could easily find a path to a professorship and researcher. She was a rare jewel. The university would benefit in many ways.

In addition, her interest and broad knowledge in terrorism completely threw him for a loop because she was just 21 years of age, yet exhibited a vast storehouse of knowledge, maturity and confidence well beyond her years. Soon, she was known to all the professors in the Department and then her reputation grew from there. The deadline for submitting her abstract was quickly approaching.

She knew that plenty of people could grow things but *managing* the soil—now that was the issue.

The next day, he saw her in the Student Center and approached her. She was wearing a pair of jeans that day, with a t-shirt sporting a Jerusalem theme. She looked plain, wearing no makeup, yet there was a magnetism about her that drew him. He invited himself to sit down. She looked at him, smiled, and disarmed him.

"So, Professor, what sort of trouble have you been into?" She asked.

"Well, you know all about our conference," Dr. Tibbets began. "We are almost ready to go... we have some very exciting speakers lined up," he said, hinting around the need for one more.

"Really? Well good for you!"

"Uh, yes, thank you. But the thing is this... we'd love for you to speak."

"What, me?! Why? What's wrong with it? Can't you get anyone else?" Mimi toyed.

"No. No one else. It's a sorry state of affairs—you're the best we could find."

"Mmmmmm," Mimi began. "I'll think about it. What subject could I do? Hfmmmm."

She knew that Dr. Tibbets could be influential. She liked him. He worked to balance the interests of the school and department with those of the staff and students. In short, he was a superb administrator in addition to being a well-known scholar in his field. He loved developing his students and she respected that because she saw it as an important leadership skill.

She worked through a number of scenarios, carefully placing each in a specific order in her mind. For soil engineering, she thought of soil components, erosion, blends, all sort of things. For desert farming, she thought of a different set of variables, each in turn building on the one before it.

"How about a survey of soil content and composition in various Middle Eastern nations with an eye to growing fruit and vegetables in a waterless desert environment?"

"I don't know, I'm still not sure."

This went on for awhile. Finally, when he had enough, and was about ready to throw up his hands, he stood up. She was not getting it.

"Ok, I confess—I submitted the abstract last week, and it's been accepted. But I wanted to change the subject. I wanted to speak on terrorism and how the Civil Engineering field needs to embrace some of my ideas," she said, a bemused smile now forming on her face.

Any other person on the planet would have sounded arrogant and self absorbed, but coming from Mimi, it was refreshing and then, he couldn't get enough of the topic, or frankly any topic she chose.

"But I also wanted to speak on Soil Management and Farming the Desert."

"Excellent, just what I was hoping to hear!" he said.

CHAPTER THIRTY-SIX: *Potential Fulfilled*   Page 205

He knew that world-class Israeli know-how combined with the latest research in the field would make the speech well received and would place Mimi in a position of the Subject Matter Expert. The ironic thing was that just across the pond, in Great Britain, Israeli scientists and lecturers were being tossed out of conference speaking engagements by the arrogant British who still catered more to the Islamists living among them. The thoroughly anti-Semitic nature of the British academic world held no respect for anything tied to Jews or Jewish causes. Unfortunately, the same mentality was working its way across the Atlantic to America. But today the gain was his.

He didn't know that much of her background, but he did know that she had experience with equipment and machinery. It was a practical set of applied skills of which few of her colleagues could boast. She was the real deal.

Professor Tibbets and his colleagues began spreading the word about the upcoming speech and made sure it was mentioned in staff meetings, newsletters, and any other method of communication within the University.

Six weeks later, the day arrived and when Mimi breezed up to the podium, all of her fellow students and professors were stunned to see a transformed young professional.

Mimi wore a stunning sky-blue two piece suit with a white blouse and a smart red, white, and blue scarf. She had applied just the right amount of makeup so as to bring the highlights of her skin tone out under the harsh lights. Her blue eyes jumped out at the audience. Her blond hair, now a little longer and curlier, was swept back in a very professional up do. She wore her diamond stud earrings, also understated. It helped to have relatives named De Beers.

The look, simple, yet elegant was breathtaking. She looked both sophisticated and stylish, though there was nothing special about her outfit. She attached a small diamond brooch on her blazer and her three-inch black pumps set off the entire ensemble perfectly. Every eye was on her. She had to fight off the butterflies as the PowerPoint slide set appeared on the screen behind her.

Since this was an international conference and the field's annual event, more than 2,000 attendees awaited her words. Two of the people in the audience were particularly intrigued by the young Israeli woman. These two in particular, a young Saudi couple, had graduated from American universities in Soil Engineering and Animal Husbandry. They were young scientists and farmers and were quite intrigued to hear the talk.

Dr. Tibbets and Dr. Gordon both moved to the podium to co-introduce her.

"Our next speaker comes to us from Israel. Miss Mimi Sullivan will complete her studies this year in both Civil Engineering and Soil Management. She is currently on leave from the Israel Defense Forces Civil Engineering Corps and is gaining a reputation as an expert in soils and farming the desert in a waterless environment. And, she knows a little about terrorism too. We are privileged to have her with us today. Mimi—thanks for joining us today."

Mimi stood and approached the speakers' lectern where she was received with polite applause.

"Thank you, Professors. Ladies and gentlemen, both of these gentlemen mean so much to me and I am honored to be here. Thanks to you, I have gained such an appreciation for my new field and look forward to collaborating with you in the future."

"As you may be aware in Israel, each and every young high school graduate, with very few exceptions, joins the military. We are a small nation facing ongoing external and sometimes internal threats. Our enemies are right next door and they are always interested in starting a fight. I do not mean to sound flippant, but we live with this every day."

"When I was a little girl, I learned all about defending our borders. Both of my parents completed their time in the army. My father just finished his reserve commitment last year and both of my brothers, my cousins, and friends—everyone I know have finished their service time too. So, we understand what commitment is all about."

"During my childhood, I watched my parents' garden and it was then I fell in love with the soil. My mother tells me I used to plant flowers and vegetables and tend them in my little corner of our farm. I still love playing in the dirt. I love to grow things and I love the smell and the feel of the soil in my hands. For some reason or other, I have learned to smell the soil and can tell you what nutrients it lacks. I can tell you what kinds of things I can grow in what soils."

"During my first year in the Army, I learned to run earth moving equipment and to prepare roadbeds. I can run all the Caterpillar and John Deere tractors and earth movers and love to train others to do so. This love of the soil and this love of new farming techniques bring me here today," The nervousness left her at this point and she climbed into the moment.

Mimi delivered a speech that took the crowd's mind with it. She wove her research and personal learning in the field with details that tickled her audience.

"I was raised on a farm and my parents taught me to drive tractors and earth moving equipment when I was 12. So, when I enlisted in the IDF, I requested the Engineering Corps and learned to drive the bigger equipment it wasn't much of a big deal—and you know what? It's not that different from driving a taxi cab in Jerusalem!" They enjoyed her stories about how she outperformed the men. That got them laughing but they didn't necessarily understand why the taxi story was so funny.

Then pausing, to capture her thoughts, she settled down and began making point after point in her lecture, pausing from time to time to reflect and drop in personal learning along the way. She covered aspects of her experiences with desert soil management and her lessons learned. She dropped in learning from her journal research and then drew conclusions that were both practical and actionable to the audience. The professors looked at each other and winked... *boy, was this a coup or what?!?*

Researchers love detail when it appeals to their particular field and she it was here where she scored a direct hit. When she concluded the speech, the audience jumped to its feet and gave her a standing ovation, a far different reception then her greeting. She was now known.

The question and answer session ran another hour with job offers coming to her as she stood there taking questions. She later looked at the business cards. She counted no less than twenty. It amused her. Her heart was in one place and one place only—the desert of Israel.

However, she would be impressed by two curious attendees—young farmers were they and though very different from her, would soon become closer than family.

> From the Good News According to Mattiahu
> The Gospel of Matthew—Chapter 5 Verse 13)
>
> "You are the salt of the earth; but if the salt has become tasteless, how can it be made salty again? It is no longer good for anything, except to be thrown out and trampled underfoot by men..."

Chapter 37

Salt of the Earth

A couple approached Mimi at the end of her talk. The extended her hand toward Mimi. "Thank you so much for your talk, today!" The woman started. "You are true breath of fresh air—an oasis in the desert. My husband and I were both educated here, but we have started a farm in Saudi Arabia. It is not far from Mecca. We have so much to learn about farming the desert. Our government has tried to develop programs and to help us learn. But we know that task is ours. We'd love to learn more."

The man beside her cleared his throat to get his wife's attention. Then he extended his hand and said, "Allow us to introduce ourselves. We are Farouk and Shabibi Ibn Nasser."

"I am pleased to meet you both," Mimi said. She shook his strong hand. "Yes... your hand and grip say farmer." Then Mimi pointed toward one of the doors and said, "I'm done here, would you like to go get something to eat? I make better conversation with a little food in my stomach."

Shabibi smiled and looked at Farouk. He nodded and said, "Of course. However, I insist that you be our guest. It is the least we can do to thank you."

"I saw a Mexican restaurant across the street," Mimi proposed. "I think I can make it that far."

The food was ordered and Mimi began, "Please, tell me about you, your education, your farm, and your challenges. I'm interested in soil, crops, livestock, current irrigation, and operation... anything really." Then she grabbed a handful of chips and added, "And please, pardon me as I work on these chips and salsa. Professors, V.I.P.s, introductions, formalities, nerves, and my final preparations all conspired to steal my lunch, breaks, and snacks. I can feel my ribs."

Farouk and Shabibi both laughed and urged Mimi to eat. Farouk began, "I'm not sure where to begin. But I am sure that I won't remember all that you asked about."

Mimi nodded, chewed, and waved him on.

"Well, our American university education prepared us for agriculture and commerce in the States. Shabibi has a business mind. She was encouraged and has already applied much of her education to our operation. The world is such a global economy... and... well... she found it useful in every way. However, I...." Farouk dropped his head and shook it back-and-forth. Farming in America's Midwest and farming in Saudi Arabia are... well, uh...."

He hit a wall, but collected his thoughts and headed in another direction.

"I have a story. Every summer at the University was spent in extensive field work... and I mean 'the field.' I spent my first summer in the fields of Iowa and Illinois. I remember my first experience like my wedding day. I stepped from the University van and was frozen in place. The others walked ahead. I couldn't. I took in the sight, savored the air, and wept. I fell where I stood."

My professor, a young lab and field instructor, came to my side. He put his arm around me and asked me, "Nasser, you okay?" I couldn't answer.

"Huh? Nasser, you hurt or something?" I couldn't respond. I buried my face in my hands and wept. My prof' stood to his feet, patted my back, and said, "Hey, man up. Get it together—then get the ph kit and specimen jars outta the van. Okay?"

"I had no embarrassment or shame. No one of them could understand or experience what I felt. I was on my knees—so I stayed to pray. It helped... some... We are taught to pray a full circle of prayer beads with a thanksgiving for each bead. It is a circle for the heart. I began on my knees with...

... I give thanks that such treasure exists on the earth.
... I give thanks that you have blessed man in this way.
... I give thanks for this sight—black dirt—moist, rich, and fertile.

"Then my heart allowed me to stand. So I stood and filled my nostrils and lungs with the air. And I continued to my thanksgiving...

> *... I give thanks for this air so sweet, thick, and full of dew.*
> *... I give thanks aroma and fragrant offering of these plants.*
> *... I give thanks for the glaciers that deposited such wealth.*
> *... I give thanks for the mighty river that divides these states.*
> *... I give thanks for the flood plain that fed and nourished.*

"And so I prayed and gave thanks. I collect the supplies, walked, and thanked God, Who alone is Great and wise in His will." Memories took Farouk's voice. He dropped his head.

Then Shabibi spoke for him. "He called me that night and shared with me the prayer he wanted to pray, but could not... the complaint of his heart. The disappointment he felt. He said he was a man with a meal of only flavorless beans. A man with so little in his bowl forced to watch another man eat a steak with all the trimmings."

Farouk found his voice and added, "I'll end my story, Mimi. You know what I'm about to say.... I wonder that day and every day of my education, *how can this help me?* But my God, blessed be He, would not allow me to leave. I heard these words in my heart and mind. He said to me, 'Do not question. Listen.'

"I did listen, and I knew that day and every day since... I cannot complain, covet, hate, or harbor envy. I must learn how to prepare, enrich, cultivate, and feed... my heart first. And then the soil that God had given us. That would be my quest.

"I learned from my professors. I challenged them with my need. I studied the lessons of America's dust-bowl. I sought and received research projects in Southern California's San Joaquin and Imperial Valleys. Later, our own high pastures taught me—in the mountains near our farm. Our arid yet fertile oases had lessons. But more, I humbled myself. I pledged to learn from any teacher sent to us. And today, kind Mimi, God brought you before us.

"You know our soil and our challenge. No glaciers left rich deposits of soil. No mighty rivers replenish. No regular rains grace our parched plains. Like your own Negev, we must bring our desert to life. We will be still now and learn from you... if you will teach."

Then Farouk yelped and leapt in his seat. Shabibi speared her elbow into his side. "This is America! I have a say, too!" Her eyes schooled and scolded her husband. Shabibi exhaled in satisfaction, turned to Mimi, and added, "You have walked this path before us. Still, I know that your heart is with ours. I sense your calling to the desert. I see your courage. You savor the challenge of so great a task. Like your God, you delight to take dirt and transform it into life. And then celebrate the moment that life takes root. You behold your work and also say, 'It is good.'"

Mimi shook herself, looked at each of them, buried her face in her hands, and muted her exclamations. Then she lifted her head, cleared her throat, and said, "Farouk, sweet Shabibi... **Will *I* teach *you*? No. *We will teach one other!*** Farouk, you had me with the story at the van. Yes, of course, I share what I can. But I have already learned from you."

The threesome chatted like old friends. They shared their farming experiences, successes, discoveries, and challenges. Mimi thought, *who would imagine that desert farming could be so exciting? And me, here with them... Saudi Arabian farmers! I don't see them as Saudis or Muslims. I see colleagues, fellow travelers, and friends—I hope. I don't want this night to end.* But Mimi's thought about the night shook her back to reality.

"Yikes! Oh my, look at the time." Mimi screamed.

"What is it?" Shabibi asked.

"I have to get to practice! I'm in the orchestra here, and we planned a practice session tonight!" Mimi spoke and searched for the bill.

"I got this," Farouk said. He jumped up and headed for the front counter.

"What do you play?" Shabibi asked.

"I'm a violinist, at least that's what I let people think," Mimi answered. "I still have so much to learn!"

"Both Farouk and I play too."

"Really? What do you play? Where?"

"We were in the university orchestra. Farouk plays violin. I play anything with strings, but I played a cello in the orchestra."

"We gotta get together and play sometime," Mimi.

"Sure," Shabibi agreed.

"When?" Mimi probed.

"We have a few more days. And we always travel with our music."

"How about Saturday evening at 6 p.m.? You can come over to my place for dinner. I love to cook for company. I'll invite some other friends who play strings, too." They all pulled out their phones to exchange emails and cell phone numbers.

"Thanks, Mimi." Shabibi spoke to and hugged her at the same time. "See you then."

Mimi climbed in her car and thought, *Maybe I should have told them that most of the other guests may be Jewish.* She stared at the steering wheel and wondered. Then she shook the idea from her mind and resolved, *No... I think... No, I know—they are both blind. O'God make me blind, too.*

When Saturday came, she found herself scurrying around getting dinner ready, tidying up her apartment, and arranging the chairs for company. She set the table and put on some music, then finished the meal, and slipped outside to smoke for a few minutes. Still fighting it, she had made a vow to herself to quit but still no progress. While her cigarette burned down, she slowly sipped a glass of the family cabernet, her favorite.

As the guests arrived, they found warmth and comfort with one another, breaking into small knots to talk. First were her friends Sheila and Stacey, two violinists, then William, a black Cello player. Finally, Tiffany, a young Asian woman who loved her viola and could really make it sing. Finally both Farouk and Shabibi arrived, instruments in hand. No introductions were needed, the musicians simply blended and slipped into an easy and informative discussions.

They talked about music, good wine, university life, vocations, and plans for life after school. *What a group here tonight,* Mimi marveled. *A young Israeli woman, two Saudis, an Asian, a Black, and two American Jewish women. And it worked.* The evening built to more than she could have hoped for.

Farouk and Shabibi shared their farming experience and the challenges they had with desert farming in Saudi Arabia. Mimi took it all in, not talking much, but listening to her friends. She had finally 'arrived' with a nice set of friends and though no boyfriend to love, still she found herself content. Graduation wasn't far off now.

When dinner concluded, she brought out a nice tiramisu from the local bakery. Tiramisu means 'Toss me up' in Italian and that brought up a conversation about language and culture. The candles were burning low by now and the young musicians sat silently, spooning the rest of the tiramisu and just drinking in what had been a most wonderful evening. Mimi also opened up a bottle of grapa—another Italian delicacy made of the grape skins... a brandy like substance that packed a wallop. They all sipped slowly, exhaling as they did.

"Where did the grapa come from? It's pretty potent," Sheila noted.

"Family," Mimi said. "I have two uncles who love to make wine. The grapa is a residual side interest, but we love it!" she said, reminiscing about the growing Israeli wine industry and the work she did on the wine country soils.

"Well, I say let's play some music!" Mimi cried. And so, a quick clearing of the table and the dishes, with everyone pitching in, the kitchen returned to order. Shabibi slipped into the kitchen and looked at Mimi for a moment, then extended her arms to her. Mimi responded with a hug and the two women from entirely different worlds cemented their friendship at that moment. Religion, faith, beliefs and what people thought made absolutely no difference to them. The two talked about some musical selections, then, when the whole group agreed, they sat down in the living room, arranged chairs and musical stands and began to play.

The music was sweet that night as they fell into the compelling rhythms of Chopin, Bach, and Beethoven. Then Mimi decided to surprise the group and brought out some Klezmer music. Normally played with clarinets, some brass, strings, and a variety of instruments, they settled on a few pieces that were more string oriented.

Even though music was culturally Jewish, there was no cultural divide. Neither Farouk nor Shabibi had ever heard Klezmer but picked it up instantly and dived in, smiling at one another as they let the music carry them away. They played for almost two hours and as the evening drew to a close, everyone agreed to stay in touch and try this again. It was close to midnight.

Farouk and Shabibi were the last to leave. Farouk returned instruments to their cases and reorganized the music. Shabibi slipped into the kitchen to help Mimi. "Thank you for the delicious meal and delightful music. You have shown us such kindness, and I...." Shabibi stopped and looked to her hands for words.

Mimi gently gripped her shoulders and said, "I feel kindness and warmth from you, as well. I don't have many friends. I'm too driven, I guess. My brothers say that I frighten most men. But that's not it... the truth is that I don't suffer fools. I won't waste time on pointless pursuits, pompous people, or frivolous friends."

"Farouk and I are the same way. Our time with you at the restaurant and here was enjoyable, but so much more. It was a dialogue of colleagues, an exchange of information, a learning experience—we were enriched. And tonight was perfect. Farouk was nervous beforehand. He feared the talk would be cotton candy conversations—no substance. Or worse, he worried about political nonsense or that some would share over-stuffed opinions on world events. Instead, our time tonight was filled with meaning and with things that matter to us. You were the perfect hostess. You gave us the gift of music and the privilege of participation with you and your friends. Mimi, you are pretty, professional, passionate, and... as Farouk told me 'practical.'"

"Shabibi, I'm not running for public office. I may be practical, and I hope I'm professional. But anything is determined by the people I'm with and projects we pursue. You made tonight special. I will be forever grateful. And I will be sad beyond measure if we don't stay in touch."

"Yes, yes, a thousand times yes. We must stay in touch. We need you in our lives, Mimi. And if I may say something else...." Shabibi paused to acknowledge Farouk at the kitchen door.

"If I may say... Mimi, you are nothing like the Jewish stereotypes that others have fed us. We both have always rejected the fanatics and fear-mongers. We have minds of our own—open and hungry to learn."

Mimi wanted to respond, but she had no words. She looked down, smiled, and shook her head—so delighted.

"I was thinking the same thing. I feel related to you in some way. I'd be honored to help you in any way I can." For a moment, she realized that they had indeed crossed cultures and prejudices that may have at one time separated them... but no longer.

Shabibi paused to allow Mimi opportunity then continued, "Like you, we have few friends. Even family say we're too dull and private. Maybe we are.... We are focused on our farm and farming. Our education has been our present priority. Our faith is personal. Our lives are filled with one another." Shabibi stepped closer to Farouk, and they put their arms around one another. She looked up into his eyes and added, "He is my best friend, my constant companion, my heart, and my soul. He is the sweet passion that fills my fantasies and the delight of my bedroom." Farouk leaned down and responded with a kiss.

Mimi's eyes were riveted on the couple, her jaw dropped, and her thoughts raced to a thousand-and-one places. "Are you all right, Mimi?" Shabibi asked.

Mimi shook herself back to sanity, thought, and then said, "Farouk, remember how you felt when you saw Iowa's rich, moist, black dirt? Something about your bowl of bland beans and the other guy's juicy steak?"

"Yes, of course, I remember."

"Well," Mimi continued, "now, I know how you felt. I just saw black dirt."

Mimi approached the couple—face straight and eyes warm. For a moment she stood and soaked in the sight of before her. Then she put her arms around them both, laid her head upon their shoulders, and said, "I am honored have you in my home and to call you my friends." She released them and stepped back. "You brought something that has been absent in my home and life. You brought real love and romance. Granted... I'm just a spectator—an envious observer. But now I know what I want... some day."

"Let's plan on another evening before you go home. We'll talk dirt," she laughed. They accepted and agreed that they would put off their trip home for another day or two.

Parting words, hugs, and final a farewell ended the evening. Each had pledged to email, text, and call. Then Mimi was alone—again. She turned off the lights and leaned back in her love-seat—alone with her thoughts and her bland bowl of beans.

> From the Prophet Isaiah
>   Chapter 60 Verse 9
>
> "Surely the isles shall wait for me, and the ships of Tarshish first, to bring your sons from far, their silver and their gold with them, to the name of the LORD your God, and to the Holy One of Israel, because he has glorified you."

Chapter 38

Ships

ZIM's best known exports were wonderful winter fruits—Haifa oranges, grapefruits, palmettos, olive oil, and flowers by the ton. Not so well known was its "other cargo," high tech weaponry, bound for America's shores. It would be ZIM's best kept secret, all manner of field weapons, Uzis, Tavors, and Flattops, rocket propelled grenades, various close battle devices, and all the ammunition to go along with it, plus, of course explosives materials, all safely hidden in boxes of those oranges and other delectables.

The ships would heave to in port, tie up, and the offloading would begin. Watching these crane operators was like watching an exquisitely choreographed ballet. Hand-picked crane operators, arranged by Dogface's contacts, maneuvered the huge cranes into position, grabbed the rust-red colored containers, and deliver them gently to the ground below. Semi-tractor trailers backed up to the docks, hooked themselves up, received their cargo containers, and began their journey overland.

Ships' manifests, shipping documents, all honoring the host country's export and import requirements would all be signed off by her contacts within the port cities, again arranged by the 'familia.' Of course, the Coast Guard couldn't inspect every inbound ship. This was only the middle point of the process.

Israel learned one thing from her past. Although certain friendships were fleeting, some friends stuck around and stayed by your side. In this case, a quiet but dependable network of longshoremen, crane operators, truckers many connected to "persons of interest" would quietly ensure expert handling and safe passage of Israeli cargo and shipments.

Old friends remembered "favors" done long ago and it was through these friends that the Israeli high command would deploy its plans. Favors and family had a way of traveling together. Many of the front lines of these contacts really had no idea for whom they worked. An oddly high percentage of them were Christians, hard working folk, who believed in saying the right things and doing the right things.

For a long while now, Israel quietly built its rescue plans for its Diaspora-living children. Grasping what was at stake, the Israeli government understood its role in protecting international Jewry. When Jews would defiantly raise their fists with shouts of 'Never Again!' through the years following the Holocaust, it was mostly in ignorance of the fact that there was a developing plan to offer protection and safe passage to the Land of Promise, to Jews living in the Diaspora.

Years of careful planning enabled the long arm of Israeli justice to prepare for this time. Known to Ben Yehuda, a small group of his compatriots at Mossad, and a few higher level contacts within the IDF, their plans were about to move from theory to planning to action.

The plans for *Operation Last* Exodus moved forward. Those friends were well placed, but invisible to the social structure. They formed what many considered almost a shadow government, often trading in things only whispered about. Some believed they existed and blamed the world's ills on them. Others denied their existence, at least publicly anyway. J. Edgar Hoover, the longtime Director of the FBI never publicly acknowledged it.

The Vicenzos however, had no doubts... or concerns. They believed shipping and garbage to be good businesses. Oh, and maybe some good ravioli and a little homemade wine, and of course, some grapa.

From Ha Yad Moshe (The Hand of Moses):
Bereshit (Genesis) 14: 10-16

Now the valley of Siddim was full of tar pits; and the kings of Sodom and Gomorrah fled, and they fell into them.

But those who survived fled to the hill country. Then they took all the goods of Sodom and Gomorrah and all their food supply, and departed.

They also took Lot, Abram's nephew, and his possessions and departed, for he was living in Sodom. Then a fugitive came and told Abram the Hebrew.

Now he was living by the oaks of Mamre the Amorite, brother of Eschcol and brother of Aner, and these were allies with Abram.

When Abram heard that his relative had been taken captive, he led out his trained men, born in his house, three hundred and eighteen, and went in pursuit as far as Dan.

He divided his forces against them by night, he and his servants, and defeated them, and pursued them as far as Hobah, which is north of Damascus.

He brought back all the goods, and also brought back his relative Lot with his possessions, and also the women, and the people.

Chapter 39

The Lessons of Entebbe

This discussion was never very far from Jewish minds. Rescuing their own was as old as the story of Lot and Abraham, way back in the Book of Genesis. When Lot and his kinsmen were taken captive by invaders, Abraham, his uncle, mustered about 400 toughened warriors and declared war on the others. In a sharp, pitched battle, Abraham's forces overwhelmed the enemy and rescued Lot and his household as well as their goods, their women, and children.

Many years later, during the years following the Prophet Samuel's death, David and his men were caught by surprise. Six hundred women and children, including both of his wives, were captured by enemy forces. David mustered his men and launched a rescue campaign to recover the people and their possessions.

Jewish religious leaders taught that it was the family's duty to rescue its own. They instructed the people to spare no expense in their effort. And the message took root. For example, in 2011 Israel paid dearly for Gilad Shalit—an Israeli IDF corporal held by Hamas for 5 years. His freedom required the release of 1,000 Hamas prisoners in Israel. And Israel agreed to the 1,000 to 1 exchange.

Jewish history tells other stories as well... Boaz, known to Jews as the Kinsman Redeemer had married the Gentile woman, Ruth, thus restoring the Messianic line to Israel. The story was perhaps one of the most interesting and beautiful to Bible scholars because it firmly and permanently welcomed a non-Jewish woman into the Messianic line. Interestingly enough, Boaz' mother was Rahab, the Jericho harlot, another Gentile, strategically placed in the lineage as well. And there they were—two non-Jews in the Messiah's lineage of David.

Ruth later became the grandmother of the future King of Israel, David. The line of the Messiah would forever be a miracle of mixed peoples. This best illustrated what happened when there really was nobody to assume the role of leadership. Boaz stepped into that void when others didn't, thus he represented a type of the coming Messiah and by taking a Gentile bride he restored the throne to the nation. He would become known as a prototype of the rescuer, or the kinsman redeemer.

CHAPTER THIRTY-NINE: Lesson of Entebbe

Ruth has become a model of faith and action. Her most quoted words stand as testament to her character and commitment:

> *Where you go, I will go,*
> *Where you live, I will live.*
> *Your people will be my people,*
> *And your God will be my God.*

Millenia later, during World War II, the worst of mankind came out to dance on Jewish graves through the work of a single madman. Hitler would enlist the help of millions to annihilate the Jewish race or people as some would call them.

But, as with virtually every epoch in human history, a redeemer or sorts would appear, perhaps even sent by God himself. Heroes such as Oscar Schindler or Raoul Wallenberg would stand up to the marching hatred and do what they could to stop it. Between them, they saved the lives of thousands of innocent Jews either by falsifying passports or visas, herding them into factories and gambling for their lives, or making up stories to protect them.

The war would bring out many Gentile heroes who would later become known as Righteous Gentiles. Israel would honor them at Yad Vashem (Hand of the Name) where trees are planted to remember their contributions. They were the ones Hollywood made movies about—others such as Irene Opdyke hardly anyone knew. There were Catholic priests and nuns who sacrificed everything risking their lives. There were committed Lutherans and other mainstream Christians too. Though the stories weren't that well known, even some Arabs felt the call and extended the hand of love.

Jewish resistance and rescue efforts from the Warsaw Ghetto or the Bielski partisans and others like them proved that the Jews were as fierce a group to contend with as any on the planet. These fighters, Jews saving Jews, preserved thousands of lives living in forests, subverting enemy plans, and carrying out guerilla war against the huge war machine.

All of this history was ingrained in the current Israeli leadership and people. Their shared cultural memory fueled preparations for the largest rescue of a dispersed people in the history of mankind.

Care and concern goes into the planning of any action on domestic soil, much more so when your forward battle space is more than 8,000 miles away. Israelis living abroad trained for many eventualities such as this and remained vigilant through their lives, half expecting the call to arms at a moment's notice.

Rescue operations are, at the core, some of the most dangerous missions a military could plan and execute. But the good news was that the Israelis had successful historical examples, though on a far smaller scale. By far, their most audacious effort was pulled off in Uganda at Entebbe in 1976. That raid required some of the most creative and gutsy planning ever done in battle. It was a masterpiece of Israeli intelligence.

That Israeli strike team flew five C-130 Hercules aircraft, plus a Boeing 707 jet converted into a flying hospital and several aircraft over half of Africa, refueling along the way, landed at a foreign airfield, deployed its soldiers into the airport while disguising one of their own as the larger-than-life Field Marshall Idi Amin in blackface, thereby fooling the Ugandan troops into believing he was one of *their* own.

If that wasn't enough, the strike team stormed the airport, shouting in Hebrew for everyone to stay down, which all did but one, and rescued their hostages. He was Yoni Netenyahu, an officer and the brother of the future Prime Minister, who died in the cross fire. An Israeli woman who had taken sick during the hijacking had been removed to a local hospital where she was later murdered in her bed. Ugandan terrorists harbored no sentiment—all manner of humanity non-existent in those with no conscience.

The real problem facing the planners now was how to round up and move close to six million people from one nation across oceans and continents to another world... not to mention managing an insurgency from across the planet. Details, details, details.

Virtually every Israeli living abroad had one thing in common, extensive military service and experience in the art of war. Most had seen action at home in one of the occasional incursion into Gaza, Judea and Samaria (known to the world as the West Bank). And others had fought in the major regional conflicts.

The outside world forced the Jews of Israel to become fighters, though they would much preferred to have retired to farms, schools, or lives of productive living among their own. Training kicked in quickly and the commanders would soon begin preparations of their own to fight Israel's first foreign war well away from its borders.

Several of her wars saw forward action in Egypt, Syria, or Jordan. Special ops had been run in Uganda during the Entebbe raid as well as secret assassination teams operating in Europe to hunt down those responsible for the Munich Olympics massacre. Jews have a long memory. But this would test the tiny nation and stretch her abilities to the breaking point.

Those paying attention began reading their Bibles to discern what was coming next. And Israel wouldn't be able to do it without help. Was Heaven listening?

By the Hand of Shlomo the King - Song of Songs
Chapter 1:2-1:11

May he kiss me with the kisses of his mouth! For your love is better than wine. Your oils have a pleasing fragrance, Your name is {like} purified oil;

Therefore the maidens love you. Draw me after you {and} let us run {together!} The king has brought me into his chambers. We will rejoice in you and be glad;

We will extol your love more than wine. Rightly do they love you. I am black but lovely, O daughters of Jerusalem, Like the tents of Kedar, Like the curtains of Solomon. Do not stare at me because I am swarthy, For the sun has burned me.

My mother's sons were angry with me. They made me caretaker of the vineyards, {But} I have not taken care of my own vineyard. Tell me, O you whom my soul loves, Where do you pasture {your flock,}?

Where do you make {it} lie down at noon? For why should I be like one who veils herself beside the flocks of your companions?

If you yourself do not know, most beautiful among women, Go forth on the trail of the flock and pasture your young goats by the tents of the shepherds. To me, my darling, you are like my mare among the chariots of Pharaoh.

Your cheeks are lovely with ornaments, your neck with strings of beads. We will make for you ornaments of gold with beads of silver.

Chapter 40

Shabbat Dinner

Danielle wasn't at all into a flashy existence but did have her eye on a new Beemer that she had seen passing by the car dealer earlier that week. She decided to ask Avram to join her when she went car shopping. *That will have to wait till Sunday,* she thought.

The past few months had been something out of a Hollywood movie for both Danielle and Avner. As all couples do, they established their favorites list. They enjoyed walking on the pier in Seal Beach, often taking in a sunset when they ended their days after long hours at work or school.

They found an excellent sushi house at the Circle in Orange, just up the street from where they met. Though their favorite ice cream shop had closed, they found another one, not far from the center of town. They discovered the El Caballo Grill, an upscale Mexican restaurant that specialized in all sorts of cuisine throughout Mexico. It was an idyllic existence and neither of them wanted it to end. Though the week was ending, her thoughts were never too far from her growing business.

Danielle's marketing firm was flourishing as she had just picked up several new clients. Her expertise in computer graphics had now turned into website design and development where she excelled in e- commerce. Her clients now did more than $500 million in annual business largely thanks to her innovative and artful design skills. She was in demand. But Friday nights were reserved for Shabbat observances.

Most of her clients were very thoughtful and just before Shabbat arrived one of them gave her a few bottles of homemade wine, a wonderful, rich cabernet, from the family's private reserve. She noticed that the bottles had a name on them, 'Shayna.'

Hmmm, cute, must be named after one of the family members, she thought She knew the name meant 'beautiful,' in Yiddish.

She had been to their family compound up in Dutch Flat, with its rolling vineyards, fruit trees, vegetable patches, relaxing family atmosphere with a back veranda overlooking a national forest, and of course the small winery downstairs under the house. She pulled out the corkscrew and slowly opened the bottle.

When the cork popped out, she set it and the bottle on the granite countertop. The wine had to breathe. It was incredibly aromatic tonight. *They got the sugar just right this wine season*, she thought. She poured a little for herself just for taste. Smooth! Everything just seemed so perfect—she felt totally in touch with her surroundings, and completely at peace with the world.

"Thank you Father," she whispered.

So, that evening, she began to prepare a full Shabbat dinner of fresh salmon which she would grill on her Blueflame gas barbeque. She fired up the grill to get it nice and hot. It reached its optimum temperature a few minutes later.

She had taught herself how to use the smoker and with the incredible spices and special rubs she found on a recent trip to the Wharf in San Francisco, it would make it a special treat. So she prepared everything and then put the fish in the special racks and then on the grill. She poked bell peppers, onions, and mushrooms onto the skewers and mixed up the 'banya,' an old Italian mixture of olive oil, butter, and garlic and then dropped them on the grill as well. The grill sizzled as the mixture dripped on the fire. She also added some asparagus. She clipped a nice sprig of rosemary off the bush in her backyard, and then patiently brushed some of the wonderful mixture onto the fish and then on the veggies. She then cracked some pepper on top along with some seasoned salt. Things smelled good... and she knew that Avner would approve. *It was a soothing aroma, a sweet savor*, she thought. *Hmmm, I think the Lord would approve too.*

With everything cooking up nicely on the grill, Danielle went into the living room and opened the drawer in her china cabinet. She pulled out the Shabbat candles and the candlestick holders.

They reminded her of the Rabbi's Triad, those candlesticks did. They had come from the same place in Europe and, though she didn't own a samovar, she smiled knowing just how meaningful their twins must have been to the previous owners, who had willed them to her. She had just polished them to a shining bronze and held them up to the light... how brightly they shined!

She thought of the museum's old curator, now well into his 70's and offered a quick prayer for him and his family. She thought about his kids who were grown now. The legend of the Triad had always remained fresh in her mind and was a reminder that there was more to the concentration camp experience and history than most Christians and Jews realized. In fact, some writers believed that there were robust Messianic Jewish congregations in Europe before the war, meaning that there were believing Jews possibly numbering in the hundreds of thousands or even in the millions, though she had her doubts about the latter number. Who knew if remnants of those fellowships started up again behind the barbed wire and Nazi guns?

Could it be possible that there was really a Messianic Jewish movement then and a large one at that? The thought boggled her mind. Why hadn't anyone acknowledged this amazing fact? Why didn't this come out in any of the Jewish stories of the Holocaust or why wasn't it mentioned by Christians? Were both sides embarrassed to discuss it?

She had no idea but wanted to know. She believed that although many Jews generally tended to label other Jews who believe in Yeshua as Christians, those Jews who had accepted the Messiah's mission in their lives saw the world quite differently. They were Jews. And no one was going to take away their identity. No one. Period. She sniffed the air. The aroma of the grill reached her.

She then went back out to the grill and checked the fish and the vegetables. They were coming along nicely. The sun was setting and it was perfect outside, so she took out her Bible and read a little, this time concentrating on Isaiah 53, the story of the suffering servant who would die for the sins of the nation Israel. That passage had caused so much controversy and had set Christian against Jew for centuries. The Believers thought it was a foretelling of Yeshua's (Jesus) death and sacrifice. The Jews believed it spoke of Israel.

It was so obvious to her about whom it spoke, but her Jewish friends still resisted her interpretations. She vowed never to give up and when she finished reading, she thought of the pain the Messiah suffered, bringing tears to her eyes.

I'm so emotional tonight, Danielle thought. She wiped away her tears, finished the reading, and felt joy at the thought of Avner's arrival.

Avner was also busy. He had gone shopping because he knew that it was time. It was time to tell Danielle how much she meant to him and it was time to make the commitment. Avner's choice of a ring wasn't based on trying to impress her. He knew that she had absolutely no expectations about jewelry (though he knew she liked fast cars and had completed a racecar driving course) but he did want to make a good impression. He had wrestled with it for a long while now. He had spoken with Ephraim who would join him at the diamond mart in L.A. So, together, he and his brother went shopping for a diamond.

That week had been a particularly challenging week for both Avner and Danielle. Avner, like his brother Ephraim, was completing his degree, though not in the same subject. His was in Leadership Development at Pepperdine University, a highly acknowledged school for this field of study.

Avner had learned much from his time in the IDF and the easy transference of that practical learning on the battlefield to the university setting gave him a leg up on other students. Where most of them could only talk theory about leaders, maybe even bring in a story or two about a contentious boss, he had sent men into battle, faced terrorists, and deactivated bombs. Yes, he had lived a lifetime for such a young man. However, one student in his class had taken some offense at his observations in battle and how they influenced Avner's perceptions of leadership.

Tewfik ibn Abdulla had immigrated to America when he was five years old. His parents had family here in America and realized that they would never be able to raise a family in Palestine. So, Tewfik, his brothers and sisters, and their parents packed up their possessions and flew to the States.

He was now 20, in his junior year, and had increasingly become bitterer about Palestine, Israel, and its occupiers. Though it had been a long time since he had come to America, he still remembered playing in the fields, his cousins, the suqs, and life at home. So much had been taken from him and even though he was now an American citizen, his heart was never very far from home.

He had grown into a handsome young man, with dark eyes and dark curly hair. His 5'6" frame was wiry though strong. He sported a thin mustache, adding to his mysterious look. Though becoming more and more fervent in his beliefs, he didn't wear any outside indicators of his beliefs such as a kiffiya or any other scarves. He seethed inside when he listened to those class discussions, growing angrier by the class.

Maybe it was that no one really understood him or maybe it really was his growing attachment to Islam, but everything that Jewish man said in the class, no matter how nice he tried to be, was irritating young Tewfik. He was done with the Jews and he knew that it was time to act.

Tewfik had also fallen in with some pro-Palestinian groups on campus. Though the university was technically a Christian school, it worked hard to accommodate all viewpoints of life including religion, sexual orientation, politics, and other social issues. The school encouraged healthy debate and always made room for dissent, as long as the dissent remained peaceful.

> **From the pen of Leonardo Di Vinci**
>
> *As every divided kingdom falls, so every mind divided between many studies confounds and saps itself.*

Chapter 41

The Census Revealed

When the general demographics from the census were announced, the American public reaction was mixed. There were those who celebrated, knowing at last that America had an identity and others who had to get used to something very new in their vocabulary, 'Islamo-Christian.'

While more than 50% of America self-identified as Christian another 15% called itself Muslim. With an increasing percentage of Muslims and a decreasing percentage of Jews, Americans would now and forever be known as an Islamo-Christian nation, twin identities with a fading sense of anything to do with Jewish culture or influence. What that meant became the hottest of topics on the talk show circuit.

The new king of the talk show circuit, Aurelio Lopes, was a well educated man born to Brazilian parents in New York City. Growing up in New York gave Lopes a very urbane perspective of the world. He was of medium height, dark, thick hair, and piercing blue eyes which came, the family believed, from their Portuguese roots. He attended the University of Pennsylvania, an Ivy League school, majoring in Political Science. After school, he snagged a position with the New York Times where he found himself writing on American culture, religion, lifestyles, and of course, politics.

His newspaper work sparked something in the American psyche. When he published his first book, it shot to the best seller list in two weeks. Within five years he would go on to publish a book every year, and increasingly he was being quoted in the media, circles of government, and then became a White House favorite. Soon afterwards, his books found audiences across the ocean and was translated into 15 different languages.

Muslims loved him, Christians loved him, and Jews loved him for he wrote of family, honesty, integrity, and values, and the integration of society in such a fashion that his followers could grasp his vision. He remained away from any issue too controversial, but some of that would soon change. He began a lecture circuit tour which got him in front of the American public.

He appeared on university campuses for commencement speeches, speaking to large profit and non-profit assemblies and conferences. These circuits eventually led to talk show appearances and then an offer for his own show. America was waiting. The show was part news, part human interest, and part comedy. He was becoming as beloved as Walter Cronkite, Johnny Carson, Oprah Winfrey, George Lopez, Jay Leno, or even Billy Mays. He was America's face.

When the census results were published, Lopes went to work and, requesting an assignment which would take him all over the country, embarked on the journalistic trip of his life. He visited synagogues, churches, mosques, and many other houses of worship for virtually every mainstream religion in America, and some not so mainstream. He learned much about America's changing landscape, particularly its struggles with the economy, high gas prices, rising inflation, and a dramatically changing religious face.

The census project took him more than a year to compile, edit, and eventually broadcast. His team assembled more than 400 interviews, and compiled more than 10,000 pages of notes, anecdotes, and research. There was a book in there somewhere. He and the producers of the show felt they knew America as well as anyone did or could. He spoke with many representing all peoples of America—blacks, whites, Native Americans, Hispanics, Asians, Jews, Muslims, and Christians, and more.

He found America a divided land. Quoting Abraham Lincoln, he commented on the nature of the fracturing of America, that "a nation divided against itself could not stand." That Lincoln delivered one of his most impactful observations during America's Civil War had more relevance than many wished to admit.

Most noteworthy was Lopes' impression of the fracturing Christian church. It was indeed America's choice. But he found in his research that Christians—though claiming that religion as their heritage—knew little if anything about it. Outside of some clergy, few knew anything about Christian history.

Few had any idea of the Reformation, the Crusades, or any knowledge of the various denominations or how they had gotten there. More disturbing, perhaps, even fewer read their Bibles though attending church weekly, during Easter, or Christmas, there was virtually nothing beyond the window dressing. It was the same for the mainstream denominations. Evangelicals or those calling themselves as such read a little more, but not that much. It all seemed so very hypocritical.

And so, Lopes brought this to the forefront—for many, believing became uncomfortable. Except for a relatively small percentage, few could articulate the premise of Christianity, or for that matter, the precepts of Judaism. Muslims weren't much better.

Further, he found that even fewer Jews, by percentage ever read their Bibles. Muslims occasionally read their Qurans and had some knowledge of Biblical characters too. He picked up the term 'Islamo-Christian' meaning that the underpinning of American faith had indeed changed to one that now excluded Judaism as a mainstream driver of its philosophical foundation. Without realizing it, the Church in America (whatever that meant) was certainly pitching in that direction.

Lopes invited a Catholic priest, a Lutheran minister, a conservative rabbi, and an imam from a mosque for a general discussion on religion in America and what it meant that Islam was increasing and Judaism was decreasing.

"Tonight, my friends we welcome you to Religion in America. We have as our special guests Father John Kemp, a Catholic cleric from Los Angeles, Reverend William Schroeder, a Lutheran pastor from Chicago, Illinois, Imam Khalid Mohammad, an Islamic leader from New York, and Rabbi Morris Greenfield from Miami, Florida."

"Gentlemen, welcome to the show. I'd like to start this discussion with our visitor from the Catholic Church. Father, welcome," he said.

"Thank you Aurelio, it's an honor to be here," he answered.

"Father, there's been a lot of discussion about Christianity in America. Our research indicates that the majority of the American people self-identify as Christians. What does this mean to you?"

"Thanks for your question. To me, as a representative of THE Church, it means that there is a higher moral code for us. What I mean by that is there is an expectation that we act as Christians are supposed to act. We treat our fellow man as we want to be treated. We give to charity. We love one another."

"So, there's an expectation of good and righteous behavior. Where does your loyalty lie"

"Well, in my opinion, there are many, many good people from many religions. You know, you will always have some problems in all faiths. We are tolerant of others' beliefs. But we live in America and our loyalty is to the nation. Americans are, by and large, good people. We believe that everyone should get along and will, provided we treat one another with respect," the priest explained.

"Ok, thanks. My next question is directed to our guest from the Lutheran Church, Reverend Schroeder. Welcome to our roundtable."

"Thank you Aurelio,"

"Reverend, what does it mean to be a Christian in America?"

"In our traditions, we led the Reformation away from the Catholic Church, not in anger so much but in enlightenment. Christians here, like Christians elsewhere, are to be loyal to the precepts in the Bible, and of course, as Americans, we honor the flag."

"How well schooled do you expect your parishioners to be? Do you expect them to read the Bible on a regular basis? Do they?"

"We'd like all of our members to read the scriptures, but we know that relatively few do. So much is open to interpretation but the basic precepts of goodness are contained within. If they come to Church on Sundays and the holidays, we feel we are somewhat ahead. Do we expect them to read everyday? Probably not, but it would be nice,"

"Thanks, very informative," Lopes said. He then turned to the Muslim cleric.

"Next, our Muslim guest is an Imam in New York. Welcome Mr. Mohammad."

"Thank you Aurelio. It is nice to be here."

"So, with all the controversy, how does Islam fit into this discussion?" Lopes asked, anticipating a direct, if not confrontive answer.

"Islam, at its core, is a peaceful religion. That some extremists from time to time choose to express their beliefs in a more violent fashion is an aberration to us. I do not support nor do I condone violence, in any form. That includes the treatment of my brothers in Palestine or anywhere else Muslims may live." The other clerics agreed with him, though missing the subtlety at the end of his comments.

The rabbi just nodded at the scholarly opinions expressed and when it was his turn to speak, he took an eloquent and non-confrontive position in his retort.

"If I may, I'd like to address the point that we all live here in America. And it is here, where all things being equal, we can safely discuss our various faiths and though some differences may exist, at the end of the day, we are all Americans. We share our celebration of such events as the

Independence Day or Memorial Day observations, even the Super Bowl or the World Series," he said, half joking, but serious as he saw events that brought people together more important than things that divided them.

The rabbi spoke of social justice for all, allowing room for his Islamic friend to speak of God's (or Allah's) goodness and single unity of being. The priest argued for sensitivity for all oppressed peoples including Palestinian refugees, most vociferously. The rabbi nodded in the affirmative and acknowledged that the Jewish state had its flaws and that Jews needed to pay attention to their neighbors' differences and celebrate them. After all, Judaism, the rabbi said, wasn't a religion of exclusion but of one that reflected the love of a great creator.

The discussion was void of any Bible-believing Christians or Messianic Jews. Of course, it was mentioned that back in the early part of the 21st Century, Bible believing Christians had been classified as potential terrorists and were to be watched as such.

But, no, they were not represented here. This gathering of clergy represented the mainstream in America. Religion was important, but loyalty to the flag trumped faith. The discussion centered on social movements, work with AIDS patients and efforts to either eradicate it or prevent further spread of the disease.

In the end, they never discussed any of the holy books or the true differences in their faiths or philosophies. But, the census had spoken. America was firmly in the 'Christian' camp with a growing new identity of an Islamo-Christian heritage. Observations on events as they were unfolding were met with some measure of restraint and even the Muslim cleric admitted that violence solved nothing.

The Muslim holy man never mentioned the Palestinian Charter or the Hamas Manifesto but did quote the Quran and the Haditha. The Rabbi never mentioned the Torah or the Old Testament but did speak to 'universal kindness and understanding.' Neither the priest nor the Lutheran pastor mentioned the Gospels. Was it any wonder why America called itself Christian but didn't know why?

And Lopes asked, "America, What does it mean to be a Christian?"

Coffee House Chatter

"Have you ever stood anyone up?" she asked.

"Yeah, once," he said, feeling rather embarrassed.

"What happened?"

"Well, I was out with some friends in the afternoon. The day sort of melted away and I completely forgot I had a date."

"What happened next?"

"Well, it was about 9 that night. The date was supposed to be for 7. When I finally remembered I called her. She didn't answer."

"Then?"

He humphed. "Well, I tried again and again, and she refused to pick up. Three days later, I get a call. She just went to Europe on a whim the next day—figured I didn't care about her."

"Did you?"

A long silence ensued.

"Maybe I didn't realize just how much. But that was nothing—especially when I found out that she was killed as a random victim in a terrorist incident in France. I never saw her again and still haunts me to this day that I was so thoughtless."

Chapter 42

Dinner Plans Missed

Avner was late.

Danielle continued to flit around the kitchen and then stepped onto the patio to do a last minute check of the grilling. Everything was done, the smell wafting out of the grill and enveloping her. She blinked away the smoke as it stung her eyes for a moment. She took her tongs and gently picked all the veggies off the grill and then with her extra-wide spatula, gathered up the asparagus, putting everything into glass serving dishes. She grabbed a thick potholder and used her special grill clamps to lift off the fish and then took everything into the kitchen to cool for a moment. She looked at the clock again and it was ten past six, and still no sign of him.

Though she wasn't too worried, she had to make sure the food didn't get cold, so she turned on the oven to 125 and gently put everything inside. Shabbat was still about 30 minutes away. She set the table—the candlesticks, the bread, and her Kiddush cup right in the center where it belonged.

Avner and Ephraim were not far away. They pulled off the freeway. Avner realized he was late. He hit speed dial to call her, but his battery was dead. He looked at Ephraim and asked for his phone. He fished for it and realized he'd left it at his apartment. Avner felt frustrated and decided to take a shortcut to drop off Ephraim at home.

Avner was distracted and didn't see the car that had pulled alongside. It was Tewfiq. He recognized Avner, but Avner's mind was elsewhere. This was the moment Tewfiq had waited for. *Allah be praised!*

In a flash, Tewfiq reached over to the passenger seat and picked up his loaded revolver. What he was doing driving around town with a loaded gun was anyone's guess, but now it was in his hands and it was time to put the Israeli in his place. The light was still red.

Tewfiq's passenger window was open—Avner's wasn't. At that moment, Avner looked over to see Tewfiq raised his weapon and squeezed off three quick shots.

Just as the two Israeli brothers looked to see the gun, the glass on Avner's side exploded. The first bullet went through the car and embedded in the door next to Ephraim. The second bullet hit Avner in the shoulder. He screamed out in pain. Then Tewfiq's final bullet fired and missed the car. Things were happening so fast now. There was glass everywhere.

"Who the heck was that?" Ephraim asked, panicking now.

Tewfiq hit the accelerator just as the light turned green. He quickly reached 50 miles per hour, and disappeared into the night his tires squealing as he made it down the block, stayed true in the fast turn he took about a quarter of a mile down the street. Meanwhile, Avner was bleeding heavily from his wound, Ephraim pulling him down in the car to protect him. Ephraim jammed the shift into park so the car wouldn't move and get caught in traffic with no driver.

Without a cell phone, there was nothing Ephraim could do. Since he couldn't see anyone, and no witnesses had come up to help, he had no other choice but to pull Avner into the other seat and take the wheel himself, which he did.

Ephraim, with blood and glass all over him quickly checked his brother. He had some medical aid training in his unit in the IDF and had learned to assess bullet wounds. Avner's shoulder was pretty torn up, the 38 bullet having hit some blood vessels but the artery wasn't hit. He uttered a quick prayer of thanks. He then staunched the wound, holding his hand on the bullet hole to try to stop the bleeding. But he knew he needed to get Avner to the hospital. He managed to shift Avner into the passenger's seat and jumped behind the wheel.

He threw it into gear, and punched the gas. Within minutes he was in the Emergency Room parking lot of St. Josephs Hospital. He picked up Avner and half dragging and half pulling him into the ER, he approached the small window inside the double glass doors. When the intake clerk saw on the two young men, she yelled that a shooting victim was in the hospital and needed immediate assistance. The doctors and nurses flew out of the ER and pulled Avner into a curtained off area, gently laying him down on one of the beds.

They quickly and adeptly cut away his shirt to assess the wound. At that point, the bullet fell onto the gurney and Avner passed out. It was 7 p.m. Thankfully, it hadn't gone that deep.

And Danielle sat, alone, in her house, in tears as the dinner sat on the table.

From the Book of Ecclesiastes
Chapter 3

There is an appointed time for everything.
And there is a time for every event under heaven—
A time to give birth and a time to die;
A time to plant and a time to uproot what is planted.
A time to kill and a time to heal;
A time to tear down and a time to build up.
A time to weep and a time to laugh;
A time to mourn and a time to dance.
A time to throw stones and a time to gather stones;
A time to embrace and a time to shun embracing.
A time to search and a time to give up as lost;
A time to keep and a time to throw away.
A time to tear apart and a time to sew together;
A time to be silent and a time to speak.
A time to love and a time to hate;
A time for war and a time for peace.
What profit is there to the worker from that
   in which he toils?
I have seen the task which God has given the
   sons of men with which to occupy themselves.

Chapter 43

The Knesset Meets

The situation was growing more urgent by the day. Most of the signs were there, but a few were missing.

It was late. The Prime Minister and the cabinet sat down around the conference table inside the Knesset. At many times through the years, the ministers, the military men, and members of the intelligence agencies would form battle plans here. Signs were appearing all over the U.S., unmistakable in the opinion of many of the ministers present in the chambers.

The clouds on the horizon looked a lot like pre-World War II Europe. Everyone around the table agreed that they were seeing the start of a second Holocaust. Though all of their forbears were now dead, this second and third generation Israeli military knew its history well. Avi Dorit, a cabinet minister who also doubled as a military advisor and would be called up when the time came, was the first to speak once the meeting was called to order.

"We are seeing something we haven't seen before which is why we need to think about worst case scenarios. Through the years, we could always count on the liberals and later the conservatives in the U.S. But it now appears our traditional blocks have receded and been replaced with an anti-Zionist sentiment.

"And more... the Christian right in the U.S. has morphed into a mystery for us. What used to be sure support for Israel is now uncertain and even sinister. It's hard to discern or sort through. Oh, sure, the tours still come through and tourists spend their money. But the churches that sponsor the travel and activities have strayed from their traditional message and support of Israel. They still preach love and salvation through Jesus saves. They still tell stories of Bible times. But they have changed something—an important element has been removed."

Avi lifted notes, scanned them, and continued, "A new term appeared and found broad use in the past few decades: *the Emergent Church*. It speaks of hope for a better world, community activism, and a more tolerant and diluted salvation message. It builds upon other terms and ideas such as a seeker-friendly and non-threatening profile. In some ways it resembles some of the Jewish movements—those not onboard with Zionist thought or goals. Still, bottom-line... a heartbeat of support of Israel beats the strongest within the more conservative evangelical congregations."

When cries for divestment in Israel's economy began in the late 20th Century, few really heeded the call. But in the past few years Dorit noted, the divestment movement had gained momentum and old friends that the Jewish state could rely on in the past, had dissolved into a very unstable network of accusers blasting them and demanding a Palestinian state with no restrictions on travel or trade or guaranteeing a Palestinian Law of Return.

This once dependable foundation found common ground with the Europeans who continued to call for a Palestinian state along with a strange cross section of Muslims, skinheads, and Black Muslims from the Nation of Islam. Much of this was driven by organizations such as the Worldwide Council of Churches and other associations like them and their American counterparts. Ecumenism was here to stay. The walls were closing in on international Jewry and the light of Biblical Christianity had dimmed.

Many of the traditional Christian denominations heralded Palestinian causes now. They were increasingly joined by what were once considered evangelicals such as some of the mega churches out in California, unthinkable a generation before. Several Popes made multiple pilgrimages to Palestine and had prayed in mosques to show solidarity with the Palestinians. They would also visit Israel and remind the Israeli government that they had been a persecuted people at one time too and should remember the refugees in their midst. Thus delivered was a subtle warning that they were being held to a higher standard.

The great irony of much of the Christmas music praising God's work in Israel or the savior being born there were simply the words in a hymnal now. The Israel of today was simply not, according to their pastors, the Israel of the Bible, nor were the Jews of today the Jews of the chosen people. The Church now claimed that mantle. Many evangelicals called it Replacement Theology.

Israel was now considered the neighborhood bully with its million man army and its reputation of brutality, at least according to CNN and the general press. The tide had turned and she was soon to be alone, much as many evangelicals had predicted would happen years before. It was against this backdrop and with this perception that the Knesset went to work.

Avi Dorit measured his words with patience as he explained to the gathering the complete reversal of fortunes that was in their midst. "As you know, many years ago, our leadership had sanctioned secret plans to prepare our defense forces to fight in foreign lands.

"We have some old friends, though the world tends to frown on them. This is the time we call in some old favors. We have begun plans to awaken those of us living abroad. As many of you know, we have more than 350,000 Sabras living expat right now, in the U.S. I speak of America with a heavy heart because we have lost their friendship."

History recorded several incidents that had eroded confidence between the two old friends including the Jonathan Pollard incident and other perceived Israeli spying operations. The Pollard incident was embarrassing for Israel as it didn't want him leaving prison, coming to Israel and writing a tell-all book about his role as a spy for Israel. But that was a long time ago and Pollard had since died in prison.

That Israel had performed any intelligence operations was taken as effrontery by America but America never admitted that, for decades, it had done similar things in Israel.

Dorit described other stories as well, including the erosion in relations between the two allies. Dorit recalled the former Vice President's visit to Israel and a dispute he had when the local housing council approved a measure to add more housing units in East Jerusalem. Angry words were exchanged between the Vice President and the Prime Minister. Later, the Secretary of State excoriated the Prime Minister in a sign of utter disrespect for another sovereign.

"Something has changed over the years. Mossad has recently completed some analysis and has been piecing together a picture for us of the last year or so, and in particular the past six months. Our Jewish Agency logistics planners are also closely watching patterns shift and are working to open up the Judea, Samaria, and the Negev for near-term future settlement. The situation has deteriorated over that time and it continues to get worse."

The ministers, many of them scribbling out notes and thoughts about the discussion, stared intently at him as he spoke.

"I've asked Avram to give us his latest assessment." Ben Yehuda slowly rose from his seat and took center stage.

"Todah rabah, (thank you very much) Avi. My friends, I cannot tell you tonight how all of this happened, but it is indeed happening right before our very eyes. In the past six months, the security situation in the U.S. has rapidly deteriorated. But, I also want to say that everything we planned for is moving along well and we need to begin preparations for what I believe to be the next step to the inevitable. We have all seen the news over the past few weeks and months.

"The protests began in the U.S. just a few weeks after Durban. Though they began as anti-racist shows of support for the oppressed of America and the world, they revealed exactly what we predicted they would. These are direct attacks on Jews and Israel, using Zionism as an excuse to further their hatred. Our assets on the ground there tell us the situation is getting worse by the day. The violence is spreading. The rhetoric sounds like Nazi Germany before the war. But as we said earlier, we do have some friends left, though not who you might think. Though we are all shocked and saddened by the current situation, we are not surprised, and we are not unprepared.

"I am here tonight to advise you that we must deliver what we believe will be enough firepower to support an insurgency such as the world hasn't seen in generations.

"The recent protests at the embassies, as you know, turned increasingly violent in the streets of New York, Washington D.C., Chicago, other cities, and at several universities, but we believe that the worst is still ahead. Though no lives were lost this time around, some people were accosted and others screamed at. We have film showing a lot of these protests. We believe these are a precursor to much more violence."

He stopped for a moment, taking out a handkerchief and wiping his sweating brow. He looked around the room to take a measure of the ministers... they were all silent, hanging on his next words. To say the room respected him was to state the obvious.

"We didn't see any killings but the tenor of the street marches was increasingly anti-Semitic and hateful. We expect things to worsen. No doubt, many of you have family living there and you are quite well aware of the situation on the ground. They haven't gone into Jewish neighborhoods with any regularity just yet nor have we seen anything resembling Kristallnacht but a pattern is a pattern. We know how to read history. We've learned that when our enemies threaten our existence, believe them."

"What disturbed us the most was that the police presence at the embassy in San Francisco did little to stop the first wave of violence. A few Jews were roughed up. There were speeches denying the *Shoah*, which we've seen for years now. We know, from history, that when mobs gain confidence, they will test their targets and continue to push out their limits. We all know what that means. It happened to our great grandparents in Germany and throughout Europe. It happened in Spain so very long ago and of course throughout Europe during the Crusades. We remember Russia, Poland, and England, And I don't have to tell you how Islam has treated our brethren."

The ministers, nodding with him in agreement as he went, possessed a common understanding of the world and saw things in the very much the same way.

"The demonstrations also had a lot of Christians marching with American Muslims along with the Nation of Islam. We are also seeing a lot of Muslims from the Middle East and Indonesia, Malaysia, and India, based on our current intelligence. The white skinheads have also jumped in. They all smell Jewish blood, like a bunch of sharks. We filmed the protests for the world to see and posted them on several social networking sites. We also filmed other things the public didn't see and we will review those films privately. We are also seeing swastikas, crosses, and Muslim symbols all together. All of them seem be of one accord on this. We estimated the crowds to be averaging at least 10,000 or so, in the larger cities" he added.

"Amazingly, we also noted several Jewish groups in the protests—anti Zionists trying to show solidarity with the protestors. The American Jews don't really seem to understand things as we do, yet. I'm not sure what it will take to wake them up. We just hope it won't get to the point that it did in Europe before World War II.

"We anticipate that the Federal Government will have to intervene soon, but what we don't know is what they will do if this spreads. They are tied down in Southeast Asia and South America. The fight is with Muslim insurgents on the surface. Yet we know the reality—these are mad attempts to cling to U.S. interests and influence.

"Our latest estimates show about a million and a half troops totally committed, mostly American, though the NATO alliance kicked in some as well. We've also been keeping our eye on Southern Mexico where Islamic evangelists are converting Mexican Catholic Indians by the droves. That may continue to compromise the U.S. border with Mexico. The drug wars are out of control there on their borders and have spilled into Arizona, New Mexico, and California. That could add to our enemies in the U.S. And, as many of you know, we have established a strong link between the drug cartels and Islamic political interests—they are now partners using one another for their own gains.

"The strange thing is that Islam has made inroads in America and seems to have replaced Judaism as part of their societal fabric, but we believe that their current 'peaceful' face will soon change," he said.

"Why America continues to court Muslim goodwill at home while simultaneously fighting insurgencies abroad, is beyond us. I suppose the world is just one great big paradox.

"Most likely we will face a local citizenry that doesn't expect much from us. Their leaders, the real rabble rousers, are pumping them full of lies that the Jews won't fight and that we are there for the hunting. Local law enforcement shouldn't be much of a problem because we have many friends among them. But there is the National Guard, and they are reasonably well trained with heavy equipment to back them up. But, our sources also tell us that we have assets there too. The big question is how loyal is the

American soldier when he faces an old friend? We understand a significant portion of the military—Marines, Army, and Navy consider themselves Christians. We just don't what to do with that kind of Christian yet.

"Some of our estimates are as much as 50% of the American Armed Forces, fire, and police" he added. The room let out a collective grunt and anyone dozing off was immediately awake. What that meant was anyone's guess but if it meant that there was an element of American Christians who were willing to step forward and help the Jews, then so much the better.

"We hope to see support but we can't depend on rumors. Once we are in position, I expect we will quickly overwhelm anything then can throw at us. We do not know how the local Jewish population will react but we expect most to join us. That would be expected if they feel safe enough. But I only worry about their willingness to forget their American citizenship and come to Israel. Some will not come and we cannot force them. Hopefully almost all of them will understand what is at stake.

"There is a Christian element that remains supportive, mostly in the stronger evangelical communities. They are increasingly calling themselves Christian Zionists—and are proud to distinguish themselves from the general Christian population. If things turn more violent, and I think they will, I believe there will be many more names added to the Avenue of the Righteous, the Righteous Gentiles," he added.

"Many of you may have read about the U.S. Census recently. You would be amazed at the new American self identity—it is Christian but evidence suggests it is really more 'Islamo-Christian'. It seems that Jews no longer figure into the national fabric of America. Many of these Christian Zionists are armed and our field officers tell us they will fight for us. We believe they will join us in the streets. Our latest estimates are that we will eventually field an insurgency of about two and a half to three million, pretty formidable by any estimation. There may even be more, we just cannot tell for sure. If the military rebels, as we believe some of them will, that will add greatly to our numbers and our firepower," he continued.

The thought of America imploding gave each of the ministers heartburn. It also made them smile for American politicians had been riding quite high in the saddle the past few decades and had become quite arrogant and preachy towards Israel. The past few administrations had treated Israel with less and less respect. But more, they flirted with and feigned before their common enemies. It made no sense to their loyal ally, Israel.

"Many in the crowds are spoiling for a fight. They are armed and many of the mosques are sitting on arsenals—we think they could be pretty hefty. But the good news for us is that we have anticipated this for some time now and we have managed to smuggle more than two and one half million weapons into the U.S. Plus, with the import of all the modular housing materials, our settlements are going up fast, and when push comes to shove, we will have housing waiting for our arrivals," he added.

"You may or may not know the details, but the 747s we send back to the States to pick up housing materials are also carrying cargo back to America. We have worked for a long while now with certain 'friends' to make sure our exports, their 'imports' arrive safely and are not detected for what they are. We've placed all the hardware to set up mechanized units on the ground. We have paid handsomely for this privilege but all of our contacts are still in place and our warehouses are filling up. When the signal goes up, our expats have their orders and know where to report. Within 24 hours of a general call up, we will have 350,000+ ready to fight. Once we add the Christian Zionists and those American servicemen who defect to our side, we will be quite a formidable force to deal with." These words were barely comprehensible to him.

What he didn't say but what was implied was a possible outpouring of trouble as Mossad intelligence had picked up rumors of mass demonstrations planned for the following 4th of July, still several months away. What wasn't evident at the moment was the exact nature of the parades or other events planned for that time. But Independence Day was certainly something to think about. Time was running out.

Israeli planners had built the infrastructure. The weapons were in place, the expat foot soldiers hadn't received any signals just yet, but the time was approaching. He knew it, the ministers knew it, and the world knew it. And so it was that the Knesset finally learned the full extent of *Operation Last Exodus*.

"Our predecessors, with almost a prophetic prescience, designed a doomsday scenario in case another Holocaust appeared imminent, and today, I believe, we must act on that plan. It is time to invoke the next phase of *Operation Last* Exodus."

He concluded his speech, sweating profusely, his breathing labored. He slowly sat down, resting his head in his hands, then running his fingers through his thinning scalp, and then looked around the room. It was silent. The ministers sat stunned but understanding, nodding.

He felt all of his 85 years in that one moment.

> From the Pen of Isaiah the Prophet
> Chapter 5 Verse 20
>
> Woe to those who call evil good and good evil;
> Who substitute darkness for light and
>   light for darkness;
> Who substitute bitter for sweet and sweet for bitter!

Chapter 44

Dallas

Team 3 touched down first in Dallas. Landing at Love Field around noon, Dallas time, the Boeing 777 landed smoothly and pulled to a stop on the runway. Several planes landed just moments before, leaving the Delta plane on the tarmac for a few extra minutes. Once cleared, it taxied to the gate and the passengers began to deplane.

Team 3's composition consisted of one Saudi, one lighter-skinned Afghani, one German-born Turk, and two Algerians. All were impeccably dressed in business attire, presumably heading for business meetings in the Dallas Metroplex. Cell phones sprang to life as everyone rushed to connect to rides or loved ones.

They reached to pull down their respective travel bags from the overhead bins. Since plans called for the teams to travel light, there would be no stop at the luggage carousels downstairs. The least exposure to the world, the better it was thought. Grabbing their carry-on luggage, they deplaned, walked up the jet way, through the airport, and headed for the car rental agency.

CHAPTER FORTY-FOUR: Dallas

As instructed, all team members donned non-descript sunglasses to further conceal their identities. Nothing was left to chance. The team leader, Mahmoud Salim, Saudi born, approached the third window of the car rental agency, as instructed. He pulled out her newly minted Texas driver's license and all the reservation documents.

"Welcome back to the U.S., Mr. Salim," the clerk said cheerfully. Dressed neatly in the agency's uniform, she eyed him. "How was your flight?" she asked.

Salim understood that question to mean that everything in the plan was working as it was supposed to, for the car rental clerk, an African American woman, well churched her whole life was the first contact in an intricate network to support the mission. She was here to welcome these new visitors to the US. Except this time, her "guests" would not be touring but would be carrying out a very different type of visit. She knew no details of the mission.

Teams 1 and 2 landed at their destinations without incident. The other teams' landings all over the U.S. found much the same experience at their destinations—smooth landings, equally efficient car rental experiences, and flawless execution of the mission's early stages. Each, like members of Team 3, held forged documents such as American drivers' licenses, Social Security cards, family pictures, and a host of items making each of them appear to be native born Americans. The documentation specialists had done their jobs. The support network, recruited and put in place by powerful individuals they would never see, was working as planned.

Teams were to have no contact with one another but through their internet email accounts would communicate with Rachman at prearranged times. Cell phones were prepaid and would be destroyed and disposed of after all calls. The less each team knew of the others the better their security would be. Besides, after all of this and even if caught and executed, there was always heaven.

And it would be the same for the other teams, as they fanned out all over the United States and closed in on their targets.

Team 3, settled into the Marriott Residence Inn. The action was a few weeks hence, but team members needed to establish a daily routine and work to blend in to the local environment. The advanced strike team placed each team member in a local business consulting arrangement, usually in the world of electronics, where they would help local businesses solve problems ranging from supply chain logistics, export issues, financials, and other business needs.

Each of them was uniquely qualified to perform such work and they toiled hard to be well liked. The three men and two women went about each day in an efficient business-like manner, blending in where they could but making efforts not to stand out.

The team members also followed a rigorous daily exercise routine. After gym workouts they partook in a daily communal meal, healthy and nutritious. There would be no alcohol, tobacco use, or any recreational drugs. Their contacts on the ground would provide every need to them. They spent their evenings pouring over local traffic patterns, entry and exit points, escape routes, and the like. Additionally, they would disappear during the weekends to local shooting ranges to practice their skills. Their hard training in the desert had prepared them for this time.

Unknown to them, their support teams were also preparing similarly, but their plans centered on the preparations, car and truck switches, and the follow up actions. It was a strange army, made up of so many former enemies, now focused on a new common enemy, a local synagogue, where an upcoming Saturday service would deliver a message to the Jews, that no matter where they went they would be hunted down like game.

Ten days before the strike, the teams began filing their twice-daily reports. The team worked out practice runs well in advance so that they would know the routine by rote. Planners threw in wild cards during practice runs to see how the team would react if some other distraction found its way into the game plan. About a week out from the strike, weather maps began to appear in the morning briefing and they worked that set of details into the operational plans.

Team 3's leader Mahmoud Salim, a Saudi by birth and a Kuwaiti by citizenship, began that morning's ritual with a cup of strong espresso along with some fruit. Once the room was swept for bugs for the umpteenth time, team members gathered around the table to discuss that day's practice run.

The advanced team had gathered a treasure trove of intelligence on the target. They pretty much knew every member of the congregation by name and sight. Using all their cyber tools and public websites, Team 3 knew every inch of the facility, what stained glass windows the 3rd Street synagogue had installed, who made them, the names of all the children and their ages, in short a total and complete scan of the target. Every other team in the other nine cities had the same set of data to initiate their actions.

"When we enter the synagogue," Salim began, "we will place ourselves at strategic locations for maximum impact." Then he pointed out spots on the enlarged floor plan of the sanctuary.

"We will carry the small machine guns with us under our suits." Salim demonstrated. "Each team member will carry three clips of ammunition and your C4 devices. The walls and ceiling must fall on the congregation once no one is standing and we're out. The timers are set—we have only a few minutes.

"I will give the signal, but no one else will speak—not a word. With it done, exit behind the stage area. There will be no talk, no looks back, and no delay.

"There will be a car waiting for us right outside of the exit. Do not delay, we have just a few minutes to do the job," he said, checking each face for understanding. They each nodded in turn. He could see the commitment and the fire in their eyes.

"My understanding is that services start at 10:00 on Saturday. The Bar Mitzvah will commence with the Bar Mitzvah boy set to begin his prayers. Remain silent until I give the order," Salim went on. The plan was well rehearsed in each member's head. But nothing could simulate the real thing, though they had come pretty close in their simulations back in the desert. What he couldn't discuss was the secondary team's role in all of this, because even he didn't know it existed.

The secondary teams were being readied as well. Their roles, even far more sinister than the primary action teams' were being discussed in hotel rooms not far from each of the primary teams.

> **From Joan D. Vinge**
> American Science Fiction Author
>
> *Fear of the unknown is a terrible fear.*

Chapter 45

Danielle

Danielle awoke with a start. It was dark, and she was disoriented. *What was that?* She thought and headed for the kitchen. It was late—she must have fallen asleep. Then the phone rang.

"Dani, this is Ephraim." The line was silent for a moment. Both their minds needed to catch-up.

"Ephi, what's, what's going on?" she asked frantically. Something was wrong and she knew it.

"Ok, calm down... look, I have something to tell you." Though it was warm her blood ran cold and she felt the shivers going up her spine.

"Is it Avner?" she asked, begging him to say something.

"Yes, there was a shooting... he was hit," Ephraim said, trying to remain calm. She screamed into the phone, but something told her to gather her wits about her.

"Where is he? Is he... is he ok?" she asked, half crying, half praying.

"Yes, he's ok. We were together, on the way home from L.A. He was going to drop me off and head to your place when we were hit by a drive-by shooting."

"The driver fired three shots at us, missed twice, but one hit him in the shoulder," Ephraim said.

"He's pretty lucky, the bullet did a little damage, but it's mostly superficial, though he lost a lot of blood."

"Where is he? Can I see him?" she pleaded.

"He's at Saint Joseph's," Ephraim answered. "I don't think they'll let you see him. Anyway, it's late, and he... well, the morning would be better."

"So come over here, now!" Dani demanded. "If I can't go, you're gonna tell me everything. Anyway, I've got a perfectly good dinner that no one has touched. I'll feed you."

"Okay. Enough said. You had me at 'dinner.'"

In minutes, Ephraim arrived. Danielle opened the door, saw Ephraim clothes, gasped, and cried out. "Oh, no, no, no! The blood!" She lunged and hugged him, and they both began to cry.

Once composed, Danielle led him to kitchen and got dinner from the oven. Just knowing he had survived seemed to calm her a little.

They ate, sipped wine, and talked. Ephraim recounted everything he could remember while Danielle fought back tears. She ached from exhaustion that demanded rest. She made a bed for him on the couch and headed for her room.

Danielle thought and prayed. She cried over Avram and the attack. But she rested easier with the knowledge that Avner had not broken their dinner date.

Coffee House Chatter

"So, there I am at my 40th high school reunion. I look across the room and see some of the kids I always looked up to and used to feel sort of intimidated by them. But I noticed that they had aged just like I had, faced many of the same struggles and were just like I was. The playing field seemed a little more level."

"How do you feel now?"

"Well, not like I did then. I mean I realized that I have done ok for myself and they have done ok for themselves, but we were all pretty much the same. Some had married, divorced, had families, some successful, some not so much... but there we were."

Chapter 46

Past Meets Present

Something was eating at Chaim. "Raphi Shachor..."

"Yeah, haven't seen him in years. Why?" Eleazer's curiosity was now peaked about an old childhood friend.

"He found me online again the other day," Chaim said. "He said he was thinking about after our chat a while ago. He's really focused on all the anti-Semitism."

"And?"

"I think I told you that he flipped a few years ago—this Jesus thing. He's concerned something big is about to happen."

"Humph! He's nuts. You remember when he'd really get into something, he'd just wear you out –talking about whatever he was into. He could be pretty convincing and really make you think he was right, sincere, and all that. I remember he really got into the JFK assassination for a few years. He read and read then he'd start preaching and if you were in the room, you had no chance."

Eleazer was chuckling now but his brother was not.

"I'm listening to him."

"You can't be serious."

"It's not that I believe him but I am intrigued by what he's saying. I'm using some of the same perspectives in the weekly Shabbos messages I've been giving in shul."

"Like what?"

"Like some of these prophecies—I think he's a little closer to the middle on the Jews second return to Israel—can't say I disagree. Not so much on the Messiah."

A silence enveloped the brothers. They eyed one another across the table, reading each other's thoughts.

"I see your point. I've had more questions on these issues. The Jesus thing—I don't know. I've heard that more and more Jews are flipping. Then I ran across some research... a whole lot of Jews believed in this nonsense before the war. The Christians called them—Christians. We called them—Christians. But they called themselves Jews."

"That concerns me. Why are they turning away from us?"

"I don't know, but there's a lot of strange stuff going on. Do you remember the story about the New Testament scrolls some archeologists found in jars buried in the desert? Just like Qumran. I think it's more than just a coincidence. There have been rumors for centuries of an authentic First Century Hebrew New Testament but no evidence—until now."

"Yes I do, why?"

"Well this discovery was different. The first textual experts reported they found a small mark akin to a signature on the top right corner of the scrolls. It closely resembled a Fe—Lamed—Pe. For *Phillip,* I think. Some kind of code maybe."

"Yeah, yeah, I wonder if that might be the evangelist who is described in the Book of Acts. He preaches about the Messiah to the Ethiopian eunuch in Gaza using Isaiah 53." Eleazer was now intrigued.

"Perfectly preserved like the Dead Sea Scrolls," Chaim said, but it was more thinking out loud.

"So, with all this 'evidence' what are you thinking?" Eleazer asked quietly.

Another silence hung between them, this one a little longer.

"After all we've been seeing and hearing about, these past few months, I'm not sure what I believe. Remember Jonathan Roberts? We've been in touch and let me tell you what we've been talking about."

"Do I want to hear this?" Eleazer now seemed agitated.

"Well, you might as well hear it. You remember the Servant Songs in Isaiah?"

"Yes, but it's been awhile since I read the prophets."

"Well Isaiah focuses a lot on this Servant. He says that His Servant will lead Israel back to God, right?"

"Well, yes, so?"

"Well, if the Servant is 'He' as in '*He* will lead ***them*** back to God,' then the '*He* cannot be the '*We*,' can He? Catch my drift?"

Eleazer fell silent. The rabbis taught that the Servant was Israel but one needed to read the context to understand fully what that meant. In this case, the Servant was a different person than Israel. This wasn't what he expected to hear from his brother, the true scholar in the family. The twins, their wizened faces beholding the other, made a deep and lasting eye contact, holding the silence between them and reading one another's thoughts.

"You know what this could mean... " It wasn't really a question as much as it was more thinking out loud. Chaim was almost paralyzed.

"Yeah, I do," Eleazer answered, taking a deep breath and slowly exhaling. "Yeah."

"What are we gonna do now?"

"Nothing just yet. We need to talk to Raphi and Jonathan before we do anything. We have to confirm this, we need to study all the prophecies before we go out and say anything.

"Can you get hold of him?"

"Yes, I think so. He's dying to see us. He'd give his eye teeth to be here in the room with us right now."

The two brothers understood that any discussion like this would result in repercussions so large and widespread; it could shake the entire rabbinical community. Jews just didn't believe in Jesus, did they?

Did they?

✡ ✡ ✡ ✡ ✡ ✡

Meanwhile, the next day, at Mossad headquarters, the planners began sifting through the day's reports, data, rumors, contacts, incoming emails and 'chatter.' News of Avner's shooting reached them somehow. Clandestine agents, many of them Bible-centered Christians, deep within the American infrastructure were paying big dividends now and the information flow was increasing by the hour.

The plans that Israel had put in place years earlier were moving ahead. The crazy thing about it was those Christians supported their Jewish friends. They believed they were placed there by God Himself, doing some sort of a cosmic favor or good deed for a chosen people who may not have really appreciated what was being done on their behalf. Israeli planners were just happy for the support and massaged the network for all it was worth. Those Bible-believing Christians-Christian Zionists-represented all walks of life from government, industry, medicine, law, academia, unions, entertainment, sciences, you name it. And the information came like a flood.

Some hinted at treason because they had "betrayed" America, but believers in those positions counted it all honor, much as those of the House of Rahab had way back in ancient days.

Rahab, the harlot, introduced to Bible readers in the Book of Joshua, gave sanctuary to two Jewish spies allowing them to spy out the land in exchange for immunity. When the invading Israelites took the city of Jericho, the Israelites spared Rahab and her family. So important was that event in Jewish history, it was recorded in the Bible, and more to the point, Rahab even makes an appearance in the lineage of David, the King of Israel. She is identified as the mother of Boaz, the future Kinsman Redeemer and future husband of Ruth, the Moabitess.

And there it was, for anyone to read, in the Tenach—the Messianic line of David had not only a former Moabitess priestess in it but, according to some, a second one, and a prostitute as well. God works in mysterious ways.

So, the Israelis began building and releasing plans to protect these, their friends. If there was one thing you could depend on, it was that the Jews remembered favors.

Ben Yehuda, after a good night's sleep, called Shoshana into his office to discuss the next phase of the operation.

"Get packed, we're inserting you into the U.S. We need somebody with a good knowledge of the States, good contacts, and with the ability to blend in. Your English is excellent and your ability to move around without detection is well known here. There are a number of contacts you must make, details to weave together with "friends" of ours.

"When do I go? I've got several projects that need my attention here."

"We've got Weinstein to step in for you, he's ready-we'll see how good your training has been," Ben Yehuda winked and smiled.

"One thing we do need to do is get with our planners before you go. Most of the material has been shipped through ZIM and a few other shipping lines. We also have other means to get things into the U.S...."

In fact, Ben Yehuda knew at that moment where every ship was on the globe. He could track every truck transporting cargo across the America. He knew where all his assets were. *Operation Last Exodus* was coming together.

More than a two and a half million weapons and all their accoutrements have been shipped to the U.S. or were currently in transit across the ocean. More waited for pick up, or were already in the warehouses. The pipeline was intact, no slips, yet. *Old friends came through,* he thought and smile in satisfaction.

He gave her a small 'mini-disk', holding trillions of terabytes of data, all properly scrambled and encrypted with software from her software house, a standard in the Land. In it were the plans of *Operation Last* Exodus.

'Now we need someone on the ground that can pull it all together. Shoshana will make it happen,' he thought.

Shoshana took the first plane out, a diplomatic flight in a small private Boeing Business Jet, usually reserved for Israeli military officials of much higher rank then hers. She would be traveling as a guest lecturer, heading to Columbia University and then down the East Coast of the United States, then across the country.

Thankfully, there was still some diplomatic immunity in place. Once in country, she would hook up with the network that would support this, the largest intercontinental and inter-oceanic rescue and extraction effort of an indigenous people in history. It was destined to fulfill Biblical prophecy.

Coffee House Chatter

"Ever had a close call—I mean one where you feared you would die?" He peered over his IPad, searching her expression.

Silence.

"Yes, a long time ago. I was at UC Irvine. Student protests ignited, and we got caught in the middle. Rocks flew, and I got hit. The crowd swarmed, and I almost got trampled. But I got lucky—a man appeared, scooped me up, and got me out of there. It was so weird... when I looked around, the guy had vanished."

Chapter 47

Things that Matter

Danielle and Ephraim entered St. Joseph's Hospital in Orange the next morning, Shabbat, as soon as visiting hours allowed. Avner had been moved from Emergency to a room of his own. The room overlooked La Veta Avenue where he could look out and see a shopping mall and medical buildings nearby. When they stepped into the room, both Avner and Ephraim exchanged a look. Danielle caught the silent communication and thought she saw Ephraim shake his head slightly. She arched her shoulders and cocked her head as if to say, *what am I missing here?*

Ephraim had the ring in his hand and stepped over to Avner for a moment. He quickly slipped it in to Avner's hand and then backed toward the door. It was a bit awkward for Ephraim so he offered to leave for a moment. When Avner stopped him, Danielle knew something was up.

"No, Ehpi, I need you here. You are as much a part of this as I am," Avner said. "Dani, come here." She stepped toward his bed and bent over to kiss him. His bandaged arm and medical devices had her eye. But Avner pulled her close with his other arm. He kissed her and clung to her, the sweet kiss lingering. Then strength failed and pain broke his grasp. He fell back, as she moved to the chair next to him.

Avner couldn't hold her and satisfy his heart. So he beheld Danielle with his eyes. His silent gaze captured, consumed, caressed, and encompassed her. She wanted to know his condition, but Avner was on another page.

"What is it?" She asked. "I've never seen you like this... not the bandages, the boy I see. Who are you?"

"You are so beautiful," Avner fawned. "I've never looked on anyone whom I've loved so much."

Danielle scooted closer and stroked his neck and face. "Got anymore of what they gave you?" She couldn't resist the humor.

"He hasn't had any pain medication this morning," Ephraim inserted. "He wanted to be clear-headed for you."

Avner cleared his throat, searched her eyes, and said, "I over-think things—life, money, relationships, the future...." He paused and collected his thoughts. "But in a moment, I saw everything. I saw my whole life past and present. I saw how little I had... until I had you." Tears brimmed and rolled down his face into his beard. The attack, the bullets, and that moment gave me clarity. Since then nothing else has mattered to me except you."

Danielle and Avner were connected—eyes, touch, heart, and mind.

"You are my beloved," Avner continued. "And I have a question for you."

Danielle's eyes filled with tears. She was captured by his intensity, passion, and sense of purpose. Her heart stopped. She held her breath and listened.

"We belong together. I have no future without you." Emotion filled his throat and choked his voice. He pushed through and asked, "Will you honor me and be my b'shert, for eternity?"

He now knew what eternity meant. So did she.

She blinked back tears, and then, since he couldn't, got down on her knees, took his hands in hers, and said, "Yes, baby, I will, my love, forever."

Both of them broke into tears, smiling, laughing holding hands, and hugging as much as they could with him in the hospital bed. Ephraim joined them at Avner's bedside.

"So," she asked, laughing through the tears, "when were you planning to do this?"

"Last night," he and Ephraim, said at the same time.

She sat stunned—replaying the evening she had planned. She pretended to hit them both, raising her fists and shaking them at the brothers.

"Well, my love, you missed the best dinner *everrrr*," she said, half joking, half overwhelmingly sad that it had to happen in this way. "Just ask your brother!"

Ephraim nodded in agreement.

"When will we do it?" she asked.

"Why wait, we both know what we want," he answered.

She agreed and knew this to be a fact. Neither of them wanted to wait. Something told them that the sooner they got married the better.

"Well, we can go to a Justice of the Peace (JOP) in the next few weeks... we have to get the license and the blood tests and all that," she said. He nodded his head but then said, "Quickly yes, JOP, no."

"At the congregation?" she asked.

"I think so, though I'm not sure how Moishe (their congregational leader) would support it."

"He knows us, I'm sure it's fine," she answered.

A week after his release, he and Dani went to see Moishe. It was as if Moishe was waiting for them, and as they entered into his study, he looked the pair over.

"Normally we'd do some counseling, but you two seem well past that," he said.

"I will not invade your privacy, but you ... " They cut him off.

"You have no worries, we've remained apart," Avner said. Moishe nodded his head and smiled, pleased and content that he was hearing the truth. He continued.

"You are entering into the biggest commitment two people can make." He proceeded to share his thoughts on marriage and the commitment it meant. They shared their feelings about marriage and upcoming plans. Though neither of them knew it at the time, there would be no real honeymoon. Holding hands, they listened to the session and answered all of Moishe's questions.

"We can do it two Sundays from now or even at the Havdalah on Saturday night," he offered. Though it seemed a little fast, he saw something different in this young couple and gave his blessings. Time was moving so fast—

blessings like this needed to be moved along quickly. He had no doubt about Danielle and Avner.

Two weeks later, *Ketuba* in hand and signed, Avner and Danielle were joined together in marriage in a small ceremony following the Havdalah. At his side, were his sister and his brother, the three Sullivans together for the first time in more than three years. Mimi had just flown in just for the wedding.

"So, this is the lovely Danielle!" Mimi spoke and stepped in to hug and kiss her. The affection was returned with thanks for Mimi's presence at the wedding. Mimi smiled.

"The honor is mine—it is so good to see my big brother happy."

Mimi and Danielle bonded immediately as Mimi recognized the intense and profound love and respect Avner felt for his bride. And it didn't hurt that Danielle could communicate in Hebrew.

Though neither Ephraim nor Mimi had considered the claims of Yeshua they respected Dani's and Avner's faith, having seen the amazing transformation in Avner's life. He had always been the rock of the siblings but he seemed now to have grown into quite a mensch.

They loved their new sister-in-law—she was now a Sullivan. Mimi promised to read the Tenach and test out their theories, though she pretty much knew what she would find. Ephraim promised to do the same.

That night, in the wedding chamber, Avner opened a nice bottle of Jordan Cabernet, an old vintage from 30 years before. He then read the *Song of Songs* to Danielle. The two of them toasted their wedding, their love, and the love of the Lord. For to them, the marriage was of three, not two.

She smiled, and with tears of joy running down both of their faces, she reached over to the lamp next to the bed and turned out the lights.

And the angels in heaven rejoiced.

> **From the Hand of Solomon the Wise (Proverbs)**
> Chapter 20 Verse 18)
>
> "Prepare plans by consultation,
> And make war by wise guidance."

Chapter 48

Shoshana Arrives

In New York, Yanit received a call from Dogface Vicenzo. He invited her to his family home again. This time they'd discuss next steps in this crazy plan. Vicenzo, his family, and their contacts weren't resting, nor was Yanit. A lot of things had happened since that first encounter several months ago.

Shoshana's plane touched down at JFK in New York City. She wasted no time. She stood on the curb in the rain and waited for a cab to see her. Her memory of the airport, and its layout came back. She noted surrounding buildings—their size, access, parking, and other details.

She snapped pictures and took videos. The images would be combined with other media to create visual aids and tools for others to follow. JFK was huge. It would take a lot of planning to bring it under control. She would need a detailed aerial view of the complex. She put a reminder in her electronic device.

Though she hadn't met either Yanit or Dogface, their paths would soon cross and would begin an association where together they would be key players in *Operation Last Exodus*. Advanced plans took time and a lot of it.

For now, attacks on Jewish targets seem to have slackened, she thought, and climbed into the cab. *Maybe it's room to breathe... or maybe just the calm before the storm.*

Nothing too serious had yet happened but the trends were indicating that something was up. She recalled Weinstein's analysis and kept it close to her heart. It seemed to her like a lull, almost like the eye of the hurricane. Most of what she was hearing was not yet a systematic plan of an evil government. The populace was a different matter—it could turn on a dime or a shekel, in a flash of an instant.

It seemed, at this juncture, that the Jews in America would learn the same lesson their forbears had but hopefully this time they would listen to the signals being sent. She knew her history and it was becoming increasingly clear that things could easily slip out of control. Of course, Israel had suffered from her neighbors' state-sponsored terrorism for decades, really from before its inception, when still either a British protectorate under the League of Nations Mandate or even before that under Ottoman rule. And of course, the Sephardic Jews had suffered for centuries as *dhimmis* in Muslim lands, she recalled. What America was seeing was child's play compared to what her nation had seen. But things could change in a heartbeat.

This was her chance to get things moving. There were so many variables, it made her head spin. She kept thinking about the earthquakes and now, most recently, a spate of volcanic eruptions all over the globe.

Hmmm, she thought, *earthquakes and volcanoes in diverse places.* There was no discernable pattern, yet, however, that there was this much seismic activity had her attention. She thought of her geologist friends who could interpret these events for her. She would place a few phone calls with time permitted.

Following this visit would be a whirlwind trip to major cities around the U.S. where the most concentrated Jewish populations were found. She reeled off the cities she would visit in her head: Chicago, Cleveland, Los Angeles, Boston, Miami, Dallas, and others. Dallas held special thoughts in her heart as her family's friendship with the Wassermans went back years. She couldn't wait to see Chaim and Esther and the family.

Her team of advanced scouts learned the inbound and outbound access routes to the airports. They studied all streets, roads, and bridges up to them. Controlling this beast was going to take some real horsepower and organizing.

Well, she thought, *I did learn how to fly a jet, didn't I?* She pulled up a Wiki on her handheld and read about the airport.

JFK was a huge airport receiving more than 50 million visitors every year. It featured four runways, one almost three miles long at 14,000 feet, and was capable of handling the largest aircraft in the world including the short-lived A380, the Wiki said. That airplane had proven a disaster to its manufacturer and after the initial rush to fly it, it had lost major market share. They had built about 200 of the huge aircraft but the market softened and never recovered.

Nearly 100 airlines from 50 countries were running operations from the facility located in the south end of Queens, most of their focus on the more recent newer models of Boeing's 787 and the new sleek blended wing body aircraft called the 'Manta Ray,' for obvious reasons. Though the plane was new, it had already garnered more than 1000 orders and the initial production runs were underway, but not enough of the planes were in service to make a difference.

JFK, was a city in itself! She did some quick calculations and figured out it would take a minimum of 5,000-10,000 troops to take and hold the location and the roads leading up to it. With anticipated help from 'friends' she surmised, they could build enough fire power to handle the challenge. She looked for and quickly found the control tower, taking into account how difficult access to the building would be. She also knew she had computing assets in place that could overcome the tower's software schemes, thus giving her and her teams the control they would need.

She quickly noted potential places to set up protective fields of fire and bunkers where her soldiers could work without fear of return fire, though she knew there was still much risk. She would need help holding the buildings near there not to mention all the other facilities. And so, the scouting of America's airports began.

She zipped a quick email to Ben Yehuda and Michael Shapiro in the Jewish Agency office telling them, in their pre-arranged code, that she was safe on the ground in New York. She sent her upcoming itinerary, again coded in software she designed herself, encrypted it, and sent it along to the planner. Her taxi pulled up and she got in.

She then let out a sigh of relief, for it had been a long flight and it was good to stretch out a little. The driver asked her where she wanted to go... she had forgotten for a moment and then said "the Manhattan Marriott."

For What It's Worth

by Buffalo Springfield—lyrics by Stephen Stills

There's something happening here
What it is ain't exactly clear
There's a man with a gun over there
Telling me I got to beware
I think it's time we stop, children, what's that sound?
Everybody look what's going down
There's battle lines being drawn
Nobody's right if everybody's wrong
Young people speaking their minds
Getting so much resistance from behind
I think it's time we stop, hey, what's that sound?
Everybody look what's going down
What a field-day for the heat
A thousand people in the street
Singing songs and carrying signs
Mostly say, hooray for our side
It's time we stop, hey, what's that sound?
Everybody look what's going down
Paranoia strikes deep
Into your life it will creep
It starts when you're always afraid
You step out of line, the man come and take you away
We better stop, hey, what's that sound?
Everybody look what's going down
Stop, hey, what's that sound?
Everybody look what's going down
Stop, now, what's that sound
Everybody look what's going down
Stop, children, what's that sound?
Everybody look what's going down

Chapter 49

Independence Day

Several weeks had passed since Shoshana's first visit to the States. Her visit was successful. Not only had she scoped out all the airports, she had also met with three of the four corridor commanders.

The Israeli leadership team now possessed detailed information on all major airports, access roads, bridges, streets, and control points. All transportation means were heavily scouted as clear pathways needed to be secured to get the Jews out. All of the intelligence gathered had made its way through analysis and was incorporated into Day 1 operations. The day was coming sooner than then could have imagined.

Jerusalem was quiet too. The American Israelis would not be caught flat-footed. Things remained quiet for now. But they wouldn't be quiet for long.

As the 4th of July, American Independence day, approached, protest organizers across America sped up their plans for the marches. In New York City, all parade permits were in place, speakers' stands were readied for maybe the biggest set of protests America had ever seen. Police expected upwards of 100,000 people in New York alone.

Unknown to the gathering crowd was a sizeable team of Israeli operatives and believing Christians mixed into the crowd. They covered every angle, street, building, block, and landmark. They would not get involved. They were there to watch and report.

The streets sprang alive that morning with festooned buntings of red, white, and blue. American flags fluttered gently in the breeze along the parade route. But that was where this Independence Day was different because this was a celebration of diversity, a very different kind of diversity.

Next to America's Old Glory proudly stood the flags of more than a dozen Islamic nations. Today in New York City, Islamic national flags outnumbered the American flags. Also visible were the green battle flags from Hamas and a variety of green and yellow flags from Hezbollah. Mixed in with those flags were others from every known terror group in the Middle East.

Tables were set up to dispense water and sun block all along the parade route. Parade planners arranged logistics centers with rest spots and tents every few blocks. Signs also popped up along the route from the various groups represented. Police, both on horseback and on foot took up positions along the route. The 'thwack thwack' of helicopter blades was heard overhead. New York City was ready.

The morning dawned grey and humid, with no expectation of rain. The march was set to begin at 9am sharp. Those planning on marching began gathering at 7 am. Local church and mosque parking lots acted as collection zones for the marchers. They unloaded protest-carry signs from trucks brought in from as far away as Connecticut, New Jersey, and Pennsylvania. Banners, signage, flags and all manner of little toy trinkets were pulled from boxes ready to be handed out along the route.

One of the giveaways was a Star of David flag bearing a Nazi swastika. Parade organizers were eager to send a message about Zionist oppression and international Jewish control. They imported more than 100,000 of these from a Chinese manufacturer, ignorant to the meaning of the flag or the symbol, but ecstatic to make the sale. Monies donated by local Muslim and Christian communities paid for the flags. Few really understood where the money came from, but those donating it did. Rachman's tentacles were everywhere.

Religious leaders gathered from all over the city. They included Imams from local mosques, Christian pastors from many ecumenical faiths and even some Rabbis opposed to Zionist rule in Israel. All of them gathered at the starting point to go over the route and then move to Central Park where the march would end and the speeches would start.

It promised to be an historic day as the work of months of planning was about to unfold. Jew, Christian, and Muslim, a true Rainbow—together at last, with the intent to protest Zionism, the greatest threat to world peace.

Marchers streamed in by plane, bus, train, subway, car, and on foot. The crowd grew quickly. More helicopters appeared overhead to track the march and provide another level of security. Children and their parents lined the sidewalks, some holding picket signs, others just out for a nice day in the summertime to see the parade.

Ben Yehuda's teams quietly slipped into place.

The clouds began to part. The steel grey sky was now broken with patches of blue appearing while white clouds formed from the remnants of the grey patches.

The bands lined up, led by an all Black jazz band, decked out in very spiffy uniforms. The first notes reached the early parade watchers.

The city-wide 'Band of the People,' an integrated jazz band prepared to play American patriotic tunes. Other bands from local communities, schools and churches gathered in order of march. Water monitors added paper hats to shield faces and heads from the soon-to-break-through sun.

At 8:55, a horn sounded followed by a bearded man dressed in Middle East garb, with a bullhorn reminding everyone why they were here.

"Today, we take back America! Today, we free ourselves from the racist policies of Israel and Zionist influence! Today, we celebrate an American Holiday but it's really about all men."

"Today, we celebrate Independence Day for our oppressed brothers in Palestine!"

"Death to the Zionist Entity!" the crowd answered.

"Death to Tyranny!"

"Free at last, Free at last! Thank Almighty Allah, We are Free at Last!"

And with that invocation, the march was off.

The marchers moved down the route slowly at first. The front band began playing an old Negro Spiritual called 'People Get Ready, There's a Train-a Comin.' That was followed up by more lively music including many well-known marching numbers. Group by group, the marchers stepped off through the streets.

Meanwhile, in the park, two miles away, final touches were made for the speakers. Coolers with ice-cold water were set by the speakers' podium. Final sound checks were completed and security personnel took up positions on the perimeter and on the podium.

The marchers continued down the street, greeted by cries of love and support from the bystanders.

"Welcome, brothers," shouted one gentleman on the roadside.

He and his family were Palestinians, brought over years before by the Obama administration as a free gift for suffering 'oppression' during the Israeli raid in Gaza back in 2009 and many other incursions since. That sponsored event, announced in the Federal Register one day, was virtually unknown to have even existed. More than $25 million was devoted to bringing them over. Yet, here they were, years later, their children and grandchildren now American citizens.

"Ah, America," one comedian and astute social commentator, used to say, "What a country."

The crowd was an interesting mix with a strong Muslim presence, really the first of its kind in the U.S. Many men and women wore traditional head dresses. The men wore long Kurta shirts, some with embroidery. Others wore colorful items, though many wore just plain white. Many of the women wore hijabs or jilbabs with appropriate head attire as well.

Muslim culture had so penetrated American consciousness that many non-Muslims had adopted the garb. It was multi-cultural and reflected their affinity for diversity. Many thought it just looked cool, not an unknown American response to new trends. Some older members of the contingent remembered when Nehru jackets became fashionable many years before.

CHAPTER FORTY-NINE: *Independence Day*

Nation of Islam (NOI) followers turned out in force for this most important day. More than 10,000 N.O.I. followers of the Prophet pushed off around 9:30 carrying signs denouncing Israel, the Jews, and the Zionist entity and promoting their agenda, virtually all focused on downtrodden conditions of the Black Man in America.

Many carried signs of their dead leader, Louis Farrakhan, now considered a prophet almost akin to Moses or Samuel. The crowd was growing larger by the minute but still no signs of anything out of the ordinary.

Following the Nation of Islam marchers was a crowd of about 100 from the local Al-Aqsa Mosque located in Manhattan. Joining them was Jamal Kareem Ibrahim, the Islamic scholar and this month, a guest lecturer at Al-Aqsa. He was seen deep in animated but friendly conversation with a Christian minister and a rabbi as they compared notes about their respective faiths and holy books.

Behind Nation of Islam members were several church groups, decked out in t-shirts with the slogan, 'Coexist-all of us.' They were joined by the small but very visible Jewish contingent, lead by a member of a Chassidic sect that did not support Israel or Zionism. This group of about 100 Jews believed that until Messiah came, any attempt to construct a Jewish state was a preposterous joke and a waste of time.

They were also joined by other less religious and far more politically active Jews. These Jews had no interest in religion and saw Zionism and Judaism in general an oppressive roadblock to progress of peace between the warring cultures.

They joined to demonstrate what they believed to be a travesty of justice, the oppression of a local native population of Arabs by Jews. They believed the Israelis were taking advantage of the Holocaust, protesting that it was used for political gain by power-hungry leaders. One of their clan was scheduled to address the crowd later that morning.

The crowd turned left after one mile and headed toward Central Park.

Bang!

Bang!

Bang!

Heads turned to see where the shots came from.

Shouts and screams came from the front of the parade. Just then, another volley of shots was heard off to the parade's right.

Police began to react and then the crowd turned unruly. The unrest seemed to move in a wave, backwards from the front of the parade to the back. Shouts turned to screams and then the first window was smashed. Just as suddenly, the police seemed to disappear, withdrawing and pulling away from the developing melee. Helicopters pulled out of their close surveillance and vanished.

What wasn't clear to authorities but was in the game plan of parade organizers all along, was that the first lists of Jewish-owned businesses, generated from the census, had appeared on the internet. The data was supposed to be held close, confidential, and not for any public release.

But parade organizers had downloaded the data as it became available from hackers placed within their ranks, and began to target the businesses, many of which were closed for the holiday. Some however, remained open and then the trouble struck. The first to go was a clothier. The shop was closed but was trashed in no time, the inventory disappearing with the crowd.

The guns were turned indiscriminately on stores aligning the streets. Glass flew through the air, cutting a swath through anyone who got in the way. Twelve lay dead, mostly Jewish shop owners and businessmen, their stores being looted and then torched.

Fires leapt around the shopping district. There was no sign of police or the Fire Department. Some later reported that they saw the police standing around, not trying to hold off the protestors, but instead choosing to join in the crowd's mayhem—some not to engage, or others just walking away. It wasn't clear if they were real police or imposters dressed for the part.

Marchers broke off from the larger crowd. They produced baseball bats and began to break windows and wreck cars. This area of town was heavily Jewish, and the crowd knew it.

What was becoming obvious to bystanders was the planning. The entire disturbance was organized as the rioters moved in a very systematic way. Many who had held rage against Jewish landowners, landlords, or shopkeepers seemed to release all of their anger at once. They dragged shopkeepers into the streets, made them strip in public, and then beat them senseless. The more violent crowd was whipped into a frenzy.

Across the street from the main group was a Jewish deli—it was the next target. Patrons were caught by surprise. Marchers streamed across the street and burst in to the establishment, began busting heads and breaking the deli case glass, while reaching in and stealing the packaged food. When patrons tried to run out they were beaten with the baseball bats.

The rioters began shouting ugly comments such as "Back to the ovens with you," and "Death to Israel and Death to the Jews!"

Many of the restaurant's customers were caught inside and as they tried to escape the swinging bats and tire irons, the rush for the door and safety causing a pileup and then a full-fledged stampede.

Seventy five restaurant customers died that day along with 100 more injured. But more, they heard curses screamed at them by the angry crowd. The restaurant burned to the ground but not before looters cleaned out the stock of the restaurant, robbed the till, and took all they could carry.

CHAPTER FORTY-NINE: *Independence Day*   Page 265

America now joined Europe in the history books.

The next targets were small cafes and pushcarts on the street. Assuming just about everyone was Jewish the mob smelled blood and went after the street vendors as well as the eating establishments.

As the mob closed in on her, one pushcart owner, a Jewish woman recently arrived from Egypt, begged for her life, pleading in Arabic to those who she thought were Arabic speakers.

She was right, for she had heard Arabic spoken, lots of it in fact. When they answered her in that language, "Die you filthy daughter of swine!" they overturned her pushcart, knocked her unconscious and then shot her in the back of the head. The rioters then stole her food and passed it around to others in the crowd. How they knew she was Jewish was unknown.

The mob spotted some Orthodox Jewish women with children. They chased after, overtook, and then beat them. One man pulled out a gun and shot some of their children before the mothers' eyes. A mother stood, screamed, and scratched at the man. But another came up with a knife and slashed her throat.

Just then, as bad as this was, the almost unthinkable happened further down the street. With gunmen now roaming throughout the area, a bookstore loomed large in front of them. And so it was— a Jewish bookstore crammed with books, religious items, with a large gift shop attached.

The crowd broke the windows, and then in a repeat of an event so hideous to the Jewish experience from some 90 or so years earlier, the rioters began pulling the books off the shelves and carried them from the store. Then, creating a huge pile in the street, someone poured gasoline on the pile, and ignited the books. More and more of them poured into the store, carrying out volumes of Bible commentaries, copies of the Talmud and many Bibles.

The crowd returned to dark ages' practice of book burning. It recalled an old weapon against the 'People of the Book' begun by the French King, Louis IX in 1240. After the 'Disputation of Paris,' he ordered the burning of the Talmud. This began a tradition of sorts, followed by the burning of 24 cartloads of Jewish holy books in 1242.

And in succession, popes would advocate more of the same. Pope Julian III, in 1552 had the Talmud burned publicly in Rome. These were followed by more public burnings in Italy and Spain. And of course, there were the book burnings by the Nazis in 1938, in the city of Nuremburg, maybe the most famous book burning of all.

As the crowd surrounded the burning pile of books, one of the Chassidic marchers turned the corner as he was still in the part of the crowd that hadn't seen the destruction just yet. He stopped, saw the books burned, and felt a fist pound into his face.

The stunned Rabbi turned to see his assailant—a young man in a *Co-Exist* t-shirt. He searched his eyes and asked, "Why? What are you doing? We are marching against the same thing!"

Without a word, the young man hit the rabbi again, this time knocking him to the ground. And then, as if demonically driven, the young Christian screamed at the rabbi. "This is what you get when you destroy the New Testament, you Christ Killer!!"

He was referring to an incident he had read about that had occurred in Israel years before, a 'fairly large' number of New Testaments were burned in Or Yehuda, Israel by some Orthodox Jews.

Information of this very strange book burning was sketchy and debated. One story, published in an online Wiki, had the deputy mayor of Or Yehuda (of the ultra-religious party), claiming to have organized the burnings.

Another account said he was trying to stop them. The mayor later admitted involvement in collecting New Testaments and 'Messianic propaganda' that had been distributed in the city. If true, the burning violated Israeli laws about destroying religious items.

However, the ugly beast had reared its head once again, but this time in America.

And then it was over, as he kicked the old rabbi in the head, killing him and leaving him for dead in the street. The rabbi's final thought was '*where did we go wrong, how come we didn't see this coming?*'

How right he was, for at that moment, the other Jewish marchers were attacked in unison by the crazy horde. Of the 100 Jewish marchers, 30 would fall dead as a result of the attacks, many more would be injured, but all the Jewish survivors realized, at that moment, that Zionism wasn't the problem and that now, they had an entirely different issue on their hands. Hundreds more Jews were either dead in the street or badly injured in stores and restaurants. Their 'friends' had turned on them.

What business establishments not touched that day were attacked in another way—huge yellow Stars of David stickers were placed on those storefront windows with the words, 'Jew-owned-Avoid Shopping Here,' while other stores received graffiti and paint. The signs were posted in English, Arabic, and Farsi. Spray cans and marking pens finished the work that the stickers started. What at the time looked like a completely spontaneous eruption of anger had been planned the entire time.

Meanwhile a few streets over in Manhattan, another mob that had broken off from the main one, closed in on a Jewish summer day school. Wielding bats, tire irons, and other heavy objects, they began wading through the crowd. Shots rang out and several children and their teachers fell dead in the courtyard.

CHAPTER FORTY-NINE: Independence Day

This was to be the case all day in New York, businesses, restaurants, large and small, were attacked, hundreds killed, and Jews chased from their businesses, dragged into the streets, and brutally beaten or killed.

Later that morning the crowds disbursed. There were no speeches in the great park that day. Word hit the media within minutes. And Ben Yehuda's teams watched. Their time was not yet.

It was, to some, a complete replay of Kristallnacht in 1938 Germany and to others the end of the mutually beneficial relationship with America. When analysts linked the two events together, all speculation went out the window... these were deliberate and planned.

The day was ending in Israel as word came across the wires that *planned and coordinated attacks* against Jewish targets were underway in America. Videos of the day's events went viral as soon as they were posted on social networking sites.

That night, a sermon was delivered in a New York mosque, two blocks from the day's events. Jamal Kareem Ibraham, the brilliant Muslim scholar was the guest Imam and what he had to say would rock the city and the world for months afterwards because it was being broadcast on not only Al Jezeera but over the internet as well. The speech would go viral within minutes and reach more than one billion people that night and the next day. Radical Islam was gaining confidence and momentum by the hour.

"Friends, what we have witnessed today," he began in his native Arabic tongue, "is the beginning of the end of the Zionist entity. That there was a small disturbance in the streets of New York speaks to the fact that the people of God have spoken. Our fighters rose up against the Jews who started it, with one voice and two fists today to teach the infidels a lesson. For we know that in the Holy Quran, it says that there is no God but Allah and Mohammed is His Prophet. The Jews deny this, the Christian Zionists deny this, but we know it is the truth!! Our arms are long and we will fight!"

The speech went on, mostly rhetoric and spoken brilliantly, for Ibraham was a gifted and eloquent speaker. Muslims the world over would now rise up against the remnant of the Jewish beast within and make their voices and actions heard.

Those fortunate enough to escape also recalled another strange phenomenon... tens of thousands of feathers floating down during the disturbance—a pogrom had come to America's shores, just the same as their ancestors had withstood generations before in Europe, in Africa, and in the Middle East.

When news of the disturbances reached Israeli leaders, the threat level was raised to red.

The great majority of American churches remained silent.

From the Hamas Charter
Article 7

The Islamic Resistance Movement is one of the links in the chain of the struggle against the Zionist invaders. It goes back to 1939, to the emergence of the martyr Izz al-Din al Kissam and his brethren the fighters, members of Muslim Brotherhood. It goes on to reach out and become one with another chain that includes the struggle of the Palestinians and Muslim Brotherhood in the 1948 war and the Jihad operations of the Muslim Brotherhood in 1968 and after.

Moreover, if the links have been distant from each other and if obstacles, placed by those who are the lackeys of Zionism in the way of the fighters obstructed the continuation of the struggle, the Islamic Resistance Movement aspires to the realization of Allah's promise, no matter how long that should take. The Prophet, Allah bless him and grant him salvation, has said:

> The Day of Judgment will not come about until Muslims fight the Jews (killing the Jews), when the Jew will hide behind stones and trees. The stones and trees will say O Muslims, O Abdulla, there is a Jew behind me, come and kill him. Only the Gharkad tree, would not do that because it is one of the trees of the Jews.

Chapter 50

Team 3 Moves

The following Shabbat after Independence Day broke warm as the sun began its slow climb into the Dallas morning sky. Although the demonstrations in the East and throughout the Midwest had targeted the streets and shopping districts, and a few Jewish schools, Chaim Wasserman and his congregation were preparing for a Bar Mitzvah, not bowing to threats to the Jewish communities. There was no guard outside his synagogue for his community had always remained tolerant and no threat existed as far as they could tell.

Team 3, as all of Rachman's attack teams were structured, was a team of five well-trained, experienced, and ruthless killers. Mahmoud Salim, a native born Saudi, led the team. Salim, a short, squat and intense looking fellow, possessed a strong background in Islamic theology or Sharia Law. He was trained in action in Afghanistan, The Philippines, and Palestine where he joined his fellow freedom fighters in actions against the Zionist oppressors. He had tasted his share of American blood as well. Among his talents was explosives handling, especially the use of C4. He was also a skilled shot and very experienced in small arms handling. He also loved to hunt with bow and arrow.

The C4, or plastique had found its way into the US through the porous Mexican borders using the skills of the 'coyotes', or special agents who smuggled people and materials into the U.S., using a panoply of adventurers, desperados, and poor families just trying to make ends meet. They were commonly known as mules.

The material is compact and deadly. It began journey to Mexico through an intricate network of international contacts that began in Pakistan with Taliban rebels. The Taliban, slowly regaining ground after initial losses to U.S. troops back in the early days of the new century, was back and as strong as ever. It had taken them close to 30 years for the full recovery as American and Coalition forces had from time to time reengaged the fight and suppressed them for a season.

After it was manufactured and packaged in the hill country, it was then carried by mules in Afghanistan through the mountain passes to warm water ports of the Persian Gulf. Next, they were met by clandestine ships, some pirate-controlled. For a price smugglers hauled the material, now well-hidden within other exports of pottery, coffee, religious icons, and bolts of fabric, plus hundreds of other commodities.

After the ocean voyage, the C4 moved overland through Mexico and was met by the network of terror agents. Next, it crossed the borders of California, Arizona, and Texas. Agents received the goods and made proper epayments. The mules, if they were lucky, were allowed to live after delivery. Sometimes, if things got hot, they would not make it across the borders. Many a shallow grave had been discovered along the borders over the years, the victims shot in the back of the head, and left for dead in those graves. Their families would be left to guess their fate.

Team 3, three men and two women, quietly slipped from their rooms that morning. Sweeper teams on the hotel staff followed within minutes of the team's departure to clean the room, removing all evidence of fingerprints, food wrappers, soap residues, sheets, towels, trash, in short any DNA. The sweeper teams were at work in each of the long-term stay hotels where the 10 strike teams had taken up residence.

They swapped cars and clothes, giving themselves a very different look that morning. In Dallas, the five terrorists dressed in appropriate Saturday morning Sabbath attire, their advance team having gathered local intelligence as to what clothes would blend in best. The men wore conservative business suits, the women wearing professional knits, each with a long skirt and moderately fashionable boots, offering the ability to hide what they could beneath them. No team member wore any jewelry or anything that could possibly distinguish them. The men adjusted their small kippas (head coverings) and the women their head scarves, all a part of the disguises, planned and arranged years ago on the desert floor in Afghanistan.

Team 3, as all teams were in the process of doing that morning, double checked their small machine guns, reviewed entry and exit plans. They reviewed back up plans, with secondary targets, and went over the synagogue's proposed morning service. This day was picked because all of the synagogues on the hit list had either a Bar or Bat Mitzvah planned thus, making the targets that much more "meaningful." They calculated that the difference in time zones wouldn't have much effect on the operation. Killing women and children wasn't an issue because these were all infidels anyway. Who would care?

A brilliant, sunny day, warming by the minute, greeted the hit team as it slowly pulled out of the parking lot. The secondary sniper team began taking up their positions across the street in high rise office buildings, in smaller business parks, and rooftops, adjacent to the facility.

There was virtually no discussion as the black Lincoln pulled into traffic. Thoughts of the action at hand gripped each team member, thoughts of only what lay ahead on their minds, so powerful was the inculcated training of Rachman's two years with them.

They were closely followed by another vehicle, assigned with the responsibility to move the car when its inhabitants began their walk to the site. The car would then be driven to a local 'chopshop,' dismantled by other members of the terror network, parts broken out, boxed, and sent to Mexico for sale, again leaving no trace of the vehicle, all evidence effectively and permanently destroyed. Teams had gotten the breakdowns down to a science and could dismantle a vehicle within 20 minutes.

A third car sat just blocks away ready to move behind the synagogue as the getaway vehicle. They had rehearsed the scenario dozens of times, every detail open to scrutiny and improvement. Not a detail was left to chance.

They moved through the neighborhood next to a business park. The Lincoln moved through traffic—no rush. They had built plenty of time in the morning's routine.

It was 9:30 a.m.

The harsh morning sun assaulted Salim's eyes as he drove eastbound on the surface streets, but was mostly blocked by his sunglasses and the visor he pulled down. Within two blocks of the target, he turned into another neighborhood adjacent to a business park.

This neighborhood of upscale housing featured three-car garages, nicely kept lawns, and lots of SUV's, a park with children's' swings, jungle gyms, and a dog walking park. Four dog owners were out walking their animals, chatting with one another on this most beautiful Saturday morning. None of them would remember a black Lincoln that morning, when questioned by police.

The terror team found the agreed parking area, away from the dog park and people. Next to the park and near another business park, closer to the target, Salim pulled alongside of the curb and parked the vehicle. Moments later, the car following Salim's disgorged a passenger who slipped into Team 3's Lincoln and pulled back out into traffic. That car would be dismantled within the hour, no trace of it left behind.

It was 9:45.

Each team member went through their mental checklists. Salim's cell phone buzzed. He pulled it out from his suit pocket.

"All clear," the disembodied voice said.

The advance scouting operation had placed two men across from the target with binoculars trained on the front entrance. The 'all clear' indicated nothing out of the ordinary on this Jewish Sabbath. People were arriving in just the order they expected, and the scouts could even, if pressed, name most of those coming in to the synagogue.

The temperature climbed to 75, nice now, but with the promise of rising higher as the day went on. Unknown to Team 3, was that the very same thing was happening in nine other American cities at virtually that same moment.

Salim and his team double-checked weapons and the small packages of explosives wrapped as presents for the Bar Mitzvah boy. There was no discussion. They crossed the street. They stepped on the sidewalk, turned left, walked past the strip mall, and entered the synagogue grounds. The getaway car appeared at a fast food restaurant across the street from the site. The driver caught sight of the team of five, though they didn't see him. Most of the moving parts were in motion.

It was 9:50

They approached the synagogue, still no interruptions, every small detail working exactly according to plan. They walked through the parking lot, mostly empty but were now joined by dozens of congregants, each nodding 'good Shabbos' greetings to one another. Little boys held onto their father's hands, the little girls, their mothers.

Some of the young teens, friends of the Bar Mitzvah, now entered the building. The five of them exchanged discrete glances. They entered the social hall and turned left into the sanctuary. They surveyed the room with a glance. The Bar Mitzvah of Stevie Goldman would start in a few moments. The five members of Team 3 took their seats. They were scattered throughout the synagogue, their packages on the floor beside them.

It was 9:55

Time seemed to slow down and speed up at the same moment. The Bar Mitzvah boy, his father, Rabbi Wasserman, and the cantor all entered the main sanctuary then, through a side door. They took their places on the podium as the rest of the congregation found seats waiting for the ceremony.

The Bar Mitzvah is an old observance meaning 'Son of the Commandment' for a boy and Bat Mitzvah, or 'Daughter of the Commandment' for a girl. Generally, though not always, the rite is performed at age 13. Some Jewish traditions make it 12 for girls but as a general rule, it's 13.

Stevie Goldman had worked hard to prepare for this day. He studied with the rabbi then took home a specially prepared compact disc to listen to the cantor's chants and learn his pieces. He faithfully practiced his portion from the Book of Numbers, Chapter 25. It was 10:20

The chapters described the zealousness of the priest Pinchas (Phineas) and how he killed a man of Israel for leading many within the camp astray and praying to the false god, Baal-Peor. He would also read from the prophets. Today's Haf'Torah portion was from the Book of Jeremiah and how He, God, had known the prophet from the womb. The service began.

The buzz of conversation began to settle down as the Rabbi rose and greeted the congregation. "Friends and guests, we welcome you in the Name of the Lord," he said. He performed the perfunctory prayers and liturgy—it was now time for the Bar Mitzvah to begin.

Rabbi Wasserman then described what the congregation would see, how the day would go. At that time, he called the first of the Torah readers, and one by one, each read their portion when, at last, Stevie's time came.

He stepped to the podium and kissing the fringes of his tallit (the prayer shawl), then to the Torah scroll rolled out before him, he began the ancient prayers...

"Barachu et Adonai, ha'mevorah."

The congregation responded with "Baruch Adonai ha'mevorah L'olam Va'ed."

He finished the opening prayer and then began to chant his Torah portion.

At that moment, time stood still. The five terrorists all stood up at the signal from Salim, their leader, "Allahu Akhbar!" (Allah is Greater) he screamed. It was 10:40.

Suddenly, there was commotion in five different areas of the synagogue. The few survivors would later recount that they saw at least three and maybe more shooters around the room. Each of the terrorists drew their weapons and began shooting, laying down a field of fire in the designated areas they had been trained to find. Bullets tore through the crowd, shouts and screams filled the sanctuary.

Rabbi Wasserman immediately threw Stevie down and covered him with his body. Stevie's father took three bullets through the chest and fell dead at the podium. Chaim took two bullets to his right leg, otherwise, he was unscathed. The Bar Mitzvah boy was shot too, and writhed in pain, shot in the shoulder and leg but remained alert while he watched everything around him. Blood and brain matter flew through the synagogue as congregants desperately scrambled for cover.

Salim's aim was a little high and his gun's ammunition took out some lights above the podium. Glass from the lights flew through the air. The two women turned slightly and aimed for the women's section, remaining calm, efficient, and devoid of emotion. The women sat too stunned to react and most fell at their positions as the bullets ripped through the pews and the congregants.

Esther, her instincts kicking in, pulled two women to the floor and lay on top of them to offer what protection she could. Although in her 70's she was still very agile, her lifelong athletic prowess paying dividends right now. Bullets pinged off the walls sending sharp shards of wood, stone, and glass through the sanctuary. At that moment, and out of view, the getaway car pulled up to the back of the synagogue, next to the door of their escape. It was 10:50.

The other two members of the team then reloaded and leveled their small portable weapons on the children's section. The kids never had a chance.

More than two hundred rounds had been fired by the terrorists. It was time to move. Salim looked around and signaled for the team to find the door and get out. The damage done, they squeezed off a few more shots as bodies moved, then fell still. No one moved now. It was 10:55.

The terror team members, stepping over bodies strewn throughout the sanctuary, made for the back door, found the car's doors open, and hopped in. The driver hit the gas and the SUV disappeared down the side alley, turned right and then disappeared into traffic. Within minutes they found the safe house. The driver drove into the open garage, the door closed, and within minutes the car was dismantled and broken down into parts. It was 10:18. There was nobody on the street to report anything amiss.

Someone in the congregation, sensing the shooting was over, peeked around a pew and noticed no further movement. Though badly wounded himself, he dialed 911. Within minutes, the sirens could be heard. The caller perished moments later, cell phone in his bloody hand, still on.

Two minutes later, with fire personnel and paramedics arriving, the five "presents" (smuggled over the Mexican border) exploded, sending a massive fireball up towards the ceiling. The ceiling tiles fell first with a tumult of wood furniture, carpeting, drywall materials, everything in one seemingly instantaneous flash. The bombs, laden with screws, nails, and sharp metal flew through the air as tiny missiles. What the guns didn't take with them, the shrapnel would.

When the rescue teams backed away from the explosions, the waiting snipers, all former military trained, began their deadly work... and one by one they picked off paramedics, fire and police personnel as they tried to minister to the dying and wounded.

Someone got off another 911 call, screaming, "Fireman and paramedics down, we are under attack!"

One of the survivors recalled later that the shots had come from out of nowhere, seemingly behind them. He was right, for the attackers had taken up positions in nearby office buildings and small offices next to and across the street from the synagogue.

Islamic justice had arrived in Middle America. Once the rescue personnel stopped moving, the support team snipers withdrew. The shooters left no indication of their whereabouts, gone without a trace. It was 10:25.

Team 3 was done. 175 dead—57 wounded. At the safe house they changed clothes, the women dyed their hair, and the men shaved their beards. They would now lay low for 24 hours and then move to the next step in their journey. Within 72 hours they would be out of the country vanishing into thin air, travelling on falsified American passports.

When the second rescue team arrived, the SWAT team joined them and took up positions in all buildings and shopping areas across from the synagogue. Since the shooters had cleaned up all traces of their attack, no physical evidence remained.

Both City fire and police came to sift through the rubble in the synagogue. But now, all was calm and quiet. The secondary team had withdrawn and vanished as had Team 3. The sun hung in the sky as the temperature reached its zenith that day. It was 90 degrees and everyone was sweating.

Against all odds, both Esther and Chaim would survive the attack. All pretenses of the Goldena Medina were no more. This was war and both of them knew it.

The paramedics found both of them under the rubble. Fire crews were able to contain the flames fairly quickly. Chaim was shot twice but not in imminent danger, looked at his wife of so many years and smiled. Esther was a little more ambulatory and walked alongside the gurney, still shaking off dust and debris as they took Chaim to the waiting ambulance.

She was covered in blood, both Chaim's and those women she was near. She took his hand and together they were loaded into the back of the vehicle. Chaim, calming now, then asked about the survivors, and when told that the Bar Mitzvah boy had made it through, he began reciting the Shema and offering thanks to God. Fifty-seven survivors would recount the terror that terrible day. The rest, who knew where they had gone?

The operation's impact and the sheer magnitude of it hadn't hit the teams until the news break on CNN 30 minutes later.

"We're getting reports of a synagogue shooting and bombing in Dallas," the announcer said. Then all hell broke loose as the reports began coming in faster than the reporter could get them in.

"There seems to be some sort of a pattern here. We're now hearing Chicago, Miami, Philadelphia, and Cleveland have all experienced attacks—near the same time.

"The first reports from Dallas indicate that there were multiple shooters. It may be that more than 100 people are dead." The reporter put his hand up to his face. He was caught up in the moment. "Oh, my God, those poor people. This is a pogrom!"

Within moments, the full brunt of the news hit the electronic media about the synagogue shootings as well. The news spread like wildfire and to many it looked as if a Jihad had been declared on the Jews of America. Between the synagogue attacks and the parade damage in New York and elsewhere, thousands of Jews lay dead, their property devastated.

Within minutes, social networking website amateurs would post videos of the day's aftermath. The videos of the synagogue massacres went viral within minutes. By the end of the day, hits on those videos would number more than a billion, and growing, largely outside of the U.S. as Muslims around the world celebrated their victories.

Unknown to the watchers around the world, but known to Rachman and his lieutenants, many of these videos were shot and posted by still other members of the killing squads, though disguised as passersby and locals. Rachman and his team sat dumbfounded as the reports began to trickle and then rush into CNN and other international news services.

More reports came in from New York, where more than 200 were reported dead, wounded, or missing. And then, there was Boston, Washington D.C., Chicago, Miami, and all the other cities he targeted. The stories were all the same. So profound was his success that he wasn't able to react at first. He was pleased to spill so much Jewish blood but was humbled by the perfect execution of his killing squads.

The Jihad was now in full effect in America, the Hamas Charter and Palestinian Manifesto well represented and being fulfilled in his day. The Independence Day parades set the stage but the synagogue massacres were icing on the cake. Rachman now believed that Jews had nowhere to hide and he would continue his war on them. He could reach them anytime and anywhere. He awaited the American response but knew they had no capability to hit him, insulated as he was in the desert.

Next to 911, it would be the worst day of terror perpetrated by a foreign enemy in American history, because, at that very moment, the full extent of the coordinated attacks was finally becoming known. Over the next few days, there would be dozens of synagogues in all, including the six in the Midwest and 4 in the East hit directly by Rachman's teams. The others were also destroyed by the marauding bands in a different fashion but with the same deadly impact.

And behind all of it was the silent, dark, sinister hand. The enemy had struck against largely unprotected targets, civilians, with no way to defend themselves. Civilian targets always made the press and were the best way to broadcast your message.

The authorities would not be able to give an account for weeks afterwards, but it was estimated that more than 2,000 Jews had paid the ultimate price that day between the shootings, explosions, and the secondary sniper teams laying in wait to pick off survivors. As far as Jewish history was concerned, it was the bloodiest day since the Holocaust in WWII... and for what, because they were Jews?

And thousands of Palestinians in Judea and Samaria, also known as the West Bank, danced in the streets. They danced in Tehran, in Damascus, in Bagdad, in Ankara, and in all the main capitals in Europe. They danced all over the Middle East, as far away as Indonesia. Children handed out candy and masked and hooded Jihadists fired their automatic weapons into the air and screamed for more Jewish blood. Allah had brought the Jews to their knees.

In Jewish circles, this day would now be known as 'the Black Sabbath and the Second Kristallnacht.' In Islamic circles, it would be known as the 'Day of our Revenge.'

And in Israel, when the news hit the wires and the internet, millions of Israeli Jews knew what was coming next.

Although sympathy was heard after the synagogue massacres, demonstrations and parades, the 'good feelings' were short-lived and international opinions quickly turned against the Jews once again. Islamo-Christian rhetoric reached back even more to paint the Zionists as the last obstacle to peace.

Cartoons appeared in the Islamic press showing rabid Jewish dogs being pursued by children with sticks and rocks in their hands saying, 'Run Jew, Run,' the analogy of the old Dick and Jane reading series not lost on those who understood such things.

Across America and in the rest of the world, most Christian churches remained silent on the matter. Some church leaders were appalled and said so, but there was no sustained outcry. It simply didn't matter to them. It was a Jewish problem, not a Christian one.

However, some church leaders sympathetic to the plight of the Palestinians and their pursuit of nationhood, remarked that the Jewish policy in the Holy Land had finally come back to bite them. It was because of the Zionist oppression that things like this could happen and they called on all sides for calm and a return to the negotiating table.

The long running third Intifada was now enjoined by many Christians in the Holy Land. The attacks in America gave it new life. It gained strength from the distant violence.

Israel had learned to manage that violence, mostly focused in and around Israel. Stone throwing youth, fueled by visions of the 72 virgins in Islamic lore, sacrificed their lives to a more modern day Moloch. Parents trained their young sons and daughters to strap on the bomb vests or blatantly challenge Israeli policemen or soldiers in the streets, at the checkpoints, anywhere really, daring them to shoot the perceived unarmed youth. It was the terrorists' way. A life sacrificed in this manner never failed to garner a biased, one-way news story, always subtly or blatantly blaming Israel for the violence.

Over time, these attacks captured the romantic imaginations of the global population. These kinds of activities were cast by Islamic sympathizers as the new David fighting the bigger, meaner, more powerful Goliath. And, through it all, the Israelis and international Jewry became the Devil incarnate, with nowhere to turn.

Once-friendly governments kicked out their diplomats, barred university professors and researchers from academic and professional conferences, boycotted Israeli products and sports teams, all in an attempt to isolate the Jews.

Sadly, this fever infected world opinion, casting Israel as a pariah nation and Jews living abroad as unwanted citizens of any nation in which they lived. It wasn't a surprise, then, when the Islamic bloc of the United Nations decided to act. They had the momentum going in their favor. Now was the time to strike. It was time to force the world's hand.

After months and months of debates, committee meetings, accusations, and negotiations a forced vote was imminent. The first General Assembly had sat in these very chambers more than 80 years prior to listen, discuss, and vote on partition, in effect dividing up the Land of Israel into a Jewish zone and a non-Jewish zone.

"Mister Secretary-General, we the undersigned, move today, to label Israel an outlaw nation from the world's community," read the U.N. Representative from Iran, Yusef Muhammad.

"We do not make this accusation lightly, but over the past 80 years or so, this nation has usurped land from those living there from time immemorial. People have lived in this land in peace but with the Jewish intruders, it has become a police state, unfriendly to all unless you are *Jewish*," he said, almost spitting out the last word.

The Israeli diplomat sat stunned. He thought, *thousands of Jews killed on the streets of America by Islamist forces, and now this?* This was a body of international diplomats. There were rules, some spoken, some not, but there was always an expected decorum which the Iranian official seemed to ignore completely.

"Our Palestinian brothers and sisters are ready to accept their nationhood. They have accepted Zionist humiliation long enough. They have a long and distinguished culture, promoting peace and brotherhood," he continued.

CHAPTER FIFTY: Team 3 Moves

The Israeli representative calmly removed his headphones and placed them down on the table in front of him. He didn't know what to do. If he sat and listened, it was an invitation to more humiliation. If he bolted, then he was no better than his antagonists were. He looked around the chamber and noticed that all the Islamic nations' representatives were smiling. The American representative looked down and away, refusing to acknowledge the Israeli.

"It is now time to banish them as the outlaws they are! This body represents the best of humanity. However, with a nation of lawbreakers, deaf to international law and dictates, it is now time for United Nations to do what is right. We demand that Israel be removed from its status as a nation and a member of this body!"

Cheers broke out all over the floor and in gallery where hundreds watched the proceedings. Chants rose in the chambers. All eyes fell on the Israeli diplomat.

At least a minute ticked by and then the Israeli stood up, turned and stared at the Iranian ambassador.

"Mr. Ambassador," he began, in a formal Farsi, for he was fluent in that tongue, "forums such as these demand that the speakers and attendees treat one another with the diplomatic respect that they have earned. I so choose to do that now." The Iranian's eyes grew big for he had no idea his adversary could understand his mother tongue. The Israeli's voice remained calm, even, and measured.

"Sir, I will not be baited into a discussion where opinions and rumor substitute for facts and history. I will not be dragged into hate for I understand what the world has become. I could recite for this body a long litany of the treatment of my people for the past centuries, culminating in recent events with the deaths of thousands more at the hands of your friends. I could recite the thousands, even the tens of thousands of Muslim on Muslim deaths at the hands of your fellow Muslims, but I will not. However, I will not tolerate the insult to my people, my Government, and the God I serve. You have now brought the curse of a curse in kind on yourself and on your houses. I shall pray for your souls."

The body sat silent as the Israeli gathered up his notes and walked slowly to the exit, leaving the remainder of the UN wondering what he meant. They would soon find out.

Coffee House Chatter

"So, believe me now?" she asked.

"Well, it's pretty convincing, I have to admit," he answered.

"Remember when we talked a while back about having your passport ready for any eventuality?" she asked.

"Yep, I do. What's your point?"

"So, did you get it yet?"

"Well, I did get the paperwork from the Post Office but I haven't filled it out yet," he said.

"What are you waiting for?" she asked.

"Well, perhaps things will get better, maybe this is just a blip," he said.

"A blip? Thousands dead in the streets and you call it a blip?" She was speechless.

Chapter 51

Chaim in the Hospital

Chaim's eyes popped open and he looked around for a moment. In the distance he heard the mournful wale of a train whistle.

Slow freight, he thought. He could hear the faint sound of the train's wheels as they click-clacked on the tracks. The whistles continued off and on for a few minutes.

There must be more than 100 cars in that train, Chaim thought. He counted them one by one. Somehow it reminded him of a Willie Nelson song. Country music was something he loved almost as much as he loved his Klezmer. It seemed that all the great musicians had a train song.

He was in the hospital, recovering from surgery where, just a few hours before, surgeons removed the bullets from his legs and stitched up his wounds suffered from flying glass from the explosives. He was sedated, yet clear at the same time.

What's Eleazer doing? Had Esther called him yet? Esther, where was she? He felt panic and felt his heart begin to race. He could feel the pain his wounds, but they weren't too bad. *Manageable,* he thought.

What seemed like visions of the future came into view as well and, though he tried putting them out of his mind, he couldn't do it.

He began recounting the day's events, then the terrible awakening of the moment of the attacks, and then the subsequent explosions. But he was somewhat cheered by the knowledge that the Bar Mitzvah boy had pulled through, shot twice but would survive. Where is he, he wondered? It all happened so fast.

Later he learned of the follow up attacks by the snipers. That hit him even harder than the initial attacks. The terrorists were laying in wait for their rescuers, something so repugnant to humankind, but something he now realized was the way things were. Hitting the weak... reminded him of the sin of Amalek when he attacked the stragglers. Any sense of tolerance for other religions, namely Islam had gone out the window.

Yes, HaShem said love one another and treat the stranger well. But that assumed that the stranger among you desired to live within your borders, join himself to your people, coexist with you in peace, and live by the term of the Tenach.

In ancient Israel, he recalled, that meant the stranger would live under your laws and join himself to your God and your people, even enduring the circumcision rite to participate in the Pesach (Passover). Many in Judaism considered Passover the holiest time of the year. The Bible certainly did. He thought of the 'Righteous Gentiles' throughout Jewish history, of the Schindlers, the Wallenbergs, and the Danes and so many more. How he longed to love others but when something like this happens, sometimes it is simply time to fight.

There was order to the universe, not THIS.

Now in his 70's, Chaim looked forward to his retirement, to teach, study, write, travel a little, and enjoy his lifelong bride, the wild redheaded Esther, who it seemed to him hadn't aged a day since he met her. Those plans, he now realized, were a distant memory. h—He still had work to do. At that moment, Esther poked her head in the door.

"Nu?", she asked.

She stepped over to the bed and kissed him gently on the lips, lingering slightly, and then bused his forehead. Esther pulled up a chair, and sat down next to him. Her red hair was disheveled and she still had blood on her clothes, but didn't want to leave Chaim's side until she was certain he was ok.

Look at her, how beautiful she looks, even like this, he thought.

She told him that "friends" had heard about the attacks and some of Dallas' finest were standing guard around the hospital and just outside his room. He was thankful for that and somewhere in the back of his mind a repugnant thought cropped up... he needed a gun now. He shivered.

She then slowly and methodically described all she had learned that day while he was in surgery. She told him of the carnage, not only in Dallas but all throughout the Midwest and the East. He stiffened at the news. She told him of the more than 2000 Jewish deaths and untold wounded. She told him that the Bar Mitzvah boy remembered everything and had given descriptions to the police, and how brave he was. He could only shake his head and wipe a tear from his eye. The world was changing around him, all at once. Thankfully he still had his bride beside him.

"Did you know that Jonathan Roberts called and offered help?"

When he shook his head, she told him that Roberts had contacted her personally and told her not to worry, that he would do whatever it took to protect his friend and the family. Roberts had made arrangements with friends of his in local law enforcement and that they had set up taking turns providing around the clock care until the rabbi recovered. That accounted, at least in part, for the stepped up police presence.

"He wants to come here to see you tomorrow," she said, eyebrows arched.

CHAPTER FIFTY-ONE: Chaim in the Hospital

He nodded his head and said, "He's a good man." And in fact, Roberts needed some time with Chaim. Chaim thought for a moment and then looked at his wife.

"I'm strong enough to see him... tell him to come as soon as he can, if he can make it," he said.

Chaim had known Roberts for years and had attended his and friend Aryeh Cohen's conferences, often speaking from the Jewish perspective to Christian audiences at Prophecy conferences. Roberts had, at his disposal, a private Gulfstream jet which was provided on as needed basis by one of his sponsors and friends. Esther dialed Roberts' phone number and got his personal assistant on the line.

"Hi, this is Esther Wasserman returning Pastor Roberts' call. I'd like to let the pastor know the Rabbi wants to see him," she said.

Weary by now, Esther nodded as the voice at the other end of the phone went over the details. She pulled out a notepad she always carried with her and jotted down a few items from the discussion. The voice at the other end was sympathetic and asked after the Rabbi's condition. Esther assured the woman that he was pretty well busted up but holding his own. And, yes, he was strong enough for a visit from Roberts.

"Eleazer also called as soon as he heard. For some reason there was no action in his neck of the woods, but everyone is watching now. They've posted 24 hour guards at his shul (synagogue). Many of the guards are Messianics and Christian Zionists. He wants to see you too."

The division and enmity between the Messianic Jewish Believers and the Orthodox didn't seem so important anymore. Both of them wondered what had happened to those Jews during the last World War who had trusted Yeshua (or Jesus) as the Jewish Messiah. Rumors persisted for years about large and robust Hebrew Christian congregations made up entirely of Jewish citizens of their respective nations. They had always treated the meshumeds (traitors) as Christians—no longer Jews. Now, he wasn't so sure that was right. A softening was coming over him and he couldn't explain it. He knew in his heart that Jews couldn't become anything else. They were still Jews even if....

Some sources numbered these Jews in the hundreds of thousands while others counted even more. Why that story wasn't known, or more importantly, understood and respected by the Christians or the Jews was another mystery. Long dormant research material began reaching those interested in connecting the different generations.

It was an uncomfortable piece of history that neither the Christians nor the Jews wanted surfaced. For now, the Jewish Believers and the Christian Zionists were pulling alongside the more traditional Jewish congregations as a show of solidarity, love, and unquestioned support. For the first time she could recall, the Orthodox Jews and Christians were working closely together in a common cause. Even allowing the Messianic Jews near to help was a statement in itself. Chaim acknowledged this with a nod of his head.

"Eleazer and I have a lot to catch up on," he said.

"You know, I was thinking, you and I might need to talk this through with him and Rifka. Remember those crazy dreams of ours? I think I know what they were about," he croaked, his throat growing dry.

She scooted her chair closer and reached out for his hand, then meeting it in silent prayer. They sat together for a long while—no words spoken. Both replayed events in their heads.

"We are hunted once again," she said, after the pause. "I have my own interpretations of the dreams too. Tell me something, do you think it's about the Diaspora and may be the time to leave for Israel?"

"That's just what I'm thinking," he answered and nodded in agreement with himself. Then he took a long pull through the straw in his water.

"The dreams had come at a time before things deteriorated so much. But now things are out of control. When the demonstrations got out of hand and those yellow Jewish stars got plastered on the windows of those businesses... well that's when it really hit me. And, then yesterday—of course." His voice trailed off as his mind took him elsewhere.

America, the Goldena Medina, had gone cold. The rabbi's wife remained silent, nodding, and knowing, for Esther always knew.

"I'm sure Eleazer sees it the same as we do," she said, just to lighten things up a bit.

"Where are the passports?"

"In the junk drawer in the kitchen."

"Good, we're going to need them soon."

Indeed, they would, but not just yet, for Chaim knew that he had work to do with his flock and with the surrounding communities. He'd be the last one to leave. He also thought that it was time to introduce Roberts and Cohen to his congregation. He knew that his lovely redheaded wife wouldn't leave his side and would rather die alongside him than leave him alone.

Many had taken his advice and had emigrated to the land. He was thankful for those who had taken his words to heart and purchased their passports. He whispered a prayer, grateful for those who took the hint got out with their funds, selling their property, and taking what they could with them.

Life was never easy in Israel, he knew, for he had spent a lot of time there. It was also home (as it would be to any Jew who returned) and he longed for Shabbat at the Wall (there was nothing on the planet to compare to Shabbat in the City of Gold and dancing with the Yeshiva boys there) and those long strolls on the beach in Haifa with his bride. His life was flashing before his eyes.

"Maybe one day we'll see Shabbat in the 3rd Temple," he said wistfully. Thoughts of rebuilding the great Temple of old were suddenly right in front of him. She sat half-listening and mind wandering.

"You know, what I'm going to miss is baseball," he chuckled. "I've heard it said somewhere that to be a good rabbi in America you needed to understand Torah and baseball."

Somewhere deep in his conscience he saw himself as a young boy playing ball in the sandlots and then going to games with his father at Yankee Stadium. He knew the game well, could cite dry statistics (which were almost as much fun as Holy Scripture) and had an intimate knowledge of the game.

He knew the history and the players as well as he knew Moshe (Moses) and the Exodus. He understood the difference between the hit and run and the run and hit. He could discuss how many ways a player could reach first base and knew what the 4th out meant.

"Maybe they will start playing ball in Eretz Yisrael," he chuckled and winked at Esther.

His mind then snapped back to the issues at hand.

For those who didn't listen, their fate would be precarious, just as their forefathers had learned for generations. He was looking forward to talking with Roberts and Eleazer about recent events. His world was changing once again.

✡ ✡ ✡ ✡ ✡ ✡

The next morning, Sunday, Jonathan Roberts boarded the Gulfstream G700, the newest generation of a high performance private aircraft owned by friends of his ministry, and headed to Dallas. Roberts traveled much of the time and was deeply indebted to owners of the donated jet.

But today, his heart was heavy for a lot of reasons. First, of course, was the senseless slaughter of thousands of American Jews at the hands of Muslims and Christians.

Second, he felt ashamed and humiliated at the behavior of those who called themselves Christians. They had given the Jews yet another reason not to trust them. And third, these weren't the Christians he knew, in fact a verse came to him just then, *I never knew you.*

When would the Christians ever learn? *Well, maybe that was the point*, he said to himself, *just a few of them got it... others never would.*' What a wasted opportunity.

May God have mercy on them on Judgment Day, he thought. He was searching hard for a sense of forgiveness but was finding it increasingly hard to find it.

He wasn't surprised at the Muslim rage in fact, he rather expected it. But America had failed to protect a once-treasured minority, her Jews. There was something about it that rang a Bell in his head. *Oh, yes, the slaughters of Native Americans so long ago*, he thought—*was this any different?*

The events of the past few weeks rattled him. He had taught it for years, lectured to stadiums full of Christians who hooted and hollered and yelled, "Amen" and "Hallelujah and Praise the Lord!"

But how many of them really 'got it?' How many of them would be willing to face what he thought was another Holocaust aimed at America's Jews, but this time demanding that Christians rise... not against the Jews, but to help them. How many of them would be willing to risk homes, cars, jobs, and their retirements? He knew the stories of those in the past who did help and what had happened to them. Could they connect today's events with Bible prophecy?

He then remembered the incredibly prophetic passage from Psalm 83:

> *O God, do not remain quiet; do not be silent and, O God, do not be still.*
> *For behold, your enemies make an uproar, and those who hate You have exalted themselves. They make shrewd plans against your people, and conspire together against your treasured ones. They have said, "Come, and let us wipe them out as a nation, that the name of Israel be remembered no more."*
> *For they have conspired together with one mind; against You they make a covenant: The tents of Edom and the Ishmaelites, Moab and the Hagrites;*
> *Gebal and Ammon and Amalek, Philistia with the inhabitants of Tyre;*
> *Assyria also has joined with them. They have become a help to the children of Lot. Deal with them as with Midian, as with Sisera and Jabin at the torrent of Kishon, who were destroyed at En-dor, Who became as dung for the ground.*
> *Make their nobles like Oreb and Zeeb and all their princes like Zebah and Zalmunna, who said, "Let us possess for ourselves The pastures of God." O my God, make them like the whirling dust, Like chaff before the wind, like fire that burns the forest And like a flame that sets the mountains on fire, so pursue them with Your tempest And terrify them with Your storm.*
> *Fill their faces with dishonor, That they may seek Your name, O LORD. Let them be ashamed and dismayed forever, And let them be humiliated and perish, that they may know that You alone, whose name is the LORD, are the Most High over all the earth.*

Could those words, uttered by King David, thousands of years ago, be any more relevant today? It didn't matter that some interpreted this Psalm as an imprecatory prayer—a prayer to ask God to help them avoid the outcome... it was real enough to him now.

He had wondered for years about the ancient Biblical prophecies and under what circumstances the Jews would feel it an imperative to leave the safe confines of America, the land that had protected them for so long. Why would they leave a land where the majority of them had become so successful, so educated, and so ensconced into the American culture and lifestyle? He remembered the immigration statistics that only 120,000 or so American Jews had emigrated to Israel but that was years ago. Maybe the Ethiopian was right, only by force and duress.

He fished around his carry-on and selected his Bible to read for a bit. That seemed the only thing able to relax him these past few months. America, his beloved, had turned on the Jewish people just as it was predicted in the Scriptures. He turned to the Book of Isaiah, the 11th Chapter, and began to read:

> *Then it will happen on that day that the Lord will again recover the second time with His hand the remnant of His people, who will remain, From Assyria, Egypt, Pathros, Cush, Elam, Shinar, Hamath, and from the islands of the sea. And He will lift up a standard for the nations and assemble the banished ones of Israel, and will gather the dispersed of Judah from the four corners of the earth.*

And there it was—the Jews would be gathered a *second* time to Israel from all over the earth. He thought about the history of this stubborn, stiff-necked people. They chased after idols, worshipped foreign gods, and did just about everything they were warned not to do.

They certainly weren't the best examples of a loyal and faithful people. They didn't need Christians or Muslims, or frankly anybody to accuse them. It was all there in the ancient Tenach for anyone to read. Their own prophets and teachers did a pretty good job of that. The record had been in their hands for millennia and so few of them were acquainted with their own history. For that matter, it wasn't much different for many Christians he knew.

Through the centuries, they tested God's forbearing spirit and yet He remained faithful to them. He recalled the Prophet Hosea describing how God would 'divorce' His bride after taking on other lovers, and then rejoin her in the holy union, a tough but sweet metaphor speaking of God's eternal love.

The promise of a regathering to the Land of Israel was as rock solid as any promise in the Bible. He remembered that the first regathering came during the times of Ezra and Nehemiah. This was the second regathering, he was sure of it. It started almost 150 years before and was revving up again. That gave him comfort.

Could this really be the time? His sense of things was that he was not only watching history but actually participating in it, a feeling that left him in awe of the Master of the Universe. He whispered a prayer thanking God that he could be used, even in his knowing sinful state.

"Why me, O Lord?" he prayed. "Hineni," he whispered. "Here I am. Use me." Then he wondered... *Could He really be using me to help?*

Roberts had, for years, been warning anyone willing to listen that if you were Jewish and in America, you were living on borrowed time and that all Jews in the U.S. would be well advised to have passports ready, arrangements made so that in case of an emergency, they would be prepared for any eventuality. It was a theme being repeated more and more often in synagogues across the nation and within churches and prophecy conferences. Once again, he felt the chills move up and down his spine and down his arms. He shivered. And now all the signs were pointing east ... to the Land of Israel.

Roberts continued reading various passages from Ezekiel, Hosea, Jeremiah, and others. The same story repeated itself, that it was God who would do the work. He would be the one doing the gathering, the plucking and the pruning.

And there would be much pruning, for Israel was a vine and He was the husbandman, ever clipping, pruning, always pruning. Israel and the whole human race would be tested, winnowed, sifted, shaken together, pressed down, and filtered and then poured out.

But the circumstances under which it would happen were too much for him to understand. He recalled from his vast historical reading how many of the Jews had a chance to escape Europe before World War II. He remembered, but most didn't take the opportunity or didn't have the opportunity at all. This time they did, and he vowed once more that he would help them as much as he was able. He set his Bible aside, offered up a prayer for holy wisdom, settled back into the comfortable seat, and within a few moments was fast asleep. His sleep was tossed and troubled.

The landing in Dallas roused Roberts from sleep. Cross winds rattled the plane offered a little excitement for touch down.

Knowing that he was safe, he relaxed once again. He had arranged a ride to the hospital to meet with Chaim and Esther, two old friends. They needed him now, and he was happy to respond. He pulled out his phone and called Esther.

"Hello?" Esther answered.

"Esther, it's me, Jonathan."

"Yoni, how good to hear your voice," she said, relieved that he was here. Esther was dog tired and it showed in her voice. But the joy at hearing an old friend revived her and she perked up a little.

"So, you're in now?"

"Yes, ma'am just landed."

"The flight was pretty smooth, I slept most of the way, but the landing got a little interesting."

"Oh, thank God you are here. We have so much to discuss."

"I'm deplaning in a few minutes. "How's Chaim?"

"OK, getting some rest now... we were very lucky."

"Luck... hmmm, well, you know what, in my book—there was no luck to it at all. The Holy One was watching over both of you," he said, trying to cheer her up a bit.

"Well, maybe, but it's been quite an ordeal, as you can imagine."

"I see the text you sent yesterday, David is picking me up, right?"

"Yes, he should be there now, so go through gate and head downstairs to the baggage claim area. He's driving a green pickup truck, a Ford F-100."

"I love Ford trucks! I have had several!" Roberts added. What he didn't tell her was that he had once been a member of the Board of Directors at Ford during his corporate career. That was a lifetime ago.

As the plane taxied up to the gate and rolled to a stop, he gathered his belongings and headed to the door. The smiling but all business flight attendant opened the cabin door and lowered the stairs for Roberts. The landing shook her a little too. She stopped him briefly, lightly touching his sleeve... "God speed to you sir."

He exited the plane, walked down the stairway, stepped onto the tarmac, and disappeared in a door next to the landing area. He headed into the airport and through the baggage claim. He emerged outside and saw David and his pickup. David got out of the truck and came up to Roberts, then threw his arms around him, a warm greeting they both needed.

The moment was overpowering for both of them. David had almost lost his parents and Jonathan his dear friends. He tossed his bags into the back of the four-door truck and settled in to the passenger seat.

They drove to the hospital. Esther was given a bed in Chaim's room. And it was at this moment she chose to go in and freshen up in the shower.

Her daughter, Shara, with help from some believing police officers, had gone to her parents' home and grabbed a change of clothes for her mother. She checked the house, brought in the mail and newspapers, and secured the house. The police chief assured Roberts that there would be a 24-hour police guard at the house. And so it was when she and the officer arrived.

> From the Prophet Isaiah,
> Chapter 54 Verse 17
>
> No weapon that is formed against you shall prosper; and every tongue that accuses you in judgment you will condemn. This is the heritage of the servants of the LORD, and their vindication is from Me, declares the LORD.

Chapter 52

A Jewish Doctor, Pickup Truck, & Christian Pastor

David Wasserman, the doctor with the pickup (and cowboy boots) had much to say to Roberts as they began the trip from the airport to the hospital. He went over the previous day's events looking for patterns, signs, anything that might help him make sense of what he was seeing. Roberts noticed the gun rack and the weapon safely stowed behind him. After all, this *WAS* Texas. And things had changed.

"You know, my father is a peaceful man, he wouldn't hurt a fly and to see this, I just can't believe it," David said. Roberts reached out and patted his shoulder.

"I know. These past weeks make me sick. And on American soil—again. "Yesterday will be seared into people's memories. Folks in past years remembered where they were for JFK, MLK, RFK, Pearl Harbor, and the Challenger. Now we will all remember Sabbath Shachor—Kristallnacht II."

"I can't hold this back any longer, David, but you need to understand what it is I think," Roberts continued.

"I think I know, Mr. Roberts," David stopped him, holding up his palm to the Pastor.

"You want to tell me that Jesus is the Messiah and that he died for our sins, and that he was resurrected on the third day," he shot back. Stunned, Roberts just let him talk.

"Well, you know what? I've had enough of this Christian message. It was the Muslims that did this... and the parade had... plenty of Christians... again!" he said, voice emotional and rising.

"David, you are one hundred percent right... and one hundred percent wrong," Roberts answered, firmly holding his ground.

"These weren't the Christians that I know. These cannot be true Bible believers, not a chance in H—," he caught himself, but both of them knew what he was about to say and they burst out laughing. In a way, it broke the tension for David felt comfortable with Roberts and began to open up to the pastor.

"My parents are both academics, they are lovers, not fighters, but my father said something to me last night after the surgery. He said that the Jews were going to put down the plowshares and pick up the swords." He explained that Chaim now knew this was war and the Jews needed to pick up arms and fight back. He had never before uttered anything like it. My father now sounds like an old general... almost like Moses or Joshua even!"

"Well, David, you should know that at this very minute, an army prepares its weapons to stand alongside of you and join the fight."

"An army? What do you mean? I've seen no friends out there, except maybe a few Christians, but just a few."

"Well, for starters we have something like 350,000 battle-trained Israelis here... and a very motivated group of Christian Zionists.

"We will have an army of *millions* within just a few days. I am in touch with some very powerful people... in fact it's already starting to happen—military men and women leaving their units and preparing to stand alongside of the Jews. Our intel tells us it could be in the *millions* when the Christian Zionists take up arms. Hey, you live in Texas. There should be no surprises here."

"I hope you are right, my goodness I hope so."

With that, David let out a big sigh. They pulled into the hospital parking lot and found a parking place right out in front, as David was on staff at the hospital. He checked the rear view mirror as he pulled in just to make sure no one was following them.

Roberts and David entered the hospital and headed up to the third floor. Roberts acknowledged the police guard, spending a few minutes with the officer outside the door. The guard, a sergeant on the force was also a strong believer and they exchanged a few observations about the previous day's events. Both knew what was at stake. They prayed together for Chaim's swift recovery and God's wisdom for them. Roberts thanked him for the support and the officer, in turn, thanked Roberts for his ministry and involving him in his work.

The pastor ducked his head in the door. Chaim turned his head and smiled at his old friend.

"Heck of a way to run a railroad, hey Yonatan?" Chaim used Roberts' Hebrew equivalent, a very special and warm gesture of greeting to his trusted friend. Roberts scooted up a chair next to the bed.

"So tell me, what happened... that is... if you feel comfortable..." Roberts asked, his countenance growing somber and his voice trailing off.

Chaim recounted the entire event. Every detail was so vivid in his mind.

"I remember looking up and realized what was happening. I saw five shooters, three men and two women. I forced Stevie down and covered him."

"I've never seen such evil in the eyes of another man. They swept the room with their guns and fired at anything that moved. I tried to remain calm and also play dead."

"Then the explosions went off. These... these... murderers were so well organized. It seemed like they had rehearsed every move—everything was so well coordinated and devastating. You know, I'm just happy to be alive, yet I almost feel that it should have been me and not them.

"Maybe the worst part was that they shot the rescuers. We heard that later—can't believe such cold-blooded killing."

Chaim had to control his anger. Roberts understood it perfectly and let the Rabbi rant a little.

"As much as I hate the act of terror, I almost understand it—but I have no room in my heart to understand such a ruthless act to follow—killing the helpers...." His voice trailed off. "This whole thing reminds me of the story of Amalek, praying on the weak at the end of the caravan."

That reference wasn't lost on Roberts as they both recalled the story from the end of Deuteronomy Chapter 25. In that story, many from the long train of marchers had fallen behind and Israel's enemy, Amalek, slaughtered the weak and helpless.

Roberts had grown used to the stories but now it was personal. He and Chaim and Chaim's family had grown closer over the years and while the Rabbi usually avoided discussions about the Messiah, the banter had suddenly become much more animated and focused on Scripture.

Roberts knew what Chaim was thinking about their many conversations over the past few years. They had debated the merits of Isaiah chapter 7 (the virgin birth), chapters 52- 53 (the suffering servant), Psalm 22 (the crucifixion), and even Zechariah 12:10 (Israel's acceptance of her pierced Messiah and the future war over Jerusalem). Each was a clear reference to the Messiah as he saw it. As expected, Chaim rejected his friend's position every time. Still, Roberts thought he could detect a softening.

"Even many of the Talmudic sources recognized many of these passages as speaking of the Messiah," Roberts said. But still Chaim remained unconvinced, though in quieter moments he had confessed to Esther that Roberts was the most convincing and kindest of the Christians he had ever met. He was no stranger to the Brit Chadasha (New Testament) having read it many times looking for clues of the Messiah's life and wasn't ignorant of 'Christian' theology.

"So, my friend, where do we go from here?" Chaim asked, hoping for a clear signal, anything that Roberts might recommend.

The pastor sat silently for a moment, drumming his fingers on the table next to Chaim's bed. The two locked eyes for a moment, holding on to a silent thought passing between them.

"You know, Chaim, I've been telling you that this was coming."

Chaim nodded and moments passed in silence. "I know, I know."

"Between you and me—I think the time has come for the Jews to go home. They must," he added.

"Well, Yoni (Johnny), we agree. Both Esther and I see it the same way. I don't know if I shared this with you, but you need to know this. Both Esther and I had these dreams about the Exodus—both of us. That was weird ... you know me—I'm not much of a mystic... yet, when I told my brother Eleazer, you'll never believe this, but he and his wife, Rifka, had the same exact dreams at the same exact time, down to the details," he said, studying Roberts and looking for his reaction.

Roberts sat and listened, nodding his head. He was fascinated by dreams and visions. *In scripture?* Sure. *But in this life?* Not likely. Still, he knew it was pure Bible.

"I wonder if this was how the prophets felt. Do you think they realized that their revelation was direct from God Himself?" Jonathan and Chaim looked at each other and wondered.

"It's magnificent! My prayers are more real than ever," Chaim confessed.

And, so it was that Chaim and Esther, who had just come back into the room after her shower, recounted the dreams to Roberts. After they finished, they just sat silent, the thick air hanging heavily between them. Roberts became aware of a fan turning in the ceiling, as it cooled the warm air.

Esther came to him. They hugged, and clung to one another. The two of them had long dropped any cultural prohibitions with Roberts as he was almost like family, thus the hugs between friends were considered safe.

Esther allowed herself to cry—finally. Roberts knew enough of this tough and resilient woman to let her go while he remained silent.

He thought of the scripture from Ecclesiastes, and in a somewhat absent-minded way said, "A time to tear apart and a time to sew together; a time to be silent and a time to speak... a time for war and a time for peace."

After her sobbing, her composure returned. Her eyes toughened at the same time, filled with determination. She looked up at him and whispered her thanks for his presence and quick response to them.

"So you think it means that it's time for the Jews to leave?" the rabbi asked, but was really just repeating what they all now saw as fact. Roberts nodded his head. They both agreed that it was the time for the departure of American Jews to their ancient homeland, whether they were ready or not.

"This sounds like it's right out of the books. Chaim, I think the Lord is speaking to you directly," Roberts said. He felt goose bumps crawling up his spine and noted them on his arms as well. Could it be these many thousands of years later?

"As I've just shared with David, you need to know, Chaim, that even at this very hour, an army is assembling to defend the Jews and help them escape. I'm hearing that many in the military are leaving their posts—that loyal Christians are stirring."

Since Roberts had planned to stay a few days, they asked David to get the spare bedroom ready for Roberts and help him with his things. Saying their good-byes, Roberts and David headed out of the room and over to the Wasserman household, still safe with its police guard.

Robert's cell phone buzzed with an encrypted text message.

"Do not return. The FBI has arrest warrants out for you."

Roberts stared at the message for a moment and then looked at Chaim. "What was it?"

"I'm now a hunted man. FBI."

Another silence enveloped them. Esther looked at Chaim, then at David.

"So, Jonathan, I'm trying to picture you with a full beard and peyos." They exchanged smiles....

And so, it was decided to 'induct' Jonathan Roberts into the community. Roberts was now "off the grid" and for the next few weeks, he grew his beard, donned a new set of clothes, and received his new identity, Rabbi Shamir Magen Yehudim (Guardian and Defender of the Jews).

But, for how long, nobody knew.

> **Coffee House Chatter**
>
> "Do you believe that history repeats itself?" She asked, looking directly at him.
>
> "I dunno... could be coincidence, could just be the times," he responded.
>
> "Feels to me that the order of the universe has been turned upside down... never thought I'd live to see this day,"
>
> "I know. What are we going to do?"

Chapter 53

Roberts & Cohen

An uneasy peace settled over America. The ripples and rumblings of violence that followed the Independence Day massacres (*Kristallnacht II*) began to subside. Jew, Gentile, Muslim, or Christian—all felt the imprint of the July 4th events and their aftermath.

The synagogue massacres were a vicious replay of century long persecutions by Muslims and Christians. Jews would be sought out—there was nowhere to hide. A land once supportive of American Jewry had turned hostile.

Jonathan Roberts (in his new identity) and Aryeh Cohen had a new sense of urgency. Their speeches and presentations took a more direct approach with a call to action. They carefully accepted invitations—large or small—to reach as many people as possible and though everyone was still reeling from the recent slaughter, they refused to pack up the tent and go home. Now was the time to fight. But Roberts now travelled with a detail who were expected to scurry him off at a moment's notice... should the FBI show up.

Roberts and Cohen had just finished a talk in New York City, when a small group approached Cohen. After a few words, he called to Jonathan, "Hey, come over and meet these folks."

Cohen pulled Roberts into the circle and said, "I think you need to hear some of this. But first meet Ayelet Simcha, a teacher at Beth Shalom Community Center and School here in New York." Roberts greeted her. "This is Nurse Jenny Del Fuego, an intensive care nurse." Roberts smiled when he heard her last name *Del Fuego*. "And this young man is Ross Evans—formerly known as Ibraham Hussein."

"Ooooh! Hallelujah!" Roberts celebrated and shook his hand. "This is a first for me."

"I'll let Ross tell you how all three of them became so close. You're gonna want to sit down." Cohen smiled with all his teeth and nodded to Ross. The circle of five pulled their chairs into a close circle and looked to Ross.

"First," Ross began, "I want to say that I'm honored to share even a few minutes with you both."

"We all are," both Ayelet and Jenny agreed.

Ross continued, "Well, let's see. Where to begin?"

Cohen and Roberts were riveted to Ross. His story captured their attention and gave them ideas for future... ideas that included Ross.

Ross retold his story once again. He concluded his comments and added, "Ross Evans was reborn in that hospital bed and these two precious women were the mid-wives. They gave me life—again." Ross went to each one with hugs, words of love, and tears.

"But there's more...." Ross raised both hands. "Since that day I have pledged my time, resources, gifts, and abilities to reverse the terrible epidemic that now sweeps through America. The day I got this bullet wound, I risked my life to save some of God's Jewish people. And I declare today with joyful resolve that should the need arise, I will die to save the Jews."

Roberts and Cohen both stood and embraced him. "We are the ones who are honored, Ross."

"And gentlemen," Jenny inserted, "let me tell you... this young man can brrrrring it!"

"He took advantage of his recovery time," Ayelet added. "He studied his Bible, the history of Israel, the plight of Jews, and the pogroms. But more, he knows the inner workings of the Nation of Islam, their tactics, and the plans they projected for the future.

"Yet most important, Ross knows how to move people. It's not that he's persuasive... don't get me wrong he is. But it's something else. He has an authority when he speaks. His words ring true. His heart is pure. And his passion is contagious."

Ross protested and deflected the praise. But Roberts jumped in, "Ross, I would like to hear you speak. I know I can help you, but more, I know you can help me and our cause. I have connections around the globe. We need you. Aryeh and I both know that our free access and opportunities to speak in public is about to change. You are an answer to our prayers... a gifted communicator able to move people and reproduce yourself."

Then Roberts took a moment to listen to his heart and study Ross' face. Then he said, "Paul's words to Timothy are important to you, aren't they, Ross? Especially 2nd Timothy chapter 2—your name is written all over it... at least in my mind."

Ross smiled, reached into his pocket, pulled out his card, and handed it to Roberts. "I think you found my frequency."

"Ross, the Lord knew I needed to meet you." Roberts rejoiced. "I needed some encouragement and hope. And I got it here you from you tonight. Let's talk more." Then he reached into his pocket, pulled out a business card, wrote on the back, gave it to Ross, and said. "This is my direct and personal contact info. Please guard it. Call me tomorrow."

Ross took the card, nodded, and said. "Yes, sir, I will."

"Del Fuego... " Roberts looked at Jenny. Your last name is a familiar name among Jews of Spain."

Jenny looked down, smiled, and then engaged Roberts, "Usually it's my looks that give rise to the Jewish comment. But my name has captured attention a few times, too. Well, I know we came from a long line of Catholics, but I left the faith a few years ago when I came to know Yeshua as the Messiah." Then she added. "I've also noted a lot of Hispanics come to our Messianic congregation... they are leaving the Catholic Churches."

Jenny paused and seemed to reboot. Then she searched Roberts' eyes and said, "I had always wondered about Jewish blood in my family. I've never told anybody this.... But a few years ago, it was Friday night and I was over at my parents' home. I fell asleep on their sofa after dinner. I awoke to sounds from the kitchen. My mother and father were bent over something on the table. I startled them and they shut whatever it was they had before them.

"I asked my mom what they were doing. She was reluctant to tell me. Instead, she told me to ask my father. I did. He seemed embarrassed. By now, I'm curious as a cat in the cupboard.

"I said, 'Papa, we've always been straight with each other. We speak the truth whatever the issue. Right?

"He nodded and said, 'Of course, Mija.'

"So tell me now... what are you and mama hiding from me?

"Tears filled his eyes. He took long moments to think. Then he said, 'Mija, I think it's time you knew.'

"So, that night, he goes to the back of the house and pulls out this really old box, sort of like a jewelry box. It's got some strange things in it. One of the things has these leather straps with these tiny boxes, a *t'fillin* with Hebrew writing on them. The other was this threadbare prayer shawl. He gently unwrapped the prayer shawl and guess what!?! It was a *tallit*! Well, I know what it is but I am really curious now and asked him where he got this thing. It looks really old, almost falling apart. I could see the Hebrew on it and the fringes and knots.

"I had never seen it before. He just started doing something that totally blew me away. He unfolded it like the men do where I attend services. He began to rock back and forth and chant prayers. They were beautiful and his voice was something like out of heaven. He spread it out a little and brought my mother and me under it. He enclosed us with it and finished his prayers.

"I've picked up some Hebrew through attendance at my congregation. So I recognized the Shema and thought, *He's chanting it in Hebrew! My Catholic dad!*

Jenny was animated and anxious to share more. "He said, 'My father received the *t'fillin, tallit,* and these mysterious chants from his father. And his father received them from his father... and so on back to the 15th Century.'

The room fell silent.

"I think it's called *L'dor v'dor* in the Hebrew," Jenny added. "It means *from generation to generation.*" Aryeh nodded in agreement. Roberts was speechless.

"I've long heard of such stories," Roberts began. "I've even read about it in books." He paused, kneaded his brow, smiled, tilted his head, and continued. "I just connected a bunch of dots. This trend of Hispanics in Messianic congregations has surged in recent years. They adopt Jewish ways of worship and leave the Catholic Church puzzled."

"Why now?" Ayelet asked.

"Well, I think they needed to know that they could worship Jesus, Yeshua, in a Hebraic context. They were primed and ready to leave because of the church. Their churches had stripped away the cultural aspects of their faith. Some went to synagogues. The majority settled in Messianic synagogues and congregations—both English and Spanish-speaking. And this has and continues to occur on both sides of the U.S. Mexican border.

Jenny jumped in, "I was moved to learn more. My research gave me names for these Hispanics with Jewish blood. They were called Crypto Jews, *Conversos*, or *Marranos*. That last term is most offensive—it means pig or swine.

"In fact, I read that Christopher Columbus was a crypto-Jew himself. Some say that the real reason he headed to the New World was to scout out a place for the Jews to live in safety.... But others disagree and say it's speculation."

"That's right," Roberts agreed. "*Marrano* was a deliberate and contemptuous term applied in Spain and Portugal to baptized Jews and their descendants from the early 15th century. And I've found the same comments about Columbus. In fact, there were many other factors in his life to support that. For example, he was a native of Genoa, Italy—an important sea port for world commerce. It's a place long associated with a Jewish influence. In fact, I've heard it said that their dialect is salt-n-peppered with words of Hebrew origin.

"Some of my research also talks about many of the Jews who escaped and became pirates and businessmen in the New World, again trying to provide shelter for their own against the Church's persecution... imagine—Jewish Pirates of the Caribbean! There are even stories about a rabbi, Samuel Palanche who moonlighted as a pirate while running the Jewish community in Amsterdam. It is said he and his crews sunk a few Spanish galleons for the booty." That evoked a laugh from the small gathering.

Roberts paused and searched his thoughts and said, "You know besides *Marranos,* there's another less familiar derogatory term for Jewish *Conversos*. It's *Chuetas* in Catalan dialect.

"*Chuetas* is used for a social group and portion of the population on the Spanish island of *Mallorca* in the Balearic Sea. *Chueta* designates to this day those stigmatized by their Jewish origins. Even the pious Catholics of Jewish blood are called *Chuetas.*

"I've read of another rabbi who was born in Palma, Mallorca," Roberts said. "His parents sought to hide their Jewish roots. In school the others cursed him with the term *Chueta.* He said that he was ten years old before discovered that he was of Jewish descent. At the same time he learned that a *Chueta* was something awful—pig in Catalan.

"These things moved him to study his Jewish origins, read, and re-associate himself with the Hebrew faith. He was born a Catholic and christened Nicolas Aguilo, but today he is Rabbi Nissan Ben Avraham. He made aliya to Israel in his mid-twenties. And he has traced the migration of Jews around the world. He has a special interest in Hispanic Jews. He's even found links to Jewish Incas in South America!"

Roberts paused to think and then said, "Here's what excites me... Hispanics sense a deep need to search out Jewish things. They have a mysterious hunger to understand Jewish traditions. And once they search, their hidden Jewish roots begin to emerge. And Jenny you are living proof."

"But I think there's more to it than human curiosity," Jenny answered. "I was drawn to seek faith within the Jewish context of a Messianic congregation. It is most magnetic. I've long had an interest in all things Jewish, but this was more—a fulfillment of some kind."

"There are doubters to be sure, and some of these ideas are a little iffy, but there is also a lot of compelling evidence to support it," Roberts added.

Jenny took a deep breath, mustered boldness, and said, "I think God is just fulfilling his promise. He's calling his people back to himself. Even those who don't know their Jewish roots like me. And even those in the farthest corners of the world. He's calling their hearts. In my spirit, I see God's people drawn to back to their historical and spiritual identity just like...." She paused, looked each one in the eyes and then asserted, "They are drawn in the same way that God drew the animals to be saved on the ark of Noah. Didn't Yeshua say, a*s in the days of Noah*?"

Roberts jumped to his feet, looked around, and said, "Now I've got goose-bumps! You gave me a rush just then, Jenny!"

"I know about being drawn or pulled toward things bigger than I," Ayelet inserted. "I've had goose-flesh ever since I met Ross and Jenny. My life has been extreme from the first day this all started. I've experienced ultimate terror, gratitude, confusion, curiosity, more fear, and then real peace."

"How did it start for you?" Roberts asked.

"So, there I am in this little gathering for our children. We were hosting a small art fair for the kids and had about a hundred or so parents and friends. We were just chatting and all of a sudden we heard all this noise outside. Then we heard the sirens and they kept getting closer and closer.

"Then, this stranger carries in Ross. Of course, we didn't know him yet but the stranger brings him in and the rumor was that he was outside with this group protesting. Some of the parents wanted to rough him up but the stranger stopped them and explained that he had actually stopped the shooter. We looked closer, found the bullet wound, and everything changed. A doctor and a nurse jumped in to help and then the ambulance came. We never found the stranger... he was just... gone, without a trace," Ayelet said. Her busy fingers twirled locks of thick, black hair, and her deep brown eyes glowed with intensity.

"I'm convinced it was a miracle," she added.

"So I followed the ambulance to the hospital. I had to see this young man who risked his life. I had to see if I could help him in any way. I stayed in the waiting room and got updates on his condition. They transferred him to ICU. So early in the morning, I snuck in and found his room."

Ayelet looked to Jenny and smiled. "My new best friend, Jenny, let me come in. She wasn't supposed to." They winked at each other.

"I left the hospital later that day to get some sleep. On the way home, I marveled at the experience and thought, *How strange.... A Christian nurse cares for a sworn enemy, a young Black Muslim. And me... I'm so drawn to the mysterious young man who stepped in to stop evil. I a Jew and he a black man associated with the Nation of Islam—yet a friendship was born. Only God. Only God.*" They all agreed.

"But, no one time thing—this was." Ayelet continued. "The three of us grew close in that hospital room and afterwards. And these two... " she said with a smile for each. "Jenny helped Ross find health and faith again. And then they both reached out to me. Jenny took me to her congregation on Shabbat. Oh, my! *A celebration or a circus,* I thought. But it didn't matter. I loved every second."

The circle of new friends laughed loud enough to draw attention—Roberts the loudest.

"Jenny was up there dancing and singing with the others. I sang... some, but clap? I made my hands red and blue—I clapped so much. Then I went back and gave Ross a report. He promised to visit when he was well enough."

"Did he?" Roberts asked.

Ross smiled, showed all his teeth, lifted his hand, and said, "My hands turned all black and blue!"

Another roar went up from the circle.

"Well," Ayelet continued. "I'd never seen love like this. Ross for us... Jenny for Ross.... and both of them for me.... the three Musketeers. I'm a Jew. I'm taught to love others—but to always be on guard. I know to do a *mitzvah* when I see the opportunity. But these two... they love all the time. Special people they are.

"I still visit on Shabbat with Jenny. I'm not sold on Yeshua. But them I like. I like their company, and they like me," Ayelet concluded.

"Nooooo, Ayelet," both Ross and Jenny mooed. They got out of their seats, pulled her to her feet, and said, "WE LOVE YOU!" Hugs all around.

"This is no coincidence," Roberts said. "We're all here by some divine appointment."

"You're right. And I think more are coming—or need to come." She pulled out her phone and sent a message to her cousin: WHERE R U?

The others took a moment to join Pastor Roberts in a prayer. He thanked God for their little circle of faith—he mentioned each by name. He prayed for their relationships to grow in love and service to one another and to God's purpose for each one. He asked God to clarify their direction and next steps. And he prayed for courage, strength, resolve, and utter abandonment to the will of God.

Ayelet's cousin sent: AT THE V's.
   CAN U LEAVE?
   WHY?
   Ayelet sent back: TRUST ME... VITAL 2 OUR CAUSE.
   WHERE?
   STARBUCKS... WEST VILLIAGE... IN SHERIDAN SQUARE ON GROVE.
   Her cousin sent: WHEN?
   Ayelet sent: NOW!!! HURRY!
   CHILL... ON MY WAY.

"Listen up!" Ayelet called out. "I'm telling you... God's not done drawin' all the animals here yet. My cousin is going to meet us for coffee. Please follow me a block or two to Starbucks down the street."

"Bless you, Ayelet!" Roberts said. "You just took the words out of my mouth. You know what they say about great minds?"

"No," Ayelet answered. "I haven't read that far yet. Come on... let's go."

"Are you coming?" Roberts asked Cohen.

"Wouldn't miss it," Cohen answered. "But I'll catch up. I think I just saw someone I know from Israel."

"Where?"

"Over there in that group of folks who came tonight. Pastor's closing up so I want to catch her before they leave."

"Gotcha," Roberts said with a thumbs-up. Then Ayelet grabbed his arm and pulled him out the door.

"Dr. Roberts, you're gonna love my cousin," Ayelet bubbled. "I'll give you a hint. Just imagine a girl like me... not as pretty, of course. But think New Yorker, university education in Israel, Jewish historian, passionate activist, connected to the city's key Italian families. That means the docks, warehouses, and the landfills. Imagine a mix of *mezuzah* and *"Familia."* Or better... *Beth L'David* and Businessmen of the Docks." Ayelet stretched her neck, got a look at Roberts' face, and poked, "Huh?"

Roberts stopped walking, grabbed Ayelet hands, looked in her eyes, and said, "Yes, I can imagine it." Then he leaned down, hugged her, and kissed her cheek. "Ayelet, your words just put the whip cream, nuts, and cherry on my sundae!"

> From the Hand of the Psalmist
> Psalm 82 Verse 4)
>
> "...Rescue the weak and needy;
>   Deliver them out of the hand of the wicked."

Chapter 54

Warriors Mingle—Hearts Unite

Cohen approached the group from the Jewish community. They stood and prepared to leave the sanctuary. That's when she turned around.

"Shoshana?!?" Cohen erupted. "How wonderful is this!" They hugged, and he asked, "What brings you here? I would not have expected to see you in a church!"

"Ha!" Shoshana shot. "Well, Aryeh, I heard about your presentation with Dr. Roberts. I was in town... had the night free.... How could I miss it?" She smiled and eyed Aryeh from head to toe. "You look good. Being famous must agree with you."

"Famous—ha! I'm just a watchman and a messenger. Somebody has to get the word out."

"Well, it must be working," Shoshana said. "You've captured the attention of some real players. Both you AND Roberts... " Then she winked at Cohen and said, "But you must know that already."

"Huh?" Cohen grunted.

"Not to worry—I'll bring you up to speed." Shoshana winked and squeezed Cohen's shoulder. "As for me... let me see.... Well, I'm here to keep the kitchen cooking and make sure nobody gets burned. That is... unless I want them burned."

"Are we at that point already?" Cohen was more serious and concerned.

"Well...." Shoshana paused and reflected on what she could say to Cohen. "Avram sent me over here for awhile. But let's keep that between you and me."

Cohen nodded and said, "Of course." He let out a troubled sigh, breathed in some better air, and asked, "Do you have a few minutes for coffee, conversation, and connection with some of our players?"

"You read my mind, Aryeh." Then she asked, "Will Jonathan be there?"

"He and the others are at Starbucks, now. Just two blocks."

Shoshana linked arm-in-arm with Cohen and said. "Lead on, Lion of God. Lead on."

Cohen and Shoshana found the coffee clutch lost in conversation. "Have you got room for two more?" Cohen asked. The welcome was unanimous. Now every eye was on Shoshana. "Oh... " Cohen jumped. "Right. Well, this is my dear friend Shoshana Bat Levy. She lives in Israel, and she's here on business. She's a cook." Cohen elbowed Shoshana and chuckled.

"Are you like a chef?" Ayelet asked.

"If I were, I'd cook up a serving of scrambled Aryeh." Shoshana answered Ayelet.

Roberts cleared his throat, scooted up in his seat, and extended his hand. "Shoshana it's an honor to meet you. I didn't realize my friend Mr. Cohen here had such distinguished friends."

The others turned to each other and whispered. "So, how do you know our friend Aryeh?" Roberts asked.

"We were in basic training together around the time of Alexander the Great. But our paths split for a time. I headed off to the Air Force, of course. My friend used his considerable brain-power to pursue communications and socio-geo-political blah, blah, blah. You know the rest.

"Still, our boy here did his time in the trenches with the grunts. I'd wave to him from high above. I've heard the biggies talk about how well he did as a battlefield commander. But I won't repeat any of it. He'd need a new fedora."

"Yeah," Cohen chimed in, "Shoshana supported my reserve unit from her perch. She kept the bees out of our hair. And her close support saved my butt more than once."

"Then let me thank you, Shoshana." Roberts said, stood, and shook her hand again. "I'm so glad his butt is here tonight."

"You're very welcome," She responded and stood to receive his hand. "But there's more." Shoshana found her seat, cast a softer gaze at Cohen, and said in quiet tones, "Sari and I were close. We worked together from time-to-time. And she saved my butt and countless others on a regular basis. I don't know how we.... I don't know how you go on without her." She reached out, hugged Cohen, and whispered something in Hebrew in his ear.

Roberts turned to the others. Jenny and Ayelet had tears and sniffles. "Sari was Aryeh's wife."

"Is Aryeh's wife," Cohen corrected him.

"So... Yonatan," Shoshana began, "tell me about your life in the blue. Your reputation has preceded you as well."

Roberts did a double-take and rebooted. He wasn't used to his name in Hebrew. But he lit up like a bulb. His warm smile and wise eyes could put anyone at ease. His physical stature, strength, and presence spawned either admiration or alarm. But Roberts' heart, passion, spiritual insight, superior mind, and real-world experience made him a great leader. He took off his glasses to wipe away some smudges.

In any field or forum, Roberts was an opponent to be feared. He kept himself combat ready, fit inside and out, practiced and familiar with weapons old and new, and well informed on current world events.

"The spiritual mentor that led me to God also taught me to fly," Roberts answered Shoshana. "He knew those in high places." Roberts pointed up. "But also had friends in Congress—one was an old Navy buddy. So... the Naval Academy was my first stop after the farm." Roberts paused, smiled, and connected with a memory.

"But before that... my mentor, who also was my truest pastor, gave me something. I netted a number of gifts at high school graduation—a pick-up truck from my parents and lots of cash in cards. But Pop Phillips gave me a gift I still carry with me today." Then he reached into his pocket and pulled a tattered and folded 3x5 card that had been laminated. He told me to drive by his place on my way out of town. I did.

"Pop Phillips admired my truck, prayed with me, gave me some needed counsel that Dad neglected, and then he gave me this. He said, 'Jonathan, God told me to pass on this gift to you. It has been God's promise and my constant confidence since I left home. Memorize it before you stop tonight. Then repeat it every day at Annapolis. And meditate on it every day till you meet the Lord.

"'I know you will face cruel combat, feel formidable fear, touch the enemy, and see unforgettable horrors. You will know war. The Lord has shown me. But Jonathan... keep this with you through it all. Keep it here.' Then Pop stepped close and put his finger on my head and on my heart. And remember, son, 'everyday in some way God will ask you in a vulnerable moment: *Do you trust me?'* Then he extended his hand and gave me this with the words 'Believe it.' We hugged, and he sent me on my way."

"So, what did he give you?" Shoshana poked. Roberts handed her the card. She unfolded it, studied the handwritten words, smiled, and said, "The *Michtam Ruach HaKodesh*—His secret treasure, indeed. This is taped in the cockpit of every jet I fly. And from the stick patch on this lamentation, I guess you do, too."

"Thank you for your patience with my story," Roberts said. "I think of Pop often and miss him very much."

"Don't apologize," Shoshana insisted. "You touched my heart... and you made me envious. I never had anyone like your Pop."

Roberts shook himself and refocused. "Well, after Annapolis... flight school, Mira Mar, and then I hoped for a carrier. But my service jacket got a *Blue Tag*. I was called in—blind. They called my name, and I stood before a review panel of three flag officers. Man, I needed new skivvies!

"Anyway, they knew everything about me—bow to stern. Then the ranking member asked, 'What's the goal of your naval service, son?'

"I repeated my mantra, 'I want to be a carrier pilot—without question. Sir.'

"Which carrier?' Another officer asked.

"I answered, 'The Harry S. Truman—the Nimitz super carrier.'

"Then the senior member said, 'Son, you have some impressive characteristics, abilities, and aptitude.' I thank him, and he continued, 'The Truman is yours. However, we need 6 to 8 months from you first.'

"I asked, 'For what purpose, sir?'

"'We'd like to send you to the Navy's War College—Special Intelligence Department. You'd been an ongoing member of the War College with the annual briefing and continuing education.'

"'Yes, sir. Of course, sir. Thank you, sir.' But I had to ask, 'Why, sir?'"

"The senior member scribbled in my service jacket, passed it down, lifted his head, and looked at me. 'Lt. Roberts... ' He paused. I stood taller and listened. He smiled and continued, '... dismissed.'

"I got to the Truman. I flew and fought in hot spots you never heard reported on the news. I was often used in joint-task-force operations with Air Force. They trained on a number of new aircraft. In my final years, I flew and even commanded a large number of missions that...." Roberts paused to rethink his words. "Well, let's just say they were *quiet missions.*"

Roberts looked at Shoshana, lifted his eyebrow, smiled, and winked. "Enough about me. Your turn."

CHAPTER FIFTY-FOUR: *Warriors Mingle—Hearts Unite*

"Ah, what's there to tell?" Shoshana replied. "We were a squadron of 24 women. We all graduated at the same time. And we all wanted to fly."

"I met Roni Zuckerman during our training. She came in as a guest lecturer and shared her experiences as the first female F-15 pilot in our air force. She's a national hero."

He noticed that Shoshana had an air to her, confident, strong, but most maternal. She carried herself with as much chutzpah (fortitude) as anyone he had met in a long time. She had education, experience, toughness, and gentleness all rolled into one.

"When I received the appointment to the first squadron of all female pilots, I was so honored and humbled. It was amazing. I was surrounded by all these beautiful Sabras, who had one thing on their minds: *defend our homes and our families.*

"They were fierce. I remember our first skirmishes with the Syrians in last two regional conflicts. I'm fortunate to be alive. They didn't know I was girl, but they knew they were out maneuvered. I shot down two of them the first day and then three a couple of days later. Battle becomes very personal when you are flying over and defending your own home and family.

"I got back, and we debriefed. Every detail is dissected and scrutinized. All of it—good, bad, wins, losses. We pulled it apart and put it back together again. We assume nothing, discard egos, shun shame, and prevent pride from any involvement. We level the field and learn everything we can. Even wins are worthless unless we can figure out why we won. It's how we prevent mistakes and save lives in the future," she explained.

"I don't think I've met the likes of you," Roberts said to her.

Ross Evans, Jenny, and Ayelet shook their heads. They were in the company of giants. All three of them recognized the moment for what it was.

Ayelet spotted her cousin and sprung to her feet. She flew off like Mercury, hugged the new arrival, and returned with a very pretty young woman.

"Hey everybody, this is my cousin. She's a lot like you guys. Serious, smart, into the news and current events.... And, oh, she's all about Israel. Then she turned to her cousin and said these two are from Israel... like war heroes or something. She pointed at Cohen and Shoshana and asked them, "Am I right?"

Ayelet and her cousin sat down. Shoshana turned to her cousin and said, "Shalom, my name is Shoshana Bat Levy. And you are... ?"

The cousin took Shoshana's hand and said, in perfect Hebrew, "I'm so glad to meet you. My name is Yanit... Yanit Silver."

> From Zechariah the Prophet
> Chapter 8:7-9
>
> Thus says the LORD of hosts, "Behold, I am going to save My people from the land of the east and from the land of the west; and I will bring them back and they will live in the midst of Jerusalem; and they shall be My people, and I will be their God in truth and righteousness."
>
> Thus says the LORD of hosts, "Let your hands be strong, you who are listening in these days to these words from the mouth of the prophets, those who spoke in the day that the foundation of the house of the LORD of hosts was laid, to the end that the temple might be built."

Chapter 55

What Time Is It?

Yanit's presence tipped the scales. Shoshana stood and said, "I propose we move the seventy feet or so over to the hotel lounge. It's larger and we can have a private corner. Please don't anyone leave. In fact, I'll buy the first round."

"And I'll buy the second," Cohen volunteered.

Roberts grabbed his things and said, "Come on gang. It's time we got down to business. Let's peel this thing back and hit it head on. I was entrusted with a message for this very group. Believe me nothing is more important than the next hour or two."

The group transitioned en mass to the lounge and found the perfect niche in the far back.

"Aryeh, wait up." Shoshana grabbed Cohen's arm. The two fell behind the rest and whispered. "I got goose-flesh when she gave me her name. I saw it in her eyes."

"You saw what?"

"You know... '*It*.' She may be a pretty girl on the outside, but I saw into her soul. And when she shook my hand.... Oh, Aryeh, I felt her strength, resolve, mettle, and more. She is just as the brief reported and forecast. I know it was all in your package."

"*It* was in my package?" Cohen wore his dunce face.

"Need I remind you that I'm armed," Shoshana jabbed.

Cohen reached into his jacket, retrieved his electronic device, and opened up his "to do" list. He showed her the screen and scrolled down the page under "New York contacts." He highlighted the words, "Interview Yanit Silver."

"What's that next to her name?" Shoshana asked.

"That's a link to my secure server where the brief on Ms. Silver is stored. And it is also updated in real time."

"Come on youz guys," called Ayelet.

The chemistry between them was immediate, irresistible, and electric. They somehow understood that their lives would forever be intertwined from this moment forward and they treated the time together with a sense of urgency and a deep respect. Each member of the small otriad now understood his or her role and was perceived by the others as an equal partner. Details were still to be worked out but there was a sense of growing confidence and trust each felt for the other.

Returning to the tables, the new friends now huddled close together and got acquainted. One by one, the others shared their backgrounds and how they had arrived at this place at this time, and for this moment. Roberts shared some of his military and corporate background, and then launched into details about his faith-based journey. He pulled no punches, sharing his beliefs that Yeshua was the Messiah, based, as he saw it, on the Hebrew Scriptures. Roberts felt compelled to share some of his thinking with them as he surveyed the small gathering.

"You know, there are moments when I just have to just step back and breathe. I can't believe all of this is happening in my lifetime—in OUR lives. Now! We are witnessing the time spoken of by the Hebrew prophets such as Isaiah, Daniel, Hosea, Moses, Ezekiel, Jeremiah, and others. When God makes a promise, He keeps it, but not necessarily in our perception of time as we know it. The Scripture says that to God a day is as a thousand years and a thousand years is as a day. It's been said that God lives outside of the time domain. He sees the beginning from the ending."

He explained his views on Jewish ownership of the Land of Israel and how he believed this was the time of the second regathering. He explained his belief that the Jews were God's chosen, not for anything they had earned or done, but from God's providence and His grace. He quoted several of the Hebrew prophets, each time describing the parallels he saw in the present time. He challenged those, including Ayelet, Yanit and Shoshana whom he knew did not share his beliefs.

"Each of you has an obligation to read your Holy Scriptures, the Tenach. I have no argument with anyone who disagrees with me as long as they know what it is they are disagreeing with. It puts us on common ground. As much as any of us understand what's going on around us, your understanding will grow geometrically when you read the prophecies about the present and future persecution and the admonition to the Jews that there is a time to return to Israel."

He believed this was indeed the time spoken by the prophets of Israel. This sparked much discussion as the unbelievers began asking questions.

"Ok, Jonathan, what specifically are you referring to?" Shoshana challenged him, not in an aggressive manner, but more out of a deep curiosity.

"Well, for starters, Shoshana, I'd point you to Ezekiel 37. I'm sure you heard of the 'Dry Bones' prophecy, right?" he parried.

"Well, yes, of course," she answered. Tell us more."

"Ezekiel explains that the dry bones, are representative of 'Am Israel,' the people of Israel, and would be brought back to life. The bones were dry, meaning dead, but God promises that the bones would live again," he explained, reading her facial expression and checking whether or not she was tracking to the discussion. She was totally dialed in to his teaching.

Roberts' words carried a certain sense of genuine excitement, almost one of wonder, and if one were perceptive, authority. It seemed that the Scriptures were coming alive to Shoshana. She watched and listened to him as he explained the story and was taken in by his enthusiasm and deep-felt commitment to her land and to her people. He made it personal and that's exactly how she took it.

Simply put, she had never heard 'her Bible' explained this way before, and by a Gentile no less. She squirmed in her chair, suddenly aware of her own discomfort. Shoshana never felt like this before, as she was one always in control of herself and the situation. Tonight, she felt neither and she didn't like it. Roberts read that too.

But, his love of the Jews and Israel was without question. She had never given much thought to the Bible, as most Jews she knew hadn't. Rather, it was a book of history, long in the past, with little relevance to today's insane world. But Roberts seemed to make it a living thing. She couldn't remember any of the rabbis she knew having the same level of enthusiasm and command of this material. It wasn't that they didn't know the Bible, but there was something special about this stranger. He knew the Bible as a living thing, not an ancient relic. He continued.

"So, the prophecy comes in stages. First, God 'resurrects' the dry bones, or the people. Next He brings them back to their land, and then 'breathes life' into the bones. He tells them, 'live,' and they begin to form a great army."

This last statement wasn't lost on Ross or Jenny as both of them, at the same time felt the goose bumps creep up their spines. They looked at each other and smiled, knowing that they were witnessing history in the making. Roberts explained the Scripture in terms that few could. He brought science, mathematics, history, and culture into the open, weaving the tale together like a great artist and his canvas. He was, in short, mesmerizing, one great story teller.

The others were listening now and very attentively nodded. Roberts explained that Ezekiel 37 was a precursor to the eventual establishment of the reconstituted nation of Israel, later born in a day after a very long time away from their land, according to the prophet Isaiah. All of them knew what May 14, 1948 meant.

"This is all interesting, but where does this Jesus of yours fit in?"

"I'm glad you asked that one!" he said, with a smile. "Remember, Jesus was a Jew. I've taken to calling Him by His real name—Yeshua. In fact, when He returns, He will come back as the greatest Rabbi the world has ever seen," Roberts explained. He was emphatic, though sensitive about this last point, though it seemed like he was being somewhat flippant. He wasn't, though, because he believed his Great Rabbi was indeed that, a Rabbi, a teacher, the best the world had ever seen. He gently described how most Christians he knew failed to put the Messiah of Israel into the proper and cultural Hebraic context.

"I must be a little self critical here... it's my belief that Christianity hasn't been particularly sensitive to its older brethren. Seems to me that God doesn't want the Jews to be anything other than what they are... Jews... who understand and love their Messiah... and remain who they are. The church has been trying to convert Jews to a foreign religion and culture for centuries. In my opinion, God didn't want them to be anybody else than who they were. I have studied this stuff for years and I can't draw any other conclusion.

"His wish is for the people to come to him as their Messiah and to remain who they are. I find it interesting that the Jews as a race or a people never seem to recognize their deliverers the *first* time but will the *second* time. Case in point: Moses. You may remember that Moses wasn't recognized by his Hebrew brothers when he killed the Egyptian way back as told in the Book of Exodus. Rather, they accused him of murder and then he flees to Median where he meets his future wife, Zipporah. He disappears for 40 years, lives with his in-laws, patiently tending sheep, and waiting for God's calling."

"Later, he meets God at the burning bush and then God calls him. But he is reluctant and eventually he and his brother Aaron stare down Pharaoh. It is then the people recognize him but even then he has to perform some of the miracles for the people first to get their attention. Then he does the same things to prove himself to Pharaoh. You might remember that even after they leave Egypt, the people begin to grumble against him but he still leads them... a stiff-necked people."

"There are other stories like this including the story of Joseph. His brothers do not immediately recognize him when they sojourn to Egypt. Remember the story? After being sold by his brothers to some Ishmaelite traders, he ends up as a viceroy in Pharaoh's house and then the world goes through a drought and famine."

"Jacob sends his sons to Egypt for food and they encounter Joseph but don't recognize him the *FIRST* time. Later, you remember, the family is reconciled to him, a *SECOND* time. I could go on and on, but this appears to be the model for the Jews... reject the redeemer first, suffer for a period of time, then recognize him the second time. You probably know where I'm going with this."

Roberts was on a roll now and he could sense that everyone was listening and absorbing his message.

"The Bible describes a time of great suffering and war before Israel recognizes her Messiah. It's called the 'Great Tribulation or the Time of Jacob's Trouble,' a time of such trouble the world has never seen. The nations will gather against Jerusalem and the Jews and Israel will suffer terribly in what we believe will be another holocaust on Jewish soil... and in some ways may already be under way if things here are put in a certain context. But in order for the great reconciliation between them and God to happen, they must be in Israel for that time. God will follow great suffering with great blessings. Are you seeing a pattern here? Wipe out the Jews, you destroy the Messiah's promise to them... makes God a liar!"

Roberts, with Aryeh jumping in now and again, lectured them on the ins and outs of Bible prophecy, especially concerning Jewish return to the land. Since Cohen understood the Diaspora so well, he added color and context to the discussion.

"There is something beginning to form in Israel. It is known as the Bible Block to insiders and it is gaining momentum, with a place for the Jews and the Bible-believing Christians too." Cohen explained.

It was an eye-opener for Yanit, Shoshana and Ayelet, all non-believers, they hadn't heard about these things but were intrigued as they could now see history, current events and the Bible intertwined in *their* lives. The Bible was a living thing, not just some dusty relic on a bookshelf.

"You know Jonathan, this is all very interesting, but right now, today, we need guns and ways to protect ourselves, your Jesus... not so much," she said, half wryly but with an added twist.

The group laughed, but it was one of those nervous laughs, less to do with humor and more to do with the uncertainty of it all. Roberts didn't take it personally, as he studied their eyes, because he knew what they were thinking. In a way, she had laid down the gauntlet and he always loved a challenge. When Roberts finished, smaller conversations bubbled to the surface and the new friends broke into smaller knots of twos and threes.

Shoshana and Yanit fell into an animated discussion all in Hebrew, leaving out the others. Some of it had to do with Roberts' comments and his Bible explanations. Some of it was just two new friends getting acquainted. Roberts was impressed with Yanit's command of Hebrew as he listened to her discussion with Shoshana. He tried to follow. For now, he just listened and captured what he could, as his Hebrew was just in the early learning stages.

Yanit shared her educational journey, her time in Israel, and her perception of recent events on the streets of America, stopping sometimes to dry her eyes as the moment overwhelmed her. She was emotional and explained that recent events were moving closer and closer to a decision point for American Jews. Shoshana understood inherently, as Yanit reminded her of one of her children. She offered her hand to Yanit, who took it and squeezed hard.

"If there is truth in what Jonathan says, then it is somewhere in the need to rescue the Jews and get them out of the United States."

Somehow he had brought many disparate elements together and woven the tapestry so perfectly she could see where the Bible met current events. It was chilling and though she didn't believe all of what he did, this set of details certainly had her thinking along those lines. She turned her attention back to Shoshana.

It was as if Yanit had found a surrogate mother. A friendship was born. When two strangers from different cultures meet there is sometimes an awkward moment or two as they get used to each other. Since culture is often transmitted through language, it can act as a barrier. However, in this case, both Yanit and Shoshana established an immediate bond through the language, the circumstances, and the respect for one another's thinking. Roberts was pleased at this connection.

The conversation was animated and deep, each of the new found friends sensing what was at stake. Recent events dictated that the cycle of more than 3,500 years of the Diaspora was about to end. It was clear the Jews didn't have much time.

Both of them agreed that it is one thing to read it in a book, an entirely different thing when it was staring you in the face. Each felt the weight of the moment. It had been supposedly attributed to Einstein that "God didn't play dice." In other words, there's no such thing as coincidence.

For the believers in the room that much was clear. For the others, it was too much to conceive at that moment. But hearts were warming and the events in the coming days, weeks, and months would confirm much of what they learned tonight.

Even now, new laws were wending their way through Congress that had a decidedly anti-Semitic tone to them. With Islamo-Christianity rising, the Jews of America were now out of options and without hope in the country of their birth. One door was closing while another was opening.

As the evening drew to a close, Yanit asked them if they could come over the next night and meet Sal and his family. "Oh, you need to meet this family, and they need to meet you," she said.

She then dialed Sal and told him to put a few more plates on for the next evening's supper.

"Tell mama that dinner's fine. Have her whip up some pasta and tomato and mozzarella salad, bread, olive oil, and some of that wonderful family wine."

There was business to attend to and it was the proper time to do it. The clock was ticking. Yanit's comfort with her Italian 'family' was so second nature by now that she felt totally comfortable dictating to Sal how the next evening's events would go. He didn't fight it because he knew how much this meant to her. Mama Vicenzo agreed to put on six more plates for dinner the next night.

As everyone got up to leave, Shoshana eyed Yanit, signaled to her with a slight tilt of her head, and pulled her out of the group for a moment.

"You know, the heavenly host is very pleased," she said, cryptically. This was the signal that Avram and the team had set up and had communicated to the Vicenzos and Yanit. Yanit, new to this but very tuned in, had been waiting for the prompt, prepared by the Vicenzos.

Yanit stopped in her tracks and eyed Shoshana, taking Shoshana's hands in hers, said, "Glory to God in the Highest."

The two women, one in her 50's, battle trained and very savvy as to the ways of the world, and the other woman, young, raw, but very perceptive and gifted, eyed one another for a long moment, apart from the crowd.

The two embraced in the most mother—daughter of hugs, for Shoshana, at that instant felt a deep kinship with Yanit. They would remain close from this point on. And in Hebrew, they began discussing the following evening's plans.

Shoshana spoke first.

"We will speak tomorrow night with the 'familia,' I like pasta."

Yanit understood that to mean something too, and answered, "You will like the food and their company very much, and the wine's not bad either."

That exchange, when translated, meant that the connection to the 'Family's' offer of support, protection, and dependability, was cemented and accepted by Shoshana's superiors.

And so it was that old friends and family, reaching back generations, would come together in helping fulfill the most ancient of prophecies, Jewish return to the Land of Israel.

> **From Dr. Thomas L. Garthwaite,**
> Under Secretary for Health in a speech
> at an Annual Awards Ceremony
>
> People may not remember exactly what you did, or what you said, but they will always remember how you made them feel.

Chapter 56

Supper with the Vicenzos

When Shoshana Bat Levy woke up that morning at 3 a.m., she immediately turned on her blackberry. After enabling her encryption shield software (self-designed by her firm in Israel), she knew access was safe and began reading emails. The first two had come from Roberts, now using a third-party name so as not to be detected. Roberts' knowledge of computing rivaled hers and so they had struck up a friendship based on their similar technical aptitudes, almost as close as their interest in 'the business at hand,' and of course their flying careers.

Roberts wanted a meeting to discuss enlisting his forces. He had Christian volunteers that would come to the aid of the Israelis. She respected his wisdom and understanding, even tolerating his belief system which focused on the Biblical end times and all that blather. Although she was now well aware of the prophecies concerning Jewish return to the land, she had more practical matters on her mind and politely would listen, but would then focus on business. She made a mental note to herself to call him as soon as she could. She'd be seeing him later that evening but would call to catch up anyway.

CHAPTER FIFTY-SIX: *Supper with the Vicenzos*

There was also an email sent from Yanit Silver. The meeting with Sal and his family, she said, was of the highest urgency. Yanit had encrypted her note with directions. 'Good girl,' thought Shoshana. She had learned the encryption software pretty quickly, a decided advantage. Well, that made sense. Yanit and Sal's contacts would provide critical contacts in the coming months. Of that she was sure.

Dinner that night held much promise. The six of them would invade the Vicenzos in a few hours and begin the arduous process of completing the battle plans and cementing any outstanding arrangements. She texted back a quick response telling Yanit that she was looking forward to seeing her again and meeting Sal's family.

Shoshana put the device away and began mapping out that day's appointments. She wondered what Roberts would bring to the table. If it was what she thought he could, then this crazy plan just might work, and with a minimum amount of casualties. Imagine transporting almost 6 million of her cousins across the planet to their new home and to safety! Imagine playing a part in the fulfillment of the ancient prophecies about bringing the Jewish people home! Though not particularly religious herself, this thought caused goose bumps to run up and down her spine and tears to fall down her cheeks. The conversation about Ezekiel 37 fluttered in her consciousness. She reminded herself to read these passages in Ezekiel before dinner. Things were moving fast. Things seemed different.

Yes, it was going to be a productive day. Dinner that night promised to be interesting too. She hadn't had any good pasta or a nice glass of wine for a while now.

That night, the six new associates gathered at the home of Sal's family. Yanit conducted the introductions to the family since she knew everyone. There was a comfortable feel to the start of the evening as each of the new friends settled into the family room which was right off the kitchen. Italian and Jewish homes often connect these two living features, and as many guests tended to remark about the Vicenzo household, 'all good parties end up in the kitchen.'

Maria "Mama" Vicenzo started the *hors d'oeuvres* around the room. Each guest was family to her. They felt it, too. The spiced Italian meatballs were a hit. And the roasted bell peppers stuffed with ricotta cheese vanished like magic. It was a houseful—just the way Mama liked it.

Conversations focused on life events, career, family, school, and the like. Shoshana was pleased to use a little of her Italian. She made easy conversation with Mama. The kitchen amazed her, and the huge Wolf stove took her breath away. Shoshana and Mama Vicenzo became fast friends. And the glass or two of private reserve cabernet helped the bonding.

Shoshana helped. She grabbed a plate of the *hors d'oeuvres* and circulated to the guests and family. She engaged in short chats, dispensed the treats, and began to feel at home. She couldn't help but wonder, *how would they treat me if they knew who I was?*

Meanwhile in the living room, a very intense conversation had begun between everyone who had met at Starbucks the previous evening. Each of them recreated the stories about how they all came together. Ross, Jenny, and Ayelet recounted the story of the shooting at the school and his subsequent hospital stay. Shoshana described her initial introduction to Yanit and Roberts' speeches. Of course, the synagogue massacres and the demonstrations were the focus of the discussion.

The elder Vicenzo updated the group on recent developments and progress—warehouse construction, teams at the docks, shipping companies, and the cyber-security company across the river in New Jersey. That conversation was important because it would be this small team that would work with Shoshana. Plans continued to disable the American infrastructure—electrical grid, water, telecommunications, city works, etc.

Yanit pulled out her wireless tablet, found the document, and scribbled a number of ideas and notes. She took the information Joe had given her and made quick calculations. Sal listened to her think out loud. Then he dropped a few things into the air.

The activity and talk prior to the meal convinced Roberts that Shoshana had an enormous amount of talent present in the room. Plus the desire and passion to support Jewish emigration from the U.S. to Israel was an obvious doubler. The group had a growing confidence that their mission could yield the results they wanted.

Members from both groups moved easily between the two and ideas brought up in each smaller discussion cross pollinated to the other. When mama called the folks into the dining room, they didn't hear her at first, so deeply engaged in conversation they were. This got the family caught up and the conversation continued over dinner. Once dinner concluded, she took a bow and went into a little speech, something she was known for.

"Ah, mia familia, it is good to share a meal, wine, and good conversation. No? But, I must turn to a serious subject here. I know why all of you are here, besides the food, of course!" She turned deadly serious.

My family and I are in this with you. We know the stories of the relationship between our two peoples. Maybe some of their dealings were, in the past, how shall we say it, a bit more 'creative' than our own. There are always going to be such things. But tonight, we confirm a covenant... we are here to help you in any way we can," she said.

Then Roberts hoisted his glass and said, "To familia."

Everyone joined his toast and responded, "A la familia!"

A Quote From Hotari's Father
—a Young Self-Detonator

My prayer is that Saeed's brothers, friends and fellow Palestinians will sacrifice their lives, too, there is no better way to show God you love him.

I wish I had done [the bombing]. My son has fulfilled the Prophet's [Mohammed's] wishes. He has become a hero! Tell me, what more could a father ask?

Chapter 57

Brainwashings

America stood isolated from any manner of suicide or homicide bombing activity until 9/11. Before the 19 young Muslim Jihadists hijacked four aircraft and ran them into the New York Trade Center Buildings, the Pentagon in the nation's capital, and a field in Pennsylvania, terrorism was virtually unknown in the United States. Oh, yes, there was the Oklahoma City Federal Building bombing and the first Trade Center attack, but America had remained virtually free from such foreign terror compared to the rest of the world.

The American Muslim population had skyrocketed in recent decades. And with it, something dangerous also appeared on the horizon. Many of America's more radical Muslim youth were learning a new trade.

Abdul Hakeem (Servant of the Wise) and Manahil Hakeem (Spring of Fresh Water) entered the university a year apart. They were a typical son and daughter of Middle East immigrants. Their parents found asylum in the U.S. They wanted to start over. Government authorities in Saudi Arabia made life difficult for them. But in America both parents played it straight and quietly slipped into the American lifestyle.

They shed their traditional clothing and adopted a western look. Both were educated in their home countries and brought the knowledge and skill sets of their training as materials engineers to the U.S. Both went to work for a major car manufacturer in Michigan. By the time of their fifth anniversary in the America, they became American citizens and celebrated the milestone with a nice dinner out with friends and family. They took the loyalty oath through misty eyes, for they believed in the American dream. For the most part, their experience wasn't that different from many other immigrants either in America or other Western nations. However, the story of their children would be different.

Both Abdul and Manahil were bright young students. Graduating within a year of one another they both scored well above average on the entry exams at the University of Michigan and took their high grades in with them. But, as sometimes happens with Muslim youth, they fell under the spell of a local Imam who would preach at the school. Slowly their ideas began to change.

"My young friends," Yusef Abdul-Qaiyoum (Servant of the Self Sustaining) began, so here you are, in America. You are the children of immigrants who, you say are successful and have come to America to live a quiet life. This is not a bad thing. But have you considered the fate of your brothers and sisters in Palestine?" he challenged them.

He wove tales of the oppression of the Muslims living under Zionist Jewish rule and how they had suffered. The Imam always tied his arguments to the oppressive policies of America and its allies, puppets really, who couldn't even exist without billions in American aid.

"America, yes, easy to live here but not so easy if you are a Muslim living under American or Zionist tyranny in the Middle East," he said.

The words dripped like honey off of his tongue and had the slow effect of luring them into his little web.

Young Abdul looked at his sister. The two of them had long ago developed their own special sibling communication. It was as if they were reading each other's thoughts. They both thought the conversation and the challenges as interesting. Two weeks later, they happened upon Abdul-Qaiyoum once again.

"So have you thought about our conversation?" he asked.

CHAPTER FIFTY-SEVEN: *Brainwashings*

Manahil looked at the Imam for a moment.

"What you say is not unfamiliar to us. We do talk at home. Our parents are not unsympathetic to your ideas. But, they escaped from a pretty difficult situation in their village in Saudi Arabia and are not willing to talk much about it. We watch the news and we too see what you see."

Her brother let her speak for them. He was the quieter of the two and would tell her later if there was anything on his mind.

Classes had ended for the day and so they headed for their car. The University had, over the years, taken on an increasingly Muslim flavor. Sharia law had grown in influence in this part of the country. Many cities that now disallowed Jews to live within their enclaves. Slowly the words of the preacher began to play on their minds.

As the end of the semester neared, they saw the preacher again. He invited them to services that Friday evening at the local mosque. After school ended that day, the two of them got into their car and headed to the religious center located near the campus. After parking the car, they went inside and were greeted by the Imam himself and two of his assistants.

The lecture covered portions of several Suras, mainly focused on helping the poor and helpless. Later the lecture turned to Zionist oppression and a growing awareness among America's Muslims that the tide of influence, once so heavily controlled by Jews and their friends in America was changing.

The Imam spoke of a new dawn in America where Sharia would be practiced not in secret but in public, a time where women would no longer act as equals but rather bow to the superior males within their families. Wearing full coverings showed Allah respect as the young women acquiesced to Muslim traditions. Manahil began wearing the scarf on a daily basis when out in public.

Over the next few months, the siblings read the Quran memorized long passages. This they did with zeal and enthusiasm. Their world view slowly changed and they began to see the rise of Islam in America and the sunset of the American ideal. Where America had controlled the world through its Jewish puppets, now the creeping shadow of Islam flowered. Islam was rising, the West was declining. Many traced Islam's rise in the West to a previous census done years before.

During the buildup to the census, Muslim communities threw their weight behind the process. It was time to vote with vigor and conviction. They would no longer simply check the 'white' box for nationality but rather 'other,' for now they would surface their greater numbers. Their leaders reasoned the more Arabs counted in the numbers meant more influence from the voting booth, and thus more attention paid to them by legislators. Eventually it would mean more money allocated for their communities and then increasing influence at the polls. Once entrenched, the Muslim population would dwarf the Jews and force its way to the forefront, putting the Jews where they belonged, where they always belonged, in the role of the Dhimmi.

The strategy worked. The census confirmed that the *suspected* number of Muslims in the U.S. was about two and one-half million. The vigorous marketing and successful results for the census, revealed that America had grown to more than 10 million Muslims. They had become a significant voting bloc that would dwarf the long-standing Jewish position and power at the polls. Islam rising—Jewish influence declining.

And so over the coming months, the radicalization of the young siblings took hold and they became part of a growing group of Islamic youth to volunteer for the most courageous act of all, martyrdom. The Imam Abdul-Qaiyoum wanted to educate his young charges and pointed them to an Islamic website that declared the following:

> "...Suicide bomber is a derogatory term invented in the West to try and describe what in Islam is known as a Fedayeen or Shahid... a martyr. The point of the bomber isn't suicide. It is to kill infidels in battle. This is not just permitted by Muhammad, but encouraged with liberal promises of heavenly reward...."

Unknown to the West with the exception of formal warfare, the *shahids* began their preparation to attack targets in and around America. The Imam explained that killing Americans was a great act but killing Jews was something special to Allah and of course to the Imams.

Their parents had no idea that their educational process had taken such a turn and though they noticed first when their daughter Manahil began wearing her scarves and traditional Muslim clothes, they began asking questions. The siblings stood together and told their parents that they had nothing to worry about. They were just returning to their roots and wanted to show the world about Islam.

The Imam continued, "So, my children let Allah be your one true guide. As the holy Quran says, '"Let those fight in the way of Allah who sell the life of this world for the other. Whoso fighteth in the way of Allah, be he slain or be he victorious, on him we shall bestow a vast reward.'"

The Abdul-Qaiyoum mosque had purchased land in the mountains of rural Vermont where the training began. The siblings flew into the state for summer camp with one expectation—preparation to die for the cause. To be a shahid meant they would be in paradise soon. Their safe, middle-class home and upbringing meant nothing now. They were now separated from their past. The spell cast by the Imam was complete. The training would harden them to the mission.

They learned hand-to-hand combat, handling explosives, preparing and setting Improvised Explosive Devices or IED's, and disguises. For 10 weeks, while their parents thought them to be at a Muslim youth camp, they were learning the fine art of urban warfare tactics and how to pick the best targets. They also learned the art of deception and how to smuggle their weapons into areas undetected. Their opportunity would come soon.

That summer, more than 200 young Muslims would attend the camp and with a growing legion of faithful followers, the numbers would soon reach the thousands, right under the noses of American authorities. With Islam gaining a toehold in America and with an increase in the numbers, Muslim influence was being felt at the ballot box as well. But while those who believed in the 'system' would support free elections and take America for what it said, those more radicalized soldiers would take matters into their own hands and force the real issue—Sharia Law or the Constitution.

Muslim watchers long understood what happened to a nation as its Muslim population begins to displace its citizens. As the 21st century unfolded, America's population hovered around one percent but would, within a generation reach two to three percent. However, if the population statistics meant anything, a geometric progression was in progress and with it, the projected Islamic population would soon reach five percent. As Muslim populations within a host nation rose, so did the level of violence. It had proven itself in France, Great Britain, and throughout Africa and Asia, until Islam became a feared minority. In time, Islam would dominate. The tables would turn.

At that critical juncture, Muslim demands for specific considerations from its host would be heard and from there, some observers believed, the early attempts to install and enforce Sharia Law would begin. In fact, it was happening as early as the first decade of the 21st century when various cities in Michigan began the process.

More states would soon follow and, as in France, many cities simply ran their own affairs with officers of the state unwilling to enter these Islamic enclaves. In other words, the Sharia-based cities became their own little independent states. America headed down a similar path. It turned against its Jews and coddled its Muslims. The social order was about to morph into something nobody could have predicted.

Michigan became the first state in the Union to issue a law first prohibiting Jews from working or attending school, and then even entering certain cities in the state. A state Constitutional Convention was called and Jews were stripped of certain rights including the right to work. Numerous lawsuits filed in Michigan courts were overturned by the Muslim-controlled State Legislature, a disturbing trend now spreading to other states in the Midwest. The Federal Government remained silent as it chose to stay out of state politics.

This trend actually reflected predictions from some Catholic social scientists years before that the Jewish influence in America would wane in favor of a closer association with Islam. Other more conservative commentators and pundits called it Islamo-Christianity. The poison was spreading throughout America's veins but America was too anesthetized to feel it.

Graduation day came, and Abdul and Manahil joined 200 other young soon-to-be *shahids*. They gathered in an old barn, long since converted to a 'classroom' and drew their assignments. Abdul-Qaiyoum expressed it a deep honor to present each of them with a symbolic bomb vest.

The planners within the Madrassa (Islamic religious school) had been busy choosing various targets throughout the United States. They focused on points of interest where the population of Jews or known Jewish-owned businesses was heaviest. However, even non-Jewish targets would do because the first aim of terrorism was to terrorize. It really didn't matter if it was a shopping center, a train station, a bus, or a school, or even an amusement park. The end game was to instill fear in the population to make your point heard. Then, you could control events around you.

After summer camp, the siblings left the safe confines of their Michigan home and caught the I-75 until it dumped onto the I-80. From there, they drove west across America to Northern California. Along the way, they stopped in several cities to sleep, eat, and refresh themselves. They took extra precaution not to reveal anything about their Muslim beliefs, wishing not to arouse any suspicions. They arrived five days later in Roseville, a small suburb of Sacramento, California. The final phase of their training began the next day.

They met in a rural area outside of the state capital, hidden from local traffic by a patch of the national forest. The planning team selected a small enclave that once acted as a family farm, nestled in the nearby hills. Six buildings stood on the site with main living quarters large enough for ten residents. The team converted the out buildings into training facilities where the residents resumed their summer work. The thick forested area provided safety and cover for the would-be martyrs. They selected seven targets that day including an amusement park, shopping malls, hospitals, and schools.

The siblings drew their assignment, an amusement park in Northern California. The target, California's Great America, was heavily attended with as many as 40,000 on any given day in summer and appealed to an international crowd. With its wild roller coasters, clear skies and perfect weather, it made for quite a summer attraction.

For months, Abdul-Qaiyoum and his planners worked to infiltrate various parks with the intent to smuggle in the bomb vests packed with explosives. When two young college girls landed jobs in the park, the plan began to mature.

Two days after their new employee orientation and training, the girls took their first assignments, operating food carts near a cluster of attractions. After work, both college students began their task. They were now sworn loyal to the Jihad declared against the Great Satan long before they were even born.

Each evening, they met with their handlers who coached them on safe assembly and handling of the bomb materials, transportation techniques, and proper disguises.

"Your covers are simple. You are both college students at local colleges studying Computer Science and Graphic Design," the trainer said.

"Your cover is perfect partly due to the proximity of Silicon Valley as well as the local international community. Many of our people who work here come from their ancestors' homelands. The presence of any professional Middle Easterner was not only unquestioned, but in this part of the country actually welcomed. Your job is to place and prepare the weapons for the *shahids* to don and complete the task at hand."

The girls would never meet the team which would allow them plausible deniability. They only knew them by description. Unknown to them, their lives would also become expendable.

During the second week of the training, each young woman began smuggling bomb vest parts into the park. When Friday of the second week came, materials for both vests were in place. Now all it would take was simple assembly of those parts into the final product.

Each of the girls was trained to handle their weapons. They quietly slipped away to find a restroom with private stalls. Once secure inside the stall, they opened up their packs and hooked up the wires, detonator device, and the package together. Bomb makers pack these weapons with bolts, nails, screws, and other metals to achieve maximum devastation, the small metal parts becoming flying death to their victims. Since both girls had no emotional attachment to their victims, they went about the smuggling and assembly processes flawlessly, remembering everything their trainers taught them. They hid the devices in the ceiling.

The entire team worked to formulate the Hakims' legends. They were students attending a conference for young computing professionals. The logistics sub team purchased several different passes for them, allowing them virtually unlimited access to the park and so that they wouldn't garner any suspicions during numerous park visits.

Additionally, the planners created several disguises so that their physical presence would change visit to visit. Meanwhile, the Hakim siblings studied the park, entry and exit points, local streets, buildings, and roads, also noting various gathering places for tourists to meet. They kept careful notes on time of day, and impact on the crowds during various kinds of weather.

Another one of the team members secured a position inside of the park as a ticket taker and from that vantage point, learned when special groups would be visiting the park. Northern California includes an expansive area from the San Francisco Bay to Sacramento to the east, and down the peninsula to Palo Alto and San Jose, where many local synagogues, Jewish youth groups, and community centers would plan special days out for their families.

When the employee learned of a Jewish Youth Day soon to visit the park, he began to ask questions of his co-workers. He discovered that more than 5,000 Jewish youth and their families were expected from a variety of Northern California synagogues, community centers, and other Jewish affiliated groups to enjoy the park during a late summer day 30 days from then.

After his shift ended, he closed out his station in the ticket booth, dutifully reported his sales for the day, turned over his cash register and all the documents within it, put on his light windbreaker jacket, and punched out on the time clock. Armed with this information, he prepared to report to his superiors.

That evening, he dialed the phone. Abdul-Qaiyoum picked up the phone. "Hello?"

"Brother Abdul-Qaiyoum, this is Benny."

"Benny, it's nice to hear from you," the Imam replied.

This simple exchange was arranged well in advance and followed a specific script worked out long before. The Imam now knew his young charge had valuable information, something he needed to know.

"Yes, I believe it is time to worship together and praise the one true God," Benny said.

"Of course, my brother. When shall I see you, my young friend?"

The two of them, through a coded language developed by their planners in a Sacramento-area mosque, made arrangements to meet that very evening. The clock was now ticking and the mission now a high priority.

Abdul-Qaiyoum then sent an encrypted email to his mentor, Abdul Aziz Rachman to arrange further instructions.

> **From the Pen of the Great Sage,
> Rabbi Hillel**
>
> *If I am not for myself, who will be for me?
> If I am only for myself, what am I?
> And, if not now, when?*

Chapter 58

Allied Forces

Urban warfare is a totally different sort of engagement from large battlefield formations where armies would face one another in the not so distant past. Fighting an urban war requires patience, superb tactical maneuverability on the ground, and in certain circumstances, the capability to support your fighting force from the air, if practicable.

As Israeli planners laid out the maps of the U.S. they quickly realized that there were four primary Jewish population centers as well as 'feeder zones.' They quickly divided the US into four major battle zones, known as Corridors.

Corridor Aleph (a rough equivalent of the letter 'A') would develop and form to provide rescue to more than 2.5 million fleeing Jews from the Eastern United States. But, as ingrained into the Israeli mentality, the goal wasn't focused on killing enemies but rather defending Jews in their attempt to seek safety in their new land, a philosophy followed by the forest partisan, Tuvia Bielski and others during World War II. With technology advancing, the IDF developed the capability in several previous wars to strike in a very surgical manner, minimizing civilian deaths.

Where the surrounding nations and cultures feasted on civilian kills, Israel always knew it must stay on the humanitarian side of any conflict. The world held it to a higher standard in war. Organizations such as CAMERA and MEMRI did everything they could to portray Israeli war fighting in a fair light while the opposing side always cast the Israelis as the new Nazis taking out of context any attempt to defend its borders and its civilian population. It was an unwinnable public relations nightmare, but the Israeli command structure knew it must continue to fight the lies, all the while knowing it would lose the battle. The war was a different thing.

The second major rescue route, Corridor Beyt, (roughly the equivalent of letter 'B') was defined as the Southeast U.S., centered in Miami and acting as a funnel for more than 1 million Jews in Florida and throughout the South. Having access to ports and waterways was a decided advantage as it was in New York and along the Eastern Seaboard.

Corridor Gimmel, (roughly the equivalent of the letter 'G') the Midwestern funnel, focused on O'Hare airport, where more than one million Jews lived in surrounding cities, counties and states. Chicago had its own issues because it would face challenges the others might not due to the nature of its population, spread out as it was and without any ocean port access.

Corridor Daleth, (equivalent to the letter 'D') centered in the Western U.S., focused on Los Angeles, Orange County, San Diego, and the Bay area, including San Francisco. One strategic advantage in the West was access to ports, shipping, either for access or for destruction. Both were on the planners' minds. The same held true for Miami and New York.

The primary targets were the airports. The ports were controlled by their 'friends' around the U.S. while IT forces, well-hidden and insulated from detection (remember who writes most of the encryption software), would provide enough disruption to keep law enforcement and any supporting infrastructure tied down and occupied.

Cyber-warfare would be the key to the grand escape and rescue operation. The planners knew and understood that Israeli software was at least two and often three generations ahead of America's. The Americans never fully understood how that was. It seemed that as long as their cell phones, video features, computers, and televisions worked without interruption, who cared where they were manufactured or designed, or what the latest release was?

From the Boy Scout Manual
Heye NachonóBe Prepared From the Modern Hebrew
Hilary Saint George Saundersí book The Left Handshake:

The Boy Scout Movement during the War, 1939-1945 had the first letter of each chapter spell out the Scout motto. The chosen words are: Bravery, Enterprise, Purpose, Resolution, Endurance, Partnership, Assurance, Reformation, Enthusiasm and Devotion.

Chapter 59

*B*uzz

At Central Command in Israel, the general staff prepared to start proceedings.

"Light 'em up!" cried General Gur Yerushalmi, Chief of Operations.

At that moment, 5,000 years of history were about to pound through the veins of 13 million Jews on all continents, nations, and cities. As communications leapt through cyberspace, flew to the satellites placed there for just this purpose, critical phone calls were placed, plans cancelled and reformulated, and preparations began moving forward at breakneck speed. The long anticipated call to an ancient people to return home was about to rock those Jews living abroad and draw them home just as the ancient Prophets declared.

Within seconds, 350,000 Israelis were alerted via wireless devices. All over America, hands grabbed cell phones, checked for coded messages, and began preparations. They would begin to leave jobs, schools, friends, families, and their lives. Plans for local defense, support, and extraction of close to six million American Jews were set in motion.

The operational phase of *Operation Last Exodus* had begun.

Families, jobs, companies, and entire industries were about to be reshaped by what would be the largest mass migration of a people in history. It would certainly be the quickest and the most elaborate, not to mention the most astonishing movement and transfer of men and wealth the world had ever seen.

Tens of thousands of documents rocketed through the electronic pipeline at that very moment. Building plans, subway system schematics, sewer systems, water systems, power stations, schools, airports, bus stations, city buildings in dozens of cities, in short the entire infrastructure of every major corridor wherever the largest Jewish populations were found... all of it available to the IDFA.

Along with that, planned escape routes previously identified, gained operational status. They would take on a distinctly Israeli flavor. The safety corridors carried code names in Hebrew from the Aleph Bet, or Alphabet and would serve to organize the regional commanders and their support teams.

In the midst of the electronic wake up call, all three Sullivans' phones buzzed as well. Ephraim's grabbed his phone from his belt and stared at the flashing message. It required a encryption key to be entered into the blinking field.

The term 'Fighting Sullivans' came to mind, reminding those who knew their history of the five brothers who were killed in service to America during World War II, thus wiping out the family bloodlines of future generations. Sacrifice was sacrifice. The message hurled all three Sullivans into the coming conflict.

Mimi's phone flashed the same message, as did Avner's and Ephraim's. Avner had pretty much recovered from the gunshot wound by now though he was still feeling some of the effects of that horrible night. The gunman was still at large, though it didn't appear anyone cared. Both Avner and Mimi keyed the codes into their phones. It was now only a matter of a few days and weeks.

Mimi's education was complete. She was ready to give herself for the task ahead. She was to assume command of Corridor Aleph in New York—the Eastern sector. And she would need to be on station within two days. She returned to her small Boston apartment and gathered her 'grab 'n go items... the small traveler packed with all her essentials. The rest wouldn't matter, she'd have a sweeper team come in and clear everything out—leaving no trace of her life there. Mimi boarded the Amtrak Acela Train in Boston bound for New York.

✡✡✡✡✡✡

Plans for a coordinated set of suicide (or homicide) bombings were in progress as well. They would soon make their first appearance in America. Self-detonating acolytes were being recruited in the mosques and madrassas and there was no shortage of them. Thousands stepped forward for the honor to strap on the bomb vests and enter into Allah's glory.

At that same moment, Manahil and Abdul boarded the light rail from Sacramento to San Jose. Since their weapons awaited them in the park, they carried nothing that would compromise their mission.

☪☪☪☪☪

Mimi's first class ticket placed her in the car behind the pilot's position. She caught up on things with her wireless assistant. She opened up an encrypted instant message from Shoshana sent just moments before. She was just back from Israel.

"Close to operational status. Need to talk asap." The note was terse, just as Mimi expected. *The time is so close,* Mimi thought. *So far, no rumblings from D.C. But the government had a way of pulling off a surprise when you weren't expecting it.*

Mimi continued through her messages with an occasional detour to see news from Israel. She hoped to glean some tidbit about her unit. She was keyed up, sensing that inner anxiety that always built up before the mission. Her thoughts now drifted more to her friends and family. She thought of her orchestra mates, of her brothers, and of course of Farouk and Shabibi. What would become of them? Would this crazy cancer of hate reach them too?

Her mind then focused on Avner. He was the big brother, the capable leader. She knew that no matter what would happen to him, he'd find a way to handle it. She found herself whispering a quick prayer for his safety and that of her sister-in-law. She missed him and ached for his wise counsel and advice.

Avner's destination was the Western U.S., Corridor Daleth—he had his instructions too. Avner sent an encrypted text to Danielle telling her to meet him at the train station. He added a Daleth symbol at the end of the encoded message, telling Danielle that there was an emergency and that they would need to move fast.

When Danielle received the encrypted text message from Avner, she stopped for a moment. Everything she had been taught and had learned about prophecy and eschatology was deeply ingrained in her thoughts but didn't necessarily control her thinking day to day. Hers was to love the Lord her God and do His will. However, this time it felt more urgent.

Several times in the past few years, she remembered wondering if the prophetic clock was closing in on midnight. Now, with all the demonstrations, the 'coming out' of the anti-Semitic/anti-Zionist movement, and blatant attacks on Jewish targets all over America, she was convinced it was so. Today was the day.

She texted him back indicating her understanding of the moment and communicating to him her willingness to do whatever it took. The stakes were never higher and she knew it.

The two young marrieds had some emergency bags always ready to go and some checklists reminding them just what items they needed to take. The emergency kits contained their critical documents, money and credit cards (though she wondered what use they would be). She needn't worry about pictures and memories, with everything backed up and stored in the clouds.

It was almost as if her very life was flashing before her eyes. She recounted her childhood and her teaching. It was hard not to take a brief trip down memory lane remembering her schooling, her parents, friends, and the rough years where she had taken some extreme liberties with her personal life. Nevertheless, those days were now behind her and her mission was never clearer, her mind focused on the task at hand. Would she see any of her loved ones again?

Avner headed to the train station where he expected to meet his young wife. So much had happened over the past few months—the shooting, the marriage, and then the pogroms. The young Israeli couldn't possibly fathom the extent of the clash just around the bend. As his train pulled into the station, he realized that life, as he once knew it was over and a new phase was beginning. The train stopped and he got out, looking for Danielle. They spotted each other and ran into one another's arms.

"We have to get to the house, there's not much time," he said to her, grabbing her arm and steering her toward the exit of the station.

"I've got all the emergency gear ready to go. All our documents are in there with some money. I think we're set."

"Do you remember when I told you that all Israelis are coded into a massive electronic communication system and that in case of a dire national emergency, there would be a call to action? Well, the call came today. Come on, we'll talk about it in the car." His sense of command and confidence was very easy to recognize. He knew the smell of battle. All of their communication would now be in Hebrew or Yiddish.

CHAPTER FIFTY-NINE: *Buzz*

In Israel, the populace drills constantly to prepare for national call ups. It is said that within 24 hours of a general call up, greater than 50% of the tiny nation is armed, on the front lines, and ready for action. With them, it is a matter of life and death. It would prove to be the case in America as the IDFA would take to the streets in defense of America's Jews.

During the ride home, he explained all the details. He described the shelters waiting for them, the preparations in place, and his first orders.

Israel considered this a general call up as the entire army was mobilizing in the homeland as well. Within 24 hours Israel would be on full alert too, though after all the events in America, they were very close to a ready state. Soon, they would be defending the lives of six million of their American brethren and helping them escape, while anticipating their arrival.

"I don't care where we go, just as long as we're together. I won't leave your side." She reached out to grasp his hand. Their hands met together and remained intertwined for the ride home.

They rode in silence. Once home, they closed the door. She reached out to him and he returned the embrace. He allowed himself to be drawn to her strength. They kissed, held each other, and hung-on to each other—just inside the doorway. Centuries of expectations, of hopes, of dreams arrived, all at once. Danielle looked at him, the love coming through the tears.

"I've read for years about God's plans for a *second return to the Land*. You know, you always wonder, how could it happen here, how could or why would anyone want to leave here?"

Her question hung between them. Leaving their successful and promising lives behind to chase the dream of millennia played on their minds.

The promises of God were never clearer and Danielle threw herself into the middle of it. She knew the answer to her own question. She began to sing a short portion of a Biblical verse. Danielle began to hum a song she knew, played during worship in her congregation.

> *Where you go, I will go, where you live, I want to live. Your people will be my people, and your God will be my God.*

In a whisper this was her promise to Avner.

Her lyric from the Book of Ruth was the sweetest thing he had ever heard, music to his ears. He pulled her close once again. And for the next short while, they enjoyed one another, not knowing what life would deal them next. The two of them then dozed off for a few minutes.

Not far away, Ephraim received his call and was instructed to contact another cell phone number, that of Shoshana Bat Levy. He knew of her prowess in the military. She knew of his prodigious computer skills—there wasn't much in this tight community that she didn't know about. She knew that his presence on her team would create a powerful staff with Dogface's cyber security teams.

Sensing that he needed to connect with his siblings, he quickly arranged a three-way conference call between himself, Mimi, and Avner. They would speak only Hebrew and then in coded terms known only to them.

Ephraim connected first, then Mimi, and then Avner, who was startled out of his quick nap and liaison with his wife. The encrypted call ensured that their conversation would be safe in case any prying eyes or ears tried to intervene.

"I'm heading east," he said simply. Mimi explained her plans as did Avner. They recognized it might be a long time before they saw one another again, if ever. The next few days, weeks, and months promised to be uncertain at best, dangerous and fraught with the unknown.

"I think we are ready," Mimi said. All three siblings had been contacted weeks before with a pre-warning. They knew and understood their assignments.

"I also have something to say to the two of you. I want both of you to know how much I love you two. I know I haven't been the easiest of sisters to deal with but neither one of you never gave up on me. Even in my darkest times, you always let me know you loved me."

Avner spoke next. "Mimi, when you came out for the wedding, I finally saw you for who you are. You're a beautiful young woman, now greatly accomplished. Long before that Ephi and I knew you were destined for greatness. We are proud to have you as our sister."

"Mimi, do you remember when you used to take me out for walks in Haifa? You would always show me the flowers and explain what they were and how they grew. I will always remember how animals would just come up to you as if they knew you. I always cherished the time with you—it was so special to me. I understood you even then and now I am so proud of you... the graduation, the music, and all you've done there. I know you are going to do great things in the East," Ephraim's voice exuded strong confidence in his sister. The call came to a quick close.

Ephraim was instructed to meet Shoshana in New York, the next day. So, he made arrangements to take the next flight out of Los Angeles and head east.

Mimi's ride to New York was in progress even as Avner and Danielle made their final arrangements for that evening. All of them traveled under assumed names and passports.

Israel went on a war footing. She prepared to receive the first massive American immigration wave, also known as the 10th Aliya. The Israeli planners working feverishly within the Jewish Agency had been tasked with the logistical piece of the operation, ensuring that each Jewish person wishing passage to Israel would have the proper arrangements and support.

The infrastructure sprang to life. Hundreds of thousands of apartments, homes, reception centers, *kibbutzim*, and *moshavim*, prepared to receive their new guests, this, the homecoming of close to an expected six million plus from America. The prophets had predicted it and now the time was at hand.

Other plans began working their way through the system. Inbound Aliya officials continued the arduous task of planning for the arriving Jews from America. Other sections of the agency had kicked things into gear for arrivals from Russia, Western Europe and into sections of Asia as well. Within months, more than thirteen million Jews, six million from America, would arrive home forever.

The Transportation Corps set to work. Part of the planning included flying the Diaspora-bound Jews out of the U.S. and into Israel. Once on the ground, a huge and tightly controlled network of ground transportation prepared to take the new arrivals to their new waiting homes.

The Leadership Team's Monday morning meeting was moments away. The ten officers in charge of this aspect of the operation discussed their response time. Israel had assembled more than six million modular housing units in the past two years. They were near their target goal. Israel could absorb its new immigrants—even deep into the Negev.

One major breakthrough, a stroke of genius really, had to do with the airborne processing centers now planned for each flight leaving the U.S. Every aircraft would clear passengers through to their destinations right on the planes. There would be little if any processing on the ground. Shapiro's plan, though not perfect, had retrofitted every wide-bodied plane in the Israeli inventory with the gear it would need to perform the electronic miracles.

And, when news reached the Jewish Agency planners that Patel and Roberts had secured the extra aircraft, Shapiro, pumping his fist, screamed, "Yes, Yes, Yes!!! We can do this now!" The inventory now numbered about 400 planes at their immediate disposal. That now meant close to 600,000 to 800,000 passengers per week, assuming the planes were flying almost 24 hours a day. The planes would be on the way within days.

As Mimi arrived in New York, the two young converts arrived at their destination in the Bay Area. Their mission approached.

Now it was just a matter of time.

Coffee House Chatter

"What happens when a nation loses its confidence?"

"Great question. I'd like to answer that with another question. Why DOES a nation lose its confidence?"

"Very thoughtful—good question. My guess is that there is either a decline in morals or a loss of focus by its leadership."

"Hmmm, good points. I would add that when political correctness supplants common sense, then it's only a matter of time before that nation loses its identity, then ceases to have influence on anything meaningful."

Chapter 60

A New Target

The date was set. The Hakims had their assignment. Everyone had completed their homework.

Well back in the previous century, a strange phenomenon gripped America. Emerging from World War II, America suddenly found herself stepping up on the stage as the leader of the western world.

Great Britain lost her grasp of the empire where the 'sun never set.' One by one, her former colonies either declared independence such as was the case in India and Pakistan or broke free from daily governance as was the case with Singapore and Hong Kong, though a strong British flavor remained.

She was virtually bankrupt now, some believed because of the way she handled affairs in Palestine. A small contingent within Christian circles who studied Bible prophecy believed it had something to do with her treatment of the Jews and the refusal to complete the promises made in the Balfour Declaration. God had a long memory, especially when it involved His chosen people, they believed.

Three years after the war, tensions reached the boiling point in Palestine where the British finally conceded they could no longer contain the Arab-Jewish powder keg. The Mandate Government declared its intention to leave the area while both Jewish and Arab regular and irregular forces prepared for what many expected to be the quick and bloody demise of the infant Jewish state.

Five Arab armies prepared for war while Jewish refugees from Europe's death camps languished in new camps built for them in Cypress. Still, tens of thousands managed to sneak in, swelling the nascent state's Jewish population to about 600,000. Internal rivalries between various Zionist factions were set aside as they pulled together to face an ancient enemy. Was it just the Arabs they faced or was there another "unseen" enemy there too?

The Jews sent emissaries around the world to find anything they could buy to conduct what they believed to be a war of independence and the very survival of the new nation. Virtually the only nation willing to sell or provide them anything was Czechoslovakia. Though America recognized Israel, she continued an arms embargo virtually assuring that the new Jewish state wouldn't make it out of infanthood. But, once again, it was a time for miracles.

Out of all this, America assumed its new role on the world's stage and during the roll call at the United Nations became the first nation to welcome Israel into the family of nations.

Excitement ran high in America's evangelical churches. After the war, she stood strong facing down the power vacuum in Eastern Europe. But, as the years passed she began her own descent into moral decline and suddenly faced a series of crises. America would have issues to deal with just as she reached the apex of her power.

After the invasion of Cuba during the Bay of Pigs, assassinations of the Kennedy brothers and Martin Luther King, and the Vietnam War, America found herself divided within. A clash of morals, values, religious ideals, and the drug culture changed America. A growing atheist movement made its imprint felt as many argued to remove any references of God from schools, government institutions, and civil agencies.

She began to doubt herself and her enemies could smell it. But, deep within, a revival of sorts began out West where a new church was forming under a tent in the brilliant California sunshine. That church and the hundreds that would spin off and form their own fellowships would carry a new message of "end times prophecy" focused on events of the Middle East, and especially Israel. Millions came to saving faith in Jesus, understanding that they were living in as exciting time as the world had ever known.

Manahil and Abdul knew it too... except for different reasons.

They had their target now and prepared to enter Allah's glory.

"Are you scared?" Abdul glanced furtively at his sister as they rode in the train. He had finally come to full realization that the mission was on. He mindlessly picked at a small scab formed from a pimple on his face. His eyes darted around the train car, avoiding the glances of others on board.

"Yes, I am. But I know what Allah expects. Are you?" Her answer calmed him a little but there was still a bit of an edge.

"We have to get this done. So much depends on us. We are carrying a message from the Imam- that these people have to pay for their sins too." She was firm but gentle with her brother.

It was a firm commitment. They knew what they had to do. This time it would be the Christians and one of their infidel churches.

> **Jeremiah the Prophet Speaks:**
> Chapter 16 Verses 14-16
>
> Therefore behold, days are coming, declares the LORD, when it will no longer be said, As the LORD lives, who brought up the sons of Israel out of the land of Egypt, but, As the LORD lives, who brought up the sons of Israel from the land of the north and from all the countries where He had banished them... for I will restore them to their own land which I gave to their fathers.
>
> Behold, I am going to send for many fishermen, declares the LORD, and they will fish for them; and afterwards I will send for many hunters, and they will hunt them from every mountain and every hill and from the clefts of the rocks.

Chapter 61

The Pilots Get Trained

Israel received Dayle Johansson's pilots as if they were family. More than 2,000 highly-skilled masters of the air joined him and his team to begin the process to fly America's Jews out of America and to the Promised Land. With more than the numbers needed, Johansson set about the training phase of the operation. Their meeting started when Ari Melnick and David Shapiro walked into the room.

It was a Shabbat, the day of rest. But work is always allowed when it means serving others in life or death situations. On this Shabbat, everyone put aside personal preferences and jumped into the work before them. They prepared to address the auditorium full of pilots.

A heavy guard ensured security for the top secret meeting just outside the undisclosed location. No family members knew where their loved ones were. Just days before, each pilot disappeared from the American landscape. Each received a new identity, and travelled a circuitous route to Israel to receive training, a crew, and their aircraft. Johansson prayed to open the conference.

Johansson prepared to introduce Melnick and Shapiro. Then two other figures walked into the back of the room. It was Jonathan Roberts and Savish Patel. Nobody could identify Roberts—they were not accustomed to his new look. The recent all-points bulletin couldn't reach Roberts here.

FBI efforts to arrest Roberts began when it was learned that he joined Christian Zionist forces. The President was so angered that he directed the FBI to ask Interpol to issue an international notice as well, which they did. Neither effort was successful, yet. The President's wish to see Roberts tried in front of a court for treason was foiled by the Wasserman twins' efforts to hide him.

The Wasserman brothers' diligent efforts to protect Roberts from the authorities were working. Joining with Israeli agents, Roberts became the invisible man. His new identity enabled him to escape the authorities—he was safe on Israeli soil for now. His now graying beard grown a little longer now and dressed as he was, he made a pretty convincing Chassidic Rabbi. Added to that were new colored contact lenses he wore.

Roberts took a seat in the back of the auditorium but when Dayle saw him, he motioned for him to come to the front. Roberts looked behind him and pulled Patel along with him. When they reached the stage, Dayle stepped away from the microphone and embraced Roberts first, then Patel. The five new friends, now partners in the largest planned mass human airlift in history, enthusiastically exchanged greetings. Dayle approached the podium to introduce his fellow workers.

"My chaverim (friends), my mishpocha (family), we are at the starting line of the greatest race in history. We have just days, or at the outside, weeks to airlift close to six million Jews from America to Israel. Europe is now emptying of its Jewish presence. Israel's population has nearly doubled in the last six months and will nearly double again when the airlift is complete. You are the engine driving this train. I have much to discuss with you. But first, I want our very dear brother to join us for a few words. Jonathan?"

Roberts approached the podium and was greeted with warm, enthusiastic applause. While there were a few Jewish members in the audience, the meeting was overwhelmingly non-Jewish. Loving Christians were reaching their hands out to the Jews in a symbol of brotherhood, respect, and love. Centuries of hate and mistrust were about to be reversed.

"Please, please, that applause is wonderful but direct it to our Lord and our God. He has brought all of you here today and by the Right Hand of His strength, may He bring His people home safely. By this time, God willing, very soon, 15 million Jewish souls will live and work in the land of their fathers. Your hard work, your toil will have made that possible."

They applauded again and yelled shouts of praise.

Roberts then went into what could be best be described as a prophetic speech, almost as if he had seen a vision. He paused for what seemed like an eternity to him. He saw his life flash before his eyes. Then, closing his eyes, he began to speak.

"I see the million dead by Roman hands in the streets of Jerusalem!"

"I see the dry bones from Ezekiel's 37th chapter!"

"I see the hundreds of thousands dead in Chmelnicki and the Crusades!"

"I see the six million dead in the camps of the *Shoah*!"

"I see the outright slaughter in the streets of America just a few months ago. It continues still!"

"I see the rise of Islamo-Christian values that honor no one but the Devil himself!"

He now lowered his voice, and paused for effect.

"I see the wonderful Christian Zionists who have stepped up and accepted the mantle of suffering to help God's chosen!"

"I see your efforts and God does too!"

"I see the true Christians, the true Bible Believers that Paul spoke of so long ago!"

"I see those sweet believers spoken of in the 10th and 11th Chapters of his letter to the Romans! We are here today to serve our Hebrew brethren!"

Roberts wrapped up his quick speech with a blessing for the pilots and the crews. He then turned it back to Johannson. The sound technicians then turned on the microphones for Melnick, Shapiro, and Patel. They stepped up to the table... now forming a panel. Patel spoke next.

"My friends, we stand at the crossroads of an historic moment. The prophets from ages past have spoken of this day. The scriptures are clear that the Jews will one day be gathered to Israel for the final time. We know much tribulation awaits them. We know there will be judgment, but we also know this is their home and it is their time."

"I cannot say what will become of them, but we stand today with a plan to bring them home. As you know, we have arranged for aircraft for this fourth major airlift. You know the others—Yemen, Iraq, and Ethiopia. But what Jonathan, Michael, or Ari didn't know until just a short time ago, is that there are not 160 aircraft available. Today I am here to tell you that we have arranged for an additional 250 planes, all twin-aisle, and capable of extended ranges! We also have acquired several more C-17's useful for conversion to medical missions as needed!! Our capacity has more than doubled-we have more than 400 aircraft in our arsenal. We can now fulfill the airlift requirements in just a few weeks!!"

The room erupted. The pilots and planners in attendance fell into animated conversations. Patel had to wrest control of the room back from the excited audience. He banged the gavel to restore order.

"This means we have to move fast. As you know, your training will be compacted to three days. By day three, you'll receive your assignments and flight crews. Each aircraft will fly with at least one physician and nurse along with some supporting medical techs. Each aircraft is equipped with enhanced Israeli avionics, electronic countermeasures, and the processing center software the best known to man. You will have Israeli air marshals on board as well."

"Our C-17's will come with experienced pilots. Most of them are retired U.S. Air Force. We have ten jets today with at least five more coming. Each major airport will have at least two C-17s assigned to it for purposes of evacuating challenging medical cases."

Patel continued his speech for another few minutes. Concluding, he looked at the audience and finished with this.

"My friends, we are on the cusp of history. It is an honor to serve with each and every one of you."

The audience rolled into another huge applause, the sound growing louder by the minute, the crowd now stomping its feet as well.

Melnick and Shapiro finished the morning session with short addresses and panel discussions. Once they finished, the pilots received their assignments for classroom and simulator time. These next three days would prove grueling but satisfying to each and every one of them.

The homecoming approached.

> Ha Yad Moshe (the Hand of Moses),
> Sh'mot (Exodus) 8:21
>
> Now the LORD said to Moses, "Rise early in the morning and present yourself before Pharaoh, as he comes out to the water, and say to him, Thus says the LORD, Let My people go, that they may serve Me...."
>
> From Ha Yad Isiyahu (the Hand of Isaiah),
> Chapter 7 Verse 18
>
> In that day the LORD will whistle for the fly that is in the remotest part of the rivers of Egypt and for the bee that is in the land of Assyria.

Chapter 62

Let My People Go

After passage of the 3rd Patriot Act and subsequent bills, tightening freedoms for them, American Jews had become pariahs in the American social structure. History was repeating itself. The press had become increasingly hostile to any Jewish presence.

The new laws had virtually extinguished any Jewish participation in the professions making it almost impossible for a Jew to attain any position of importance. American businesses closed the doors to Jewish applicants. To students of history, it was a repeat of the past, most recently from Nazi Germany and the Nuremburg Laws. When the Germans enacted the laws, it was with the express purpose of pushing the Jews out of Germany and extorting their money. What didn't make sense to the Jews was that they had been there for generations and were deeply ingrained into the social, educational, and professional infrastructure. Now the American Jews faced the same scenario.

The universities and colleges were turning away Jewish students, now known by addresses due to the census. With an increasing phenomenon known as Islamo-Christianity, the first states passed anti-Jewish legislation prohibiting them from holding jobs or in some cases barring them from living in certain communities.

As Islam grew in power and size in these states and drew more mainstream Christians to its cause, economic conditions worsened. Some believed there to be a direct correlation between treatment of the Jews and encroaching Islamo-Christian attacks. Others denied anything of that nature even possible, especially in America, which had a Constitution, democracy, and freedom.

That was no longer the case, at least for the American Jews.

The spate of violence and the rounding up of the first Jewish citizens where many simply disappeared had finally convinced most of America's Jews that the time had come to leave. Getting out now would be challenging but doable. Though awareness of the current situation grew among the Jewish communities, there was still small remnant that denied any of it.

Many punished themselves in remorse and anger. They didn't think this could happen in America. They hadn't listened. They hadn't taken advantage of the open window to leave. Now, they remembered the lessons of the Jewish Germans (or German Jews). The prudent ones got out in time. The foolish ones delayed, doubted, and....

Chaim was sufficiently recovered from the shooting—though he needed his cane. But he gathered enough strength to travel to Washington with his brother. They still had access to the President—they were childhood friends. The Wassermans and the President grew up together.

The two rabbis had made multiple trips to the White House to plead the case of the Jews to the President. Each time he promised them that no harm would come to their people. But every time another "action" occurred, he turned and railed against the Jews and America's Jewish leadership. He complained that they had corrupted America with their greedy ways, controlled the financial world, and influenced all manner of government—local or national. The rabbis grew more and more confused. Still, they had hope that some sense could be talked into the President's head. Maybe he would listen this time.

Chaim finally issued his first warning during that last meeting that the Jews would have no choice but to fight back. They both noticed the marked difference in the President's appearance, as they were ushered into the Oval Office. He was decidedly more drawn, his hair rapidly graying, and his demeanor more agitated.

"We know our history, Mr. President, and we know enough that history tends to repeat itself and is doing so at this very hour."

"We also know that God will avenge his people."

The President was not easily intimidated.

"Really? Are you threatening me with God?"

"No, Mr. President. We are old friends. We played baseball together as children, we went to school together. We were practically brothers. You came to our house and we went to yours. I don't know what's happened to you these past few years, but you must realize, sir that things have changed. America has turned its back on my people."

"We have learned that when an enemy threatens our very existence, then we must believe him. You've no doubt read or at least know of *Mein Kampf*. If you have not, then you must certainly know the story of the book. Hitler laid out the plan for my ancestors' destruction then simply followed the plan. He was but the next one in a long line of 'Hamans,' out to destroy the Jewish people. Now, today, of course, there are the Muslim and Christian threats which they always carry out. The more recent anti-Semitism coming out of the Middle East and from Islam and Christianity here in America and Europe underscores the point that it's happening again, now, today, here in America. The Jews of Europe should have seen it coming. They did not. We now see it taking deeper roots here," Chaim continued. They had indeed learned the lessons of history.

The President remained silent.

"Sir, you have professed your support for a diverse and integrated America. In that vision, which we supported by the way, you have afforded followers of the Islamic faith a home here. Under any other circumstances that would be fine. But in the last 10 years, things have increasingly gone wrong, badly wrong. Tens of thousands of my people have been killed in the past three months alone—in our streets, in our schools, in our shops, and in our synagogues. You must allow my people free passage to their true home, Israel. And, yet you still refuse to let my people go!" he cried, pounding the floor with his staff-like cane.

This gained the attention of the secret service officers who were visibly offended that someone was yelling at their chief. They moved a step closer but backed off when the President waved them off.

"Mr. President, you must understand that this time our people will fight back. Right now, even now, we are prepared to do what we have to do to protect ourselves. The time for talking is over. In the next few days, there will be a disaster in the U.S., which you must account for if it occurs as I say it will. You, alone, will bear the brunt of that event."

The President sat, stunned. Did this old friend dare threaten him? Here, in the Oval Office? His secret service cohort sensing physical confrontation, and seeing a threat when it was stated, moved closer but did not react just yet. The intense debate between the President and the Rabbi left both of them wiping their brows, panting, and working hard to control any outburst of anger.

The President stood up and rose to his full six foot, five inch height. He towered above the two rabbinical brothers as did his secret service cohort. The two Rabbis were no physical threat, though everyone in the room was feeling uncomfortable. Eleazer spoke next.

"Mr. President, do you remember the oath you swore during your inaugural? You promised that anti-Semitism would be met with the harshest of responses and that you could not, would not, tolerate any indication of such an act. You have still yet to condemn the synagogue attacks or the aftermath of the marches in any hard terms. Our enemies are sharpening their knives to carve us up and finish us off," he said, picking a metaphor that seemed eloquent and expressive. Now it was the President's turn to respond.

"Losing five to six million Jews at this point will drain the country of much of the medical, financial and technical know-how America needs to overcome the challenges it faces," the President answered, sounding like he had regained his calm and collected manner.

"In fact, both of you must know that it is here in America where Jews, Christians, and Muslims can form the true brotherhood of man, only here in America," he said emphatically.

This sounded like so much political posturing to the brothers but sounded even more like something the Pharaoh would have said thousands of years ago. It hit both brothers at the same time.

The meeting ended with an exchange of handshakes and promises by the President to quell the violence. Neither of the brothers reacted to his words. The clock was ticking now, time was running short. The two rabbis had to act but were in a quandary.

Chaim caught the next plane out of Reagan International and headed back to Dallas. Eleazer had to wait another hour before catching a plane to L.A.

After visiting with the President, Chaim had never felt as depressed as he had at this moment. Was this how Moses felt after his confrontations with Pharaoh? At the airport, he looked at Esther and just shook his head.

As always, she correctly perceived his mood and probed gently, especially when he began rubbing his beard and his forehead.

"So, I take it the President wasn't exactly open to your request." Esther reached out and took Chaim's hand.

"You could say that again."

"Eleazer and I are at a loss. We believe we know where this is going, but I can't see how it will work out."

"What do you want to do?" She asked.

"Well, here's a crazy thought." Chaim sat up straight and found Esther's eyes. "I'd love to be able to have the same kind of power over circumstances that Moses did."

"Can you imagine what that would do for us?" Chaim wondered aloud.

"What, a repeat of the plagues or something?" she parried. He didn't react as if it went right over his head.

"Well, think about it, could you imagine us having the ability to do something like that?" he answered.

"My b'shert," she continued. "Do you remember when we met?"

"Of course I do, it was the most amazing day of my life."

"Well, you might remember that I fell in love with you but wasn't all that thrilled about the Bible or your thinking. I was a student and wannabe scientist, or at least I thought of myself as a scientist. Maybe more like a snot-nosed kid with a dream."

"But when I got into my Entomology research, I discovered something far more beautiful about this amazing planet where we live. I discovered a whole other life on and under the ground, and in the air," she said, slowly and patiently awaiting his reaction.

"Bugs—pests like flies, gnats, and fleas—all that became my new world. You have always given me the room to grow and learn. I have always appreciated and admired you for that. And through the years your sermons, my Tenach reading, and the writings of sages have revealed God and a bit of His creation to me. And, in turn, also to the family of researchers with whom I have worked. The tiny animals I study are a fascination and wonder—**living evidence of design and the Designer."**

Esther and her husband, a learned rabbi, had many discussions, some bordering on outright arguments about creation or evolution. She, at least at the beginning argued for evolution, he, of course argued for creation.

"When pheromones were discovered back in the late 19th century, all the scientists could figure out was that 'nature' had a way of communicating within each species. Even an ant, a tiny little ant, has a very elaborate and complex system of communicating to others in the anthill and along the ant trail."

"When small insects communicate it also may be over long distances. We have proven that these tiny little creatures can even fly miles into wind and find their mates when the female puts out her mating signal. I've come to love all of them, even the pests, because they help declare the Glory of God," she said. Esther, over the years had come to believe in the creation, though she still had a million questions.

"So, what does this have to do with our situation," the rabbi asked.

"Well, we may have a lot more power in our hands than we think. Tell me, my love, do you remember the 10 plagues?"

"Who me? ***Do I remember the 10 plagues?***" he asked, in a self-mocking, incredulous manner.

"Well, then, you must know what my research has done. You've read some of my papers and seen me speak, but you may not know about the latest research. Not only do they have well-developed communication systems and capabilities, we've been working with Israeli scientists and they have taken the process even further, basically leaving American research in the dust."

The rabbi was now sitting on the edge of his seat and leaning forward. His interest suddenly engaged with his wife.

"Tell me more, this is all very new to me." It wasn't that he didn't listen to all of her stories over the years but there was so much he couldn't absorb it all, despite his tremendous intellect.

"Well, our Israeli friends can now reconstruct the entire communication code within most of the common species of insects and many small animals, frogs and the like. They've got computing assets there that we don't have here. Remember that most of the newly designed chips that find their way into any computing device have probably been designed in Israel, right?

"Their scientists are working closely with Electrical engineers and communications specialists to identify the algorithms associated with the electrical impulses and chemical transmitters the insects use. They have recorded all the transmissions and mapped them out electronically, electromagnetically, and chemically into various patterns pertinent to that particular insect or animal family. They can *see* the outgoing and incoming messages from the sender and differentiate it from the receiver. And today, they claim, they can communicate with them. You know, it's strange, there's something I remember reading about in Bereshit, (Genesis) that seems to indicate that man could, at one time, communicate with animals."

"So, let me see if I understand. The scientists in Israel can communicate with insects and amphibians? Is that what I'm hearing?"

"Yes, and other species too—and not only that, but they can now duplicate the signals and shape their behaviors." In other words, we may have more 'tools' at our disposal than you think. God has set up the system and didn't I read somewhere that humans are to be masters of the earth?"

"This sounds like genetic engineering gone crazy. And to think that I teach communication skills to adults who have trouble talking to each other." He just shook his head from side to side, staring at the floor.

"Well, if it's used for an evil purpose, I suppose so. But you surely remember.... Israel, in the last major regional conflict, packed up some hornet egg cases. They sent them into and behind enemy lines. They drove the enemy into the open field. How many Jewish lives were saved? And how human shields were saved as well?" Muslim fighters were well known to use human shields when fighting in street battles.

Chaim stroked his beard. "I am very impressed with this interesting history of the kingdom of the bugs but how can it help us?" he asked. It wasn't sinking in yet.

She then explained a developing idea. The idea was so out of his way of thinking she decided to call in the heavy guns. She dialed her sister and then called for a family get-together. She and Chaim would fly to LA and the two identical couples would spend the weekend together. She quickly made arrangements for the trip.

The following weekend, they touched down at LAX. It was a warm, breezy day. When they were all in the car, Esther managed the discussion. She then explained all that she had told Chaim about her learning in the field and her personal research as well as her observations on the Scripture.

"You know, I've always wondered if the staff Aaron had in his hand had special powers—something like a radio transmitter or something like that. Almost like a special rod that could send out signals to animals or maybe even bugs."

Chaim and Eleazer looked at each other and as the thought hit them at the same moment.

"**Recreate the plagues**?!?" Are you *messhugah?*"

The full extent of his wife's ideas finally hit him and his brother at the same time.

Esther looked at Rifka and the identical twin sisters just smiled at each other, nodding, knowing, and understanding what the other was thinking. Rifka's background in Physics and Engineering made the perfect counterbalance to her sister's wisdom and understanding of the plant and animal kingdoms. Rifka had designed satellites and elaborate artificial intelligence systems for both commercial and military applications over the years but wasn't at liberty to discuss them. This might be the time, though it would put her at great risk.

"With God, all things are possible," Esther said.

"Remember, He designed the system, all we would be doing is using His equipment," she said, wryly, shooting a wink in her twin's direction.

The room fell silent. The twin brothers looked at each other, each reading the other's thoughts.

"Well it won't be easy, but it's doable," Esther continued. In fact, she was aware of Israeli efforts to export some of the technology for pest control and other uses but it wasn't as well received in the U.S. as it was in Israel.

Rifka nodded in agreement and added, "We have the technology to do something that will get the President's attention."

Chaim leaned over and began rocking back and forth, putting his elbows on his knees and holding his head in his hands. All they could hear were some unintelligible prayers being uttered from the back of his throat, mixed with "Oy, oy, oy." Eleazer put his hand on his brother's knee, patting it to calm him.

Coffee House Chatter

"What do you think of genetic engineering? She asked.

"What, like growing drought-resistant corn, wheat, or fruit?"

"Yes and maybe more—controlling bugs, animals, that sort of thing."

"Well, that's all sci-fi stuff… straight out of Spielberg."

"Ya think?"

Chapter 63

Consensus on Critters

Over the next several weeks, the twin sisters grew their plans. They spent the next few days contacting associates and colleagues in both in the Entomological and Biological Sciences and the Engineering disciplines from Israel to arrange the first meetings and were on an airplane the following Sunday.

Arriving in Israel, they hailed a sherut (taxicab) and headed to Haifa where a research conference on entomology and pest control was set to begin the following day.

Scientists had proven the capacity to communicate with larger species of animals such as great sea creatures and simians. Man had, through history domesticated previously wild animals but had never been able to either control or even contain the smaller creatures in the kingdom. But that was changing.

All manner of pests continued to wreak havoc on crops, deliver deadly disease through fleas, mosquitoes, flies, and other pests as well. But with recent scientific breakthroughs in communication theory using electrical and chemical analysis, Israeli scientists had decoded many of the communication systems of common pests. With the intent to maximize understanding of various species for the betterment of mankind, they had begun the process of reestablishing a long lost relationship with the animal kingdom that was blocked shortly after the creation.

The scientists and engineers began to put their plan together. Esther and Rifka now found themselves right in the middle of unfolding events. The twins now realized that a lifetime of study was coming down to one huge experiment, though largely proven but still with many unknowns to work through.

The top secret conference was in the midst of final preparations and the two American sisters were invited to speak and help lead several of the breakout sessions. As delegates, they also had voting privileges so that when the time came, they could help lead the discussions and eventually the vote.

The first meetings between American and Israeli scientists were somewhat contentious. There was disagreement on the point whether or not unleashing various insects and animals on an unsuspecting population constituted serious manipulation of natural forces. Someone in the room brought up a past libel, something that caused everyone in the room to stop in their tracks.

"We've all read our history books—you know how the Jews were blamed for the plagues in the middle ages and for causing massive amounts of The Black Death throughout Europe. Jews died too but that never is mentioned. This is serious though because we will be accused of the same thing again," noted one American Jewish scientist.

"True, true, but what is the alternative?" countered a well-known Israeli entomologist, who had a large family contingent living in America.

"We all know what's coming. We've already seen the pogroms, the synagogue massacres and the parade murders, not to mention the appearance of Jewish Stars of David on the windows in New York and elsewhere. Isn't it plainly obvious that America doesn't want the Jews anymore?"

Esther and Rifka looked at each other, reading the other's thoughts. It didn't happen all the time, but at certain times it did... like now.

"Look, time is running out for academic debate. We have the technology to reproduce several of the original plagues. We cannot sit here and debate this forever," Rifka's voice carried through the hall with conviction and a sense of urgency, snapping the others to attention. She continued.

"The way it looks from our perspective is that we have to deliver our 'weapons' in the next three to six weeks, sooner if possible. Both of our husbands have access to the White House. They will continue to plead for the safety and release of American Jews but we don't have much hope the President will support us."

For the next three days, the conference of 350 scientists and engineers hotly debated the pros and cons of this most dramatic development. For years genetic engineering had been the topic of arguments on both sides of the scientific community. Yet, those debates, centered on whether or not manipulating the genes within crops and determining whether or not the food itself was safe. Those debates were mostly academic and the genetic engineered foods appeared on market shelves anyway.

This debate, however, had to do with the lives of millions of innocents. Their survival was first and foremost on the minds of the conference attendees. But others weren't at risk like the Jews of America and elsewhere.

On Day Two the first article that appeared on the conference agenda came to a vote. *Would the conference support the use of electronic and biological weapons on a civilian population?* It was understood: no direct attack on people. Rather the animal kingdom would carry the battle—as described in the Bible. The difference, of course, the Biblical plagues were delivered by the hand of God. These would be delivered as a result of man's learning about God's "mechanisms" and then using the technology accordingly.

Was God involved?

The Conference President had everyone seated. More than 350 attendees, representing more than 100 nations, waited in the main hall while the chosen delegates took their seats for the first vote. The air was alive and the mood in the hall was electric.

"Mr. Chairman," the moderator/facilitator, began, "we are ready to take the first vote. Mr. Sergeant- at -Arms, please read the proposal."

"The issue on the table reads thus: 'It is resolved that the International Union of Life Sciences supports the use of non-violent natural means to wage a _defensive_ war on an aggressor with the intent of doing no harm to the host human population," the proposal read.

The room was stunned into silence. Never had such a bold and aggressive proposal been brought forth for debate to this body or any other scientific group like this. Years of scientific research were now coming to a head. Israeli scientists, always in search of a non-violent way to help defend their nation, now held their breath. A democratic approach to such a provocative issue like this was virtually unheard of in the civilized world.

"We will now vote," declared the chairman. "We will begin with the State of Israel," he said. "I must remind you of the confidentiality of this issue and the news of the succeeding vote."

There was no outside press present so the security of the vote was assured. The members were all Jewish so there were no outside influences present either, although there were plenty of dissenting opinions.

Rifka squirmed in her seat as her moment had come. As the voting began, Esther and Rifka leaned in to one another whispering about events as they unfolded.

"Israel votes aye."

"Italy votes no."

"What was that about?" Why did the Italians vote no?"

"Strange, but all I can figure is that it may have less to do with the status of America's Jews and more to do with the secular nature of the Italian Jewish community," Rifka countered. Some people just didn't get it.

"I wonder," Esther answered.

Switching topics for a minute she started another line of questions for her sister.

"Exactly what will we need?" Esther asked. She had developed the biological angle to the plan but it was Rifka who was working on the engineering and electronics angles.

"The computers aren't very big... we can actually run most of this off of handhelds. We've programmed all of your experimental data into the servers. Your models tested perfectly. Some good software engineering there," said Rifka.

"From there, we've networked all the field pieces into the main source. We can see every piece we have in the field and can hear them too. We have this mapping software I'll show you later... simply amazing. We can track the swarms as they come in whether they are flies, gnats, beetles, anything."

"The field equipment is the miracle is in all this. When we tested the call for the various species, we did it remotely from more than a mile away. We placed sensors on the riverbanks in Missouri—and fortunately attracted no attention. Later, we extended our reach to two, then five, then ten miles. Then we released the pheromones and the enhanced electronic signals. In less than 10 minutes we drew hundreds of frogs out of the Missouri River and even stopped traffic for a bit. But the amazing thing was the insects... you can't even imagine. And, as you can probably guess, we had plenty of alibis and good cover stories."

"In this case, we will work throughout the Tidal Basin area and up and down the Potomac and of course all the lakes in the area. There are a good number of rivers and streams too. The sensors are no larger than small coins. I've even seen some that resemble flowers and plants. The Israelis have mastered the art of miniaturization. I love their "fly on the wall" technology where they can plant something almost anywhere. They can attach them to trees or just drop them in bushes. They will be virtually indistinguishable from the local plant life. They are even working on shutdown technology that will silence the device if it knows it's being watched," Rifka explained.

The sisters stared at each other as more votes were added to the total. Esther nodded at her sister. It seemed that their thoughts now moved between them with no effort to do so.

"I remember our early experiments with the technology. We actually were able to draw fish out of the water. Boy did that stink!"

"Well, yes, of course. The smaller creatures," said Rifka, now beginning to show some anxiety. The vote was coming to a final tally.

"The Netherlands votes aye."

"I count 50 for, 10 against," Rifka whispered. Her sister nodded her head as she acknowledged it.

"I think we're going to need more votes," Esther said, somewhat disconsolately. Rifka agreed, but then placing her hand on her twin's knee, reassured her. "It will be alright," she said. "Remember who's in charge?"

CHAPTER SIXTY-THREE: *Consensus on Critters*

"Great Britain abstains."

The momentum was building. The delegates continued their votes. Although they were short of the 85% they sought, the gap had closed. They now had 80%, where it had been at less just a few moments before.

"Argentina votes, Aye."

Rifka let out an audible sigh and then sank back in her chair, her heart beating wildly as she ran her hands through her red hair. She could feel the sweat beads running down her back as every nerve stood on end. She had never felt so alive, yet so frightened. It was both thrilling and terrifying because she knew what was soon to happen.

"France votes aye."

"Spain votes aye."

"Australia votes aye."

The time came for the United States. Esther, the delegate leaned forward to the microphone.

"America votes aye," she said confidently.

The votes continued—consensus was building. The buzz in the hall grew as well. *Would the scientists come to agreement to unleash biological technology on America's capital? Would they deliver a powerful message without the loss of human life?*

The last vote was cast and a team of three accountants collected the data and began to tally the numbers. A few minutes to compare their totals and the percentages—then the team leader, a Physicist from South Africa, cleared his throat and asked for silence.

"Ladies and gentlemen, the Union has spoken with a firm and loud voice here today. All 100 votes are now counted-the totals are 87 aye, 10 nay, and 3 abstentions. The measure carries!"

The room sat stunned into silence, and then it seemed that everyone began shouting at once. The room bursting into a cacophony of sound. But everyone knew just what this meant. The chairman struck the gavel on the dais and then commanding the meeting back to order.

"Everyone in this room is remanded to silence. There cannot be a single word of this to leak out. We have each taken an oath to protect this vote. The safety of the American Jewish population may well rest on your shoulders."

> From the Hand of Moses (Sh'mot-Exodus)
> Chapter 7 Verse 17
>
> "Thus says the LORD, "By this you shall know that I am the LORD: behold, I will strike the water that is in the Nile with the staff that is in my hand, and it will be turned to blood."

Chapter 64

Bloody Water

Two weeks later, the first agents landed in the States. Armed with innocuous looking small handheld devices the Washington D.C. team headed for the Potomac to begin their first reconnaissance. The Israelis carried newly minted passports and traveling documents from the forging masterminds in Jerusalem. Mimi's D.C. commander in the field met them in the Library of Congress, a heavily traveled tourist site.

The long hours of hard coding were about to pay off. Ephraim and the cyber security team arranged by Dogface Vicenzo had been at it nonstop for about 36 hours. They broke up the time by short breaks for food and an occasional catnap.

But time was short and Ephraim had pretty much run out of options. Then, to his complete surprise, he found himself looking right into the DC Water System's intranet. He blinked he eyes in wonder—he couldn't believe it. But there it was! All those long hard hours at the keyboard paid off!

"We're in! We're in!" Ephraim rejoice. "I've got the site. Check this out, you guys."

CHAPTER SIXTY-FOUR: *Bloody Water*

The other six members of the team who had been working different aspects of the puzzle, spun in their chairs and focused on the wall-sized projection of the DC water system. The cyber team began exploring the puzzle in front of them. It was all so familiar.

There wasn't much time so they had to work fast and more importantly, Ephraim needed to communicate with Mimi directly to explain what they had. He blasted a short text to her explaining what they were doing. He sent the live link to Mimi on an encrypted channel known only to their teams.

Mimi's small device buzzed on her hip. She grabbed it and looked at the message.

"I've just received word that we have penetrated the Water Authority's firewalls. The cyber team is in and is now reprogramming the system," she told her team in the bunker.

She texted Ephraim right back expressing her encouragement. Her team dialed into the link and could follow Ephraim's progress. The hours seemed like minutes. But they were in.

This was indeed great news because it put her forces on the offensive now giving them some much needed breathing room and the upper hand in this battle of wits with the White House.

She then turned her attention to matters closer at hand.

"We don't have much time. I understand you are almost ready to go."

"We need about two days to position everything. Our research tells us that the amphibian population is robust this year. We also know that the various insects are mating as well so there shouldn't be too long a delay from the time we put out the signals and the chemicals. Our electronic equipment is working as designed," the scientist answered.

So the plans were set. The nations' capital was about to experience a set of plagues of Biblical proportions.

The D.C. water system is huge. The Authority manages more than 1,200 miles of pipes, includes five pumping stations and reservoirs, four elevated storage tanks, and tens of thousands of valves, not to mention almost 9000 fire hydrants.

Commando teams formed at midnight with the intent of disabling the pumping stations at the Dalecarlia and McMillan Water Plants. It was midnight and the well-trained and drilled mixed teams of Israeli commandos and local Christian Zionists were ready to roll. Many of the water treatment personnel had abandoned the sites and joined forces with the strike teams. Success would depend on local insider knowledge.

The teams assembled at midnight, checked out their gear, and climbed into their vehicles for the short ride. Each team's journey would end by disembarking about one mile from the sites. They carried small radios to stay in touch with the others. There were five strike teams.

At just the right moment, Ephraim's cyber team turned off the water flow to the city. The team had two hours to work.

"Yarden (Jordan) 1, come in," whispered the team coordinator.

"Yarden 1 here," the voice answered. "We are in position."

"Move in," the commander dictated.

"Moving now," the team leader answered, then clicked off.

The guard station in front of the Dalecarlia facility was manned by one guard. Two team members crept to within 30 yards of the guardhouse.

It was quiet. They could see the guard reading a newspaper and sipping coffee. The two forward strikers then created a muffled diversion to draw out the guard.

The guard heard the sound, which to him sounded like an animal snuffling around in the bushes. He put down his paper and coffee and headed out of the shack to investigate the noise. Without ever seeing his attackers, he tripped on a wire which had been placed in just that location and down he went.

The Israeli commandos quickly silenced him, tied him up, muffled his mouth, and administered knock out drops, then continued to penetrate the facility. Two of the Christian Zionists, workers from the treatment facility, joined the Israelis. The strike team was now in control of the water system of Washington D.C.

The smaller strike team was on the move. The plant hummed though there were few workers on duty. The team moved to the next phase of the silent attack. The next two-woman team moved in dark silence to encounter the first member of the water treatment plant. They ambushed him from behind, first knocking him down to the ground, then silencing him with a knockout chemical. He would awake in the morning with a tremendous headache, not remembering what happened.

Their target was the valve system. Their intent was to ensure the red compound soon to be dropped in the water by their cohorts, made it to the main. They set to work on the equipment, tapping their small handheld devices into the main computer system, as they were shown in training. Within minutes, the equipment showed circulation, working well. They exited the same way they came in.

The other teams copied their fellow strikers. Each target was neutralized in turn and now the D.C. system was putty in the hands of the invaders.

It was early Sunday morning. At 1 a.m. from an isolated wooded area not far from the main Washington D.C Water supply, a Christian Zionist mortar team lobbed the first of 10 shells of a rust oxide-like compound into the basin. The water would turn a deep blood red within minutes, and thus the first of the "plagues" would be underway. It would take just a few hours to reach all the taps in the city.

✡ ✡ ✡ ✡ ✡ ✡

About 4 a.m. the President awoke and headed into the shower. He had tossed and turned all night, the air-conditioning drying him out. The water felt good, waking him up a little. He closed his eyes and drank in some of the refreshing water. Then it happened.

As the shower began spitting and choking out its new water stream, the President noticed the blood red water. At first he thought he was bleeding and began frantically searching all over his body for a cut or some sort of injury, though he felt no pain.

Once he realized it was the water, he was stunned and angry then instantly thought of the two rabbis. His screams and cursing must have been pretty loud because the First Lady burst into the bathroom and could see steam but not much else until she opened up the shower door and all she could see was red. It looked just like blood. She began to scream until her husband stopped her. He looked like he had been in a knife fight.

"Get Bill up here," he growled. He was in no mood for calming at that moment, so she threw a robe around herself, grabbed the phone and dialed up the Chief of Staff.

"On my way," the President's aide said groggily, being awakened from a deep REM sleep. He had just gotten to bed one hour before after helping the President on some urgent White House business late the prior evening.

The Chief found the President in a foul mood.

"I want to know what's going on. Call a press conference for noon today. Let's get this out in the open."

Bill worked to notify the press that the President would meet them at noon. Just before the conference started, Bill received a text: *Church bombing in California... 10 minutes ago. Hundreds dead or hurt.*

Bill just stared at his little monitor. *How much worse was this going to get?* He had to find the President and alert him of the San Francisco bombing.

The day flew by with more and more reports about the red water attack and, then, almost by the hour another mention of suicide attacks against Christian churches. By the time of the news conference, there would be more than 12 church attacks.

The President entered the small ante-chamber next to the Press Room. The Chief of Staff intercepted him just in time with the news. The President just hung his head and the two of them exchanged a look of sadness.

"Ladies and Gentlemen, the President of the United States." The President gathered his thoughts, working hard to contain his anger and his sadness at the attacks. But as he was to take the podium, his training kicked in.

"Good afternoon to all of you. We have just been informed that there has been another church bombing in San Francisco, making 12 in all today. Details are sketchy at this hour but we are monitoring the events there. I can only offer my deepest sympathies to the families." He then switched topics to the tainted water.

"Many of you awoke this morning expecting to take clean showers and drink clean water. I did too. But when I stepped into my shower the water turned a very deep red, like blood. We have since determined that terrorists have tainted the water supply but that there are no toxins within the water, so it is safe. We have beefed up security at all water treatment facilities and pumping stations. My science and environmental staff tell me the water should cycle clean in the next 24 hours or so. I am told that the damage was confined to local sources. I will now take a few questions but cannot stay long."

The first question came from New York Times reporter.

"Mr. President, who do you think has done this?"

"We don't know just yet, but we do know this... there were several intruders at the Water Works very early this morning. Whoever it was dropped a coloring agent into the water. Several guards were attacked. They didn't hear or see anything and were disabled when taken by surprise. We are investigating now."

The conference lasted for 30 minutes. The President then ended it by looking into the cameras and issuing a warning.

"We will find whoever did this. And when we do, we will prosecute to the fullest extent of the law... that I will promise."

Neither the President nor his staff mentioned that no mainstream Christian church was attacked.

From the Palestinian Charter

Article 19: The partition of Palestine in 1947 and the establishment of the state of Israel are entirely illegal, regardless of the passage of time, because they were contrary to the will of the Palestinian people and to their natural right in their homeland, and inconsistent with the principles embodied in the Charter of the United Nations, particularly the right to self-determination.

Article 20: The Balfour Declaration, the Mandate for Palestine, and everything that has been based upon them, are deemed null and void. Claims of historical or religious ties of Jews with Palestine are incompatible with the facts of history and the true conception of what constitutes statehood. Judaism, being a religion, is not an independent nationality. Nor do Jews constitute a single nation with an identity of its own. They are citizens of the states to which they belong. Where Would the Jews Go?

Article 22: Zionism is a political movement organically associated with international imperialism and antagonistic to all action for liberation and to progressive movements in the world. It is racist and fanatic in its nature, aggressive, expansionist, and colonial in its aims, and fascist in its methods. Israel is the instrument of the Zionist movement, and geographical base for world imperialism placed strategically in the midst of the Arab homeland to combat the hopes of the Arab nation for liberation, unity, and progress.

Israel is a constant source of threat vis-a-vis peace in the Middle East and the whole world. Since the liberation of Palestine will destroy the Zionist and imperialist presence and will contribute to the establishment of peace in the Middle East, the Palestinian people look for the support of all the progressive and peaceful forces and urge them all, irrespective of their affiliations and beliefs, to offer the Palestinian people all aid and support in their just struggle for the liberation of their homeland.

Chapter 65

Drones

The 'Italian' connection was paying off in spades. Along with state-of-the-art weaponry and other war-fighting material inbound from Israel, the local support network arranged by the Vicenzo family and friends, had purchased and installed large quantities of electronic gear such as hand held devices, personal computers, and small, lightweight projectors with 3D display capabilities which could project hologram-type imagery.

This latest technology, developed first by Israel for the battlefield then, for the movie making industry to enhance the moviegoer's experience, gave the viewer the ability to see virtually any film in dazzling 3D. To the urban war fighter, any and all 2D drawings, blueprints, and technical diagrams could be converted into a 3D experience. This gave the war planners the ability to virtually walk inside, around, and through the potential targets and help fully understand any and all challenges they might face.

As far as their Israeli counterparts knew, this technology remained only within their capabilities and had not reached the outside world. This might be the competitive advantage they would need to turn the tables on their American hunters. The world was inverting. The Israelis knew they had the better software, at least two and sometimes three generations ahead of anything now operated by her enemies.

The warehouse conversion process was in the advanced stages now and drawing to full operational capability. The crews, hired and paid by the Vicenzos and their connections, were the best in the business. The virtual war rooms were fitted with GPS secure conference capabilities and huge, wall-sized widescreens capable of simultaneously viewing different urban locations, allowing planners to shift troops, change plans, and react to changes on the ground in a moment's notice.

What the satellites couldn't see would be picked up by the thousands of mini drones soon to be deployed. Construction crews, soon to take on new duties as soldiers and support teams, laid in sleeping arrangements, foodstuffs, and exercise facilities which could sustain those living within for months, though none of them expected to be there that long.

CHAPTER SIXTY-FIVE: Drones

Israelis had a hand in latest generation flying drone technology. The latest developments included small, flying devices virtually impossible to detect due to their tiny size and elusive nature. One of their electronic masterpieces gave those 'flying' them the ability to be literally a fly on the wall. The technology had become so good that tiny cameras could fly into a battle zone and carry small, virtually undetectable packages into the area with them.

One such invention was a biological weapon using insect cases. Remote pilots could launch the drone with a small case of insects attached and then drop it into the hot zone. Then the drone dispersed its cargo into a field, a building, or into water sources, depending on the requirement.

Remote Israeli pilots sent hundreds of cases of freshly hatched hornets into the enemy's camp in the last regional conflict. The buzzing troops flushed the enemy into the open. Thus it was open season on the opposition. Israeli gunners and infantry easily swept the field and ensured a total victory. And for some strange reason, the hornets never attacked the Israelis.

The border had remained relatively calm since then. The enemy never knew what hit them. Israeli scientists and planners never released *that* technology and kept it a closely held secret. And more surprises were on the way.

When asked about rumors of a 'hornet brigade', Israeli military spokesmen denied any knowledge of the story. As far as they were concerned, the facts that any insects attacked merely underscored the fact that bad fortune could happen to anyone at anytime. On that particular day, Hezbollah and their Lebanese friends happened to be on the wrong end of contrary winds.

From the Prophet Yerimijahu (Jeremiah) 51:27

Lift up a signal in the land,
Blow a trumpet among the nations!
Consecrate the nations against her,
Summon against her the kingdoms of Ararat,
Minni and Ashkenaz;
Appoint a marshal against her,
Bring up the horses like bristly locusts

Chapter 66

Battle Plans Forming

A secure phone call and teleconference was set and the four regional commanders dialed in to teleconference on their personal computers. They were greeted that morning by General Gur Yerushalmi. Looking grave and not at all his usual affable self, the general stepped to the podium in Israel and the international meeting got under way. Yerushalmi, a close confidant of Shoshana Bat Levi, was picked to deliver the message.

"Boker Tov, and shalom, chaverim, (Good morning and peace, my friends) you no doubt have never expected to be facing circumstances like these. However, the IDF and the Mossad had been planning various scenarios for years in case something like this ever happened. You may not be aware of the details of these plans, but each of you knew that you could be called on in case something like this could happen."

"As tragic as the past few months have been, we are not, however, without resources. At this very hour, you have much help on the way. Our forward intelligence teams have paved the way with some rather impressive firepower and help from old and new friends."

At that very hour, squads of IDFA soldiers had secured warehouses all over the nation as provided by their Italian friends. More than 2.5 million weapons awaited their new owners as well as tons of explosives, supplies, and food.

Mechanized units, well hidden from the public due to crafty transportation, stood ready to roll into action. Supplies contained clothes with special RFID sensors to help the soldiers recognize one another. Night vision goggles, provided by "friends" would enable them to move at night and early in the morning in the dark where they could feel a little safer. The long arm of the IDF was about to undergo its most important test.

Several reports, rumors really, had reached the commanders' ears. The rumors concerned themselves with stories of fracturing American military units, facing one another with weapons as mutineering soldiers left their bases. These Christian Zionist soldiers faced the most difficult decision of their lives, that of remaining sworn loyal to the flag of the United States of America or choosing the Bible, and defending America's Jews as they attempted to escape, as their 'higher authority.'

American officers and enlisted personnel were, at that moment, making life-changing decisions that in one way or another would not only weaken the American social structure but potentially cause it to crumble. The rule of law only works if certain deterrents remain in place and now even those were threatened by a growing mutiny of American forces, at least those residing stateside. Once a citizenry loses confidence in its government, that government becomes weak and cannot enforce its own laws. Anarchy can follow.

The increasing Muslim presence in the U.S. military made things even more complicated. The strange irony wasn't lost on those remaining in the military: American Muslims fighting a domestic disturbance against American Jews and Christian Zionists while the very same military was engaged in fighting their brethren abroad.

It was becoming the American government's worst fear—Americans facing Americans, brothers in arms against one another. There were also reports of fire fights on military bases, with disappearing material and aircraft. This particularly intrigued the Israeli brain trust as it had understood this to be a possibility and with their intelligence officers working closely with friends, it was now coming true. It reminded some of the Civil War, fought almost two hundred years before.

The IDFA regional commanders received their first set of orders. The inbound transmission directed them to secure four key international airports by any means necessary: JFK in New York, Miami International in Miami, Florida, O'Hare in Chicago, Illinois, and Los Angeles International (LAX) in California. If it were necessary and practicable, regional airports could be captured if they were strategic in nature. John Wayne Airport, in Orange County California was considered strategic because of its proximity to local transportation arteries. Many Jews lived in Orange County, San Diego, and points north. Each would be a feeder center to the main point of departure, Los Angeles International.

The Israeli commander continued.

"Remember, the goal is not war with America, but to save Jews. We invoke the memory of great Jewish fighters such as the Bielski partisans or those who fought to defend the Warsaw Ghetto and others like them, who fought the Germans, but would rather have been saving lives than killing their enemies. We remember the brave resistance fighters in the Warsaw Ghetto who fought the Nazis sometimes with their hands and little else. We must keep our priorities in order. But, if need be, we must be prepared to strike quickly. Our forward intelligence has penetrated U.S. military bases near each of these major regional airports."

The commander continued, "We have also learned that about half of the American soldiers willing to support us, a far greater percentage that we dared even believe. They support Israel and are willing to do whatever it takes to help the Jews. They have told us time and time again that they are willing to die for our cause if need be. If we extrapolate that number, it could run a million or more in the Western Corridor alone, just from the military, not counting police and firemen and others like city workers, and who knows who from the population.

"We do know that a Christian minister named Jonathan Roberts has joined us. He believes he can pledge another two or three million armed supporters, maybe more. These Christians are sympathetic and supportive. We have had our theological battles over the years with them, but as it turns out they are about the only friends we have left.

What he didn't say, but all of them now understood, was the long-time perceived friend, the United States of America, was no longer a friend in any way.

"We have met in emergency sessions over the past few weeks and we believe his promises are rock solid. We are currently assessing American military strength and will to fight a war on its own soil, against its own citizens. You may remember that America has not fought a foreign invader since the War of 1812, or if you consider the border skirmishes during the Mexican American War in 1846-1848. If you factor in the Southern Confederacy as a foreign invader during their Civil War, then it is 1865." The short history lesson put into context a concept that nobody could have dreamt of this a few short months ago.

"Islam invaded the U.S. with the World Trade Center bombings in 1993 and 2001 and is strangling the freedoms America once knew and cherished through manipulation of American law," he continued

"Then of course there were the recent Independence Day protests turned into bloodbaths later the well-coordinated synagogue massacres, and most recently the church bombings. As security measures continued to increase on America's streets, freedoms are evaporating there." He also observed that a growing percentage of the U.S. military was now Muslim.

Islam was a stateless, faceless enemy and hardly could be called an invader, or at least as far as the American Government was concerned. And since that time, the U.S. had tried to balance Muslim civil rights with ongoing wars against their religious compatriots in foreign lands. It was one great big paradox. With the growing influence of Islam in U.S. politics, economics, and social issues, America faced something it never had to worry about—a distinct threat to its internal security while at the same time trying to appease and placate more vocal members of the Islamic community domestically. This wasn't like the perceived Communist threats in the 1920-1950's.

The internal Islamic threat grew more insidious. Young American-born Muslims joined the military and embraced radical elements of their religious faith. Lines between religion and the Constitution blurred. These were American citizens but loyalty to U.S. institutions grew increasingly fuzzy as time went on.

"We have spent a lot of resources to provide safe coverage to the Jewish refugees to get them to the airports and safely to Israel. We must hold not only the airports but all the streets and boulevards leading to the airports, as well as many key buildings, bridges, and other urban infrastructure. This may include the expressways and freeways, the main arteries of their public transportation systems. We don't have much time," he added.

"There are trains and in some areas, the monorails, to consider as well. In the Midwest and the east, much of the transportation is underground, which poses another issue. Our demolition teams are training now and we expect them to be in place within a few days. They will sabotage certain key parts of any theater where we operate, if need be. We also have a team of cyber warriors who are prepared to attack the electronic infrastructure and take down the communications and public works. We may need to cripple communications, police, fire, and the American military. We want to avoid any massive airbursts to completely destroy U.S. military communications, but we can also deliver those if need be," he explained.

America was severely weakened by its prolonged presence in the Middle East, the Philippines, and in Indonesia, plus other regional wars in Central and South America. The Mexican border war, fought over drugs, illegal immigration, and perceived territorial rights had most recently claimed the lives of thousands of American soldiers. The American public was nervous and rightly so.

More than 1.5 million troops were deployed internationally either in close combat or as peacekeepers. The only homeland defense at the President's disposal was local law enforcement and National Guard troops. As good as they were, they would be no match for a battle-hardened and well- trained urban guerilla insurgency especially if joined by others not yet counted in the mix.

If things went according to plan, more than 350,000 battle-trained and tested Israelis, defecting American Bible-believing Christians and defecting American military from the remaining Christian Zionists in America would complete a formidable fighting force. The true believers would soon make their presence known. Organizing them and synching their operations with the IDFA would be another matter.

Jonathan Roberts would soon discover that entire units of U.S. Army, Navy, and Marines would join forces in support of Israel and the Jews. It meant the loss of everything dear to them. They risked family, home, life, and freedom.

It was the toughest personal dilemma Roberts had ever faced. He loved and treasured America. But his beloved nation had turned on its Jewish citizens. And many of America's Christians had turned on them, too.

He believed that an attack on Jews was also an attack on Christians, though most Christians were oblivious to this opinion. His followers and students believed this as well but many others did not. He knew what his calling was and he was prepared to pay the ultimate price. His heart was broken, for the America he signed up to protect and defend had abandoned her ideals.

Roberts' team was also running supporter lists against known terrorists to ensure, as best as they were able, that no "unfriendlies" were able to access his plans. He had the connections and the resources to do so. The lists would soon be culled to remove any names that were suspected as potential enemies.

Unknown to the main body of his readers but known only to a very small inner circle of closest advisors was an internal list of about 100,000 of his closest associates. These individuals he knew were closer, more trusted compatriots to whom he would turn if things got out of hand. They were generous with donations, willing to take on burdens not considered by others on the general mailing list.

For all practical purposes, it would be the end of the Jewish presence in America. They fought in all of her wars, served in her governments, taught in her schools, and worked in her factories. They defended the guilty and the innocent in her courts, healed her sick, contributed to her inventions and innovations in all manners of life.

And in some ways, it would be the end of the current underpinning of Bible-believing Christians willing to lay their lives down for their friends. And, in a way, something very special about America would die too.

Jonathan Roberts remained a hunted man with a price on his head. He just looked different.

> **From the Hand of Moses, Sh'mot - Exodus**
> **Chapter 8 Verse 21**
>
> "For if you do not let my people go, behold, I will send swarms of flies on you and on your servants and on your people and into your houses; and the houses of the Egyptians will be full of swarms of flies, and also the ground on which they dwell."

Chapter 67

Let My People Go
—Pestilence

The next day, Chaim and Eleazer were again summoned into the President's chambers. By this time, the bloody water supply was the biggest news item in the capital and all over the nation, in fact all over the world. Hydrologists and biochemists, and all manner of scientists had begun sampling the water all over the District with the intent to determine the danger to the public.

There was no conclusive proof but it appeared that some sort of terror attack was to blame and the President was hopping mad. It didn't help the matter when his science advisors informed him that thousands of fish, some dead, some live had washed up on the shores of the Potomac and the surrounding rivers, lakes, and other local bodies of water.

The church bombings, mostly out west were news but not as big, even though they involved a massive death toll, more than 1,000

"I suppose you two have something to do with this?"

"Mr. President, we can only tell you this. It is time to let our people go! This is what God expects of you."

"The two of you need to deliver a message to the Jews. I mean no one any harm- this little trick of yours is very clever, but no one is laughing. If you think for a moment I don't know what you are up to, then you are sadly mistaken."

Now, he needed to turn to more urgent matters and told the Wasserman brothers that he would tolerate no further parlor tricks played on him.

"There is evidence of an international Jewish conspiracy regarding the financial troubles, the run on the banks, and the collapse of order in some of the larger cities in some way rests with you. It is the Jews who have brought this calamity on America," he said to them, pointing a finger in Chaim's midsection.

"Mr. President, you know very well it's not the Jews who are the cause of the nation's troubles. Yes, we heard how the water system was compromised but you have much bigger problems on your hands than two rabbis like us. This nation's irresponsible management of its money supply, the unsustainable public programs and the unethical banking practices, not to mention how you have treated America's Jews, have done more than all the Jews combined could have possibly done."

"Chaim, the Jews stay. Period."

"Mr. President, I can only say this- there is more coming. But we must again try to convince you to open up the cities around America and let the Jews out peacefully, safely, and calmly. I am certain these events will stop," he cautioned the Chief Executive.

The perception of the Goldena Medina evaporated into the mists of history. America would soon join Spain, England, France, Germany, Eastern Europe, and Russia as comfort zones gone badly. America had turned into Egypt and the Jews into makers of bricks... they just weren't building pyramids.

Chaim and Eleazer knew exactly what was coming.

The President also knew that suicide bombers were loose on American soil. Things were out of control.

Meanwhile, Mimi had other business on her mind.

Mimi's covert strike teams had delivered the first blow... now came the next test. Her field agents reported that the electronic and chemical devices were ready and fully functioning. An encrypted text message buzzed on her hip.

"We are operational. The time is now," said the text. It was from another field team, Yarden 2, and it meant the second plague was imminent.

By this time, the entire city of Washington was up in arms about the blood-red water but was assured that it was just an old parlor trick—that someone had contaminated the water with some sort of food coloring. In a way, they were partially right as the color was generally harmless but it put a good scare into the population. Within two days, the last of the bloody water was through the system and things returned to some sort of normal state.

That night, Chaim and Esther had another dream. In the dream, they saw an army of frogs covering the ground. Esther's text reached Rifka just as Rifka was texting her. Though she had an idea of what was to come, the dreams still came.

"Tzfardim?" (Frogs), the text said.

Yarden 2 was in place. The team of 26 scientists and forward agents had 'wired' the trees, riverbanks, the D.C. Tidal Basin, the Potomac and smaller lakes and streams near the Capitol and the White House.

The equipment was programmed and the chemists released the pheromones.

The teams waited. The sights and sounds would be etched in their memories forever.

The first frog climbed out of the water—drawn by some primal force. It seemed confused—out of its comfort and away from water. Still, it followed the call. Then more frogs came. Tens of thousands followed close behind. They crept, hopped, croaked, and came in an endless procession—now in the hundreds of thousands.

The President was holding a cabinet meeting when his chief of staff entered the room. The slimy green army was overrunning Washington D.C. CNN, Fox News, and all the major networks stopped programming to broadcast the scene. One commentator said it was like something out of the Bible while another raised the possibility that eco-terrorists were at work. Only when the other major networks followed Al-Jazeera's coverage did anyone blame the Jews.

Mimi's team had all the stations up on the wall besides their battlefield maps and real time video feeds. This was truly something to see. Everything stopped in command headquarters as her team gathered around the monitors.

Esther fired off a text message to Rifka.

"I can't believe this is happening. We had a dream last night—the same as the Exodus. But I had no idea what it was we were unleashing… if Pharaoh experienced anything like the Scripture describes, then it must have been hell on earth for him and his household." The angst was evident in her note.

By now, there were millions of frogs. They covered the ground, finding their way into restaurants, offices, homes... everywhere. They invaded the airport and took up residence inside airplane engines and landing gear. They found busses, trains, cars, and all manner of public transportation including the Metro.

Upon wakening, families discovered them in their kitchens, bathrooms, pantries, ovens, and anywhere where there was an opening, they came in. They came from every body of water around and sometimes seemed to come from nowhere at all. The strange invasion set all the city's dogs to barking so the racket was overwhelming. Cats didn't know what to do.

That night Chaim and Esther had another dream. They both woke up at midnight and then the explanation came to them. Now they had no doubt—it was God who spoke. Still, they wondered at how and why He chose *them* to carry the message.

The message was clear: *Go to the President and say:* **Let my people go!**

Chaim's phone rang and the clock read 12:10 a.m. It was Eleazer. "Did the two of you just have another dream?"

"Yes!" Chaim shouted. "And I assume you too?"

Chaim and Eleazer didn't have to ask to see the President. He summoned them the next day. "Make this stop!" The President demanded.

"Mr. President," Ephraim began, "we are not responsible for *all* of this trouble."

"We will do our best to look into all this, Mr. President," Eleazer pledged. "We will share what we know when we know it."

"But for now, Mr. President... " Ephraim paused, looked to his brother, and then back to the president. "Sir, a force far greater than any man or government is at work here. And He has a single issue on His agenda. His people must have freedom to choose their own destiny."

The president snarled in distain and barked, "Get 'em outta here!"

The next day, without water, the frogs began to die. Great heaps piled up all over the city and surrounding suburbs. The smell was indescribable. People appeared on the streets wearing paper hospital masks. Some wore respirators, bought from local hardware stores. But the smell was so overpowering, nothing really worked. Traffic stopped. Restaurants closed as did all public and private business establishments.

Still, the President remained stiff-necked. He would not release the Jews.

Ephraim and Eleazer knew what was next. The Bible described the dust of the earth turning into lice, meaning the plague would be so horrendous on the population that the lice would completely inundate the city, people, animals, and get into everything.

Meanwhile, the field teams began to initiate the electronic and chemical sequences to 'activate" the lice. The scientists had thus far identified more than 1,500 communication codes of the more than 3000 different species but they wouldn't need all of them. They would make contact with 200 species, easily enough to deliver the message.

The blood-sucking parasites began to hear and smell the call. Slowly the tiny army began to grow until thick clouds formed over the Capitol, the White House, and all manner of public structures. Even Mr. Lincoln, Mr. Washington, and Mr. Jefferson received visits. The pests descended into homes, businesses, fields, everywhere. Head and body lice attacked both humans and animals, the buzzing driving them almost insane, everyone, anyway except the Capitol's Jews.

Administration scientists, who were able to explain all the previous 'plagues,' couldn't figure out a way to replicate or explain this one. Apparently, their equipment hadn't reached the level of sophistication that Israeli science had. One scientist even said that this was the 'finger of God Himself.'

His colleagues laughed at him derisively but he was the only one who was even close. When a small team of scientists captured some of the pests and looked at them under the microscope, they noted that the small pests possessed a very unusual wing structure—each wing appeared to be an inverted triangle and when the insect closed its wings, they appeared to form tiny stars of David.

The President refused to budge. It was now becoming more and more personal to him and his usually confident demeanor wavered. His long career in public service proved him to be able to defeat virtually any enemy, but this one. This in turn, brought out anger and hostility.

Chaim and Eleazer shuddered to think what was coming next.

Seven days later, the Israeli strike teams delivered the next message.

Washington D.C. and surrounding counties woke up to swarms of insects, strange, huge biting flies, and unseen in this part of the nation until now. Not only that, but local hospitals began seeing thousands of patients reporting blisters and boils breaking out on their bodies.

The blisters and boils, tender to the touch, required painful lancing to provide any relief. With antibiotics for this disease running low, patients were then increasingly prone to infections. No matter how fast the doctors worked, they couldn't stem the infections from spreading. Medications began running out. The authorities were powerless.

The swarms of flies were so thick that car traffic moving through the area had to keep their windshield wipers constantly on along with their wiper fluid as the flies hit the cars and created blinding driving conditions.

Windshields smeared with a bloody and thick slime-like substance. From the flies came maggots, crawling into everything and covering every surface available. If the sight of this was disgusting, the smell was even worse.

Strangely, none of the pestilence seemed to reach Jewish or Christian Zionist households.

The rabbis again returned to the White House, pleading for the Jews' safe passage to Israel.

"Sir, the people just wish religious freedom, some sense of liberty."

Still the President remained stiff-necked and hard hearted.

"The Jews must stay. Don't you understand that you cannot just come in this place and dictate your wishes!?!"

"Mr. President, you are fighting against forces, kingdoms, fortresses, principalities and powers that you cannot possibly imagine." Chaim, trying a little diplomacy, was referring to something that was even more powerful than even he could imagine.

How much more could the nation's capital take?

They would soon find out on the following Saturday when thick, dark clouds moved in on the city. The President woke up very early that morning. It was quiet, though a steady rain was falling. Then the hail began.

Within minutes a drenching hailstorm pelted the White House. Baseball-sized hailstones fell all over the city, again focused directly on the nation's capital, and falling even more heavily on the President's residence. The building shook from thunder and lightning.

The President went to his bedroom window. It was surreal sight—like a cinematic scene. Lightning scorched the ground. Just a few feet from his window fire licked the ground and consumed the grass.

The Israeli scientists also awoke to the pounding rhythm of the hailstones. They watched in stunned surprise. This was far beyond their plan, power, or capability—and certainly wasn't in the game plan.

Intelligence fielded by Mimi's agents told tales of dead animals, crushed ripening crops, ruined bridges, roadways, street lights, and all manner of destroyed vehicles caught in the downpour.

The hailstorm's devastation inside the beltway and in surrounding states would reach into the hundreds of billions of dollars. Somehow the television and radio transmission towers survived the terrible tragedy. And no Jews or Christian Zionists were harmed nor were their residences damaged.

News reports that evening supported what the Israelis already knew: tens of thousands of animal deaths as the poor beasts were caught in fields on local farms and ranches, unable to find safety. Sadly, many died in piles, evidence of stampedes, as they tried to find their way into their barns or other shelters.

When the next day dawned, all manner of crops were found destroyed as the hailstones smashed everything in their path. Perhaps more telling was the anti-Semitic rhetoric pounding the airwaves, blaming Jewish leaders for bringing this on the U.S. Capital.

The beltway was under siege from a storm that nobody saw coming. The rain continued through the next four days, flooding great parts of the eastern seaboard. Transportation came to a standstill with the Capitol virtually shut down. When the President summoned Chaim and Eleazer, the two brothers managed to find their way to the White House. They found the President reduced to a state they couldn't describe. It hovered somewhere between depression and rage.

"I am not that religious of a man per se, though I consider myself a Christian—but I am directing both of you to ask this God of yours or whoever is responsible for all of this, to spare this city and the surrounding areas. I know you people are doing something to cause these disasters so pray to your God to stop this!"

The Wasserman brothers did as they were asked. They prayed and the storms abated. The Capital and now the Western U.S. had suffered several terrible blows with such a sudden swiftness that religious stations and authorities had to sit up and take notice.

Although the secular press ignored any possible connection with a religious connotation, the possibility of biblical-style calamities wasn't lost on the faith-based press. The Vatican issued a statement in sympathy with America while other religious figures from the Islamic world declared that it was Allah's will that America suffer because of its Jews. Nothing was making sense anymore. At the same time, to others, everything was making sense.

Evangelical stations began running 24 hour a day programming focused on the stories contained in the Book of Exodus and the aftermath impact on Egypt.

The rains, thunder, lightning, and hail slowed then stopped. And the president reversed course—again. He hardened his heart. The Jews would remain in America.

Esther, Rifka, and the scientist soldiers began to plan the next wave of attacks. Locusts were called to consume the crops.

Sunday morning, seven days after the hailstorms, many prepared to attend church. Instead, preparations were interrupted by enigmatic noise. A shrill, wind, and whirl sounded from the south... the wind—the whisk and whorl of locusts wings. Countless millions whipped the air in wave after wave.

The skies turned dark. The sun was blocked. The locusts swarmed on every green plant and tree, not felled by the devastating hailstorms.

Not long after, the earth looked stripped, bare, and naked to the world. In a thousand churches a thousand pastors, priests, and other church leaders decided to change their sermons to a study of chapter 10 of the Book of Exodus. In the few synagogues brave enough to open for regular morning minion services, that day's Torah portions were suspended for another look at what the Christians were reading.

The chief of staff entered the room and found the President glued to the news. Reporters all over the East told of the total devastation all around the city and outlying counties. The damage seemed to be isolated near the Beltway, Washington proper, and into Virginia. His top aide could see the President's demeanor and then thought, 'this may not be the best time.'

"Bill, this looks pretty bleak, doesn't it?" he asked, more of a statement than a question.

"Yes sir, it does," he responded, quietly and with the utmost reverence for the moment. His aide remained silent, awaiting more from his chief.

"Mr. President, the press is hoping for a statement. I've held them off all morning. Do you want to say anything?"

"No, not right now. I need to meet with the Secretary of Agriculture for starters and then maybe the National Weather Service. We need answers and we need them quickly. Why don't you schedule something for this evening for us? I don't want to get into this with the press but the residents living in the area deserve to know what we are doing."

"Yes, sir, I'll let them know. I'll get Dan on it right now," the aide said. Dan Schuster was the White House Press Secretary.

"Also, get a hold of those rabbis. I want to see them too, sooner than later," he added.

When Chaim and Eleazer were summoned, the President asked his secret service agents to make themselves ready for either an arrest or perhaps a little 'education.'

The rabbis entered the Oval Office.

"Chaim, Eleazer, I need to ask for your forgiveness. You may think me a fool for being so hard-headed. I recognize my shortcomings regarding the Jews. Please, if you have any power over this, can you take away the locusts?"

The rabbis inherently knew the plagues ran for short durations, but so much of this was a mystery to them as it happened so quickly and seemingly without warning. Even though their wives understood the details, it was still a mystery to them.

They prayed while at the same time the scientists behind all of the 'natural disasters' switched off the equipment.

When a strong Nor'easter blew into the city later that day, the locusts were swept away and drowned in the Potomac. The fish would eat well that week as the Chesapeake and all local bodies of water were inundated with the flying creatures. A few days later, the rabbis appeared at the White House once again.

"Mr. President, don't you see what harm you are bringing about on this great nation of ours?"

"What are you saying?"

"Only this, do you know the story of the Exodus?"

"Well, apart from an old myth in the Bible about the Jews... "

"Mr. President, that was no myth! Maybe a better way to put it is this: It IS NOT a myth."

"Oh, come now, Chaim. All that Bible stuff is just a bunch of stories. Myths made up by superstitious men. You're an educated man. You can't believe that stuff!" The President answered in a very condescending manner.

"Mr. President, as much as you disparage *that Book*, sir, I am amazed that you still call yourself a Christian."

"What do you mean?"

"Well, the Christians I know believe what their Bible says. They also try to live their lives in accordance to its words and ways."

The President was getting testy now and Chaim and Eleazer could both sense it. He had a habit of pulling the skin at his thumbs' edge and then biting off the tiny residual flaps, sometimes causing himself to bleed. He was working on both thumbs now in this battle of wills.

"Let me lay it out for you sir. Do you remember the story of Gush Katif in August of 2005?"

The President shook his head.

"No? Let me help you remember that nearly 10,000 Israelis were forced out of their homes and off their land by the Israeli military and police departments, through the direction of the Prime Minister of Israel. But it was virtually directed by extraordinary pressures brought to bear on them by one of your predecessors from this very office. Israel was promised all kinds of support through the Roadmap to Peace, but all they got was more trouble from the Arabs and a cold shoulder from America... and later 8,000 rockets from Gaza."

"Just a few days later, Hurricane Katrina hit America and the similarities are too coincidental to be ignored. Everything from the financial ruin brought to bear on Israel's economy from lost crops and revenue to the displacement of local populations. New Orleans residents suffered similar population displacement, and if my math is right, both were displaced in similar numbers percentage-wise. You simply do not divide up God's land, and I don't care if you are a Jew or a Gentile, it simply doesn't matter."

"Then in early 2006, five months later, Israel's prime minister was struck down with a massive stroke. He remained in a vegetative state for years before he died. The timing is no coincidence, for I believe that God doesn't play dice," the rabbi said, with increasing confidence and power.

"America is in the midst of its own set of plagues much like the devastation that hit Egypt 3500 years ago. Mr. President, I can guarantee you one thing, that forces are at work so powerful that you cannot stop them. Just in the past year, America has experienced unprecedented horrors including six hurricanes that have taken thousands of lives and caused billions of dollars worth of damage. We've had tornados too numerous to mention and the earthquakes—and, Mr. President, when do you last remember three simultaneous active volcanoes in America?"

"Additionally, the cost to insurance and then through the population by means of hiked premiums and the fact that the government cannot make up for this by just printing more money, puts this nation on the edge."

"Sir, the U.S. is under judgment. Anyone who tries to divide up the land of Israel as you have advocated will pay a tremendous price—let me correct myself, The U.S. *is paying* a tremendous price for its treatment of Israel, the Jews, and the Land itself. And let me underscore the point... anyone, anyone, sir who causes the Jews grief will pay for it many times over—it's called a Curse for a Curse in Kind. You, Sir, are poking your finger in the eye of God."

Then Chaim jumped in, "From President Carter to your term, Mr. President, America has pushed an increasingly hostile policy towards Israel. This policy has been met with natural disaster after natural disaster hitting the U.S. with unprecedented consequences. Just like Eleazer said, several American and European insurance firms have suffered tremendous financial loss and many have gone out of business. The total costs have not been fully absorbed by the U.S. Treasury but they soon will. The government has had to step in and pay for a lot of the damage and as a result, we are virtually bankrupt," Chaim told him.

It was clear the President was becoming more and more agitated. He saw where this was headed. He was done with the conversation.

"Get out of my office, the two of you!" cried the President, feeling the hair on the back of his neck bristle and his blood pressure rising.

At that moment, the secret service officers rose and somewhat roughly escorted the two rabbis out of the Oval Office. What they didn't see was the President drop down heavily in his chair, once the rabbis were out of sight, and spin around to look out over the White House lawn and gardens.

CHAPTER SIXTY-SEVEN: Let My People Go—Pestilence

"How dare they throw these... these... *these myths and legends* at me," the president shouted to the ceiling. "It's like blackmail—threats! And right here in my own office—the Office of the President!"

Still, once the immediate threat was quashed, the President returned to his resistance. The Jews would remain.

Later that night, both rabbis settled into a deep sleep. At exactly midnight, Chaim, Eleazer, Rifka, and Esther were awakened by another dream. This time, they dreamt of a dark terror spreading across the area, darkness so thick that the four of them couldn't even describe it. And this time, even the President awoke at exactly the same time as the rabbis and their wives, the terror consuming him as well.

About noon the next day, astronomers from all over the nation gathered in the capital to witness a solar eclipse of the sun. Scientists at the National Observatory became extremely excited when the eclipse began. The moon slowly moved through its position in the heavens and as it did, it blocked the sun's light. One minute turned into ten, then twenty, and then an hour. Was this like the long day of Joshua only reversed?

Minutes passed and angst mounted among the crowd. The sun's light never appeared. Instead, greater darkness encroached. It was darker than any starless, moonless night. And, though summer, it grew cold and colder, still.

Fear gripped the crowd. The masses were bewildered and lost. No one could explain it. And no one could manage or control it. Flashlights didn't work. Electronic devices died. Street lights went dark. Vehicles were void of power. Nothing worked. The only activity was the fear that worked in the minds of the people.

Once more—this event stretched well beyond what Israeli scientists were able to do.

Ok, stay calm, the President thought.

He reached for the phone and tried to call his aid. No dial tone, nothing. Now he began feeling a sense of rising terror, for nothing was working.

The darkness lasted three days, during which nothing moved in the capital. But, the plague was stayed and eventually the light returned. Strangely, there was no darkness in Jewish or Christian households.

That next evening, the President turned on the news. He was calmer now, the tension releasing as the lights came on. He poured himself a glass of wine and fired up a Cuban cigar (now legal with recent ties to Cuba thawed), as he watched the news. A story came and went so fast that he wasn't sure he actually saw it. After all he'd seen, this last item was the straw that broke the camel's back.

The news item had to do with yet another pestilence story of fire ants from South America invading the Texas panhandle. They were moving quickly to surrounding states. The story mentioned that contrary *east to west winds* were to blame for carrying the fire ant queens towards the west coast. In fact, he remembered hearing something from his youth about these ants that were so destructive to livestock, leaving them very sick once they attacked in swarms as they were apt to do. But this attack was different—the attacks also spread eastward.

"For some reason," the reporter said, "a very select number of animals from each herd is dying. This latest pestilence seems to affect all manner of livestock. And the individual animals taken defies explanation. They are often the strongest in the herds."

The President shook his head to clear it. Then he thought, *This has to be a bad dream. If it's serious, I'll see it in the morning news.*

"Something else that has been noted is that none of these infestations seem to be hitting Jewish families or neighborhoods."

Historians later noted inexplicable occurrences that impacted America. It seemed that the events tied directly to the way the Administration was treating its Jewish citizens. The coincidences were uncanny. However, the newspapers and electronic media of the time were blind to any spiritual connection. They kept the stories as separate front page fodder. A million blogs lit up with the story.

America continued to absorb natural and man-made disasters. A series of earthquakes, volcanoes, fires, floods, hurricanes, and tornados followed one after another. Autumn fires in California are often arson-related but the cause of these fires was less certain. And their explosive spread was pushed by fierce Santa Ana winds. The forces of nature ran wild. Damage rose into the multi-billions of dollars. Insurance companies collapsed—one after another.

The onslaught of natural events wasn't lost on the Israelis. Press reports appeared in the Israeli press. The nation was stunned by what it saw. The Rabbinate began wondering aloud in the press whether these were indeed plagues being visited on America for the escalating harsh relations between the two nations.

Later that evening, the First Lady screamed. The President rushed to find her in their son's bedroom. She hovered over the bed and held their 13-year-old son's lifeless body. Also, by his bed lay his dog—dead. Both firstborn. And on the bed and floor were tens of thousands of dead red fire ants.

From the Pen of the Prophet Isaiah
Chapter 12 Verse 3

O My people!
Their oppressors are children,
And women rule over them.
O My people!
Those who guide you
Lead you astray and
Confuse the direction of your paths.

Chapter 68

Let My People Go—Remix

The President was called *The Deal-Maker.* He was a player in countless circles of influence. So he could get whatever he wanted and make everyone else think they got a deal. He'd developed the skills from youth. He was an expert at how to make himself comfortable and happy. He built a fortune and then grew bored with the lifestyle, later to head to public office where he decided his expertise would best be used.

Later he ran for a seat in the House of Representatives. He ran clean campaigns and won with superior deal-making. He never stopped fieldwork. He was connected to some social network 24/7. He could be seen everywhere online. He built loyal grassroots organizations out of thin air.

He served eight years in Congress—three landslide reelections. Then he set his sights of the Senate and won. He served twelve years—reelection was a cakewalk. His popularity was still on the rise. So he sensed the calling to the White House. So he formed an exploratory committee to run for the presidency.

The committee responded with the precision expected of his campaign teams. Within a few months, fundraisers raised the tens of millions for his expected announcement. Once he announced, the party came alongside of him to move to the big stage. He stormed through the Iowa caucus with more than 70% of the vote. By the time he reached New Hampshire, the race, for all practical purposes, was over.

His opponents realized quickly that the real race was for the vice presidency and those plum positions on his future cabinet. All the while, a quiet shadow began to grow casting about stories of Jewish control of the media, financial institutions, and education. It was faint but it was there, whispered in cocktail party conversations, water cooler discussions, never blatant, but it was out there and growing. Again.

The election was almost comical. The other party threw whatever it could against him but his campaign remained at the highest ethical standards, something the public hadn't seen in years. The election was a sight to see as he swept through the evening with almost 70% of the vote and 90% of the electoral tally. It was a landslide, the most popular president in history.

Through the next few years, his presidency was stellar. Legislative efforts to combat illegal immigration, welfare fraud, rising pensions, and out of control medical costs were met with success after success. Talk show hosts had little to say except in his praise. Slowly, his leadership gained momentum and the confidence and swagger that America once knew began to return. Nevertheless, with all the advances, circumstances beyond his control began to erode the gains the nation had experienced.

It began innocently enough with a quivering in the stock market, which had largely recovered from its wild economic gyrations earlier in the decade. Investors, never a stable group anyway, were growing increasingly nervous over rising gas prices, now reaching $200 a barrel and upwards of $8 a gallon. Stocks, bonds, and precious metals were beginning to behave in ways not seen in years. With the advent of a nationalized health care policy years before, the rampant inflation predicted began to gain a toehold in the economy. When inflation hits hard, money shrinks and that became the tipping point. Underlying all economics is the behavior of people. Comparisons to post World War 1 Germany appeared in the press.

It was increasingly difficult for the average family to make ends meet. In order to meet expected profit targets, companies large and small began the inevitable cycle of layoffs, and benefit cuts. Shareholder pressure increased with investors seeking shelter from losses and demanding action from their corporate boards of directors.

High profile stories of economic and ethical wrongdoing, bank foreclosures, investment scams, and out-of-control public and private pensions drained taxpayers to the breaking point. Single income earners became overly stressed and began putting off basic household purchases to take care of the simple bare necessities of life. Feeding one's family trumped buying the new car, going to the movies, or even taking a meal out. Where dinner and a movie used to cost a family of three maybe $50, now it was well north of $200. The dollar's value was shrinking and the American taxpayer was growing increasingly edgy.

The road ahead would as difficult for him as any of his predecessors had faced. And the faint whispers of who was responsible could be heard in social circles, churches, mosques, and on the beltway. He was not immune to them and vowed to dig in deeper to the economic problems. He called his advisers to a special meeting that morning.

As his economic advisors began to arrive, a story broke about a bank failure in California. Just a few short years before The Bank of the Nation was a top performer in most financial portfolios. The bank's collapse had his team worried. They were well aware of the news before the President was.

They also knew that the President had many close Jewish personal advisors whom he had come to trust. There it was again, the Jews in the midst of a financial crisis. However, these advisors held no loyalty to anyone other than the U.S. and this president, actually viewing Israel with disdain. It was not an unknown phenomenon—Jews who had totally assimilated and chose to downplay their Jewish roots while attaching themselves to the nation of their birth. The question remained, however, how loyal would that nation be to them when conditions deteriorated?

The meeting was held in the conference room of the White House. There would be no press coverage today. They needed the time to plan for the announcements. The President needed his privacy and his closest advisors to hear it from him first.

"Ladies and Gentlemen, word has reached me this morning that we've had another bank failure," he opened.

"I've been in touch with regulators. It seems like we're headed for another crisis like we saw back in the early part of the century," he continued.

"We have incurred tremendous debt, which in the past few years we've begun to pay off. Much of this was due to heavy overspending by previous administrations. But this situation will require something pretty spectacular to resolve."

He was right. Income and social security taxes on Americans had reached close to 50% of gross income with those participating states not far behind, averaging something like an additional 10%. The American taxpayer was drowning and they were looking for someone to blame. The president continued.

"In times like these America has always risen to meet the challenge. I cannot say for sure, but this one looks like we may be in for quite a rough ride. Revenues are not going to meet our expenditures and with the promises we made years ago between pensions and health care, America could face a situation called 'sovereign insolvency."

The advisors sat stunned... they couldn't believe what they were hearing. Did he say *insolvency*? *Like Greece suffered years before?* Did that mean the Government was bankrupt? What did it mean, exactly?

"There are forces operating in our midst that do not have American interests foremost in their minds. I do not have to tell you what the people are saying or what they believe. I read the polls and listen to the news talk shows just like you do. I don't want to believe it myself but it would appear that Jewish influences, so long denied, are at work here and we are about to feel the worsening effect of that influence."

The president had never broached this topic, but he did today. And his opinions made their way to the media. At that point, all bets were off. To this point, he was completely supported by his Jewish advisors and more than 60% of the Jews in America, as strange as that sounded. However, some were now beginning to hear a different message.

He was well aware of the worsening attitude towards Jews and some of the random attacks aimed at them. It wasn't personal to him—just business. What the future held, he hadn't a clue. He was mad at what he perceived to be the self-righteous attitude of Jewish financiers, business leaders, and Jewish lobbyists. And he'd lost patience with Israel's greedy hand-out cry for military aid and help with who knows what else.

His advisors tried to absorb this innuendo. *Was the president laying blame for the economic crisis at the feet of America's Jews?* Were that so, things would get ugly fast. It wasn't long after Hitler assumed the leadership, than state sponsored terror took hold in Germany.

It had been building before Hitler's rise to power. Jewish members of Germany's radical left hadn't exactly endeared themselves to the population either. It almost gave Hitler an excuse. The Russian revolution led by many of Jewish blood, gave him another reason to hate the Jews. Then again, there was always that arrogant sense of 'chosenness,' an idea so out of context to reality that it was just downright annoying.

Once the government sanctioned such thinking, the populace would explode in anger, mindlessly looking and finding the proper scapegoat. Combined with the governmental bureaucracy and an increasingly wild population, the Jews fell smack dab into the crosshairs of destiny.

America had its scapegoat.

> From the Book of Bereshit (Genesis),
> Chapter 12, verses 1-3
>
> Now the LORD said to Abram,
> Go forth from your country,
> And from your relatives and from your father's house,
> To the land which I will show you;
> And I will make you a great nation,
> And I will bless you, and make your name great;
> And so you shall be a blessing;
> And I will bless those who bless you,
> And the one who curses you I will curse.

Chapter 69

Mutiny

American military might projects globally. In virtually any crisis, American troops may fight in distant corners of the world, presumably to defend others or to defend American interests. However, when a foreign invader infiltrates the Homeland, it's another matter entirely.

The U.S. military re-instituted the draft several years before and with it came an expected sense of resentment among those drafted. Though the majority of the armed forces were still volunteer-based, it was increasingly difficult to recruit and retain, despite incentives such as fully paid college tuition, a new GI Bill that virtually guaranteed housing, and increased retirement and medical benefits.

All GI's were now guaranteed lifetime medical benefits even if only serving for a four-year hitch. But still, with the thousands coming home in boxes and an unclear understanding why America continued to fight all these distant wars that never seemed to end it was having an impact on the military. A burgeoning peace movement gained momentum.

One valuable piece of information reaching Israeli planners in the Jewish Agency was Evangelical Christian representation in those forces. While many had absolutely no interest in anything dealing with Jewish events, other committed Christian soldiers saw the world differently. However, they had never been tested in this way before.

Experience told the Israeli intelligence teams that slightly less than half of this Christian subgroup would fight with the Jews. They correctly perceived that a readily available, trained army might cross the line and identify themselves as American Christians, not as Christian Americans, and thus switch their loyalty from the Stars and Stripes to Israel and its Star of David, or more precisely, to the God of Israel. Provocative as it seemed, many began seeing this choice as more and more obvious.

Pastors embedded within those military communities became fond of citing the chapters ten and eleven of the Epistle to the Romans. In that letter, written by the Rabbi Shaul (aka the Apostle Paul), Gentile believers are explicitly directed to cause the Jews to become jealous for the faith by living their lives in sacrifice, love and service to the very people whom were called the 'chosen.' They are directed to love the Jewish people and remember that they were grafted in to the root, not the other way around.

The Christian mission was to the 'Jew first and then to the Gentiles, with no mention of tearing the Jews from their culture or way of life. Loyalty to the American flag was a matter of personal conscience. However, when following the flag opposed Holy Scripture and trampled on God's chosen, then the believer had to choose between the two... not an easy choice.

These men and women, the Israeli planners believed, weren't anti-American and didn't hate the country of their birth. Rather, they felt a higher calling-namely that of helping the Jewish people as their Bible dictated. Roberts and others like him also remembered the dictates of the 13th Chapter of Romans requiring Christians to put themselves under the authority of elected officials because God Himself had willed their election. The conflict was obvious.

These Christians could not allow themselves to target the Jewish people—that would have violated Scripture as they understood it. Roberts taught the critical scriptures. He began with Genesis 12:3: *I will bless those who bless you and curse those who curse you.* Then the Epistle to the Romans 11:13-24. Rav Saul commanded the Gentile believers to support and love the Jewish people. But many never got the message. Their leaders misunderstood the role of the Jews and Israel... and from that a sense of arrogance crept into Christian teaching.

Carefully examined, it instructed Christians to respectfully share what they knew but never lord it over the Jews. Gentile believers were warned

CHAPTER SIXTY-NINE: Mutiny

not to be arrogant. The Bible warned them that God could just as easily cut them off if they weren't careful and add the Jews back into the tree. Roberts quoted it accurately and often to his listeners:

> *But I am speaking to you who are Gentiles. Inasmuch then as I am an apostle of Gentiles, I magnify my ministry, if somehow I might move to jealousy my fellow countrymen and save some of them. For if their rejection is the reconciliation of the world, what will their acceptance be but life from the dead? If the first piece of dough is holy, the lump is also; and if the root is holy, the branches are too.*
>
> *But if some of the branches were broken off, and you, being a wild olive, were grafted in among them and became partakers with them of the rich root of the olive tree, do not be arrogant toward the branches; but if you are arrogant, remember that it is not you who supports the root, but the root supports you.*
>
> *You will say then, 'Branches were broken off so that I might be grafted in.' Quite right, they were broken off for their unbelief, but you stand by your faith. Do not be conceited, but fear;* ***for if God did not spare the natural branches, He will not spare you, either.***
>
> *Behold then the kindness and severity of God. To those who fell, severity, but to you, God's kindness, if you continue in His kindness; otherwise you also will be cut off. And they also, if they do not continue in their unbelief, will be grafted in, for God is able to graft them in again. For if you were cut off from what is by nature a wild olive tree, and were grafted contrary to nature into a cultivated olive tree, how much more will these who are the natural branches be grafted into their own olive tree?*

A difficult choice faced them and their families, something the Israeli planners had to take into account. They simply couldn't take up arms against God's chosen, no matter what their orders were. It was risky but worth the chance. And, they had a friend who could and would help them, Jonathan Roberts.

None of them believed it would come to this, figuring that American governmental officials would step in and combat growing anti-Semitism. With an increasing stream of anti-Semitic vitriol now coming from many churches and mosques, not to mention within the Government itself, the electronic and the dwindling print media, the battle lines were being drawn.

The first military defectors came from a small training base near Long Beach, California. Other groups would join in the mutiny soon and once they came, the fighting forces would take on a much more disciplined approach, a very military look.

Six army pilots and weapons officers and fifty infantry commandeered the first three aircraft: 2 Apache AH-64 gunships and 1 Chinook CH-47 helicopter. The Apaches took to the skies first, jumping up and hovering above the airfield. The Apaches, armed with Hellfire missiles and cannon hovered at the ready.

The Chinook began spinning up, its twin turbo-shaft engines roaring to life. It then lifted off slowly with the troops anxiously awaiting orders. The hulking beast took its position between the Apaches for protection, a battlefield lesson learned years ago. The pilots and weapons officers scouted the area below and above them looking for any signs of trouble. The troop transport began its slow climb into the sky, flying them up to the airport, just 15-20 minutes away.

They had just returned from an adventure in southern Mexico where they had taken on Muslim insurgents in treacherous mountainous terrain. Now the battle was on their home turf, the U.S.A. None of them relished this but understood the order of things. It was decision time... these American Christians understood that there was no turning back.

The theft would normally have been reported to Colonel Dutch Ellison, the commander of the base, but he was on board one of the helo's and in command of the mission.

"Let's get these things up to LAX... go, go, go!!" he urged his men. The Apaches and the Chinook jumped forward and formed a tight battle formation, ready for the short flight up the freeways to the Los Angeles Airport complex. Word was out that thousands of other believing soldiers abandoned their posts at various bases in Southern California and were heading to the airport as well.

Confusion reigned as base personnel didn't know what was happening, most of their leadership siding with the insurrection. The renegades had masked their movements to look like a training mission. They would soon be followed by others, forming the first all Christian Zionist attack teams. Within minutes more choppers joined Ellison and his men—every serviceable vehicle was flying in the formation. Seconds later, the entire communication system on the ground went blank, dead, with remaining operators completely isolated. Diversionary explosions around the base and surrounding area would keep the soldiers at the bases busy for hours.

Immediately, the pilots made direct contact with the Israeli commander of air traffic, located in one of the warehouses at LAX, as arranged beforehand through contacts developed by advance Israeli advance scouts and Jonathan Roberts. The Israeli commanders in the air traffic control teams were using the encrypted software package designed by Shoshana Bat Levi's firm allowing for secure transmissions.

The Battle for LAX was underway.

Many of these supporters had fought hard to hold on to their Second Amendment rights to keep and bear arms—some even had memorized the promise in the document.

> "A well regulated Militia, being necessary to the security of a Free State, the right of the people to keep and bear Arms, shall not be infringed."

This amendment drew tremendous attention in the late 20th Century and early into the 21st Century. No one could argue the intent—that of a free state guaranteeing the right of a well regulated militia to help defend the nation in times of external threat. But this was bound to raise the hackles of even the staunchest of defenders for in this case, the 'rights' of those citizens were potentially turning their weapons against the nation they loved. However, to those joining the Israeli forces, it now became clear to them why the 2nd Amendment was so important... for a time such as this.

The Scripture never really counseled on these kinds of situations but killing Jews and turning ones' back on Israel seemed the bigger offense. Many would weep when they began cleaning their weapons. They knew that Scripture was about to become the sword that divided families, friends, and compatriots. What would Jesus do? What would Jesus say?

Many good Christians would find themselves fighting other Christians—those who believed that Israel and modern-day Jews had little, if anything to do with the Biblical Jews or Israel or prophecy for that matter. It would be a matter of personal choice and one that was ripping the nation apart.

✡ ✡ ✡ ✡ ✡ ✡

Meanwhile, Vicenzo's warehouses in and around L.A. became beehives of activity. They began to map their first targets. Planning teams projected the street grids on massive screens linked up to the three satellites code named Hananiah, Mishael, and Azariah. Another wall projected the underground maze of tunnels, utilities, and support city facilities. Another wall displayed the schematic plan for the control tower that would be the first stage of the battle plan.

LAX is a huge complex covering a vast area within Southwest Los Angeles. The airport grew to be one of the most heavily used in the world and covered more than five square miles and 3,500 acres of prime Los Angeles real estate. The prize was control of the four main runways.

Taking the airport and then defending it would be tough but doable. The primary goal was setting up the rescue corridor, allowing ground transportation to bring the fleeing refugees to the airport. That meant all forms of transportation. Just getting the Jews close and helping them to make a run for the airport would be a challenge but it had to be done. Since L.A. included such a vast area, that meant that speedy and dependable communication and support would be essential.

The maps and the holograms showed them how the enemy could command the high ground and fire on the airport from above. Major streets included Sepulveda and Century, with several entry points funneling into the two major streets, thus making up the perimeter. There were high buildings all around the airport and that meant neutralizing any threat from those areas as well.

Planners met in other rooms to discuss control of the streets, bridges, and freeway overpasses. Israeli eyes were everywhere and friends were coming alongside her efforts to extract the American Jews. Christians with strong Bible backgrounds joined them. An increasingly large number of Jews were showing up willing to do what was necessary to make *Operation Last Exodus* a reality. There were fewer disbelievers among them now.

One of key issues the battlefield commanders faced was how far out to set the perimeter. The commanders noted the 405 and the 105 freeways were key arteries to the airport. They decided that they needed the freeways and all the overpasses to remain intact as well as the side streets. Explosives didn't solve the problem. The commanders knew they needed to control and keep them clear of snipers, and anyone else who decided to interrupt their plans. There was so much that could go wrong and in urban warfare, the complications were even more evident.

The first Israeli squad deployed 2 miles from Los Angeles International Airport. The 20,000 ground troops were supported by the first units of supportive American GI's. A slow trickle at first, it quickly grew into a formidable fighting force. The small army swelled to more than 50,000 troops in days. This group was joined by the Christian citizen soldiers.

Within another week, the Los Angeles / Orange County fighting force would number 250,000 with all manner of weaponry and invaluable local knowledge of the surroundings. The Israeli military teams were astonished at the outpouring of support. It would soon grow to more than one million in Southern California alone. Roberts' predictions and promises were all coming true.

When squad leaders made contact with the first American cells to defect, they exchanged battle codes, communication signals, and order of battle plans, and passed out the permanent RFID stickers marking them as comrades rather than enemies. The mechanized units shipped in for so many months and painstakingly assembled in dozens of warehouses around the Southland began to appear. They included jeeps, armored personnel carriers, and small but extremely fast attack tanks. The commander wondered aloud how residents of LA would react to the presence of an enemy's vehicles on the streets of their city. Citizens of LA would have a field day with their digital and movie cameras.

Of course, not completely known was the expected response of American armed forces. With so many committed to foreign deployments, this was the only time Israeli forces could expect to do any damage. It was a short window of time.

The Government was slow to respond. The commanders continued to emphasize that they were not here to do America any harm at all. The true goal was to save Jewish people from another impending Holocaust. The second *Shoah* had already taken too many Jewish lives and the Israeli invaders had no intent to spill any more blood than necessary. At this point, more than 100,000 American Jews had been sacrificed to the Islamo-Christian enemy.

From Ha Yad Moshe (the Hand of Moses)
Sh'mot (Exodus)
Chapter 3:21-22 & Chapter 12:35-36

I will grant this people favor in the sight of the Egyptians; and it shall be that when you go, you will not go empty-handed. But every woman shall ask of her neighbor and the woman who lives in her house, articles of silver and articles of gold, and clothing; and you will put them on your sons and daughters. Thus you will plunder the Egyptians.

Now the sons of Israel had done according to the word of Moses, for they had requested from the Egyptians articles of silver and articles of gold, and clothing; and the LORD had given the people favor in the sight of the Egyptians, so that they let them have their request. Thus they plundered the Egyptians.

Chapter 70

Taking Plunder

Readers of history understand that the wealth of nations is usually controlled by powerful interests within that nation's power structure. Wealthy families may control vast empires simply by sitting on various corporate boards, owning stock, or managing the entity that does. For years, the Rothschild family was known for such control of money in Europe. But there was no controlling Jewish family or group of families in America with quite that much wealth or control.

However, no matter how much evidence was brought to bear, people believed what they wanted to and acted accordingly. If the internet was to be believed, the Jews owned and controlled everything from Hollywood to the Communications industry from the banks to insurance. It was an old argument.

However, to say that the Jews had done well in America was an understatement. But success isn't always measured in just economic terms. For the American Jew, however, it was a combination of factors that defined its collective wealth. For example, from the 1970's and beyond, well over 60% of American Jews graduated college. The American population never understood what kind of national treasure it really had. Jews may not have controlled the financial world, medicine, the educational institutions, or the scientific communities, but they certainly had an influence on them.

The problem on the table now was how to extract the Jewish financial capital and move it to Israel. Michael Shapiro worked to rescue the human capital. These other analysts set to rescue the financial capital.

The toughest thing was that most of Jewish financial capital was invested in real estate, retirement accounts, not to mention pensions, social security, securities, bonds, and other financial instruments. In other words, much of it was held in illiquid accounts. Shapiro's colleagues developed financial models of Jewish families, businesses, and singles. There were so many variables to consider among them estimates of how much the typical Jewish family was worth not to mention Jewish business valuations.

They began with a family model constructed of several assumptions, one of which was that most adult Jews were married and remained so. If there were close to 5.5 million, and the typical family had between one and two children, the general estimator was about 1.75 million Jewish families living in the U.S. What would a transfer of that much money do to the American economy... to Israel's economy?

Next, they began scanning Jewish college graduation rates and looked at income tables associated with those graduation rates. It had been proven over the years that the more education one attained, the higher income he/she usually could expect. Balancing that was how many were working in the professions such as medicine, law, engineering, education, or manufacturing. Working with census data, social science studies, and historical data, the planners pegged the average American Jewish family wealth (meaning net worth) at somewhere between one half million to one million dollars. If the estimate was close, that meant that American Jewish wealth was somewhere north of 1.75 trillion dollars... *or more.*

Estimates of about one-half million dollars per family totaled $875 billion. Estimates of $1 million per family came out to $1.75 trillion. Some of those holding a little more awareness of their Biblical knowledge recalled that Moses had the Israelites take Egyptian wealth with them by *plundering* their neighbors, *by request and not by pressure or extortion. If the account is to be believed, the Egyptians were only too happy to participate in the transfer of wealth.*

This didn't even consider European, Australian, or Central or South American Jewish wealth. Rumors circulated for years that stolen art treasures from World War II were known as well. What would they be worth in current market?

When the team met to prepare their presentation, they recognized the irony. Most Israelis were barely making ends meet, whether or you had an education or not. Massive demonstrations swept through Israel protesting the high cost of living. That this much Jewish wealth existed was something to behold. Before the executive team entered the room, the planners intensely discussed what that kind of capital would mean to an Israeli economy so ravaged over the years.

Imagine what the nation could do with that money. There would be enough to feed every Israeli child and any group living within their borders. With some decent investing, they could pay off all their nation's loans and still have plenty left over. Now, how could they do it?

The leadership team entered the room to listen to the financial team's presentation. They included the leaders of government and industry.

The presenters laid out all the numbers plus a lot more. They provided detailed summations of Jewish business interests, levels of education and professional qualifications of the inbound immigrants, and of course the financial status of the average person expected to make Aliya.

Included in the briefing was a talk about Jewish innovation, inventions, patents, and the Nobel Peace Prize recipients over the years. Jewish ingenuity drove Israel's entrepreneurial mindset and global achievements. More Israeli businesses were launched per capita than anywhere in the world. One after another, the presenters made their cases.

"We have completed the programming for wealth transfer. Our software teams are ready to release electronic "bots" capable of attaching themselves to every Jewish account, no matter the type. Each bot carries electronic DNA that "sniffs out" and links to the census data and finds the online equivalent account in that person's or family's name. This includes 401K's, pension information, you name it," the speaker concluded.

By the time the briefings concluded, the Leadership team sat stunned and silent. This would not just be a transfer of wealth but would also include a transfer of immense intellectual capital. Jewish brainpower, technical knowhow and the financial means to back it up meant that Israel would take its place among the world's elite.

It was *funny* how the world may have hated the Jews but had no trouble taking from them the wonderful and profound inventions, medical breakthroughs, and technology developed in the tiny nation. Everywhere you looked, Israeli and Jewish technology and innovation drove power plants, computers, aircraft, medicine, water management, and a host of other things. What America would lose in the transfer of wealth, financial means, and brainpower, Israel would gain. There was no way to measure it.

The second discussion, still in development when the Leadership team re-entered the meeting focused on the Jewish art treasures of World War II Europe. Rumors circulated for years that the Germans had hidden the art deep in caves throughout the continent. Back at the turn of the century, financial records kept in a meticulous fashion by the Swiss were finally brought to light and the long cold trail to more stolen Jewish wealth warmed up again.

Israel recognized this as an extremely sensitive matter and proceeded with the utmost caution. There were those who doubted Switzerland's neutrality when in fact, all of the combatants of World War II kept offices in the nation and in some cases traded gold, armaments, oil, and other commodities with one another, keeping an eye to the post-war world order. When this fact came to light many years later, it went virtually unnoticed... until now.

One of the art committee members was an art historian who remembered Moses' ancient command to the Israelites. He was also a scholar in the lost Holocaust art treasures and had gathered stories for years. Towards the end of the second day of the meeting, he rose and addressed the panel assemblage.

"Many of you know that stolen art treasure is nothing new. History records victorious armies looting vanquished nations. How far back do we wish to go? Jerusalem was looted as far back as the kingship of Rehoboam, Solomon's son. After destroying Jerusalem and the Temple in 70 C.E., the Romans, carried the gold from the Temple all the way to Rome. We observe this sacking of the city at Tish B'Av every year. Various legends exist as to where the gold went and who may have taken it after that. Throughout history, the conquerors always took the loot with them. Even our own Moses and Joshua, according to Biblical accounts saw fit to capture some precious treasures after military victories.

"But the Nazis were a different story. Hermann Goring and others systematically stole art treasures from innocent civilians with the intent to fatten their personal fortunes but also to buttress their claims as a legitimate government. If a government has gold, it has wealth.

"In addition to the art, they stole silverware, candlesticks, and any household items they could carry. And they stripped the dead bodies of eyeglasses, gold teeth, and other personal items. Tons of gold from the victims were melted into gold bars and transferred to Switzerland where enemy combatants actually did business with one another during the war. Later, tens of thousands of these items were discovered after the war by the Allies. Many of the treasures were bought by private collectors. Some were returned to their owners, if they could be found. Others remained in storage while some governments made attempts to find the rightful owners." The speaker gained the rapt attention of everyone in the room.

"One story I know of makes me wonder if this is why we still try. At the end of the 90's, a part of the Art Provenance and Claims Research Project, a Jewish woman in her 90's was contacted by authorities and was told she was the heir of some of the confiscated art. She was the last one left as the remainder of her family perished in the *Shoah*. Several art pieces found their way back to her family, meaning her alone. One of the pieces, an impressionist painting, she later sold for $135 million. Imagine if the owners and that wealth had survived!"

The money was one thing, but the legacy of the dead was quite another.

But, as with any of these stories, the price paid for any of this was still too high. He stopped for a moment to let the amazing fact sink into the audience's mind. He continued—the six million on his mind.

"That the art was stolen was one thing, but now almost 100 years later, we must re-invigorate the effort to bring the art and accompanying wealth back to where it belongs... to the Jewish people. It belongs to the commonwealth of Israel and if we cannot trace it back to the original owners, it should, *it must*, rest with the nation. We are closer than ever to finding the remainder. Today, we call on our Swiss friends to reveal what they know. We ask every civilized nation to return the stolen art to the rightful owners." The art historian sat down and looked around the room.

His comments elicited no perfunctory applause nor did they even acknowledge his speech. But the impact of what he had said would be with them in the days ahead.

The financial planners set to work on plans to transfer the wealth from America to Israel. Draining that much money from a nations' coffers and transferring it to another was something so monumental they couldn't even imagine the impact. Israeli bankers and their IT teams worked doggedly around the clock making plans to receive the monies and then ensuring that the money would be matched to those claiming it. It promised to be an arduous task but a necessary one. There was no room for failure.

Israeli electronic capabilities had made tremendous progress over the past few months mapping out the general Jewish wealth picture. The bankers and their supporting teams had many surprises up their sleeves. Much still remained to be done. Meanwhile, Israel continued preparations to receive her sons and daughters.

The modular housing boom was nearly complete. With Israeli ingenuity in the science of hydroponics and other innovative uses of water, solar energy, and its rapidly improving new electrical grid technology, Israel progressed to become the world's first 'green nation.' Events from the past few decades with nations declaring five to ten percent reductions in greenhouse gas emissions were almost a thing of the past in the tiny nation. This was disruptive technology at its finest—something the world would be clamoring for in time. More to the point, each new modular home was capable of becoming its own power station and could generate tremendous amounts of solar power by the virtue of being where it was, in the middle of the desert. Combined with advances in personal transportation, Israel was now at the top of the heap in alternative energy technology.

Better Place, an Israeli start up designed and mastered smart-grid technology by setting up car battery charging and changing stations all over Israel. The new science allowed drivers to pull into a changing station, and receive a newly charged battery, all within three minutes. In time, some predicted, cars would be dirt cheap and drivers would pay for miles just as they paid for minutes with cell phones. Within a few years, the Israelis exported the technology to North America where the car-driving culture thrived.

Virtually free of any need of Mid-East oil, Israel had done her small part to reduce terrorism internally at the source... the funding. And, with recent rich discoveries of natural gas and oil deposits under the Israeli soil and under the Mediterranean, Israel could now meet all of its power needs. Potential surpluses of these resources intrigued the more entrepreneurial-minded and made her enemies even more envious. It was the unknown wild card.

> From 2nd Samuel
> Chapter 22 Verse 35
>
> He trains my hands for battle,
> So that my arms can bend a bow of bronze.

Chapter 71

Strike in the OC

The Christian Zionists were coming to the side of Southern California Jews in droves. Among the first to bolt his military assignment and join the IDFA was Billy Glass, an Army captain and ace Apache helicopter pilot. Most of his superior officers from his helicopter group joined him as well.

They met in haste, planning "training missions" with the intent of "borrowing" the aircraft and using them to defend the defenseless. Logistics and maintenance crews quickly 'arranged' fuel supplies and weapons caches. Israeli maintenance crews handled the spare parts and the supply requirements. The pilots and their supporters hoped that the battles would be short with less need for extended maintenance. The Apaches and Ospreys in Orange County were ready to rumble.

He had just returned from a tour of duty in the Philippines, seeing action all over the islands where he battled Islamic insurgents in the jungles of Mindanao and other islands. Glass had gained a reputation for demonstrating no fear in battle. He and his weapons officer, Steven 'Beau' Beauregard, a Louisiana Cajun with a long brown mustache, half a dozen tattoos, and a reputation for accuracy, had flown together for several years. Both had come to saving faith in the Bible just a year before and were familiar with Jonathan Roberts' teachings. The handwriting was on the wall and they saw unfolding events as part of God's great plan. That they happened to be a part of it was both thrilling and humbling to them.

He and Beau had been through a lot together and they realized what was at stake. They knew that there was no turning back now... this was for keeps. If they were caught, it meant a firing squad for treason, if shot down, it meant a scramble for their lives, if they even survived the impact. Death even had its benefits too—being ushered into the arms of a loving God.

There was no middle ground here. Identity was an easy one—they were *American Christians*, always willing to die for the flag but not to challenge God's eternal law as they saw it. God's rules trumped their orders. They believed the Jews, for whatever reason were chosen and recognized that they needed to help them or die trying. They would leave the details to the Master of the Universe.

IDFA commanders picked up intelligence that three local mosques had just received shipments of small arms, explosives, ammunition and were planning to attack Jewish targets in and around the County.

The Christian contingent's first target was the Islamic Learning Center mosque located in Anaheim, about 10 minutes north of the airport as the crow flew. The pilots and their weapons officers met for a quick prayer, as did the others, then climbed into their choppers, strapping in for the short journey north. It was one thing to fly with a partner—it was an entirely different experience flying with a friend. These Apache crew members were closer than brothers. Glass and Beau would be joined by two other aircraft for this morning's mission.

Four other Apaches would head south to Newport Beach for one of the larger Islamic teaching centers. Ground intelligence had learned that local plans for Jewish targets were stored there. So the plan wasn't to destroy the target but to capture it. Its booty of intelligence was valuable. The Apache helicopters escorted four V-22 Ospreys with 20 paratroopers each.

The Israeli ground commander in Orange County screamed the order, "Scramble the Apaches and Ospreys!" Then seven Apaches, their General Electric turbo-shaft engines whined, warmed, and then leaped into the early morning sky at John Wayne Airport in Orange County. The first mission of the IAFA's (Israeli Air Force of America) Southern California Battle Group was underway.

The Apaches headed northwest over the 405 and then up the 55 Freeway, banking low into Santa Ana, then skittering even lower over the area, encountering no challenges just yet. It was a clear day pushed by Santa Ana winds with not a cloud in the sky. The air temperature would hit 105 degrees by noon that day. They could see Disneyland in the distance out to the northwest, its various attractions gleaming in the morning sun.

Just then, off to the northeast and coming in hot, Glass saw three aircraft approaching him. Trained for battle, he instantly recognized the signatures and profiles of the aircraft... they were fellow Apache gunships just like his. His heart was about to pound out of his chest. From the looks of things, they had angled in from Camp Pendleton but then headed north... friend or foe? Time was flying and time was standing still, like the long day of Joshua. He yelled into his mic, asking the approaching aircraft to identify themselves.

"Identify yourselves—we don't want any trouble, we harbor no anger towards you!"

Just then, a Hellfire missile headed for him, its smoke trailing behind. He had to make a split second decision and just as he began evasive maneuvers, the missile flew slightly above and behind him. It headed into a business park across just north of the airport and exploded in a brilliant orange fireball. *That was close,* he thought.

He yelled in the mic, "Beau, buddy, it's on, it's on—this here's for real!"

The other Apache wasn't done just yet either. He heard the warning signal go off again and realized he was in the path of another inbound missile. That one missed too, just below and to the right of them. He was now bracketed but he couldn't for the life of him understand why any fellow Army pilot would do that.

His wing man, JJ Johnson, another Christian Zionist and his weapons officer, known as Lonesome Dave, both who mutinied with this group of pilots, unloaded the first volleys of their cannon. They hit the other Apache and it began to spin out of control towards the ground. It smashed into the ground near the hotel complex across the 405 slightly northeast of the airport and exploded into a huge fireball.

"Nice shot JJ! I owe you one, buddy!" he said into his mic.

"Hey, man, we got your backsides!" JJ yelled back.

He took a quick glance down the freeway and could see the Hyatt Hotel in flames. One down, two to go. Just then, the second Apache enemy fired off its first Hellfire missile, again a near miss. This wasn't going to be easy. Some force seemed to be shielding him and his compatriots from inbound weapons. He believed it was God. Beau whispered a prayer, just to make sure.

At that point, the other helos moved into position and fired one Hellfire each at the attackers. The remaining two choppers exploded in bursts of orange and yellow, falling into another business complex and setting off several fires at the same time. Now it was time to go to work.

"Sad to see good Boeing product wasted that way," he said to Beau.

Two of the Apaches peeled off heading towards Long Beach and another mosque just identified by field intel. But Glass and Beau, joined by another AH-64, continued heading northwest towards the target. Urban warfare over America wasn't exactly what they signed up for, but the stakes were higher now and they knew that there wasn't much time to think about things. It was time for action.

The two choppers encountered no other resistance as they headed up the 55, then turned west over the 22 Freeway, then angled up the 57. 'Better to head in from the east, with the sun behind us,' thought Glass. He looked slightly west and his ground spotter came on the box.

"Samson 1, note the golden dome off to the west, you should be closing in on the target now," the voice said. Glass and his weapons man scanned the horizon, looking out of the twin windows on the flying tank, for that is what the Apache is.

"You will see some trucks in the parking lot and other vehicles to the immediate west on State College Boulevard, they should be coming right into view about now," the controller said.

"Copy that," he said, calmly, his steely nerves steady.

His weapons officer nervously fingered the triggers of his missiles and guns. In the distance, they could see the sun glinting off the huge brass dome, causing a bright reflection in their vision.

"As you circle around, you will have a pretty clear shot. They are unloading the trucks now and we can see the rocket propelled grenade launchers and a whole lot of ammo boxes... we have no idea what else may be inside," the controller explained.

"Thanks, I got 'em now... permission to engage," Glass asked.

"Permission granted," the voice immediately said. His heart was beating out of his chest.

Beau fingered his Hellfires, ready to fire. This little weapon packed a big punch and a few local mosques were about to find out how much.

Beau released the first Hellfire and as it streaked towards the dome, the helicopter bucking underneath them at release. Neither one of them could have anticipated the blast.

The missile reached the dome, penetrating the bronze structure, burying itself into the weapons cache hidden under the first floor in a secretly built, concrete enforced bunker. Nothing would stop these new bunker-buster missiles.

In an instant, the mosque exploded as the blast turned the sky a brilliant orange and the accompanying explosion sent debris more than 500 feet into the air, the blast wave rocking the helicopter. The smoke could be seen for more than 60 miles on this most brilliant and beautiful of days. As amazing as that explosion was, the real fireworks were about to begin.

Just then, a secondary explosion headed in five directions at once, and with it, half the city block virtually dissolved before their eyes. With video cameras rolling, the transmission was reaching the spotters and commanders on the ground. What wasn't apparent from the ground but immediately became clear was that this little Muslim enclave had jihadists living in the area, hell bent on their mission, to destroy Orange County's Jews.

Tunnels connecting their homes in all directions, had acted as underground transporting corridors shielding the weapons runners from the street. The tunnels exploded as did most of the homes, businesses and vehicles all up and down the street.

As the mosque, buildings, homes, and surrounding streets were burning, the two Apache officers in the second aircraft also asked permission to fire on the trucks in the parking lot. Events slowed for the pilots and their weapons officers. Everything seemed to be moving in slow motion.

"Permission to engage secondary targets," the pilot asked.

"Permission granted, Samson 2."

With permission secured, they sent a torrent of 30-mm automatic cannon fire and a Hellfire right behind it. The trucks exploded one at a time, leaping into the air in a grotesque scene of twisting aerial acrobatics, each truck explosion in turn setting off the others. The blast tossed the men loading them into the air like ragdolls, blown to bits.

The helicopters now headed west looking for more targets. As they left their primary targets in flames, they hovered over several small strip malls. Suddenly an RPG headed for the second Apache. Using quick evasive tactics, the pilot avoided the shoulder-fired missile and then unloaded on the storefront. What was once a hookah bar and lounge exploded right in front of them, silencing the warriors inside and causing a massive secondary explosion a few stores down from the bar, including a hallal meat market. The meat store had just received a supply of fresh beef and lamb, and a whole lot more including hundreds of weapons, ammunition, and explosives.

"Nice work, Samson 2," the voice said.

"I guess they're in for some nice barbeque tonight," the weapons officer chided, referring to the meat market, but then feeling remorse as he said it. There was no joy in this mission and both soldiers felt it.

The Newport Beach team headed low over the 405 Freeway and then turned south along Jamboree Boulevard. They caught the mosque's domed structure in the distance and made a few adjustments for their final approach. As the air strike team approached the target, they noticed that a small crowd had gathered outside the mosque.

This posed a problem for them, as they wanted minimum contact with the ground. Because this wasn't just a search and destroy mission, they needed to exercise extreme caution. How would they be able to take the mosque and get the intelligence materials they needed without loss of civilian life?

"Gideon 1, this is Right Arm," the spotter said.

"Right Arm, this is Gideon 1," the lead helicopter pilot answered.

"We have a situation here, civilians on the target grounds," he said.

"Copy that, Right Arm," answered the pilot. What to do now? They were 30 seconds from the target.

"Where are our ground forces?" the pilot asked. The ground forces referred to were a small company of approximately 150 Israelis that had deployed to the south part of the county.

"Gideon 1, I see them! Here they come!"

Within a moment, the Apache pilot and his compadres in the V-22's could see the armored column approaching from the west and the south.

"How many at the mosque?" he asked.

"I see about 75 or so, looks like a mixed group, women, children, and some men," the voice answered.

"Ok, how close are our men?" the Apache pilot asked.

"Hold on... "

The spotter directed his next transmission to the ground commander, a woman named D'vorah Rafaeli. She had assumed command of this unit just a few days before when she got the call from home.

"Right Arm, this is Kelev Gadol (Big Dog), we are about one minute out from your position," she said. The heat was on and everyone tensed as the moment approached.

"All helos, hold your fire, we are going to approach from the ground first," the spotter said.

At that moment, all six aircraft took higher positions and began a slow circling dance over the mosque, each about 1500 feet above the domed structure, each with weapons trained on ground targets.

On the ground, those on the grounds of the mosque looked up upon hearing the noise of the Apaches and the Ospreys. Just then, there was a flash of light as someone hidden in the bushes behind the mosque sent a rocket-propelled grenade flying towards one of the Ospreys....

The pilot dodged the missile. But as he did so, the strange looking beast began gyrating wildly. The pilot and co-pilot fought to bring it under control. Then a second RPG headed for the V-22, striking the flank of the half plane, half helicopter.

The Osprey began spiraling downward. About 300 feet above the ground, the pilots pulled it out of its downward rotation and managed to slow the descent. The ground was coming up fast.

It hit hard, jostling the paratroopers quite a bit, stunning them for the moment. Though not totally destroyed, the aircraft was damaged and when the pilots finally brought it down, it was across the street and now out of the action. Though somewhat shaken up, the paratroopers gathered their gear and headed into the action across Jamboree. Motorists were stunned as they happened upon the action. A few Christians with the attack team managed to divert traffic and turn it around. There was no sign of local police or National Guard units.

As the second RPG was fired, the third Apache in the attack team, Gideon 3 let out a ferocious burst of cannon fire, killing the shooter and a few others in the courtyard of the mosque. The others hit the ground trying to find cover near cars, behind walls, anywhere to avoid the incoming fire. The RPG missed and embedded itself in a Mercedes dealership across the street. The showroom exploded into shredded glass and flames—cars ignited one after the other. Within minutes the dealership and three other businesses were destroyed.

At that same moment, the Israeli ground team rammed the front gate of the mosque knocking it off its hinges and pushing through to the courtyard while the three remaining Ospreys lowered themselves into hovering position over the mosque. The loading ramps opened, rappelling ropes descended, and the Osprey began disgorging its troops on top of the mosque's rooftop. The Apaches continued their protective dance around the perimeter ensuring no interference.

The ground forces all arrived safely, quickly deployed, and joined the paratroopers. They stormed the building and headed for the document center. Muslim personnel on the ground quickly realized what they were up against and surrendered, with several soldiers holding weapons on them. With the courtyard now subdued and under control, the paratroopers went to work to capture the intelligence treasures awaiting them. Arabic and Farsi speaking troops trained their weapons on the enemy—calming them and explaining to them to do nothing rash.

Inside, all was chaos. The soldiers approached the doors from three sides. The key here was to avoid any civilian casualties. Helmet-mounted cameras recorded the assault. If any accusations came out of the skirmish, there would be multiple sets of tape to refute the stories, should they differ from official records. The Israelis learned their lessons from the Gaza blockade incident years before.

Major Dov Pinsky, a former Israeli reservist and 10 year Orange County resident was in second in command to Rafaeli. The Israelis knew an Islamic Day School was chartered for the mosque there so they approached cautiously, weapons live but guarded.

There were now 175 troopers on the ground and five flying machines hovering slightly above the mosque. The other Osprey was out of action but all its troops had joined the fight. The troops cautiously approached the six-room school, which was located towards the back of the property. Just then, several machine guns from the school opened up on the Israelis.

"Right Arm, Right Arm, we are under fire," screamed Rafaeli. Pinsky's troops are pinned down—gunfire over their heads. Then the guns abruptly stopped.

"We need to determine if there are any children inside," she yelled.

"We are checking right now," Right Arm replied.

"We'll hold fire for now," she transmitted back.

"Hold your fire everyone," she directed. The teams stood down.

"D'vorah, we're in touch with the Director of the school. He's in the group that surrendered. He says there are children inside."

"Ok, let me think for a second." D'vorah went silent and then ordered her troops to fall back out of range.

"We don't know who or what is in there. But we know it's a prize. They are defending it like Mohammed's bones. So I want it," she demanded.

"We need to get word inside the school for them to stand down... need to tell them they are outnumbered and outgunned. For God's sake, I don't want a slaughter. Can we get him to talk to them? I have some Arabic and Farsi speakers with me," she said.

"I've got him here with me. He says there are six rooms each with 20 children. There is a teacher in each room," Right Arm replied. Her worst nightmare was unfolding before her.

"Oh, great... they are using the children as human shields. We've got the drawings for the facility with us... it's a holographic image so we can see the inbound and outbound access points. We can do this a couple of ways. We can mount up a V-22 and go in from above or try to fire tear gas into the windows and flush them out. I'd rather have some stinging eyes then dead bodies," she said.

"Copy that. Let me see if I can reason with him," Right Arm answered. "Hang on for a minute," he answered.

"He says there are telephones in each room. Let's try dialing in," he offered.

"I'll do anything not to kill any kids... the shooters are another matter," she said, matter-of-factly.

Six phones went off in the mosque's classrooms simultaneously. Each was answered by a male adult, each vowing not to surrender, and hurling oaths at the Israelis.

The Israeli technicians managed to create a party line so that their commander was able to speak with each room at the same time.

"Look, we want no harm to the children. Surrender your weapons and you will not be harmed either. You have one minute to give up your weapons and come out," Rafaeli shouted.

"No! We will die with our children. We will all die for Allah!" the leader said. That answered at least one of D'vorah's questions—they spoke English well enough.

"You have 30 seconds," she answered, calmly but firmly. She hated this. But her training took over.

Meanwhile, a V-22 dipped lower and prepared to come over the roof. The paratroops had the school surrounded, tear gas at the ready. The next 30 seconds were the longest of D'vorah's life. She thought about her three children, now all but grown. She remembered all at once about rocking them to sleep at night, holding them when they were sick, singing Psalms to calm them. Her mind snapped back to the present.

"Ten seconds" She was cool—calm.

Silence from the targets.

As the clock ticked down, there was silence all around them. When the team completed its debrief later that evening, each of them commented on something they all noted, a peaceful and awesome silence that none of them could explain. They remained laser-focused on the situation at hand, but had an incredible peace surround them, almost protecting their presence there. No one offered an explanation. No one had to.

"Team 1, approach slowly, stay covered as best you can, but come as close as you are able, and then fire the canisters into the window. The gas and the flash bangs will stun them, then team 2 can follow in," she said.

"Everyone, this is for real... there are 120 kids inside. Gas masks on!" she firmly directed her soldiers.

With their gas masks on, Team 1 moved to within a few feet of the door. The terrorist's voices and guns were silent for the moment.

"Gideon 1, prepare to enter from the top," she whispered into her microphone. Command now shifted between her and the Osprey pilot.

"Copy that D'vorah."

Valuable seconds ticked by... the V-22 now in position, the back loading ramp fully deployed and the soldiers now on the roof, ready to rumble.

"Go!!!!" Rafaeli shouted.

Team members fired flash-bang grenades first and then tear gas. The soldiers burst into each of the classrooms and those on the roof came crashing into the rooms from above.

The children screamed. There was noise and confusion everywhere. Within moments, the troops found the children and the shooters. The scene was chaotic. The rooms quickly filled with smoke and the tear gas.

As the troops entered the rooms they immediately encountered the most horrifying situation and the one they dreaded most—gunmen with guns and knives drawn and ready to kill the kids. The Muslim shooters had begun to tie up the kids and had drawn knives with the intent to slit their throats, rather than allow them to be taken prisoner by the Israeli soldiers. It didn't matter that this signified Muslim on Muslim violence but rather as with all terror, it was meant to project the outrageous and the inexplicable. Two of the kids were seriously wounded as the tear gas permeated the rooms. Everyone was coughing, crying, and sneezing.

Rafaeli and her commandos cared about preserving life at any cost no matter who the children were.

All six teams were now in the rooms facing similar situations.

The commander followed in on her troops' tail. She shouted in Arabic at the Muslim gunmen. "Put down your weapons!"

All of the soldiers had their guns drawn. No response.

"You have five seconds," she yelled again. Her voice cut through the chaos and commanded attention. The schoolhouse went silent. Thoughts and visions of Islamic terror focused on Jewish schools in Israel flashed through her mind. She had seen it all.

"No! We will die here with our children!" One of the knife-wielders screamed.

"Put the knife down!"

He was defiant. Then a muffled scream came from the next room. Shots were fired—one, two, three.

More children screamed. The Israeli troops did their best to prevent a massacre.

After the gunfire, the room fell silent. Precious moments passed.

The leader had two kids tied up. One bled from a slashing he had administered minutes before. He held the knife at the throat of a little girl. Rafaeli judged her to be about seven or eight years old. She coughed and gagged from the tear gas.

Rafaeli began to bargain and plead with the man. "Please, please don't hurt her—you can take me as a hostage. Just leave her alone."

All guns in the room were trained on him but any small slip up could take the young child's life, something that the Israeli commander couldn't bear.

"No, she dies, we all die—you filthy Jew!"

Rafaeli dropped her weapon and put her hands up. She felt no fear. She was full of torment and anguish for the child. *How could someone do this to a child?* She wondered. *What a vile monster!*

She took a step toward him. He tightened his grip on the child. She struggled to breath.

"Please—I beg you—drop the knife."

"Never..."

CRACK! A bullet pierced his forehead and took his brain and the back of his skull to the wall. The monster dropped, and the girl fell in a heap. Rafaeli scooped her up and took to safety. The scene was repeated in an instant with every hostage taker.

The siege ended. Five terrorists were in Jewish custody—their brothers littered the blood stained floor. Medics flew to the injured. And evacuation was enroute for wounded.

The hostages were safe and the scene secure. But silence was not to be. Little ones hurt or frightened wailed like sirens.

The Israeli troops had prevented a massacre. Jewish commandos are known for their precise, swift, and severe use of deadly force. They are also known for fierce conviction, concern, and care to protect the innocent.

With the fog of battle cleared, the collection of intelligence was priority. D'vorah and Dov sent eyes and hands in search of documents and materials.

Dov called out, "Check every classroom, office, restroom, trash container, cabinets, closet, cupboard, and void. You know what we need. Send it outside to the analysts—they'll search and sort."

In minutes the analysts gave the commanders more reason to celebrate. They found the attack plans against Jewish targets for all of South Orange and San Diego Counties. Congratulations all around..brief but heartfelt. She congratulated them on a job well done.

"Look at this," Dov said, "they have attack plans for Jewish schools, synagogues, museums, community centers, and other Jewish interests including some neighborhoods. We saved children today, but we will also avert the potential massacre of tens of thousands of other lives!"

D'vorah lifted documents and cried out, "My God, the census logo is on almost every document here. These contain addresses and information on Jews living all over the area. What a nightmare!"

"What a miracle!" Pinsky added.

D'vorah, Dov, and the analyst stared in silence at the documents and one another. Then the analyst said, "I pray that these are the only hard copies. I'll know more after I get the computer and media to my lab."

Then he lifted a handful of documents to the sky and prayed, "H'Shem You have shown us Your great power and mercy this day. May Your favor continue upon us. Blind our enemies and guard Your people. Your eyes never fail. You who keep Israel shall neither slumber nor sleep."

Those who stood by and overheard the analyst report to D'vorah and Dov said, "Amen."

> From the Prophet Isaiah
> Chapter 29 Verses 5-6
>
> But the multitude of your enemies will become
>   like fine dust,
> And the multitude of the ruthless ones
>   like the chaff which blows away;
> And it will happen instantly, suddenly.
> From the LORD of hosts you will be punished
>   with thunder and earthquake and loud noise,
>   with whirlwind and tempest and
>   the flame of a consuming fire.

Chapter 72

The Ground Shakes

When Farouk Ibn Nasser woke up that morning he heard something strange. Rather, it was what he didn't hear that caused him some concern for he was a farmer, used to hearing the noise of his farm animals just before dawn broke. Raised in a small farming community in Saudi Arabia, he had gone to school in the West and gained a fair understanding of agricultural techniques learned at the university and making things grow in the desert, even meeting and enjoying his time with Israeli Agricultural instructors. He had no trouble with them nor did they with him. His animals provided much for his family—butter and eggs, milk, beef, and lamb, his favorite. But this morning was different for his animals were silent.

He rolled over in bed, kissed his wife, got dressed, brushed his teeth, and after spending a few minutes in prayer on his prayer rug and reading his Quran, he headed for the front door, curious to see why things were so

CHAPTER SEVENTY-TWO: *The Ground Shakes*

quiet. When he stepped out the front door, there was a certain dryness in the air, but nothing else that he could detect. But something wasn't right and he knew it. He couldn't find his English Sheepdog, normally at his side as soon when he entered his gardens and fields. He was different from others he knew in that he enjoyed the presence of his dogs and they helped him around the farm.

Hmmm, strange, he thought. He went to the barn and found the door open and the animals gone. Concern crept into his mind.

He walked into the cornfield where the corn was swayed lazily in the gentle breeze. Seeing nothing unusual but the sensing the silence around him, he moved deeper into the corn and there he noticed something strange. As he cast his eyes south, he saw it – a gentle puff of steam rising in the distance. He decided to investigate.

When Nasser walked to where he thought he had seen the steam, it occurred to him that he was standing in the middle of his cow pasture. The area didn't look any different but he did notice that a small puddle of hot water had broken through the surface of the ground and appeared to be bubbling up from below.

This is interesting. I wonder if there's a hot water spring under the ground, he thought. Nasser turned around and headed back to his house, still looking for his animals. It was interesting, indeed and would get even more interesting in the coming days.

He heard a bleating sound and recognized the noise as one of his sheep. The noise was coming from the cornfield he had been in just a few minutes before. When he walked deeper into the stalks, he saw the gentlest of his sheep that he had named Daisy, his wife Shabibi's favorite. She was with her two little ewes and seemed to be a scared. He reached out to stroke behind her ears—which seemed to calm her a little.

He heard more rustling and when he went even further into the field he began to find more of the animals. Now why they had decided to head further into the corn he had no idea. But, the thought intrigued him. He recalled from his research that animals could sense something about to happen before humans could. A few minutes later he had located his other animals and then saw his dog. None of this was making sense. Still, he'd ask his wife and then place a few calls to his animal husbandry friends and run this by them.

He led his animals back to the barn—cautious and curious. He looked over his shoulder at the steam that rose in the distant fields. With the his livestock back in the barn, he took a deep breath and went to work. But the animals were unsettled. They ran in circles and then bolted back out of the barn and into the fields. Then he felt it.

It started as a very small rumble, almost a groan from the earth.
Earthquake? He wondered?

The animals were now back in the safety of the fields. He reached for his cell phone and called his wife, Shabibi. "Come out here. I need you to try and figure this out.."

"Why are the animals out of the barn and running in circles out there?" She asked.

Shabibi had also attended school in the West and specialized in raising farm animals. Her long flowing black hair was tied in a bun this day. She wore simple farm clothes for the work was hard and she wasn't out in public, otherwise she would be wearing a burkha.

She was tall for her tribal affiliations, taller than her husband, with a flashing white smile and dark warm eyes. She was a friend to all, even the Jews and Christians she met while in school. The sun had darkened her a little more with long hours spent outdoors caring for her sweet animals. Her eyes showed the beginnings of crow's feet, and though she was young they gave her the look of a woman of wisdom.

She sometimes fretted over her facial lines, but her husband would hear none of it. He loved her as he loved this farm. She loved the land, her flocks, and her husband. It was a tough life but one she wouldn't trade for the world. She was doing exactly what Allah had called her to do and she was content.

Her keen sense of things was that the animals were scared and something was coming. The brief shaking stopped and the young married couple looked at each other with raised eyebrows, shoulder shrugs, and surprise.

"Did you feel that?" Farouk asked her—his voice shaky.

"Yes... earthquake? I don't remember anything like that ever... not here anyway."

"I wonder...."

"Well, it certainly got the animals' attention didn't it?"

The animals calmed down after a few minutes with her singing to them. For some reason her soft, gentle, and reassuring voice always seemed to relax her four-footed friends. They followed her into the barn.

Once the animals were safe in the barn, she headed back to the house to make some breakfast and Farouk headed into the barn, once again, to get the morning's proceedings started. The rest of the day went according to plan and the whole incident was pretty much forgotten by lunch.

What neither of them noticed was that their well, the only source of drinking water for miles, was drying up quickly. The water level had receded by more than two feet in the past 24 hours.

The next morning, upon awakening, both Farouk and Shabibi felt the rumbling and the animals were agitated again. They both went out to the barn and noted the animals had taken off into the fields once more. Farouk remembered his walk to the pastures to see the steam and this time, he noticed something he hadn't the day before.

"You've got to see this... " he said, leading the way to where the hot water and rose from the ground. The water had spread a little wider and there was a small, though noticeable hump coming up from the ground.

"Strange."

"Smell that?"

"Phew... stinky—smells like sulpher! Maybe there are springs underneath—bubbling up," Shabibi said. They move a little closer to the rising steam.

When they approached, the slight rumbling stopped but they also noticed that the air smelled worse.

"We need to call the neighbors to check this out," he said.

"I wonder what they might think... maybe we can build a bathhouse out here—I hear that mineral hot springs can have healing powers. We can share it with the others and have a place to relax!" He and Shabibi then speculated on what the farmers and ranchers might think of this new treasure of theirs.

The next day, Farouk came back to the same spot and noted nothing changed from the day before. And so it went for a few more days, the water and steam receding into the earth. With no changes and the animals seemingly settled down, he and Shabibi went about their business with no further thought about the strange goings on in the pastures and fields.

What Farouk and his wife didn't know was that this area had a history of both seismic and volcanic activity. Though the immense sand piles in the desert act as a buffer for most seismic events, it didn't mean that Saudi Arabia was immune to catastrophic earthquakes or volcanoes.

In fact, in 1256, Medina, the second holiest site in Islam was rocked by tremors and though not generally known, the land between Medina and Mecca held some of the world's largest fields of volcanic rock, home to huge lava fields (harraat in Arabic). The area was twice the size of Lebanon. Much of the western region of Saudi Arabia contained volcanic rock lurking just beneath the soft desert sand. This area, known by geologists as the 'Arabian Shield' spanned the entire west coast of Saudi Arabia.

Deep under the surface, huge continental plates were on the move. Ancient submerged volcanoes were disrupted and all manner of materials were being stirred up, causing openings in the surface of the crust and inviting those materials to make their escape. But for the next few days, things had returned to normal.

About two weeks later, the young couple and other farmers near them awoke to braying animals, barking dogs, and squawking birds. The ground began to shift that early morning and the residents of the small farming community were literally tossed out of their beds by the early morning earthquake. The shaking built slowly until the two farmers and their neighbors realized they were in the middle of one of the biggest seismic events in Saudi history. It would be the first of more than 100 separate earthquakes and aftershocks in the coming days.

Registering more than 7.0 on the Richter Scale, the locals gathered that morning to another sight they would never forget. For in Farouk Ibn Nasser's pastures stood a 100 foot cylinder cone, pushing out of the ground and growing by the hour. The volcano had chosen his field to erupt that morning. This was no random hot springs. The air smelled foul with all the gasses released from the earth.

As the farmers looked on, the small volcano grew first to 150 feet, then to 200 and so on. By the end of the day, the volcano now stood more than 400 feet high and began to belch out hot ash, molten lava, and huge rocks that rocketed into the sky and began to fall around them.

'We need to get the animals out of here and to safety," Farouk yelled. Shabibi agreed and began to round them up.

"I'll get into the safe, grab the cash and all of our documents," he said. So, Farouk raided the little safe in the kitchen and grabbed gold and other jewelry, bank cards, computer and electronic equipment, and cash.

Three days later, the volcano began a full-on eruption, slowly at first, but violently gathering momentum.

Volcanologists arrived to study the phenomenon. This volcano, similar to the Mexican Paricutin explosion in 1943, was really heating up now. As the cone grew, so did the lava, sending its pyroclastic flow to overtake Farouk's and the other locals' fields. The lava was moving at more than 100 feet per hour and closing fast on the house and barnyard as well as the fields, which were overtaken first.

But what had Saudi officials most worried was the fact that the Hajj was only days away and the volcano appeared capable of far more damage, its reach now extending beyond the new lava fields. What had originally appeared to be a tiny new hot springs finding its way to the surface through a fissure in the earth, now potentially threatened Islam's holiest site.

And, almost like Lot's wife, Farouk knew he shouldn't look back as he left his family's property. When he did, his heart broke, for his house, fields, and everything he and his wife had worked for were now in flames.

From the Brit Hadasha—Hab'sorah HaK'dosha

> al pi Mattai (The Gospel of Matthew)
> Chapter 24 Verses 7-8
>
> For nation will rise against nation, and kingdom against kingdom and in various places there will be famines and earthquakes. But all these things are merely the beginning of birth pangs.
>
> Chapter 73

Mecca & the Hajj

Mecca is the holiest site in Islam and, for centuries, has been the site of the Hajj. The city, about 2 million strong had a long and storied history, having been founded, according to Muslim traditions by Abraham and his eldest son, Ishmael. Mecca sits in Western Saudi Arabia, and had become known for its commerce with its skilled merchants and traders.

Over time, Mecca drew many traders and merchants, often becoming the preferred overland trade route because sea lanes had increasingly become more and more dangerous due to piracy and violence. This, in turn, encouraged more trade and slowly, over time, made Mecca an increasingly important city as it became a safe haven from untoward elements. Since Mecca occupied such a strategic place, it drew local tribes in an annual declaration of a ceasing of hostilities and an accompanying pilgrimage to the holy site of the Kabbah.

It was there that local tribesmen arbitrated disputes and resolved debts. This, in turn, presented opportunities for enhanced trading and commerce at local fairs, giving all parties a sense of common identity, further increasing Mecca's importance to the region. But none of this would matter without the growing presence of the Prophet.

Mecca sits in a triangle of three great cities and with access to the Zamzam well, became even more prominent as a major source of water, which, in the arid desert is the very source of life itself. It was no surprise that it became a major stop along the way of the great caravans of yesteryear. The area became known as the Hejaz.

According to Muslim sources, when pagan influences invaded the 'one true faith,' it took the Prophet Mohammed and his followers years to defeat them. During that time, Mohammed began to receive divine revelations from the Angel Jibrail (Gabriel) which helped him and his followers to overthrow the pagan influences that had corrupted Abraham's religion.

Severe and long-suffered persecution by opposing tribes, led Mohammed to migrate to Medina. There his troops would overcome his foes, and he would give birth to Islam. Medina was the second holiest city in Islam and not far from Mecca. And so, the Hajj, the annual gathering of the tradesmen, merchants, and tribesmen, gained in importance to the growing faith.

The Hajj is commanded in the Quran. Muslim tradition says it was one of the last acts of public worship performed by Muhammad. The Hajj and the subsequent visit to Mecca is one of Five Pillars of Islam. All Muslims are supposed to attend at least once in their lives. It is said to be a commemoration of the stories of all the Islamic faithful such as Abraham (Ibrahim), Hagar (the mother of Ishmael, Abraham's firstborn), and Ishmael. The event brings all Muslims together, rich and poor, to worship in unity, part of which shows in the pilgrims' dress. This year, however, the Hajj would not be remembered for the unifying effect of the event. Instead it would be remembered for something much different.

When the first 100-pound rock fell just a mile from the Kabbah within the main site, Hajj officials anxiously looked to the skies for answers. Just what was Allah, the Merciful, doing?

Over the next few days, the volcano calmed down a little, as did the earth's temblors, and officials rested with assurance that the events of the past few days were winding down. The day of the Hajj arrived and so did the pilgrims.

When the faithful enter the state of ihram (purity) they remain so throughout the event. Hajj devotees from all over the Muslim world and numbering more than one million, were in full effect, the men wearing the ihram garments (two seamless white sheets wrapped around the body) and sandals. The women were dressed in white, exposing only their faces and hands. During the ihram, the attendees may not cut their nails or hair, engage in any sexual relations, argue, fight, or hunt. This was a holy time and this was Muslim worship at the pinnacle of its existence. The focus was on trying to please Allah and the rituals designed to draw them to the Hajj.

For now, the volcano remained dormant and the pilgrims began their circular 'counter ambulation' movements around the Kaaba. Reporters and bloggers began writing about Allah's mercy citing the fact that the volcano, currently the biggest story on the internet, had calmed down and was going inactive once again. Then all hell broke loose.

About 10:00 a.m. on the third day of the pilgrimage, the volcano sprang to life once again. This time flying debris reached the outskirts of the city, and then, with one huge blast equivalent to a multiple nuclear explosions, some said, millions of tons of molten rock, lava, and ash fell on the worshippers.

The effect blocked out much of the sunlight. A cataclysm of Biblical proportions fell on them. Fire and brimstone-like material rained down day and night. Like a focused artillery barrage, the strike zone narrowed.

Then a massive earthquake lurched and rolled through the area. The 8.5 quake rocked everything for miles. The violent upheaval and mortars of molten rock terrorized more than a million Hajj participants. They panicked but found no place to run. The earth gyrated for almost two minutes.

The pilgrims were trapped and then began to run into one another. Screams and pleadings to Allah the Just, emanating from the center of the circle and closest to the Kabbah reached those on the outside. Once the crowds began moving in the opposite direction of the 'counter ambulation,' all semblance of order broke down and then the trampling began. The Hajj was famous for stampedes. Cries for calm went unheeded.

It was like a scene from a horror movie. Those furthest from the center and able to get away escaped the tumultuous crowd but were hit by falling debris. Fiery boulder after fiery boulder struck the Kabbah, the huge windowless stone cube so symbolic to the faithful.

Within minutes the stone was reduced to rubble and then buried in a fiery pile. The hopes and dreams of more than one billion of the earth's inhabitants were dashed on the rock. Followers of the Prophet wept as one who would weep for an only child.

The trembling, gyrating earth was so strong that no one could stand its force. Allah had awakened and was angry. The shaking seemed to go on for an eternity especially to those trapped in the middle of the crowd. The worshippers self-combusted from the falling fire. They rolled and piled into one another in agony in their attempts to extinguish the flames and get away from this burning hell. Those enveloped by the flames and utter chaos around them, pleaded for a merciful death from their creator, screaming for mercy to an unresponding Allah.

A huge dust storm materialized out of nowhere. It hovered over the horizon and then within seconds fell upon the worshippers amidst the fiery rocks and the rolling, bucking earth. Howling winds of dust and sand enveloped the entire city, turning the day into night. The dust was everywhere and into everything. The storm seemed of cataclysmic proportions and its ferocity literally cut into the skin of the faithful.

The shaking finally slowed and then stopped. The hot flaming ash and rock continued its deadly rain. The winds ceased. Mecca had become a deathtrap. Dust covered everything. Flames leapt everywhere as worshippers' clothes exploded in fire. It was a veritable hell on earth. An eerie, deathly silence then enveloped the site.

And then the unthinkable happened... slowly at first, and then with what those few survivors would later describe as something akin to hell itself—the ground opened up into an enormous cavern, a screeching, groaning sound, and with it Mecca, with its pilgrims began falling into the growing chasm.

The screams were unbearable. Within just a few seconds, the earth swallowed the entire complex with upwards of one million pilgrims falling silent all at once.

CNN, Fox, Al-Jazeera, and other media recorded the event. Transmissions of the cataclysmic event suddenly went black. The video feed was turned off by event organizers. They didn't want the world to see. However, some forgotten cameras continued to roll. Satellite pictures transmitted again when the winds subsided. The world could now see the utter destruction and flattened holy site. Images of the belching volcano and its deadly fiery rain also escaped. The event could be seen from space, interestingly, the smoke and flames as well as the tremendous dust storm. Who was to blame?

☪☪☪☪☪☪

Within minutes, the press picked up the story....

"This just in... and with all that has happened over the past few months... I cannot fathom this... a huge earthquake and immense volcanic eruption has struck Mecca in Saudi Arabia. The information coming in is sketchy but it appears that hundreds of thousands of Muslim faithful may be dead. This is too much to bear!" The reporter fell speechless as the station went to a station break.

In the days that followed, Christian commentators heard on radio, television, print media, and the internet likened the events as similar to Sodom and Gomorrah or the rebellion of Korah, and other Biblical cataclysms.

It didn't take long for Israel and the Jews to receive blame for the disaster. Many Islamic clergy claimed the Jewish state had launched an unprovoked nuclear strike during the Hajj, purposely targeting the crowd and destroying Islam's holiest site. Otherwise how could you explain the huge crater left behind and the intense flames and smoke?

Mecca was gone.

As the story flashed across CNN, Shoshana stopped in her tracks, completely glued to the screen. She had just dug into her favorite 'Pete's Grilled Chicken' dinner and was ready to relish the savory flavor. She recalled her recent discussion with Weinstein and Ben Yehuda and instantly she knew and understood the earthquakes, and all that was happening. And, now volcanoes just popping up in farmers' fields and then destroying the centerpiece of the world's largest religion? *What was that all about?* She took a couple of bites, but was not hungry anymore. She then pushed away the dish.

Though not particularly religious, she made a mental note to herself to pick up her new copy of the Tenach she had just purchased, hoping to find some sort of meaning in all this. The world was going nuts all around her. It just seemed too weird for these were the exact kinds of things she and Jonathan Roberts had just discussed. She yanked her cell phone out of her pocket and dialed up her young colleague at the Mossad.

✡ ✡ ✡ ✡ ✡ ✡

And as news reached the bunker of the destruction in Saudi Arabia, a great fear consumed Mimi. She had to find Shabibi and Farouk... but how... with all that was going on. She was paralyzed. She fired off an encrypted text message.

"Shabibi, are you there? News is coming in now. Oh, God, please answer me!!!"

✡ ✡ ✡ ✡ ✡ ✡

In the next few days, dozens of C-17 aircraft flew in humanitarian aid, equipment, food, water, and for those who did survive the events, Muslim holy articles, prayer rugs, and Qurans. The United Nations declared it as an international Day of Mourning.

Sympathy poured forth from the international community. One of the first responders was the World Wide Ecumenical Association of Churches who pledged both money and aid to the few surviving victims and their families. Governments leaped in to do the same. Israel, despite the libels thrown at her, offered aid which was promptly rejected by any and all Islamic and Christian entities and charities.

A talk show host on a religious channel in America actually wondered aloud whether this was some sort of judgment on Islam itself. That brought howls of protest from the international Islamic community. There were more vociferous calls for international Jihad against the Jews and the West. And with it came a rebuke from Western political leaders—ever vigilant not to upset their Islamic citizens and guests. These protests were reminiscent of Muslims who had focused their anger on the obscure pastor who had threatened to burn the Quran years before.

This in turn heated up Islamic-Christian debate so much that a retraction was soon run and apologies made. Things settled down a little in America, mostly because the Muslim voices forced the issue. One of the voices, the Council on American Islamic Relations (CAIR) published a statement condemning the comment. It was not nice or safe to criticize Islam or even speculate as to the meaning of the most important geological event in the past 100 or maybe 1000 years or maybe ever. The talk show host resigned the next day. He would later be found dead in his home, run through by a sword, his tongue cut out and laid on his chest.

It reminded some of the worldwide Muslim reaction when cartoons of Mohammed were published years before or the Muslim threats and *fatwas* uttered against Salmon Rushdie when he published the Satanic Verses. Islam's international reach was not to be ignored.

☾ ☾ ☾ ☾ ☾ ☾

Not far away, Medina next felt the earth's next gyrations. As the volcano erupted in Mecca, Medina also began to feel the tremors.

Medina, Islam's second holiest site, lies directly north of Mecca and not far from dormant volcanoes. Settled by Jews as a desert oasis about the year 135, Medina later became the home of the Prophet when he fled from Mecca. Later, those Jews who did not convert to Islam or didn't flee the area were killed by Muslim forces. Centuries later, in about 661, Medina became the capital of the Islamic state. Earthquakes were also known to frequent the area.

Centuries later, in 1804, Medina was overrun by the Wahabi sect, an ultra conservative branch of Islam. A few years later, in 1812, Egyptian and Ottoman forces recaptured it. Once Turkish rule collapsed at the close of World War I, forces loyal to the Ibn Saud family then conquered it just a few years later in 1925.

A series of quakes began that week and increased in intensity. With the great rolling earthquakes came a shifting instability to the earth and though the desert sand did provide some sort of shock absorber for the incredible waves of energy generated by the quake swarms, several mosques began to feel the effects of the shaking.

The earthquakes subsided for a short time, then, on the third day of the Hajj, at virtually the same moment of the huge volcanic eruption near Mecca, the tomb of Mohammed began to shake violently. Within minutes, Medina, too was virtually flattened and with it, a huge loss of life. The mosques crumbled all over the city, the holy sites falling in on themselves. Within minutes, thousands were dead and the second holiest site in Islam lay in ruins.

In one day Islam would lose its two holiest sites, leaving Jerusalem and the Dome of Rock and its smaller cousin, the Al Aqsa Mosque, as the final place of its heart's desire.

The Prophet Zechariah - Speaks on Jerusalem—Chapter 12 Verses 2-5

Behold, I am going to make Jerusalem a cup that causes reeling to all the peoples around; and when the siege is against Jerusalem, it will also be against Judah.

It will come about in that day that I will make Jerusalem a heavy stone for all the peoples; all who lift it will be severely injured. And all the nations of the earth will be gathered against it.

In that day, declares the LORD, I will strike every horse with bewilderment and his rider with madness. But I will watch over the house of Judah, while I strike every horse of the peoples with blindness.

Then the clans of Judah will say in their hearts, 'A strong support for us are the inhabitants of Jerusalem through the LORD of hosts, their God.'

The Prophet Micah
Predicts the Birth of the Messiah—Micah 5:2

But as for you, Bethlehem Ephrathah,
Too little to be among the clans of Judah,
From you One will go forth for Me to be ruler in Israel.
His goings forth are from long ago,
From the days of eternity.

Chapter 74

Dome of the Rock, Jerusalem (Al Aqsa)

The destruction of both Mecca and Medina left Islam the Al Aqsa mosque and the Dome of the Rock as the only holy remnant remaining from the three stars of Islam. Muslims would now turn to it, further escalating tensions between them and the Jewish state for control of the city, the eternal Jewish capitol, and now Islam's holiest site. Diplomatic discussions for the establishment of a Palestinian state had for years stalled on this point. Now it was all coming down to a battle for Jerusalem and everyone knew it.

The whole world wondered at the recent events in Mecca and Medina. Fear gripped the nations as they worried about what was to come next. Prophecy writers, teachers, speakers, and self-proclaimed experts were abuzz, as were the Imams and Jewish leaders. Every new world event or catastrophe fed the frenzy.

The public was hungry for information. And the press was only too happy to feed them. The mainstream print, broadcast, and online media pounced on every event that provided any prophetic perspective. They covered events and chased down angles on prophecy, pagan cultures, medieval seers, alien intervention, the Kabala, and more.

Still, the public events, prophecy experts, and published materials that ignited the greatest interest and hunger were related to the Bible—both Jewish and Christian sources.

Bibles and commentaries flew off the shelf. Purveyors of online study materials scrambled to pace demand.

Churches burst at the seams. Religious leaders everywhere were challenged by their flocks. Many were hard-pressed to understand, provide insight, or offer perspective on current events. Those with real knowledge and biblical study on the topic of prophecy were in great demand.

The annual *International Bible Prophecy Symposium* was scheduled to begin in Chicago. The symposium was a big draw for end-times teachers, scholars, authors, prophecy experts and enthusiasts. This year was a bigger draw than ever before, and for good reason.

Current events were turning heads for more than one reason. Bible scholars have long declared the central role Jerusalem and Israel would play in the end times. They had also long debated the reasons why Islam and the world had developed such an unfavorable attitude toward Israel. *And, they asked, why such concern over Jerusalem?*

Past discussions noted that Islam already had its two holy sites. Jewish and Christian leaders challenged Islam's claims about any Quranic mention of Jerusalem. Islam countered those claims explaining that Mohammad visited the city in his night visions. Though it was challenged as obscure, the Muslim faithful held on to it for dear life. But now, it was a moot point.

Everyone who followed Bible prophecy recognized recent events like puzzle pieces falling into place. The doubters remained outside the circle, as they pointed accusing fingers at the religious authorities. But the world's attention was now focused on a small patch of land in the Middle East and the small city within it.

Organizers set up a press conference for the first time in symposium history. They wanted to sample and share the speakers' thoughts prior to the opening session. Jonathan Roberts was a clear yet controversial speaker on this topic. He was also of particular interest to the press. Roberts had been promoted as a workshop and plenary session speaker. And the organizers assured the press that he'd be there for them. But there was a problem—Roberts was now on every law enforcement watch list, including Interpol.

Symposium speakers were seated at a long line of tables in front of the press. Few were used to this kind of frenzy and most had never been in a press conference. They hid behind their name cards, mics, and water bottles.

The press coordinator stood at the center podium, smiled, and said, "I'm Ms. Scott, your facilitator today. I'd like to welcome all of you today to the 51st annual *International Bible Prophecy Symposium.* A few speakers applauded, but most looked wary of the press. The press corps already shouted questions, moved toward the tables, and waved their arms for recognition. The coordinator raised her voice, "We'll take one question at a time. I have assistants with microphones. Please wait until you're recognized and have a mic.

"Yes, Ms. Dulberg. To whom is your question?"

"Denise Dulberg, CNN. My question is for you," she answered. "Where is Jonathan Roberts?"

"Oh, right.... I'm sorry." The coordinator turned to an assistant, exchanged words, and then returned to the reporter. "Thank you, Ms.

CHAPTER SEVENTY-FOUR: *Dome of the Rock, Jerusalem*

Dulberg. We are expecting...." She was interrupted.

Loud squeals, thumps, and amp-static feedback crackled through the air. The center white screen that had displayed the symposium's title and logo was covered with snow or diagonal lines. Then a clear voice broke through. "Yes, D.D. I hear you. *Yom tov!* What's your question?" Dulberg turned three shades of red—then cast a sheepish expression at her immediate colleagues. She was clearly not prepared for this.

She cleared her throat and began, "Yes, uh... thank you, uh, Dr. Roberts. *Boker tov.*" She bit her lip to punish herself, dropped her head to her notes, adjusted her glasses, then straightened up and looked at the screen. "Dr. Roberts, why are you not here?"

"I'm talkin' to you, right?"

"Uhmm... yes, of course, but sir... I mean, why aren't you here with us in Chicago?"

"D.D., aren't you from Israel?" Roberts asked.

"I'm sorry, Dr. Roberts," Ms. Scott, the coordinator, interrupted. "I don't see where Ms. Dulberg's personal vita is of any relevance here. The question is for you." Symposium insiders knew that Ms. Scott had strong opinions about Roberts. In the past she called him a pseudo-intellectual fear-monger.

Members of the press expressed their disapproval with Ms. Scott. Some heckled, "Let her answer." Or "Give it a rest, Scott." Other reporters just murmured and groused among themselves. The male correspondents let D.D. have all the floor time she wanted. It gave them opportunity to look at her without suspicion or idle stares.

D.D.s shoulder length hair was a rich red like a California Redwood. Her face and other features were striking and shapely. The camera loved her and every cameraman did too. But D.D. was no princess. Her beauty was easy to see, but she was not. She didn't have a social side—always serious, always on a mission. Someone she respected once told her, "D.D., you have a pretty poker-face. I'd like to see the real one someday."

She stood straight and spoke for herself. Her voice cracked a bit from the attention, but she always had something to say. "Dr. Roberts, I agree with Ms. Scott, but I respect you... and to answer your question... I'm from Chicago, born on the Southside." Then she paused and looked down to collect her courage. "However, not long after I was born, my parents made *Aliya* to Israel. It is where I went to school—even university. But I did my graduate work in journalism here at the University of Chicago. I chose to stay, and I maintain my dual citizenship in both countries. I am fluent in both English and Hebrew.

"Now," she said with a breathy huff. "Dr. Roberts, speakers, and fellow press—I answered that question and gave my vita because of the critical state of our world at this moment. Although, I am not ashamed of who or what I am, I am here for CNN. I am here for the countless people who are afraid... afraid for all of us. So, I want answers from whatever reliable person, source, or prophecy there is.

"Now, Dr. Roberts, on to my questions. I have two I think you will allow. First, why are you not in Chicago?"

"God bless, you, D.D. I'm glad you were the one to ask that question." Roberts, paused, gazed down, contorted his face a bit, then lifted his head and answered. "D.D. I'm not in Chicago because there is a international warrant for my arrest."

"Hmmf!" Ms. Scott snorted in satisfaction.

"But I am here with you in voice and image to speak what truth I know. I'm here to share what knowledge I have. And I'm here to leave you with more questions than answers. What's your other question?"

"Dr. Roberts, the events of the past few months have shaken the world. No pun intended. People are unsettled all over the planet. Please tell us how you interpret the seismic, meteorological, and geological events around the globe. Are these things related to Bible prophecy? Also, you are a man of many letters with a keen scientific mind... are there other explanations? Thank you."

"The real prize in all of this is Jerusalem. First, we must remember the prophecy of Micah who predicted the birth of the Messiah in Beyt-Lechem (Bethlehem). And of course, the chilling prophecies uttered by Zechariah about Jerusalem are stunning in their accuracy. I believe that the yearning for Jerusalem is deeply ingrained within every Jew's DNA, whether or not they even believe in God," he said. Roberts was just warming up.

"Why is that?" D.D. asked.

"Let me explain. The Bible foretells a time where the nations will become so obsessed with Jerusalem that they will do anything to control it and destroy its true and rightful tenants, the Jews. However, those nations that wish to conquer the city will pay a heavy price. We couldn't figure it out all these years —with Mecca and Medina as the two crown jewels in the Muslim world, why Islam would want Jerusalem so much? Seems like it's a no-brainer now.

"We also read the blogs, vlogs, and the Middle East press. There are several excellent sources I'd add to the press—Jihad Watch, CAMERA and MEMRI. They explain that any Jewish presence without Muslim dominance is an affront to Islam. The Islamic mind cannot fathom Jews in control of anything in that part of the world.

"From what I've read, it would appear that the world's interest in Jerusalem is about to explode. This isn't merely academic. Our teaching institute, *The Learning House,* continues to receive requests for our materials from all over the world. Our team of speakers is booked out for the next six months. It seems many have woken up to the fact that the Bible really is worth reading. We are also finding ourselves in increasing dialog with many traditional atheists, mostly from the scientific community who want to debate evolution and the existence of intelligent life beyond our earth. As some of you know, I have a deep interest and personal interest in current research in the world of science.

"The vast majority of inquiries for our materials are focused on the Books of Daniel, Revelation, the Gospels, and the importance of Jerusalem. They want to know what all the hoopla is about the Jews, the Bible, Islam, Christianity... people have awakened—they see a connection between current events and the Bible."

Roberts switched gears and incorporated another recent topic of interest, the volcano and earthquake activity in Saudi Arabia... the hottest trending topic on the internet.

"I love the accessible information on the internet and particularly some of the better 'wiki's' that are out there. I recently found something on the Ring of Fire, which happens to be the area of the Pacific Ocean basin where about 75% of the world's active volcanoes are. Though the eruption in the desert is removed from that area on the map, it all seems to be tied in together.

"We've been following volcanic activity in the Pacific. We've recently been hearing about more swarms of earthquakes in the Ring of Fire and are seeing more earthquake and volcanic activity in the Philippines and Indonesia as well. Have you noticed that wherever there is an Islamic insurgency, or pressures brought on Israel for land concessions, or large concentrations of Muslim population, there seems to be corresponding volcanic and seismic activity as well?

"The ring of fire has more than 450 volcanoes within it. We expect even the dormant volcanoes to get busy soon. And if the earthquakes are any indication, we may be in for more of the same.

"More than a dozen volcanoes had recently sprung to life, spewing hundreds of millions of tons of pollutants into the air. A great irony in all this is the fact that what man may have contributed to global warming pales in comparison to the seismic and volcanic events the past few years. Scientists debated whether they would warm or cool the earth. Included were Pinatubo in the Philippines, Mount Hood in Oregon, and Mt. St. Helens in Washington State. The Three Sisters in eastern Oregon had begun to awake, too.

This hit a nerve with the news crews and they began shooting questions at him in a rapid fire manner.

"Pastor Roberts, what, if anything, do the earthquakes and volcanoes have to do with Bible prophecy?" The question came from a Filipino reporter.

"Well, in my opinion, wherever you have the enemies of the Jews actively fighting against Israel and the Jewish nation, whether or not is in the land of Israel or it is in the Diaspora, or frankly anywhere on the planet, there will be consequences for those who participate. The records that Pharaoh and his legions paid a dear price for not letting God's people go, even after ample warnings by Moses and Aaron.

"As you know, there is more and more anti-Semitic activity around the world, but it has seriously intensified in America. The Jews have suffered numerous murderous attacks on their synagogues, schools, cemeteries, neighborhoods, and businesses. Thousands are now dead and the threat is growing. Most of it is coming from Islamic forces as well as anti-Semitic Christians, two of the Jews' ancient enemies.

"In my opinion, you can see that God works to defend His ancient people. I'm not going to sugarcoat this... America is on the brink, and there have been and will continue to be larger and more destructive natural disasters—soon—mark my words. This will make the recent spate of hurricanes, tornadoes, volcanoes, earthquakes, and other similar events will seem like child's play. Our research also indicates that every time the U.S. or, frankly, anyone tries to force land concessions on Israel, well, that nation suffers horrendous consequences.

"And let me remind you," Roberts added, "that doesn't exclude Israel either. When their leaders have traded land for peace, they have suffered similar consequences. If you read the stories of Israel's and Judah's ancient kings, the same patterns seemed to follow them too. If a king or the priests did evil, they were punished as was the nation. If a king did well, the nation was blessed. Some even blame assassinations and health problems of some of Israel's leaders on the fact that they bargained away land for peace.

"For example, many of you may not know this but when Gush Katif (Israeli forced evacuations in Gaza) was evacuated in 2005, the Jewish population displacement closely matched the American population displacement, by percentage, of New Orleans. Hurricane Katrina almost destroyed the city. What most people don't do is put the clues together—connect the dots. In this case, the hurricane occurred within days of that forced evacuation.

"The two events may not directly correlate but there seems to be an association between the two. You can tie these natural disasters in America to the actions of the United States government vis-a-vis Israel. Whenever America has meddled in Israel's affairs and forced it to give away land, she's paid a dear price. We must never forget that the Land of Israel is God's land... period."

Roberts was laser focused on his topic and could feel his blood pressure surge. This was his passion and for a moment he paused, took out a handkerchief, and wiped his brow. The intensity in his voice rose to another level and he continued.

"When it comes to terror, there is, in my mind, a direct relationship between those who perpetrate such horrors, the nations that offer them sanctuary, and the damage and suffering they will incur. Scripture says, "I will bless those who bless you and curse those who curse you." The reporters returned a blank stare—his comments lost on all but a few.

"I don't know about you, but doesn't this look like judgment of some sort?

"Now, I need to attend to other business. You have a well-informed and respected panel of speakers and scholars before you. I know they're anxious to continue this discussion. Shalom."

> From the Pen of Ha Melech Shlomo
> (King Solomon) Proverbs
> Chapter 17 Verse 17
>
> A friend loves at all times,
> And a brother is born for adversity.

Chapter 75

Friends

Mimi remained absorbed in her battle and logistics plans. Things were heating up in New York.

Shabibi's phone alerted her—a new text message.

It was Mimi. "R U OK?" It was the 10th message sent and the one that finally reached her friends.

"Yes. Shaken not harmed. But all is lost... except our animals."

"Soooo sorry. We are hearing 1 million dead? Really?"

"Yes. Or more."

Mimi had no idea how to comfort such loss. "My tears & prayers... all for you, Shabi."

"Thank you."

"What's next?" Mimi texted.

"States... maybe. Until we sort things out."

"Can you get here? I think I can help."

Shabibi answered, "I need to hear your voice."

Mimi responded, "Me too."

Now Mimi had another problem. She had to remain on station but needed to extend help to her friends. Then the idea hit her. Mimi thought, *we have the world's best document specialists. If we can work up a set of documents for Shabibi and Farouk, we can at least get them out of Saudi and to safety... maybe the safe house. This just might work.*

✡ ✡ ✡ ✡ ✡ ✡

Mimi put her phone away and found a quiet space to be alone. Emotions shook her and upset her stomach. She was nauseous and lightheaded. She ran to the toilet and lost her breakfast.

She felt sick and scrambled. She needed rest. But the bed and dark room didn't give rest—too much on her mind. The current operation, her friends Farouk and Shabibi, the roars from the earth, and her own busy yet empty life—all this filled her mind.

She stroked the scars on her cheeks. That seemed so long ago. The memories came flooding back. She thought of all the sadness she had caused, the drugs, the family disagreements, the boys she hurt—all of it.... The tears came again—and the gnawing feeling....

I feel so empty... success—achievement, all fine... but then this. I feel so helpless. Those poor people in Mecca... and the killings here. What am I not seeing?

She thought of her family, friends, and her unit in Israel. She missed all of them very much. She felt grateful for them. She thought of God too, though in more of an abstract way. Her mind drifted to her brother and sister-in-law, and Avner's newfound faith. *Was all of this happening for a reason?* She couldn't answer that but it sure did intrigue her logical and scientific mind.

Three hours had passed. Mimi called and Shabibi answered.

"You sound tired," Mimi said. "Are you okay?"

"Safe for now, but no... it's hell on earth here. We are living out of our suitcases trying to figure out what we are going to do. And when we heard about the synagogue attacks and the demonstrations, and all that... we thought.... Are YOU ok?"

Mimi hadn't even thought about herself, so concerned was she with her friends' fate.

"I'm okay. But it was close. I know people who were killed. Extremism in any form is dangerous."

"I know, Mimi, I know. The earthquakes woke us up, literally tossed us out of bed," Shabibi explained, her voice filled with both awe and horror.

"And then the advancing volcanic lava and ash. My poor animals were so scared—they had to run for their lives. How we ever managed to herd and gather them is a miracle," she said. The sheer terror and sadness echoed in her voice.

Then there was Mecca and the Hajj.

"My brother was at the Hajj. We have no word. I worry, Mimi. I fear that he is...." Shabibi's words stopped—sobs began. The gasps and groans of grief filled Mimi's ear. Mimi could hear Farouk's soothing voice—the voice of a husband's comfort.

Mimi shared in their pain and sighed in sympathy. She thought of her own brothers. That fed her fears and fueled her sorrow. *So much tragedy and death these past few weeks,* she thought. *Losses on both sides of the world. It's just so much to deal with.* The gnawing feeling came again.

"How soon can you two get back here?"

"That's our only real choice and desire. We've tried to book a flight, but things are in chaos here. We'll keep trying."

"No," Mimi insisted. "Stop trying. I can do it. Double-check your visas for clearance. Give me a few days. Then I'll have tickets in your names waiting at the airport for you. They'll even be 1st class. I have friends in the right places.

"I'll make sure you are met at the destination— look for someone with a sign for Minnie and Mickey."

"Oh, Mimi, we couldn't have you do that." Shabibi protested with what little strength she had.

"Nonsense. It's done. I want to do this for you. I can hear how exhausted you are. This is one less worry. Besides...." Mimi hesitated and thought. She continued in a quiet voice. "Shabi, there's a lot about me that I haven't told you." Another pause. "And I'm not sure I can ever tell you, but know this...."

Emotion seized Mimi. She coughed to cover her quiver and find her voice again. "Know this, Shabi, you are my sister. You can... you must... trust me." She cleared her throat again and turned tears into a chuckle. "My father once told me that I was the most courageous son he had. It was his way. Still, he said, "Mimi, I don't think that you're afraid of anything." Shabi, he was wrong. I know that now... because I'm afraid of losing the two of you."

CHAPTER SEVENTY-FIVE: Friends

Three days later, Farouk and Shabibi arrived at Westchester County airport north of the city. Two members of Mimi's security team met them with the appropriate signs.

"How was your trip?"

"Where is the nearest tomb?" Farouk groaned.

She said, "Don't mind him. First class wore him out."

"Naw, the flight was fine," Farouk answered. "It's the trouble, terror, and trials of these last days and events. They have chased us down and stolen our strength."

"Are we going to have a chance to see Mimi?"

"In time, meanwhile we've arranged a safe house for you. Every need will be taken care of by friends of ours." The escort answered. He then notified Mimi that her guests were safely on the ground.

Coffee House Chatter

"Do you believe that the Jews are the chosen people?" he asked.

"Yes, I do, but why do you ask?" she answered.

"Well, I'm tired of this. I mean, the Jews aren't any more special than any other people. They make mistakes, are sometimes arrogant, and remain mostly separate from the rest of the society where they live," he said.

"And your point is?" she asked.

> From the Hand of Moses Bereshit (Genesis)
> Chapter 12 Verse 3—The Abrahamic Convenant
>
> I will bless those who bless you
> and curse those who curse you.

Chapter 76

The Underground Express

The Jews were on the run.

Ross Evans, the former Ibraham Hussein, had undergone intense healing—body, heart, soul, and mind. In time he felt well enough to get out and share his experience. He began to share his story and speak at Black congregations during his recovery.

His natural ability combined with God's anointing made him a power speaker. Soon he was in demand all over the area. And it wasn't long before news of Ross Evan spread across the country. People wanted to hear from this former Christian turned Muslim turned Christian again. They wanted to hear the story of a bona-fide hero who took a bullet for others. Churches all over the country began to invite him to speak. And he answered the calls. He knew it wasn't about the churches or himself—he had been given a mission.

His energy had pretty much returned, though he still felt some of the effects of the shooting. Evans was very directed at helping the Jews find a way out of the country and back to the land of their fathers. His conversion back to the God of his mother had taken hold. He was a changed man. His initial efforts, though slow to gather momentum, were met with an increasingly overwhelming outpouring of Black support within certain communities.

Much of the support came from Black Baptist congregations, something he remembered from his childhood. The congregants took their church seriously, dressing in 'Sunday Best' always and reading their Bibles faithfully. Many other churches around the nation lined up speaking engagements for him. Some of his lectures ended up on a slew of video posting services.

The new Black Underground Railroad, now known as the Underground Expressway, was moving ahead. Stations were set up along the way. The rescuers opened their arms and hearts to the frightened Jews. They remembered the stories of their ancestors during the Civil War and those who helped shepherd them out of the South and into the North.

From community to community, state to state, it also reminded some of the historical rescue efforts of the tiny village of Le Chambon sur Lignon in France. There in the south part of France, 5,000 villagers and their pastors hid 5,000 Jews, both adults and children, from the eyes of the Nazis.

They hid them in cellars, basements, inside walls, underground, in the fields, everywhere they could think the Germans would not look. None was lost. It became a model of what could happen when a community took its direction from the Bible seriously and acted on it with no questions asked.

Ross' reading uncovered this story and others of 'Righteous Gentiles' who had come to the aid of Jews during World War II and he began seeing links to the same types of activities now in the Bible Belt of the Southern United States. He learned of the Raoul Wallenbergs and the Oscar Schindlers, of the Irene Opdykes and many others who provided shelter for the chosen.

That truly remarkable story was virtually unknown to the Black congregations but the results were the same and they were learning fast. Of course, for years faithful Blacks who knew their Bibles could see the connection between them and God's people, for obvious reasons.

He added this to his story-telling repertoire because it resonated with the congregations to whom he spoke. Evans scheduled a number of speaking engagements in the Deep South, beginning with the Black Baptist church of Reverend Charles Graham.

When Reverend Charles Graham, a hulk of a man, began his sermons on Messianic prophecies, he left out very little. The scripture would speak for itself. The Reverend had a huge television and webcast following. He was known for his pacing, sweat pouring down his deep ebony face, his radiant smile, his eyes of fire, with that easily identifiable gap between his front teeth.

Graham had memorized tremendous passages of scripture—often teaching for hours without having to refer to the text. He rarely missed a quote. He had a working knowledge of Hebrew and Greek, and had always had a soft spot for the Jews about whom he found himself speaking more and more these days. He began Sunday's talk with the Book of Ezekiel, the 37th chapter, and went from there.

"Yes, brothers and sisters, we must look to the Scripture for our salvation," he thundered.

"Say it Brother," and "Hallelujah!"

The congregation was on its feet within moments as he read down the key prophecies concerning the Children of Israel and their return home.

"The Bible tells us that the Jews were a stiff-necked people, but we must love them!"

"The Bible tells us that the Jews are chosen, but it was God who did the choosing!!"

"The Bible tells us the Children of Israel will be brought back to the Land a second time where God himself will renew their spirits and rebuild their land."

"The Bible says to the Jew first, then to the Greek!" he thundered.

"The Bible tells us that The Messiah will return to His People, He will rescue them!"

"The Bible tells us we must love the Jews—help them because we are grafted in to the tree!"

"And the Bible tells us we must love those who persecute us! We must replace hate with love!"

Each statement was met with "Amens!" and "Hallelujahs" by the congregation. The last exhortation was met with the loudest response of all. These believers were solid and they knew their Bibles—and they were ready to serve... and ready to die, in love, for their beliefs.

These were most solid and dependable believers. It didn't matter where they fit into the political or social spectrum. Poor or rich, well to do or down on their luck, each member of the congregation was prepared for service to the God of Abraham, Isaac, and Jacob. The families knew and understood what was at stake and they stepped up to help. There was little of the formality of the organizing that usually goes with something like this.

There were no edicts issued forth from the pulpit, no speeches given, no fund raisers or bake sales. It was just true Bible-believing Christians following the dictates of their Bibles. And follow them they did, like the French citizens of Le Chambon. Graham had them whipped up into a frenzy and by the end of the sermon, they were ready to help where ever they could.

The next weekend, it was Evans' turn to speak to Graham's congregation. Five million people would be watching on international television and internet audience accompanied by a world-wide radio network as well.

"Friends, I so much appreciate you and what you represent at this most difficult time in our history. For years, we have battled so much together. Our parents and grandparents lived through the Civil Rights days. We've battled for our freedom and for our right to vote. You know my history... my mother, who lived among you, loved and cherished the Jews more than I could ever possibly do. I didn't listen to her, but rather went on my own journey and became a member of the Nation of Islam." The crowd kept its silence.

And he related his testimony to them, retelling the story of the shooting, his encounters in the hospital with Jenny Del Fuego, Ayelet Simcha, and later Jonathan Roberts.

"When I met Pastor Roberts a while back I told him I was ready to lay my life down for the Jewish people. I do not do this for any personal gain, but rather because I am directed by the Lord Himself," he said.

This statement was met with thunderous applause, for the congregation appreciated his personal journey and felt at one with him. He was on a roll now. It was hot and he mopped his brow, the sweat pouring off him just like his friend Charles Graham.

"We now face that time, I believe, predicted so long ago by the Hebrew prophets. The Jewish return to the land of Israel is imminent—it is time for the Jews to go home. We must help them. For, the Bible tells us, 'I will bless those who bless thee, and curse those who curse thee,'" he said, his voice rising, and then falling silent.

Again, his mother's tender words and face came to him. Those in the front rows could see the tears rolling down his cheeks.

And at that moment, Evans clutched his chest and fell to his knees, arms raised in holy prayer to his Creator.

> **From the Hand of Rav Shaul**
> Egeret Polous Ha Shalicha—Epistle to the Romans
> Chapter 11 Verses 17-18
>
> But if some of the branches were broken off, and you, being a wild olive, were grafted in among them and became partaker with them of the rich root of the olive tree, do not be arrogant toward the branches; but if you are arrogant, remember that it is not you who supports the root, but the root supports you.

Chapter 77

Comfort, Comfort Ye My People

As the next few weeks would show, the Israeli planners finalized arrangements to spirit the Jews out of America and to a safe place in Israel. Hooking up with a growing 'Underground Express' would prove fruitful because now the Jews had allies to help them out of their neighborhoods and hide them wherever and whenever they needed. Many Christian churches would sacrifice much, members laying their lives on the line to help the Jewish refugees. The message from the all-Black churches spread throughout the nation.

Spurred on by Evans and Graham, these churches silently and efficiently found ingenious ways to hide the Jews as they sought passage out of the U.S. The churches formed receiving houses to protect the Jews while they awaited transportation to the airports. Busses, small shuttles, and family cars appeared out of nowhere to aid the cause. Some communities devised elaborate schemes to hide the Jews underground in sewer systems, and utility bunkers, thus evading peering eyes.

Black Baptist congregations formed an intricate system of safe passage to move the more than 500,000 Southern Jews to the Miami International Airport. Using the lists from the census, they spirited the Jews away in the dead of night. They stuffed the Jews into car trunks, provided disguises when needed, and secreted them out of hot areas.

Racial divisions vanished as Christians across the South banded together to work a modern day miracle. Believing whites and blacks recognized the Biblical significance of the event and bonded with one another in a way no social welfare program could manage. This effort, impossible to conceive of just a few short months before broke down racial barriers in a way that more than 175 years of Civil Rights legislation couldn't.

The Christian Zionists formed small militias to assist the Jewish dash for the homeland. They came from the military, the National Guard, local law enforcement, fire departments, construction crews, city works, schools, law firms, hospitals, and everywhere, from all walks of life, and they came to fight and they came to help. And they came to save the Jews.

Militias in America were nothing new. During the years and months leading up to the Revolutionary War, each state formed its own militia. Through the years, a formal American military formed but each state maintained its citizen soldiers or home guards. Later still, those groups formed into the National Guard which rotated soldiers into the nation's military, as conditions dictated.

Many National Guard soldiers from all walks of life and from all 50 states, defected to the Jewish/Christian Zionist side, bringing their weapons with them when they could and depleting America's last bastion of internal defense.

These Christians would do their part to reverse historical Christian antagonism and, in so doing, would make the Jews realize what a Christian could be or should be. They prepared to fulfill the expectations made of them millennia before when God challenged them to make the Jews jealous for the faith, not at the end of a sword, whip or a gun but through the Love of the Messiah. They lived out the Epistle to the Romans.

They were now ready to die a martyr's death to help God's people achieve what the prophets spoke of so many years ago. The Apostle Paul (also known by his Hebrew name, Rav Shaul) would be proud as his heart's desire was to see his brethren saved from death to life eternal. They were now one step closer.

Jewish doubts vanished as Christians began forming protective enclaves in virtually nearly every city and township across America. They risked everything because they believed the Jewish Diaspora was ending and it was time to help these ancient people back to their ancestral homeland.

They acted with love and didn't worry whether or not the Jews themselves believed the words in their own Bibles. Those churches preached the Word of God with a clear sense of purpose.

With this approach, the churches saw their numbers double then double again within weeks. Money poured into the offerings and much of that money found its way to the defense efforts of the Jews. The defending Christians were motivated and directed by the teaching of Roberts, Evans, and Graham. They brought food, water, clothes, and other life-sustaining aid to the Jewish refugees who had no other means of support.

In contrast, many of the mainstream churches saw declines in attendance. Though a few joined Jewish relief efforts, it was not a systematic support effort. Church leadership in these denominations buckled at the challenge before them. Much as history had explained, especially in World War II, most of them didn't see this as their fight and so they stayed away.

As bad as things had gotten financially, putting in with the Jews or the Christian Zionists would make matters even worse or so they thought. With the exception of a small minority, others jumped into the fray with the Islamo-Christian side. The Spirit was moving but only in certain places.

Islamic money flowed too, directly from the Middle East, mostly from Iran, a traditional funding source for terror directed at Israel and the West. Tremendous amounts of money flowed into terrorist coffers from Saudi sources over the years but more recently, the money was coming in from Iran.

Strangely, Saudi involvement in terror was slowing. Roberts, though, believed he knew why. He began his radio address by describing the role of Iran.

"When we read about the massive invasion of Israel described by the Prophet Ezekiel in the 38th and 39th chapters, Sheba and Dedan, longtime tribal names associated with the Arabian Peninsula, will stand off to the sidelines, unwilling to support the invasion to wipe out Israel."

"When the invasion begins, it will be led by Iran and accompanied by many other nations, apparently all Islamic countries from the African continent."

His point was not lost on his listeners. For years now, Israel's neighbors were building massive weapons caches in anticipation of a future conflict. Though no large buildup of troops was yet detected, tens of thousands of rockets and missiles laid in by the Syrians and Iranians was a known fact. And, still Israel hadn't budged. The time clock advanced again as America's Jews were heading home.

The next battle for the streets started as a small altercation just outside of Chicago where a mosque and a church sat across the street from one another. But the real focus was just down the street where a synagogue stood, its sanctuary filled with both congregants and fear. Though many Jews still refused to put this latest wave of anti-Semitism into historical context, this reformed synagogue, Temple Beth Zion did so.

The synagogue hadn't seen its sanctuary filled in years. It was packed today. Even those Jews generally professing little belief in their holy books had come to attend services. The Jews didn't know where to turn and so the synagogue seemed a safe and natural place to be. When a carful of young Muslims slowly drove by, it was with mal intent.

Slowly, the new BMW cruised by the synagogue, its four young inhabitants just checking things out. The small attack squad had been drilling for weeks and was now ready to strike.

Jameel Hassan Nasrallah was born in America of Jordanian parents. About a block down the street he skillfully executed a U-turn and headed back down the street. At that moment, his three co-riders lowered their windows, pulled their small automatic weapons out and began firing at the synagogue in short bursts with deadly accuracy.

Screams could be heard, and in spite of guards stationed in front of the building, the bullets shattered glass and ripped into the building. Both guards were hit and did not return fire.

Nasrallah gunned the accelerator after taking a quick glance inside the synagogue, He turned left at the next intersection, heading westbound. Unknown to him and his co-conspirators was that another car with four Christians witnessed the entire event and began following them. No other bystanders stepped in to help.

Nasrallah blew the red light. The Christians followed close behind. The young Christians weren't armed. They knew they had witnessed a hate crime. But a confrontation with the shooters seemed like a bad idea. *Was it up to them to exact revenge?* They had always been law abiding Americans. The driver, Wilson Benedict, and his three companions talked it out and tried to figure what to do.

"We have to chase them and identify them to the police," Benedict shouted. "Somebody call the cops now! Explain what happened and report our location."

His co-riders all dialed their cells to report what they saw to other friends and family. They received no response.

Benedict had just completed his senior year in History at the University of Illinois, Urbana. Having been raised a Christian, but in a traditional mainstream Christian church, he had come to saving faith in Jesus during his years in college, realizing that just because you were raised in a Christian home didn't mean you were one. What being a Christian meant may have been one of the least understood things they knew.

So, he began reading the Bible faithfully and then attended a Jonathan Roberts conference on Bible Prophecy when invited by a close friend. What he heard there stunned him. With his keen sense of the subject, he soon changed his major to Ancient History. He then decided to add Hebrew and Greek courses to his degree path. It was all very strange... everything he was seeing in the press and the media was dovetailing exactly with what he was reading in the Bible. It was all so clear now.

He then began making plans for seminary. The Scripture had never been emphasized in his home church as it had by these Christians. He even met some Jews who believed as he did, something he never thought could happen.

It was weird to him—Jews who believed in his savior. How could you be both a Jew and a Christian? But, as his reading of the Scripture revealed, virtually all of the early believers were Jewish and remained so until their deaths. Were they actually Christians too? Oh, how history had turned.

Now he was excited to help the Jews and support Israel. It had never occurred to him that he might actually be a player in any of the events leading up to the Jews' departure from America. It dawned on him that he was now 'in the game,' and as a result, a player in Biblical prophecy.

He recalled the words of the Epistle of Jacob (or James) that said, "Faith without works is dead." He and his friends now understood just what that meant.

Nasrallah and his companions began hunting more prey. As night fell that Saturday evening, he knew where he wanted to go—to a nearby neighborhood, heavily populated by Jewish residents. The census data had even reached these tough young men. They knew where they were going and who they wanted to hunt. It was time to make the Jews in the area realize who now owned the streets. The BMW crept down the street, turned right into the quiet, mostly Jewish neighborhood. Benedict and his friends watched as Nasrallah's car worked its way down the street.

They found their target, for just down the street was a birthday party for a young Jewish girl of 16. She and her family had planned the event for about 7 that evening and as guests began to arrive, Nasrallah and his gunmen struck again.

They each fired six quick bursts into the house and the crowd that had gathered near the front door. As they unloaded, Benedict and his companions could only watch the carnage in horror. Their screams of anguish filled the evening air. Fourteen people fell dead in the front yard with many more wounded. Nasrallah hit the gas and about two blocks up turned and disappeared, leaving a long skid mark behind.

Benedict and his companions called 911 again to report the second shooting. And still no police response. When the shooting stopped, they headed for the house to offer what help they could. For an hour they waited and when the police finally showed up, more than 20 were now counted dead at the house alone.

As the paramedics collected the victims and tried to aid the wounded, Benedict could only watch and then screamed into the night, not realizing he and his friends had just witnessed some of the first shots that would soon embroil America's neighborhoods. America would soon turn on itself, a virtual civil war. He vowed to himself that he would never be a bystander again. Not if he could help it.

Nasrallah and his comrades killed or wounded 35 Jews that afternoon and evening. As they headed back home, they heard the first report of the shootings. Even though a clear description of the car was given, it didn't concern him because his car was now in a chop shop, waiting dismantling, the parts heading for shipment out of the state. The shooters then disbursed and agreed to not be in contact for at least another month. Their handler was a former Marine. He was tied to the Islamo-Christian terror network in his fight against Zionism and the Jews. He promised to be in touch.

In tears and anguish, Benedict and his friends did what they could to bring comfort to the grieving families and then huddled together to pray for direction and to offer themselves to God's service. These four young men's lives would never be the same again. The battle to save the Jews was on and they were now soldiers, fighting in a war that many would later call a 'spiritual civil war.'

Later that night, Benedict and his friends learned that what they witnessed weren't isolated events. Gunfire had erupted all over the city and into the surrounding communities. Police were undermanned and outgunned. They simply couldn't respond. Police and local hospitals accounted for hundreds of victims. The attacks were being trumpeted by local mosques and a few churches who simply 'had enough' of the Jews.

Many Christian Zionists found their way to Israeli planners through Jonathan Roberts and his contacts. Roberts and his teams began organizing local defense units of both Jews and Christians to defend their neighborhoods. With the seemingly impotent police response, it was becoming clearer to the Jewish citizens of Chicago and the surrounding states in the Midwest that they were alone and at the mercy of the surrounding population. But this time, unknown to most of them, they would never be alone again.

Militias are often associated with cultic or extremist groups. But this was nothing other than a group of concerned citizens interested in defending their homes and protecting innocent life from internal or external threats. In this case, there was no call for insurrection against the Government. But if the Government tried to dispense with the Jews as the Nazis did, then all bets were off. The growing militia prepared to fight.

The Christian Zionists began going door to door to offer their help. Squads began nightly patrols in the area. They built small arsenals and could be seen carrying their weapons on the streets and in the neighborhoods, to the chagrin of law enforcement agencies.

There was a growing perception that police had lost control of the streets, even in the 'nice' and 'safe' areas of the suburbs. Until the Jews made their escape, these new soldiers would stand guard and defend their Jewish neighbors, blessing those whom God had chosen.

Three weeks after the synagogue and neighborhood shootings, several more bands of young Muslims and some of their Christian friends, climbed into their cars for more attacks. Feeling empowered by the success of the first drivebys, they fanned out to different parts of the city. What they couldn't possibly know was that they were heading into a trap that would not only surprise them but put fear into their superiors.

Benedict's small defense unit grew to more than 1,000. The first street battle with real opposition was about to spring into the American consciousness. The Christian supporters of Israel were now ready. The past weeks of defense and tactical training was about to pay off.

The first car, a dark, late model SUV, pulled into a small neighborhood with tree lined streets. It was just after 8 p.m., and the summer sun was making its slow descent into the west. As darkness descended on the area, one of the local militiamen dropped a two-tone radio signal to Benedict, who had taken up residence in a command post not far up the street. Cameras from three angles found the car, one they didn't recognize.

"Command Central, go... " said Benedict.

"Command Central, we see a dark model SUV making its way up Madison Street." The scout described the car and who was in it.

"We see him, teams please check in."

And one by one, each team of three defenders clicked their codes into their radios. The terrorists were heading into a trap.

When the car slowed, the four shooters began pulling their weapons out and took aim at one of the the homes.

"Permission to fire, Command leader?" The snipers were ready to defend the attack.

Benedict yelled into his mic, "Permission granted. Fire!!"

All at once, a huge burst of blinding light from a spotlight found the SUV and was followed by a cacophony of sound. The large, four-door

Suburban tried to maneuver out of the trap but the driver was blinded and soon realized, in a moment too quick to discern, that three cars had been placed in his path. He had no way out.

The four terrorists never got off a shot for they were hit by half a dozen sharpshooters who formed a triangulated zone of fire around the car. As the bullets tore into the car, glass exploded and upholstery burst forth from the intense fire. The young terrorists tried to hide but were completely surrounded. The defenders' bullets found their mark, spattering blood all over the inside of their vehicle.

Benedict could hear their screams on his radio. Within moments they were silenced, the car now a stark testimony as to what had happened in the street. He cringed, realizing he and his teams had now taken human life. That it was defensive and for a cause he believed in didn't matter at that moment. He was now a changed young man.

Moments later, feeling overwhelmingly nauseated, he stumbled out of the house he occupied with his supporters, fell on his knees and threw up on the lawn. Feeling completely drained, he began to cry and pray, asking God for forgiveness, knowing what he had done, no matter what the reason.

The defenders melted into the night, leaving the young, now dead terrorists alone in their car. Many other cars in different areas of the city, met a similar fate, with only one shooter getting off any shots and taking one Christian Zionist defender with him.

About an hour later, the police and paramedics arrived to begin the grim task of clearing the area. They removed the dead, and eliminated all traces of the attack. But the police were puzzled when they discovered that no witnesses stepped forward who had seen the attack or heard any gunfire.

News stations were slow to pick up the story, and when they did, the street scene was unrecognizable. But that didn't mean that there was no record of the assault. Youtube watchers saw the feed about an hour later. This continued a growing trend where cameras were rolling everywhere, all the time. In another two hours several short videos appeared all over the internet on the incidents in Chicago and elsewhere in the nation.

The police forces faced their own battles, being stripped of personnel daily as many Christians left their ranks to support the Christian/Jewish resistance. Local law enforcement couldn't respond to all the 911 calls throughout the city. Some left for the Islamo-Christian side as well, while others remained on the force.

The local police captain addressed his officers at the incident debrief with something very strange to report: there was no record of any distress call made.

"It has come to our attention that we received no 911 calls on this shooting or any others tonight. The only thing we did receive was a call from one of the residents in the neighborhood who called to complain that there was a big SUV blocking the street and no traffic could pass. That was it, no report of violence, no emergency calls, nothing amiss."

"People, it's no surprise that we're running short of personnel. Many of our fellow officers have chosen sides in this situation but for those of us who remain, we must do our best. Do you have any questions?"

"Yes, Captain. How can we prepare if nobody is calling 911? How can we be everywhere at once?" The question was one that everyone had on their minds but nobody was willing to admit it in public.

"My only answer is to trust your instincts. Keep working your street contacts—keep your ears to the ground. I know we are outgunned and outmanned, but we do have the law on our side. Starting tonight, we will reassign patrols to the heavier Jewish areas and may have to decrease some other areas. Hopefully this will be temporary. Where Jewish residents are in small numbers, they are on their own." No one could predict whether or not this tactic would be successful.

The neighborhood, as many across the nation would soon learn, had simply turned away from law enforcement, no longer trusting the police force's ability to defend a defenseless populace. Many perceived that law enforcement was impotent to fix anything. America and all it stood for hung precariously in the balance.

The Bible-believing sectors supporting the Jews had now taken up their own defense and were only too happy and honored to do it. As many of them would later confess to one another, 'it was time to turn the tables and do the right thing.' Years of anti-Semitic history was about to be reversed, at least in this community, and soon others across the Land of the Free and the Home of the Brave.

And so it was that the first street battles between 'the Sunday People' and Allah's best were fought in the streets of Chicago. These skirmishes were over quickly but it would serve as a harbinger of things to come. More battles loomed just over the horizon. Except this time, the stakes were far higher and the results weren't exactly what the young Muslims and their Christian counterparts expected.

Word soon reached local mosques that a number of their foot soldiers had been slaughtered by brutal Jewish gangs who, unprovoked, had shot these innocent young community leaders to death. The truth didn't matter because at this juncture those with malice on their minds were content to invent their own truths. A Muslim cleric held a news conference at an Islamic Learning Center near the downtown section of Chicago.

"You are doing nothing to stop this slaughter of Muslims! The Jews and their Christian friends are murdering us in the streets and all you can do is appeal for peace?" The Muslim cleric was angry and prepared to turn up the heat. His incendiary speech spread through the community quickly revving up further hatred.

When the story hit the press the next day, Muslim families screamed for recompense and revenge. Threats of Jihad were amplified in mosques all over America. Since there were few, if any witnesses, it became a battle of words and opinions. Muslim youth and an increasing number of Jew-hating Christians began finding common ground with one another in the same fashion that the Bible-believing Christians would with their Jewish counterparts. The battle lines were being drawn. Who was right, who was wrong?

Many mainstream Christian denominations continued distancing themselves from the Jews and other 'renegade, apostate' Christians.

This action drew Rome to the table, where the Pope appealed for calm and peace. He finally had enough and decided to call a special council to take care of the rising tensions between the different religious bodies once and for all.

Rome convened the session in the Vatican with several other Christian denominations and invited all North and South American bishops. Their intent was to arrive at a theology for a 'New Order' which everyone could understand and accept. He had to find a way to bridge the gap between Christians and Muslims.

Also invited to the two-week conclave were Islamic clerics. With international pressures mounting and the Palestinians calling for a national homeland for themselves, the Islamo-Christian coalition continued to cement its relationships and continued to reach out to others to form this new association. Together they would focus on a common enemy.

By the end of the conference they issued a joint statement which would direct ecumenical Christians around the world to finally divest all holdings from Israel, form closer ties with those Arab Christians living in Palestine and elsewhere in the Middle East, and last, to issue a veiled condemnation of Israel and the Jews. There was even some time devoted to the events in America.

It had finally come out into the open. The time had come to embrace a closer relationship with Islam. Islam was rising on the world stage and Judaism was receding. The Church's leaders saw and recognized the trend, rightly so, they thought. Political correctness and social acceptance counted for far more than an ancient antagonist. Other mainstream denominations weren't far behind. There was some history to all of this as was noted in the final conference circular released on the internet.

The former Pontiff, Pope John Paul II spent a great deal of time working to build bridges to Islam. The Vatican documented more than 60 different meetings with Muslims, one of which featured the Holy Father appearing at a pop star-type rally with Muslim youth in Africa. Many would say this was Catholicism's effort to reach out to the Islamic masses. Others disagreed and said it more closely resembled a pact with the devil.

At that rally, the Pope would declare, "We believe in the same God, the one God, the living God, the God who created the world, and brings his creatures to perfection."

His opponents within the greater Evangelical community disagreed.

Later he would meet with Yassir Arafat, leader of the Palestinian Authority, more than a dozen times to draw the two closer together. Later still, his successor, Pope Benedict, joined Turkish Muslims in a mosque to pray together. The Christian community remained split on the symbolism.

All of this was a mystery to international Jewry and Bible-believing Christians who couldn't understand why the many mainstream Christian denominations would cozy up to a religion so opposed to Judeo-Christian values and that sponsored terror and death as a cultural value. It just didn't make sense.

The churches openly turned on the Jews and aligned themselves with Islam. They based much of this position on theological differences and social economics. For years many of the mainstream denominations skirted the issue but now the path was clear.

"Christians today see the world differently than our brethren two thousand years ago. Israel and the Zionist principles for which it stands have failed their Palestinian brothers. They oppress them, forcing them to live in squalor," stated a Vatican spokesman after the latest council meeting.

"Israel continues to deny international efforts to intervene. This is Apartheid at its worst. The wall of separation now symbolizes a new and more virulent form of racism. With the 2009 Goldstone Report and others like it, we can see clear evidence of Jewish intransigence. Israel is the roadblock to true peace in the region."

The spokesman's speech set off protests in Israel but nowhere else. This statement caused further splits within Christian circles as many decided they were no longer represented by the mainstream faiths. This left Israel and the Jews virtually isolated from the nations, especially as economic divestment efforts continued.

These actions were, at the time, a culmination of dozens of meetings between the Holy See, leadership councils of other ecumenical churches, and Islamic leadership. The leadership conferences and meetings were often followed up by group 'fact-finding' tours made up of ranking Bishops and

Church leaders to the Holy Land where the perfunctory visits would be held with Israeli leadership, then followed by more visits to cities like Bethlehem or to the Palestinian refugee camps. No one seemed to find it ironic that the Palestinians now controlled Bethlehem, the hometown of the one they worshipped.

When the leadership councils spoke about their visits, they normally couched their communiqués in diplomatic language, spiking those messages with thinly veiled references to Israeli persecution of the Palestinians, and of course the border fence which Israel had built decades before to stop terror. Though few outside were willing to accept it, terror incidents plummeted in Israel after it built its security fence.

And, over time, the 'new order theology' slowly infused the Churches, particularly specific denominations with a twist on 'Replacement Theology.' This time, Christians and many Muslims, from both Shia and Sunni backgrounds, were setting a new course for the faiths. This historical backdrop formed a framework for rising tensions in America where the world would see the first fruits of the new Islamo-Christian relationship. Some of this growing cooperation found a fertile home in the U.S.

Soon, Islamo-Christian militias formed within neighborhoods too, joining forces to make war on the 'Saturday People,' as the Jews were known. Allah, they felt would sanction such an action. After all, according to the Pope, they served the same God. Even the Eastern Orthodox traditions fell in line with Rome.

Those Muslims and the Christians joining them simply didn't see the Jews in any other way than the criminals they were. They brutalized Palestinians in Palestine and they killed Muslims all over the world. They controlled the banks, Hollywood, the insurance and medical industries, and who knew what else? Though an official edict had been issued years before exonerating the Jews from killing Christ, many within the Church still believed it and continued to hold the Jews responsible. The Jews were the cancer that needed to be expunged from the face of the earth. However, one church stepped up to challenge the rising tide.

One of the mainstream churches that did not allow itself to be pulled into this direction was a robust Lutheran congregation in Orange County. The pastor, Thomas Brandenburg, was a former college athlete who, after graduation, felt a calling to the pulpit. Once he graduated, this thickly built, blond, blue-eyed young man with a winning personality and a charming smile, entered the seminary with intentions to build a solid Lutheran community, honoring the last three generations of his forefathers as pastors in the faith. Thomas knew his Bible well—he was well grounded in his beliefs. Later, after graduation and ordination, he found his home in Orange.

Through the years, Pastor Tom's congregation grew. The school attached to the church also expanded and continued to draw more and more families. Test scores were solid, the school's reputation growing with an outstanding faculty of teachers and many compelling activities for families. They were missing only one thing, that of anything resembling Jewish ministry. But change was in the air.

Pastor Tom had recently learned about a controversial but respected Christian minister who had taught extensively on eschatology (study of the Last Days). It was an area in which he lacked knowledge. For some reason he had been studying some of these topics for a brief time now but wasn't quite sure how it all fit together. One congregant gave him a book from this minister and he began reading it. He made a note to himself to track down more of these materials.

And then it hit him early one morning in a devotional he was studying. This week's sermon placed him into the middle of a controversy his church had debated for years-Jewish ministry. With the spreading battles throughout America creeping more and more into the news, and his own community, his attention was now piqued.

He could point with pride to church missionary activity aimed at Africa, Central and South America, but not Israel. He knew he had few if any Jews in the congregation, though he did know of at least one Jewish family in the school. But this week's passage from the Jewish evangelist, Saul of Tarsus, or Paul the Apostle, had him tied up in knots. The passage from Romans, chapter 1 boldly declared:

> *For I am not ashamed of the gospel, for it is the power of God for salvation to everyone who believes, to the Jew first and also to the Greek.*

Saul's letter to the believers in Rome became a foundational text in Christian circles but it was something that Pastor Tom wrestled with. It hit him right in the gut—he had never before felt this conviction. He was a Lutheran Seminary graduate and saw his brand of Christianity through that lens. This was the very same Martin Luther that had almost single handedly ushered in the Reformation when he nailed his 95 Theses to the church door in Germany. Luther was at the forefront to bring the Holy Scriptures into the light once again after so many centuries of darkness.

Yet he also knew the history how Luther, the namesake of his church, had, later in life, hurled invectives against the Jews, but that was so long ago and at a time closer to the end of Luther's life and when he supposedly wasn't in his right mind. He had no reading of his congregation on this issue, but if he were a betting man, he believed they would do the right thing when pressed.

This however was now, and it hit him hard. He was well aware of current events. He even has spoken out against recent acts of terror aimed at the synagogues. Now it all seemed so logical. He read and reread similar texts in the various letters of Paul, Peter, and other New Testament writers. He went back and reacquainted himself with the entire scripture, both Old and New Testaments.

But the clear message to Pastor Tom was that the Jews were still the central focus of God's plan, no matter what history or men said. He called the eldership and arranged for two weeks off as he had some 'personal business,' to attend.

One morning, after intense prayer and devotion, the pastor broke into tears. How could he have missed this most simple admonition to the Christians and in particular his own flock? He got on his knees and then on his face as he sought his creator and confessed his sins and his growing revelation and understanding of the Bible.

He wept as he pounded the floor in repentance and now vowed to make amends. After his personal devotional time was over, he headed over to the local Starbucks and as he was ready to order his double Espresso, he met an extraordinary young man who would later become known to him as the Warrior. This was the very same Starbucks where Danielle and Avner had met.

The Warrior was a tall, strapping young man of mixed racial background. A former US Army soldier, He knew and understood how it was that the Jews occupied a place in God's plan and was now in the crosshairs of history. Discussion soon turned into more thoughtful study.

They soon began an intensive daily meeting at the coffee house that turned around the Pastor's thinking. They formed a close fellowship and it was from the Warrior that he began gaining a new sensitivity to Israel and the Jewish people. It all happened one morning as the Pastor ordered his drink. He pulled out his Bible and began reading from the Book of Isaiah.

"What are you reading?"

"Isaiah 52 and 53."

"Great passages, some of my favorites."

That began a passionate discussion. As schooled as the Pastor was, there was something about this young man that drew him closer. As they talked, the conversation turned to the Jews, Israel, the second return, and the prophetic time clock.

"Do you really believe this is the time?"

"No doubt. From what I can see, all the signs are in place now. The scripture is clear with multiple references to the second return. The Diaspora is ending."

"The Diaspora? What's that?"

"It's the great dispersion. Remember the Assyrian and Babylonian captivities spoken of in the Old Testament? That began the process to scatter the Jews to the four corners of the earth, largely due to their disobedience. This was all predicted by Moses in the later portions of Deuteronomy and other prophets of course."

"And then, what?" the Pastor asked, as if hearing this history for the first time. In fact, he had heard it before, but it was from the mandatory Old Testament History course and a few dusty old history books, now largely forgotten. Old Testament history wasn't the real meat of his profession, the New Testament was. But the Warrior was casting new light and new context on the material and the Pastor was feeling a deep stirring inside himself.

"Rome took care of the rest. Sometime around 70 A.D., you might remember from your studies that the Romans burned Jerusalem to the ground and killed something like one million Jews. The Messianic Jews, or early Christians as some called them, fled the city, remembering Yeshua's words."

"Yeshua?"

"Oh, I'm sorry... Yeshua is Jesus' Hebrew name. I attend a congregation where we call him Yeshua. It's part of our perspective that we live in the end times... complete with signs pointing to the conclusion of the prophetic clock." The Warrior's presence was firm, convicted, and very intense.

"What signs in particular do you mean?" the Pastor probed. It was now dawning on him that his congregation wasn't ready, wasn't prepared to deal with this news. Neither was he and he could only imagine what the elders and the Board of Directors might have to say.

"Well, a whole lot of it deals with the end times. I usually start this conversation with relatively recent events such as the discovery of the Dead Sea Scrolls, the creation of the Jewish state after World War II, the taking of Jerusalem in 1967. Also, it's worth noting some of the more recent regional wars and the recent attacks on Jews in America and all over the world... and a host of other events." The Warrior made his case compelling. His ability to blend in both ancient and modern day history clarified several points of interest for the Pastor.

"Well, specifically I always think of 1948—the year Israel declared independence. They had no real defense against five invading armies and a world that was pretty much disinterested about their plight," the Warrior explained. He was lucid, easy to follow, and Pastor Tom was running to keep up.

"During that war, the Jews were outgunned, outmanned, and out-everything-ed, But, something else was operating... the spirit of the people, and of course, the Spirit of the Lord Himself."

"Through the years, the Jews have been faced with wars, rumors of wars, international hatred that I think is satanically inspired, and they have won every one, though they have taken quite a beating. God simply will not let them become extinct, because His promises are forever."

"Think about it, they are surrounded by more than 300 million of their immediate enemies yet have been preserved for this time. The Egyptians or Assyrians couldn't do it, or the Babylonians, or the Persians, or the crusaders—no nation could wipe them out. The Russians or the local populations throughout history failed too, though they tried. Pogroms always fell short and even though the Nazis tried, and more recently, the Muslims, they couldn't do it either."

And so, they talked late into the night. They swapped scriptures, stories, and discussed the current political landscape. The Pastor's thinking was turning rapidly. The thought occurred to him that he had missed all of this and had become so theologically focused on the Christian message, he missed its context—a Jewish book written by Jews and for Jews—66 books written by 40 authors over a 3,500 year span, a fabulously intricate and coded message system. When the Warrior brought Matthew 23 and 24 into the discussion and explained the Hebraic context of the passage, the Pastor just shook his head.

"So the Messiah's return is for the Jews... meaning He cannot return until Israel recognizes Him, do I have it right?" The Pastor was completely into the story now.

"That's as I see it," the Warrior responded.

"You know, I might recommend grabbing some of Jonathan Roberts' teaching materials. You can download them or request CD's, but in any event, get your hands on them. This guy gets it. I believe that before Yeshua comes to reign on earth, He will return for His Church, that much we know as the rapture, but He will not return to establish the millennium on earth until the Jews, collectively, and as a nation, confess their sin and then recognize Him as their Messiah. Take a look at Zechariah, the 12th Chapter to see my point,"

"You are the third or fourth person to tell me to listen to his stuff. I've heard a little about him. What you're talking about is pretty scary."

"It is scary, unless you really know the scripture and the Lord... so many Christians don't know their own Bibles as well as they should. Roberts used to speak a lot in the area but now there is an international manhunt out for him."

"So I've heard... " Pastor Tom pondered aloud.

The Pastor's Messianic education was just beginning.

Seeking the only Jews he knew at all, the family from his school, he sought counsel. However, he discovered that the family had disappeared. The Warrior, who had also mentioned Moshe, Avner and Danielle's congregational leader, found out that he was gone too. The war was now on his back door.

The Warrior took the Pastor under his wing and educated him on the basics. So the next few nights, armed with some help from his new friends, he launched into a detailed and intensive study of Messianic prophecy and Jewish return to the Land of Israel.

Everything seemed so fresh as if he were reading it for the very first time. He learned about the dispersion of the Jews predicted by Moses, just as the Warrior taught him, then the numerous promises made to this ancient people about returning to their land, each, in turn, told a little differently by the ancient prophets. He had read it before but now the information was jumping off the pages of the Bible and the history books. It was all making sense now.

The message was clear, consistent, and painful. The fire of his heart was turning and it was towards Israel. Growth and learning are sometimes difficult, but the rewards are infinitely greater than the pain. This went on for more than two weeks and when he emerged, he was a new man. The direction of his church was about to change.

And now, he had to reach out to his community's Jews and help them get home.

From Ha Yad Shaul (the Hand of Paul) —2nd Timothy
Chapter 4 Verse 2

Preach the word; be ready in season and out of season; reprove, rebuke, exhort, with great patience and instruction.

Chapter 78

A Curse or Blessing in Kind

Roberts' teams had been working for months to ensure each battle group was equipped to handle local action. With the exception of a few members of each group few of the localized Christian militias were formally trained. But, then, few of the Israelis were well trained when stepping into the breach during the War of Independence in 1947-1948.

Armies find a way to fight and defend themselves and can learn quickly if they have decent leadership and an understanding and belief in the mission. In this manner, few Americans were hardened soldiers when the Revolutionary War began either, nor were their grandchildren fully prepared for the butchery of what would become the Civil War where more than 600,000 Americans would die in America's most devastating war, just 80 years later. That war, as historians wrote years later, took more American lives with it than all of her wars combined. Once they 'they saw the elephant,' America's Civil War soldiers grew into some of the toughest fighters ever seen on a battlefield.

Though the Christian Zionist militias seemed green at the beginning of their defense of America's Jews, they would soon gain valuable experience in the field, especially with the help they would receive from the Israeli commanders on the ground.

The Israeli commanders, mostly young but very experienced in battle, would provide that leadership. And, each member of the local 'Messianic Militias' would have one huge advantage working in his/her favor, that of 'local knowledge.'

In many ways, the local Christian Zionists and those Jews fighting alongside of them knew their areas well. This would prove hugely beneficial as they made their plans to help Jewish families escape the madness that had taken over America's streets and neighborhoods.

The militias were highly motivated, neighbors finding neighbors, church members finding other like-minded members. Secure electronic networks sprung up seemingly out of nowhere to protect data, also helping hook up individuals and small fighting units, making them impervious to searching eyes. The quick forming militias used the various social networking tools strategically, but sparingly, ensuring they didn't become too vulnerable.

A huge black market for all manner of weaponry and ammunition sprung up almost overnight. Guns exchanged hands, ammunition found its way to the defenders as well as enemies. All manner of bartering became the mainstream source of trade. Combined with Israeli firepower, this fighting force would be formidable and operational quite soon.

Tens of thousands of gold coins, diamonds and precious metals now spoke far more loudly than a checkbook or credit card. So far, local law enforcement all over the U.S. continued falling into a pattern of general denial of their circumstances and believed, at least publicly, they could handle any disturbances no matter who started them. However, in private, they knew they were outgunned and vulnerable, especially in light of the fact that many law enforcement and firefighting personnel followed their military brethren and deserted their local units as well.

Whether or not the FBI knew the extent of the desertions wasn't clear, but there had been no indication of any movement by the nation's leading law enforcement agency. It was almost like it was content to let local law enforcement handle its own problems. But the sheer numbers of the combatants and the quickly deteriorating situation on the ground would soon push the authorities into action. It reminded some of the absolute lawless state that Mexico became decades earlier when law and order broke down and the drug cartels controlled the streets.

Soon thereafter, Roberts, through Bat Levi's network of Israeli commandos began directing his street teams to the Israeli commanders on the ground. His intent was to organize them into efficient fighting units, capable of providing the support needed.

And, almost as if an ancient Bible prophecy had been spoken into a modern fulfillment, the Jews began asking for support and help from their Christian neighbors, when completely by surprise, much of their neighbors' gold and silver jewelry and coinage found new homes in Jewish households. The Christian Zionists poured out their love and their wealth on the Jews. The Jews benefiting from this completely unexpected windfall would later carry much of their newfound riches to their new homeland, giving them a fresh start in life and the ability to pay their mounting bills as the electronic transfer of Jewish wealth was still being worked out.

Roberts' trained army of pastors across the nation taught to larger and hungrier audiences, moving them to action. They began fervently teaching the words of the Apostle Jacob (known for generations of Bible believers as James, the brother of Yeshua), that 'faith without works is dead.' The call to arms and defense was met with an outpouring of support, both monetarily, militarily, and spiritually.

CHAPTER SEVENTY-EIGHT: A Curse or Blessing in Kind

The Pastors and their flocks believed and taught that a great spiritual war was in progress and the battleground was for Jewish hearts and minds. Any blood spilled would be for the defense of God's ancient chosen.

Pastor Tom prepared to deliver his weekly address. This one would be different because it had a Jewish theme to it. It was Purim. This Lutheran Church was about to change its entire direction.

"Friends and neighbors, you have no doubt heard it taught from one of the most prolific Messianic scholars in modern times, that God deals with blessings and curses in kind. What that means is this: If someone curses the Jews with a specific threat, that curse will be turned on the one doing the cursing." The congregants this Sunday morning sat up... this message was different.

"We have seen this in ancient times and in modern history. In the book of Esther, Haman, the chief commander of the Persian army wanted to murder the Jewish leader, Mordechai. In short, he built a gallows to hang the Jewish man, but in so doing, he brought the curse back on himself. Haman was hanged a few days later on the very gallows he'd built for Mordechai."

"In similar fashion, ancient Assyria, Egypt, the Philistines, Babylon, the Persian empire, the Seleucids, Greeks, Romans, Byzantines, Crusaders, Spain during the Inquisition, Hitler, Saddam Hussein, Stalin, and others, have paid a similar price, with God returning a curse for a curse in kind." They paid for their curse of the Jews with their own lives... and sometimes their entire civilizations.

"And now... sadly and unbelievably America is in the same place. She is riddled with debt, saddled with obligations she'll never be able to pay. The great ecological disasters of recent years have damaged the oceans and killed untold sea life. Her armies have exhausted themselves fighting for decades overseas. She has now turned away from the Jews as has the rest of the world."

He then explained the corollary.

"When someone decides to bless the Jews, he will return a blessing for a blessing in kind. For centuries, America protected her Jews, then when, in the fullness of time, the Nation of Israel was born, came to her side, even in the midst of tremendous opposition from enemies and friends alike, and stood her ground. Even her staunchest ally, Great Britain stood opposed to Jewish statehood."

"In the years after World War II, with the rest of the world struggling, America rose to perhaps her greatest stature, all the while, providing the most visible support of her Jews and Israel. But, once she began listening to the voices of Islam and some within Christianity, she grew cold and over time, we can see the results. God once blessed this nation, making it the richest nation on the planet. But I believe He is reversing that blessing."

"Purim provides a great example of that story. We can learn from the story of Haman and Josef Stalin. Some say Stalin died on Purim as he prepared to destroy the Jews of Russia. I stand before you and the nation to declare that we must band together and support the Jews and Israel, most likely at great price and sacrifice to many of us and our families."

Though skeptical at the beginning, the speech struck a chord with his listeners. Almost as if on cue, another wave of support rolled in. Brandenburg's followers searched out other friendly congregations and plans formed to support the Jewish exodus from America. The speech immediately went viral online with millions of hits within days. Almost as if on cue, a completely unexpected block of Christians turned on tradition. This congregation and others like it began preparations to help the Jewish escape plans.

The ancient Biblical model of blessings too—a blessing for a blessing in kind rolled through the Christian community. With the encroaching series of economic setbacks and calamities, the believing Christians found themselves in the middle of history. What became a topic of great discussion was that as soon as the Christian families began 'blessing' the Jews, reports came in of great blessings coming back to them. Blessing after blessing poured into the Christian Zionist households and communities. Sick relatives became well almost overnight. Prayers became more fervent, skilled, and faith-bound. The congregants dusted off their Bibles.

Those Christians unemployed for months suddenly found jobs with salaries far above what they had expected. Personal debt vanished, the sick regained health, businesses began to grow in the midst of economic chaos, friendships were restored, and marriages healed, all in all great blessings were being poured out on the believers who had decided to jump in to help the Chosen People of God. The pantry, an ongoing community ministry to the homeless bulged with extra food offerings. Money rolled in and the community began building homeless shelters with no strains on finances.

The blessings swept the nation, community to community, state to state. Former enemies found peace together as warring factions within certain parts of the great assembly (the Church) buried old hatreds and worked toward reconciliation, thus fulfilling the words of Yeshua and Rav Shaul. This had its effects in more traditional and organized Christianity as well.

Many organized parts of the great assembly, broke from traditional ties and gravitated towards support of the Jews and their escape. Hundreds of Catholic priests ignored the pleas from Rome to build and support growing Islamic ties. Instead they chose to steer their flocks towards Israel and the Jews. They reversed history in the process. Some other ecumenical churches did too, including Presbyterians and Methodists, and Lutherans. The demarcation point became the support of the Jews and Israel. But they were in the minority.

For those churches choosing not to support the ancient people of God, they found themselves in the midst of church splits where bitter rancor over these choices severed friendships, divided families and congregations, and caused enormous emotional damage with their parishioners. Finances suffered, long standing friendships fractured, and a spirit of contentiousness prevailed.

For those not considering Israel and the Jews, the events around them made no sense. Fear controlled much of their thinking as few of them had sound Biblical educations or teaching from their leadership to explain what they saw. To those who were paying attention, there was no need of explanation. The Spirit was indeed moving, but not necessarily in the ways many anticipated. The Bible did all the talking.

In Catholic circles, the bell tolled loudly and with such intense emotions that the Holy Father became personally involved with the deteriorating situation. The Vatican had for centuries been at loggerheads with Judaism, though casting peace feelers from time to time as well.

During World War II, many Catholic priests and nuns gave their lives in sacrifice to defend and protect Jews from the annihilation of the German onslaught. At great personal risk, many hid Jewish children inside monasteries and convents, believing they were doing God's work, which according to Scripture, they were. They also died in numbers too great to count. Many of these 'Righteous Gentiles,' both living and dead, were honored at Yad VaShem in Jerusalem.

But, through the years much debate split the Catholic Church as to whether or not the Jews had any relevance in modern times. Disagreements and conflicts were not unknown between the two for centuries. Over time, Jewish leaders held the Church accountable for not confronting Hitler and resisting with greater tenacity during the war years.

The great Roman Church defended these onslaughts with explanations that the Church was doing all it could to help. It didn't want to risk a worse situation as it had millions of its own to protect and defend. It had so many assets to protect that the risk was too much to bear.

And now, with newly emerging trends in Catholicism, it was becoming apparent another great split was about to cleave the assembly in pieces. And at the center of the division was the small, but growing schism in Central and South America, best exemplified by a single priest in Mexico.

> **From the Hand of Samuel the Seer, 1st Samuel**
> Chapter 15 Verse 22
>
> Samuel said, Has the LORD as much delight in burnt offerings and sacrifices as in obeying the voice of the LORD? Behold, to obey is better than sacrifice, and to heed than the fat of rams?

Chapter 79

Father Gregor

Father Gregor De Toledo pastored a modestly-sized Catholic church near Mexico City. The padre came from a long line of priests, where in each generation, at least one brother or sister entered into Church service. He was a tall, kind, circumspect, semi-balding and lighter complexioned man than his flock was used to seeing. Years before, De Toledo completed a Geology degree in Spain. Later, he finished a doctorate in the field with an emphasis in oil exploration where he worked for a few years.

As time went on, he sensed a call to join the priesthood, entered the seminary, and then became a Dominican priest. His special skills with language (he was fluent in Spanish, Hebrew, Aramaic, Latin, and Greek, and passable, though rough English) gave him a very worldly perspective and moved him towards great scholarship. But De Toledo had a secret, something the family had locked away for centuries. Something stirred within his veins and he was about to find out just what it was.

Father De Toledo's flock consisted of more than 500 occasional attendees and 250 or so regulars. His congregation, nestled in the hills of a small Mexican agricultural community near the capital seemed like a small Shangri-La. The village received a well-balanced amount of rain and sunshine, mixed with cooling summer ocean breezes, making the area a very pleasant place to live. The rich, dark, and fragrant soil yielded large vegetables and fruits such as squash, corn, beans, and amazing fruits such as guavas, papayas, pineapples, and mangos, all with minimal pest damage.

De Toledo loved this community, the small farms, the gentle people and the life he lived. But he had a problem, something that he realized wasn't anything he could fix but rather was so much bigger than anything he had ever known.

Early one morning, De Toledo, a devotee of various Church readings of the visions of the Blessed Mother, was reading through the Old Testament and stumbled upon some of the prophecies concerning cataclysmic battles in Israel and the entire world.

It was Thursday morning. While he was preparing his sermon for the upcoming Sunday he began to compare some of the visions of Our Lady of Fatima and the visions from the prophets described in the Bible. He was well schooled in all the Church history including those visions of the Blessed Mother.

Along with his reading, and being a student of the physical world around him, the scientist within began 'triangulating' these events with what had just occurred in Mecca and Medina. He read the prophecy of Ezekiel 37 and many other related 'return to Zion' scriptures.

Strangely, he thought, *events in the world seem to be correlating to the Bible and the Jews in particular. It must be a coincidence.*

The geologist in him was drawn to the recent flurry of earthquakes in diverse places not to mention the accelerating pace of volcanic eruptions. The Geologist in him sat up and took notice. He was aware of the encroaching anti-Semitism growing in America, and the world though it wasn't readily apparent to him where he lived. Of course, there were new rumors of wars all over the world. The rumors seemed almost daily. He was well aware of the long-standing divisions between his church and the Jews. Then all of it hit him with a force that he knew must have been from the Hand of the Lord Himself.

Where the visions of the Virgin spoke of all sorts of disasters, nothing seemed was mentioned of the Jews or for that matter, Jesus Himself. There was a lot about the Virgin Mother, but little about her son, Jesus, the Head of the Church. It seemed the recent visions totally ignored the Bible and the words of the prophets and even Jesus himself. This put everything in opposition to what he thought the truth to be.

He looked at the clock and realized it was almost dawn—he had stayed up all night in study and prayer and he needed to get some rest. The rising sun had brought him into a new day, filled with questions and curiosity. There was something else too.

Recently, his parishioners had been peppering him with questions about the Jewish people, Israel, and certain messianic prophecies as well as prophecies focused on the return of the Jews to Israel.

When several of his parishioners came to him the next morning, they were again full of questions about the Bible, something that was so new to him that he was caught off guard. The priest was well schooled in Catholic lore, the history of the Church, and all the learning that a Dominican priest must know. But this? He was unprepared for any of it. He shook the cobwebs from his head to start the day.

"Father, tell us about these prophecies! We hear from our family and friends in America that something big is happening now and more is soon to happen. Tell us about the Jews and why all of this is so important!" There was a sense of urgency in their pleas.

He sensed they were excited for good reason, but didn't know what it was.

Since not all of the villagers could read or write, they naturally came to the priest for information. It was the village way. In his 15 years here, he baptized their children, presided over their weddings, funerals, and any other special events such as Quinceñeras and the like. But he wasn't prepared for these biblical questions. So, he began to study and what he found disturbed him because none of it appeared very high on the list of things he needed to know.

"My children, why is this so important?" he asked, half hoping they would drop their curiosities.

"Father, we are hearing from our families that much change is occurring. Many of our relatives in America Del Norte (North America) are leaving the Church. They are learning Jewish ways, reading the Bible... and they tell us we must do the same!"

"Well, so have I. I think I am beginning to understand what they are saying." Right then, they agreed to begin meeting another day for Bible study. The following Wednesday, the study began. Ten of the villagers showed up and the priest began to teach.

"We will begin with a little background for all of you which will acquaint you with some of the things that will help you understand the context of the Scriptures."

"Since you are so interested in Israel and in the Jewish people all of a sudden, I thought we could begin with the concept of why the Jews are chosen and what they will encounter in the last days."

He pointed out many scriptures, some of which were strange to the gathering but they absorbed it with rapt intent. The little gathering wanted to know. The little gathering demanded to know.

"We can start with the concept of the chosenness of the Jews. We see it mentioned in the first five books of Moses. However, it occurs all through the Old Testament.

"We should begin with the Books of Genesis and Exodus, the first and second books of the Torah. The Jews were chosen, yes, but being chosen didn't mean it came without huge responsibilities. There are several characters and passages that describe how the line of the Messiah would travel through Abraham, Isaac, and then Jacob. Abraham's first son, Ishmael, though blessed, does not inherit the promised line," he explained.

"In Exodus 19, Moses told us that the Jews would be God's own possession and a kingdom of priests:

> *Now then, if you will indeed obey My voice and keep My covenant, then you shall be My own possession among all the peoples, for all the earth is Mine; and you shall be to Me a kingdom of priests and a holy nation. These are the words that you shall speak to the sons of Israel.*

"And again, Moses wrote in Deuteronomy 7:7-8,

> *For you are a holy people to the LORD your God, and the LORD has chosen you to be a people for His own possession out of all the peoples who are on the face of the earth.*

"Then, much later, the Prophet Amos in the 3rd chapter and verse 2 warned them that even though they were chosen if they sinned they would suffer consequences:

> *"You— only have I chosen among all the families of the earth. Therefore I will punish you for all your iniquities.*

"Father, what about the Gentiles and especially the world's Catholics?" One of his parishioners asked the question with such passion and perception that the priest was taken aback.

"All of God's children were special to Him but the Jews were chosen for a special mission, that of being a light to the nations, according to the Prophet Isaiah, and carrying the message of a loving God to the world. Whether or not they accomplished the mission as explained by the Prophet Isaiah was up for debate. Some believe they did, others believe the opposite."

The priest explained that while the Jews had blessed the world through untold contributions in medicine, finance, science, education, the arts, and more, some argued they had largely failed their spiritual mission, though they had brought the Messiah to the world. It didn't mean God had cast them off but it meant that He now extended the Kingdom to a people who were not originally called by His name. The Gentiles would now be included in the Kingdom of Heaven.

"Remember, the Jews delivered the Messiah to the world. I must admit, this reading is taking me to places I never knew about in the Bible and with the current situation in the world growing darker by the day, I am now thinking that a lot more is to come. It seems to me that current events and events in Bible prophecy are on a collision course."

"The Jews remain chosen because God is the same yesterday, today, and forever. He does not go back on His promises. But it doesn't mean He doesn't love others too, and that is why, I believe your hearts are stirred up as they are today."

It was a small gathering—his office fit everyone. It would be the last time that would happen, for the next week, the group doubled in size. The following week, it doubled again and within a month, he was speaking to more than 100 of his parishioners and some neighbors from other local villages. The word was spreading about his teaching.

Something else happened, too. Those who couldn't read had someone read to them. In many cases, children read to parents and other family members. Then the children expressed an interest in the Bible.

As each session ended, Father De Toledo blessed them and encouraged them to read these things for themselves. This was not something that most Catholics he knew were used to doing, but there was something happening he couldn't explain.

He then began to speak of the salvation of the Lord. They'd heard the words a million times—still, it seemed new and fresh. The villagers asked many questions and wondered why this hadn't been taught before. The priest covered all the main scriptures predicting Jewish return to the Land of Israel, though for the life of him he couldn't figure out why they wanted to know.

The little congregation was abuzz at the new learning. And strangely, there was no talk of the traditional teachings of the Church. The congregants only wanted to hear the Bible. And though they still loved the stories about Mary, there was precious little discussion about her now. And when he taught them a key prophecy in the Gospel of Matthew, they sat at rapt attention.

"Jesus said that in the last days, there would be wars and rumors of wars, earthquakes in diverse places, and the love of many would grow cold," he said, reading from the Gospel of Matthew.

Hands shot up and the questions came with vigor and with a surprisingly deep insight, considering this was all new to them. Recent events brought to them by increased access to the internet and television convinced them they were witnessing bible prophecy coming alive right before their very eyes.

CHAPTER SEVENTY-NINE: Father Gregor

At the conclusion of the fifth session, he closed up his backpack and headed to his little cottage next to the church. It was very warm and he paused to wipe his sweating pate.

When he came up the small garden walkway to his home, he stopped at the mailbox and opened it. Pulling the envelopes out, Father De Toledo stopped to find a letter addressed from America in a hand he didn't recognize. He thought of some relatives there but wasn't close to them, in fact hadn't he heard from them in years.

The letter was from a distant cousin inviting him to an all expenses paid Spanish language conference in the U.S. The conference was to address the Jews of the Southwest United States and their relations in Mexico and throughout Central and South America on the subject of the mass exodus of Hispanics from the Catholic Church and into synagogues and Messianic congregations. Now THIS he had to see.

Apparently, what he experienced over the past few weeks was spreading like wildfire throughout the villages of Central and South America and it now explained to him, at least in the short term, why the Bishop and the Archbishop had seemed so edgy lately.

The timing couldn't have been more perfect nor could it have been more puzzling. Why him, why now, and how had they found him? The next day another letter arrived, this time with only a phone number and an admonition for him to call the number, for it was urgent.

The day after that, the telephone rang in the Del Fuego residence in New York. Jenny Del Fuego happened to be at her parents' home for dinner and picked up the phone. The person at the other end began chattering in Spanish a little too quickly for her to understand.

She called her father to the phone. For the next 2 hours an intense conversation ensued between the long lost cousins.

"Gregor, it is so good to hear your voice," David Del Fuego said excitedly.

"David, it's good to hear yours too... how long has it been?"

"Gotta be at least 20 years, 30 maybe. I think we were last down there when we were children," Del Fuego answered. His cousin, now found and confirmed from a genealogy search on the internet had paid off.

"Gregor, I have something to say to you... do you remember my parents and how when your parents would visit, and when we came in the room, they would go silent?"

"Hmmm, yes, I recall," the priest said. "Why do you ask?"

"Well, I've finally come to grips with all of this. Did you know our families are Jewish?" The other end of the phone fell silent, and the Del Fuegos thought they heard weeping.

"Are you sure? How did you find out?" De Toledo asked, now completely confused yet somehow calmly comforted and getting agitated and excited all at the same time.

"We did a genealogy on the family," David answered.

"We found that we descend directly from the Crypto Jews and the Conversos from Spain. The families escaped during the Inquisition and made it to the New World. They went underground with their faith and adopted Catholic ways for protection. But the Jewish ways, the secret rituals remained buried deep within the families."

"That explains what I've been seeing in the past few months... and explains why our leadership is so agitated. The Bishop and Archbishop, whom we never see, suddenly appeared the week before last. They asked all kinds of questions about the congregation, about if we knew about any Jewish blood in the parishioners, all very strange, and now you show up in my life. I also received an invitation to a conference about this subject," he said as he fished out the conference brochure and read it to the Del Fuegos.

"Well, cousin, guess what? Our names, are both old Spanish Jewish names. It's all beginning to fall into place. So there you have it, and you, a Jewish priest!" Del Fuego said. They all laughed, the irony hanging thick in the air.

Del Fuego's last comment sent chills up and down the priest's spine. The secret was out. *The villagers are going to love this,* he thought.

It will explain a lot and probably make them ask more questions, the internal discussion continuing within.

"Are you going to attend the conference?" the priest asked his cousin.

"Yes, can you come?"

"I am now!" the priest said. "I've got to see you!"

"Good because there's something I need to show you," said Del Fuego.

"I can't wait," said the priest.

The next two weeks seemed to drag on forever. But the time came and when the cousins met at the conference registration desk, the reunion was sweet, hugs and tears dissolving the years of separation. Their new adventure was about to begin.

"My cousin!" said Del Fuego. His excitement was difficult to contain.

"Let me look at you. You've hardly changed, except for maybe what you are wearing," he said.

"Well, it's all in how you look at it," the Padre replied. Clothes aren't that important to me. And, of course, a little less hair," he said, laughing, running his hand over the balding head.

"OK, let's go up to my room because I have something I want you to see," Del Fuego urged.

CHAPTER SEVENTY-NINE: Father Gregor

The cousins walked onto the elevator for the ride to the 7th floor. They got off and turned right, went past the ice and soda machines, and then past the gym. They arrived at Del Fuego's room.

Del Fuego switched on the light and motioned for his cousin, the priest, to sit down.

"You are going to need to sit down when you see this," his cousin said.

Del Fuego opened up his suitcase roller, reached in a pulled out a soft felt green bag with a silver cup, very old with intricately designed Hebrew writing. Next, he pulled out a red bag, threadbare, but still holding up. He reached into the bag and extracted a worn but clearly well made set of Tfillin or phylacteries. The phylacteries were missing one of the small boxes that comprise the pieces of the set.

The priest was spellbound. When Del Fuego handed the items to his cousin, the two of them fell silent.

"Where did you get these?" De Toledo asked.

"Well, as far as I can tell, they've been in the family for years. Judging by the worn nature of the items, I can only guess they've been with us for generations. My father gave them to me and his father gave them to him. My guess is that they have been in the family for maybe as long as 400-500 years, maybe longer," Del Fuego explained.

"Wow, this is indeed providential... and I have something for you too."

From his suitcase, he too had brought some items for his cousin to see, touch, and behold. De Toledo pulled out a small satchel wrapped in newspaper and then untied the twine. Del Fuego watched intently as his cousin carefully unwrapped the package.

It was a full *tallit*, a Jewish prayer shawl, worn during Shabbat services. It was clear the garment had seen better days but it remained intact, complete with its complex network of fringes and knots, totaling, some said, 613, to remind the wearer of the commandments of God Himself.

"I think this has been in our family for about 500 years." De Toledo and Del Fuego, cousins going back generations didn't realize it then, but these two religious artifacts had left Spain with their common ancestors, some 500+ years before and were now in the presence of one another for the first time since they left the Kingdom of Ferdinand and Isabella during the dark days of the Inquisition.

Neither of them could believe this strange twist of fortune, but they both knew what it meant. Neither of the cousins believed in sheer accidents or unexplained coincidences. There was meaning here and both of them understood that something was afoot.

"I have something else to show you too...."

Father Gregor reached into the little bag and extracted a small box, and gently laid it in the hand of his cousin. Tears ran down Del Fuego's face. The missing box... the *tallit* and *t'fillin* sets were together for the first time in 500 years.

The long-lost relatives attended seminars together over the next three days. The organizers were more interested in inclusion so they invited all manner of people, Jews, non-Jews, Church officials, and anyone expressing an interest in the subject. This also included both mainstream Jewish and Messianic leaders.

There was an unspoken agreement to leave prejudice at the door and learn more about why so many Hispanic Catholics were leaving Catholicism and flocking to a Jewish lifestyle and learning, with focus on the Bible.

The conference drew more than 5,000 attendees. The heaviest representation came from Mexico and the Southwest United States where some of the heaviest concentrations of Hispanic Jewry existed. One of the speakers, a Jewish woman from European stock revealed her story of grandparents escaping the Nazis during the War and living in Toledo, Spain, an old Jewish town.

"My family lived in a small village protected from the soldiers by the local townspeople. They didn't exactly have it easy but the Spaniards shielded them from the Fascist troops and ensured their safety. This ironic twist of fate was made even sweeter when someone commented on the fact that some 500+ years before the Spanish crown chased the Jews from Spain and 500 years later the Jews returned to relative safety."

"This was an exquisite reversal of fortune that resulted in virtually no loss of Jewish life in Spain during the War. Life wasn't exactly a party, but Franco never caved in to Hitler either." Her storytelling avarice was riveting and the audience hung on every detail.

The story brought tears to the cousins' eyes as they began to compare notes. Their parents had told them similar stories about their own families. The pieces were coming together.

The padre now understood the panic in the Church in Mexico. It had been a bastion of Catholic strength and power for centuries. Hundreds of thousands of Catholics just like his parishioners were leaving the Church in droves and forming new congregations, focused on Bible study and Jewish approaches to worship. There was a new and profound outward expression of love for the Jewish people and Israel, where there had been little if any in their past.

They were shedding the traditional Catholic practices and if the local Church didn't go along, they just left. He was receiving answers to his prayers and learning about himself all at once. As the people left their

CHAPTER SEVENTY-NINE: Father Gregor

parishes, so did their financial support. Religion or faith, suddenly felt more personal, more like a relationship between a loving father and his children.

The Vatican was interested and worried which was obvious because the leaders in each area suddenly appeared at the churches, testing the climate and the loyalty of the people. Their interest in the conference had more to do with trying to understand the phenomenon they were seeing around them.

The conference was a life changer for De Toledo. Change was in the air. As the conference closed, the cousins now reunited and closer than ever, agreed to keep in touch through the internet. The priest then caught a taxi to the airport and prepared to return home, books, CD's, and new contacts filling his suitcase.

While sitting in the airport, his cell phone buzzed with a text message asking him when he was returning. The priest now stood at a crossroads because he could now see where all of this appeared to be heading. Rather than texting back, he dialed the phone and the church's secretary answered.

"Senior, Padre are you coming home soon?" There was worry in her words.

"Si, I am coming home now... how are you, mija?" Something was wrong and he could sense it. "Are you ok?"

"The Archbishop and the Bishop were here again this week. They want to see you." But he felt she was still holding something back.

"I'll be home by tomorrow. I'm in the airport—we leave in an hour."

Once he boarded the plane, Father De Toledo fished out some of the conference documents and began to read about the role of the Jews in end times.

He noted that many scriptures with which he was familiar were explained in a very different context to what he was used to teaching. Later, when he grew somewhat sleepy, he put his head back and dozed off. He awoke upon landing. His plane had arrived on time to Mexico City.

Shaking the cobwebs from his head and blinking several times to wake up, he prepared to grab his bags and deplane. A moment later, he pulled out his cell phone and placed a call to his ride.

He exited the terminal and looked for the blue Ford Escort. When he spotted Rosa, his secretary, he waved to her and she pulled over to pick him up. Ford's recovery, in part, was due to the new factories they had set up in Mexico and this car was a local product from that factory. He even felt some pride for that because several of his parishioners worked at the factory and it was a source of pride for the community.

She opened up the trunk and the back door. The priest threw his bags in and climbed in the car. He looked at her for a moment and sensed something that he couldn't quite explain.

"You seem different, Rosa, what's going on?"

"They were here again, Father. The Archbishop and the Bishop."

"What did they want? What did they say?"

"They seemed very angry. I've not seen them like this." She seemed frightened and he sensed it.

"Did they threaten you or anyone?"

"Not directly, but they said they would be back to see you."

She drove out of the airport. The priest didn't know what to think. He had no idea what they were thinking, let alone what they might be planning.

He feared for his parishioners and he feared for his friends. They drove awhile. Then he saw the smoke rising in the distance from somewhere near the village.

From the Hand of the Psalmist
Chapter 8 Verse 24

Rescue the weak and needy;
Deliver them out of the hand of the wicked.

Chapter 80

Operation Last Exodus
—Fully Engaged

The Los Angeles commander of operations was Yigal Davidson, a young 25 year old Israeli Captain. Davidson had fought in the last regional conflicts and was comfortable and competent in his role. He personally led a battalion of paratroops behind enemy lines and cut communications, utilities, and had managed to disrupt their operations without any of his team being killed. He was known for his quick, decisive and wise decision making on the battlefield. He now had far more firepower under his command than he had in Israel and he wasn't afraid to use it.

Meanwhile, the Israeli battle teams continued to join up with their Christian Zionist defenders. Each contact was precarious because the Jewish defenders didn't always know who they could trust. There were some indications of operational penetration into their plans. The Israelis realized that anyone who approached them was a risk till proven otherwise.

Traitors and spies were dealt with harshly. Some of the penetrators were executed in military fashion while still others were moved to secure facilities and incarcerated. Rumors abounded that Dogface's garbage dumps kept secrets but nothing had been proven. The Rule of Law was breaking down. Chaos always had a way of asserting its own path.

Davidson's plan called for the tens of thousands of Christian Zionist militiamen to secure strategic high ground. That meant all high rise office complexes and hotels along roads leading into the airport. Still other Christians, shut down the freeways to allow safe passage to fleeing Jews. Busses, 'borrowed' or just taken from their storage yards, showed up in various neighborhoods to provide transportation to the airport. Israeli teams exchanged secure codes with their allies.

Aircraft Retrofitting neared completion. Israeli aircraft teams worked feverishly to install electronic countermeasures (ECM) and chaff systems designed to decoy any missile fired at the planes. Turn around crews trained and prepared for restocking of amenities for the long flights. Israeli ground crews prepared the planes for final checks at the various airports in the small country. The first wave of wide-bodied aircraft would soon arrive with their crews aboard.

But much lay ahead. The streets were not yet totally secured.

Operation Last Exodus was underway in Los Angeles.

On the West side of the city, Avner and now Dani were busy securing the passageways to the airport, specifically LAX and John Wayne in Orange County. The Christians, well armed, and volunteering to take even the most undesirable work in a very undesirable situation were proving themselves every bit the fulfillment of the Jews' friends, a stunning reversal of history.

Normally reticent and distrustful of Christians, the Jews of America had no choice as they were now at the mercy of these new friends, longtime historic enemies. The first wave of deployments began as troop transports arrived at various gathering points around West Los Angeles.

Christian militiamen and women received their provisions, RFID identifications and took up defensive positions on the streets, buildings, and utility facilities. Those not carrying weapons were not allowed into the fight just yet. They would receive training, though it would be short. Dogface's contacts spent the better part of two weeks stepping these new soldiers through a basic training course in urban warfare at their garbage dumps. It wasn't thorough, but it would have to do.

Squads of Israelis and Christian Zionist soldiers quickly seized hotels and other buildings near the airport on Century and Sepulveda Boulevards and closer to the water. Attack teams captured other buildings and converted them into critical operational centers. Israeli commanders knew that two weeks of training was not altogether dissimilar to what arriving refugees from Europe received when taking on defense of the Yishuv during Israel's War for Independence. Good leadership always knew how to make adjustments in battle.

Battle plans fell into place. Israeli and Christian Zionist soldiers fanned out and took up positions on rooftops and in hotel rooms overlooking the streets. For miles around, parts of LA became an armed camp. Since many of those joining themselves to the Jewish cause were already trained in handling weapons, the remainder of the drills dealt with crowd control, vehicle inspections, and supply chain logistics.

Deserting Christian military and law enforcement were arriving every hour and were forming into an army of defenders such as had never been seen on American soil. Even the largest of the Civil War battles, Gettysburg had 150,000 troops combined facing one another in a relatively confined area covering about 25 square miles. These battles would cover hundreds of square miles with hundreds of thousands of defenders involved until the final Jew was lifted to safety and taken home to Israel.

Davidson called an early morning meeting with his key leaders.

"We have to get control of the communication facilities including radio,

TV, and print media. I don't wish to alarm anyone but unless we either knock them out or fail to control them, we will be in serious trouble."

Israeli planners anticipated this contingency and when Davidson pulled up the plans, those in the room gasped. The plan called for a storming of every major television and radio station in the LA area. The plans called for the communications specialists to broadcast both in code as well as in plain English, Spanish, Arabic, Farsi, Tagalog, Vietnamese, and any other language deemed necessary. The code had been pre-arranged.

He called both Avner and Danielle to his side and explained what he needed. The young couple had one advantage—Danielle had contacts all through the industry and knew who she could trust and who she couldn't. The three of them broke off from the rest of the meeting and huddled in a conference room. The key would be the Christian Zionists because they would need the muscle but also her friends who could bend the wills of the station managers to her side.

Another area of concern was the internet. If radio and TV could be controlled, which would be difficult at best, they knew the internet could not. Israeli planners considered the possibility of taking out communication satellites. The idea had merit. But if they could turn the internet into a advantage, it may be worth the effort. Their enemies would be at it as well. It could turn into a battle for cyberspace and working with the Vicenzos contacts would help ensure success. On the other hand, dropping enough misinformation into the public airwaves could work to their advantage through subterfuge and confusion.

Next, Avner then put the squads of commandos together and through the network already established by Roberts and his allies, they had what they needed. Avner put a call out to the numerous warehouses where armored units awaited his command. The troops were ready to go into action. His leadership skills would be sorely tested from communication and media to power and water facilities. He gathered his subordinates to explain the planning.

"Water and power are critical. We need to control these if for no other reason is that they give us some bargaining chips. Remember that the goal isn't to destroy anything but rather to rescue refugees. We are starting to see Jews gathering for the trip to the airport. We have to make the trip safe for them."

In the next few days, under Avner's command, Israeli teams trained to storm every communications facility they could.

The idea wasn't to control communication as much as it was to dispense crowd control and safety information and to ensure that people understood what was happening. Mixed teams of Jews and Christians prepared broadcasts and internet warnings, also tapping into 911 systems, Megan Alerts, and any other public notifications available. Plans called for any and all electronic media to carry the messages.

About twelve million Los Angeles residents would hear that the streets weren't safe and to stay indoors. Those venturing out would be at risk. The Israelis knew that they would have to restore some sort of order and with their Christian allies aboard, they worked to do so. With some command of the air, the task would be more doable. They needed the streets open, uncluttered, and safe, peacefully if possible. But if they needed to fight, they would do that too.

The various teams fanned out across the city bursting into the studios and commandeering the broadcast facilities of LA's radio and television stations. One of Avner's squads, led by defecting Green Beret soldiers captured the flagship station from Clear Signal, a huge radio and television conglomerate. Within minutes the station was under control of the former marine team leader. With regular programming interrupted, the soldiers, with guns trained on the technicians to ensure the signal continued to broadcast, made the following speech.

"Fellow citizens, please remain calm. Our mission is to help rescue the Jewish citizens in your communities while maintaining order at all costs in the community. We will not attack anyone in anger unless we are fired on first. Your instructions are simple-conduct your business in as normal a fashion as you are able but do not approach our troops on the streets. Further advisories will be posted on this station and on all news casts."

Identical messages were broadcast that day from every station in the LA area. Coupled with them were messages for more than a dozen major languages in the area.

Once the initial communiqués went out and a general order began to form on the streets, the commanders would be able to allow minimal movement for shopping necessities and medical needs. With the hundreds of thousands of Christian Zionist allies providing support this aspect of the operation took a slow but measured step forward.

For now, a general shutdown was the only way to conduct business. With overwhelming firepower available, and control of the air tipping in their direction, local law enforcement wasn't as much of a threat as it once was. Helicopters were in the air.

Additionally, crack teams of Israeli commandos stormed every major water and power facility as well. Avner and his mixed squadron of 250 men and women commandeered the headquarters of the Los Angeles Department of Water and Power. Israeli commandos now controlled the electrical and gas company grids, with programming designed to shut down the greater Los Angeles basin should they be challenged.

Danielle now assumed her duties ensuring no disruption in battle space communications occurred. Her expertise with electronics and the software would soon pay off handsomely. Israeli and Christian Zionist squads seized control of the main roads.

Appeals for help were made to the Governor. Local police admitted they were outgunned and outmanned. City officials realized that local law enforcement was not able to help. Under Israeli direction, they issued warnings to local citizens to stay indoors as much as possible. Other communication was issued to law enforcement that no harm was intended. They wanted no confrontation, just clear and safe passage to the airport.

But things spiraled out of control. The citizenry not able to sit by and do nothing. The Governor was now drawn in and realized he would need to call in National Guard troops to quell the disturbances hitting the streets. Many other neighborhoods struggled under Islamo-Christian militias with those areas promising death to the Jews and Christians who dared oppose them.

Once the census information was leaked, enemies attacked Jewish neighborhoods or any districts where they suspected Jews lived. Islamo-Christian forces killed thousands of Jews in the process and ransacked their homes. Gun battle after gun battle erupted, driving most indoors. Israeli planners and their Christian counterparts knew they couldn't be everywhere at once, but began a systematic plan to surround those areas not in their control.

In defense, the Christian Zionists began forming Neighborhood Watch and Defend Teams, much as Chicago defenders did just weeks earlier. Neighborhood after neighborhood was hit and it now it was time for the 100,000 Israeli defenders and their Christian Zionist allies to push the campaign to the enemy and join the fight.

Sporadic gunfire was heard in various neighborhoods but a bigger battle was forming and the Israelis knew it. Intelligence had been pouring in for weeks through a variety of communication channels. Unless it was a feint, West LA looked to be the next target, where hundreds of thousands of Jews lived. Rumors of thousands of armed Muslims and Christians were assembling at a number of mosques and churches, and then deploying to hit the Jewish communities and take as much Jewish life with them as they could.

"We have some assets on the ground. Let's do this!" Davidson's senior commanders scrambled to execute his orders.

His graphics teams had the heaviest Jewish neighborhoods displayed on the walls in their 3D maps, each with entry and exit points. Local churches and the tens of thousands of Christian Zionists were combing their neighborhoods for individual Jewish families as well. The three satellites, Hananiah, Mishael, and Azariah, now dialed into LA and other major cities across the American landscape, beamed real time pictures of the situation on the ground.

"Get those guys in the air and get the recon units up now!"

They would be ready within the hour to deploy. The believing soldiers readied themselves to defend, transport, and if need be, strike back.

"This is not a mission of destruction but rather of rescue. But that doesn't mean we don't fight." Davidson's message reflected the Israeli line... no engagement with the enemy unless absolutely necessary.

They prepared to sweep the streets and get the Jews to safety. Davidson had several mechanized units at his command, a unit of a dozen Apache helicopters, some V-22 Ospreys, a number of Chinook troop transport helicopters as well as two Chinooks converted for evacuation requirements.

His fellow Israelis stood ready to do their work. Joining them would be more than 600,000 Los Angeles area Jewish citizens, a third of them armed and willing to help defend the exiting masses. Additionally there was an infusion of about 500,000 Christian Zionists and defecting U.S. military members, most of whom had seen action in the jungles of the Philippines or in Central and South America chasing Islamic and Hispanic drug gangs. Estimates ran close to one and half to two million friendly troops.

The Governor placed an urgent call to the White House that evening.

"Mr. President, the situation on the ground here is worsening by the hour. It's confusing sir. There are some Christians who have joined the Muslims and some who are helping the Jews. It's hard to tell the good from the bad guys. I am close to calling the Guard."

"Get your Guardsmen down there and do what you can to the two sides apart. We're going to get some observers down there and get you some help from the local bases." The President was agitated and short with the Governor.

"Sir, I mean no disrespect but we are not talking about a few gang members here. These are heavily armed and dangerous *armies* not a bunch of hoodlums. We are completely outgunned and outmanned. I am afraid that we are going to have a bloodbath here. Several Jewish neighborhoods are surrounded by Muslims, skinheads, and their Christian friends. Everybody is armed to the teeth."

The President fell silent on the phone. He knew that at least four major airports had been taken by the IDFA. He knew that his best and most capable troops were not on U.S. soil and that any help would not be able to defuse the situation. The Federal government was virtually helpless. Nobody believed the situation would become so desperate.

"I can call a National Emergency right now and order reserves up from Pendleton or from March but it won't be enough. You've got to get the Guard down there and do what you can."

The situation worsened by the hour. Running gun battles could be heard in many areas of greater Los Angeles, from Downtown to the Valleys north to San Fernando and east to San Gabriel. In the West side of the city, most notably in the Mar Vista area and other heavily populated Jewish enclaves, L.A. Jews and their friends formed armed bands to fend off the enemy. The heavily Jewish area near Wilshire and Fairfax was under siege.

Davidson's drones were up now and he and his staff could see the area well. A complex of buildings was held jointly by Islamo-Christian forces and two skinhead squads numbering several hundred. They were well-trained soldiers, many with previous military experience.

Islamo-Christian forces seized a hospital on the West side as well as several office buildings overlooking some residential areas. Several of the buildings had flat roofs, which provided easy launching pads for mortars and larger portable rockets.

Opposing forces smuggled the rockets in through the porous Mexican border, another payoff from the drug cartels. Though the government never went public with it, it wasn't a real surprise to see Muslim gunmen teaming with the Mexican drug cartels to form dangerous enemies. The drug border war seemed unwinnable at this point, with free passage of contraband and personnel coming into the U.S. from above and underground.

The mortar barrage began with a pounding of the Jewish residential areas, then with supplemented with machine guns and rifles. This group of 250 fighters had the high ground but didn't know what they faced. All they knew was that orders coming from a West-side mosque had them facing Jewish targets in a nearly all Jewish neighborhood. They cherished the moment. Dozens of homes were in flames, as were cars and other vehicles. All the words of their heroes, from Hitler to Farrakhan rang in their ears.

Anyone roaming around outside was a sitting duck and for that matter, anyone in a home within range was little better off. The barrage set house after house on fire, and when any of the residents sought to evade the flames by running outdoors, they were cut down by machine gun fire from the windows of the closer buildings.

"We've got some radio traffic coming in now, office buildings in Santa Monica, north of Montana taking heavy fire. What are our drones telling us?"

"We're up... we see the shooters now," the drone commander answered. Looks like they have five buildings that are housing the shooters... we can see the mortar launchers too."

"Ok, we have to neutralize the threat. He pulled his secure radio out and found Avner.

"Avner where are you?"

"We're closing in on the hospital... do you have the drone feed yet?"

"Yes, looks like they are using the hospital for cover."

"I think so... ok, take your team with you... do we have any air support?"

"Let me see what I can do," Davidson said. "Gideon 3, come in."

"Gideon 3 here." Gideon 3, another Apache commander, was within 2 miles of the group of buildings

"We need to shift focus here, I need you over the hospital as soon as you can... there's a complex of office buildings across from there."

"I see them now... I see the shooters.... I can lay some cannon in there and kill the rockets... there goes another one now!" the Apache pilot exclaimed.

"Permission to engage!"

"Permission granted, hit 'em hard Gideon!"

Gideon 3's weapons officer released his cannon and the rocketeers dissolved in a pink mist, the rocket launchers falling silent.

The neighborhood of about 200 homes was badly damaged, flames everywhere. Who knew what had come of the residents of those homes?

The Apache then deftly turned—the pilot and the weapons officer assessing the hospital. The pilot realized he had a difficult situation on his hands.

The terror team had taken rooms on the west wing of the facility. No one knew it then, but their assault on the hospital left a bloody trail with patients dead or wounded in their rooms and the entire wing in shambles. The helicopter backed off a little, searching for the shooters in the windows.

Suddenly, and without warning a rocket propelled grenade came heading their way from behind them, across and down the street. The Apache tried to evade the inbound missile but it was too late for evasive maneuvers.

The helicopter's warning dweedled on, its high pitched tone almost deafening the pilot and his weapons man. "

"Incoming!"

"Get out of there Gideon!" The RPG streaked towards the helicopter.

He hit the throttle and tried pulling out of his hover position. The RPG screamed toward the Apache and hit the rotor blades, sparks and flames leaping out of the rotor's housing.

The helicopter bucked and shook, then began to lose altitude, and spun towards the ground.

"Ground, we are hit, we are hit!! We are losing altitude... we need to put this thing down but we've lost our blades!!"

The chopper continued to fall. The pilots tried every maneuver they could think of but nothing worked. The Apache hit the ground at an awkward angle and then rolled over, broken and twisted blades beneath them. The safety features of the crew cabin saved the pilot and his weapons officer, for now.

But they were upside down and the smell of fuel permeating the downed aircraft. The two crewmen were shaken but otherwise unharmed, but now vulnerable and within range of the window shooters.

"Ground, we are down, and the chopper is flipped."

Just then, the shooters in the hospital windows opened fire on the Apache. So far, no explosions even thought the automatic weapons fire was hot.

"We're taking fire from the hospital!" He blasted into the mic. Though down, they maintained radio contact.

"Gideon, I've got help on the way. Hang on!"

At that moment, Avner's team turned the corner and saw the action in front of them. His armored vehicle had a 50 caliber machine gun mounted atop the personnel carrier. His gunner aimed then fired at the windows. Cement, metal, and glass exploded in every direction as the small cannon unloaded, tearing great holes in the facing of the building. Six shooters returned fire from the window but were quickly neutralized.

The hospital was heavily damaged. Twelve hospital patients were dead, caught in the crossfire while dozens lay wounded. But the terrorists were dead, taken out by Avner's team. With the immediate threat now under control, medical personnel were finally free to attend the wounded. The dead would have to wait for now. Avner and his squad had the helicopter crew to save next. Just then another threat appeared.

About two dozen Islamo-Christian troops crept up to the disabled Apache. Avner's men watched with horror as they began crawling over the wreckage and toward the crew members. The crewmembers only side arms, but knew they were in a bad position. They couldn't shoot if they had to.

Slowly drawing their weapons, they inched closer toward the downed pilots, aware that Christian Zionist and Israeli forces were present. There would be no taking of prisoners here. This war was not about gaining ground nor was it about controlling territory. It was about total war, something defined long ago in a very distant war.

Avner split his squad into two smaller teams of six each. They had to strike quickly. Though outmanned, they had superior firepower but had to be careful not to hit the helicopter for fear of any fuel leaks and a subsequent explosion. They quickly reassessed their targets. Avner barked out a quick command to his team.

"Ok, we've got less guys but we have more power. We need to hit these guys from two directions." Avner's calm was evident but his voice reflected urgency.

But the Islamo-Christian fighters had other ideas. They reached the two crew members and crudely cut them out of their harnesses. Instead of shooting them, they decided to take the two as hostages.

But Avner was having none of that now. He knew he was out of time. This was a no-win situation unless he and his men could free the Apache crew.

His teams split off and found good cover. The terrorists dragged the shaken helo crew out of the chopper and roughly pushed them into a Humvee they had hijacked earlier in the afternoon.

Avner's first strike team made up of four Israelis trained for urban combat and two Christian Zionist allies took aim at the tires of the vehicle. As the skinhead driver began to negotiate his way into traffic, Avner's other team of six pushed a car into their path. As the car swerved, Avner's men shot out all four tires.

Meanwhile, the other 20 opposing soldiers took aim at Avner's teams. Disappearing behind some cars, Avner's men managed to pick off seven of the enemy, dropping them in the street while losing none themselves.

The Humvee, with the Apache crew and the terrorists was now dead in the street. The unmoving SUV was now Avner's target but things would be difficult as they enemy had both cover and the hostages. Avner knew he would need help. He radioed Davidson at HQ for help.

"Come out now and you will not be harmed," he yelled at the captors.

Just then, enemy forces jumped out from behind some cars. Avner's men took aim.

A vicious firefight ensued. Avner's men were still outmanned but had better position. His men hit four more Islamo-Christian gunmen, wounding them by a nearby home. Avner's men remained hidden, now behind a small retaining wall next to the buildings.

A car door opened and one of the Apache crew members was shoved out. He had a knife sticking out of his neck and he was not moving.

Avner was infuriated and ordered his men to take the car. It was obvious now that someone was going to die. He had come too far and had seen too much to let these evil men do any more damage.

Three of his men were mutineers and military sharpshooters. They quickly brought the Humvee into view on a battlefield computer and found the four hostage takers and the remaining hostage in the car. His two teams brought their weapons to bear on the Humvee. Time was running out.

He gave the order.

CHAPTER EIGHTY: Operation Last Exodus—Fully Engaged

The next few moments were some of the fiercest Avner would see. Shots were fired from several positions and when it appeared the hostage takers were no longer moving, Avner's men moved to the Humvee.

"You have one more chance to release the hostage."

"Never! We will all die together!"

Tension gripped Avner. He'd been through so much these past few months and now this. It all came down to 16 dead terrorists in the street and 4 hostage takers.

Avner, exhausted but calm, stopped for a moment and prayed, a response unknown to him just a few short months ago.

"Lord God, I have absolutely no control over this. I pray for your wisdom and guidance."

The car, stopped cold in the street, remained in the sight of his shooters. The hostage was in the back seat, squeezed between two of the terrorists.

The moments ticked by.

Avner, needing a better assessment of what the situation was in the car, radioed Davidson.

"Can you get one of the smaller drones in here?"

"Copy that, we'll zip something to you in a moment."

Another technological marvel, the insect-sized drone appeared almost instantly. It hovered unseen and near the SUV, running video directly to Avner and his men's hand held devices.

The hostage was still alive, with the others inside. They had one weapon trained on the helo pilot. They were trapped and they knew it.

Suddenly the passenger's door opened. One of the hostage takers slowly emerged from the car, his hands extended in the air. His small machine gun was in the air but he was not acting aggressively.

"Lay it down and slowly go down on your knees." Avner's voice had the authority of command.

Just as he was about to kneel down, the driver of the car aimed and fired at him, hitting him square between the shoulder blades. He was down now, blood streaming out of the wounds in his back. There were three enemy soldiers, one hostage, and now 12 Israeli and Christian Zionists watching them.

"Can you guys get a bead on the three gunmen?" Avner whispered into his mic.

One by one, each of his men replied in the affirmative. There was no other choice.

"Ok, click once if you have a clear field of fire."

The first click came back... then a second, a third, until all 12 of his sharpshooters responded back.

"May God help us. Fire when ready."

"Engage!!"

The shooters opened up. The blasts blew out all the windows in the SUV. In a flash, it was over.

Avner led the team to the car. The helo pilot had taken two bullets, one to the shoulder and one to his neck, but was still alive.

The hostage takers were dead. The car was a mess. The weapons officer was still alive, though appeared to be in worse shape. Avner called in his field medical unit. Within minutes they appeared, stabilized the crewmembers, and were on the way to the hospital, just a block away.

Off in the distance, one of Davidson's drones picked up movement in an adjacent Jewish neighborhood. More than 2,500 Islamo-Christian forces had massed on the perimeter, preparing to move on the homes. Jewish residents were trapped with no apparent help in sight.

"We have the neighborhood surrounded and are ready to move in. Asking permission to engage," asked the Muslim commander to his superior.

"May Allah be with you," came the answer.

The battle group, comprised of members of the Nation of Islam, hundreds of volunteers from a local mosque, a squad of skinheads, and more than 500 self-described Christians prepared to burn the Jews out of their homes and force them into the open. It was a strange army to say the least but hatred of the Jews was a common bond.

"We are moving now."

The commander clicked his headset to notify a smaller attack team to move on the street. His troops had cordoned off the area now and there was no traffic moving in the residential area.

The Jewish residents were mostly blind as all phone lines and television feeds had been cut by the enemy. Cell phone towers had been taken down as well so there was little outbound communication. Local residents tried desperately to call out or use computing power were unsuccessful in doing so. They were sitting ducks, or so the Islamo-Christians believed.

Davidson's forces were about a mile away... the hospital and surrounding neighborhoods now under Israeli control. This new hotspot was not going down easily.

The Islamo-Christian forces slowly tightened the vice. This was a ten square block area with upscale homes, businesses, offices, more medical centers and two synagogues. Unknown to any of the opposing forces was that many of the local residents gathered in the synagogues, barricading themselves inside. Those fortunate enough to get out of their homes were scared, but for some reason everyone remained fairly calm.

The Islamo-Christian soldiers had acquired some rather exotic weapons including some flamethrowers, plastic explosives, and some heavy guns, some stolen from National Guard armories years before and some smuggled through the porous Mexican border tunnels.

Their commander, Glenallen Brown, was a former green beret and political radical, now an outspoken opponent of anything to do with Israel or Zionist thought.

He saw Zionism the same as apartheid, an old argument foisted upon Palestine by the Zionists decades before. Though not adopting a formal Muslim name, he saw his political and social aims the same as Islam and chose to spend his time with Muslims whenever he could.

Heavily decorated, his military record was stellar, having received the Silver Star and the many honors for bravery in the field. Fighting Islamic insurgents in the Philippines years before, he was captured, tortured, and then, once discharged refuted his American heritage and took up against America. He now saw common ground with those he used to fight.

His forces now had the neighborhoods squeezed in a vice and began going house to house to flush anyone out into the open. His special skills were quite pertinent as he had led troops in identical close fighting in the Philippines years before.

"When I give the signal, move into the first street of homes, you know the drill."

"Got it," answered his lieutenants, one by one.

Brown then put a call out to his intel team. He referred to them as his hawkeyes.

"Hawkeye 1, report in," he ordered.

"Hawkeye 1 here. Perimeter looks secure for...." Hawkeye 1 never finished his transmission for suddenly a huge blast rocked the entire area. Smoke and debris filled the sky.

"What the... ??"

"Hawkeye 1, what was that?"

There was no response.

"Hawkeye 2, report in," he yelled.

No response either. What he didn't know but would soon find out was that Avner's teams had penetrated his security shield and were moving fast into the firefight. The blast was from a small fast action tank which had taken out his three field leaders and virtually flattened a business building complex. He was now operating blind, his intel teams down.

Meanwhile, house to house fighting was heating up. Avner's teams were closing in on the Islamo-Christian forces and with their drones up and hovering over the battle zone, they could see who was where. Avner's electronic warfare specialist also emitted a signal to confuse the enemy while at the same time allowing his teams to remain connected to one another. The mini drones were performing beyond expectation.

His first squad found a group of invaders and hit them with all they had. Pouring small arms fire into a small group of homes, the homes burst into flames, flushing out the Muslims and their allies.

Now with more than 200 of the enemy exposed, Avner had to think fast and act faster. His instincts were to kill them all. But something else was operating deep within. Since he spoke fluent Arabic, he chose to try to get them to surrender. He pulled out a megaphone and addressed the enemy soldiers, who recognized they were surrounded.

"We have you surrounded. We wish you no further harm... nobody here wins. Please put down your weapons and we will spare you."

"No! We will fight to the death," the Muslim commander shouted back.

At that moment, several of the Jihadists reached into their shirts and pulled self detonating cords. The simultaneous explosions could be heard more than a quarter mile away.

Avner shielded his eyes as the flames flew from the Muslims. Fortunately for Avner and his troops, they were well shielded from the force of the blast but several local residents trying to flee were hit by flying shrapnel. Dozens lay wounded in the street. Avner's troops began their advance, going house to house now. As they cleared out each home, they left at least one of their own to guard the home and protect the civilians inside.

Brown's troops began their retreat out of this neighborhood. Avner still had about 500 of his team spread out and advancing.

Slowly, Avner and his forces turned the tide and the battle began to slow. A few hours later, the streets returned to a peaceful quiet. But the damage was real enough.

The firefight had been intense and bloody, but the threat was neutralized by quick acting Israelis and Christian Zionists. Another 500 Jews lay dead either in their homes or in the streets. Hundreds of Muslims and enemy Christians lay dead in between houses, on lawns, and on the streets of the local business districts.

Other battles like this continued to rage in various parts of the city.

Things quieted down for now, but a strange phenomenon began. Busses, trains, and cars appeared almost out of nowhere, filled with Christian drivers, soldiers, and their Jewish passengers. *Operation Last Exodus* to LAX was now in full effect. Almost as if drawn by some invisible spiritual beacon, thousands, then tens of thousands of Jews began rolling to the airport.

The corridors began to clear.

Chapter 81

Financial Collapse

The press picked up the action in Los Angeles and around the nation. The unstable situation created tremors around the world. The first indicator was a huge drop in Asian stock markets. The economic virus spread—Europe felt the next shockwaves. That morning the Dow opened down more than 2,500 points. It was a mystery as to why the markets were so slow to respond to the disturbances. But once it began, experts wondered if there was any way to stop it.

This was just what the markets didn't need as other economic indicators had begun signaling trouble as well. Oil skyrocketed through $300 a barrel while gold flew through the $3,000 barrier and many brokerage houses began watching as their complex network of investments dissolve. Stocks retreated to levels not seen in decades. Within hours, all the indicators were going in the wrong direction and the situation accelerated.

With the economy rapidly moving toward the brink, inflation indicators, in check for years finally responded to the massive amounts of debt the U.S. faced. Inching upward, it quickly reached a gallop. The nation teetered on the edge of a major meltdown. The first signs of local domestic trouble were seen in a run on a Bank of America in San Diego. It began late in the afternoon.

With stunning speed, panic set in as frightened depositors swarmed bank after bank. Police were powerless to stop the bank runs. Street gangs then got into the action and began robbing the customers as they left the banks. Random gunfights broke out all over the city.

In pockets, it was beginning to look like an insurrection and a complete breakdown of law and order. San Francisco followed Los Angeles and the major Jewish population centers as law enforcement left their respective departments and their brethren left theirs further north.

Within two hours of the bank runs came news that bands of thieves, reacting to a web story of food shortages, stormed a large supermarket to steal food. Next to go was bottled water. Alcohol and tobacco products (always good black market bets), and drugs of all kinds were next. Local residents caught the fever and followed the thieves into the store. They cleaned out the store's pharmacy. When police arrived, the damage was done. There was little they could do. The looters vanished into the night. They stripped the market clean by 10 p.m.

This lethal combination of circumstances brought out street gangs who offered their muscle at a price. This taxed police to their limits as gun battles raged all over LA, Orange County, and San Francisco and the Bay Area. Both the Bay Bridge and the Golden Gate were taken over by street thugs who demanded extortion money from passengers going both directions. Again, law enforcement was powerless as about half of their numbers had joined Christian Zionist and Jewish troops. Some joined their enemies.

Almost overnight, paper money gave way to a barter system where tobacco, alcohol, medicines, diapers, virtually any kind of commodity became currency for other goods and services. Gold climbed to $4,000 an ounce within days.

Guns, ammunition, and other weapons commanded steep prices. Keeping the peace was virtually impossible and any National Guard lagged. Besides many of the Guardsmen were deployed on foreign soil, leaving the units compromised. Others split off to join Jewish resistance or their enemies.

✡ ✡ ✡ ✡ ✡ ✡

In an open field in Queens, New York, teams of Israeli paratroopers loaded up into three Chinook Ch-46's and 47's with an Apache Ah-64 and a V-22 Osprey troop/gunship for backup, for the quick trip to JFK and the airport control tower. Each transport chopper held 75 soldiers supporting the ground operations already underway at airport. Thousands more Christian Zionist defenders would soon follow and would secure the perimeter of the airport. The team commander checked in with the control tower at JFK.

"We are ready to go."

"Copy that. We see you on our screens. It's time to move." Mimi's voice carried authority and anticipation.

As the Chinooks climbed into the sky, mechanized units began to converge from all directions on the airport. The vehicles expertly hidden, all assembled over the past year and a half in Dogface's and Yanit's warehouses were finally turned loose in the streets. Those units were manned by both Israelis and Christian Zionists, mostly defecting American military personnel, working together at long last. Loaded with crack paratroops, they set down the choppers just yards from the control tower.

And for now, Shabibi and Farouk remained in the safe house under the protection of close friends.

> From the Book of Job
> Chapter 38 Verse 25
>
> As often as the trumpet sounds he says, 'Aha!'
> And he scents the battle from afar,
> And the thunder of the captains and the war cry.

Chapter 82

The Battle for Brooklyn

Christian Zionist troops worked with Israeli teams to secure the outer boundaries of the airport. Within a few hours the troops had secured the airport and established a perimeter around the control tower. They moved to control all inbound routes to the facility—streets, bridges, and railroads.

The dreams and visions of Jonathan Roberts, Michael Shapiro, Shoshana Bat Levi, Dogface Vicenzo and Yanit Silver, had finally come to fruition. Their first objective was to control all inbound and outbound traffic from the main airport roads and bridges to the airport.

They were now airborne. The Israeli commander called out, "Ok, you know the drill. We put down about 50 yards from the control tower. We are placing men on top of the terminals and will have snipers placed throughout the area. Once we are out of the chopper, we will surround the building and blow the doors. We need everyone inside alive. I want you to look at each other because your lives and the lives of your fellows here depend on one another."

The choppers hovered over the airport after the short flight. The gunships hovered nearby looking for any inbound threats. So far, there was nothing.

The Chinooks came in low and slow. The ramps opened in the back and the paratroops ran out the doors. All in all, 5 of the huge troop carriers landed one by one. Each carrying 75 soldiers disgorged their men. With lightening speed, they had the building surrounded and were ready to assault the tower.

They expected stiff resistance but encountered little as nobody expected an airport takeover. They were joined by mutineering Army troops from nearby military bases where many of them commandeered other helicopters and headed to JFK.

Mimi's numbers swelled by the hour. The Israelis were now firmly in control of the outer ring of the airport. It took more than 10,000 to take and hold the facility.

Meanwhile, thousands of troops and other defenders lined the expressways, streets, and access roads leading to the terminal. Pro-Zionist forces now controlled the trains and busses, though the word wasn't widely broadcast just yet. There were still hotspots around the greater New York area and the Jews remained largely afraid to come to the surface. The window of time would be short. The word spread to the Christian friends of the Jews, largely through the ministry of Jonathan Roberts' lieutenants. In turn, the Jews learned of the escape routes and the safe houses.

With Israelis in control of the tower, the air traffic controllers diverted all inbound flights to Newark, La Guardia, or Boston. They offered no resistance, and as it turned out were friendly to the cause. Miraculously, there were few casualties at the airport as the strike teams had used the element of surprise to their advantage.

Christian Zionist forces took up defensive positions in support of the Jews. They occupied neighborhoods, business parks, and controlled the roadways and were working on the train systems. But opposing forces were digging in too and open urban warfare was about to erupt on a grand scale, something not seen on the streets of America for almost 200 years. The American infrastructure was about to collapse. A critical battle for iconic Jewish neighborhoods was about to begin.

The next major area of concern to the defense efforts was the Borough of Brooklyn, home to nearly a half million Jews who had lived there for more than 150 years. It was a gathering place for the Chasidim but in the past 30 years, a rapidly growing contingent of Muslims had moved in and was causing havoc for the Jews.

Jewish neighborhoods in this city included Washington Heights, Williamsburg, Midwood, Crown Heights, Sheepshead Bay and Brighton Beach among others, but these were the key areas and housed close to half of Brooklyn's Jews. Protecting and defending Brooklyn and these neighborhoods was critical to the success of the operation. But it wasn't going to be easy.

Although there were certain areas within Brooklyn where Muslims and Jews lived in reasonable peace, it was also home to many radicalized Pakistani Muslims. Recent experience taught the Jewish residents not to discuss such issues as religion or politics as those topics were flashpoints to the peace of the community. So, the residents lived at a relative calm with their neighbors, exercising restraint wherever possible, essentially hiding their collective heads in the sand.

However, recent Muslim arrivals seemed to coincide with increasing street beatings, vandalism against Jewish property, public denouncements, demonstrations, and intimidation tactics. These Muslims tended to be from other religious strongholds including members from well-known terror groups such as the Islamic Brotherhood, Islamic Jihad, and Al-Qaida. They were more confrontive with their Jewish neighbors.

When one Islamic leader attempted to declare Sharia law in the area, though he had no real power to do so, tensions jumped, even among those of non-religious backgrounds. His followers decided to enforce what they could and Brooklyn quaked in the increasingly threatening environment.

And here, too, Rachman had his allies.

"Salaam alaikum," the Imam greeted the commander in the mosque.

"Alaikum Salaam," came the response.

"How are the plans coming?" the Imam controlling this sector of Brooklyn needed to know.

"We are nearly ready. The Independence Day parade was just the prelude. I estimate more than 10,000 in our little army, mixed with Christians who see the world as we do. The Zionists are in for a surprise. We will make them pay for their crimes both here and in Palestine."

As Islamo-Christian plans to target the Chassidic community neared completion, loyal followers volunteered in droves. To join the jihad meant glory, both here on earth and in the heavenlies if they died in the line of duty.

Leaders stockpiled weapons, smuggled in all matter of guns, explosive devices, and other war tools over the Canadian border. Logistics specialists hid the weapons in several remote rural areas including acreage secretly purchased through friendly third parties complete with delivery plans to their various drop-off points. By the time they completed their actions, the battle would be concluded and the Jewish community would be eradicated, the trail to find them cold. If they died in the action, so much the better as dying for the cause was the ultimate service to Allah. Taking Jews was a bonus.

Civil authorities, unwilling to interfere in religious matters between communities expressed platitudes of empathy for oppressed minorities and support for multi-culturalism but did nothing to stop the Islamic strong-armed tactics. Since multi-cultural communities only work when all sides decide to let others live in peace, there was bound to be trouble.

The first wave of attacks planned for two neighborhoods near the Chassidic worship center, began with a seemingly random confrontation in a nearby park. A young Islamic woman began screaming that she had been attacked by two Yeshiva students from the nearby synagogue.

It didn't take long for the story to spread and mutate throughout the borough and when it did, emotions spilled over. The Imam stationed his troops throughout the area, prepared to initiate the offensive as soon as the synagogue filled to its normal numbers.

It was a Shabbat evening and the sun began its slow descent in the western sky. The faithful began arriving in small groups until the synagogue received its full contingent of Friday night worshippers. The young men arrived in traditional Chassidic clothing with their long black frocks, hats, and trousers set off by their white shirts.

Just then, an angry mob of 100 or so young Muslims formed several blocks down from the Center. Another group, now forming about 250 in number, soon joined them. The march toward the Center was picking up steam.

"Things are going as planned. They don't suspect anything," the commander radioed his superior in the mosque. Their numbers grew.

"Our numbers have now reached close to 1000, we are armed and ready to go," the commander continued. Other battalion-sized groups began combing the local neighborhoods, awaiting the signal for the main attack.

"Pick your moment," the Imam answered.

The commander positioned his attackers across the street and on rooftops around the neighborhood. They were well-placed. If anyone noticed them, there had been no reaction. As the service approached, the crowd grew larger.

The first action came against a small jewelry store a block away from the Center. Though more a diversion, it was meant to inflict enough damage to business infrastructure so as to be taken seriously. About 20 of the young Muslims broke the store's window and jumped inside the small business to do what damage they could. Not much merchandise was visible since the owner had closed for the weekend. Within moments, a huge fireball knocked out the remaining glass while the building exploded in flames. It was a classic diversionary tactic.

As the building burned, another small knot of the mob broke away. They headed to the parked cars up and down the street and began setting them on fire. Within minutes, dozens of cars burned and as they did, the gas tanks exploded, taking more and more cars with them. Eastern Parkway looked like a war zone.

By this time, the crowd, now with visible weapons drawn grew to more than 2,500 and headed towards the Jewish worship center. Inside were more than 250 worshippers, still oblivious to the events just outside their door.

The mob fanned out like a gang before a street fight. They carried guns, knives, and bats and incendiary devices. They torched business after business, with an efficiency that pleased the Imam and the commander. They expected no resistance tonight.

But not far from the heart of Brooklyn a mixed force of Christian Zionist fighters and Israeli commandos was heading their way. The defenders headed toward the Muslim insurgents. A colossal street fight lay just ahead.

Islamo-Christian forces continued to gain strength in other areas. Mosques and supporting churches became recruiting grounds for them. They would soon be heard from soon around the city.

From the Hand of Rav Shau
Epistle to the Romans
Chapter 12:6-8

Since we have gifts that differ according to the grace given to us, each of us is to exercise them accordingly: if prophecy, according to the proportion of his faith; if service, in his serving; or he who teaches, in his teaching; or he who exhorts, in his exhortation; he who gives, with liberality; he who leads, with diligence; he who shows mercy, with cheerfulness.

From the Pen of Shlomo—King Solomon the Wise
Proverbs 11:14

Where there is no guidance (leadership) the people fall, but in abundance of counselors there is victory.

Chapter 83

On Wings of Eagles

It felt good to be on the stick again.

The 787 felt solid and safe underneath him. The cargo section was loaded. Three doctors and nurses sat in first class for takeoff along with Special Forces trained for urban combat. Once airborne, medical staff would head back and prepare the cabin for any medical cases. The soldiers continued to review battle plans. The customs teams prepared their computers to process all the inbound immigrants. Flight 777 was ready and Dayle Johannson was grinning from ear to ear. Months and months of preparation were about to pay off.

"Tower, Flight 777, *Operation Last Exodus,* awaiting your go."

"777 Operation Last Exodus, you are cleared for takeoff. God speed, my friend, may His grace be with you."

Then Johannson winked at his co-pilot and gave her the thumbs up. In the right seat sat Avishag Bat-Levy, Shoshana's youngest daughter. She was fresh out of flight school and anxious to serve.

Behind them was the first wave of rescue planes. Flight plans called for one takeoff per minute, allowing the jet wash to clear enough for the next flight until all 80 of the first wave of rescue planes were in the air. For the next hour and a half from Ben Gurion Airport in Tel Aviv and five other air fields around Israel, the same scenario was unfolding. Within two hours more than 400 aircraft would be airborne.

Johannson knew this was their only shot. He and his pilots had to make this work. Affairs on the ground were as complete as they could be. Conditions were hot on the ground in all four corridors. They were at the point of no return. He and the various crews received information from Israeli intelligence about the situation on the ground in the various rescue corridors.

He had more than 4,000 men and women under his command now, pilots and flight crews from all over the world focused on one thing-get to the Jews who wanted to come to Israel.

With engines winding up, the 787 leaped forward, straining to take to the air. This airplane wanted to fly. This latest version of a long line of workhorses from Boeing was now well into the maturity phase of its production run. Though it had some initial problems during its development and flight test years, once the plane took to the skies, it blew away the competition.

Johannson's aircraft began its long roll down the runway and at 7,000 feet, pulled the stick back. The plane began its graceful climb into the early morning sky, her wings flexing gently like a graceful bird. Tel Aviv was quiet below, the sea sparkling below like a field of diamonds.

The rescue fleet was retrofitted with the latest electronic countermeasures installed by the Israeli Air Force. The planes could handle almost any inbound threats including shoulder fired missiles and something more fired from the air.

The lead pilot and commander of the entire operation felt a warm satisfaction that in about 12 hours he'd be on the ground loading the first American Jews on his plane. Each flight carried two crews. Specially constructed crew quarters built for this mission included showers, bunks, and a separate galley to keep the crews fresh. This would help minimize any disruptions or delays. Plans called for the inbound crews to go below decks to the rest area and sleep most of the way back, leaving time for a meal, a shower, and some planning.

The medical section included room for 10 beds and another 10 special recliners. Ground crews trained for quick turnaround times. If all went well with the fleet, there would be no more than a 30 minute wait time to refuel, run preflights, and board. Cargo was all specially marked and prepared for quick unloading and reloading to whatever battle zone required it.

The plane reached its first cruising altitude of 40,000 feet and the crew settled in for the flight. Johannson looked out his windows and noted the twin JSF's escorting them up. Airspace was safe here but who knew what awaited them as they approached the U.S.?

Within two hours, all 400 planes were in the air, a flying armada capable of flying about 150,000 Jewish immigrants home to Israel in the first wave. Another 50 aircraft would be airborne from various international capitals as backup planes, should mechanical problems be discovered.

Operation Last Exodus was now fully operational.

Chapter 84

Eastern Corridor–
Mimi Takes Command

NYC found itself in the throes of a collapsing infrastructure. The city was paralyzed, the surrounding communities ground to a halt. There were reports of backed up sewer systems, malfunctioning electrical systems, water, and other utilities all having gone down in the past few hours.

Parts of the sprawling city now looked like an armed camp, with 100,000 Israelis moving on the airport and surrounding streets, tunnels, and trains and subways. Tens of thousands of armed and unarmed Christian Zionists were arriving by the hour.

Mimi Sullivan was in firm command of the Eastern Corridor command. She now had the chance to prove her mettle. When the pre-signal came in, she had just returned from her brother's wedding in California. The last few weeks were a blur. She slipped into her uniform, side arm in her holster, and Uzi nearby. Though the Uzi was fading as a weapon of choice, she liked the weapon's size and handling. She knew it well.

The once rebellious teen, now a freshly graduated civil and geological/soil engineer with a passion for people would now have the chance to demonstrate her leadership skills. She knew and understood the tremendous weight on her shoulders.

Local forces loyal to Mimi prepared for a six to twelve week occupation of the streets plus rescue efforts. Protection depended on help from their Christian friends. The latest calculations run by Shapiro and the Agency estimated rescue traffic at about 294,000 passengers a week from JFK. She didn't know if she had that much time but she couldn't concern herself with such matters. She had a job to do.

Mimi powered up her own laptop. It was a lightweight affair weighing less than one pound and capable of handling just about anything thrown at it. She and her support staff had a crack team of fellow Israelis ready to take up the defense and rescue of the eastern seaboard's Jewish population.

Battles raged around the city, and former American forces now joined to the IDFA were busy everywhere. The situation on the ground was intensifying by the minute. Mimi was located in the command center—

one of Dogface's warehouses about a mile from the airport. The electronic maps and visuals filled the walls. All manner of security was in place to guard inbound and outbound communications and the flow of people.

Ephraim and his teams, fresh from the nation's capital, were busy with other business, namely control of New York's essential transportation services. Finished with his work in D.C. he turned up in New York to lead efforts to ensure Israeli control of the Metropolitan Transportation Authority and making sure New York's Jews had safe passage on trains and busses to the airport. Mimi's troops were working to clear the streets and create open passageways to JFK.

Ephraim's team prepared to take control of city services. He discovered that more than 60% of the subway's operators were behind him and the efforts to help the Jews. They would find a way to manage the other 40%. For those wishing to leave, they were granted that option. Fortunately, he faced no clear opposition as Israeli troops and their sympathizers stormed the command centers to wrest control. Many came from the transit authority itself, either outspoken believers or hidden for years in fear of their jobs and their lives. It didn't hurt the more than 60% of the city's key service providers, police, fire, and transportation workers threw in their lot with the *Operation Last Exodus*.

Hundreds of drivers appeared to drive the busses needed to provide rapid transit to the airport. Combined with control now asserted over the trains and subways, Israeli forces were slowly gaining ground and control of local transportation. But there were still battles to be fought.

✡ ✡ ✡ ✡ ✡ ✡

It was 3 a.m. The first train prepared to move out toward JFK anticipating its first few stops before it made it to the airport. Without warning, as the driver was preparing to step into pilot's seat, she was spun around by a homeless person, or at least she thought so. So quick was the move, that she was shoved into the small compartment, quickly bound and gagged, then made to sit on the floor.

The 'mugger' turned out to be a female Israeli soldier, trained for this very mission. She quickly dropped a two-tone code into her radio and her fellow team members, pulling out their weapons, stepped onto the platform and assumed their positions. She was joined by several Christian Zionists, recruited by the Roberts Network. Placing three soldiers in each car, they hoped to fend off any efforts to redirect the train.

"Go, Go, Go!"… came the order from the team's commander who was located in the front car, guarding the pilot's cabin. The empty train headed

CHAPTER EIGHTY-FOUR: *Eastern Corridor—Mimi Takes Command*

out to its first stop to gather up fleeing Jews attempting to escape who had gathered at Howard Beach Station, Sutphin Blvd., and the Long Island Railroad (LIRR). They needed to keep these trains under control and running through the city. Many New Yorkers would have to walk today and their Jewish neighbors would take the train to the airport—that was if anyone was willing enough to brave the streets.

At the same time, Muslim and Christian insurgents moved on the Long Island Railroad Jamaica Station link to the Airtrain. Islamo-Christian planners believed if this train service were disrupted, it would cause havoc with the escaping Jews. And right they were. However, Zionist forces were prepared.

A squad of 50 Israelis and their supporters rushed the first train out of JFK that morning. The first of several running gun battles began shortly after dawn. And quickly, pro-Israel Christians and their Israeli allies moved on the subway system and any trains they could commandeer.

The opposition was busy too as the battle for New York spread. As in Los Angeles and other major cities around the country, loyalty was at a premium. Many Bible-believing Christians, true supporters of Israel and the Jews, were peeling off in stupendous numbers in New York. Joining with their fellow believers from the military and from the civilian population, they began building a formidable army to protect the soon departing émigrés.

Supporters and defenders created safe houses in all five boroughs, Long Island, and outside the city. The believers were at the vanguard of this new human shield. Rather than hiding behind innocent civilians in their quest to bring death and destruction as their Muslim enemies had done for years, they stepped in front of the chosen, providing the protective shield. Like Le Chambon, the tiny community in World War II France, less of this was planned or organized as it may have seemed These Christians who saw this as their Biblical duty stepped up and assumed their rightful place as the Righteous of the Nations.

Bands of defenders formed all over the city, and now reports circulated that their enemies were targeting the subways, bent on taking as much Jewish life as possible. The subway was important to the Israeli defenders because it represented a crucial transportation link out of the city and to the airport.

Knots of young Islamo-Christians headed underground. Shia and Sunni, NOI, Skinheads, along with the more radical sects put aside their differences in pursuit of their common enemy. They were armed, dangerous, and were not afraid to die. Their first target was Grand Central Terminal.

The first reported skirmish took the passengers and subway workers in Grand Central by surprise. Gun battles erupted all over the terminal.

About 2500 Islamo-Christian forces were inside and barricaded near Grand Central Terminal. Outside, Israeli and their Christian Zionist allies numbered about 1,000 but their numbers were swelling by the hour. Innocent civilians were helpless, caught in the crossfire. The shooters targeted passengers as they disembarked the subway cars, mowing down dozens of innocents in the process. There appeared to be no way out.

✡ ✡ ✡ ✡ ✡ ✡

Just then, a rumbling sound came from well below the ground. As it grew in intensity near 42nd Street, the ground at street level seemed to sway, buckle, and then cave in. The noise was deafening. A coordinated set of explosions, timed for maximum destruction, hit five trains within seconds of one another.

Mirroring the London and Madrid subway attacks decades before, the tracks and trains lifted into the air in a horrible display of twisted metal and human suffering. A tremendous amount of smoke and debris rained down on those inside caught in the maelstrom. Islam had struck again, this time at the heart of New York's subway system.

✡ ✡ ✡ ✡ ✡ ✡

Just then a transmission came in from another field commander inside the subway tunnels. His words were broken and garbled.

"We've got... situation... here. Gra... five... many d...."

Mimi shouted, "Say again! Say again!" You're breaking up. Retransmit." She had the transmission on the squawk box. All of the monitors turned on at once to listen to the exchange.

"Five trains hit, hundreds dead, we are pinned down," came back the voice. Apparently, most communication was out in the tunnels, the lights as well.

Just then, news of the Brooklyn attacks reached the command center.

✡ ✡ ✡ ✡ ✡ ✡

Five trains now lay in ruins, the screams of the wounded reached the street. The traps were strategically laid as Islamo-Christian soldiers erected more makeshift barricades to hide themselves. The destruction was horrifying. Two tunnels lay in ruins and the stations collapsed. The Israelis and their allies were trapped below, several dead and wounded. Survivors had to quickly shake off the effects of the blasts while their hunters closed in.

CHAPTER EIGHTY-FOUR: *Eastern Corridor—Mimi Takes Command*

Mimi's situation boards lit up... simultaneous attacks being reported all over the city.

Along one of the tracks lay the wreckage of the A, B, and C line trains along with two others. These trains carried thousands of New Yorkers at the morning rush hour and now the trains lay in ruins, blocking the tracks and creating havoc for rescuers.

As firefighters arrived the Islamo-Christian forces began picking off the rescue workers just as they had in Dallas and the other cities during the Kristallnacht II synagogue attacks. They meant business and were here to prey on their victims. Life meant nothing.

"Get some help down here now!"

"We're coming!"

Smoke and debris filled the air but the Israelis and Christian Zionist soldiers poured in from several entrances. They took up positions on the staircases and behind some of the wreckage... enough so that they began to return fire.

✡ ✡ ✡ ✡ ✡ ✡

"We are under siege!!!" The transmission pierced through the other noise in the command center.

"What is your situation?"

"We are trapped by the Chassidic Center, 770 Eastern Parkway," came back the voice. Mimi had teams in Brooklyn but most everything seemed under control until that moment.

"Get me Yosi," she barked.

Yosi Abraham, the Brooklyn team leader came on the line.

"We are heavily here."

"What do you have?"

"We've got several Fast Attack Vehicles and about 1,000 in the battle group with me but we have other assets nearby."

"Yosi, I need you to hold at all costs. We're getting some support for you. We have assets not far from you... hold on!!!!"

Mimi stopped for a moment, composing herself in the middle of terrible chaos. She found herself uttering a short prayer which startled her, measuring her breathing.

"God, if you are there, please help us and help our soldiers. PLEASE!!!"

Her commanders were ready and awaiting orders here in the command center. Thankfully, Ephraim had ensured that communications were functioning fine and were as secure as they could be. She clicked on and got Yosi back.

"We're on it... We've got air support coming your way— inbound V-22 and an Apache." Yosi looked up to the sky, hoping, hoping....

"We're looking at a battalion sized force here. We're encountering return fire, but we are taking back some ground.... We are taking a lot of fire... this was well planned."

"Ok, keep me informed," she answered. She turned her attention back to the airport and the arrival of the planes. The first wave was just minutes away.

✡ ✡ ✡ ✡ ✡ ✡

"What are you seeing?" she asked her airport commander.

"The refugees are coming in. We have opened up all of the main roadways coming in. Supporting Christians are arriving every minute and the deserting service men are bringing a lot of their own firepower. We are pushing out the perimeter."

"Good, very, very good. Get me the Air Traffic Controllers," she ordered her communications officer, Hunni Lieberman. All of her air traffic controllers were in place, but there was still much to do.

"Air Traffic is online now, Mimi."

"Where are our planes?"

"Inbound, about five minutes out. We have 120 aircraft inbound, so within a few minutes we'll begin landing about 2 a minute, one on each runway. Then, in about two hours we will have the first contingent out of here."

She looked at some of the camera feeds on the wall. The tent cities were pretty much complete... sufficient for the quick stay they expected. A little hardship would be a small price to pay while they waited. *But no worries*, she thought. *They will be well provisioned for the short stay.*

The airport was now filled-more than 50,000 desperate people crammed into every inch of space awaiting their ticket to safety. The tents would hold upwards of a quarter-million. It looked like Woodstock. If the locals could hold out for just a short time, an orderly departure could be assured.

The airport was secure for now. Loyal Air Traffic Controllers and their Israeli counterparts assumed full control of all inbound and outbound traffic. The growing army in and outside the airport spread out and controlled all roads, bridges, and thoroughfares near the airport.

Mossad intelligence nailed it. The Roberts' militias were quick to learn, were mostly in place and doing their jobs. She knew that more than two million Christian Zionists in the East were fighting to help the Jews reach Israel. She and Roberts had met a few times to discuss plausible and possible

CHAPTER EIGHTY-FOUR: Eastern Corridor—Mimi Takes Command

scenarios and from his estimates (not far off from Mossad's and the Jewish Agency's) she pretty much knew what to expect.

She checked with her Air Traffic Controllers again to get a sense of where the inbound aircraft were. It was nervous time until the first aircraft landed.

Thousands of refugees packed the airport, with hundreds of thousands more right behind them. A growing issue now was crowd control. Would the refugees be willing to wait? The massive tent city on and around the airport grounds would have to work for a short time. If anything went wrong, they had no contingency plans.

"Mimi! Mimi! We see them! Here they come!"

"Oh, thank God," she whispered. Indeed the first three aircraft, two 747's and one 787 were just now lining up for final approach. They would soon be on the ground. More refugees were coming too, carrying little more than one or two bags with them. Many carried important family documents, escaping with whatever cash, silver, or gold they could carry or that their neighbors gave them.

She called a quick meeting. It was down to tightly-executed tactics now. Most everything was in place, due to the meticulous and well thought out planning in the months leading up to this event. The planners saw it coming. Once the synagogue attacks and the demonstrations on the 4th of July grabbed the headlines, it became pretty obvious that time was short.

Roberts himself now joined the discussions, albeit from the Jerusalem Command Center. His military experience in the air as well as in cyberspace would prove to be an invaluable link in the process.

Also online were Shoshana and Ephraim. They were running the cyber side of the operation.

"Boker Tov everyone," (good morning), Mimi said, her accent more pronounced than before. It always came out in stressful times. Her confidence was sharp, she felt in command.

"We have secured the major airports in the area (referring to John F. Kennedy and La Guardia, as well as Newark across the Hudson River) and many of our anticipated friends are joining us—increasing by the hour. Our first refugees, or should I call them the 'new pioneers' have reached JFK. Our first inbound flights will be here within a few minutes. Our field teams are now in operation on the streets and in the neighborhoods. We've got the Eastern Seaboard divided into subzones each with a commander forming small corridors of safety to get the people out. Yanit Silver and Sal Vicenzo are online with us. Are you ready with your report?" Yanit spoke first.

"Yes. We've got pretty much everything in place. Most of our work is done. I did a sweep of all our sub-regional commanders this morning... all the mechanized units are deployed on the streets and neighborhoods. We're still working on more fuel supply but we have enough for about 10 weeks of action. Dogface is here with me... he's been working with the ports and the customs people. All of them have held their end of the bargain."

"We've gained control of the roadways and the expressways here in New York. Our demolition teams have most of the major bridges and tunnels mined and ready to blow if we need to do so. But that's a last resort... we don't want to do any more damage than we need to do," explained Dogface.

"We are picking up some street intelligence that skirmishes are breaking out all over New York, Boston, Philadelphia, and the DC-Baltimore areas. Increasing numbers of Jews are disappearing... virtually vanishing overnight and we believe are headed to the airports now or are hiding underground until transportation can be arranged. We're also receiving a goodly amount of human traffic at the dumps. We have reason to believe that loyal Christians have been active in this area and have secured most of the Jews."

And one by one, each of the street teams checked in. The subways were critical and with several lines down, it would complicate things further.

The camera went back to Mimi, dressed in her camouflage uniform with her hair swept and pulled back and under her beret. She now had full command of the entire Eastern Seaboard with more than 100 teams like hers in warehouses all over the East. Her leadership impact was immediate... cool under pressure, firm, yet willing to listen to others as the events unfolded.

She was operating true to the Israeli style of command, allowing, even encouraging troops in the field to improvise and make field decisions. She brought up the map of New York City to illustrate what they had secured and what still needed to be brought under control. Everything was color coded with information streaming in 'real time.' Communications specialists were running in and out constantly to bring new information on street battles or movement of the authorities. Yanit spoke next.

"We've got all the major expressways under control, though there are still some areas of resistance. We're encountering some Islamo-Christian forces forming in the mosques and madrassas. They control a couple of train stations but we are rushing forces to counter them, but only in the interest of keeping the trains safe for Jewish travel. We have Friendlies at all the stops so we feel we have the upper hand. So far, we've been able to contain the enemy but they are forming more and more battle teams. We

CHAPTER EIGHTY-FOUR: Eastern Corridor—Mimi Takes Command

are pretty spread out but our Christian Zionist friends are stepping in to fight too."

Mimi broke in, "I've just checked with our ATC's. The first planes are landing now. Each plane can take some medical cases. I'm told we have about 200 infirm, disabled, elderly in our first group. Thankfully we have those hospital planes coming in too. We have two C-17's inbound as well."

This last issue was particularly sensitive to her. She knew that the mentally challenged, aged, and sick were particularly vulnerable, as they could not defend themselves. The C-17's would go a long way towards taking care of the medical cases.

"We are going to land one every couple of minutes or so. Once they are on the ground, our ground crews will refuel... stock the planes up, and begin the escorting. We have assets on the ground and around the airport so we are as secure as we can be right now. Thankfully we have medical and care-giving personnel in place as well."

Her voice had taken on a hoarse quality in the past few days as she had had little sleep and was in constant meetings with her staff. She felt an urge to smoke, but it quickly passed as she focused her attention on the briefing.

"I know rumors are circulating that we are negotiating to purchase several cruise ships to transport them, but still nothing. Though it would be efficient to transport thousands at a time in ships, it would make the ships sitting ducks on the water, unless they were clearly marked with the hospital ship markings and even then the Islamic enemy had never shown anything but disdain for the helpless.

"I worry about another Leon Klinghoffer," Mimi said, recalling one of the more infamous Islamic terror attacks years before. After radical Islamists, led by the infamous terrorist Abu Nadal, had commandeered the Achille Loro, a cruise ship, wheelchair-bound passenger, Leon Klinghoffer, was shot and then dumped overboard with his wheelchair. It redefined the term 'heinous crime.' The Israelis understood these types of crimes... the Olympic athletes in 1972, the Entebbe story, numerous bus bombings in the Homeland, the list just went on and on.

The phones in the command center continued to receive inbound communication. Yosi's brigade was dug in and now began its counterattack.

✡ ✡ ✡ ✡ ✡ ✡

"The V-22 and an Apache are here now and is providing some close air support. The Chassidic center is surrounded and the enemy is moving around the flanks... they have a good part of the neighborhood surrounded," Yosi spoke into his radio.

"Ok, what are they bringing to the fight?" Mimi asked.

"Some of our scouts saw AK-47s, a lot of rifles, and we're hearing a good number of RPG's," he answered. "I also see some Humvees—loaded with machine guns."

"Ok, I can see our troops on the monitors. We have to roll up their left if we can. Get your guys over to the small shopping center and then move out. I've got some armored vehicles inbound... they are just a few blocks from you. Hold on!"

"We see them now... they're moving quickly."

"Good, see if you can flush the enemy out into the open... and get them to surrender... I don't want any more bloodshed than we need."

The Islamo-Christian soldiers re-opened the attack against the synagogue but as they did they were met by a surprise as defending gunmen placed on the rooftops of several surrounding buildings answered back. The defenders then poured a steady stream of fire down on the invaders but since they were undermanned, all they could do at this point was try to delay the enemy. Slowly, the 2,500 enemy fighters closed in on the Chassidic Center, now about 200 yards out. Inside, the hundreds of worshippers huddled together in fear, some nearing panic. Snipers manned the windows and the roof.

As the defenders closed ranks, the armored vehicles approached the center. The firefight gained in intensity with shooting now breaking out all around the building and surrounding structures. Flames leapt out of a mini mall near the center. Just then, the Islamo-Christians moved towards the synagogue.

The vehicles, manned by former U.S. Military soldiers, moved into position. Gunners using night vision goggles spotted several enemy soldiers and opened fire, taking down about 50 fighters. The Islamo-Christian forces answered with a torrent of hot lead.

"I'm hit, I'm hit!" screamed one of the gunners. His mates pulled him down to safety and while doing so, the enemy continued its attempt to take the Chassidic center. Yosi, now alarmed but staying calm, redirected the vehicle around the corner.

At this point, about 500 of the enemy were poised to storm the building. Their commander knew as did the soldiers that this was now a suicide mission as there would be no way for them to escape. With the doors locked and barred, entrance would not be easy.

As they approached the door a second time, they were met with a hail of small arms fire, the first wave of them cut down near the entrance. A hundred or so of them closed in on the back of the facility but were met with shooters placed in the windows. The enemy pitched several hand grenades through the windows. Moments later, several explosions were heard inside. The second floor was in danger of being engulfed by flames.

The fighting's intensity increased. Israeli and Christian Zionists had several smaller units pinned down in a nearby apartment complex and realized that some of this was going to be either house to house or even room to room. They had several apartment buildings surrounded but the Islamo Christian forces had already taken the building. Things were happening so quickly now that the ground commander realized he had several battles on his hands.

"Yosi, what's the situation?" Mimi asked.

"We've got about 500 of them surrounding the center. It's getting hot here," he answered.

Just then, Mimi's chief of staff came up.

"The first planes are landing now!" she said.

"Ok, the rest?"

"Inbound, we can see them all on the screens... we'll have more than 125 planes on the ground within the hour."

Mimi breathed a sigh of relief. At least part of her plan was working.

✡ ✡ ✡ ✡ ✡ ✡

The moments ticked by. A short lull engulfed the combatants. Just then, the sound of rotors could be heard overhead of the combatants.

"I see the V-22's about a mile out. They should be there in a moment or two... hang on," Mimi shouted, agonizing with her teams on the ground in Brooklyn.

The Islamo-Christian forces advance had stalled. Just as they began their final assault, the V-22 appeared overhead. The gunner locked on the closest assault teams, drew her bead and fired. The 30 caliber gun unloaded and stopped the assault dead in its tracks.

"Yosi, is that the V-22 I hear?!?" Mimi inquired.

"Yeah!! The Osprey is hitting them hard!! We have our guys moving around their flanks. I think we can roll them up."

And roll them up, they did. More than two thousand Israeli and Christian Zionists swarmed into the action. The Chassidic Center wasn't out of danger just yet but the tide was beginning to turn.

As the Israeli forces moved into the fight, several smaller attack teams appeared and surrounded the Islamo-Christian fighters. Realizing they were surrounded, they threw down their weapons and surrendered. But a few resistors refused to give up. When ordered to put down their weapons, they advanced on the Israeli teams.

In a last-gasp effort, more than 100 of them attacked the worship center and opened fire on the front windows. Glass flew everywhere as they unloaded their automatic weapons. Jewish and Christian Zionist defenders returned fire. This time it was the AH-64 Apache that jumped into the action. It turned its attention on this latest hotspot. The door gunner took aim on the enemy troops, found his mark and let fly. The effect was deadly. The 30 caliber machine gun cut the enemy to pieces, instantly killing more than half of the squad.

The remainder continued to advance on the worship center but just as they did, a squad of 200 Israelis appeared from behind an adjoining building and emptied their weapons on the offenders. The battle drew to a quick close, with the remaining 50 enemy falling either dead or seriously wounded. Once the battlefield fell silent, shouts of "hold your fire" were given to the Israeli and Christian defenders. The ground seemed to be a living thing as the wounded from both sides crawled on the ground to avoid being hit.

The Islamo-Christians couldn't face capture from their enemies, so many of the wounded acted as if they were dead. Slowly and cautiously, several Christian Zionist defenders approached the bodies and were met with fresh bursts of gunfire. Three of them fell mortally wounded, again drawing fire from the Israeli troops. It was over.

The battle for the Chassidic center ended with 144 Jewish dead, more than 1,500 Islamo-Christian dead, and more than 1000 captured. Now the Israelis had to decide what to do with the prisoners. Other battles around Brooklyn ended with both sides suffering heavy casualties.

✡ ✡ ✡ ✡ ✡ ✡

Israeli and Christian Zionist forces set up a makeshift prison at a nearby school putting 250 of their number in charge. Each prisoner was stripped to the waist, patted down for any weapons, and then transported to the school.

As the battlefield commanders in Brooklyn wrote their preliminary reports and emailed them in, the tallies were horrific. Brooklyn would see more than 10,000 civilian Jewish dead and wounded. The Muslims suffered, but their losses were mostly combatants. Some reports said 25,000 Islamo-Christian dead and wounded. Israeli and Christian Zionist forces lost 250 with 1000 wounded. This went beyond any pogrom.

Though the bloodletting was heavy, Godly Christian citizens managed to hide and protect Brooklyn's remaining Jews and then began the transport them to JFK. As in Los Angeles, and the other major corridors around the nation, busses, trains, subways, cars, and any transportation means possible, just appeared to escort their human cargo to safety.

CHAPTER EIGHTY-FOUR: Eastern Corridor—Mimi Takes Command

✡ ✡ ✡ ✡ ✡ ✡

As the planes landed and refueled, restocked, and prepared for turnaround flights, their flight crews prepared the cabins for the first emigrants. The crews fired up their onboard computers, completed final security checks, and begin loading their passengers. It was a sight to see... the first 350 new Israeli citizens were cleared through to Ben Gurion Airport by the time the first flight reached it final cruising altitude of 40,000 feet.

> **From the Babylonian Talmud, Sanhedrin 4:8 (37a)**
>
> Whoever destroys a soul, it is considered as if he destroyed an entire world. And whoever saves a life, it is considered as if he saved an entire world.

Chapter 85

Chicago

Within a few weeks, a very quiet movement began in the suburbs of Chicago. Jews, who had lived in their neighborhoods for generations, began disappearing. Slowly the Jewish neighborhoods emptied out. The underground express led by Christian Zionist forces, quietly snatched away their Jewish neighbors, hiding them in walls, cellars, basements, garbage dumps, and anywhere they could to avoid authorities.

With an increasingly active Christian Zionist movement growing and asserting itself, the Jews slowly began to realize that there really were good Christians, ones who really followed their Savior's words.

For Sale signs popped up in Jewish neighborhoods near Chicago. The big city wouldn't be far behind.

As the neighborhoods emptied, an eerie sense of foreboding began gripping Chicago's citizenry. Many residents reported a sense of loss, not only of their neighbors, but a missing culture. The Jewish presence, so long a strong underpinning of the city's culture and the underpinning of business, medicine, education, politics, engineering, and a host of other fields simply vanished.

CHAPTER EIGHTY-FIVE: Chicago   Page 507

As strange as the absence of the Jews was, something else seemed to coincide with it—the homes began selling so quickly, that demand quickly outstripped supply, thus driving prices even higher. No one could explain this strange turn of events, especially in light of the multi-decade real estate slump where prices seemed to stay low for an interminably long time.

Housing prices skyrocketed, in complete contradiction to the market, and as transactions completed, Jewish money was held in escrow accounts, the sellers unable to complete the sales deals. At first the numbers seemed insignificant, but over the coming months hundreds, then thousands of homes turned over. The escrow companies held astronomical amounts of cash, now approaching billions. Not only was this evident in Chicago and surrounding communities, it spread to all of Illinois and then across the country.

Jewish residents in Miami senior communities saw their values almost double overnight. Real Estate agents, smelling profits, moved in full force. Though, as in Chicago and other Jewish population centers, the Jews were in hiding but what appeared to be a secret hand in all this seemed to be guiding events as they unfolded.

Israeli planners did not foresee this particular event, but in their zeal to ensure Jewish wealth was captured and directed to the Jewish state, they made contingencies to ensure that the money would find its rightful owners. Armed with the census records and with the ability to track all real estate transactions in the U.S. the financial information technology professionals set to work. Writing mind-numbing algorithms, years in testing, they managed to identify each real estate transaction. This, in turn, somewhat guaranteed that if and when the Jews were able to escape America, they would have a stake in the game as soon as they landed in Israel and as they did so, their accounts would start off in positive territory.

Waiting for the appropriate moment, they released the bots....

✡ ✡ ✡ ✡ ✡ ✡

As loyal Christian Zionist forces continued to cast a wide safety net for Jewish friends and acquaintances, the blessings increased for them as well. For some reason, their presence and work appeared very much in the background and went undetected. With O'Hare airport under control of 15,000 combined forces, the busses began arriving. The Midwest commander reported that morning to the planning meeting.

"We have 60 planes inbound this morning. Jewish refugees are arriving now. We've cleared and are holding all roads leading to the airport. We've got assets in the air, circling to find any hotspots and to protect the inbound vehicles."

The battles in Chicago's streets had been fierce. Thousands lay dead, the burial teams sweeping the streets almost daily to collect their victims. Jewish death rates were slightly lower in Chicago then the other corridors. Israeli troops asserted general control of the streets. Most of Chicago's Jewish population would soon be moving to O'Hare, and on to Israel. Others from nearby states and cities were making plans to get to Chicago as well. But nobody believed it would be without incident.

Local church groups stepped up to provide aid and comfort. Hiding the Jews in homes, schools, warehouses, farms, ranches, and virtually anywhere they could, they had made good on their promises. Here again, Dogface's garbage dumps provided temporary shelters when needed. Jonathan Roberts had a very loyal following in this Midwest citadel and the locals continued to prove their mettle. But Roberts remained in hiding, his teams managing events around the nation.

The local commander was known to Mimi in New York and had served with Avram during their mandatory service time in Israel. Her one and one half million street soldiers carried the battle to the enemy. Their task was similar to that in the other major corridors... the police force was decimated, as was the local fire department. More than half of their numbers had joined the Christian Zionist forces, even counting many Catholics, Lutherans, and other Christian denominations as well.

The mainstream denominations seemed more supportive in Chicago. And their congregations began to experience untold blessings with many reporting strange spiritual awakenings and new desire to read the Bible. There was a turning of the heart among the clergy in many of the Windy City's churches.

It was reported that bickering and disagreements between the various schisms faded when they focused on Jewish needs. The blessings rolled in to the defenders as family rifts seemed to heal, children once estranged to families began returning, and most amazing of all, those fighting addictions such as drug, alcohol, and gambling abuse were cured almost overnight. The blessings came in so many different ways, that one pastor in a small *Believers' Chapel* summed it up best:

CHAPTER EIGHTY-FIVE: Chicago

Friends, though none of us really can say we were ready for this, the greatest test of our faith, it is with God's blessings that we rise to the occasion. God's promises to the Jews carry blessings for the gentiles too. It's been a good long while since we have visited the Old Testament book of Genesis. But today, we focus on the 12th chapter where God promises Abraham that those blessing the Jewish people will be blessed themselves. I quote verse 3: *I will bless those who bless thee and curse those who curse thee.*

✡ ✡ ✡ ✡ ✡ ✡

And on came the jets. Ground crews feverishly performed the necessary service as the jets awaited their passengers for their long nonstop flights to Israel. They would haul more than 40,000 out in the first cycle. Everything was working according to plan. With planning and some good fortune, the first of Chicago's Jews would be on their way within the hour.

An estimated 300,000 Jews were streaming to the airport. Shapiro's planning teams arranged for tens of thousands of tents to be erected near the airport and on airport grounds for those who couldn't find room inside the airport. O'Hare could hold upwards of 50,000 passengers but now the population in and around the facility swelled to more than 250,000. This would take a little less than a week, if everything worked correctly. And like New York, tent cities popped on the airport grounds as a temporary holding station for the escaping Jews. Tens of thousands now calling the airport their temporary home.

The first loadings went without incident. In two minute increments, the jets streaked into the sky, each carrying 400 refugees, headed home to the Land of their Fathers.

Within days, Chicago would be Judenfrei (free of its Jews).

✡ ✡ ✡ ✡ ✡ ✡

> From the Hand of Paul, the Letter to the Galatians
> Chapter 5, Verses 22-23
>
> But the fruit of the Spirit is love, joy, peace, patience, kindness, goodness, faithfulness, gentleness, self-control; against such things there is no law

Chapter 86

Shabibi's Gift

New York's Jewish population, once numbering in the millions was almost gone. Like Chicago, Miami, and Los Angeles, New York was virtually *Judenfrei*. Though small pockets of Jewish Americans remained behind, well over 95% of America's Jews were gone and now called Israel home. The fate of the remainder was still to be determined.

Mimi was exhausted... 10 weeks of nonstop action took its toll. How do you measure casualties when one death seems too much? Thousands of Israeli fighters and former American Jews were dead or wounded, thousands of their Christian Zionist brethren as well. Islamo-Christian forces suffered heavier losses. No body counts were available, but the estimates ran into the tens of thousands.

Mimi had one more thing she needed to do. Time was running out and she had to find Shabibi and Farouk get them out of the country. She fired off a text to Shabibi.

"Things are settling down here. Need to see you."

No answer.

Mimi waited for 10 minutes and texted Shabibi again.

CHAPTER EIGHTY-SIX: *Shabibi's Gift*

"R U there?"

No answer.

Mimi calmed herself. She stepped out to smoke.

✡ ✡ ✡ ✡ ✡ ✡

Where could they be?

Mimi called the head of the airport detail.

"Can you get me up to Westchester Airport?"

"Yes, of course, but things are still hot in some areas. I am not confident that I can guarantee your safety."

"Well, I appreciate your candor, but let me be the judge of that. I have two dear friends up there. I fear for their lives."

Thirty minutes later, Mimi and a small security team boarded a V-22 and headed up to Westchester. For good measure, an Apache accompanied the small party. It was Mimi's first over flight in more than a week. She couldn't believe the city. It looked so calm especially after the crazy street battles over the past few weeks. Still, there was a lot of wreckage, destruction... and the ever present berms of dirt that ringed the airport providing safe cover for the Jews she was protecting. Her training of the construction teams and their quick work was perhaps the coup d'état of her applied Civil Engineering prowess.

She fired off another text to Shabibi.

"I'm coming in. Are you there?"

Still no answer. Something was wrong.

Mimi looked at her watch. They had been the air about 30 minutes.

The choppers landed on the helo pads outside the main complex. Mimi grabbed her bag and headed to the house from the back. Just then, she spotted something in the wooded area near the home—a glint of steel. And then came the gunfire.

"Get back! Get back!" Mimi yelled to her security detail. "Get those choppers up!" Since the rotors still hadn't stopped spinning, the pilots managed to get airborne once again.

Meanwhile on the ground, Mimi and her contingent were pinned down near the heliport. She had 30 highly trained soldiers, men and women sworn to her safety. Mimi took the safety off her weapon.

The commander who was heading up the mission radioed the V-22.

"What are you seeing up there?"

"Looks like the shots came from the trees—but they are well hidden."

"Ok, circle over and keep it hot."

Meanwhile Mimi and her fellow combatants spread around the grounds—unaware of happenings inside the house.

Mimi pulled her radio from her waistband....

"What are you seeing in the front?"

"No movement... but we see 3 vehicles hidden in the woods."

"Ok, don't approach just yet. Do they have plates?"

"Uh, negative."

Mimi's mind was spinning... *3 vehicles, no plates, one fusillade of shots fired... they want to draw us in the house....*

"Reuven, take five of the men with you and see if you can flush out the shooters in the woods... meanwhile, send 3 of the men around back and get an insect drone into the house."

"Got it Mimi... " He clicked off.

Just then, as the AH-64 came directly overhead, an RPG headed for the chopper... missing high.

The AH-64 opened fire on the woods in the same direction... the cannon fire ripped a huge swath into the trees and silencing the shooter...

Mimi looked up to hear more shots now coming from the house.

"They have Shabibi and Farouk hostage inside!"

"Mimi, we have a live feed from inside the house... we see about 10 men, heavily armed with assault rifles. They have your two friends in the center... they are tied up, bound and gagged."

"How the hell did they find us here?"

Just then, another round of shots came from another forested area near the house. Mimi sent three more snipers around the house to quiet those shooters.

"Mimi we see the shooters in the woods... "

"Engage them... "

"Ok...."

Just then, the Apache let fly another torrent of shells into this new wooded area... the shooters fell silent. The snipers held fire.

Precious moments ticked off the clock.

"Ok, I need all of you in the back woods... now!"

Silently, the 30 soldiers crept towards the woods... and gathered there. Mimi, making sure they were hidden, drew up the assault plans.

"Ok this is not going to be easy... we need to draw them out... I don't want a street fight... been there and done that! "I know this home... we'll cut the power off first and...." Just then, a bullhorn screeched on.

"We have your friends here... and we have demands. Nobody gets hurt but you have to follow our directions." The speaker spoke with no accent... puzzling Mimi for a moment.

"Who is that?"

"We think he's a former New York cop... we ran the video feed through our computers and found a hit... he's in there with some former SWAT team members." Reuven was well trained in house to house fighting.

"Tough guys, huh? Ok, well, there's 30 of us, about 10 or so of them... but they are holding the cards."

"Yeah, but we have an advantage...." Mimi cracked a grin... maybe the first time she smiled in weeks.

"This little smart phone has all the house's codes inside it. I can monkey with the lights, the heat, the air, everything... even the sprinkler system. We have flash bangs and smoke grenades so we can confuse them first... remember, they are used to being in OUR position, not the other way around. Let's see what they have to say...."

"Ok, we're listening."

"Get that V-22 down here and let us load up... with your friends and nobody gets hurt. We will release them when we get to our destination."

Mimi now silently positioned her 30 man contingent around each entrance... each of them armed with the flash bangs and smoke grenades.

Minutes ticked by.... By now the video feed revealed the men inside posted by windows, though the shades were drawn.

"Ok, on "3," begin tossing in the flash bangs and the smokers... but I will get things started by turning on the heat and the sprinklers at the same time... it will take a few minutes for them to react."

On went the heat and the sprinklers.... The soldiers could hear yelling in the house.

"One-Two————Three!!!! Go!"

One by one, each of Mimi's team hurled in the grenades... shots were fired then Mimi's team stormed the house....

Yelling... screaming... shots inside....

Seconds turned into an eternity when Mimi jumped through the bedroom window and headed into the living room.

Everything was chaos... Shabibi and Farouk were on the floor. All ten SWAT team members were either wounded or dead... it was a mess. Her team took light casualties... two wounds. The room was smoky, more than 90 degrees and everything was soaked.

Mimi rushed to her friends... and got her soldiers to untie them... both of them were ok... but very shaken and scared. Once untied, they saw Mimi and reached out to her....

Once order was somewhat restored, they opened windows to clear the air and laid down towels to soak up the water. Mimi had her aides bring some bottled water to the former captives. The clean-up crews made quick work of the house restoring it to some level of normalcy.

It was over.

✡ ✡ ✡ ✡ ✡ ✡

All three found it hard to fight back the tears. They fell into an animated conversation, falling over each other to tell the details of the past few weeks... and the hostage situation.

"Mimi, we can't even describe the horror... the earthquake knocked us off our feet and when the volcano finally blew, we had to take off with just the clothes on our backs... we had just enough time to grab some essentials from the house before we got out of there. The animals made it through and they are at another friend's farm about 15 miles from our place... we walked them all the way there. We still haven't heard from my brother... and my feet still hurt!"

Mimi sat dumbfounded... she understood loss and she understood friendship.

"I cannot even describe what the past few weeks have been like... after we arranged everything, I didn't know if you had gotten here safely... and being out of touch because of the war... I don't know... I just can't believe you are here with me..." Mimi said.

"Mimi, we know... and feel the same way." They described the pickup at the airport and the arrival at the house.

"It was perfect here... after all the chaos in Saudi. After a week here, there was a delivery for some clothing or something. We thought nothing of it until about an hour later when another delivery came... then the men...." Shabibi's voice trailed off.

Farouk spoke next.

"After all we'd been through... we thought we were safe here. And we were, for a time... then the invasion... they just broke in here." He buried his head in his hands.

Mimi just blew some air out of her cheeks. *How did they find out? She wondered...*

In the midst of talk over troubles, Shabibi, now calmed down, pulled out a small wrapped gift. She handed it to Mimi and said, "My mother sends this to you. She wants you to have it... for your kindness to us."

Mimi unwrapped the gift. It was a brilliant multi-colored scarf of blues, reds, and greens. "It's breathtaking," Mimi cried. "It's so beautiful." She lifted the scarf, held it to her cheek, and caressed it like a loved one's face.

"It likes you," Shabibi said. "The colors light up your face."

"I love it, Shabi. Thank you! Thank your mother."

"In our family, when tragedy strikes, we find it helpful to do something for others. We give and in turn it reduces our pain. We were taught to find joy in our gifts to others. So, Mimi, you have given me joy and my mother, too."

"Can you help me wrap it correctly?" Mimi asked— her voice fragile and emotion still near the surface. She turned around to Shabibi.

"Of course. Here, let me help you."

She took the scarf, created an elegant wrap for Mimi, and tucked her hair underneath. The effect was stunning.

"This scarf has been in the family for generations. My mother knows how much you mean to us. So, welcome to our family!"

"Well," Mimi said with all teeth and smile. "I have a surprise for you...."

Farouk and Shabibi looked at each other—surprised and with suspicious glares.

"Anyway," Mimi bubbled. "You saw from my talk in Boston how I can be a celebrity to some of those V.I.P. old-timers, right?" Both nodded.

"Well, one supportive gentleman and his wife are especially dear to me. This is their place and I wanted to come and spend some time here with you.... But then the circumstances changed. They are away. They know all about you and would love to have you house-sit in their absence. You're invited to be their guests even upon their return—as long as you need."

> From the 2nd Letter to Timothy
> by the Hand of Rav Shaul
> 2 Timothy Chapter 2 Verses 3-4
>
> I thank God, whom I serve with a clear conscience the way my forefathers did, as I constantly remember you in my prayers night and day, longing to see you, even as I recall your tears, so that I may be filled with joy.

Chapter 87

Shabbat at Papa G's

"Well, like I said," Mimi began, "Shabbat begins tonight. And...."

"C'mon Mimi, we are ready for your Shabbat," Shabibi assured her.

"Well, I don't know," Mimi blushed—then looked at the couple. "Still, I'd be honored if you'd join us tonight. I'll light the candles. I'll teach you the Hebrew prayers—blessings over the bread and the wine. We'll share the bread and wine, and much more."

Mimi looked to the floor, listened to her heart, and then lifted her gaze. "To be honest... I'm not that religious. But there's something about *this* Shabbat, the burdens of my job, world events, your presence, my love for you, and my concern for Shabi's.... Well, uh... I mean... the unsettled state of affairs and fragile emotions that we all feel."

Shabibi looked to Farouk. He took a moment to collect his thoughts and said, "In my youth, I grumbled and complained over every hardship I faced. My wise and patient Imam would listen to my pain or injustice. But he said the same thing—every time.

CHAPTER EIGHTY-SEVEN: Shabbat at Papa G's

To sink in sorrow, to sit in sadness, to stand in fire, and to dwell in darkness is to choose affliction and torment. But a greater truth reminds me of this: In God there is no sorrow, no suffering, no darkness, no affliction, and no torment. In God is light and joy—a high and holy view. To be free of all afflictions, I hold fast to God. I turn wholly to Him. I go to no one else. I take refuge of His love.

My young brother, all your suffering comes from this: *you do not turn toward God alone.*

"I heard those words many times. Yet I did not live those words until I left home. I sought property, found our farm, labored hard, and lived alone. That is when I learned to pray. I came to know God's presence. And I found the means to ascend above affliction.

"But in these days, I have been surrounded by sorrow and suffering. Pain has displaced prayer. Disaster has stolen my devotion. Confusion has claimed my prayer beads—they are lost.

"And so, Mimi, I say to you, yes. Bring us to prayer, bring us to devotion, and bring us to joy and light. We look to you this evening to bring us to God... YOUR GOD."

"My... My God??! What—what are you telling me?" Mimi cried.

"Mimi, we have something to say... and we don't want you to misunderstand anything we are about to say." Shabibi's voice was firm, yet there was a very obvious tone of tenderness to her friend.

"We have forsaken Islam... and...." She couldn't finish.

Mimi looked back and forth at Farouk and Shabibi.

"What's going on? What is this? I never expected you to forsake anything... for me anyway," Mimi said, in a halting manner.

"Mimi, this isn't about you... it isn't about religion, it's about the one you call Yeshua."

"Well, I don't, well, I mean... uh, what about Yeshua?"

"This is crazy, is it not? Farouk and I have been through a lot... come here, honey...." Farouk came alongside her.

"This is beyond anything I have ever experienced. I can't believe what I'm about to say... "

Mimi was lost...

"Mimi, we accepted the Messiah of the Jewish people! Do you remember when you told us about your brother Avner? We listened and we learned that this Yeshua of the Bible answers everyone's questions. Islam was close in some ways... there would be a coming deliverer... but the Jesus of Islam is not the Jesus of the Bible."

"Go on... this is intriguing."

"We finally realized it as we were herding the animals away from the volcano. I prayed that God Himself would send us a sign as to what we should do... I asked him to shake things up in our lives... I didn't mean it literally!" Shabibi laughed and as she did, the others in the room joined her.

"Mimi, this isn't that complicated.... He died for all of us... Muslims, Jews, Gentiles, no matter who you are. This Shabbat you are about to have reminds us that we are heading into a resting period with God... and it is tonight we wish to rest in His light and rest in your presence."

Mimi made preparations in the dining room. Farouk, Shabibi, and Mimi came together to the kitchen.

"Oh, my those smells! Reminds me of home!" Farouk looked at peace as did his wife.

"Oh, hummus, tabouli, lentil soup, roasted lamb... and more! I'm keeping it warm till later. Come on." Then Mimi called in the security contingent... to join them. They each snitched a knish.

They entered the room—darkened except for daylight that peeked around the drawn curtains. Mimi was at the head of a small serving table covered in pure linen overlaid with lace. Upon the linen was a colorful collage of flowers, candles, bread, wine, and all that was required for their Shabbat Seder. Mimi wore an embroidered black dress with her new gift covering her head. Shabibi saw the scarf and smiled.

Mimi lit the candles. She waived her hands over the flames three times to welcome Shabbat and *Ruach H'Kodesh*. She brought her hand to cover her eyes. With eyes covered she prayed:

Baruch Ata Adonai, Elohenu Melech HaOlam,
Asher Kidshanu B'Mitzvotav, V'tzivanu, l'chadlich Ner Shel Shabbat.

Blessed art Thou, O Lord our God, King of the Universe,
Who commanded us to kindle the Sabbath lights.

Mimi dropped her hands, and all heard a noise from the kitchen. It was followed by a gust of wind. The flames bowed over with the breeze—none extinguished. Then they lifted up again.

A special hush and holiness had entered. The air was thick and sweet. Mimi had never looked so beautiful. The candles put an amber glow upon her face. Everyone saw it. And they saw her eyes—they filled, she blinked, and tears ran down her cheeks to drop on lace below.

Mimi lifted her eyes and smiled at each one there. Then she lifted her glass of wine and spoke. Her voice was small and soft and shaken with emotion. "Please, repeat the prayer after me. I'll go slowly.

Baruch Ata Adonai,
Elohenu
Melech HaOlam,
B'oray P'ri
HaGafen.

Blessed art Thou, O Lord our God, King of the Universe,
Who created the fruit of the Vine.

Mimi drank from the *Kiddush* cup and passed it around the table.

Then Mimi came full stop. She rested her folded hands on her stomach, look at each one, and said, "This next step is very meaningful to me, and probably no one else on the planet. It's called *Netilat Yadaiyim*—washing hands. Some say it's meaningless now. One rabbi, some say a great teacher and more, changed it. He chose instead to wash feet, but not his own. He washed the feet of others—his disciples. Ever since I heard that about that rabbi, I've changed my own *Netilat Yadaiyim*.

"I wash my hands. *Why?* Since youth, I've been troubled by deeds I've done with these hands. I imagine marks and stains on these hands." She lifted and opened her hands. "Even though we weren't that religious, the Shabbat felt so holy in youth. In the *Netilat Yadaiyim* I imagined my hands as clean... the marks removed and gone. Maybe a child's fantasy—still, I felt better, cleansed. But now I do more. You'll see. Follow my actions or not. I do this for me.

Baruch Ata Adonai, Elohenu Melech HaOlam,
Asher Kidshanu B'Mitzvotav, 'al V'tzivanu, Netilat Yadaiyim.

Blessed art Thou, O Lord our God, King of the Universe,
Who commanded us about washing the hands.

Mimi poured water over her right hand and her left. Then with her hands still wet she touched her eyes and with both hands her mouth. She dried her hands, eyes, and mouth. And she lifted her hands, nodded, smiled, and gave thanks.

All four followed her every move. Farouk wept when he was done.

Next Mimi lifted the *challah*, the traditional bread, and looked at each one. "Repeat after me."

Baruch Ata Adonai,
Elohenu Melech HaOlam,
Ha Motzi, Lechem
Min Ha Aretz.

Blessed art Thou, O Lord our God, King of the Universe,
Who brings forth bread from the earth?

Mimi broke the bread and handed a piece to each of them. Then she dipped it in a common dish of sea salt in the center and ate. All followed.

"It's amazing to me," Mimi said, "Bread crosses all cultures and peoples. We broke bread together. We are now *mishpocha*—family!" She smiled, clapped, and spun around like a little girl.

Mimi still stood over the table with candles lit. "I don't want this time to end. I love you all so much. And I just can't...." At that moment a much different sound—blown leaves and flowing water. Mimi turned. The breeze blew her scarf and hair. And they looked down to find the candles extinguished. Farouk spoke next.

"In my land there are many winds. We must learn each one, know what it does, and call it by its name. I've heard the stories. But I had never experienced His wind... until we left our farm land.

"We bid our land good-bye. It held all our hopes, our sweat, our blood, our future, and our very lives. Grief poured from us like water from a sponge. The sorrow took our strength—the weeping left us weary. Without the life to speak or to stand—we sat hopeless and broken in the sand.

"Then He came. Unlike any other... His holy breath lifted our heads, filled our hearts, renewed our minds, strengthened our bodies, and gave us hope." He wept again.

"From that moment," Shabibi began, "I knew... we knew that it was going to be okay. And we had the strength and courage to follow the steps that brought us here."

"And just now," Farouk continued, "as He left us, He whispered words that we both heard." Shabibi wept and laughed all at once.

✡ ✡ ✡ ✡ ✡ ✡

When Israelis woke up the next morning... Saturday, the first planes were landing... bringing tens of thousands of new immigrants. The return had begun. This went on for weeks. Shuvah Yisrael.

✡ ✡ ✡ ✡ ✡ ✡

Weeks later, on Sunday, the first workday of the new week, the nation's chief financier, a cabinet minister in Tel Aviv, fired up his computer and looked at the bank's reserves that morning. He blinked, closed his eyes and blinked again at the nation's capital strength. Overnight, more than $3 trillion had been transferred into Jewish hands from America. Israel was now one of the wealthiest nations on earth and that was without counting the newly discovered oil reserves *under Jewish soil.*

✡ ✡ ✡ ✡ ✡ ✡

In America, the head of the Federal Reserve received a phone call telling him that all identifiable American Jewish wealth, including real estate, retirement plans, corporate holdings, everything—was gone. America's banks were on the verge of collapse.

The chairman felt the tremors coming, then fell off his chair. He was dead before he hit the floor.

✡ ✡ ✡ ✡ ✡ ✡

The small Jewish enclave was quiet that very same morning. There was a knock on the door. "Mr. Roberts? Please come with us."

✡ ✡ ✡ ✡ ✡ ✡

From the Pen of Amos the Prophet,
Chapter 3:6-7

Thus says the LORD,
For three transgressions of Gaza and for four,
I will not revoke its punishment,
Because they deported an entire population,
To deliver it up to Edom.
So I will send fire upon the wall of Gaza
And it will consume her citadels.

From the Pen of David the Psalmist
Chapter 88:8

You have removed my acquaintances far from me; you have made me an object of loathing to them; I am shut up and cannot go out.

Coffee House Chatter

"So, you're a Christian, right?" she asked.

"Well, yeah, isn't everybody? I mean I do good deeds, never stolen anything, y'know, I'm a good Christian, right? I go to church, I read my Bible sometimes, and am a good person," he said.

"Not what I meant. Let me ask you this. If this nation turned its guns on the Jews, or got into a shooting conflict with Israel, what would you do?" she asked.

"That would never happen, you know that," he said.

"But if it did, what would you do?" she asked.

"Well, I'm a loyal American, so I guess if I had to I'd follow orders," he said.

"Exactly," she said.

Chapter 88

Attack at Sea—
The Turning Point

In the middle of the operation, the Turks raised an American flag.

Though the tide had turned against America's Jews, an all-out disregard for Israel hadn't yet come to fruition. But all of that was about to change.

For years, Palestinians and their sponsors continued to bait the Israelis into a provocative action. Most attempts to set the bait for Israel had failed but a new set of players was about to enter the fray.

Year after year, peace activists carrying humanitarian aid into Gaza attempted to break through Israeli blockades of Gaza. The power of internet video services was sure to show the Israelis in an unfavorable light. Israel continued to hope for international understanding knowing it would be a miracle to receive it. The Palestinians continued to hope for international pressure and regional hatreds to drive a stake into the heart of the Jewish state, once and for all.

Recalling that the aim of terror is twofold, Israeli spokespersons continued to remind an increasingly deaf international community that the twin purposes of terror were not only to turn the victims into the perpetrators but also to provoke a response so over the top that the real victims would be seen as monsters and the terrorists would be seen as the victims.

Israel, sensing that hostilities were certain to be blamed on her, held back using full force and for years and continued its policies of restraint that few nations would acknowledge publicly but would privately recognize as honorable. Ships were diverted to the port of Ashdod where Israeli, then later, international inspectors, would clear the cargo for overland passage just a few klicks south into the Gaza strip.

Muslim claims that Gaza was being starved met with Israeli counterclaims that the Gazans enjoyed a better standard of living than many in the area. Millions of tons of aid reached the small enclave of a million and a half, meaning that each resident of Gaza received close to one ton of aid per person.

As international pressures mounted, a former ally turned on Israel and jacked up the threat meter to a new level. The latest flotilla to leave Cypress included a six ship contingent, led by two Turkish frigates, two fast attack craft, and two missile boats. As they moved into the Mediterranean Sea, Israeli intelligence picked up this new threat on radar. Israeli agents had been watching the growing threat in the harbor there for days, but now the flotilla was under power. Other agents in place reported a growing defiance and threat to the Jewish state.

The new wrinkle in this operation was the fact that Turkey led the flotilla with unknown intent. Israel's first response was to survey the skies to see if any other threats existed. When it was discovered that a Turkish AWACS plane had taken to the air, the Israelis knew that this international high stakes game of poker was heating up.

Israel then launched a reconnaissance aircraft of its own, a C-130. The Israeli spy plane, like its 747 counterpart, was loaded with a massive amount of electronics gear. Israeli officers on board immediately detected other aircraft in the vicinity and radioed in to the local airbase on a secure connection. Other threats would soon appear.

"We are now picking up six more vessels, frigates, missile boats, and attack craft and they are flying the Turkish flag," the Israeli captain warned.

"We are tracking through our satellites. They've also launched four aircraft, which appear to be F-15s," the commander answered.

The possibility that Turkish F-15s, built by Boeing, could actually face Israeli F-15s was an interesting irony that the Israelis could appreciate.

Israel's fighters remained superior to other aircraft in the region but that was changing. They now flew the 5th generation F-15s and Joint Strike Fighters or JSF's.

The ships were now less than 75 miles off the coast and in just a few hours would be well within the blockade zone. The aircraft remained mostly outside of range but were certainly noticeable... and menacing.

"Establish contact with the Turkish ship," the captain ordered his communications chief. She tapped the codes into her computer and received the protocol.

"This is the captain of the Israeli ship Magen Avraham (the Shield of Abraham). You are ordered to direct your ship to our port city of Ashdod."

"Our destination is Gaza," the Turkish captain answered.

"Do we know who is on board any of the ships? Any 'dignitaries' or 'peace activists?' Depending on who's on board, it could mean trouble. If the Turkish ships fire on us and we answer, that puts this firmly into a NATO situation, something that nobody wants," the captain said to his second in command, and the ground commander. They recalled the earlier blockade runners and the fate that awaited them.

CHAPTER EIGHTY-EIGHT: Attack at Sea

He was right, for any attack against one member of NATO meant that other members of the alliance could well step into the fray to defend one of their own. And that, as everyone on board the Israeli naval vessel knew, meant the United States, Great Britain, or other NATO members. This was uncharted territory and the Israeli captain knew he needed to go up the chain. And the captain was flying an American flag... adding insult to injury.

"We need direction," he told his superiors.

Israeli Central Command connected into the U.S. Embassy in Jerusalem. Israel's ambassador to the United States was now awake and dialed in on the call as well.

"We have the U.S. ambassador on the phone right now," the Israeli ambassador said.

"We have explained the situation to him. He is contacting his superiors right now."

"Sir, the ships will be here within the hour."

"Affirmative. We are scrambling four JSF's for backup." The situation was heating up by the minute.

The American ambassador reached the legation in Jerusalem. What instruction he was about to receive would transform relations between the two long time allies. The U.S. ambassador had his answer.

"Sir, any attack on a Turkish vessel will be perceived as an act of war on NATO, and thus on the United States of America. My orders are directly from the President," the ambassador warned.

The Israeli ambassador was suddenly faced with a decision that he could not make. One sovereign nation was face-to-face with another. Not only that, but a long-term friendship hung in the balance. He had no choice but to contact the Prime Minister. His hot line connected to the PM's chief of staff.

"Mr. Prime Minister, the Turks' flotilla is bearing down on our ships. We have virtually no time left. We must either let them pass or face them down at sea," he said, his voice wavering, the disbelief showing in his voice.

"I'm calling the cabinet together right now," the PM said. "I will have an answer for you in a few moments. Please stay on the line with me," he said firmly and resolutely.

The Turks and the other ships in the flotilla knew the NATO agreement and the rules of engagement. It was time to act. All of this had been rehearsed before so game theory experts had worked through all the scenarios. The calculated gamble was about to be tested.

The minutes ticked by.

The Israeli aircraft were now airborne, minutes from the sea and their targets carefully chosen. The Turkish AWACS aircraft remained over international waters but only a few minutes away from the flotilla and the Israeli Navy. They could see the Israeli planes now. Beyond them lurked the American 5th Fleet.

In the back of the mind of every Israeli seaman and the American 5th Fleet Admiral was the ghost of the U.S.S. Liberty.

From the Pen of the Prophet Ezekiel: 34:12-16

For this is what the Sovereign Lord says: I myself will search for my sheep and look after them. As a shepherd looks after his scattered flock when he is with them, so will I look after my sheep. I will rescue them from all the places where they were scattered on a day of clouds and darkness. I will bring them out from the nations and gather them from the countries, and I will bring them into their own land.

The Players

Elijah Abdul—A leading member of the Nation of Islam and speaker at the Conference on Racism in Durban, South Africa. Delivers an extremely anti-Semitic / anti- Zionist message at the plenary session. Is modeled a bit after Louis Farakkhan.

Tewfik ibn Abdulla—A young Palestinian man who attends classes with Avner. He immigrated from Palestine as a youth. He harbors anger and bitterness towards Jews and Israelis. He lies in wait for Avner.

Yusef Abdul-Qaiyoum (Servant of the Self Sustaining)—Imam of the mosque that Abdul and Manahil attend. He will recruit them into the Suicide Bomb tradition where they will self detonate in a church.

Yosi Abraham—The Brooklyn ground commander. He and some of his are trapped in the Chassidic Center.

Jocelyn Anderson—Owner of a hi tech modular housing company who will sell her company to the Israelis.

Mrs. Anderson—Elderly woman who witnesses a brutal murder of a Jewish couple in Indiana. D.D. Dulburg reports on the crime and is largely ignored by the station management team.

Shoshana Bat-Levi—Levi is Ben Yehuda's right hand. A trained F-15 fighter pilot, trained agent, and owner of a software firm that creates encryption software. She is fluent in several languages and tasked to coordinate defense for the Jews leaving America. She and Aryeh Cohen are old friends from their early military training.

Steven "Beau" Beauregard—Billy Glass' weapons officer. He's a Louisiana Cajun with a long brown mustache, half a dozen tattoos, and a reputation for accuracy. Beau and Billy have flown together for years and know each other's minds and hearts. They are new in their beliefs but recognize the gravity of the situation. They are heartbroken as they take up arms against fellow soldiers.

Wilson Benedict—College age Christian from Chicago. He and his friends witness the synagogue attack, and call in a 911 to the police. He also witnesses the massacre at the neighboring home. He vows to help the Jewish people defend themselves from future attacks and later forms and heads up a Neighborhood Watch to do so.

Avram Ben-Yehuda—Director of Operations of the Mossad. Now 85, he's from the first generation born after the State of Israel declared independence. A veteran of many of Israel's wars, he oversees foreign operations and will help with defending America's Jews with the intent of extracting them to Israel. He's the co-architect of *Operation Last Exodus*.

Pastor Thomas Brandenburg—Young Lutheran pastor and former college athlete. Influencial in Orange, California congregation. He studied scripture about end times prophecy and the Jewish people and stumbled across verses that convicted his soul and changed his thinking. He realized the Jews are still chosen and cherished by God and his ministry did little to teach that message from the Book of Romans. He repents and rededicates his life to minister to the Jews in his community and to help the Jews in any way he can.

Sholom Braun—(Pronounced Sholum)—Summer camp acquaintance of Chaim. They share a cabin and become friends. He and his friend Sheila Mishkan, will introduce Esther and Chaim, though Esther and Chaim have been checking each other out for a week. He likes Rifka but is too insecure to say anything. She suspects as much but is patient until he figures things out for himself.

Glenallen Brown—A former green beret and political radical, now an outspoken opponent of anything to do with Israel or Zionist thought. Brown had soured on the US after his capture and torture years by before. A highly skilled and decorated soldier, he now leads Islamo-Christian forces into a street battle in Los Angeles.

Aryeh Cohen—An Israeli writer, lecturer, former Israeli government spokesmans, and friend of Jonathan Roberts. He lectures on the encroachment of Islam among nations. Married to an Egyptian Jewish woman who did sensitive work for the Israeli government. Powerful communicator— he warns Jews to always have their passports ready.

Lonesome Dave—Believing Army officer flying with JJ Johnson as his weapons officer.

Yigal Davidson—The Los Angeles commander of operations, a young Israeli Captain, 25 years of age. Will head up the Western Corridor defense and will be joined by Danielle and Avner Sullivan.

David Del Fuego—He is the father of Jenny Del Fuego and long lost cousin of Gregor De Toledo, the Mexican priest. They both discover their common Jewish roots, descendents of the Spanish Jews who left the Inquisition, interest in Jewish worship, history, and current Jewish affairs.

Jenny Del Fuego—The night nurse who cares for Ross Evans and helps him shed his Muslim beliefs and return to the faith of his childhood. Accepted the Lord a long time ago and wears a Star of David to speak of her support for the Jewish people. Has a family secret that will be told.

Father Gregor De Toledo—A priest who pastors a modestly-sized Catholic church near Mexico City. De Toledo comes from a long line of Catholic priests and church functioinaries. He discovers his Jewish roots and leads his church and other congregations from rigid Catholic views on Jewish affairs to a movement more supportive Israel and the Jews. All this is done at great risk to himself and his parishioners, but the growing interest of his flock encourage the change.

Johnny DiMattea—A trusted friend of the Vicenzos and was one of those guys who just 'took care of things.' Johnny's phone calls the next day would set many things in motion.

Avi Dorit—An Israeli cabinet minister who also doubles as a military advisor. He will introduce Ben Yehuda who will in turn, announce that *Operation Last Exodus* needs to be invoked.

Denise Dulberg—Very astute reporter who picks up the story about a murdered couple in Indiana. Later, she interview Jonathan Roberts via international hookup at the Prophecy Conference.

Colonel Dutch Ellison—The believing commander of a military base near Long Beach, California. He and his fellow Christian Zionist comrades heist several helicopters and make a run up to Los Angeles to capture and control LAX airport in support of the Jews.

Dolores Esquivel—A census taker in Los Angeles, she notices the high number of Muslims in her district as she goes door to door to complete her portion of the census.

Billy Glass—An Army captain and Apache helicopter pilot who defects from the U.S. military with many other believers to help the Jews escape. His skill with the helicopter will result in the attacks on several mosques, taking out huge weapons caches targeted for the Jews in Southern California.

Reverend Charles Graham—Black Baptist church Pastor in the Southern U.S. He and his followers will provide relief, comfort, and safety to fleeing Jews in his area. He will later host Ross Evans who will be speaking at his church.

Rabbi Morris Greenfield—A rabbi from Miami, Florida who joins Aurelio Lopes on his talk show.

Abdul Hakeem (Servant of the Wise)—Young college student who had entered the university a year apart from his sister, Manahil. They were a typical son and daughter of Middle East immigrants who have been recruited for a suicide mission.

Manahil Hakeem (Spring of Fresh Water)—Young college student who had entered the university a year apart from her brother, Abdul. They were a typical son and daughter of Middle East immigrants.

Ibraham Hussein (formerly and again, Ross Evans)—A young African-American man raised by a Christian mother who loved the Jews. In college he was persuaded by campus Muslims to join the Nation of Islam. He is well-read and educated at the University of California. Still, the influence of radical Islamic teaching moves him to join a rally near a Jewish school/community center in New Jersey. The mob turns violent, but he acts in selfless abandon to save Jewish lives. His hospital recovery goes far beyond his physical wounds. A Christian nurse and a young Jewish woman befriend, bless, and speed his healing and transformation. Ross Evans leads part of the rescue effort, speaks in African American churches, and helps plan the Jews' escape.

Jamal Kareem Ibraham—Mentor of Abdul Rachman and Imam. He's a brilliant scholar. Born in Iran, he is an expert in Sharia law. Plays 10 instruments, speaks 6 languages, and writes poetry. Loves working the recruiting tables at the universities. Ibraham also taught at the university. He has a PhD in Mathematics.

Dayle Johannson—The leader of the Christian pilot's group who will volunteer their services as pilots for the airlift. By the time the airlift begins, there will be close to 400 of them.

JJ Johnson—JJ is a Christian-Zionist and an Apache helicopter pilot. His weapons officer is Lonesome Dave. He's the wingman in Glass' flying squadron of AH-64s. He becomes engaged in action near John Wayne Airport. His ship faces two Apaches from the opposition.

William Jones—A newly elected U.S. Senator from Missouri who authors a bill to establish whether or not America is a Christian nation. It will be attached as a rider to an appropriations bill and get passed later. He later writes an editorial for the New York Times about the new legislation.

Father John Kemp—A Catholic cleric from Los Angeles who joins Aurelio Lopes on his talk show.

Hunni Lieberman—Hunni is Mimi's communications officer who coordinates battlefield communications between the various field commanders and headquarters.

Aurelio Lopes—Talk show host, writer, expert on the census and learns much about Christians in America. Discovers that while many identify themselves as Christians, few read their Bibles and fewer still understand what being a Christian means. Reports on the deep divisions within American culture. Promotes the term, 'Islamo-Christian,' which is becoming more and more popular, replacing Judeo-Christian when speaking about American ethics and religious values.

Ari Melnick—A flight engineer who has immigrated to Israel from France. He works for Michael Shapiro and is a logistics specialist. Multi talented as a painter, cartoonist, and writer, Ari also helps plan for eventualities such as this.

Sheila Mishkan—She is summer camp roommates with Esther Handle and, along with Sholom Braun acts as a go-between for Chaim and Esther. They have been friends since childhood. She is crushing on Sholom a bit. He's clueless. She hopes.

Imam Khalid Mohammad
An Islamic leader from New York who joins Aurelio Lopes on his talk show.

Moishe—Danielle's and Avner's Messianic Congregational Leader.

Yusef Muhammad—Iranian representative to the UN who files the documentation to declare Israel a pariah state, an outlaw. His sinister goal is to have Israel removed from the family of nations.

Jameel Hassan Nasrallah—Nasrallah is a young Muslim born in America of Jordanian parents. He and three others conduct a drive-by shooting of a Chicago synagogue. They also attack a nearby Jewish neighborhood.

Farouk Ibn Nasser—Young Saudi farmer, educated in the U.S. He and his wife, Shabibi, meet Mimi at a conference where she delivers a speech. They become fast and close friends, despite the cultural and religious barriers. Their farm will be destroyed by the volcano and subsequent earthquakes. They will reach out to Mimi for help. They become Mimi's best friends and cross an ancient bridge in the process.

Shabibi Ibn Nasser—Young Saudi animal specialist, educated in the U.S. She and her husband, Farouk, meet Mimi at a conference. They become fast and close friends, despite the cultural and religious barriers. She and her husband are also violinists.

Penelope Patel—Wife of Sarvish, an accomplished engineer, savvy businesswomanand, and a former model. This Brazilian woman is 6'4" in height (6'8" in her heels). She is a foot taller than her husband, who she advises in business affairs.

Sarvish Patel—Sarvish runs the world's largest aircraft leasing agency. He has more than 800 aircraft in his inventory with access to more. He provides aircraft for Jonathan Roberts to support the airlift.

Dov Pinski—Second in command in the South Orange County action behind D'vorah Rafaeli. He figures out where the OC Muslim battle plans are being hidden.

Afraima Rachman—Mother of Abdul Aziz Rachman, an Iraqi businesswoman working for the Geneva Corporation. After tiring of conflicts in her native country, she immigrated to Great Britain. They have 3 children, one of whom becomes a terror mastermind.

Abdul Aziz Rachman—Terror mastermind living in a cave in Afghanistan. Engineers the synagogue massacres one week after the Independence Day Parade and protest march.

Rachman is the son of Iraqi immigrants and was radicalized on campus in England by Jamal Kareem Ibraham where he studied Engineering.

Mohammad Rachman—Father of Abdul Aziz Rachman, an Iraqi businessman working for the Geneva Corporation. After tiring of conflicts in his native country, he immigrated to Great Britain.

D'vorah Rafaeli—Israeli female ground commander calling in air support to take a mosque with loads of intelligence information.

Jonathan Roberts—Christian minister, teacher, and supporter of Israel. A man of unique intelligence—Annapolis graduate, decorated fighter pilot, military stategist, businessman, and respected Christian leader. A believer in Genesis 12:3—he has sought to bless Israel and Jews and has worked to ensure their security and perception among American evangelicals. He has used his abilities to motivate and organize Americans supportive of the Jews. He has worked to hid Jews at risk and to facilitate their airborne escape to the Land of Israel. He understands himself to be an instrument of God in fulfillment of ancient prophecies for Israel's restoration.

Danielle Rogers—Lovely African American woman with a very sensitive heart prepossessed for Israel and the Jewish people. Speaks passable Hebrew, Yiddish, and studies the languages constantly. Meets Avram in a Starbucks in Orange County California and they begin a romance on the spot... love at first sight. She owns a successful marketing and graphics firm.

Mahmoud Salim—Team 3 squad leader, Saudi by birth and a Kuwati by citizenship, selected by Rachman to lead the synagogue attack in Dallas. He is ruthless and deals in heroin and the weapons black market as well.

Reverend William Schroeder—A Lutheran pastor from Chicago, Illinois who joins Aurelio Lopes on his talk show.

Dan Schuster—Schuster is the White House Press Secretary.

Raphi Shachor—A childhood friend of the Wasserman twins. He contacts them after a number of years to discuss the Bible and Messianic prophecy. For a long time they thought him a little crazy for his beliefs but now they are not so sure.

Michael Shapiro—Chief Director of the Jewish Agency of Logistics and Planning in Jerusalem. He along with Ari Melnick and his team of 50 help plan many practical aspects of *Operation Last Exodus*. They coordinates plans for the extraction of Jews from America, arrange for aircraft airlifts, organize local ground transportation, and plan housing for the new immigrants.

Ziva Shemesh—Ziva is a young Messianic Jewish woman and artist. She meets Michael Shapiro while he's on a visit to America. She shares her faith, biblical insights, and her profound love of Israel with him. She creates a painting using scriptures from the Book of Ezekiel and sends it to him. The painting has a deep and lasting effect on him. She secretly falls in love with him, hoping that he comes to the same realization of the Messiah she has.

Sheila—Young Jewish violinist and friend of Mimi's. She will join the group for dinner at Mimi's where they will all play music after dinner. Plays in the orchestra with Mimi and the others.

Yanit Silver—American-born Jewish woman who completed her college degree in Israel, learned Hebrew and a lot of Jewish history there as well. She becomes a central figure in the rescue of the American Jews. Has extraordinary organizational skills useful when material and facilities must be coordinated. Childhood friend of the Vicenzos.

Ayelet Simcha—Ayelet is a young Jewish woman who was in the community center where the Nation of Islam mob attacked and Ross intervened. She visited Ross in the hospital, has a part in his change, and witnesses his tranformation and healing. Ayelet, Nurse Jenny, and Ross become and stay friends. Her cousin Yanit is another key player in *Operation Last Exodus*.

Sterling Smith—Sterling is a news anchorman—first to report the synagogue shootings. He's a Bible believing Christian and knows the shootings are akin to the a pogrom and will lead to another holocaust.

Stacey—Young Jewish violinist and friend of Mimi's. Plays in the orchestra with Mimi and the others. She joins the group for dinner at Mimi's where they will play music after dinner.

Avner Sullivan—A young Israeli man who travels to America after his military service concludes. He is the oldest brother in a family of three siblings, the others being Mimi and Ephraim. Avner is a gifted leader. Meets and eventually marries an African-American woman, Danielle Rogers. Later finds himself defending the Jews' flight from Los Angeles.

Ephraim Sullivan—The third of the "Fighting Sullivans" and is a gifted computer programmer and software designer. Attends University of California, Irvine where he endears himself to several professors. Ephraim will eventually hook up with Shoshana Bat Levi as they attempt to take down parts the American infrastructure and help rescue American Jews from another Holocaust.

Mimi Sullivan—A young Israeli woman who travels to America during her military service, on an educational assignment. Brilliant, she sports a 200 IQ. Is gifted in civil engineering and soil engineering as well. Accomplished violinist who befriends two young Arab farmers from Saudi Arabia after they meet at a conference at which she speaks. She is tough and has survived two knife attacks in her younger years. Eventually graduates from MIT with a double engineering major and leads the Eastern Corridor rescue efforts.

The Warrior—He is a tall young man of mixed racial heritage. He knows and understands the Jews' place in history and God's future plan. He's a former special forces soldier and becomes a mentor to Pastor Tom through the scriptures helping him understand the role of Israel and the Jews.

Tiffany—Tiffany, a young Asian woman who loves her viola and is a friend of Mimi's. She will join the group for dinner at Mimi's where they will all play music after dinner. Plays in the orchestra with Mimi and the others.

Joe Vicenzo—Head of the Vicenzo family and father to Sal. Compassionate man, focused on 'la familia.' Majority stockholder of garbage companies across America and has influence in trucking, ports, warehouses, customs, and cyber security. He and Sal will play a crucial part in the story as they are well-connected to many people who will be called upon to help rescue America's Jews and help get them to the promised land.

Maria Vicenzo—"Mama" to those who know her, she is a compassionate and loving Italian mother who serves as the rock of the Vicenzo family. She runs a tight home and is a tremendous cook. She will host a dinner later in the story where the major players come together to cement the planning for the eventual rescue of America's Jews.

Sal "Dogface" Vicenzo—Close friend of Yanit Silver, Sal and his family live in New York and own interests in garbage and warehouses. They will figure into the story as friends who will provide vital services and facilities to help the Jews defend themselves and will aid in the rescue efforts with heavy logistical support. Earned his nickname when he was called a Dogface by a 4th grade classmate and knocked out the kid's teeth. Nobody ever messed with him again.

David Wasserman—Chaim's and Esther's son, a Doctor. He drives a green Ford truck with a gunrack in the back. He also wears cowboy boots.

Esther Handel Wasserman—Chaim's wife of his youth. Gifted amateur athlete when younger, they meet in a summer camp before she goes away to Grad school that Fall. She is extremely bright and does research in 'the kingdom of the bugs,' which later becomes a central theme. Her identical twin sister, Rifka is an engineer.

Rabbi Chaim Wasserman—Orthodox rabbi married to Esther, the wild redhead who has a PhD in Entomology. Chaim and his twin brother Eleazer have a series of prophetic dreams about the ancient Exodus, and spend a good part of the story trying to figure out what it means.

Rabbi Eleazer Wasserman—Twin brother of Chaim. He and his wife Rifka have the same set of dreams. He is a trusted advisor to his identical twin brother.

Rifka Handel Wasserman—The identical twin sister of Esther's. Smart in her own right, she is an accomplished engineer—scientist and together with her identical twin sister will help deliver some surprises to Washington D.C.

Shara Wasserman—Chaim's and Esther's daughter. She is a University Professor.

Daniel Weinstein—Brilliant, young Mossad analyst supporting Avram Ben Yehuda and Shoshana Bat Levi. He finds many different, seemingly disconnected events and ties them together in a pattern, thereby helping his superiors identify the first signs of the approaching holocaust and helps them make tough decisions.

William—Young Black cellist and member of the orchestra with Mimi.

Michael Wilson—Jewish Agency Director who is buying up a number of modular housing businesses which will be merged into one large entity. The company will build modular housing with the latest environmental designs in anticipation of housing the fleeing Jews from America and the nations.

General Gur Yerushalmi—Chief of Operations of the IDF in Israel. He's coordinating things from Tel Aviv while Shoshana handles the U.S. Operation.

Key Words & Concepts

Aliya: going up—ascent to Jerusalem; exaltation; a lofty place.

Allahu Akhbar: The Arabic term for "God is Great."

Apache AH-64: attack helicopter manufactured by the Boeing Company as an helicopter—has seen action in several theaters of battle and is a preferred weapon for dozens of nations.

B'rit HaChadashah: A Hebrew term for "the New Covenant," and the name which the Messianic believers give the New Testament.

B'shert or Besert: Yiddish for fated or meant-to-be.

Boker Tov: Good Morning.

C-130: Four engine aircraft manufactured by the Lockheed Martin Corporation. It is used as a troop transporter, for cargo, reconnaissance, and sometimes as a gunship.

CAMERA: Committee for **A**ccuracy for **M**iddle **E**ast **R**eporting in **A**merica. A watchdog group that often refutes official news accounts and brings the rest of the story out to the public.

C.A.I.R.: America's largest Islamic civil liberties group. Since its establishment in 1994, CAIR has worked to promote a positive image of Islam and Muslims in America.

Chanakah: The Feast of Dedication described in the Book of Maccabees. There is one clear reference to this Jewish holiday in the New Testament from the 10th Chapter of John.

Conversos: From the word for conversion in Spanish, Jews from Spain who had received Yeshua (or Jesus) as their Messiah. Scholars debated for centuries whether or not they were really Jews. Some maintained their new Christian faith while others secretly practiced Judaism. Also called New Christians or Crypto Jews.

Crypto Jews: Jews from Spain who outwardly practiced Christianity but actually secretly maintained their Jewish traditions. Scholars debated for centuries whether or not they were really Jews. They often kept secret Jewish rituals within their families.

Dhimmi: Subservient status for anyone living under Muslim rule. Supposedly it protects the minority, but historically the truth was often the opposite. Reference the website Dhimmi Watch or From Time Immemorial by Joan Peters for further details.

Diaspora (or the Jewish Diaspora): The English term used to describe the *Galut* (Yiddish: *Golus*) or exile of the Jews from the region of the Kingdom of Judah and Roman Iudaea and later emigration from wider *Eretz Israel*.

Eid: An Arabic term meaning "festival" including any number of holidays.

Eretz Israel: Hebrew for "Land of Israel."

Expat: Expat or Ex-patriate status meaning a person temporarily or permanently living away from home in a country and culture other than that of the his upbringing or legal residence. 350,000 Israelis were living expat in America in the early 21st Century.

Ferklempt: Sweaty or a little clammy.

Gibbor (or Gibbowr): A Hebrew word for "mighty" or "mighty man."

Goldena Medina: America, a safe place for Jews; almost like the promised land. Nicknamed by the 19th century European Jews as they escaped pogroms for the safety of America's shores.

Goy: A gentile. The technical Hebrew term is the Nations. The word is sometimes used in derogatory manner when speaking of Gentiles. The plural form is ***goyim.***

HaShem: It is a respectful term for God, without pronouncing His name. Hebrew expression for the Name of God—HaShem literally means "The Name."

HaShomer: Hebrew for "Watchman" or "Guardian"—a Jewish defense organization in *Eretz Israel* founded out of *Bar-Giora* in April 1909. It ceased to operate after the founding of the *Haganah* in 1920. The purpose of Hashomer was to provide guard services for Jewish settlements in the *Yishuv,* freeing Jewish communities from dependence upon foreign consulates and Arab watchmen for their security.

Hellfire Missile: Manufactured by the Lockheed Martin Corporation and has a television-guided weapon that can reach speeds of 900 miles per hour. Each Hellfire weighs about 100 pounds, includes a 9 kg / 20 pound warhead, with a range of about 8,000 meters. Thousands of Hellfires had reached customers as diverse as Israel, Great Britain, Egypt, France, and others. Unit price: $80,000.

Hijabs / Jilbabs / Kurta: Woman's and Men's traditional Muslim wear, often white and sometimes stitched with embroidery.

IDF: Israeli Defense Forces.

IDFA: Israeli Defense Forces of America. The American branch of Israel's army that will defend the Jews as they escape America and go to Israel.

Imam: An Arabic term for an Islamic leadership position, often the worship leader of a mosque and the Muslim community.

Judaizers: Believing Jews who try to foist Jewish practices on the Christians. Sadly, they have been largely misunderstood and the Christians, by forcing Jews to convert or ignore their heritage, have lost much of their Hebraic roots and adopted quasi-pagan practices into their churches.

Ketuba: Jewish marriage contract usually detailing pre-nuptial agreements between the bride and the groom. It is considered protection for the wife and acted as a replacement of the price paid by the groom for his bride. Once the Ketuba was signed, the bride was protected in the event of the cessation of marriage, either by the death of the husband or divorce.

Kibbutz(im): Collective farming community usually founded on Socialist principles in the early days of Israel's settlement.

Klezmer: "Jewish Jazz" imported from Europe. A rich and productive Yiddish culture was wiped out during the war. Klezmer was an important part of that culture.

Kristallnacht: *Night of Broken Glass* (Germany 1938) and also Reichskristallnacht, Pogromnacht, and November pogrom, where a sanctioned pogrom was brought to bear on the Jews of Germany. Storefronts were broken with glass everywhere, dozens of Jews beaten or killed, and many more taken from homes and businesses and sent to concentration camps. This event would serve as a backdrop of Kristallnacht 2, when a street protest spins out of control and the Jews of New York are picked as targets. Jewish homes were ransacked, as were shops, towns and villages, as SA stormtroopers and civilians destroyed buildings with sledgehammers, leaving the streets covered in pieces of smashed windows—the origin of the name "Night of Broken Glass." Ninety-one Jews were killed, and 30,000 Jewish men—a quarter of all Jewish men in Germany—were taken to concentration camps, where they were tortured for months, with over 1,000 of them dying. Around 1,668 synagogues were ransacked, and 267 set on fire. In Vienna alone 95 synagogues or houses of prayer were destroyed. Martin Gilbert writes that no event in the history of German Jews between 1933 and 1945 was so widely reported as it was happening, and the accounts from the foreign journalists working in Germany sent shock waves around the world. The Times wrote at the time:

> No foreign propagandist bent upon blackening Germany before the world could outdo the tale of burnings and beatings, of blackguardly assaults on defenseless and innocent people, which disgraced that country yesterday.

The attacks were triggered with the assassination of German diplomat Ernst von Rath by Herschel Grynszpan, a German-born Polish Jew in Paris, France. *Kristallnacht* was followed by further economic and political persecution of Jews. It is viewed by historians as part of Nazi Germany's broader racial policy—the beginning of the Final Solution and the Holocaust.

Legend: In intelligence work, a legend is a created alias for the agent. The agent will use the legend to act out his or her identity in the interest of completing the mission for which he or she is sent.

Madrassa: Islamic religious school focused on teaching Sharia Law to its students.

Marranos: Meaning "pig" in Spanish, these were Jews who 'converted' to Christianity but it was suspected they retained Jewish practices in the home.

Messhugah: A Yiddish term meaning "crazy."

Messhugahners: A Yiddish term meaning "crazy people."

Memri: Middle **E**ast **M**edia and **R**esearch **I**nstitute. MEMRI bridges the language gap which exists between the West and the Middle East, providing translations of main Middle Eastern tongues such as Arabic, Persian, Urdu-Pashtu, and Turkish media, as well as original analysis of political, ideological, intellectual, social, cultural, and religious trends in the Middle East. Much of what comes out of that part of the world is hidden in the language. MEMRI attempts to decode much of what is said and make it understandable to a wider world.

Mensch: A Yiddish (German) term for "man" but really means someone who is a dependable and straight forward person. (*uber-mensch* is "super-man").

Mezuzah: A Hebrew term for "door-post." The *mezuzah* is a piece of parchment—often within a decorative case. The written inscription contains verses from the Torah— often the words of the Jewish prayer *Shema Yisrael*.

Midrash: The transliteration of a Hebrew word meaning "story." But *midrash* has also come to mean a shared study, exposition, historical record, or writings of a didactic nature.

Moshav(im): Collective farming community often individually owned but of fixed and equal size. Crops and goods are produced through individual and/or pooled labor. Moshavim are governed by an elected council.

Nuremburg Laws: A series of anti-Semitic laws aimed at the Jews designed to strip them of all civil rights, ability to work, and live in a peaceful manner with their neighbors.

Otriad: In the Polish and Russian resistance a word describing the forest partisans who fought the Nazis using guerilla warfare tactics. The otriad was a group that could number from a few dozen to hundreds.

Protocols of the Learned Elders of Zion: A document published in the early 20th century blaming international Jewry for a world-wide financial conspiracy. The text was later proven a hoax but remained alive in anti-Semitic circles as proof of the Jews' plans for world domination.

Purim: An annual remembrance of the events recorded in the Tenach—Esther 9.

Quran: Spelled Quran, Qu'ran, or Koran, it is considered Holy Scripture to Muslims.

Replacement Theology: The teaching and doctrine among certain Christian denominations that the Church has replaced Israel and the Jews as the chosen people.

Ruach HaKodesh: The Hebrew term for "The Holy Spirit" of God.

Sabra: Native born Israelis.

Seder: A Hebrew word meaning "order" or "sequence." It is commonly used to describe the ritual ceremony on Friday evening beginning Shabbat. And it refers to the Passover dinner ritual.

Shabbat (or Shabbos): Shabbat is the Jewish Sabbath or day of rest. Shabbos is the Yiddish expression of the same. Wishing someone "Good Shabbos" or Shabbat Shalom, is to wish them Peace of/on the Sabbath for them, family, and their households.

Shahid: Martyr, usually declared so after a suicide bombing.

Sharia: Islamic Law—Sharia is the comprehensive body of Islamic laws that regulates the public and private aspects of the lives of the Muslims. Sharia is not a single code of laws—rather, it consists of four sources that legal experts refer to.

Sherut: Israeli service taxicab—more of a small minibus.

Shoah: The Hebrew term for the Holocaust.

Shul: A Yiddish reference to the place and activities for the Jewish congregation. Germans saw the study practices of the Jews and referred to their participation as "school" or *shul* in German.

Shtetl: A Yiddish word meaning small village where the European Jews lived.

Suq: An Arab marketplace much like an open farmers' market.

Tenach: The entirety of the Hebrew Scriptures.

Tish B'Av: The 9th of Av, the Hebrew month. It is believed that many Jewish disasters such as the destruction of the Temple happened on Tish B'Av.

Viral Marketing: An internet concept based on rapid spread of news or some sort of publicity campaign. The numbers tend to progress geometrically and spread like a virus would... the more people that are exposed, the more they, in turn will expose others.

Yeshua: The Hebrew name for Jesus.

Yiddish: The *lingua franca* of most European Jews before the Holocaust. Largely a dead language now but is spoken and preserved within many of the Orthodox communities.

Yishuv: A term used in Hebrew referring to the body of residents in the Land of Israel before the establishment of the State of Israel. Residents and new settlers were referred to collectively as "The Yishuv."

Yom Tov: Good Day.

Yom Ha'Shoah: The Hebrew term for the annual Holocaust day of remembrance.

Noted Resources

The following list of resources and published materials are some of the materials used to write this story. Some of the books are hard to find and may either be out of print, available online, or in used bookstores. Others are in print and are readily available. Since I believe that a positive approach to life is important, I have included many heartwarming stories of rescue efforts. I think they speak to the kinder and gentler nature in all of us. I believe that many Christians will fulfill that role in the future.

Abandonment of the Jews by David Wylie: Among the controversial perspectives that Wylie lays out (he is a Protestant minister) is that America and the British Foreign Office had no intention of rescuing the Jews during the Holocaust. He chronicles how both allied nations actually feared that hundreds of thousands (if not more) of Jews would be dumped on the allies by Germany with nowhere to go. Interesting to consider in this equation is what England's immigration policy was for the Jews and Palestine. When the latter is overlaid with this story, it becomes evident that Great Britain and the United States did relatively little to provide safe haven for Europe's Jews, thus becoming silent partners in the eventual slaughter and attempted genocide of the Jewish people. Also discussed in detail is American immigration law, quotas, and other details.

A History of Christianity by Paul Johnson—A controversial take on Christianity, Johnson does leave the reader with much to think about, especially the tension between the Papacy and the Protestant wings of the faith. The book also has some interesting things to say about the early Jews who formed what would later become known as Christianity.

A History of Israel Howard Sacher by A comprehensive account of Zionism and the rise of the Jewish state mostly taken from the 1800's through the late 20th century. Sachar gives detailed accounts of battles and wars plus a treasure trove of behind the scenes details explaining how the modern Jewish state came to be. Excellent backdrop for anyone wishing to understand the current situation in the Middle East as it now stands.

A History of the Jewish People by H.H. Ben Sasson—Comprehensive history of the Jewish people and their migrations throughout Europe and the world. Excellent references to some rather obscure events. A must for any library.

A Peace to End All Peace by David Fromkin—Fromkin discusses the fall of the Ottoman Empire and the creation of Modern Middle East. This book is critical if the reader wants to understand politics in this part of the world. He gives an excellent history of World War I and the sudden presence of the British in Palestine, which then frames what happens in the next 30 or so years. He also discusses the "Great Game" which is a chronicle of British-Russian interests in areas such as Afghanistan and India. Many of the mistakes made by those nations involved then are being made again today. If you read this in conjunction with the Rape of Palestine, you will become quite knowledgeable about Middle Eastern affairs in a short time.

A Time for Trumpets, Not Piccolos by Frank Eiklor—Eiklor is an evangelist and is passionate for Israel. This book and a companion pamphlet (Israel, Front Page, the Untold Story) describe the nature of anti-Semitism and anti-Zionism, a very close cousin.

Camera Website—This is an investigative website that picks up stories where the general press leaves off. In many instances what is reported in the press gives half truths and Camera goes deeper to expose them or outright lies. It is well documented and worth a look. Go to by http://www.camer.org/.

DebkaFile Electronic Newsletter—Excellent newsletter that delves deep into the Middle East and presents short articles exposing anti-Semitism, anit-Zionism from all over the world. They seem to have intelligence sources that nobody else has. Excellent reading and provocative insights. You may acquire DebkaFile news by visiting the website. Go to http://www.debka.com/search/tag/Israel/.

Defiance Nachma Tec by The Bielski Partisans rose up against the Nazis during WWII in an attempt to rescue as many Jews as possible. The story revolves around Tuvia Bielski who was responsible for saving close to 1200 Jewish lives. Amazing read. A movie was released in 2008 that brings the book to life.

Eye to Eye (Facing the Consequences of Dividing Israel) by William Koenig—This book is truly unique in all the research available. It maps natural disasters in the United States and places them side-by-side against political pressures brought to bear on Israel, specifically when the U.S. forces Israel to exchange land for peace. The book is controversial and will challenge the reader to ask whether the events so described within are coincidence or predictable based on the author's thesis. The evidence is compelling though the book can be a little tedious.

For Zion's Sake Electronic Newsletter—This newsletter runs a variety of articles from various sources, many with Biblical connotations. This weekly publication also includes some very interesting videos often from the world of Islam. Excellent compilation of news sources on a number of topics of interest regarding Israel, the Middle East, and Bible prophecy. Go to: http://forzion.com/.

From Time Immemorial by Joan Peters, 1984—This book is a must read for anyone wishing to challenge Muslim claims to the land of Israel. She started her research sympathetic to the Palestinians but changed her opinions when delving into the facts. She finds that modern-day Israel wasn't populated by Arabs "from time immemorial" as claimed, but that Arab immigration to Israel is a relatively recent phenomenon. She discusses movement of various peoples in the region and chronicles the role of the Turks and the Ottoman Empire. Not easy reading, but worth the time. Excellent sources in the index.

Haaretz website—Israeli news site packed with articles on a number of provocative topics. Go to: http://www.haaretz.com/.

Hamas Charter by Ditto above. This document is provocative and to the point. To many Muslims, there is no room for a Jewish state and these documents prove it.

Historical Atlas of Judaism by Dr. Ian Barnes and Josephine Bacon—A wonderful coffee table book with excellent maps and graphics telling the story of the Jews. Wonderful resource for population trends, migration stories, wars, the Holocaust, and a lot more.

If Not Now, When? by Primo Levi—A fictional account of the true story of the partisans who fought back and derailed the German Army at every opportunity. Levi poses many questions about our existence and the life of the suffering Jews.

Islamic Invasion by Robert Morey—Morey is the Executive Director of the Research and Education Foundation. He describes Islam's rise in the West, compares essential passages from the Bible to the Qur'an and steps the reader through the main differences of the faiths. The life of Mohammad is also highlighted. This is an excellent overview of Islam and its goals.

Jerusalem Post website—Up to the minute news on Israel and the world. The site features a very balanced view of Israeli politics and features some excellent writers. Go to http://www.jpost.com/.

Jewish Pirates of the Caribbean by Edward Kritzler—The title brings to mind the Disney movies. But that is where the similarity ends. This book chronicles the history of the Jewish Conversos and Marranos. As it turns out, these people headed to the New World with the likes of Columbus and other well-known explorers and built trading routes and shipping companies. They set up much of the business infrastructure of Spanish, Portuguese, and Dutch New World adventurism. It fills in a lot of gaps as to what happened to those forced into Catholic conversions and how they handled their Jewish identities once they escaped the Inquisition.

Jews, God, and History by Max Dimont—Though somewhat dated, Dimont delves into Jewish history and brings some interesting discussion about civilization to the table. Israel, the Jews, and their enemies all play a part. The book emphasizes how the Jews have integrated into all main social systems and how they have influenced them at the same time while trying to maintain their Jewish identity. It is a secular history and I do have some disagreements with his attempt to explain away spiritual matters. Nonetheless, it's an excellent historical overview.

Jihad Watch website—Formerly known as Dhimmi Watch, this website features an ongoing blog and articles about International Islam. It holds no punches and is quite controversial but very good. Go to: http://www.jihadwatch.org/.

K-House—Koinonia House is the ministry and online resource of Chuck and Nancy Missler. The character of Jonathan Roberts was loosely based upon the life of Chuck Missler, an Annapolis graduate and an administrative staffer to President Reagan. Go to http://www.khouse.org/.

My Life by Golda Meir– An excellent first-hand account of the birth of Israel and those events leading up to it. She is a superb storyteller and a woman who exemplified what living in peace with her neighbors was all about. But when it came time to fight, she understood that too. No understanding of the nation of Israel or its struggle for independence can be understood without this book.

O Jerusalem by Dominique La Pierre and Larry Collins by One of the best accounts of the founding of the Jewish state told from several perspectives. These writers are among my favorites and the reader will not be disappointed. The movie does not do the book justice.

One Palestine, Complete by Tom Segev—A member of the HaAretz Staff, Segev writes a revisionist perspective of Palestine's history under British control. It gives another look at behind the scenes relationships between the Arabs, the British, and the Jews.

Our Hands Are Stained with Blood by Michael L. Brown—The story of how the Christian Church has persecuted the Jews down through the years. Brown is a Jewish Believer in the Messiah and is very clear in the message. Sad as it is to say, many Christians do not know or care about the Church's history and its relationship to anti-Semitism. It is not an easy read but it is something that every Christian needs to know.

Palestinian Manifesto by Ditto. This document is must reading for anyone interested in the current conflict. After you read it, there can be no doubt about the Arab's intentions.

Paper Walls by David Wylie, 1968, 1985: So, what was America up to during the Holocaust and what did it know, when, and what did it do about it? Sadly, America knew plenty about the death camps, the mass slaughter, and Germany's hostility towards the Jews and chose to do virtually nothing, at least as far as official government policy. According to Wylie, the U.S. erected "Paper Walls" to keep the Jews out, actually mimicking the British policy in Palestine. This is a dark chapter in America's history and proves beyond a doubt that America cared little for the plight of the Jewish refugees.

Righteous Gentile by John Bierman—This is the story of Raoul Wallenberg, Swedish diplomat, who signed visas and other documents to protect as many Jews as he could. He saved countless lives but was captured at the close of the war by the Soviet Union and never heard from again. It is a great mystery what happened to him and why the Russians did what they did.

Safe Haven by Allis and Ronald Radosh, 2009—The story of Harry Truman and his response to the pressures brought to bear on him during the three years from WWII to the U.N. Vote of Partition and Israel's Declaration of Independence. Truman put up with hostility from a number of places including a split American Jewish community, some in favor of statehood and some not. Added to this was the Department of State which ran counter to White House policy, thereby creating some very embarrassing situations for the President. This is a terrific history with many stories of the intransigent Arabs unwilling to allow any Jewish presence in that part of the world and Great Britain's attempt to hold on to its dying empire.

Saving Remnant by Herbert Agar—Agar discusses the rescue efforts of the American Jewish Joint Distribution Committee. This courageous group smuggled in food, clothing to the refugees of Europe, and managed to bring comfort to as many as it could.

Schindler's List by Thomas Keneally. Schindler proved that one person could make a difference in the life of the persecuted. This book chronicles his rise as an industrialist and then the realization of what the Nazi death machine meant. He then lays his life down for the Jews and protects thousands of them in his factory. The movie is tough to watch but encouraging at the same time. He is remembered at Yad Va' Shem in Israel.

Start up Nation by Dan Senor and Saul Singer—Published in 2009, Start up Nation provides an insider's glimpse into the amazing Israeli business engine and the spirit of innovation. Israel's infrastructure is driven by its military veterans who carry on lifetime relationships through their networking. These relationships drive the entreprencurship so prevalent in the tiny state.

The Exodus by Leon Uris—Fictionalized account of the "illegal" immigration of Jews to Palestine after World War II. This classic tale follows the Jews from Europe to the deportation camps in Cypress through the confrontation with Britain to enter the Land.

The Future Church by John L. Allen—The author covers ten trends that are revolutionizing the Catholic Church today. The book has much to say about Catholicism's relationship with Islam and Judaism and portends some interesting possibilities.

They Have Conspired Against You by Olivier Melnick—The book delves deeply into modern day Anti-Semitism and the causes for it. The author spent seven years in research and has produced a fine work that ties Biblical Prophecy and truth to the question of Anti-Semitism. Well worth the read.

The Holocaust, The French, and The Jews by Suzanne Zuccotti—Though many Jews from France died in the *Shoah*, she shows another side to the French people—stories of courage, defiance, and hope. She gives an excellent overview of Le Chambon Sur Lignon and many other stories like it.

The Hope by Herman Wouk—A fictional account of the founding of the Nation of Israel. As most good writers of historical fiction, he takes real characters and blends them into the story. Excellent reading by an excellent writer.

The Mezuzah in the Madonna's Foot by Trudy Alexi—She writes a very compassionate personal story of escaping Nazi persecution, passing through Spain, and then finding her way to America. She tells several short stories about the Spanish Jewish connection, one of which talks about an increasing number of Hispanic Catholics from the Southwest USA who seem to keep strange Jewish rituals in their homes for no apparent reason.

The Politics of Heroin by Alfred McCoy—A forthright history of how drugs move between nations and those who are responsible for it. America's role is explained and it's not necessarily what we might think it is. The drug problem in Afghanistan today is every bit as serious as it was in the early 1990's and long before. In fact, many believe that America's enemies depend to a large extent on drug sales to help raise funds for terrorist activities.

The Qur'an—Used for a number of quotes and backdrop. The old adage is to keep your friends close and your enemy closer.

The Rape of Palestine by William Ziff, 1938: Written when Nazi Germany was in ascension, Hitler was in power, and before WWII began, this book is a must read for any true student of the Holocaust and the subsequent events leading to Israel's independence. The book takes on British authorities and challenges them on the White Paper, the Mandate, and their lack of sensitivity to the Jews and their plight. It chronicles business and property transactions in an unfiltered light, challenging what to many today is the right of Arabs' claim to the Land of Israel. Ziff provides excellent, unbiased insight and analysis that portended today's events. Messianic believers and those associated with them will find the final chapter, "Am I my Brother's Keeper" particularly stunning and cogent, as the author refers to European "Hebrew Christians" in huge numbers, and clearly counts them as fellow Jews and part of the National Restoration of Israel, 10 years before Israel was re-founded and established. He speaks of the Christian Church's role and responsibility regarding their Jewish brothers.

The Secret War Against the Jews by John Loftus and Mark Aarons—The book discussed how Western espionage has betrayed the Jews. It is of note that Jonathan Pollard continues to languish in an American jail for spying on the U.S., while this sort of thing is suspected of being conducted by Americans on Israel all the time. A lesser known account of U.S.S. Liberty is given. Though this story will probably spark some anger from Navy vets, it's worth considering, especially in light of the heat of battle during the Six Day War.

The Source by James Michener—The book is a fictional account of the Jewish nation and is an excellent novel written by one of my favorite authors. Michener poses the interesting idea in the last chapter about Israelis coming to America to help fight attacks on a synagogue. The Source is the spark for this story. Though the book is slow to get started, when it warms up, it is tough to put down.

The Terror Network by Claire Sterling—This book came out in the early 1980's and was immediately translated into more than a dozen languages. It is somewhat dated in that the main terror groups such as Germany's Baader Meinhof gang or the Japanese Red Army (and many others) seem to have been replaced by Islamic fundamentalists. In any event, she explains terror's purpose and how its perpetrators carry it out. The rules of terror remain the same. She discusses the purchase and shipment of armaments, how the various groups collaborate, and how both the left and the right often tap the same resources for help. Must reading to understand the psychology of terror by either the right or the left.

Trading With the Enemy by Charles Higham—A stunning indictment of World War II Allied secret financial relationships with the Axis. That America would or could trade with the Nazis during the war isn't exactly well known. The book also traces American industrial giants such as IBM and ITT and others who helped build Hitler's infrastructure before and amazingly, during the war.

Understanding the Arab Israeli Conflict (What the Headlines Haven't Told You) by Michael Rydelnik—An up to date Biblically oriented book that explains many of the mysteries of anti-Semitism and Islamic Jew hatred. Tracks nicely to Why the Jews and goes a long way to explain further the mysterious hatreds that seem to dominate Islam today.

When Being Jewish was a Crime by Rachmiel Frydland—This autobiography, written by a Messianic Jewish survivor of the Holocaust, tells the story of life in the concentration camps and how he makes it through. It is a testimony to faith in G-d when many of his fellow survivors turned away he found newfound strength through his Messiah.

Why the Jews by Dennis Prager and Joseph Telushkin, 1983—Cogent analysis of the causes and effects of anti-Semitism through the years. The book is not long, only 198 pages with a long list of sources. The authors discuss Christian and Muslim anti-Semitism as well as perspectives from the Left such as Communism and Socialism. Also mentioned is the perspective from the Enlightenment. Contains a comprehensive list of sources if you wish to continue your research.

About the Author

Robb Schwartz holds two masters degrees— one in Human Resources & Organization Development and the other a Masters in Business Administration (MBA). Before landing his current position in the aerospace industry, he was self-employed as the Southern California Director of the Institute of Reading Development. He also spent seven years as a member of the *Board of Examiners of the California Awards for Performance Excellence* and two years as a member of the *Board of Examiners of the Malcolm Baldrige National Quality Award Program*.

Robb is a student of Bible prophecy and the history of Israel. His interests range from American political assassinations, the American Civil War, historical anti-Semitism, baseball, and reading. He lives in Southern California with his wife Nancy and teenage daughter Shayna.

Operation Last Exodus is Robb's first published novel, but a sequel to this one is on the fast-track, now.

Operation Last Exodus is also available as an ebook and coming soon as an audiobook at http://www.spiritofhopepublishing.com.